More Praise for SARA PARETSKY and. . . .

. . . INDEMNITY ONLY

"What really continues to amaze and impress about this series is V.I. herself, undoubtedly one of the best-written characters in mystery fiction."
—*The Baltimore Sun*

"Compelling. . . . A thoroughly convincing, gritty tale."
—*The New Republic*

"Not since crime-fiction masters Raymond Chandler and Dashiell Hammett has a mystery writer integrated a character and an environment so seamlessly, to such telling, vibrant effect." —*Chicago* Magazine

. . . BLOOD SHOT

"Her best and boldest work to date. . . . A criminal investigation that is a genuine heroic quest." —*The New York Times Book Review*

"Purely and simply, this is a splendid whodunit." —*Chicago Sun-Times*

"A gripping, entertaining story." —*Publishers Weekly*

. . . BURN MARKS

"Warshawski's reputation for recklessness gets her into more than hot water in *Burn Marks*. . . . Nobody buys off V.I. Warshawski and nobody can scare her into silence." —*San Francisco Chronicle*

"Bang-up . . . one gritty good read . . . V.I. is a worthy heir to Marlowe!" —*Daily News* (New York)

"Superb plotting and strong characterization . . . *Burn Marks* is one of the best of the series. V.I. ('Don't call me Vicky') is tough on crooks. . . . Her stubbornness may not make her a convivial dinner partner, but she's great company in a mystery." —*Houston Chronicle*

SARA PARETSKY

THREE COMPLETE NOVELS

SARA PARETSKY

THREE COMPLETE NOVELS

INDEMNITY ONLY
BLOOD SHOT
BURN MARKS

WINGS BOOKS

NEW YORK • AVENEL, NEW JERSEY

This 1995 edition is published by Wings Books,
distributed by Random House Value Publishing, Inc.,
40 Engelhard Avenue, Avenel, New Jersey 07001,
by arrangement with Dell Publishing,
a division of Bantam Doubleday Dell
Publishing Group, Inc.

Random House
New York • Toronto • London • Sydney • Auckland

Printed and bound in the United States of America

Library of Congress Cataloging-in-Publication Data
Paretsky, Sara.
   [Selections]
   Three complete novels / Sara Paretsky.
      p.   cm.
   Contents: Indemnity only — Blood shot — Burn marks.
   ISBN 0-517-14801-3
   1. Warshawski, V. I. (Fictitious character)—Fiction. 2. Private investigators—Illinois—Chicago—Fiction. 3. Women detectives—Illinois—Chicago—Fiction. 4. Detective and mystery stories, American. 5. Chicago (Ill.)—Fiction. I. Title.
PS3566.A647A6 1995
813'.54—dc20   95-10833
                                              CIP

8 7 6 5 4 3 2 1

Contents

INDEMNITY ONLY

For Stuart Kaminsky. Thanks.

A NOTE FROM THE AUTHOR

On New Year's Eve, flushed with champagne, I made a secret resolution to write a novel in 1979 or send that fantasy packing along with my daydreams of singing at La Scala or dancing with Nureyev. The next day I began:

> I looked hopefully in my wallet, but found only the two greasy singles which had been there in the morning. I could get a sandwich, or a pack of cigarettes and a cheap shot of scotch. I sighed and looked down at the Wabash Avenue el tracks.

Nine months later, I'd added about fifty pages to this unpromising opening and thought I should resign myself to a life of selling computers to insurance agents. At that point a co-worker named Mary Hogan, who knew about my efforts, showed me the Northwestern University fall extension catalog. Stuart Kaminsky was teaching an evening course called "Writing Detective Fiction for Publication." I felt like Alice finding the mushroom—just what I needed to get to be the right size.

Stuart read my puny story with great care. He gave me essential advice for thinking about my character and my story. In the process V.I. stopped smoking and took up my whiskey, Black Label. Most important, Stuart became the voice I needed to hear, the voice that said, "You can write. You can do this thing." Without Stuart I would not have had the confidence to push the story through to the end. That is why *Indemnity Only* is dedicated to him.

Whenever I read the memoirs of a writer like Sartre, who says he knew from childhood he was "destined for words," or Bellow, who knew he "was born to be a performing or interpretive creature," I wonder what unacknowledged voice spoke to them as children. Sartre actually tells us it was his mother and his grandfather who bound his childish effusions as novels and passed them with much outspoken pride around the neighborhood. Without his family creating in him that vision of himself, young Jean-Paul could not have grown up with such a sense of destiny. His cousins, told at the same age they were fated to be engineers, became engineers.

I wrote from my earliest childhood, but for myself only. Like the heroine of *Dream Girl*, I spent vast amounts of my waking hours imagining myself inside different stories; when they acquired some kind of shape, I wrote them down. But I thought my stories were a sign of the sickness afflicting the woman in the play, and that true love would cure me as it did her, for I grew up in a time and place where little girls were destined to be wives and mothers.

I did find true love, but my husband, Courtenay Wright, convinced me that my stories were worth telling, that my dreams signaled not sickness but a lively mind. His support has not wavered from that cold New Year's Day to the present hot June in which I struggle with my seventh V.I. novel. I have had some terrible pain and disability in between; Courtenay has held on to me and kept me from losing that essential core from which my stories come. In a way, every word I write is dedicated to Courtenay.

When I finished the manuscript in May 1980, with the first weak paragraph and limp chapter exchanged for the current one, Stuart Kaminsky sent it to his agent, Dominick Abel, in New York. Dominick took on V.I. and me and has stuck with us ever since. I don't want to turn this introduction into a volume of the Talmud, so I'll only say of Dominick, in the old Chinese words, that I would send him for horses.

It took him a year to find a publisher for *Indemnity Only*. Indeed, when I'm getting too conceited with myself, I pull out the file of rejection letters from that year and read that I'm "too talky"; have "wooden characters"; wrote a "derivative story"; and that *Indemnity Only* was a "marginal book which we can't afford to take on." The file is a nice fat one and a good antidote for vanity. In the face of so much negativism, I'm especially grateful to Nancy van Itallie and the Dial Press for taking the gamble on publishing me.

The Dial Press is no more, and this is sad. But after almost a decade of wandering I've found my proper home at Delacorte. Jackie Farber and Carole Baron provide the kind of editorial and publishing support most writers only dream about.

Indeminity Only came to life so precariously that it remains very precious to me. Sometimes I look at it with amazement—amazed that I did find the strength to write a book, amazed that someone actually published it. And now that Delacorte is bringing out a new edition I look at it with a lot of pride. I was tempted to go through and polish up the writing, change those flaws I wasn't alert enough to see in 1979. But I decided it would be unethical to tamper with the text. With the exception of two very small corrections this is the same book I sent to Dominick Abel ten years ago.

Sara Paretsky
Chicago
June 1990

(This letter was written to accompany the 1990 Delacorte reissue.)

1 SUMMERTIME

The night air was thick and damp. As I drove south along Lake Michigan, I could smell rotting alewives like a faint perfume on the heavy air. Little fires shone here and there from late-night barbecues in the park. On the water a host of green and red running lights showed people seeking relief from the sultry air. On shore traffic was heavy, the city moving restlessly, trying to breathe. It was July in Chicago.

I got off Lake Shore Drive at Randolph Street and swung down Wabash under the iron arches of the elevated tracks. At Monroe I stopped the car and got out.

Away from the lake the city was quieter. The South Loop, with no entertainment beyond a few peepshows and the city lockup, was deserted—a drunk weaving uncertainly down the street was my only companion. I crossed Wabash and went into the Pulteney Building next to the Monroe Street Tobacco Store. At night it looked like a terrible place to have an office. The hall's mosaic-tiled walls were chipped and dirty. I wondered if anyone ever washed the scuffed linoleum floor. The lobby must create a reassuring impression on potential clients.

I pushed the elevator button. No response. I tried again. Again no response. I shoved open the heavy stairwell door, climbing slowly to the fourth floor. It was cool in the stairwell and I lingered there a few minutes before moving on down the badly lit hallway to the east end, the end where rents are cheaper because all the offices look out on the Wabash el. In the dim light I could read the inscription on the door: "V. I. Warshawski. Private Investigator."

I had called my answering service from a filling station on the North Side, just a routine check on my way home to a shower, air conditioning, and a late supper. I was surprised when they told me I had a caller, and unhappy when they said he'd refused to give a name. Anonymous callers are a pain. They usually have something to hide, often something criminal, and they don't leave their names just so you can't find out what they're hiding ahead of time.

This guy was coming at 9:15, which didn't even give me time to eat. I'd spent a frustrating afternoon in the ozone-laden heat trying to track down a printer who owed me fifteen hundred dollars. I'd saved his firm from being muscled out by a national chain last spring and now I was sorry I'd done it. If my checking account hadn't been so damned anemic, I'd have ignored this phone call. As it was, I squared my shoulders and unlocked the door.

With the lights on my office looked Spartan but not unpleasant and I cheered up slightly. Unlike my apartment, which is always in mild disarray, my office is usually tidy. I'd bought the big wooden desk at a police auction. The little Olivetti portable had been my mother's, as well as a reproduction of the Ufizzi hanging over my green filing cabinet. That was supposed to make visitors realize that mine was a high-class operation. Two straight-backed chairs for clients completed the furniture. I didn't spend much time here and didn't need any other amenities.

I hadn't been in for several days and had a stack of bills and circulars to sort through. A computer firm wanted to arrange a demonstration of what computers could do to help my business. I wondered if a nice little desk-top IBM could find me paying customers.

The room was stuffy. I looked through the bills to see which ones were urgent. Car insurance—I'd better pay that. The others I threw out—most were first-time bills, a few second-time. I usually only pay bills the third time they come around. If they want the money badly, they won't forget you. I stuffed the insurance into my shoulder bag, then turned to the window and switched the air conditioner onto "high." The room went dark. I'd blown a fuse in the Pulteney's uncertain electrical system. Stupid. You can't turn an air conditioner right onto "high" in a building like this. I cursed myself and the building management equally and wondered whether the storeroom with the fuse boxes was open at night. During the years I'd spent in the building, I'd learned how to repair most of what could go wrong with it, including the bathroom on the seventh floor, whose toilet backed up about once a month.

I made my way back down the hall and down the stairs to the basement. A single naked bulb lit the bottom of the stairs. It showed a padlock on the supply-room door. Tom Czarnik, the building's crusty superintendent, didn't trust anyone. I can open some locks, but I didn't have time now for an American padlock. One of those days. I counted to ten in Italian, and started back upstairs with even less enthusiasm than before.

I could hear a heavy tread ahead of me and guessed it was my anonymous visitor. When I got to the top, I quietly opened the stairwell door and watched him in the dim light. He was knocking at my office door. I couldn't see him very well, but got the impression of a short stocky man. He held himself aggressively, and when he got no answer to his knocking, he opened the door without hesitation and went inside. I walked down the hallway and went in after him.

A five-foot-high sign from Arnie's Steak Joynt flashed red and yellow across the street, providing spasms of light to my office. I saw my visitor whirl as I opened the door. "I'm looking for V. I. Warshawski," he said, his voice husky but confident—the voice of a man used to having his own way.

"Yes," I said, going past him to sit behind my desk.

"Yes, what?" he demanded.

"Yes, I'm V. I. Warshawski. You call my answering service for an appointment?"

"Yeah, but I didn't know it would mean walking up four flights of stairs to a dark office. Why the hell doesn't the elevator work?"

"The tenants in this building are physical fitness nuts. We agreed to get rid of the elevator—climbing stairs is well known as a precaution against heart attacks."

In one of the flashes from Arnie's I saw him make an angry gesture. "I didn't come here to listen to a comedienne," he said, his husky voice straining. "When I ask questions I expect to hear them answered."

"In that case, ask reasonable questions. Now, do you want to tell me why you need a private investigator?"

"I don't know. I need help all right, but this place—Jesus—and why is it so dark in here?"

"The lights are out," I said, my temper riding me. "You don't like my looks, leave. I don't like anonymous callers, either."

"All right, all right," he said placatingly. "Simmer down. But do we have to sit in the dark?"

I laughed. "A fuse blew a few minutes before you showed up. We can go over to Arnie's Steak Joynt if you want some light." I wouldn't have minded getting a good look at him myself.

He shook his head. "No, we can stay here." He fidgeted around some, then sat in one of the visitors' chairs.

"You got a name?" I asked, to fill in the pause while he collected his thoughts.

"Oh, yeah, sorry," he said, fumbling in his wallet. He pulled out a card and passed it across the desk. I held it up to read in a flash from Arnie's. "John L. Thayer. Executive Vice-President, Trust, Ft. Dearborn Bank and Trust." I pursed my lips. I didn't make it over to La Salle Street very often, but John Thayer was a very big name indeed at Chicago's biggest bank. Hot diggity, I thought. Play this fish right, Vic, I urged myself. Here come de rent!

I put the card in my jeans pocket. "Yes, Mr. Thayer. Now what seems to be the problem?"

"Well, it's about my son. That is, it's about his girl friend. At least she's the one who—" He stopped. A lot of people, especially men, aren't used to sharing their problems, and it takes them a while to get going. "You know, I don't mean any offense, but I'm not sure I should talk to you after all. Not unless you've got a partner or something."

I didn't say anything.

"You got a partner?" he persisted.

"No, Mr. Thayer," I said evenly. "I don't have a partner."

"Well, this really isn't a job for a girl to take on alone."

A pulse started throbbing in my right temple. "I skipped dinner after a long day in the heat to meet you down here." My voice was husky with anger. I cleared my throat and tried to steady myself. "You wouldn't even identify yourself until I pushed you to it. You pick at my office, at me, but you can't come out and ask anything directly. Are you trying to find out whether I'm honest, rich, tough, or what? You want some references, ask for them. But don't waste my time like this. I don't need to argue you into hiring my services—it was you who insisted on making an appointment for the middle of the night."

"I'm not questioning your honesty," he said quickly. "Look, I'm not trying to get your goat. But you are a girl, and things may get heavy."

"I'm a woman, Mr. Thayer, and I can look out for myself. If I couldn't, I wouldn't be in this kind of business. If things get heavy, I'll figure out a way to handle them—or go down trying. That's my problem, not yours. Now, you want to tell me about your son, or can I go home where I can turn on an air conditioner?"

He thought some more, and I took some deep breaths to calm myself, ease the tension in my throat.

"I don't know," he finally said. "I hate to, but I'm running out of options." He looked up, but I couldn't see his face. "Anything I tell you has to be strictly in confidence."

"Righto, Mr. Thayer," I said wearily. "Just you, me, and Arnie's Steak Joynt."

He caught his breath but remembered he was trying to be conciliatory. "It's really Anita, my son's girl friend. Not that Pete—my son, that is— hasn't been a bit of a problem, too."

Dope, I thought morosely. All these North Shore types think about is dope. If it was a pregnancy, they'd just pay for an abortion and be done with it. However, mine was not to pick and choose, so I grunted encouragingly.

"Well, this Anita is not really a very desirable type, and ever since Pete got mixed up with her he's been having some peculiar ideas." The language sounded strangely formal in his husky voice.

"I'm afraid I only detect things, Mr. Thayer. I can't do too much about what the boy thinks."

"No, no, I know that. It's just that—they've been living together in some disgusting commune or other—did I tell you they're students at the University of Chicago? Anyway, he, Pete, he's taken to talking about becoming a union organizer and not going to business school, so I went down to talk to the girl. Make her see reason, kind of."

"What's her last name, Mr. Thayer?"

"Hill. Anita Hill. Well, as I said, I went down to try to make her see reason. And—right after that she disappeared."

"It sounds to me like your problem's solved."

"I wish it was. The thing is, now Pete's saying I bought her off, paid her to disappear. And he's threatening to change his name and drop out of sight unless she turns up again."

Now I've heard everything, I thought. Hired to find a person so her boyfriend would go to business school.

"And were you responsible for her disappearance, Mr. Thayer?"

"Me? If I was, I'd be able to get her back."

"Not necessarily. She could have squeezed fifty grand out of you and gone off on her own so you couldn't get it back. Or you could have paid her to disappear completely. Or you may have killed her or caused her to be killed and want someone else to take the rap for you. A guy like you has a lot of resources."

He seemed to laugh a little at that. "Yeah, I suppose all that could be true. Anyway, I want you to find her—to find Anita."

"Mr. Thayer, I don't like to turn down work, but why not get the police —they're much better equipped than I for this sort of thing."

"The police and I—" he started, then broke off. "I don't feel like advertising my family problems to the police," he said heavily.

That had the ring of truth—but what had he started to say? "And why were you so worried about things getting heavy?" I wondered aloud.

He shifted in his chair a bit. "Some of those students can get pretty wild," he muttered. I raised my eyebrows skeptically, but he couldn't see that in the dark.

"How did you get my name?" I asked. Like an advertising survey—did you hear about us in *Rolling Stone* or through a friend?

"I found your name in the Yellow Pages. And I wanted someone in the Loop and someone who didn't know—my business associates."

"Mr. Thayer, I charge a hundred and a quarter a day, plus expenses. And I need a five-hundred-dollar deposit. I make progress reports, but clients don't tell me how to do the job—any more than your widows and orphans tell you how to run the Fort Dearborn's Trust Department."

"Then you will take the job?" he asked.

"Yes," I said shortly. Unless the girl was dead, it shouldn't be too hard to find her. "I'll need your son's address at the university," I added. "And a picture of the girl if you have one."

He hesitated over that, seemed about to say something, but then gave it to me: 5462 South Harper. I hoped it was the right place. He also produced a picture of Anita Hill. I couldn't make it out in the spasmodic light, but it looked like a yearbook snap. My client asked me to call him at home to report progress, rather than at the office. I jotted his home number on the business card and put it back in my pocket.

"How soon do you think you'll know something?" he asked.

"I can't tell you until I've looked at it, Mr. Thayer. But I'll get on the case first thing tomorrow."

"Why can't you go down there tonight?" he persisted.

"Because I have other things to do," I answered shortly. Like dinner and a drink.

He argued for a bit, not so much because he thought I'd change my mind as because he was used to getting his own way. He finally gave up on it and handed me five hundred-dollar bills.

I squinted at them in the light from Arnie's. "I take checks, Mr. Thayer."

"I'm trying to keep people at the office from knowing I've been to a detective. And my secretary balances my checkbook."

I was staggered, but not surprised. An amazing number of executives have their secretaries do that. My own feeling was that only God, the IRS, and my bank should have access to my financial transactions.

He got up to go and I walked out with him. By the time I'd locked the door, he had started down the stairs. I wanted to get a better look at him, and hurried after him. I didn't want to have to see every man in Chicago under a flashing neon sign to recognize my client again. The stairwell lighting wasn't that good, but under it his face appeared square and rugged. Irish-looking, I would have said, not what I would have thought of as second-in-command at the Fort Dearborn. His suit was expensive and well cut, but he looked more as if he'd stepped from an Edward G. Robinson movie than the nation's eighth largest bank. But then, did I look like a detective? Come to think of it, most people don't try to guess what women do for a living by the way they look—but they are usually astounded to find out what I do.

My client turned east, toward Michigan Avenue. I shrugged and crossed the street to Arnie's. The owner gave me a double Johnnie Walker Black and a sirloin from his private collection.

2
DROPPING OUT
OF SCHOOL

I woke up early to a day that promised to be as hot and steamy as the one before. Four days out of seven, I try to force myself to get some kind of exercise. I'd missed the previous two days, hoping that the heat would break, but I knew I'd better get out this morning. When thirty is a fond memory, the more days that pass without exercise, the worse you feel going back to it. Then, too, I'm undisciplined in a way that makes it easier to exercise than to diet, and the running helps keep my weight down. It doesn't mean I love it, though, especially on mornings like this.

The five hundred dollars John Thayer had given me last night cheered me up considerably, and I felt good as I put on cutoffs and a T-shirt. The money helped take my mind off the thick air when I got outside. I did five easy miles

—over to the lake and around Belmont Harbor and back to my large, cheap apartment on Halsted. It was only 8:30, but I was sweating freely from running in the heat. I drank a tall glass of orange juice and made coffee before taking a shower. I left my running clothes on a chair and didn't bother with the bed. After all, I was on a job and didn't have time—besides, who was going to see it?

Over coffee and some smoked herring I tried to decide how to approach Peter Thayer about his missing girl friend. If his family disapproved of her, he would probably resent his father hiring a private detective to look into her disappearance. I'd have to be someone connected with the university— maybe in one of her classes wanting to borrow some notes? I looked pretty old for an undergraduate—and what if she wasn't registered for the summer quarter? Maybe I'd be from an underground journal, wanting her to do an article on something. Something on labor unions—Thayer had said she was trying to push Peter into being a union organizer.

I stacked my dishes by the sink and eyed them thoughtfully: one more day and I'd have to wash them. I took the garbage out, though—I'm messy but not a slob. Newspapers had been piling up for some time, so I took a few minutes to carry them out next to the garbage cans. The building super's son made extra money recycling paper.

I put on jeans and a yellow cotton top and surveyed myself in the mirror with critical approval. I look my best in the summer. I inherited my Italian mother's olive coloring, and tan beautifully. I grinned at myself. I could hear her saying, "Yes, Vic, you are pretty—but pretty is no good. Any girl can be pretty—but to take care of yourself you must have brains. And you must have a job, a profession. You must work." She had hoped I would be a singer and had trained me patiently; she certainly wouldn't have liked my being a detective. Nor would my father. He'd been a policeman himself. Polish in an Irish world. He'd never made it beyond sergeant, due partly to his lack of ambition, but also, I was sure, to his ancestry. But he'd expected great things of me. . . . My grin went a little sour in the mirror and I turned away abruptly.

Before heading to the South Side, I walked over to my bank to deposit the five hundreds. First things first. The teller took them without a blink—I couldn't expect everyone to be as impressed with them as I was.

It was 10:30 when I eased my Chevy Monza onto the Belmont entrance to Lake Shore Drive. The sky was already bleached out, and the waves reflected back a coppery sheen. Housewives, children, and detectives were the only people out this time of day; I coasted to Hyde Park in twenty-three minutes and parked on the Midway.

I hadn't been on campus in ten years, but the place hadn't changed much, not as much as I had. I'd read somewhere that the dirty, poverty-stricken collegiate appearance was giving way to the clean-cut look of the fifties. That movement had definitely passed Chicago by. Young people of indeterminate sex strolled by hand-in-hand or in groups, hair sticking out, sporting tattered cutoffs and torn work shirts—probably the closest contact any of them had with work. Supposedly a fifth of the student body came from homes with an annual income of fifty thousand dollars or more, but I'd hate to use looks to decide which fifth.

I walked out of the glare into cool stone halls and stopped at a campus phone to call the registrar. "I'm trying to locate one of your students, a Miss Anita Hill." The voice on the other end, old and creaky, told me to wait. Papers rustled in the background. "Could you spell that name?" I obliged. More rustling. The creaky voice told me they had no student by that name. Did that mean she wasn't registered for the summer quarter? It meant they had no student by that name. I asked for Peter Thayer and was a little surprised when she gave me the Harper address—if Anita didn't exist, why should the boy?

"I'm sorry to be so much trouble, but I'm his aunt. Can you tell me what classes he might be in today? He's not home and I'm only in Hyde Park for the day." I must have sounded benevolent, for Ms. Creaky condescended to tell me that Peter was not registered this summer, but that the Political Science Department in the college might be able to help me find him. I thanked her benevolently and signed off.

I frowned at the phone and contemplated my next move. If there was no Anita Hill, how could I find her? And if there was no Anita Hill, how come someone was asking me to find her? And why had he told me the two were students at the university, when the registrar showed no record of the girl? Although maybe he was mistaken about her being at the University of Chicago—she might go to Roosevelt and live in Hyde Park. I thought I should go to the apartment and see if anyone was home.

I went back to my car. It was stifling inside and the steering wheel burned my fingers. Among the papers on the backseat was a towel I'd taken to the beach a few weeks ago. I rummaged for it and covered the steering wheel with it. It had been so long since I'd been in the neighborhood that I got confused in the one-way streets, but I eventually made it to Harper. 5462 was a three-story building that had once been yellow brick. The entryway smelled like an el station—musty, with a trace of urine in the air. A bag labeled "Harold's Chicken Shack" had been crumpled and thrown in a corner, and a few picked bones lay near it. The inner door hung loosely in its frame. It probably hadn't had a lock for some time. Its paint, once brown, had chipped and peeled badly. I wrinkled my nose. I couldn't blame the Thayers too much if they didn't like the place their son lived in.

The names on the bell panel had been hand-printed on index cards and taped to the wall. Thayer, Berne, Steiner, McGraw, and Harata occupied a third-floor apartment. That must be the disgusting commune that had angered my client. No Hill. I wondered if he'd gotten Anita's last name wrong, or if she was using an assumed name. I rang the bell and waited. No response. I rang again. Still no answer.

It was noon now and I decided to take a break. The Wimpy's I remembered in the nearby shopping center had been replaced by a cool, attractive, quasi-Greek restaurant. I had an excellent crabmeat salad and a glass of Chablis and walked back to the apartment. The kids probably had summer jobs and wouldn't be home until five, but I didn't have anything else to do that afternoon besides trying to find my welching printer.

There was still no answer, but a scruffy-looking young man came out as I was ringing. "Do you know if anyone in the Thayer-Berne apartment is home?" I asked. He looked at me in a glazed way and mumbled that he hadn't seen any of them for several days. I pulled Anita's picture from my pocket and told him I was trying to track down my niece. "She should be home right now, but I'm wondering if I have the right address," I added.

He gave me a bored look. "Yeah, I think she lives here. I don't know her name."

"Anita," I said, but he'd already shuffled outside. I leaned against the wall and thought for a few minutes. I could wait until tonight to see who showed up. On the other hand, if I went in now, I might find out more on my own than I could by asking questions.

I opened the inside door, whose lock I'd noticed that morning was missing, and climbed quickly to the third floor. Hammered on the Thayer-Berne apartment door. No answer. Put my ear to it and heard the faint hum of a window air conditioner. Pulled a collection of keys from my pocket and after a few false starts found one that turned the lock back.

I stepped inside and quietly shut the door. A small hallway opened directly onto a living room. It was sparsely furnished with some large denim-covered pillows on the bare floor and a stereo system. I went over and looked at it—Kenwood turntable and JBL speakers. Someone here had money. My client's son, no doubt.

The living room led to a hallway with rooms on either side of it, boxcar style. As I moved down it, I could smell something rank, like stale garbage or a dead mouse. I poked my head into each of the rooms but didn't see anything. The hall ended in a kitchen. The smell was strongest there, but it took me a minute to see its source. A young man slumped over the kitchen table. I walked over to him. Despite the window air conditioner his body was in the early stages of decomposition.

The smell was strong, sweet, and sickening. The crabmeat and Chablis began a protest march in my stomach, but I fought back my nausea and carefully lifted the boy's shoulders. A small hole had been put into his forehead. A trickle of blood had come out of it and dried across his face, but his face wasn't damaged. The back of his head was a mess.

I lowered him carefully to the table. Something, call it my woman's intuition, told me I was looking at the remains of Peter Thayer. I knew I ought to get out of the place and call the cops, but I might never have another chance to look over the apartment. The boy had clearly been dead for some time—the police could wait another few minutes for him.

I washed my hands at the sink and went back down the hall to explore the bedrooms. I wondered just how long the body had been there and why none

of the inmates had called the police. The second question was partially answered by a list taped up next to the phone giving Berne's, Steiner's, and
Harata's summer addresses. Two of the bedrooms containing books and
papers but no clothes must belong to some combination of those three.

The third room belonged to the dead boy and a girl named Anita
McGraw. Her name was scrawled in a large, flowing hand across the flyleaves
of numerous books. On the dilapidated wooden desk was an unframed photo
of the dead boy and a girl out by the lake. The girl had wavy auburn hair and
a vitality and intenseness that made the photo seem almost alive. It was a
much better picture than the yearbook snap my client had given me last
night. A boy might give up far more than business school for a girl like that. I
wanted to meet Anita McGraw.

I looked through the papers, but they were impersonal—flyers urging
people to boycott non-union-made sheets, some Marxist literature, and the
massive number of notebooks and term papers to be expected in a student
apartment. I found a couple of recent pay stubs made out to Peter Thayer
from the Ajax Insurance Company stuffed in one drawer. Clearly the boy had
had a summer job. I balanced them on my hand for a minute, then pushed
them into my back jeans pocket. Wedged behind them were some other
papers, including a voter registration card with a Winnetka address on it. I
took that, too. You never know what may come in handy. I picked up the
photograph and left the apartment.

Once outside I took some gulping breaths of the ozone-laden air. I never
realized it could smell so good. I walked back to the shopping center and
called the twenty-first police district. My dad had been dead for ten years, but
I still knew the number by heart.

"Homicide, Drucker speaking," growled a voice.

"There's a dead body at Fifty-four sixty-two South Harper, apartment
three," I said.

"Who are you?" he snapped.

"Fifty-four sixty-two South Harper, apartment three," I repeated. "Got
that?" I hung up.

I went back to my car and left the scene. The cops might be all over me
later for leaving, but right now I needed to sort some things out. I made it
home in twenty-one minutes and took a long shower, trying to wash the
sight of Peter Thayer's head from my mind. I put on white linen slacks and a
black silk shirt—clean, elegant clothes to center me squarely in the world of
the living. I pulled the assortment of stolen papers from my back jeans pocket
and put them and the photograph into a big shoulder bag. I headed back
downtown to my office, ensconced my evidence in my wall safe, then
checked in with my answering service. There were no messages, so I tried the
number Thayer had given me. I rang three times and a woman's voice answered: "The number you have dialed—674-9133—is not in service at this
time. Please check your number and dial again." That monotonous voice
destroyed whatever faith I still had in the identity of my last night's visitor. I

was certain he was not John Thayer. Who was he, then, and why had he wanted me to find that body? And why had he brought the girl into it, then given her a phony name?

With an unidentified client and an identified corpse, I'd been wondering what my job was supposed to be—fall girl for finding the body, no doubt. Still . . . Ms. McGraw had not been seen for several days. My client might just have wanted me to find the body, but I had a strong curiosity about the girl.

My job did not seem to include breaking the news of Peter's death to his father, if his father didn't already know. But before I completely wrote off last night's visitor as John Thayer, I should get his picture. "Clear as you go" has ever been my motto. I pulled on my lower lip for a while in an agony of thought and finally realized where I could get a picture of the man with a minimum of fuss and bother—and with no one knowing I was getting it.

I locked the office and walked across the Loop to Monroe and La Salle. The Fort Dearborn Trust occupied four massive buildings, one on each corner of the intersection. I picked the one with gold lettering over the door, and asked the guard for the PR department.

"Thirty-second floor," he mumbled. "You got an appointment?" I smiled seraphically and said I did and sailed up thirty-two stories while he went back to chewing his cigar butt.

PR receptionists are always trim, well-lacquered, and dressed in the extreme of fashion. This one's form-fitting lavender jumpsuit was probably the most outlandish costume in the bank. She gave me a plastic smile and graciously tendered a copy of the most recent annual report. I stuck on my own plastic smile and went back to the elevator, nodded beneficently to the guard, and sauntered out.

My stomach still felt a little jumpy, so I took the report over to Rosie's Deli to read over ice cream and coffee. John L. Thayer, Executive Vice-President, Trust Division, was pictured prominently on the inside cover with some other bigwigs. He was lean, tanned, and dressed in banker's gray, and I did not have to see him under a neon light to know that he bore no resemblance to my last night's visitor.

I pulled some more on my lip. The police would be interviewing all the neighbors. One clue I had that they didn't, because I had taken it with me, was the boy's pay stubs. Ajax Insurance had its national headquarters in the Loop, not far from where I was now. It was three in the afternoon, not too late for business calls.

Ajax occupied all sixty floors of a modern glass-and-steel skyscraper. I'd always considered it one of the ugliest buildings downtown from the outside. The lower lobby was drab, and nothing about the interior made me want to reverse my first impression. The guard here was more aggressive than the one at the bank, and refused to let me in without a security pass. I told him I had an appointment with Peter Thayer and asked what floor he was on.

"Not so fast, lady," he snarled. "We call up, and *if* the gentleman is here, he'll authorize you."

"Authorize me? You mean he'll authorize my entry. He doesn't have any authority over my existence."

The guard stomped over to his booth and called up. The news that Mr. Thayer wasn't in today didn't surprise me. I demanded to talk to someone in his office. I was tired of being feminine and conciliatory, and made myself menacing enough that I was allowed to speak to a secretary.

"This is V. I. Warshawski," I said crisply. "Mr. Thayer is expecting me."

The soft female voice at the other end apologized, but "Mr. Thayer hasn't been in all week. We've even tried calling him at home, but no one answers."

"Then I think I'd better talk to someone else in your office." I kept my voice hard. She wanted to know what my business was.

"I'm a detective," I said. "Something rotten's going on which young Thayer wanted to talk to me about. If he's not in, I'll talk to someone else who knows his job." It sounded pretty thin to me, but she put me on hold and went off to consult someone. Five minutes later, the guard still glaring at me and fingering his gun, the soft-voiced female came back on the line, rather breathless. Mr. Masters, the Claim Department vice-president, would talk to me.

The guard hated letting me go up—he even called back up to Ms. Softy, in hopes I was lying. But I finally made it to the fortieth floor. Once off the elevator, my feet sank deep into green pile. I made my way through it to a reception area at the south end of the hall. A bored receptionist left her novel and shunted me to the soft-voiced young woman, seated at a teak desk with a typewriter to one side. She in turn ushered me in to see Masters.

Masters had an office big enough for the Bears to work out in, with a magnificent view of the lake. His face had the well-filled, faintly pink look a certain type of successful businessman takes on after forty-five, and he beamed at me above a well-cut gray summer suit. "Hold my calls, Ellen," he said to the secretary as she walked out.

I gave him my card as we exchanged firm handshakes.

"Now what was it you wanted, Miss—ah—?" He smiled patronizingly.

"Warshawski. I want to see Peter Thayer, Mr. Masters. But as he's apparently not in and you've agreed to see me, I'd like to know why the boy felt he needed a private detective."

"I really couldn't tell you that, Miss—ah—do you mind if I call you—" He looked at the card. "What does the *V* stand for?"

"My first name, Mr. Masters. Maybe you can tell me what Mr. Thayer does here."

"He's my assistant," Masters obliged genially. "Jack Thayer is a good friend of mine, and when his boy—who's a student at the University of Chicago—needed summer work, I was glad to help out." He adjusted his features to look sorrowful. "Certainly if the boy is in the kind of trouble that it takes a detective to solve, I think I should know about it."

"What kinds of things does Mr. Thayer do as your assistant? Settle claims?"

"Oh, no," he beamed. "That's all done at our field locations. No, we handle the business side of the business—budgets, that kind of thing. The boy adds up figures for me. And he does good staff work—reviews reports, et cetera. He's a good boy—I hope he's not in trouble with those hippies he runs around with down there." He lowered his voice. "Between you and me, Jack says they've given him a bad idea of the business world. The big point about this summer job was to give him a better picture of the business world from the inside."

"And has it?" I asked.

"I'm hopeful, Miss—ah—I'm hopeful." He rubbed his hands together. "I certainly wish I could help you. . . . If you could give me a clue about what was bothering the boy?"

I shook my head. "He didn't say . . . Just called me and asked if I could stop by this afternoon. There wouldn't be anything going on here that he'd feel would require a detective, would there?"

"Well, a department head often doesn't know what's going on in his own department." Masters frowned importantly. "You're too remote—people don't confide in you." He smiled again. "But I'd be very surprised."

"Why did you want to see me?" I asked.

"Oh, I promised Jack Thayer I'd keep an eye on his boy, you know. And when a private detective comes around, it sounds kind of serious. Still, I wouldn't worry about it too much, Miss—ah—although maybe we could hire you to find out where Peter's gone." He chuckled at his joke. "He hasn't been in all week, you know, and we can't reach him at home. I haven't told Jack yet—he's disappointed enough in the boy as it is."

He ushered me down the hall and back to the elevator. I rode down to the thirty-second floor, got off, and rode back up. I strolled back down the hall.

"I'd like to see where young Thayer sits," I told Ellen. She looked at Masters's door for guidance, but it was shut.

"I don't think—"

"Probably not," I interrupted. "But I'm going to look around his desk anyway. I can always get someone else to tell me where it is."

She looked unhappy, but took me over to a partitioned cubicle. "You know, I'm going to be in trouble if Mr. Masters comes out and finds you here," she said.

"I don't see why," I told her. "It's not your fault. I'll tell him you did your best to force me off the floor."

Peter Thayer's desk was unlocked. Ellen stood watching me for a few minutes as I pulled open the drawers and sorted through the papers. "You can search me on my way out to see if I've taken anything," I told her without looking up. She sniffed, but walked back to her own desk.

These papers were as innocuous as those in the boy's apartment. Numerous ledger sheets with various aspects of the department's budget added up, a sheaf of computer printouts that dealt with Workers Compensation case estimates, correspondence to Ajax claim handlers—"Dear Mr. So-and-So, please verify the case estimates for the following claimants." Nothing you'd murder a boy for.

I was scratching my head over these slim pickings, wondering what to do next, when I realized someone was watching me. I looked up. It wasn't the secretary.

"You're certainly a lot more decorative than young Thayer," my observer remarked. "You taking his place?"

The speaker was in his shirt-sleeves, a man in his thirties who didn't have to be told how good-looking he was. I appreciated his narrow waist and the way his Brooks Brothers trousers fit.

"Does anyone around here know Peter Thayer at all well?" I asked.

"Yardley's secretary is making herself sick over him, but I don't know whether she knows him." He moved closer. "Why the interest? Are you with the IRS? Has the kid omitted taxes on some of the vast family holdings deeded to him? Or absconded with Claim Department funds and made them over to the revolutionary committee?"

"You're in the right occupational ball park," I conceded, "and he has, apparently, disappeared. I've never talked to him," I added carefully. "Do you know him?"

"Better than most people around here." He grinned cheerfully and seemed likable despite his arrogance. "He supposedly did legwork for Yardley—Yardley Masters—you were just seen talking to him. I'm Yardley's budget manager."

"How about a drink?" I suggested.

He looked at his watch and grinned again.

"You've got a date, little lady."

His name was Ralph Devereux. He was a suburbanite who had only recently moved to the city, following a divorce that left his wife in possession of their Downers Grove house, he informed me in the elevator. The only Loop bar he knew was Billy's, where the Claim Department hung out. I suggested the Golden Glow a little farther west, to avoid the people he knew. As we walked down Adams Street, I bought a *Sun-Times*.

The Golden Glow is an oddity in the South Loop. A tiny saloon dating back to the last century, it still has a mahogany horseshoe-shaped bar where serious drinkers sit. Eight or nine little tables and booths are crammed in along the walls, and a couple of real Tiffany lamps, installed when the place was built, provide a homey glow. Sal, the bartender, is a magnificent black woman, close to six feet tall. I've watched her break up a fight with just a word and a glance—no one messes with Sal. This afternoon she wore a silver pantsuit. Stunning.

She greeted me with a nod and brought a shot of Black Label to the booth. Ralph ordered a gin-and-tonic. Four o'clock is a little early, even for the Golden Glow's serious-drinking clientele, and the place was mostly deserted.

Devereux placed a five-dollar bill on the table for Sal. "Now tell me why a gorgeous lady like yourself is interested in a young kid like Peter Thayer."

I gave him back his money. "Sal runs a tab for me," I explained. I thumbed through the paper. The story hadn't come in soon enough for the front page, but they'd given it two quarter columns on page seven. RADICAL BANKING HEIR SHOT, the headline read. Thayer's father was briefly mentioned in the last paragraph; his four roommates and their radical activities were given the most play. The Ajax Insurance Company was not mentioned at all.

I folded the paper back and showed the column to Devereux. He glanced at it briefly, then did a double take and snatched the paper from me. I watched him read the story. It was short and he must have gone through it several times. Then he looked up at me, bewildered.

"Peter Thayer? Dead? What is this?"

"I don't know. I'd like to find out."

"You knew when you bought the paper?"

I nodded. He glanced back down at the story, then at me. His mobile face looked angry.

"How did you know?"

"I found the body."

"Why the hell didn't you tell me over at Ajax instead of putting me through this charade?" he demanded.

"Well, anyone could have killed him. You, Yardley Masters, his girl friend . . . I wanted to get your reaction to the news."

"Who the hell *are* you?"

"My name's V. I. Warshawski. I'm a private detective and I'm looking into Peter Thayer's death." I handed him a business card.

"You? You're no more a detective than I am a ballet dancer," he exclaimed.

"I'd like to see you in tights and a tutu," I commented, pulling out the plastic-encased photostat of my private investigator's license. He studied it, then shrugged without speaking. I put it back in my wallet.

"Just to clear up the point, Mr. Devereux, did you kill Peter Thayer?"

"No, I goddamn did not kill him." His jaw worked angrily. He kept starting to talk, then stopping, unable to put his feelings into words.

I nodded at Sal and she brought us a couple more drinks. The bar was beginning to fill up with precommute drinkers. Devereux drank his second gin and relaxed somewhat. "I'd like to have seen Yardley's face when you asked him if he killed Peter," he commented dryly.

"I didn't ask him. I couldn't figure out why he wanted to talk to me, though. Was he really very protective of Thayer? That's what he intimated."

"No." He considered the question. "He didn't pay much attention to him. But there was the family connection. . . . If Peter was in trouble, Yardley'd feel he owed it to John Thayer to look after him. . . . Dead . . . he was a hell of a nice boy, his radical ideas notwithstanding. Jesus, this is going to cut up Yardley. His old man, too. Thayer didn't like the kid living where he did—and now, shot by some junkie . . ."

"How do you know his father didn't like it?"

"Oh, it wasn't any secret. Shortly after Pete started with us, Jack Thayer came storming in showing his muscle and bellowing around like a vice-president in heat—how the kid was betraying the family with his labor-union talk, and why couldn't he live in a decent place—I guess they'd bought a condo for him down there, if you can believe that. I must say, the boy took it very well—didn't blow up back or anything."

"Did he work with any—well, highly confidential—papers at Ajax?"

Devereux was surprised. "You're not trying to link his death with Ajax, are you? I thought it was pretty clear that he was shot by one of those drug addicts who are always killing people in Hyde Park."

"You make Hyde Park sound like the site of the Tong Wars, Mr. Devereux. Of the thirty-two murders in the twenty-first police district last year, only six were in Hyde Park—one every two months. I don't think Peter Thayer is just the neighborhood's July–August statistic."

"Well, what makes you think it's connected with Ajax, then?"

"I don't think so. I'm just trying to eliminate possibilities. . . . Have you ever seen a dead body—or at least a body that got that way because of a bullet?" He shook his head and moved defensively in his chair. "Well, I have. And you can often tell from the way the body lies whether the victim was trying to fight off the attacker. Well, this boy was sitting at his kitchen table in a white shirt—probably ready to come down here Monday morning—and someone put a little hole smack in the middle of his head. Now a professional might have done that, but even so, he'd have to bring along someone whom the boy knew to get his confidence. It could've been you, or Masters, or his father, or his girl friend. . . . I'm just trying to find out why it couldn't be you."

He shook his head. "I can't do anything to prove it. Except that I don't know how to handle a gun—but I'm not sure I could prove that to you."

I laughed. "You probably could. . . . What about Masters?"

"Yardley? Come on! The guy's one of the most respected people you could hope to find at Ajax."

"That doesn't preclude his being a murderer. Why don't you let me know more about what Peter did there."

He protested some more, but he finally agreed to tell me about his work and what Peter Thayer had done for him. It just didn't seem to add up to murder. Masters was responsible for the financial side of the claim operation, reserving and so on, and Peter had added up numbers for him, checking office copies of issued drafts against known reserves for various claims, adding up overhead items in the field offices to see where they were going over budget, and all the dull day-to-day activities that businesses need in order to keep on going. And yet . . . and yet . . . Masters had agreed to see me, an unknown person, and a detective besides, on the spur of the moment. If he hadn't known Peter was in trouble—or even, maybe, known he was dead—I just couldn't believe his obligation to John Thayer would make him do that.

I contemplated Devereux. Was he just another pretty face, or did he know anything? His anger had seemed to me the result of genuine shock and bewilderment at finding out the boy was dead. But anger was a good cover for other emotions too. . . . For the time being I decided to classify him as an innocent bystander.

Devereux's native Irish cockiness was starting to return—he began teasing me about my job. I felt I'd gotten all I could from him until I knew enough to ask better questions, so I let the matter drop and moved on to lighter subjects.

I signed the bar tab for Sal—she sends me a bill once a month—and went on to the Officer's Mess with Devereux for a protracted meal. It's Indian, and to my mind one of the most romantic restaurants in Chicago. They make a very nice Pimm's Cup, too. Coming on top of the Scotch, it left me with a muzzy impression of dancing at a succession of North Side discos. I might have had a few more drinks. It was after one when I returned, alone, to my apartment. I was glad just to fling my clothes onto a chair and fall into bed.

3

THAT PROFESSIONAL TOUCH

Peter Thayer was protesting capitalist oppression by running wildly up and down the halls at Ajax, while Anita McGraw stood to one side carrying a picket sign and smiling. Ralph Devereux came out of his office and shot Thayer. The shot reverberated in the halls. It kept ringing and ringing and I tried seizing the gun from Devereux and throwing it away, but the sound continued and I jerked awake. The doorbell was shrilling furiously. I slid out of bed and pulled on jeans and a shirt as a loud knock sounded. The fuzziness in my mouth and eyes told me I'd had one or two Scotches too many too late in the evening before. I stumbled to the front room and looked through the peephole as heavy fists hammered the door again.

Two men were outside, both beefy, with jacket sleeves too short and hair crew-cut. I didn't know the younger one on the right, but the older one on the left was Bobby Mallory, Homicide lieutenant from the twenty-first district. I fumbled the lock open and tried to smile sunnily.

"Morning, Bobby. What a nice surprise."

"Good morning, Vicki. Sorry to drag you out of bed," Mallory said with heavy humor.

"Not at all, Bobby—I'm always glad to see you." Bobby Mallory had been my dad's closest friend on the force. They'd started on the same beat together back in the thirties, and Bobby hadn't forgotten Tony even after promotions had moved him out of my dad's work life. I usually have Thanksgiving dinner with him and Eileen, his warmly maternal wife. And his six children and four grandchildren.

Most of the time Bobby tries to pretend I'm not working, or at least not working as an investigator. Now he was looking past me, not at me. "This is Sergeant John McGonnigal," he said heartily, waving his arm loosely in McGonnigal's direction. "We'd like to come in and ask you a few questions."

"Certainly," I said politely, wishing my hair weren't sticking out in different directions all over my head. "Nice to meet you, Sergeant. I'm V. I. Warshawski."

McGonnigal and I shook hands and I stood back to let them into the small entryway. The hallway behind us leads straight back to the bathroom, with the bedroom and living rooms opening off to the right, and the dining room and kitchen to the left. This way in the mornings I can stumble straight from bedroom to bathroom to kitchen.

I took Bobby and McGonnigal to the kitchen and put on some coffee. I casually whisked some crumbs off the kitchen table and rummaged in the refrigerator for pumpernickel and cheddar cheese. Behind me, Bobby said, "You ever clean up this dump?"

Eileen is a fanatical housekeeper. If she didn't love to watch people eat, you'd never see a dirty dish in their house. "I've been working," I said with what dignity I could muster, "and I can't afford a housekeeper."

Mallory looked around in disgust. "You know, if Tony had turned you over his knee more often instead of spoiling you rotten, you'd be a happy housewife now, instead of playing at detective and making it harder for us to get our job done."

"But I'm a happy detective, Bobby, and I made a lousy housewife." That was true. My brief foray into marriage eight years ago had ended in an acrimonious divorce after fourteen months: some men can only admire independent women at a distance.

"Being a detective is not a job for a girl like you, Vicki—it's not fun and games. I've told you this a million times. Now you've got yourself messed up in a murder. They were going to send Althans out to talk to you, but I pulled my rank to get the assignment. That still means you've got to talk. I want to know what you were doing messing around with the Thayer boy."

"Thayer boy?" I echoed.

"Grow up, Vicki," Mallory advised. "We got a pretty good description of you from that doped-out specimen on the second floor you talked to on your way into the building. Drucker, who took the squeal, thought it might be your voice when he heard the description. . . . And you left your thumb-print on the kitchen table."

"I always said crime didn't pay, Bobby. You guys want some coffee or eggs or anything?"

"We already ate, clown. Working people can't stay in bed like sleeping beauty."

It was only 8:10, I noticed, looking at the wooden clock next to the back door. No wonder my head felt so woolly. I methodically sliced cheese, green peppers, and onions, put them on the pumpernickel, and put the open-faced sandwich under the broiler. I kept my back to Bobby and the sergeant while I waited for the cheese to melt, then transferred the whole thing to a plate and poured myself a cup of coffee. From his breathing I could tell Bobby's temper was mounting. His face was red by the time I put my food on the table and straddled a chair opposite him.

"I know very little about the Thayer boy, Bobby," I apologized. "I know he used to be a student at the University of Chicago, and that he's dead now. And I knew he's dead because I read it in the *Sun-Times.*"

"Don't be cute with me, Vicki; you know he's dead because you found the body."

I swallowed a mouthful of toasted cheese and green pepper. "Well, I assumed after reading the *Sun-Times* story that the boy was Thayer, but I certainly didn't know that when I saw the body. To me, he seemed to be just another corpse. Snuffed out in the springtime of life," I added piously.

"Spare me his funeral oration and tell me what brought you down there," Mallory demanded.

"You know me, Bobby—I have an instinct for crime. Where evil flourishes, there I will be, on my self-appointed mission to stamp it out."

Mallory turned redder. McGonnigal coughed diffidently and changed the subject before his boss hemorrhaged. "Do you have a client of some kind, Miss Warshawski?" he asked.

Of course I'd seen this one coming, but I still wasn't sure what I wanted to do. However, she who hesitates is lost in the detective biz, so I opted for partial disclosure.

"I was hired to get Peter Thayer to agree to go to business school." Mallory choked. "I'm not lying, Bobby," I said earnestly. "I went down there to meet the kid. And the door to his apartment was open, so I—"

"When you got there or after you'd picked the lock?" Mallory interrupted.

"So I went in," I continued. "Anyway, I guess I failed in my assignment, since I don't think Peter Thayer will ever go to business school. I'm not sure I still have a client."

"Who hired you, Vicki?" Mallory was talking more quietly now. "John Thayer?"

"Now why would John Thayer want to hire me, Bobby?"

"You tell me that, Vicki. Maybe he wanted some dirt to use as a lever to pry the kid off those potheads down there."

I swallowed the rest of my coffee and looked at Mallory squarely. "A guy came to me night before last and told me he was John Thayer. He wanted me to find his son's girl friend, Anita. Anita Hill."

"There's no Anita Hill in that setup," McGonnigal volunteered. "There's an Anita McGraw. It looks like he was sharing a room with a girl, but the whole setup is so unisex you can't tell who was with who."

"Whom," I said absently. McGonnigal looked blank. "You can't tell who was with *whom*, Sergeant," I explained. Mallory made explosive noises. "Anyway," I added hastily, "I was beginning to suspect that the guy had sent me on a wild-goose chase when I found there was no Anita Hill at the university. Later I was sure of it."

"Why?" Mallory demanded.

"I got a copy of Thayer's picture from the Fort Dearborn Bank and Trust. He wasn't my client."

"Vicki," Mallory said. "I think you're a pain in the butt. I think Tony would turn in his grave if he knew what you were doing. But you're not a fool. Don't tell me you didn't ask for any identification."

"He gave me his card and his home phone and a retainer. I figured I could get back to him."

"Let me see the card," Mallory demanded. Suspicious bastard.

"It's his card," I said.

"Could I please see it anyway." Tone of father barely restraining himself with recalcitrant child.

"It won't tell you anything it didn't tell me, Bobby."

"I don't believe he gave you a card," Mallory said. "You knew the guy and you're covering for him."

I shrugged and went to the bedroom and got the card out of my top drawer. I wiped it clean of prints with a scarf and brought it back to Mallory. The Fort Dearborn logo was in the lower left-hand corner. "John L. Thayer, Executive Vice-President, Trust" was in the middle, with his phone number. On the bottom I had scribbled the alleged home number.

Mallory grunted with satisfaction and put it in a plastic bag. I didn't tell him the only prints on it at this point were mine. Why spoil one of his few pleasures?

Mallory leaned forward. "What are you going to do next?"

"Well, I don't know. I got paid some money to find a girl and I feel like I ought to find her."

"You going to ask for a revelation, Vicki?" Mallory said with heavy humor. "Or do you have something to go on?"

"I might talk to some people."

"Vicki, if you know anything that you're not telling me in connection with this murder—"

"You'll be the first to know, Bobby," I promised. That wasn't exactly a lie, because I didn't know for sure that Ajax was involved in the murder—but we all have our own ideas on what's connected to what.

"Vicki, we're on the case. You don't have to prove anything to me about how cute or clever you are. But do me a favor—do a favor for Tony—let Sergeant McGonnigal and me find the murderer."

I stared limpidly at Bobby. He leaned forward earnestly. "Vicki, what did you notice about the body?"

"He'd been shot, Bobby. I didn't do a postmortem."

"Vicki, for two cents I'd kick you in your cute little behind. You've made a career out of something which no nice girl would touch, but you're no dummy. I know when you—got yourself into that apartment—and we'll overlook just how you got in there right now—you didn't scream or throw up, the way any decent girl would. You looked the place over. And if something didn't strike you straight off about that corpus, you deserve to go out and get your head blown off."

I sighed and slouched back in the chair. "Okay, Bobby: the kid was set up. No dope-crazed radical fired that shot. Someone he knew, whom he would invite to sit down for a cup of coffee, had to be there. To my mind, a pro fired the shot, because it was perfectly done—just one bullet and right on the target—but someone he knew had to be along. Or it could have been an acquaintance who's a heck of a marksman. . . . You looking into his family?"

Mallory ignored my question. "I figured you'd work that out. It's because you're smart enough to see how dangerous this thing could be that I'm asking you to leave it alone." I yawned. Mallory was determined not to lose his temper. "Look, Vicki, stay out of that mess. I can smell organized crime, organized labor, a whole lot of organizations that you shouldn't mess with."

"You figure because the boy's got radical friends and waves some posters he's glued into organized labor? Come on, Bobby!"

Mallory's struggle between the desire to get me out of the Thayer case and the need to keep police secrets to himself showed on his face. Finally he said, "We have evidence that the kids were getting some of their posters from a firm which does most of the printing for the Knifegrinders."

I shook my head sorrowfully. "Terrible." The International Brotherhood of Knifegrinders was notorious for their underworld connections. They'd hired muscle in the rough-and-tumble days of the thirties and had never been able to get rid of them since. As a result most of their elections and a lot of their finances were corrupt and—and suddenly it dawned on me who my elusive client was, why Anita McGraw's name sounded familiar, and why the guy had picked me out of the Yellow Pages. I leaned farther back in my chair but said nothing.

Mallory's face turned red. "Vicki, if I find you crossing my path on this case, I'm going to run you in for your own good!" He stood so violently that his chair turned over. He motioned to Sergeant McGonnigal and the two slammed the door behind them.

I poured myself another cup of coffee and took it into the bathroom with me where I dumped a generous dollop of Azuree mineral salts into the tub and ran myself a hot bath. As I sank into it, the aftereffects of my late-night drinking seeping out of my bones, I recalled a night more than twenty years ago. My mother was putting me to bed when the doorbell rang and the man who lived in the apartment below us staggered in. A burly man my dad's age, maybe younger—all big men seem old to little girls. I'd peeped around the door because everyone was making such a commotion and seen him covered with blood before my mother rounded on me and hustled me into the bedroom. She stayed there with me and together we heard snatches of conversation: The man had been shot, possibly by management-hired thugs, but he was afraid to go the police officially because he'd hired thugs himself, and would my dad help him.

Tony did, fixing up the wound. But he ordered him—unusual in a man usually so gentle—to leave the neighborhood and never come around to us again. The man was Andrew McGraw.

I'd never seen him again, never even connected him with the McGraw who was now president of Local 108 and hence, in effect, of the whole union. But he'd obviously remembered my dad. I guessed he'd tried to reach Tony at the police and, when he'd learned my dad was dead, had pulled me out of the Yellow Pages, assuming I would be Tony's son. Well, I wasn't: I was his daughter, and not the easygoing type my dad had been. I had my Italian mother's drive, and I try to emulate her insistence on fighting battles to the finish. But regardless of what kind of person *I* was, McGraw might be finding himself now in trouble of the kind that not even easygoing Tony would have helped him out of.

I drank some more coffee and flexed my toes in the water. The bath shimmered turquoise, but clear. I peered through it at my feet, trying to figure out what I knew. McGraw had a daughter. She probably loved him, since she seemed dedicated to the labor movement. Children usually do not espouse causes or careers of parents they hate. Had she disappeared, or was he hiding her? Did he know who had killed young Peter and had she run away because of this? Or did he think she'd killed the boy? Most murders, I reminded myself, were committed between loved ones, which made her statistically the odds-on favorite. What were McGraw's connections with the hired muscle with whom the International Brotherhood lived so cozily? How easily could he have hired someone to fire that shot? He was someone the boy would let in and talk to, no matter what their feelings for each other were, because McGraw was his girl friend's father.

The bathwater was warm, but I shivered as I finished my coffee.

4

YOU CAN'T SCARE ME (I'M STICKING TO THE UNION)

The headquarters of the International Brotherhood of Knifegrinders, Shear Edgers, and Blade Sharpeners is located on Sheridan Road just south of Evanston. The ten-story building was put up about five years ago, and is sided with white Italian marble. The only other building in Chicago built with such opulence is the headquarters for Standard of Indiana; I figured that put the brotherhood's excess profits on a par with those of the oil industry.

Local 108 headquarters was on the ninth floor. I gave the floor receptionist my card. "Mr. McGraw is expecting me," I told her. I was shunted down the north corridor. McGraw's secretary was guarding the entrance to a lakeside office in an antechamber that would have done Louis XIV proud. I wondered how the International Brothers felt when they saw what their dues had built for them. Or maybe there were some beaten-up offices lower down for entertaining the rank-and-file.

I gave my card to the secretary, a middle-aged woman with gray sausage curls and a red-and-white dress that revealed an unlovely sag in her upper arms. I keep thinking I should lift five-pound weights to firm up my triceps. Looking at her, I wondered if I would have time to stop at Stan's Sporting Goods on my way home to pick up some barbells.

"I have an appointment with Mr. McGraw."

"You're not in the book," she said abruptly, not really looking at me. I had on my navy raw silk suit, with the blouson jacket. I look stunning in this outfit and thought I deserved a little more attention. Must be those sagging triceps.

I smiled. "I'm sure you know as well as I do that Mr. McGraw conducts some of his business on his own. He arranged to see me privately."

"Mr. McGraw may sometimes take up with whores," she said, her face red, her eyes on her desk top, "but this is the first time he's ever asked one up to his office."

I restrained an impulse to brain her with her desk lamp. "Good-looking lady like you in his front office, he doesn't need outside talent. . . . Now will you please inform Mr. McGraw that I'm here?"

Her shapeless face shook under the thick pancake. "Mr. McGraw is in conference and can't be disturbed." Her voice trembled. I felt like a creep—I couldn't find a girl or a murderer, but I sure knew how to rough up middle-aged secretaries.

McGraw's office was soundproofed, but noise of the conference came into the antechamber. Quite a conference. I was about to announce my intention of sitting and waiting when one sentence rose above the din and penetrated the rosewood door.

"Goddamnit, you set my son up!"

How many people could possibly have sons who might have been set up in the last forty-eight hours and be connected with the Knifegrinders? Maybe more than one, but the odds were against it. With the sausage curls protesting loudly, I opened the door into the inner office.

Not as large as Masters's, but by no means shabby, it overlooked Lake Michigan and a nice little private beach. At the moment it was none too peaceful. Two men had been sitting at a round table in the corner, but one was on his feet yelling to make his point. Even with his face distorted by anger I didn't have any trouble recognizing the original of the picture in the Fort Dearborn Trust's annual report. And rising to his feet and yelling back as I entered was surely my client. Short, squat without being fat, and wearing a shiny gray suit.

They both stopped cold as they saw me.

"What the hell are you doing in here!" my client roared. "Mildred?"

Sausage curls waddled in, her eyes gleaming. "I told her you wouldn't want to see her, but no, she has to come barging in like she's—"

"Mr. McGraw, I am V. I. Warshawski." I pitched my voice to penetrate the din. "And you may not want to see me, but I look like an angel compared to a couple of homicide dicks who're going to be after you pretty soon. . . . Hi, Mr. Thayer," I added, holding out a hand. "I'm sorry about your son—I'm the person who found the body."

"It's all right, Mildred," McGraw said weakly. "I know this lady and I do want to talk to her." Mildred gave me a furious look, then turned and stalked out, shutting the door with what seemed unnecessary violence.

"Mr. Thayer, what makes you think Mr. McGraw set your son up?" I asked conversationally, seating myself in a leather armchair in a corner.

The banker had recovered himself. The anger had smoothed out of his face, leaving it dignified and blank. "McGraw's daughter was going out with my son," he said, smiling a little. "When I learned my boy was dead, had been shot, I just stepped in to see if McGraw knew anything about it. I don't think he set Peter up."

McGraw was too angry to play along with Thayer. "The hell you say," he yelled, his husky voice rising. "Ever since Annie started hanging around with that whey-faced, North Shore pipsqueak, you've been coming around here, calling her names, calling me names. Now the kid is dead, you're trying to smear her! Well, by God you won't get away with it!"

"All right!" Thayer snapped. "If that's the way you want to play ball, that's how we'll play it. Your daughter—I saw the kind of girl she was the first time I set eyes on her. Peter never had a chance—innocent young kid, high ideals, giving up everything his mother and I had planned for him for the sake of a girl who'd hop into bed with—"

"Watch what names you call my daughter," McGraw growled.

"I practically begged McGraw here to leash his daughter," Thayer continued. "I might as well have saved my pride. This type of person doesn't respond to any human feeling. He and his daughter had earmarked Peter for some kind of setup because he came from a wealthy family. Then, when they couldn't get any money out of him, they killed him."

McGraw was turning purple. "Have you shared this theory with the police, Mr. Thayer?" I asked.

"If you have, Thayer, I'll have your ass in court for slander," McGraw put in.

"Don't threaten me, McGraw," Thayer growled. John Wayne impersonation.

"Have you shared this theory with the police, Mr. Thayer?" I repeated.

He flushed slightly under his careful tan. "No, I didn't want it blurted all over the newspapers—I didn't want any of my neighbors to see what the boy was up to."

I nodded. "But you're really convinced that Mr. McGraw here—and/or his daughter—set up Peter and had him shot."

"Yes, I am, damnit!"

"And have you any evidence to support this allegation?" I asked.

"No, he doesn't, goddamnit!" McGraw yelled. "No one could support such a goddamn asshole statement! Anita was in love with that North Shore snot. I told her that it was a colossal mistake. Get involved with the bosses and you get your ass burned. And now look what's happened."

It seemed to me that the bosses had been the ones to get burned in this case, but I didn't think it would do any good to mention it.

"Did you give Mr. McGraw one of your business cards when you were here before?" I asked Thayer.

"I don't know," he said impatiently. "I probably gave one to his secretary when I arrived. Anyway, what business is it of yours?"

I smiled. "I'm a private investigator, Mr. Thayer, and I'm investigating a private matter for Mr. McGraw here. He showed me one of your business cards the other night, and I wondered where he got it."

McGraw shifted uncomfortably. Thayer stared at him with a look of disbelief. "You showed her one of my cards? Why the hell did you do that? For that matter, why were you talking to a private investigator at all?"

"I had my reasons." McGraw looked embarrassed, but he also looked mean.

"I bet you did," Thayer said heavily. He turned to me. "What are you doing for McGraw?"

I shook my head. "My clients pay for privacy."

"What kinds of things do you investigate?" Thayer asked. "Divorces?"

"Most people think of divorce when they meet a private detective. Frankly divorce is pretty slimy. I do a lot of industrial cases. . . . You know Edward Purcell, the man who used to be chairman of Transicon?"

Thayer nodded. "I know of him anyway."

"I did that investigation. He hired me because his board was pressuring him to find out where the disposable assets were going. Unfortunately he didn't cover his tracks well enough before he hired me." Purcell's subsequent suicide and the reorganization of a badly damaged Transicon had been a ten-day wonder in Chicago.

Thayer leaned over me. "In that case, what are you doing for McGraw?" He lacked McGraw's raw menace, but he, too, was a powerful man, used to intimidating others. The force of his personality was directed at me and I sat up straight to resist it.

"What business is it of yours, Mr. Thayer?"

He gave me the frown that got obedience from his junior trust officers. "If he gave you my card, it's my business."

"It didn't have anything to do with you, Mr. Thayer."

"That's right, Thayer," McGraw growled. "Now get your ass out of my office."

Thayer turned back to McGraw and I relaxed slightly. "You're not trying to smear me with any of your dirty business are you, McGraw?"

"Watch it, Thayer. My name and my operation have been cleared in every court in this country. In Congress too. Don't give me that crap."

"Yeah, Congress cleared you. Lucky, wasn't it, the way Derek Bernstein died right before the Senate hearings began."

McGraw walked right up to the banker. "You SOB. You get out of here now or I'll get some people to throw you out in a way that'll pop your high-and-mighty executive dignity for you."

"I'm not afraid of your thugs, McGraw; don't threaten me."

"Oh, come on," I snapped. "Both of you are tough as all get out, and you're both frightening me to pieces. So can you cut out this little-boy stuff? Why do you care so much about it, Mr. Thayer? Mr. McGraw here may have tossed a business card of yours around—but he hasn't tried to smear your name with his dirty business—if he's got dirty business. You got something on your conscience that's making you so upset? Or do you just have to prove you're the toughest guy in any crowd you're in?"

"Watch what you say to me, young lady. I've got a lot of powerful friends in this city, and they can—"

"That's what I mean," I interrupted. "Your powerful friends can take away my license. No doubt. But why do you care?"

He was silent for a minute. Finally he said, "Just be careful what you get into with McGraw here. The courts may have cleared him, but he's into a lot of ugly business."

"All right; I'll be careful."

He gave me a sour look and left.

McGraw looked at me approvingly. "You handled him just right, Warshawski."

I ignored that. "Why did you give me a fake name the other night, McGraw? And why did you give your daughter a different phony one?"

"How'd you find me, anyway?"

"Once I saw the McGraw name, it began stirring in the back of my mind. I remembered you from the night you were shot—it came back to me when Lieutenant Mallory mentioned the Knifegrinders. Why'd you come to me to begin with? You think my dad might help you out the way he did back then?"

"What are you talking about?"

"Oh, can it, McGraw. I was there. You may not remember me—but I remember you. You came in absolutely covered with blood and my dad fixed up your shoulder and got you out of the building. Did you think he'd help you out of whatever trouble you're in this time, until you found out he was dead? Then what—you found my name in the Yellow Pages and thought maybe I was Tony's son? Now, why did you use Thayer's name?"

The fight died down in him a bit. "I wasn't sure you'd do a job for me if you knew who I was."

"But why Thayer? Why drag in the senior guy in Chicago's biggest bank? Why not just call yourself Joe Blow?"

"I don't know. It was just an impulse, I guess."

"Impulse? You're not that dumb. He could sue you for slander or something, dragging his name in like that."

"Then why the hell did you let him know I'd done it? You're on my payroll."

"No, I'm not. You've hired me to do some independent professional work, but I'm not on your payroll. Which brings us to the original question: what'd you hire me for, anyway?"

"To find my daughter."

"Then why did you give her a false name? How could I possibly look for her? No. I think you hired me to find the body."

"Now, look here, Warshawski—"

"You look, McGraw. It's so obvious you knew the kid was dead. When did you find out? Or did you shoot him yourself?"

His eyes disappeared in his heavy face and he pushed close to me. "Don't talk smart with me, Warshawski."

My heart beat faster but I didn't back away. "When did you find the body?"

He stared at me another minute, then half-smiled. "You're no softie. I don't object to a lady with guts. . . . I was worried about Anita. She usually calls me on Monday evening, and when she didn't, I thought I should go down and check up on her. You know what a dangerous neighborhood that is."

"You know, Mr. McGraw, it continues to astonish me the number of people who think the University of Chicago is in an unsafe neighborhood. Why parents ever send their children to school there at all amazes me. Now let's have a little more honesty. You knew Anita had disappeared when you came to see me, or you would never have given me her picture. You are worried about her, and you want her found. Do you think she killed the boy?"

That got an explosive reaction. "No, I don't, goddamnit. If you must know, she came home from work Tuesday night and found his dead body. She called me in a panic, and then she disappeared."

"Did she accuse you of killing him?"

"Why should she do that?" He was bellicose but uncomfortable.

"I can think of lots of reasons. You hated young Thayer, thought your daughter was selling out to the bosses. So in a mistaken fit of paternal anxiety, you killed the kid, thinking it would restore your daughter to you. Instead—"

"You're crazy, Warshawski! No parent is that cuckoo."

I've seen lots of kookier parents but decided not to argue that point. "Well," I said, "you don't like that idea, try this one. Peter somehow got wind of some shady, possibly even criminal, activities that you and the Knifegrinders are involved in. He communicated his fears to Anita, but being in love he wouldn't welch on you to the cops. On the other hand, being young and idealistic, he had to confront you. And he couldn't be bought. You shot him—or had him shot—and Anita knew it had to be you. So she did a bunk."

McGraw's nerves were acting up again, but he blustered and bellowed and called me names. Finally he said, "Why in Sam Hill would I want you to find my daughter if all she'd do is finger me?"

"I don't know. Maybe you were playing the odds—figuring you've been close and she wouldn't turn on you. Trouble is, the police are going to be making the connection between you and Anita before too long. They know the kids had some tie-in with the brotherhood because there was some literature around the house created by your printer. They're not dummies, and everyone knows you're head of the union and they know there was a McGraw in the apartment.

"When they come around, they're not going to care about your daughter, or your relationship with her. They've got a murder to solve, and they'll be happy to tag you with it—especially with a guy in Thayer's position pressuring them. Now if you tell me what you know, I may—no promises, but *may*—be able to salvage you and your daughter—if you're not guilty, of course."

McGraw studied the floor for a while. I realized I'd been clutching the arms of the chair while I was talking and carefully relaxed my muscles. Finally he looked up at me and said, "If I tell you something, will you promise not to take it to the police?"

I shook my head. "Can't promise anything, Mr. McGraw. I'd lose my license if I kept knowledge of a crime to myself."

"Not that kind of knowledge, damnit! Goddamnit, Warshawski, you keep acting like I committed the goddamn murder or something." He breathed heavily for a few minutes. Finally he said, "I just want to tell you about— you're right. I did—I was—I did find the kid's body." He choked that out, and the rest came easier. "Annie—Anita—called me Monday night. She wasn't in the apartment, she wouldn't say where she was." He shifted a bit in his chair. "Anita's a good, levelheaded kid. She never got any special pampering as a child, and she grew up knowing how to be independent. She and I are, well, we're pretty close, and she's always been union all the way, but she's no clinging daddy's girl. And I never wanted her to be one.

"Tuesday night I hardly recognized her. She was pretty damn near hysterical, yelling a lot of half-assed stuff which didn't make any sense at all. But she didn't mention the kid's murder."

"What was she yelling?" I asked conversationally.

"Oh, just nonsense, I couldn't make anything out of it."

"Same song, second verse," I remarked.

"What?"

"Same as the first," I explained. "A little bit louder and a little bit worse."

"Once and for all, she didn't accuse me of killing Peter Thayer!" he yelled at the top of his lungs.

We weren't moving too quickly.

"Okay, she didn't accuse you of murdering Peter. Did she tell you about his being dead?"

He stopped for a minute. If he said yes, the next question was, why had the girl done a bunk if she didn't think McGraw had committed the murder? "No, like I said, she was just hysterical. She—Well, later, after I saw the body, I figured she was calling because of—of, well, that." He stopped again, but this time it was to collect some memories. "She hung up and I tried calling back, but there wasn't any answer, so I went down to see for myself. And I found the boy."

"How'd you get in?" I asked curiously.

"I have a key. Annie gave it to me when she moved in, but I'd never used it before." He fumbled in his pocket and pulled out a key. I looked at it and shrugged.

"That was Tuesday night?" He nodded. "And you waited 'til Wednesday night to come to see me?"

"I waited all day hoping that someone else would find the body. When no report came out—you were right, you know." He smiled ruefully, and his whole face became more attractive. "I hoped that Tony was still alive. I hadn't talked to him for years, he'd warned me off good and proper over the

Stellinek episode—didn't know old Tony had it in him—but he was the only guy I could think of who might help me."

"Why didn't you call the cops yourself?" I asked.

His face closed up again. "I didn't want to," he said shortly.

I thought about it. "You probably wanted your own source of information on the case, and you didn't think your police contacts could help you." He didn't disagree.

"Do the Knifegrinders have any pension money tied up with the Fort Dearborn Trust?" I asked.

McGraw turned red again. "Keep your goddamn mitts out of our pension fund, Warshawski. We have enough snoopers smelling around there to guarantee it grade A pure for the next century. I don't need you, too."

"Do you have any financial dealings with the Fort Dearborn Trust?"

He was getting so angry I wondered what nerve I'd touched, but he denied it emphatically.

"What about the Ajax Insurance Company?"

"Well, what about them?" he demanded.

"I don't know, Mr. McGraw—do you buy any insurance from them?"

"I don't know." His face was set and he was eyeing me hard and cold, the way he no doubt had eyed young Timmy Wright of Kansas City Local 4318 when Timmy had tried to talk to him about running a clean election down there. (Timmy had shown up in the Missouri River two weeks later.) It was much more menacing than his red-faced bluster. I wondered.

"Well, what about your pensions? Ajax is big in the pension business."

"Goddamnit, Warshawski, get out of the office. You were hired to find Anita, not to ask a lot of questions about something that isn't any of your goddamned business. Now get out and don't come back."

"You want me to find Anita?" I asked.

McGraw suddenly deflated and put his head in his hands. "Oh, jeez, I don't know what to do."

I looked at him sympathetically. "Someone got you in the squeeze?"

He just shook his head but wouldn't answer. We sat it out in silence for a while. Then he looked at me, and he looked gray. "Warshawski, I don't know where Annie is. And I don't want to know. But I want you to find her. And when you do, just let me know if she's all right. Here's another five hundred dollars to keep you on for a whole week. Come to me when it runs out." It wasn't a formal apology, but I accepted it and left.

I stopped at Barb's Bar-B-Q for some lunch and called my answering service. There was a message from Ralph Devereux at Ajax; would I meet him at the Cartwheel at 7:30 tonight. I called him and asked if he had discovered anything about Peter Thayer's work.

"Look," he said, "will you tell me your first name? How the hell can I keep on addressing someone as 'V.I.'?"

"The British do it all the time. What have you found out?"

"Nothing. I'm not looking—there's nothing to find. That kid wasn't working on sensitive stuff. And you know why—V.I.? Because insurance companies don't run to sensitive stuff. Our product, how we manufacture it, and what we charge for it are only regulated by about sixty-seven state and federal agencies."

"Ralph, my first name is Victoria; my friends call me Vic. Never Vicki. I know insurance isn't your high-sensitivity business—but it offers lots of luscious opportunities for embezzlement."

A pregnant silence. "No," he finally said, "at least—not here. We don't have any check-signing or authorizing responsibility."

I thought that one over. "Do you know if Ajax handles any of the Knifegrinders' pension money?"

"The Knifegrinders?" he echoed. "What earthly connection does that set of hoodlums have with Peter Thayer?"

"I don't know. But do you have any of their pension money?"

"I doubt it. This is an insurance company, not a mob hangout."

"Well, could you find out for me? And could you find out if they buy any insurance from you?"

"We sell all kinds of insurance, Vic—but not much that a union would buy."

"Why not?"

"Look," he said, "it's a long story. Meet me at the Cartwheel at seven thirty and I'll give you chapter and verse on it."

"Okay," I agreed. "But look into it for me, anyway. Please?"

"What's the *I* stand for?"

"None of your goddamn business." I hung up. *I* stood for Iphigenia. My Italian mother had been devoted to Victor Emmanuel. This passion and her love of opera had led her to burden me with an insane name.

I drank a Fresca and ordered a chef's salad. I wanted ribs and fries, but the memory of Mildred's sagging arms stopped me. The salad didn't do much for me. I sternly put French fries out of my mind and pondered events.

Anita McGraw had called up and—at a minimum—told her father about the murder. My bet was she'd accused him of being involved. Ergo, Peter had found out something disreputable about the Knifegrinders and had told her. He probably found it out at Ajax, but possibly from the bank. I loved the idea of pensions. The Loyal Alliance Pension Fund got lots of publicity for their handling, or mishandling, of Knifegrinder pension money, but twenty million or so could easily have been laid off on a big bank or insurance company. And pension money gave one so much scope for fraudulent activity.

Why had McGraw gone down to the apartment? Well, in the first place, he knew whatever discreditable secret Thayer had uncovered. He was afraid that Anita was probably in on it—young lovers don't keep much to themselves. And if she called up because she'd found her boyfriend with a hole in his head, McGraw probably figured she'd be next, daughter or no daughter.

So he went racing down to Hyde Park, terrified he'd find her dead body too. Instead she'd vanished. So far, so good.

Now if I could find Anita, I'd know the secret. Or if I found the secret, I could publicize it, which would take the heat off the girl and maybe persuade her to return. It sounded good.

What about Thayer, though? Why had McGraw used his card, and why had this upset him so much? Just the principle of the thing? I ought to talk to him alone.

I paid my bill and headed back to Hyde Park. The college Political Science Department was on the fourth floor of one of the older campus buildings. On a hot summer afternoon the hallways were empty. Through the windows along the stairwell I could see knots of students lying on the grass, some reading, some sleeping. A few energetic boys were playing Frisbee. An Irish setter loped around, trying to catch the disk.

A student was tending the desk in the department office. He looked about seventeen, his long blond hair hanging over his forehead, but no beard —he didn't appear ready to grow one yet. He was wearing a T-shirt with a hole under the left arm and was sitting hunched over a book. He looked up reluctantly when I said hello but kept the book open on his lap.

I smiled pleasantly and told him I was looking for Anita McGraw. He gave me a hostile look and turned back to his book without speaking.

"Come on. What's wrong with asking for her? She's a student in the department, right?" He refused to look up. I felt my temper rising, but I wondered if Mallory had been here before me. "Have the police been around asking for her?"

"You ought to know," he muttered, not looking up.

"You think just because I'm not wearing sloppy blue jeans I'm with the police?" I asked. "How about digging out a departmental course list for me?"

He didn't move. I stepped around to his side of the desk and pulled open a drawer.

"Okay, okay," he said huffily. He put the book spine up on the desk top. *Capitalism and Freedom,* by Marcuse. I might have guessed. He rummaged through the drawer and pulled out a nine-page list, typed and mimeographed, labeled "College Time Schedule: Summer 1979."

I flipped through it to the Political Science section. Their summer schedule filled a page. Class titles included such things as "The Concept of Citizenship in Aristotle and Plato"; "Idealism from Descartes Through Berkeley"; and "Super-power Politics and the Idea of *Weltverschwinden.*" Fascinating. Finally I found one that sounded more promising: "The Capitalist Standoff: Big Labor Versus Big Business." Someone who taught a course like that would surely attract a young labor organizer like Anita McGraw. And might even know who some of her friends were. The instructor's name was Harold Weinstein.

I asked the youth where Weinstein's office was. He hunched further into

Marcuse and pretended not to hear. I came around the desk again and sat on it facing him, and grabbed his shirt collar and jerked his face up so that I could see his eyes. "I know you think you're doing the revolution a great service by not revealing Anita's whereabouts to the pigs," I said pleasantly. "Perhaps when her body is found in a car trunk you will invite me to the party where you celebrate upholding your code of honor in the face of unendurable oppression." I shook him a bit. "Now tell me where to find Harold Weinstein's office."

"You don't have to tell her anything, Howard," someone said behind me. "And you," he said to me, "don't be surprised when students equate police with fascism—I saw you roughing up that boy."

The speaker was thin with hot brown eyes and a mop of unruly hair. He was wearing a blue work shirt tucked neatly into a pair of khaki jeans.

"Mr. Weinstein?" I said affably, letting go of Howard's shirt. He stared at me with his hands on his hips, brooding. It looked pretty noble. "I'm not with the police—I'm a private detective. And when I ask anyone a civil question, I like to get a civil answer, not an arrogant shrug of the shoulders.

"Anita's father, Andrew McGraw, hired me to find her. I have a feeling, which he shares, that she may be in bad trouble. Shall we go somewhere and talk about it?"

"You have a feeling, do you," he said heavily. "Well, go feel about it somewhere else. We don't like police—public or private—on this campus." He turned to stalk back down the corridor.

"Well executed," I applauded. "You've been studying Al Pacino. Now that you've finished emoting, could we talk about Anita?"

The back of his neck turned red, and the color spread to his ears, but he stopped. "What about her?"

"I'm sure you know she's disappeared, Mr. Weinstein. You may also know that her boyfriend, Peter Thayer, is dead. I am trying to find her in the hopes of keeping her from sharing his fate." I paused to let him absorb it. "My guess is that she's hiding out someplace and she thinks she won't be found by whoever killed him. But I'm afraid she's crossed the path of an ugly type of killer. The kind that has a lot of money and can buy his way past most hideouts."

He turned so that I could see his profile. "Don't worry, Philip Marlowe —they won't bribe me into revealing her whereabouts."

I wondered hopefully if he could be tortured into talking. Aloud, I said, "Do you know where she is?"

"No comment."

"Do you know any of her good friends around here?"

"No comment."

"Gee, you're helpful, Mr. Weinstein—you're my favorite prof. I wish you'd taught here when I went to school." I pulled out my card and gave it to him. "If you ever feel like commenting, call me at this number."

Back outside in the heat I felt depressed. My navy silk suit was stunning, but too heavy for the weather; I was sweating, probably ruining the fabric under the arms. Besides, I seemed to be alienating everyone whose path I crossed. I wished I'd smashed in Howard's face.

A circular stone bench faced the college building. I walked over to it and sat down. Maybe I'd give up on this stupid case. Industrial espionage was more my speed, not a corrupt union and a bunch of snotty kids. Maybe I'd use the thousand dollars McGraw had given me to spend the summer on the Michigan peninsula. Maybe that would make him angry enough to send someone after me with cement leggings.

The Divinity School was just behind me. I sighed, pulled myself to my feet, and moved into its stone-walled coolness. A coffee shop used to serve overboiled coffee and tepid lemonade in the basement. I made my way downstairs and found the place still in operation. There was something reassuring in this continuity and in the sameness of the young faces behind the makeshift counter. Kindly and naive, they preached a lot of violent dogma, believed that burglars had a right to the goods they took because of their social oppression, and yet would be rocked to their roots if someone ever required them to hold a machine gun themselves.

I took a Coke and retired to a dark corner with it. The chairs weren't comfortable, but I pulled my knees up to my chin and leaned against the wall. About a dozen students were seated around the wobbly tables, some of them trying to read in the dim light, most of them talking. Snatches of conversation reached me. "Of course if you're going to look at it dialectically, the only thing they can do is—" "I told her if she didn't put her foot down he'd—" "Yeah, but Schopenhauer says—" I dozed off.

I was jerked awake a few seconds later by a loud voice saying, "Did you *hear* about Peter Thayer?" I looked up. The speaker, a plump young woman with wild red hair, wearing an ill-fitting peasant blouse, had just come into the room. She dumped her book bag on the floor and joined a table of three in the middle of the room. "I was just coming out of class when Ruth Yonkers told me."

I got up and bought another Coke and sat down at a table behind the redhead.

A thin youth with equally wild but dark hair was saying, "Oh, yeah, the cops were all over the Political Science Office this morning. You know, he was living with Anita McGraw, and she hasn't been seen since Sunday. Weinstein really told them off," he added admiringly.

"Do they think she killed him?" the redhead asked.

A dark, somewhat older woman snorted. "Anita McGraw? I've known her for two years. She might off a cop, but she wouldn't shoot her boyfriend."

"Do you know him, Mary?" the redhead breathed.

"No," Mary answered shortly. "I never met him. Anita belongs to University Women United—that's how I know her. So does Geraldine Harata, her other roommate, but Geraldine's away for the summer. If she wasn't, the cops would probably suspect her. They always pick on women first."

"I'm surprised you let her into UWU if she has a boyfriend," a bearded young man put in. He was heavy and sloppy—his T-shirt gaped, revealing an unlovely expanse of stomach.

Mary looked at him haughtily and shrugged.

"Not everyone in UWU is a lesbian," the redhead bristled.

"With so many men like Bob around, it's hard to understand why not," Mary drawled. The fat youth flushed and muttered something, of which "castrating" was the only word I caught.

"But I never met Anita," the redhead continued. "I only started going to UWU meetings in May. Has she really disappeared, Mary?"

Mary shrugged again. "If the pigs are trying to put Peter Thayer's death off on her, I wouldn't be surprised."

"Maybe she went home," Bob suggested.

"No," the thin youth said. "If she'd done that, the police wouldn't have been around here looking for her."

"Well," Mary said, "I, for one, hope they don't catch up with her." She got up. "I have to go listen to Bertram drone on about medieval culture. One more crack about witches as hysterical women and he'll find himself attacked by some after class."

She hoisted a knapsack over her left shoulder and ambled off. The others settled closer to the table and switched to an animated discussion of homo-versus heterosexual relationships. Poor Bob favored the latter, but didn't seem to get many opportunities for actively demonstrating it. The thin boy vigorously defended lesbianism. I listened in amusement. College students had enthusiastic opinions about so many topics. At four the boy behind the counter announced he was closing. People started gathering up their books. The three I was listening to continued their discussion for a few minutes until the counterman called over, "Hey, folks, I want to get out of here."

They reluctantly picked up their book bags and moved toward the stairs. I threw out my paper cup and slowly followed them out. At the top of the stairs I touched the redhead's arm. She stopped and looked at me, her face friendly and ingenuous.

"I heard you mention UWU," I said. "Can you tell me where they meet?"

"Are you new on campus?" she asked.

"I'm an old student, but I find I have to spend some time down here this summer," I answered truthfully.

"Well, we have a room in a building at fifty-seven thirty-five University. It's one of those old homes the university has taken over. UWU meets there on Tuesday nights, and other women's activities go on during the rest of the week."

I asked her about their women's center. It was clearly not large, but better than nothing at all, which was what we'd had in my college days when even women radicals treated women's liberation as a dirty phrase. They had a women's health counseling group, courses on self-defense, and they sponsored rap groups and the weekly University Women United meetings.

We had been moving across campus toward the Midway, where my car was parked. I offered her a ride home and she flung herself puppylike into the front seat, talking vigorously if ingenuously about women's oppression. She wanted to know what I did.

"Free-lance work, mostly for corporations," I said, expecting more probing, but she took that happily enough, asking if I would be taking photographs. I realized she assumed that I must be a free-lance writer. I was afraid if I told her the truth, she would tell everyone at UWU and make it impossible for me to find any answers about Anita. Yet I didn't want to tell glaring lies, because if the truth did come out, these young radical women would be even more hostile. So I said "no photographs" and asked her if she did any photography herself. She was still chattering cheerfully when we pulled up in front of her apartment.

"I'm Gail Sugarman," she announced as she struggled clumsily out of the car.

"How do you do, Gail," I replied politely. "I'm V. I. Warshawski."

"Veeyai!" she exclaimed. "What an unusual name. Is it African?"

"No," I answered gravely, "it's Italian." Driving off, I could see her in the rearview mirror, scrambling up the front steps of her apartment. She made me feel incredibly old. Even at twenty I had never possessed that naive, bouncing friendliness; and now it made me feel cynical and remote. In fact, I felt a bit ashamed of deceiving her.

5

GOLD COAST BLUES

Lake Shore Drive, long one, large pothole, was being dug up and repaired. Only two northbound lanes were open and the traffic was backed up for miles. I decided to cut off onto the Stevenson Expressway going west, and then back north on the Kennedy, which went up the industrial North Side toward the airport. The rush-hour traffic was exacerbated by the load of people trying to get out of town on a stifling Friday night. It took me over an hour to fight my way to the Belmont exit, and then fifteen blocks east to my apartment. By the time I got there, all I could think of was a tall, cool drink and a long, soothing shower.

I hadn't noticed anyone coming up the stairs behind me, and was turning my key in the lock when I felt an arm on my shoulder. I'd been mugged once before in this hallway. Whirling reflexively, I snapped my knee and kicked in one motion, delivering directly onto my assailant's exposed shinbone. He grunted and backed off but came back with a solid punch aimed at my face. I ducked and took it on the left shoulder. A lot of the zip was gone, but it shook me a little and I drew away.

He was a short, stocky man, wearing an ill-fitting plaid jacket. He was panting a little, which pleased me: it meant he was out of shape, and a woman has better odds against an out-of-shape man. I waited for him to move or run away. Instead he drew a gun. I stood still.

"If this is a holdup, I only have thirteen dollars in my purse. Not worth killing for."

"I'm not interested in your money. I want you to come with me."

"Come with you where?" I asked.

"You'll find out when we get there." He waved the gun at me and pointed down the stairs with his other arm.

"Beats me why well-paid hoods always dress so sloppily," I commented. "Your jacket doesn't fit, your shirt's untucked—you look like a mess. Now if you were a policeman, I could understand it; they—"

He cut me off with an enraged bellow. "I don't need a goddamn broad to tell me how to dress!" He seized my arm with unnecessary force and started to hustle me down the stairs. He was holding me too close, though, I was able to turn slightly and bring my hand up with a short, strong chop under his gun wrist. He let go of me but didn't drop the gun. I followed through with a half-turn that brought my right elbow under his armpit and made a wedge of my right fist and forearm. I drove it into his ribs with my left hand, palm open, and heard a satisfying *pop* that told me I'd hit home between the fifth and sixth ribs and separated them. He yelled in pain and dropped the gun. I reached for it, but he had enough sense to step on my hand. I butted him in the stomach with my head and he let go, but I was off balance and sat down hard. Someone was clattering up the stairs behind me and I only had time to swing my foot and kick the gun away before turning to see who it was.

I thought it might be a neighbor, roused by the noise, but it seemed to be a partner, dressed nearly to match the first hood but bigger. He saw his buddy leaning against the wall, moaning, and hurled himself onto me. We rolled and I got both hands under his chin, forcing his neck back. He let go, but clobbered me on the right side of my head. It shook me all the way down my back, but I didn't give in to it. I kept rolling and leaped up with my back to the wall. I didn't want to give him time to draw a gun, so I grasped the paneling behind me for leverage and swung my feet at his chest, knocking him off balance, but falling on top of him. He got another good punch in, to my shoulder, just missing the jaw, before I wiggled away. He was stronger, but I was in better shape and more agile, and I was on my feet way in advance of him, kicking him hard over his left kidney. He collapsed at that, and I was hauling back to do it again when his partner recovered himself enough to pick up his gun and clip me under the left ear. My kick connected at the same time and then I was falling, falling, but remembering to fall rolling, and rolling off the edge of the world.

I wasn't out long but long enough for them to hustle me downstairs. Good work for two partially disabled men. I guessed any neighbors alerted by the sound had turned up their TVs to drown it out.

I regained a sickly sort of consciousness as they pushed me into the car, fought to hold it, threw up on one of them, and went under again. I came back more slowly the second time. We were still moving. The one with the separated ribs was driving; I'd thrown up on the other one, and the smell was rather strong. His face was very set and I thought he might be close to tears. It's not nice for two men to go after one woman and only get her after losing a rib and a kidney, and then to have her vomit down your jacket front and not be able to move or clean it off—I wouldn't have liked it, either. I fumbled in my jacket pocket for some Kleenex. I still felt sick, too sick to talk and not much like cleaning him up, either, so I dropped the tissues on him and leaned back. He gave a little squeal of rage and knocked them to the floor.

When we stopped, we were close to North Michigan Avenue, just off Astor on Division, in the area where rich people live in beautiful old Victorian houses and apartments or enormous high-rise modern condominiums. My right-hand partner flung himself out the door, took off his jacket, and dropped it in the street.

"Your gun's showing," I told him. He looked down at it, then at his jacket. His face turned red. "You goddamn bitch," he said. He leaned into the car to take another poke at me, but the angle wasn't good and he couldn't get much leverage behind his arm.

Ribs spoke up. "Come on, Joe—it's getting late and Earl don't like to be kept waiting." This simple statement worked powerfully on Joe. He stopped swinging and yanked me out of the car, with Ribs pushing me from the side.

We went into one of the stately old houses that I always thought I'd like to own if I ever rescued an oil-tanker billionaire from international kidnappers and got set up for life as my reward. It was dull red brick, with elegant wrought-iron railing up the steps and around the front windows. Originally built as a single-family home, it was now a three-flat apartment. A cheerful black-and-white patterned wallpaper covered the entry hall and stairwell. The bannister was carved wood, probably walnut, and beautifully polished. The three of us made an ungainly journey up the carpeted stairs to the second floor. Ribs was having trouble moving his arms, and Joe seemed to be limping from his kidney kicks. I wasn't feeling very well myself.

The second-floor apartment was opened by yet another gun-carrier. His clothes fit him better, but he didn't really look like the class of person that belonged in this neighborhood. He had a shock of black hair that stood up around his head in a wiry bush. On his right cheek was a deep red scar, cut roughly like a Z. It was so dark that it looked as though someone had painted him with lipstick.

"What kept you two so long? Earl's getting angry," he demanded, ushering us into a wide hallway. Plush brown carpet on the floor, a nice little Louis Quinze side table, and a few pictures on the walls. Charming.

"Earl warned us this goddamn Warshawski bitch was a wise-ass, but he didn't say she was a goddamn karate expert." That was Ribs. He pronounced my name "Worchotsi." I looked down at my hands modestly.

"Is that Joe and Freddie?" a nasal tenor squeaked from inside. "What the hell took you guys so long?" Its owner appeared in the doorway. Short, pudgy, and bald, he was familiar to me from my early days in Chicago law enforcement.

"Earl Smeissen. How absolutely delightful. But you know, Earl, if you'd called me up and asked to see me, we could have gotten together with a lot less trouble."

"Yeah, Warchoski, I just bet we would've," he said heavily. Earl had carved himself a nice little niche on the North Side with classy prostitution setups for visiting conventioneers, and a little blackmail and extortion. He had a small piece of the drug business, and the rumor was that he would arrange a killing to oblige a friend if the price was right.

"Earl, this is quite a place you've got. Inflation must not be hurting business too much."

He ignored me. "Where the hell's your jacket, Joe? You been walking around Chicago showing your gun to every cop on the beat?"

Joe turned red again and started to mutter something. I intervened. "I'm afraid that's my fault, Earl. Your friends here jumped me in my own hallway without introducing themselves or saying they had come from you. We had a bit of a fracas, and Freddie's ribs got separated—but he pulled himself together nicely and knocked me out. When I came to, I was sick on Joe's jacket. So don't blame the poor fellow for ditching it."

Earl turned outraged to Freddie, who shrank back down the hall. "You let a goddamn dame bust your ribs?" he yelled, his voice breaking to a squeak. "The money I pay you and you can't do a simple little job like fetch a goddamn broad?"

One of the things I hate about my work is the cheap swearing indulged in by cheap crooks. I also hate the word *broad*. "Earl, could you reserve your criticisms of your staff until I'm not here? I have an engagement this evening —I'd appreciate it if you told me why you wanted to see me so badly you sent two hoods to get me, so I can get there on time."

Earl gave Freddie a vicious look and sent him off to see a doctor. He motioned the rest of us into the living room, and noticed Joe limping. "You need a doctor, too? She break your leg?" he asked sarcastically.

"Kidneys," I replied modestly. "It all comes from knowing how."

"Yeah, I know about you, Warchoski. I know what a wise-ass you are, and

I heard how you offed Joe Correl. If Freddie knocked you out, I'll give him a medal. I want you to understand you can't mess around with me.''

I sank down into a wide armchair. My head was throbbing and it hurt to focus on him. "I'm not messing around with you, Earl," I said earnestly. "I'm not interested in prostitution or juice loans or—''

He hit me across the mouth. "Shut up." His voice rose to a squeak and his eyes got smaller in his pudgy face. In a detached way I felt some blood dribbling down my chin—he must have caught me with his ring.

"Is this a general warning, then? Are you hauling in all the private eyes in Chicago and saying 'Now hear this—don't mess around with Earl Smeissen!'?"

He swung at me again, but I blocked him with my left arm. He looked at his hand in surprise, as if he wondered what had happened to it.

"Don't clown with me, Warchoski—I can call in plenty of people to wipe that smirk off your face."

"I don't think it would take very many," I said, "but I still don't have any idea what part of your turf I'm messing in."

Earl signaled to the doorman, who came and held my shoulders against the chair. Joe was hovering in the background, a lascivious look on his face. My stomach turned slightly.

"Okay, Earl, I'm terrified," I said.

He hit me again. I was going to look like absolute hell tomorrow, I thought. I hoped I wasn't shaking; my stomach was knotted with nervousness. I took several deep diaphragm breaths to try to relieve the tension.

The last slap seemed to satisfy Earl. He sat down on a dark couch close to my chair.

"Warchoski," he squeaked, "I called you down here to tell you to lay off the Thayer case."

"You kill the boy, Earl?" I asked.

He was on his feet again. "I can mark you good, so good that no one will ever want to look at your face again," he shouted. "Now just do what I say and keep your mitts outta that."

I decided not to argue with him—I didn't feel in any shape to take on both him and the doorman, who continued to hold my shoulders back. I wondered if his scar had turned redder with all the excitement but voted against asking him.

"Suppose you do scare me off? What about the police?" I objected. "Bobby Mallory's hot on the trail, and whatever his faults, you can't buy Bobby."

"I'm not worried about Mallory," Earl's voice was back in its normal register, so I concluded the brainstorm was passing. "And I'm not buying you—I'm telling you."

"Who got you involved, Earl? College kids aren't part of your turf—unless young Thayer was cutting into your dope territory?"

"I thought I'd just told you not to pry into my affairs," he said, getting up again. Earl was determined to pound me. Maybe it would be better to get it over with quickly and get out, rather than let him go on for hours. As he came at me, I pulled my foot back and kicked him squarely in the crotch. He howled in anguish and collapsed in a heap on the couch. "Get her, Tony, get her," he squealed.

I didn't have a chance against Tony, the doorman. He was trained in the art of working over loan defaulters without showing a mark. When he finished, Earl came hobbling over from the couch. "This is just a taste, Warchoski," he hissed. "You lay off the Thayer case. Agreed?"

I looked at him without speaking. He really could kill me and get away with it—he'd done it to others. He had good connections with City Hall and probably in the police department too. I shrugged and winced. He seemed to accept that as agreement. "Get her out, Tony."

Tony dumped me unceremoniously outside the front door. I sat for a few minutes on the stairs, shivering in the heat and trying to pull myself together. I was violently ill over the railing, which cleared my headache a bit. A woman walking by with a man said, "Disgusting so early in the evening. The police should keep people like that out of this neighborhood." I agreed. I got to my feet, rather wobbly, but I could walk. I felt my arms. They were sore, but nothing was broken. I staggered over to the inner drive, parallel to Lake Shore Drive and only a block away, and hailed a taxi home. The first one pulled off after a look at me, but the second one took me. The driver clucked and fussed like a Jewish mother, wanting to know what I'd done to myself and offering to take me to a hospital or the police or both. I thanked him for his concern but assured him I was all right.

6

IN THE COOL
OF THE NIGHT

I'd dropped my purse by my door when Freddie and I were scuffling, and asked the cabdriver to come upstairs with me to get paid off. Living at the top of the building, I was pretty confident that my bag would still be there. It was, and my keys were still in the door.

The driver tried one last protest. "Thanks," I said, "but I just need a hot bath and a drink and I'll be all right."

"Okay, lady.," He shrugged. "It's your funeral." He took his money, looked at me one last time, and went downstairs.

My apartment lacked the splendor of Earl's. My little hallway had a small rug, not wall-to-wall carpeting, and an umbrella stand rather than a Louis Quinze table. But it also wasn't filled with thugs.

I was surprised to find it was only seven. It had been only an hour and a half since I had come up the stairs the first time that evening. I felt as though I'd moved into a different time zone. I ran a bath for the second time that day and poured myself an inch of Scotch. I soaked in water as hot as I could bear it, lying in the dark with a wet towel wrapped around my head. Gradually my headache dissipated. I was very, very tired.

After thirty minutes of soaking and reheating the tub, I felt able to cope with some motion. Wrapping a large towel around me, I walked through the apartment, trying to keep my muscles from freezing on me. All I really wanted to do was sleep, but I knew if I did that now I wouldn't be able to walk for a week. I did some exercises, gingerly, fortifying myself with Black Label. Suddenly I caught sight of a clock and remembered my date with Devereux. I was already late and wondered if he was still there.

With an effort I found the restaurant's name in the phone book and dialed their number. The maître d'hôtel was very cooperative and offered to look for Mr. Devereux in the bar. A few minutes passed, and I began to think he must have gone home when he came onto the line.

"Hello, Ralph."

"This had better be good."

"If I tried explaining it, it would take hours and you still wouldn't believe me," I answered. "Will you give me another half hour?"

He hesitated; I guessed he was looking for the pride to say no—good-looking guys aren't used to being stood up. "Sure," he said finally. "But if you're not here by eight-thirty, you can find your own way home."

"Ralph," I said, controlling my voice carefully, "this has been one absolute zero of a day. I'd like to have a pleasant evening, learn a little bit about insurance, and try to forget what's gone before. Can we do that?"

He was embarrassed. "Sure, Vicki—I mean Vic. See you in the bar."

We hung up and I looked through my wardrobe for something elegant enough for the Cartwheel, but loose and flowing, and found a string-colored Mexican dress that I'd forgotten about. It was two-piece, with a long full skirt and a woven, square-necked top that tied at the waist and bloused out below. The long sleeves covered my puffy arms and I didn't have to wear pantyhose or a slip. Cork sandals completed the costume.

Surveying my face under the bathroom light made me want to reconsider going out in public. My lower lip was swollen where Earl's pinky ring had sliced it, and a purple smudge was showing on my left jaw, extending veinous red lines like a cracked egg along my cheek to the eye.

I tried some makeup; my base wasn't very heavy and didn't conceal the worst of the purple but did cover the spidery red marks. Heavy shadow took the focus from an incipient black eye, and dark lipstick, applied more strongly than my usual style, made the swollen lip look pouty and sexy—or might if the lights were dim enough.

My legs were stiffening up, but my daily runs seemed to be paying off—I negotiated the stairs without more than minor tremors. A taxi was going by on Halsted; it dropped me in front of the Hanover House Hotel on Oak Street at 8:25.

This was my first visit to the Cartwheel. To me it typified the sterile place where bright, empty North Siders with more money than sense liked to eat. The bar, to the left of the entrance, was dark, with a piano amplified too loudly, playing songs that bring tears to the eyes of Yale graduates. The place was crowded, Friday night in Chicago. Ralph sat at the end of the bar with a drink. He looked up as I came in, smiled, sketched a wave, but didn't get up. I concentrated on walking smoothly, and made it to where he sat. He looked at his watch. "You just made it."

In more ways than one, I thought. "Oh, you'd never have left without finishing your drink." There weren't any empty stools. "How about proving you're a more generous soul than I and letting me have that seat and a Scotch?"

He grinned and grabbed me, intending to pull me onto his lap. A spasm of pain shot through my ribs. "Oh, Jesus, Ralph! Don't!"

He let go of me at once, got up stiffly and quietly, and offered me the barstool. I stood, feeling awkward. I don't like scenes, and I didn't feel like using the energy to calm Ralph down. He'd seemed like a guy made for sunshine; maybe his divorce had made him insecure with women. I saw I'd have to tell him the truth and put up with his sympathy. And I didn't want to reveal how badly Smeissen had shown me up that afternoon. It was no comfort that he would limp in pain for a day or two.

I dragged my attention back to Ralph. "Would you like me to take you home?" he was asking.

"Ralph, I'd like a chance to explain some things to you. I know it must look as though I don't want to be here, showing up an hour late and all. Are you too upset for me to tell you about it?"

"Not at all," he said politely.

"Well, could we go someplace and sit down? It's a little confusing and hard to do standing up."

"I'll check on our table." When he went off, I sank gratefully onto the barstool and ordered a Johnnie Walker Black. How many could I drink before they combined with my tired muscles and put me to sleep?

Ralph came back with the news that our table was a good ten-minute wait away. The ten stretched into twenty, while I sat with my uninjured cheek propped on my hand and he stood stiffly behind me. I sipped my Scotch. The bar was over-air-conditioned. Normally the heavy cotton of the dress would have kept me plenty warm, but now I started to shiver slightly.

"Cold?" Ralph asked.

"A little," I admitted.

"I could put my arms around you," he offered tentatively.

I looked up at him and smiled. "That would be very nice," I said. "Just do it gently, please."

He crossed his arms around my chest. I winced a little at first, but the warmth and the pressure felt good. I leaned back against him. He looked down at my face, and his eyes narrowed.

"Vic, what's wrong with your face?"

I raised an eyebrow, "Nothing's wrong."

"No, really," he said, bending closer, "you've gotten cut—and that looks like a bruise and swelling on your cheek."

"Is it really bad?" I asked. "I thought the makeup covered it pretty well."

"Well, they're not going to put you on the cover of *Vogue* this week, but it's not too awful. It's just that as an old claims man I've seen lots of accident victims. And you look like one."

"I feel like one too," I agreed, "but really, this wasn't—"

"Have you been to a doctor about this?" he interrupted.

"You sound just like the cabbie who took me home this afternoon. He wanted to rush me to Passavant—I practically expected him to come in with me and start making me chicken soup."

"Was your car badly damaged?" he asked.

"My car is not damaged at all." I was beginning to lose my temper— irrationally, I knew—but the probing made me feel defensive.

"Not damaged," he echoed, "then how—"

At that moment our table was announced in the bar. I got up and went over to the headwaiter, leaving Ralph to pay for drinks. The headwaiter led me off without waiting for Ralph, who caught up with us just as I was being seated. My spurt of temper had infected him; he said, "I hate waiters who haul off ladies without waiting for their escorts." He was just loud enough for the maître d' to hear. "I'm sorry, sir—I didn't realize you were with madame," he said with great dignity before moving off.

"Hey, Ralph, take it easy," I said gently. "A little too much ego-jockeying is going on—my fault as much as yours. Let's stop and get some facts and start over again."

A waiter materialized. "Would you care for a drink before dinner?"

Ralph looked up in irritation. "Do you know how many hours we've spent in the bar waiting for this table? No, we don't want a drink—at least, I don't." He turned to me. "Do you?"

"No, thanks," I agreed. "Any more and I'll fall asleep—which will probably ruin forever any chance I have of making you believe that I'm not trying to get out of an evening with you."

Were we ready to order? the waiter persisted. Ralph told him roundly to go away for five minutes. My last remark had started to restore his native good humor, however. "Okay, V. I. Warshawski—convince me that you really aren't trying to make this evening so awful that I'll never ask you out again."

"Ralph," I said, watching him carefully, "do you know Earl Smeissen?"

"Who?" he asked uncomprehendingly. "Is this some kind of detective guessing game?"

"Yeah, I guess so," I answered. "Between yesterday afternoon and this afternoon I've talked to a whole lot of different people who either knew Peter Thayer or his girl friend—the gal who's vanished. You and your boss, among others.

"Well, when I got home late this afternoon, two hired thugs were waiting for me. We fought. I was able to hold them off for a while, but one of them knocked me out. They took me to Earl Smeissen's home. If you don't know Earl, don't try to meet him. He was just starting to muscle to the top of his racket—extortion, prostitution—when I was with the Public Defender ten years ago, and he seems to have kept right on trucking since then. He now has a stable of tough guys who all carry guns. He is not a nice person."

I stopped to marshal my presentation. From the corner of my eye I saw the waiter shimmering up again, but Ralph waved him away. "Anyway, he ordered me off the Thayer case, and set one of his tame goons on me to back it up." I stopped. What had happened next in Earl's apartment was very raw in my mind. I had calculated it carefully at the time, decided that it was better to get everything over at once and convince Earl that I was scared than to sit there all evening while he took increasingly violent shots at me. Nonetheless, the thought of being so helpless, the memory of Tony beating me, like a disloyal whore or a welching loan customer—to be so vulnerable was close to unbearable. Unconsciously, my left hand had clenched, and I realized I was slicing it against the tabletop. Ralph was watching me, an uncertain look on his face. His business and suburban life hadn't prepared him for this kind of emotion.

I shook my head and tried for a lighter touch. "Anyway, my rib cage is a little sore—which is why I winced and yelled when you grabbed hold of me in the bar. The question that's exercising me, though, is who told Earl that I'd been around asking questions. Or more precisely, who cared so much that I'd been around that he asked—or paid—Earl to frighten me off."

Ralph was still looking a little horrified. "Have you been to the police about this?"

"No," I said impatiently. "I can't go to the police about this kind of thing. They know I'm interested in the case—they've asked me to get off, too, although more politely. If Bobby Mallory—the lieutenant in charge of the case—knew I'd been beaten up by Earl, Smeissen would deny the whole thing, and if I could prove it in court, he could say it was a million things other than this that made him do it. And Mallory wouldn't give me an earful of sympathy—he wants me out of there anyway."

"Well, don't you think he's right? Murder really is a police matter. And this group seems pretty wild for you to be mixed up with."

I felt a quick surge of anger, the anger I get when I feel someone is pushing me. I smiled with an effort. "Ralph, I'm tired and I ache. I can't try explaining to you tonight why this is my job—but please believe that it is my job and that I can't give it to the police and run away. It's true I don't know specifically what's going on here, but I do know the temperament and reactions of a guy like Smeissen. I usually only deal with white-collar criminals—but when they're cornered, they're not much different from an extortion artist like Smeissen."

"I see." Ralph paused, thinking, then his attractive grin came. "I have to admit that I don't know much about crooks of any kind—except the occasional swindlers who try to rip off insurance companies. But we fight them in the courts, not with hand-to-hand combat. I'll try to believe you know what you're up to, though."

I laughed a little embarrassedly. "Thanks. I'll try not to act too much like Joan of Arc—getting on a horse and charging around in all directions."

The waiter was back, looking a little intimidated. Ralph ordered baked oysters and quail, but I opted for Senegalese soup and spinach salad. I was too exhausted to want a lot of food.

We talked about indifferent things for a while. I asked Ralph if he followed the Cubs. "For my sins, I'm an ardent fan," I explained. Ralph said he caught a game with his son every now and then. "But I don't see how anyone can be an ardent Cub fan. They're doing pretty well right now—cleaned out the Reds—but they'll fade the way they always do. No, give me the Yankees."

"Yankees!" I expostulated. "I don't see how anyone can root for them—it's like rooting for the Cosa Nostra. You know they've got the money to buy the muscle to win—but that doesn't make you cheer them on."

"I like to see sports played well," Ralph insisted. "I can't stand the clowning around that Chicago teams do. Look at the mess Veeck's made of the White Sox this year."

We were still arguing about it when the waiter brought the first course. The soup was excellent—light, creamy, with a hint of curry. I started feeling better and ate some bread and butter, too. When Ralph's quail arrived, I ordered another bowl of soup and some coffee.

"Now explain to me why a union wouldn't buy insurance from Ajax."

"Oh, they could," Ralph said, his mouth full. He chewed and swallowed. "But it would only be for their headquarters—maybe fire coverage on the building. Workers Compensation for the secretaries, things like that. There wouldn't be a whole lot of people to cover. And a union like the Knifegrinders—see, they get their insurance where they work. The big thing is Workers Comp, and that's paid for by the company, not the union."

"That covers disability payments, doesn't it?" I asked.

"Yes, or death if it's job-related. Medical bills even if there isn't lost time. I guess it's a funny kind of setup. Your rates depend on the kind of business you conduct—a factory pays more than an office, for instance. But the insurance company can be stuck with weekly payments for years if a guy is disabled on the job. We have some cases—not many, fortunately—that go back to 1927. But see, the insured doesn't pay more, or not that much more, if we get stuck with a whole lot of disability payments. Of course, we can cancel the insurance, but we're still required to cover any disabled workers who are already collecting.

"Well, this is getting off the subject. The thing is, there are lots of people who go on disability who shouldn't—it's pretty cushy and there are plenty of corrupt doctors—but it's hard to imagine a full-scale fraud connected with it that would do anyone else much good." He ate some more quail. "No, your real money is in pensions, as you suggested, or maybe life insurance. But it's easier for an insurance company to commit fraud with life insurance than for anyone else. Look at the Equity Funding case."

"Well, could your boss be involved in something like that? Rigging phony policies with the Knifegrinders providing dummy policyholders?" I asked.

"Vic, why are you working so hard to prove that Yardley's a crook? He's really not a bad guy—I've worked for him for three years, and I've never heard anything against him."

I laughed at that. "It bugs me that he agreed to see me so easily. I don't know a lot about insurance, but I've been around big corporations before. He's a department head, and they're like gynecologists—their schedules are always booked for about twice as many appointments as they can realistically handle."

Ralph clutched his head. "You're making me dizzy, Vic, and you're doing it on purpose. How can a claim department head possibly be like a gynecologist!"

"Yeah, well, you get the idea. Why would he agree to see me? He'd never heard of me, he has wall-to-wall appointments—but he didn't even take phone calls while we were talking."

"Yes, but you knew Peter was dead, and he didn't—so you were expecting him to behave in a certain guilty way and that's what you saw," Ralph objected. "He might have been worried about him, about Peter, because he'd promised Jack Thayer that he'd be responsible for the boy. I don't really see anything so surprising in Yardley's talking to you. If Peter had been just a stray kid, I might—but an old family friend's son? The kid hadn't been in for four days, he wasn't answering the phone—Yardley felt responsible as much as annoyed."

I stopped, considering. What Ralph said made sense. I wondered if I had gotten carried away, whether my instinctive dislike of over-hearty businessmen was making me see ghosts where there were none.

"Okay, you could be right. But why couldn't Masters be involved in a life-insurance fiddle?"

Ralph was finishing off his quail and ordering coffee and dessert. I asked for a large dish of ice cream. "Oh, that's the way insurance companies are set up," he said when the waiter had disappeared again. "We're big—third largest in total premiums written, which is about eight point four billion dollars a year. That includes all lines, and all of the thirteen companies that make up the Ajax group. For legal reasons, life insurance can't be written by the same company that writes property and casualty. So the Ajax Assurance Company does all our life and pension products, while the Ajax Casualty and some of the smaller ones do property and casualty."

The waiter returned with our desserts. Ralph was having some kind of gooey torte. I decided to get Kahlua for my ice cream.

"Well, with a company as big as ours," Ralph continued, "the guys involved in casualty—that's stuff like Workers Comp, general liability, some of the auto—anyway, guys like Yardley and me don't know too much about the life side of the house. Sure, we know the people who run it, eat with them now and then, but they have a separate administrative structure, handle their own claims and so on. If we got close enough to the business to analyze it, let alone commit fraud with it, the political stink would be so high we'd be out on our butts within an hour. Guaranteed."

I shook my head reluctantly and turned to my ice cream. Ajax did not sound promising, and I'd been pinning hopes to it. "By the way," I said, "did you check on Ajax's pension money?"

Ralph laughed. "You are persistent, Vic, I'll grant you that. Yeah, I called a friend of mine over there. Sorry, Vic. Nothing doing. He says he'll look into it, see whether we get any third-hand stuff laid off on us—" I looked a question. "Like the Loyal Alliance people give some money to Dreyfus to manage and Dreyfus lays some of it off on us. Basically though, this guy says Ajax won't touch the Knifegrinders with a ten-foot pole. Which doesn't surprise me too much."

I sighed and finished my ice cream, feeling suddenly tired again. If things came easily in this life, we would never feel pride in our achievements. My mother used to tell me that, standing over me while I practiced the piano. She'd probably disapprove of my work, if she were alive, but she would never let me slouch at the dinner table grumbling because it wasn't turning out right. Still, I was too tired tonight to try to grapple with the implications of everything I'd learned today.

"You look like your adventures are catching up with you," Ralph said.

I felt a wave of fatigue sweep over me, almost carrying me off to sleep with it. "Yeah, I'm fading," I admitted. "I think I'd better go to bed. Although in a way I hate to go to sleep, I'll be so sore in the morning. Maybe I could wake up enough to dance. If you keep moving, it's not so bad."

"You look like you'd fall asleep on a disco floor right now, Vic, and I'd be arrested for beating you or something. Why does exercise help?"

"If you keep the blood circulating, it keeps the joints from stiffening so much."

"Well, maybe we could do both—sleep and exercise, I mean." The smile in his eyes was half embarrassed, half pleased.

I suddenly thought that after my evening with Earl and Tony, I'd like the comfort of someone in bed with me. "Sure." I said, smiling back.

Ralph called to the waiter for the bill and paid it promptly, his hands shaking slightly. I considered fighting him for it, especially since I could claim it as a business expense, but decided I'd done enough fighting for one day.

We waited outside for the doorman to fetch the car. Ralph stood close to me, not touching me, but tense. I realized he had been planning this ending all along and hadn't been sure he could carry it off, and I smiled a little to myself in the dark. When the car came, I sat close to him on the front seat. "I live on Halsted, just north of Belmont," I said, and fell asleep on his shoulder.

He woke me up at the Belmont-Halsted intersection and asked for the address. My neighborhood is just north and west of a smarter part of town and there is usually good parking on the street; he found a place across from my front door.

It took a major effort to pull myself out of the car. The night air was warm and comforting and Ralph steadied me with shaking hands as we crossed the street and went into my front hallway. The three flights up looked very far away and I had a sudden mental flash of sitting on the front steps waiting for my dad to come home from work and carry me upstairs. If I asked Ralph to, he would carry me up. But it would alter the dependency balance in the relationship too much. I set my teeth and climbed the stairs. No one was lying in wait at the top.

I went into the kitchen and pulled a bottle of Martell from the liquor cupboard. I got two glasses down, two of my mother's Venetian glasses, part of the small dowry she had brought to her marriage. They were a beautiful clear red with twisted stems. It had been a long time since I had had anyone up to my apartment, and I suddenly felt shy and vulnerable. I'd been overexposed to men today and wasn't ready to do it again in bed.

When I brought the bottle and glasses back to the living room, Ralph was sitting on the couch, leafing through *Fortune* without reading it. He got up and took the glasses from me, admiring them. I explained that my mother had left Italy right before the war broke out on a large scale. Her own mother was Jewish and they wanted her out of harm's way. The eight red glasses she wrapped carefully in her underwear to take in the one suitcase she had carried, and they had always held pride of place at any festive meal. I poured brandy.

Ralph told me that his family was Irish. "That's why it's 'Devereux' without an *A*—the *A*s are French." We sat for a while without talking, drinking our brandy. He was a bit nervous, too, and it helped me relax. Suddenly he grinned, his face lighting, and said, "When I got divorced I moved into the city because I had a theory that that's where you meet the chicks—sorry, women. But to tell you the truth, you're the first woman I've asked out in the six months I've been here—and you're not like any woman I ever met before." He flushed a little. "I just wanted you to know that I'm not hopping in and out of bed every night. But I would like to get into bed with you."

I didn't answer him, but stood up and took his hand. Hand-in-hand, like five-year-olds, we walked into the bedroom. Ralph carefully helped me out of my dress and gently stroked my puffy arms. I unbuttoned his shirt. He took off his clothes and we climbed into the bed. I'd been afraid that I might have to help him along; recently divorced men sometimes have problems because they feel very insecure. Fortunately he didn't, because I was too tired to help anyone. My last memory was of his breath expelling loudly, and then I was asleep.

7
A LITTLE HELP
FROM A FRIEND

When I woke up, the room was full of the soft light of late morning, diffused through my heavy bedroom curtains. I was alone in the bed and lay still to collect my thoughts. Gradually the memory of yesterday's events returned, and I moved my head cautiously to look at the bedside clock. My neck was very stiff, and I had to turn my whole body to see the time—11:30. I sat up. My stomach muscles were all right, but my thighs and calves were sore, and it was painful to stand upright. I did a slow shuffle to the bathroom, the kind you do the day after you run five miles when you haven't been out for a couple of months, and turned the hot water in the tub on full blast.

Ralph called to me from the living room. "Good morning," I called back. "If you want to talk to me, you'll have to come here—I'm not walking any farther." Ralph came into the bathroom, fully dressed, and joined me while I gloomily studied my face in the mirror over the sink. My incipient black eye had turned a deep blackish-purple, streaked with yellow and green. My unin-jured left eye was bloodshot. My jaw had turned gray. The whole effect was unappealing.

Ralph seemed to share my feeling. I was watching his face in the mirror; he seemed a little disgusted. My bet was that Dorothy had never come home with a black eye—suburban life is so dull.

"Do you do this kind of thing often?" Ralph asked.

"You mean scrutinize my body, or what?" I asked.

He moved his hands vaguely. "The fighting," he said.

"Not as much as I did as a child. I grew up on the South Side. Ninetieth and Commercial, if you know the area—lots of Polish steelworkers who didn't welcome racial and ethnic newcomers—and the feeling was mutual.

The law of the jungle ruled in my high school—if you couldn't swing a mean toe or fist, you might as well forget it."

I turned from the mirror. Ralph was shaking his head, but he was trying to understand, trying not to back away. "It's a different world," he said slowly. "I grew up in Libertyville, and I don't think I was ever in a real fight. And if my sister had come home with a black eye, my mother would have been hysterical for a month. Didn't your folks mind?"

"Oh, my mother hated it, but she died when I was fifteen, and my dad was thankful that I could take care of myself." That was true—Gabriella had hated violence. But she was a fighter, and I got my scrappiness from her, not from my big, even-tempered father.

"Did all the girls in your school fight?" Ralph wanted to know.

I climbed into the hot water while I considered this. "No, some of them just got scared off. And some got themselves boyfriends to protect them. The rest of us learned to protect ourselves. One girl I went to school with still loves to fight—she's a gorgeous redhead, and she loves going to bars and punching out guys who try to pick her up. Truly amazing."

I sank back in the water and covered my face and neck with hot wet cloths. Ralph was quiet for a minute, then said, "I'll make some coffee if you'll tell me the secret—I couldn't find any. And I didn't know whether you were saving those dishes for Christmas, so I washed them."

I uncovered my mouth but kept the cloth over my eyes. I'd forgotten the goddamn dishes yesterday when I left the house. "Thanks." What else could I say? "Coffee's in the freezer—whole beans. Use a tablespoon per cup. The grinder's by the stove—electric gadget. Filters are in the cupboard right over it, and the pot is still in the sink—unless you washed it."

He leaned over to kiss me, then went out. I reheated the washcloth and flexed my legs in the steamy water. After a while they moved easily, so I was confident they would be fine in a few days. Before Ralph returned with the coffee, I had soaked much of the stiffness out of my joints. I climbed out of the tub and enveloped myself in a large blue bath towel and walked—with much less difficulty—to the living room.

Ralph came in with the coffee. He admired my robe, but couldn't quite look me in the face. "The weather's broken," he remarked. "I went out to get a paper and it's a beautiful day—clear and cool. Want to drive out to the Indiana Dunes?"

I started to shake my head, but the pain stopped me. "No. It sounds lovely, but I've got some work to do."

"Come on, Vic," Ralph protested. "Let the police handle this. You're in rotten shape—you need to take the day off."

"You could be right," I said, trying to keep down my anger. "But I thought we went through all that last night. At any rate, I'm not taking the day off."

"Well, how about some company. Need someone to drive you?"

I studied Ralph's face, but all I saw was friendly concern. Was he just having an attack of male protectiveness, or did he have some special reason for wanting me to stay off the job? As a companion he'd be able to keep tabs on my errands. And report them to Earl Smeissen?

"I'm going to Winnetka to talk to Peter Thayer's father. Since he's a neighbor of your boss, I'm not sure it would look too good for you to come along."

"Probably not," he agreed. "Why do you have to see him?"

"It's like the man said about Annapurna, Ralph: because he's there." There were a couple of other things I needed to do, too, things I'd just as soon be alone for.

"How about dinner tonight?" he suggested.

"Ralph, for heaven's sake, you're beginning to act like a Seeing Eye dog. No. No dinner tonight. You're sweet, I appreciate it, but I want some time to myself."

"Okay, okay," he grumbled. "Just trying to be friendly."

I stood up and walked painfully over to the couch where he was sitting. "I know." I put an arm around him and gave him a kiss. "I'm just trying to be unfriendly." He pulled me onto his lap. The dissatisfaction smoothed out of his face and he kissed me.

After a few minutes I pulled myself gently away and hobbled back to the bedroom to get dressed. The navy silk was lying over a chair, with a couple of rents in it and a fair amount of blood and dirt. My cleaner could probably fix it up, but I didn't think I'd ever care to wear it again. I threw it out and put on my green linen slacks with a pale-lemon shirt and a jacket. Perfect for suburbia. I decided not to worry about my face. It would look even more garish with makeup in sunlight than as it was.

I fixed myself Cream of Wheat while Ralph ate toast and jam. "Well," I said, "time to head for suburbia."

Ralph walked downstairs with me, trying to hold out a supporting hand. "No, thanks," I said. "I'd better get used to doing this by myself." At the bottom he won points by not lingering over his good-byes. We kissed briefly; he sketched a cheerful wave and crossed the street to his car. I watched him out of sight, then hailed a passing cab.

The driver dropped me on Sheffield north of Addison, a neighborhood more decayed than mine, largely Puerto Rican. I rang Lotty Herschel's bell and was relieved when she answered it. "Who's there?" she squawked through the intercom. "It's me, Vic," I said, and pushed the front door while the buzzer sounded.

Lotty lived on the second floor. She was waiting for me in the doorway when I made it to the top of the stairs. "My dear Vic—what on earth is wrong with you?" she greeted me, her thick black eyebrows soaring to punctuate her astonishment.

I'd known Lotty for years. She was a doctor, about fifty, I thought, but with her vivid, clever face and trim, energetic body it was hard to tell. Sometime in her Viennese youth she had discovered the secret of perpetual motion. She held fierce opinions on a number of things, and put them to practice in medicine, often to the dismay of her colleagues. She'd been one of the physicians who performed abortions in connection with an underground referral service I'd belonged to at the University of Chicago in the days when abortion was illegal and a dirty word to most doctors. Now she ran a clinic in a shabby storefront down the street. She'd tried running it for nothing when she first opened it, but found the neighborhood people wouldn't trust medical care they didn't have to pay for. Still, it was one of the cheapest clinics in the city, and I often wondered what she lived on.

Now she shut the door behind me and ushered me into her living room. Like Lotty herself, it was sparely furnished, but glowed with strong colors—curtains in a vivid red-and-orange print, and an abstract painting like fire on the wall. Lotty sat me on a daybed and brought me a cup of the strong Viennese coffee she lived on.

"So now, Victoria, what have you been doing that makes you hobble upstairs like an old woman and turns your face black-and-blue? I am sure not a car accident, that's too tame for you—am I right?"

"Right as always, Lotty," I answered, and gave her an abbreviated account of my adventures.

She pursed her lips at the tale of Smeissen but wasted no time arguing about whether I ought to go to the police or drop out of the case or spend the day in bed. She didn't always agree with me, but Lotty respected my decisions. She went into her bedroom and returned with a large, business-like black bag. She pulled my face muscles and looked at my eyes with an ophthalmoscope. "Nothing time won't cure," she pronounced, and checked the reflexes in my legs and the muscles. "Yes, I see, you are sore, and you will continue to be sore. But you are healthy, you take good care of yourself; it will pass off before too long."

"Yes, I suspected as much," I agreed. "But I can't take the time to wait for these leg muscles to heal. And they're sore enough to slow me down quite a bit right now. I need something that will help me overlook the pain enough to do some errands and some thinking—not like codeine that knocks you out. Do you have anything?"

"Ah, yes, a miracle drug." Lotty's face was amused. "You shouldn't put so much faith in doctors and drugs, Vic. However, I'll give you a shot of phenylbutazone. That's what they give racehorses to keep them from aching when they run, and it seems to me you're galloping around like a horse."

She disappeared for a few minutes, and I heard the refrigerator door open. She returned with a syringe and a small, rubber-stoppered bottle. "Now, lie down; we'll do this in your behind so it goes quickly to the bloodstream. Pull your slacks down a bit, so; great stuff this, really, they call it 'bute' for short, in half an hour you will be ready for the Derby, my dear." As she talked, Lotty worked rapidly. I felt a small sting, and it was over. "Now, sit. I'll tell you some stories about the clinic. I'm going to give you some nepenthe to take away with you. That's very strong, a painkiller; don't try to drive while you're taking it, and don't drink. I'll pack up some bute in tablets for you."

I leaned back against a big pillow and tried not to relax too much. The temptation to lie down and sleep was very strong. I forced myself to follow Lotty's quick, clever talk, asking questions, but not debating her more out-landish statements. After a while I could feel the drug taking effect. My neck muscles eased considerably. I didn't feel like unarmed combat, but I was reasonably certain I could handle my car.

Lotty didn't try to stop my getting up. "You've rested for close to an hour—you should do for a while." She packed the bute tablets in a plastic bottle and gave me a bottle of nepenthe.

I thanked her. "How much do I owe you?"

She shook her head. "No, these are all samples. When you come for your long-overdue checkup, then I'll charge you what any good Michigan Avenue doctor would."

She saw me to the door. "Seriously, Vic, if you get worried about this Smeissen character, you are always welcome in my spare room." I thanked her—it was a good offer, and one that I might need.

Normally I would have walked back to my car; Lotty was only about eight blocks from me. But even with the shot I didn't feel quite up to par, so I walked slowly down to Addison and caught a cab. I rode it down to my office, where I picked up Peter Thayer's voter card with the Winnetka ad-dress on it, then flagged another cab back to my own car on the North Side. McGraw was going to have quite a bill for expenses—all these cabs, and then the navy suit had cost a hundred and sixty-seven dollars.

A lot of people were out enjoying the day, and the clean fresh air lifted my spirits too. By two I was on the Edens Expressway heading toward the North Shore. I started singing a snatch from Mozart's *"Ch'io mi scordi di te,"* but my rib cage protested and I had to settle for a Bartok concerto on WFMT.

For some reason the Edens ceases to be a beautiful expressway as it nears the homes of the rich. Close to Chicago it's lined with greensward and neat bungalows, but as you go farther out, shopping centers crop up and indus-trial parks and drive-ins take over. Once I turned right onto Willow Road, though, and headed toward the lake, the view became more impressive—large stately homes set well back on giant, carefully manicured lawns. I checked Thayer's address and turned south onto Sheridan Road, squinting at numbers on mailboxes. His house was on the east side, the side where lots face Lake Michigan, giving the children private beaches and boat moorings when they were home from Groton or Andover.

My Chevy felt embarrassed turning through twin stone pillars, especially when it saw a small Mercedes, an Alfa, and an Audi Fox off to one side of the drive. The circular drive took me past some attractive flower gardens to the front door of a limestone mansion. Next to the door a small sign requested tradesmen to make deliveries in the rear. Was I a tradesman or woman? I wasn't sure I had anything to deliver, but perhaps my host did.

I took a card from my wallet and wrote a short message on it: "Let's talk about your relations with the Knifegrinders." I rang the bell.

The expression on the face of the neatly uniformed woman who answered the door reminded me of my black eye: the bute had put it out of my mind for a while. I gave her the card. "I'd like to see Mr. Thayer," I said coolly.

She looked at me dubiously, but took the card, shutting the door in my face. I could hear faint shouts from beaches farther up the road. As the minutes passed, I left the porch to make a more detailed study of a flower bed on the other side of the drive. When the door opened, I turned back. The maid frowned at me.

"I'm not stealing the flowers," I assured her. "But since you don't have magazines in the waiting area, I had to look at something."

She sucked in her breath but only said, "This way." No "please," no manners at all. Still, this was a house of mourning. I made allowances.

We moved at a fast clip through a large entry room graced by a dull-green statue, past a stairway, and down a hall leading to the back of the house. John Thayer met us, coming from the other direction. He was wearing a white knit shirt and checked gray slacks—suburban attire but muted. His whole air was subdued, as if he were consciously trying to act like a mourning father.

"Thanks, Lucy. We'll go in here." He took my arm and moved me into a room with comfortable armchairs and packed bookcases. The books were lined up neatly on the shelves. I wondered if he ever read any of them.

Thayer held out my card. "What's this about, Warshawski?"

"Just what it says. I want to talk about your relations with the Knifegrinders."

He gave a humorless smile. "They are as minimal as possible. Now that Peter is—gone, I expect them to be non-existent."

"I wonder if Mr. McGraw would agree with that."

He clenched his fist, crushing the card. "Now we get to it. McGraw hired you to blackmail me, didn't he?"

"Then there is a connection between you and the Knifegrinders."

"No!"

"Then how can Mr. McGraw possibly blackmail you?"

"A man like that stops at nothing. I warned you yesterday to be careful around him."

"Look, Mr. Thayer. Yesterday you got terribly upset at learning that McGraw had brought your name into this. Today you're afraid he's black-mailing you. That's awfully suggestive."

His face was set in harsh, strained lines. "Of what?"

"Something was going on between you two that you don't want known. Your son found it out and you two had him killed to keep him quiet."

"That's a lie, Warshawski, a goddamned lie," he roared.

"Prove it."

"The police arrested Peter's killer this morning."

My head swam and I sat down suddenly in one of the leather chairs. "What?" My voice squeaked.

"One of the commissioners called me. They found a drug addict who'd tried to rob the place. They say Peter caught him at it and was shot."

"No," I said.

"What do you mean, no? They arrested the guy."

"No. Maybe they arrested him, but that wasn't the scene. No one robbed that place. Your son didn't catch anyone in the act. I tell you, Thayer, the boy was sitting at the kitchen table and someone shot him. That is not the work of a drug addict caught in a felony. Besides, nothing was taken."

"What are you after, Warshawski? Maybe nothing was taken. Maybe he got scared and fled. I'd believe that before I'd believe your story—that I shot my own son." His face was working with a strong emotion. Grief? Anger? Maybe horror?

"Mr. Thayer, I'm sure you've noticed what a mess my face is. A couple of punks roughed me up last night to warn me off the investigation into your son's death. A drug addict doesn't have those kinds of resources. I saw several people who might have engineered that—and you and Andy McGraw were two of them."

"People don't like busybodies, Warshawski. If someone beat you up, I'd take the hint."

I was too tired to get angry. "In other words, you are involved but you figure you've got your ass covered. So that means I'll have to figure out a way to saw the barrel off your tail. It'll be a pleasure."

"Warshawski, I'm telling you for your own good: drop it." He went over to his desk. "I can see you're a conscientious girl—but McGraw is wasting your time. There's nothing to find." He wrote a check and handed it to me. "Here. You can give McGraw back whatever he's paid you and feel like you've done your duty."

The check was for $5,000. "You bastard. You accuse me of blackmail and then you try to buy me off?" A spurt of raw anger pushed my fatigue to one side. I ripped up the check and let the pieces fall to the floor.

Thayer turned white. Money was his raw nerve. "The police made an arrest, Warshawski. I don't need to buy you off. But if you want to act stupid about it, there's nothing more to say. You'd better leave."

The door opened and a girl came in. "Oh, Dad, Mother wants you to—" She broke off. "Sorry, didn't know you had company." She was an attractive teen-ager. Her brown, straight hair was well brushed and hung down her back, framing a small oval face. She was wearing jeans and a striped man's shirt several sizes too big for her. Maybe her brother's. Normally she probably had the confident, healthy air that money can provide. Right now she drooped a bit.

"Miss Warshawski was just leaving, Jill. In fact, why don't you show her out and I'll go see what your mother wants."

He got up and walked to the door, waiting until I followed him to say good-bye. I didn't offer to shake hands. Jill led me back the way I'd come earlier; her father walked briskly in the opposite direction.

"I'm very sorry about your brother," I said as we got to the greenish statue.

"So am I," she said, pulling her lips together. When we got to the front of the house, she followed me outside and stood staring up at my face, frowning a little. "Did you know Peter?" she finally asked.

"No, I never met him," I answered. "I'm a private investigator, and I'm afraid I'm the person who found him the other morning."

"They wouldn't let me look at him," she said.

"His face was fine. Don't have nightmares about him—his face wasn't damaged." She wanted more information. If he'd been shot in the head, how could his face look all right? I explained it to her in a toned-down, clinical way.

"Peter told me you could decide whether to trust people by their faces," she said after a minute. "But yours is pretty banged up so I can't tell. But you told me the truth about Peter and you're not talking to me as if I was a baby or something." She paused. I waited. Finally she asked, "Did Dad ask you to come out here?" When I replied, she asked, "Why was he angry?"

"Well, he thinks the police have arrested your brother's murderer, but I think they've got the wrong person. And that made him angry."

"Why?" she asked. "I mean, not why is he mad, but why do you think they got the wrong person?"

"The reasons are pretty complicated. It's not because I know who did it, but because I saw your brother, and the apartment, and some other people who've been involved, and they've reacted to my seeing them. I've been in this business for a while, and I have a feel for when I'm hearing the truth. A drug addict wandering in off the streets just doesn't fit with what I've seen and heard."

She stood on one foot, and her face was screwed up as if she were afraid she might start crying. I put an arm around her and pulled her to a sitting position on the shallow porch step.

"I'm okay," she muttered. "It's just—everything is so weird around here. You know, it's so terrible, Pete dying and everything. He—he—well—" She hiccuped back a sob. "Never mind. It's Dad who's crazy. Probably he always was but I never noticed it before. He's been raving on and on about how Anita and her father shot Pete for his money and dumb stuff like that, and then he'll start saying how it served Pete right, like he's glad he's dead or something." She gulped and ran her hand across her nose. "Dad was always in such a stew about Peter disgracing the family name, you know, but he wouldn't have—even if he'd become a union organizer he would have been a successful one. He liked figuring things out, he was that kind of person, figuring things out and trying to do them the best way." She hiccuped again. "And I like Anita. Now I suppose I'll never see her again. I wasn't supposed to meet her, but she and Pete took me out to dinner sometimes, when Mom and Dad were out of town."

"She's disappeared, you know," I told her. "You wouldn't know where she's gone, would you?"

She looked up at me with troubled eyes. "Do you think something's happened to her?"

"No," I said with a reassurance I didn't feel. "I think she got scared and ran away."

"Anita's really wonderful," she said earnestly. "But Dad and Mother just refused even to meet her. That was when Dad first started acting weird, when Pete and Anita began going together. Even today, when the police came, he wouldn't believe they'd arrested this man. He kept saying it was Mr. McGraw. It was really awful." She grimaced unconsciously. "Oh, it's been just horrible here. Nobody cares about Pete. Mother just cares about the neighbors. Dad is freaked out. I'm the only one who cares he's dead." Tears were streaming down her face now and she stopped trying to fight them. "Sometimes I even get the crazy idea that Dad just freaked out totally, like he does, and killed Peter."

This was the big fear. Once she'd said it, she started sobbing convulsively and shivering. I took off my jacket and wrapped it around her shoulders. I held her close for a few minutes and let her sob.

The door opened behind us. Lucy stood there, scowling. "Your father wants to know where you've gone to—and he doesn't want you standing around gossiping with the detective."

I stood up. "Why don't you take her inside and wrap her up in a blanket and get her something hot to drink: she's pretty upset with everything that's going on, and she needs some attention."

Jill was still shivering, but she'd stopped sobbing. She gave me a watery little smile and handed me my jacket. "I'm okay," she whispered.

I dug a card out of my purse and handed it to her. "Call me if you need me, Jill," I said. "Day or night." Lucy hustled her inside at top speed and shut the door. I was really toning down the neighborhood—good thing they couldn't see me through the trees.

My shoulders and legs were beginning to hurt again and I walked slowly back to my car. The Chevy had a crease in the front right fender where someone had sideswiped it in last winter's heavy snow. The Alfa, the Fox, and the Mercedes were all in mint condition. My car and I looked alike, whereas the Thayers seemed more like the sleek, scratchless Mercedes. There was a lesson in there someplace. Maybe too much urban living was bad for cars and people. Real profound, Vic.

I wanted to get back to Chicago and call Bobby and get the lowdown on this drug addict they'd arrested, but I needed to do something else while Lotty's painkiller was still holding me up. I drove back over to the Edens and went south to the Dempster exit. This road led through the predominantly Jewish suburb of Skokie, and I stopped at the Bagel Works delicatessen and bagel bakery there. I ordered a jumbo corned beef on rye and a Fresca, and sat in the car, eating while I tried to decide where to get a gun. I knew how to use them—my dad had seen too many shooting accidents in homes with guns. He'd decided the way to avoid one in our house was for my mother and me to learn how to use them. My mother had always refused; they gave her unhappy memories of the war and she would always say she'd use the time to pray for a world without weapons. But I used to go down to the police range with my dad on Saturday afternoons and practice target shooting. At one time I could clean and load and fire a .45 police revolver in two minutes, but since my father had died ten years ago, I hadn't been out shooting. I'd given his gun to Bobby as a memento when he'd died, and I'd never needed one since then. I had killed a man once, but that had been an accident. Joe Correl had jumped me outside a warehouse when I was looking into some inventory losses for a company. I had broken his hold and smashed his jaw in, and when he fell, he'd hit his head on the edge of a forklift. I'd broken his jaw, but it was his skull against the forklift that killed him.

But Smeissen had a lot of hired muscle, and if he was really pissed off, he could hire some more. A gun wouldn't completely protect me, but I thought it might narrow the odds.

The corned beef sandwich was delicious. I hadn't had one for a long time, and decided to forget my weight-maintenance program for one afternoon and have another. There was a phone booth in the deli, and I let my fingers do the walking through the Yellow Pages. The phone book showed four columns of gun dealers. There was one not too far from where I was in the suburb of Lincolnwood. When I called and described what I wanted, they didn't have it. After $1.20 worth of calls, I finally located a repeating, mediumweight Smith & Wesson on the far South Side of the city. My injuries were really throbbing by this time and I didn't feel like a forty-mile drive to the other end of the city. On the other hand, those injuries were why I needed the gun. I paid for the corned beef sandwich and with my second Fresca swallowed four of the tablets Lotty had given me.

The drive south should have taken only an hour, but I was feeling light-headed, my head and body not connected too strongly. The last thing I wanted was for one of Chicago's finest to pull me over. I took it slowly, swallowed a couple more tablets of bute, and put all my effort into holding my concentration.

It was close to five when I exited from I-57 to the south suburbs. By the time I got to Riley's, they were ready to close. I insisted on coming in to make my purchase.

"I know what I want," I said. "I called a couple of hours ago—a Smith & Wesson thirty-eight."

The clerk looked suspiciously at my face and took in the black eye. "Why don't you come back on Monday, and if you still feel you want a gun, we can talk about a model more suited to a lady than a Smith & Wesson thirty-eight."

"Despite what you may think I am not a wife-beating victim. I am not planning on buying a gun to go home and kill my husband. I'm a single woman living alone and I was attacked last night. I know how to use a gun, and I've decided I need one, and this is the kind I want."

"Just a minute," the clerk said. He hurried to the back of the store and began a whispered consultation with two men standing there. I went to the case and started inspecting guns and ammunition. The store was new, clean, and beautifully laid out. Their ad in the Yellow Pages proclaimed Riley's as Smith & Wesson specialists, but they had enough variety to please any kind of taste in shooting. One wall was devoted to rifles.

My clerk came over with one of the others, a pleasant-faced, middle-aged man. "Ron Jaffrey," he said. "I'm the manager. What can we do for you?"

"I called up a couple of hours ago asking about a Smith & Wesson thirty-eight. I'd like to get one," I repeated.

"Have you ever used one before?" the manager asked.

"No, I'm more used to the Colt forty-five," I answered. "But the S&W is lighter and better suited to my needs."

The manager walked to one of the cases and unlocked it. My clerk went to the door to stop another last-minute customer from entering. I took the gun from the manager, balanced it in my hand, and tried the classic police firing stance: body turned to create as narrow a target as possible. The gun felt good. "I'd like to try it before I buy it," I told the manager. "Do you have a target range?"

Jaffrey took a box of ammunition from the case. "I have to say you look as though you know how to handle it. We have a range in the back—if you decide against the gun, we ask you to pay for the ammo. If you take the gun, we throw in a box free."

"Fine," I said. I followed him through a door in the back, which led to a small range.

"We give lessons back here on Sunday afternoons, and let people come in to practice on their own during the week. Need any help loading?"

"I may," I told him. "Time was when I could load and fire in thirty seconds, but it's been a while." My hands were starting to shake a bit from fatigue and pain and it took me several minutes to insert eight rounds of cartridges. The manager showed me the safety and the action. I nodded, turned to the target, lifted the gun, and fired. The action came as natually as if ten days, not ten years, had passed, but my aim was way off. I emptied the gun but didn't get a bull's-eye, and only two in the inner ring. The gun was good, though, steady action and no noticeable distortion. "Let me try another lot."

I emptied the chambers and Jaffrey handed me some more cartridges. He gave me a couple of pointers. "You obviously know what you're doing, but you're out of practice and you've picked up some bad habits. Your stance is good, but you're hunching your shoulder—keep it down and only raise the arm."

I loaded and fired again, trying to keep my shoulder down. It was good advice—all but two shots got into the red and one grazed the bull's-eye. "Okay," I said. "I'll take it. Give me a couple of boxes of ammo, and a complete cleaning kit." I thought a minute. "And a shoulder holster."

We went back into the store. "Larry!" Jaffrey called. My clerk came over. "Clean and wrap this gun for the lady while I write up the bill." Larry took the gun, and I went with Jaffrey to the cash register. A mirror was mounted behind it, and I saw myself in it without recognition for a few seconds. The left side of my face was now completely purple and badly swollen while my right eye stared with the dark anguish of a Paul Klee drawing. I almost turned to see who this battered woman was before realizing I was looking at myself. No wonder Larry hadn't wanted to let me in the store.

Jaffrey showed me the bill. "Four hundred twenty-two dollars," he said. "Three-ten for the gun, ten for the second box of cartridges, fifty-four for the holster and belt, and twenty-eight for the cleaning kit. The rest is tax." I wrote a check out, slowly and laboriously. "I need a driver's license and two major credit cards or an interbank card," he said, "and I have to ask you to sign this register." He looked at my driver's license. "Monday you should go down to City Hall and register that gun. I send a list of all major purchases to the local police department, and they'll probably forward your name to the Chicago police."

I nodded and quietly put my identification back in my billfold. The gun took a big chunk out of the thousand dollars I'd had from McGraw, and I didn't think I could legitimately charge it to him as an expense. Larry brought me the gun in a beautiful velvet case. I looked at it and asked them to put it in a bag for me. Ron Jaffrey ushered me urbanely to my car, magnificently ignoring my face. "You live quite a ways from here, but if you want to come down and use the target, just bring your bill with you—you get six months' free practice with the purchase." He opened my car door for me. I thanked him, and he went back to the store.

The bute was still keeping the pain from crashing in on me completely, but I was absolutely exhausted. My last bit of energy had gone to buying the gun and using the target. I couldn't drive the thirty miles back to my apartment. I started the car and went slowly down the street, looking for a motel. I found a Best Western that had rooms backing onto a side street, away from the busy road I was on. The clerk looked curiously at my face but made no comment. I paid cash and took the key.

The room was decent and quiet, the bed firm. I uncorked the bottle of nepenthe Lotty had given me and took a healthy swallow. I peeled off my clothes, wound my watch and put it on the bedside table, and crawled under the covers. I debated calling my answering service but decided I was too tired to handle anything even if it had come up. The air conditioner, set on high, drowned out any street noises and made the room cold enough to enjoy snuggling under the blankets. I lay down and was starting to think about John Thayer when I fell asleep.

8
SOME VISITORS DON'T KNOCK

I came to slowly, out of a sound sleep. I lay quietly, not sure at first where I was, and dozed again lightly. When I woke up the second time, I was refreshed and aware. The heavy drapes shut out any outside light; I switched on the bedside lamp and looked at my watch—7:30. I had slept more than twelve hours.

I sat up and cautiously moved legs and neck. My muscles had stiffened again in my sleep, but not nearly as badly as the previous morning. I pulled myself from the bed and made it to the window with only minor twinges. Looking through a crack I pulled in the drapes, I saw bright morning sunlight.

I was puzzled by Thayer's account of a police arrest and wondered if there would be a story in the morning paper. I pulled on my slacks and shirt and went down to the lobby for a copy of the Sunday *Herald-Star*. Back upstairs I undressed again and ran a hot bath while I looked at the paper. DRUG ADDICT ARRESTED IN BANKING HEIR'S MURDER was on the lower right side of the front page.

Police have arrested Donald Mackenzie of 4302 S. Ellis in the murder of banking heir Peter Thayer last Monday. Asst. Police Commissioner Tim Sullivan praised the men working on the case and said an arrest was made early Saturday morning when one of the residents of the apartment where Peter Thayer lived identified Mackenzie as a man seen hanging around the building several times recently. It is believed that Mackenzie, allegedly addicted to cocaine, entered the Thayer apartment on Monday, July 16, believing no one to be at home. When he found Peter Thayer eating breakfast in the kitchen, he lost his nerve and shot him. Commissioner Sullivan says the Browning automatic that fired the fatal bullet has not yet been traced but that the police have every hope of recovering the weapon.

The story was continued on page sixty-three. Here, a full page had been devoted to the case. Pictures of the Thayer family with Jill, another sister, and a chic Mrs. Thayer. A single shot of Peter in a baseball uniform for New Trier High School. A good candid picture of Anita McGraw. An accompanying story proclaimed LABOR LEADER'S DAUGHTER STILL MISSING. It suggested "now that the police have made an arrest, there is hope that Miss McGraw will return to Chicago or call her family. Meanwhile, her picture has been circulated to state police in Wisconsin, Indiana, and Michigan."

That seemed to be that. I lay back in the water and closed my eyes. The police were supposedly hunting high and low for the Browning, questioning Mackenzie's friends, and searching his hangouts. But I didn't think they'd find it. I tried to remember what Earl's goons had been carrying. Fred had had a Colt, but I thought Tony might have had a Browning. Why was Thayer so willing to believe Mackenzie had killed his son? According to Jill, he'd been insisting at first it was McGraw. Something nagged at the back of my mind, but I couldn't put a finger on it. Could there possibly be any proof that Mackenzie had done it? On the other hand, what proof did I have that he hadn't? My stiff joints, the fact that nothing had been touched in the apartment. . . . But what did it really add up to? I wondered if Bobby had made that arrest, whether he was among those diligent policemen whom Police Commissioner Sullivan unstintingly praised. I decided I needed to get back to Chicago and talk to him.

With this in mind I got dressed and left the motel. I realized I hadn't eaten since those two corned beef sandwiches yesterday afternoon and stopped at a little coffee shop for a cheese omelette, juice, and coffee. I was eating too much lately and not getting any exercise. I surreptitiously slid a finger around my waistband, but it didn't seem any tighter.

I took some more of Lotty's pills with my coffee and was feeling fine by the time I pulled off the Kennedy at Belmont. Sunday morning traffic was light and I made it to Halsted by a little after ten. There was a parking place across from my apartment, and a dark, unmarked car with a police antenna on it. I raised my eyebrows speculatively. Had the mountain come to Mohammed?

I crossed the street and looked into the car. Sergeant McGonnigal was sitting there alone with a newspaper. When he saw me, he put the paper down and got out of the car. He was wearing a light sports jacket and gray slacks and his shoulder holster made a little bulge under his right armpit. A southpaw, I thought. "Good morning, Sergeant," I said. "Beautiful day, isn't it?"

"Good morning, Miss Warshawski. Mind if I come up with you and ask you a few questions?"

"I don't know," I answered. "It depends on the questions. Bobby send you?"

"Yes. We got a couple of inquiries in and he thought I'd better come over to see if you're all right—that's quite a shiner you've picked up."

"Yes, it is," I agreed. I held the door to the building open for him and followed him in. "How long have you been here?"

"I stopped by last night, but you weren't home. I called a couple of times. When I stopped by this morning I just thought I'd wait until noon to see if you showed up. Lieutenant Mallory was afraid the captain would order an APB on you if I reported you missing."

"I see. I'm glad I decided to come home."

We got to the top of the stairs. McGonnigal stopped. "You usually leave your door open?"

"Never." I moved past him. The door was cracked open, hanging a bit drunkenly. Someone had shot out the locks to get in—they don't respond to forcing. McGonnigal pulled out his gun, slammed the door open, and rolled into the room. I drew back against the hall wall, then followed him in.

My apartment was a mess. Someone had gone berserk in it. The sofa cushions had been cut open, pictures thrown on the floor, books opened and dropped so that they lay with open spines and crumpling pages. We walked through the apartment. My clothes were scattered around the bedroom, drawers dumped out. In the kitchen all the flour and sugar had been emptied onto the floor, while pans and plates were everywhere, some of them chipped from reckless handling. In the dining room the red Venetian glasses were lying crazily on the table. Two had fallen off. One rested safely on the carpet, but the other had shattered on the wood floor. I picked up the seven whole ones and stood them in the breakfront and sat to pick up the pieces of the other. My hands were shaking and I couldn't handle the tiny shards.

"Don't touch anything else, Miss Warshawski." McGonnigal's voice was kind. "I'm going to call Lieutenant Mallory and get some fingerprint experts over here. They probably won't find anything, but we've got to try. In the meantime, I'm afraid you'll have to leave things the way they are."

I nodded. "The phone is next to the couch—what used to be the couch," I said, not looking up. Jesus, what next? Who the hell had been in here, and why? It just couldn't be a random burglar. A pro might take the place apart looking for valuables—but rip up the couch? Dump china onto the floor? My mother had carried those glasses from Italy in a suitcase and not a one had broken. Nineteen years married to a cop on the South Side of Chicago and not a one had broken. If I had become a singer, as she had wanted, this would never have happened. I sighed. My hands were calmer, so I picked up the little shards and put them in a dish on the table.

"Please don't touch anything," McGonnigal said again, from the doorway.

"Goddamnit, McGonnigal, shut up!" I snapped. "Even if you do find a fingerprint in here that doesn't belong to me or one of my friends, you think they're going to go all over these splinters of glass? And I'll bet you dinner at the Savoy that whoever came through here wore gloves and you won't find a damned thing, anyway." I stood up. "I'd like to know what you were doing when the tornado came through—sitting out front reading your newspaper?

Did you think the noise came from someone's television? Who came in and out of the building while you were here?"

He flushed. Mallory was going to ask him the same question. If he hadn't bothered to find out, he was in hot water.

"I don't think this was done while I was here, but I'll go ask your downstairs neighbors if they heard any nose. I know it must be very upsetting to come home and find your apartment destroyed, but please, Miss Warshawski—if we're going to have a prayer of finding these guys we've got to fingerprint the place."

"Okay, okay," I said. He went out to check downstairs. I went to the bedroom. My canvas suitcase was lying open but fortunately had not been cut. I didn't think canvas would take fingerprints, so I put it on the dismantled box springs and packed, going through the array of clothes and lingerie on the floor. I put the wrapped box from Riley's in, too, and then called Lotty on the bedside phone.

"Lotty, I can't talk right now, but my apartment has been ravaged. Can I come and stay a few nights?"

"Naturally, Vic. Do you need me to come get you?"

"No, I'm okay. I'll be over in a while—I need to talk to the police first."

We hung up and I took the suitcase down to the car. McGonnigal was in the second-floor apartment; the door was half open and he was talking, with his back to the hallway. I put the suitcase in my trunk and was just unlocking the outer door to go back upstairs when Mallory came squealing up to the curb with a couple of squad cars hot behind him. They double-parked, lights flashing, and a group of kids gathered at the end of the street, staring. Police like to create public drama—no other need for all that show.

"Hello, Bobby," I said as cheerily as I could manage.

"What the hell is going on here, Vicki?" Bobby asked, so angry that he forgot his cardinal rule against swearing in front of women and children.

"Not nice, whatever it is: someone tore my place up. They smashed one of Gabriella's glasses."

Mallory had been charging up the stairs, about to muscle me aside, but that stopped him—he'd drunk too many New Year's toasts out of those glasses. "Christ, Vicki, I'm sorry, but what the hell were you doing poking your nose into this business anyway?"

"Why don't you send your boys upstairs and we'll sit here and talk. There's no place to sit down up there and frankly, I can't stand to look at it."

He thought about it for a minute. "Yeah, why don't we go sit in my car, and you answer a few questions. Finchley!" he bellowed. A young black cop stepped forward. "Take the crew upstairs and fingerprint the place and search it if you can for any clues." He turned to me. "Anything valuable that might be missing?"

I shrugged. "Who knows what's valuable to a ransacker. A couple of good pieces of jewelry—my mother's; I never wear them, too old-fashioned —a single diamond pendant set in a white gold filigree with matching earrings. A couple of rings. There's a little silver flatware. I don't know—a turntable. I haven't looked for anything—just looked and looked away."

"Yeah, okay," Bobby said. "Go on." He waved a hand and the four uniformed men started up the stairs. "And send McGonnigal down to me," he called after them.

We went to Bobby's car and sat together in the front seat. His full, red face was set—angry, but not, I thought, with me. "I told you on Thursday to butt out of the Thayer case."

"I heard the police made an arrest yesterday—Donald Mackenzie. Is there still a Thayer case?"

Bobby ignored that. "What happened to your face?"

"I ran into a door."

"Don't clown, Vicki. You know why I sent McGonnigal over to talk to you?"

"I give up. He fell in love with me and you were giving him an excuse to come by and see me?"

"I can't deal with you this morning!" Bobby yelled, top volume. "A kid is dead, your place is a wreck, your face looks like hell, and all you can think of is getting my goat. Goddamnit, talk to me straight and pay attention to what I say."

"Okay, okay," I said pacifically. "I give up: why did you send the sergeant over to see me?"

Bobby breathed heavily for a few minutes. He nodded, as if to affirm that he'd recovered his self-control. "Because John Thayer told me last night that you'd been beaten up and you didn't believe that Mackenzie had committed the crime."

"Thayer," I echoed, incredulous. "I talked to him yesterday and he threw me out of his house because I wouldn't accept his word that Mackenzie was the murderer. Now why's he turning around telling you that? How'd you come to be talking to him, anyway?"

Bobby smiled sourly. "We had to go out to Winnetka to ask a few last questions. When it's the Thayer family, we wait on their convenience, and that was when it was convenient. . . . He believes it was Mackenzie but he wants to be sure. Now tell me about your face."

"There's nothing to tell. It looks worse than it is—you know how it is with black eyes."

Bobby drummed on the steering wheel in exaggerated patience. "Vicki, after I talked to Thayer, I had McGonnigal go through our reports to see if anyone had turned in anything on a battered woman. And we found a cabbie had stopped at the Town Hall Station and mentioned picking up a woman at Astor and the Drive and dropping her at your address. Quite a coincidence, huh? The guy was worried because you looked in pretty bad shape, but there wasn't anything anyone could do about it—you weren't filing a complaint."

"Right you are," I said.

Mallory tightened his lips but didn't lose his temper. "Now, Vicki," he continued. "McGonnigal wondered what you were doing down at Astor and the Drive looking so bloody. It's not really a mugger's spot. And he remembered how Earl Smeissen owns a condo down there on Astor, in from State Street—or Parkway they call it when it gets into the tony part of town. So now we want to know why Earl wanted to beat you up."

"It's your story. You're saying he beat me up, you give me a reason why."

"He probably had a bellyful of your clowning," Bobby said, his voice rising again. "For two cents, I'd black your other goddamn eye for you."

"Is that why you came over, to threaten me?"

"Vicki, I want to know why Earl beat you. The only reason I can think of is that he's tied to the Thayer boy—maybe had him shot when someone else fingered him."

"Then you don't think that Mackenzie is responsible?" Mallory was silent. "You make the arrest?"

"No," Mallory said stiffly. I could see this hurt. "Lieutenant Carlson did."

"Carlson? I don't know him. Who's he work for?"

"Captain Vespucci," Mallory said shortly.

I raised my eyebrows. "Vespucci?" I was beginning to sound like a parrot. Vespucci had been a colleague my father was ashamed to talk about. He'd been implicated in a number of departmental scandals over the years, most of them having to do with police bought off by the mob, or turning the other cheek to mob activities in their territory. There'd never been enough evidence to justify throwing him off the force—but that, too, the rumors said, was because he had the kind of connections that made you keep quiet.

"Carlson and Vespucci pretty close?" I asked.

"Yes," Bobby bit off.

I thought for a minute. "Did someone—like Earl, say—bring pressure on Vespucci to make an arrest? Is Donald Mackenzie another poor slob caught in a trap because he was wandering around the wrong part of town? Did he leave any prints in the apartment? Can you find the gun? Has he made a confession?"

"No, but he can't account for his time on Monday. And we're pretty sure he's been involved in some Hyde Park burglaries."

"But you don't agree that he's the killer?"

"As far as the department is concerned, the case is closed. I talked to Mackenzie myself this morning."

"And?"

"And nothing. My captain says it's a defensible arrest."

"Your captain owe anything to Vespucci?" I asked.

Mallory made a violent motion with his torso. "Don't talk like that to me, Vicki. We've got seventy-three unsolved homicides right now. If we wrap one up in a week, the captain has every right to be happy."

"All right, Bobby." I sighed. "Sorry. Lieutenant Carlson arrested Mackenzie, and Vespucci told your captain, who told you to lay off, the case was closed. . . . But you want to know why Earl beat me up." Mallory turned red again. "You can't have it both ways. If Mackenzie is the killer, why would Smeissen care about me and Peter Thayer? If he beat me up—and I mean *if* —it could have been for lots of reasons. He might've made a heavy pass I turned down. Earl doesn't like ladies who turn him down, you know—he's beaten a couple before. First time I ever saw Earl was when I was a starry-eyed rookie attorney on the Public Defender's roster. I was appearing for a lady whom Earl beat up. Nice young prostitute who didn't want to work for him. Sorry, I just committed slander: she alleged that Earl beat her up, but we couldn't make it stick."

"You're not going to ask for charges, then," Mallory said. "Figures. Now tell me about your apartment. I haven't seen it, but take it as read that it was torn apart—McGonnigal gave me a brief description. Someone was looking for something. What?"

I shook my head. "Beats me. None of my clients has ever given me the secret to the neutron bomb or even a new brand of toothpaste. I just don't deal with that kind of stuff. And anytime I do have volatile evidence, I leave it in a safe in my office . . ." My voice trailed off. Why hadn't I thought of that sooner? If someone had torn the apartment apart looking for something, they were probably down in my office now.

"Give me the address," Bobby said. I gave it to him and he got on the car radio and ordered a patrol car to go up and check. "Now, Vicki, I want you to be honest with me. This is off the record—no witnesses, no tapes. Tell me what you took out of that apartment that someone, call him Smeissen, wants back so badly." He looked at me in a kindly, worried, fatherly way. What did I have to lose by telling him about the picture and the pay stub?

"Bobby," I said earnestly, "I did look around the apartment, but I didn't see anything that smacked remotely of Earl or any other person in particular. Not only that, the place didn't look as though anyone else had searched it."

Sergeant McGonnigal came up to the car. "Hi, Lieutenant—Finchley said you wanted me."

"Yeah," Bobby said. "Who came in and out of the building while you were watching it?"

"Just one of the residents, sir."

"You sure of that?"

"Yes, sir. She lives in the second-floor apartment. I was just talking to her —Mrs. Alvarez—said she heard a lot of noise about three this morning, but didn't pay any attention to it—says Miss Warshawski often has strange guests and wouldn't thank her—Mrs. Alvarez—for interfering."

Thanks, Mrs. Alvarez, I thought. The city needs more neighbors like you. Glad I wasn't home at the time. But what, I wondered, was whoever ransacked my place looking for so desperately? That pay stub linked Peter Thayer to Ajax, but that was no secret. And the picture of Anita? Even if the police hadn't connected her to Andrew McGraw, the picture didn't do that, either. I had put them both in my inner safe at my office, a small bomb- and fireproof box built into the wall at the back of the main safe. I had kept current case papers in there ever since the chairman of Transicon had hired someone to retrieve evidence from my safe two years ago. But I just didn't think that was it.

Bobby and I discussed the break-in for another half hour, touching occasionally on my battle wounds. Finally I said, "Now you tell me something, Bobby: Why don't you believe it was Mackenzie?"

Mallory stared through the windshield. "I'm not doubting it. I believe it. I'd be happier if we had a gun or a fingerprint, but I believe it." I didn't say anything. Bobby continued to look forward with unseeing eyes. "I just wish I'd found him," he said at last. "My captain got a call from Commissioner Sullivan Friday afternoon saying he thought I was overworked and he was asking Vespucci to assign Carlson to help me out. I went home under orders —to get some sleep. Not off the case. Just to sleep. And next morning there was an arrest." He turned to look at me. "You didn't hear that," he said.

I nodded agreement, and Bobby asked me a few more questions about the missing evidence, but his heart wasn't in it. At last he gave up. "If you won't talk, you won't. Just remember, Vicki: Earl Smeissen is a heavy. You know yourself the courts can't nail him. Don't try to play hardball with him —you're just not up to his weight at all."

I nodded solemnly. "Thanks, Bobby. I'll keep it in mind." I opened the door.

"By the way," Bobby said casually, "we got a call last night from Riley's Gun Shop down in Hazelcrest. Said a V. I. Warshawski had bought a small handgun down there and he was worried—she looked rather wild. That wouldn't be anyone you'd know, would it, Vicki?"

I got out of the car, shut the door, and looked in through the open window. "I'm the only one by that name in my family, Bobby—but there are some other Warshawskis in the city."

For once Bobby didn't lose his temper. He looked at me very seriously. "No one ever stopped you when you had your mind set on something, Vicki. But if you're planning on using that gun, get your ass down to City Hall first thing tomorrow morning and register it. Now tell Sergeant McGonnigal where you're going to be until your place is fixed up again."

While I was giving McGonnigal my address, a squawk came in on Mallory's radio about my office: the place had been ransacked. I wondered if my business-interruption insurance would cover this. "Remember, Vicki, you're playing hardball with a pro," Bobby warned. "Get in, McGonnigal." They drove off.

9
FILING A CLAIM

When I got to Lotty's it was afternoon. I had stopped on the way to call my answering service—a Mr. McGraw and a Mr. Devereux had both phoned, and left numbers. I copied them into my pocket phone book but decided not to call until I got to Lotty's. She greeted me with a worried head shake. "Not content with beating you, they beat your apartment. You run with a wild crowd, Vic." But no censure, no horror—one of the things I liked in Lotty.

She examined my face and my eye with her ophthalmoscope. "Coming along nicely. Much less swelling already. Headache? A bit? To be expected. Have you eaten? An empty stomach makes it worse. Come, a little boiled chicken—nice Eastern European Sunday dinner." She had eaten, but drank coffee while I finished the chicken. I was surprised at how hungry I was.

"How long can I stay?" I asked.

"I'm expecting no one this month. As long as you like until August tenth."

"I shouldn't be more than a week—probably less. But I'd like to ask the answering service to switch my home calls here."

Lotty shrugged. "In that case, I won't switch off the phone by the guest bed—mine rings at all hours—women having babies, boys being shot—they don't keep nine-to-five schedules. So you run the risk of answering my calls and if any come for you, I'll let you know." She got up. "Now I must leave you. My medical advice is for you to stay in, have a drink, relax—you're not in good shape and you've had a bad shock. But if you choose to disregard my professional advice, well, I'm not liable in a malpractice suit"—she chuckled slightly—"and keys are in the basket by the sink. I have an answering machine by my bedroom phone—turn it on if you decide to go out." She kissed the air near my face and left.

I wandered restlessly around the apartment for a few minutes. I knew I should go down to my office and assess the damage. I should call a guy I knew who ran a cleaning service to come and restore my apartment. I should call my answering service and get my calls transferred to Lotty's. And I needed to get back to Peter Thayer's apartment to see if there was something there that my apartment smashers believed I had.

Lotty was right: I was not in prime condition. The destruction of my apartment had been shocking. I was consumed with anger, the anger one has when victimized and unable to fight back. I opened my suitcase and got out the box with the gun in it. I unwrapped it and pulled out the Smith & Wesson. While I loaded it, I had a fantasy of planting some kind of hint that would draw Smeissen—or whomever—back to my apartment while I stood in the hallway and pumped them full of bullets. The fantasy was very vivid and I played it through several times. The effect was cathartic—a lot of my anger drained away and I felt able to call my answering service. They took Lotty's number and agreed to transfer my calls.

Finally I sat down and called McGraw. "Good afternoon, Mr. McGraw," I said when he answered. "I hear you've been trying to get in touch with me."

"Yes, about my daughter." He sounded a little ill-at-ease.

"I haven't forgotten her, Mr. McGraw. In fact, I have a lead—not on her directly, but on some people who may know where she's gone."

"How far have you gone with them—these people?" he demanded sharply.

"As far as I could in the time I had. I don't drag cases on just to keep my expense bill mounting."

"Yeah, no one's accusing you of that. I just don't want you to go any further."

"What?" I said incredulously. "You started this whole chain of events and now you don't want me to find Anita? Or did she turn up?"

"No, she hasn't turned up. But I think I flew off the handle a bit when she left her apartment. I thought she might be wrapped up in young Thayer's murder somehow. Now the police have arrested this drug addict, I see the two weren't connected."

Some of my anger returned. "You do? By divine inspiration, maybe? There were no signs of robbery in that apartment, and no sign that Mackenzie had been there. I don't believe he did it."

"Look here, Warshawski, who are you to go around questioning the police? The goddamn punk has been held for two days now. If he hadn't done it, he'd have been let go by now. Now where the hell do you get off saying 'I don't believe it'?" he mimicked me savagely.

"Since you and I last talked, McGraw, I have been beaten and my apartment and office decimated by Earl Smeissen in an effort to get me off the case. If Mackenzie is the murderer, why does Smeissen care so much?"

"What Earl does has no bearing on anything I do," McGraw answered. "I'm telling you to stop looking for my daughter. I hired you and I can fire you. Send me a bill for your expenses—throw in your apartment if you want to. But quit."

"This is quite a change. You were worried sick about your daughter on Friday. What's happened since then?"

"Just get off the case, Warshawski," McGraw bellowed. "I've said I'll pay you—now stop fighting over it."

"Very well," I said in cold anger. "I'm off the payroll. I'll send you a bill. But you're wrong about one thing, McGraw—and you can tell Earl from me —you can fire me, but you can't get rid of me."

I hung up. Beautiful, Vic: beautiful rhetoric. It had just been possible that Smeissen believed he'd cowed me into quitting. So why be so full of female-chismo and yell challenges into the phone? I ought to write, "Think before acting" a hundred times on the blackboard.

At least McGraw had agreed to knowing Earl, or at least to knowing who he was. That had been a shot—not totally in the dark, however, since the Knifegrinders knew most of the hoods in Chicago. The fact that he knew Earl didn't mean he'd sikked him onto my apartment—or onto killing Peter Thayer—but it was sure a better connection than anything else I had.

I dialed Ralph's number. He wasn't home. I paced some more, but decided the time for action had arrived. I wasn't going to get any further thinking about the case, or worrying about intercepting a bullet from Tony's gun. I changed out of the green slacks into jeans and running shoes. I got out my collection of skeleton keys and put them in one pocket, car keys, driver's license, private investigator license, and fifty dollars in the other. I fastened the shoulder holster over a loose, man-tailored shirt and practiced drawing the gun until it came out quickly and naturally.

Before leaving Lotty's, I examined my face in the bathroom mirror. She was right—I did look better. The left side was still discolored—in fact it was showing some more yellow and green—but the swelling had gone down considerably. My left eye was completely open and not inflamed, even though the purple had spread farther. It cheered me up a bit; I switched on Lotty's telephone answering machine, slipped on a jean jacket and left, carefully locking the doors behind me.

The Cubs were playing a doubleheader with St. Louis, and Addison was filled with people leaving the first game and those arriving for the second. I turned on WGN radio just in time to hear DeJesus lead off the bottom of the first inning with a hard drive to the shortstop. He was cut down easily at first, but at least he hadn't hit into a double play.

Once clear of Wrigley Field traffic, it was a quick twenty-minute drive downtown. It being Sunday, I was able to park on the street outside my office. The police had left the area, but a patrolman came over as I entered the building.

"What's your business here, miss?" he asked sharply but not unpleasantly.

"I'm V. I. Warshawski," I told him. "I have an office here which was broken into earlier today and I've come to inspect the damage."

"I'd like to see some identification, please."

I pulled out my driver's license and my private investigator photo-ID. He examined them, nodded, and gave them back to me. "Okay, you can go on up. Lieutenant Mallory told me to keep an eye out and not let anyone but tenants into the building. He told me you'd probably stop by."

I thanked him and went inside. For once the elevator was working and I took it rather than the stairs—I could keep fit someday when I wasn't feeling quite so terrible. The office door was closed, but its upper glass half had been shattered. When I went inside, though, the damage wasn't as severe as to my apartment. True, all my files had been dumped onto the floor, but the furniture had been left intact. No safe is totally entry-proof: someone had been into the little one in back of the big one. But it must have taken five hours at least. No wonder they'd been so angry by the time they got to my apartment —all that effort for nothing. Fortunately I hadn't had any money or sensitive papers in the place at the time.

I decided to leave the papers where they were: tomorrow I'd get a Kelly Girl to come in and file them all for me again. But I'd better call a boarding service for the door, or the place would be ransacked by thieves. I'd lost one of Gabriella's glasses; I didn't want the Olivetti to go as well. I got a twenty-four-hour place to agree to send someone over, and went downstairs. The patrolman wasn't too happy when I explained what I'd done, but he finally agreed to check it with the lieutenant. I left him at the phone and continued on my way to the South Side.

The bright, cool weather was continuing, and I had a pleasant drive south. The lake was dotted with sailboats along the horizon. Nearer the shore were a few swimmers. The game was in the bottom of the third, and Kingman struck out. 2-0, St. Louis. The Cubs had bad days, too—in fact, more than I did, probably.

I parked in the shopping center lot behind the Thayer apartment and reentered the building. The chicken bones had disappeared, but the smell of urine remained. No one came out to question my right to be in the building, and I had no trouble finding a key to open the third-floor apartment.

I should have been prepared for the shambles, but it took me by surprise. When I'd been here before, there had just been the typical disorder of a student apartment. Now, the same hand or hands that had been to my place had done a similar job here. I shook my head to clear it. Of course. They were missing something, and they had been here first. It was only after they hadn't found it that they had come to me. I whistled a bit between my teeth —the opening bars to the third act of *Simon Boccanegra*—and tried to decide what to do. I wondered what was missing and thought it most likely to be a piece of paper of some kind. It might be evidence of fraud or a picture, but I didn't think it would be an actual object.

It didn't seem too likely that it was still in the apartment. Young Thayer might have given it to Anita. If she had it, she was in worse danger than she seemed to be already. I scratched my head. It looked as though Smeissen's boys had covered all the possibilities—sofa cushions ripped, papers and books dumped on the floor. I decided to believe that they had gone through everything page by page—only if my search didn't turn up anything would I take that job on. In a student apartment with several hundred books it would take a sizable chunk of time to examine each one in detail. The only things that were still intact were appliances and floors. I made a methodical search of all the rooms for loose boards or tiles. I found a few and pried them up, using a hammer I found under the kitchen sink, but didn't turn up anything more interesting than some old termite damage. Then I went through the bathroom fixture by fixture, taking down the shower rod and looking into it, and the toilet and sink pipes. That was quite a job; I had to go to my car for tools and break into the basement to turn off the water. It took me more than an hour to get the rusted fittings loose enough to open them. I wasn't surprised to find nothing but water in them—if anyone had been into them, they would have opened more easily.

It was 6:30 and the sun was going down when I returned to the kitchen. The chair where Peter Thayer had been sitting had had its back to the stove. It was possible, of course, that the missing thing had not been hidden deliberately, but had dropped. A piece of paper might float unnoticed under the stove. I lay on my stomach and shone a flashlight under it. I couldn't see anything, and the opening was pretty small. How thorough did I want to be? My muscles were aching and I had left my phenylbutazone at Lotty's. But I went to the living room and got some bricks from a brick-and-board bookcase. Using the jack from my trunk as a lever and the bricks as a wedge, I slowly pried the stove off the floor. It was an impossible task; the jack would catch and raise the thing, and just as I was kicking a brick under the side, down it would slip again. Finally, by dint of pulling the table over and wedging the jack underneath it, I was able to get one brick under the right side. After that the left came up more easily. I checked the gas line to make sure it wasn't straining, and carefully raised the stove by another brick. I then got down on my stomach again and looked underneath. There it was, a piece of paper stuck by grease to the bottom of the stove. I peeled it slowly off in order not to tear it, and took it over to the window to examine.

It was a carbon copy about eight inches square. The top left corner had the Ajax logo on it. In the center it read, "Draft only: not negotiable," and it was made out to Joseph Gielczowski, of 13227 South Ingleside in Matteson, Illinois. He could take this to a bank and have it certified, at which point Ajax would pay the sum of $250 to the bank as a Workers Compensation indemnity payment. The name meant nothing to me and the transaction sounded perfectly straightforward. What was so important about it? Ralph would know, but I didn't want to call him from here—better get the stove down and leave while the leaving was good.

I levered up the stove, using the table again as a wedge, and pulled the bricks out. The stove made a dull thud as it dropped—I hoped the downstairs neighbors weren't home or were too self-engrossed to call the police. I gathered up my tools, folded the claim draft and put it in my shirt pocket, and left. A second-floor apartment door opened a crack as I went by. "Plumber," I called. "There won't be any water on the third floor tonight." The door closed again and I left the building quickly.

When I got back to my car, the game was long over and I had to wait for the eight o'clock news to come on to get the score. The Cubs had pulled it out in the eighth inning. Good old Jerry Martin had hit a double; Ontiveros had singled, and wonderful Dave Kingman had gotten all three of them home with his thirty-second homer of the season. And all this with two out. I knew how the Cubs were feeling tonight, and sang a little *Figaro* on the way home to show it.

10

BEAUTIFUL PEOPLE

Lotty lifted her thick eyebrows as I came into the living room. "Ah," she said, "success shows in your walk. The office was all right?"

"No, but I found what they were looking for." I took out the draft and showed it to her. "Make anything of it?"

She put on a pair of glasses and looked at it intently, pursing her lips. "I see these from time to time, you understand, when I get paid for administering to industrial accident victims. It looks totally in order, as far as I can tell— of course, I don't read them for their content, just glance at them and send them to the bank. And the name Gielczowski means nothing to me, except that it is Polish: should it?"

I shrugged. "I don't know. Doesn't mean anything to me either. I'd better make a copy of it and get it stowed away, though. Have you eaten?"

"I was waiting for you, my dear," she answered.

"Then let me take you out to dinner. I need it—it took a lot of work finding this, physical I mean, although the mental process helped—nothing like a university education to teach you logic."

Lotty agreed. I showered and changed into a respectable pair of slacks. A dressy shirt and a loose jacket completed the outfit, and the shoulder holster fitted neatly under my left arm. I put the claim draft in my jacket pocket.

Lotty scrutinized me when I came back into the living room. "You hide it well, Vic." I looked puzzled and she laughed. "My dear, you left the empty box in the kitchen garbage, and I knew I had brought no Smith & Wesson into the house. Shall we go?"

I laughed but said nothing. Lotty drove us down to Belmont and Sheridan and we had a pleasant, simple dinner in the wine cellar at the Chesterton Hotel. An Austrian wine store, it had expanded to include a tiny restaurant. Lotty approved of their coffee and ate two of the rich Viennese pastries.

When we got home, I insisted on checking front and back entrances, but no one had been around. Inside, I called Larry Anderson, my cleaning friend, and arranged for him to right my apartment. Not tomorrow—he had a big job on, but he'd go over with his best crew personally on Tuesday. Not at all, he'd be delighted. I got hold of Ralph and agreed to meet him for dinner the next night at Ahab's. "How's your face?" he asked.

"Much better, thanks. I should look almost presentable for you tomorrow night."

At eleven I bade Lotty a very sleepy good night and fell into bed. I was instantly asleep, falling down a black hole into total oblivion. Much later I began dreaming. The red Venetian glasses were lined up on my mother's dining-room table. "Now you must hit high C, Vicki, and hold it," my mother said. I made a tremendous effort and sustained the note. Under my horrified eyes, the row of glasses dissolved into a red pool. It was my mother's blood. With a tremendous effort I pulled myself awake. The phone was ringing.

Lotty had answered it on her extension by the time I oriented myself in the strange bed. When I lifted the receiver, I could hear her crisp, soothing voice saying, "Yes, this is Dr. Herschel." I hung up and squinted at the little illuminated face of the bedside clock: 5:13. Poor Lotty, I thought, what a life, and rolled back over to sleep.

The ringing phone dragged me back to life again several hours later. I dimly remembered the earlier call and, wondering if Lotty were back yet, reached for the phone. "Hello?" I said, and heard Lotty on the other extension. I was about to hang up again when a tremulous little voice said, "Is Miss Warshawski there?"

"Yes, speaking. What can I do for you?" I heard the click as Lotty hung up again.

"This is Jill Thayer," the little voice quavered, trying to speak calmly. "Can you come out to my house, please?"

"You mean right now?" I asked.

"Yes," she breathed.

"Sure thing, honey. Be right out. Can you tell me the trouble now?" I had shoved the receiver between my right shoulder and my ear and was pulling on some clothes. It was 7:30 and Lotty's burlap curtains let in enough light to dress by without my having to fumble for the lamp switch.

"It's—I can't talk right now. My mother wants me. Just come, *please.*"

"Okay, Jill. Hold the fort. I'll be there in forty minutes." I hung up and hurriedly finished dressing in the clothes I'd worn last night, not omitting the gun under my left shoulder. I stopped in the kitchen where Lotty was eating toast and drinking the inevitable thick Viennese coffee.

"So," she said, "the second emergency of the day? Mine was a silly hemorrhaging child who had a bad abortion because she was afraid to come to me in the first place." She grimaced. "And the mother was not to know, of course. And you?"

"Off to Winnetka. Another child, but pleasant, not silly." Lotty had the

Sun-Times open in front of her. "Anything new about the Thayers? She sounded quite panicked."

Lotty poured me a cup of coffee, which I swallowed in scalding gulps while scanning the paper, but I found nothing. I shrugged, took a piece of buttered toast from Lotty, kissed her cheek, and was gone.

Native caution made me check the stairwells and the front walk carefully before going to the street. I even examined the backseat and the engine for untoward activity before getting into the car. Smeissen really had me spooked.

Traffic on the Kennedy was heavy with the Monday morning rush hour and people staggering home at the last minute from weekends in the country. Once I hit the outbound Edens, however, I had the road chiefly to myself. I had given Jill Thayer my card more to let her feel someone cared than because I expected an SOS, and with the half of my mind that wasn't looking for speed traps I wondered what had caused the cry for help. A suburban teen-ager who had never seen death might find anything connected with it upsetting, yet she had struck me as essentially levelheaded. I wondered if her father had gone off the deep end in a big way.

I had left Lotty's at 7:42, and turned onto Willow Road at 8:03. Pretty good time for fifteen miles, considering that three had been in the heavy city traffic on Addison. At 8:09 I pulled up to the gates of the Thayer house. That was as far as I got. Whatever had happened, it was excitement in a big way. The entrance was blocked by a Winnetka police car, lights flashing, and as far as I could see into the yard, it was filled with more cars and many policemen. I backed the Chevy down the road a bit and parked it on the gravel verge. It wasn't until I turned the motor off and got out that I noticed the sleek black Mercedes that had been in the yard on Saturday. Only it wasn't in the yard, it was tilted at a strange angle off the road. And it was no longer sleek. The front tires were flat, and the front windshield was a series of glass shards, fragments left from radiating circles. My guess was that bullets, and many of them, had caused the damage.

In my neighborhood a noisy crowd would have gathered to gape over the sight. This being the North Shore, a crowd had gathered, but a smaller and quieter one than Halsted and Belmont would have attracted. They were being held at bay by a lean young policeman with a mustache.

"Gee, they really got Mr. Thayer's car," I said to the young man, strolling over.

When disaster strikes, the police like to keep all the news to themselves. They never tell you what happened, and they never answer leading questions. Winnetka's finest were no exception. "What do you want?" the young man said suspiciously.

I was about to tell him the candid truth when it occurred to me that it would never get me past the herd in the driveway. "My name is V. I. Warshawski," I said, smiling in what I hoped was a saintly way. "I used to be

Miss Jill Thayer's governess. When all the trouble started this morning, she called me and asked me to come out to be with her."

The young cop frowned. "Do you have any identification?" he demanded.

"Certainly," I said righteously. I wondered what use a driver's license would be in proving my story, but I obligingly dug it out and handed it to him.

"All right," he said after studying it long enough to memorize the number, "you can talk to the sergeant."

He left his post long enough to walk me to the gate. "Sarge!" he yelled. One of the men by the door looked up. "This is the Thayer girl's governess!" he called, cupping his hands.

"Thank you, Officer." I said, imitating Miss Jean Brodie's manner. I walked up the drive to the doorway and repeated my story to the sergeant.

He frowned in turn. "We didn't have any word about a governess showing up. I'm afraid no one is allowed in right now. You're not with a newspaper, are you?"

"Certainly not!" I snapped. "Look, Sergeant," I said, smiling a bit to show I could be conciliatory, "how about just asking Miss Thayer to come to the door. She can tell you if she wants me here or not. If she doesn't, I can leave again. But since she did ask for me, she's likely to be upset if I'm not allowed inside."

The upsetness of a Thayer, even one as young as Jill, seemed to concern the sergeant. I was afraid he might ring for Lucy, but instead he asked one of his men to fetch Miss Thayer.

Minutes went by without her appearance, and I began to wonder whether Lucy had seen me after all and set the police straight on my governess story. Eventually Jill arrived, however. Her oval face was pinched and anxious and her brown hair had not been brushed. Her face cleared a little when she saw me. "Oh, it's you!" she said. "They told me my governess was here and I thought it was old Mrs. Wilkens."

"Isn't this your governess?" the patrolman demanded.

Jill gave me an anguished look. I moved into the house. "Just tell the man you sent for me," I said.

"Oh, yes, yes, I did. I called Miss Warshawski an hour ago and begged her to come up here."

The patrolman was looking at me suspiciously, but I was in the house and one of the powerful Thayers wanted me to be there. He compromised by having me spell out my name, letter by laborious letter, for his notebook. Jill tugged on my arm while I was doing this, and as soon as we were through spelling, before he could ask more questions, I gave her a little pat and propelled her toward the hall. She led me to a little room near the big green statue and shut the door.

"Did you say you were my governess?" She was still trying to figure that one out.

"I was afraid they wouldn't let me inside if I told them the truth," I explained. "Police don't like private detectives on their turf. Now suppose you tell me what's going on."

The bleak look reappeared. She screwed up her face. "Did you see the car outside?" I nodded. "My father—that was him, they shot him."

"Did you see them do it?" I asked.

She shook her head and wiped her hand across her nose and forehead. Tears were suddenly streaming down her face. "I heard them," she wailed.

The little room had a settee and a table with some magazines on it. Two heavy-armed chairs stood on either side of a window overlooking the south lawn. I pulled them up to the table and sat Jill in one of them. I sat in the other, facing her. "I'm sorry to put you through it, but I'm going to have to ask you to tell me how it happened. Just take your time, though, and don't mind crying."

The story came out in little sobs. "My dad always leaves—leaves for work between seven and seven thirty," she said. "Sometimes he goes earlier. If something special—special is—going on at the bank. I'm usually asleep when he goes. Lucy makes—made him breakfast, then I get up and she makes another breakfast. Mother has toast and coffee in her room. She's—she's always on a—a diet."

I nodded to explain not only that I understood these details but why she was reporting them. "But today you weren't asleep."

"No," she agreed. "All this stuff about Pete—his funeral was yesterday, you know, and it shook me up so I couldn't—couldn't sleep very well." She'd stopped crying and was trying to control her voice. "I heard Daddy get up, but I didn't go down to eat with him. He'd been so strange, you know, and I didn't want to hear him say anything terrible about Pete." Suddenly she was sobbing, "I wouldn't eat with him, and now he's dead, and now I'll never have another chance." The words came out in great heaving bursts between sobs; she kept repeating them.

I took her hands. "Yes, I know, it's tough, Jill. But you didn't kill him by not eating with him, you know." I patted her hands but didn't say anything else for a while. Finally, though, as the sobs quieted a bit, I said, "Tell me what did happen, honey, and then we can try to figure out an answer to it."

She worked hard to pull herself together, and then said, "There's not much else to tell. My bedroom is above here and I can see the side of the house. I sort of—of wandered to the window and watched him—watched him drive his car down to the road." She stopped to swallow but she had herself in hand. "You can't see the road because of all the bushes in front of it, and anyway, you can't see all the way down to the bottom from my room, but I knew from the sound that he'd gotten down and turned onto Sheridan." I nodded encouragingly, still holding her hands tightly. "Well, I was sort of going back to my bed, I thought I might get dressed, when I heard all these shots. Only I didn't know—know what they were." She carefully wiped two new tears away. "It sounded horrid. I heard glass shattering, and then this squeal, you know, the way a car sounds when it's turning a corner too fast or something, and I thought, maybe Daddy had an accident. You know, he was acting so crazy, he could have gone charging down Sheridan Road and hit someone.

"So I ran downstairs without taking off my nightgown and Lucy came running from the back of the house. She was yelling something, and trying to get me to go back upstairs and get some clothes on, but I went outside anyway and ran down to the drive and found the car." She screwed up her face, shutting her eyes and fought against her tears again. "It was terrible. Daddy—Daddy was bleeding and lying all spread out on the steering wheel." She shook her head. "I still thought he'd been in an accident, but I couldn't see the other car. I thought maybe they'd driven off, you know, the ones with the squealing tires, but Lucy seemed to guess about the shooting. Anyway, she kept me from going over to the car—I didn't have any shoes on, and by then a whole lot of cars had stopped to stare at it and she—Lucy—made one of them call the police on his CB. She wanted me to come back to the house but I wouldn't, not until the police came." She sniffed. "I didn't like to leave him there all by himself, you know."

"Yeah, sure, honey. You did real well. Did your mother come out?"

"No, we went back to the house when the police came, and I came upstairs to get dressed and then I remembered you and called you. But you know when I hung up?" I nodded. "Well, Lucy went to wake up Mother and tell her, and she—she started crying and made Lucy get me, and she came in just then so I had to hang up."

"So you didn't get a glimpse of the people who killed your dad?" She shook her head. "Do the police believe he was in the car you heard taking off?"

"Yes, it's something to do with shells. I think there weren't any shells or something, so they think they must be in the car."

I nodded. "That makes sense. Now for the big question, Jill: Did you want me to come out for comfort and support—which I'm happy to provide—or to take some kind of action?"

She stared at me through gray eyes that had seen and heard too much for her age lately. "What can you do?" she asked.

"You can hire me to find out who killed your dad and your brother," I said matter-of-factly.

"I don't have any money, only my allowance. When I'm twenty-one I get some of my trust money, but I'm only fourteen now."

I laughed. "Not to worry. If you want to hire me, give me a dollar and I'll give you a receipt, and that will mean you've hired me. You'll have to talk to your mother about it, though."

"My money's upstairs," she said, getting up. "Do you think the same person killed Daddy who killed Pete?"

"It seems probable, although I don't really have any facts to go on."

"Do you think it's someone who might—well, is someone trying to wipe out my family?"

I considered that. It wasn't completely out of the question, but it was an awfully dramatic way to do it, and rather slow. "I doubt it," I said finally. "Not completely impossible—but if they wanted to do that, why not just get you all when you were in the car together yesterday?"

"I'll go get my money," Jill said, going to the door. She opened it and Lucy appeared, crossing the hall. "So that's where you are," she said sharply. "How can you disappear like that and your mother wanting you?" She looked into the room. "Now don't tell me that detective woman got in here! Come on, you," she said to me. "Out you go! We've got trouble enough around here without you stirring it up."

"If you please, Lucy," Jill said in a very grown-up way, "Miss Warshawski came up here because I invited her, and she will leave when I ask her to."

"Well, your mother will have something to say about that," Lucy snapped.

"I'll talk to her myself," Jill snapped back. "Can you wait here, please, while I get my money," she added to me, "and then would you mind coming to see my mother with me? I don't think I can explain it to her by myself."

"Not at all," I said politely, giving her an encouraging smile.

After Jill had gone, Lucy said, "All I can say is that Mr. Thayer didn't want you here, and what he would say if he could see you—"

"Well, we both know he can't," I interrupted. "However, if he had been able to explain—to me or to anyone else—what was on his mind, he would very likely be alive this morning.

"Look. I like Jill and I'd like to help her out. She called me this morning not because she has the faintest idea of what I can do for her as a private detective, but because she feels I'm supporting her. Don't you think she gets left out around here?"

Lucy looked at me sourly. "Maybe so, Miss Detective, maybe so. But if Jill had any consideration for her mother, maybe she'd get a little consideration back."

"I see," I said dryly. Jill came back downstairs.

"Your mother is waiting for you," Lucy reminded her sharply.

"I know!" Jill yelled. "I'm coming." She handed me a dollar, and I gravely wrote out a receipt on a scrap of paper from my handbag. Lucy watched the whole thing angrily, her lips shut in a thin line. We then retraced the route I'd taken Saturday through the long hall. We passed the library door and went clear to the back of the house.

Lucy opened the door to a room on the left, saying, "Here she is, Mrs. Thayer. She's got some terrible detective with her who's trying to take money from her. Mr. Thayer threw her out of the house on Saturday, but now she's back."

A patrolman standing beside the door gave me a startled look.

"Lucy!" Jill stormed. "That's a lie." She pushed her way past the disapproving figure into the room. I stood behind Lucy, looking over her shoulder. It was a delightful room, completely windows on three sides. It overlooked the lake out the east side, and a beautiful lawn, complete with a grass tennis court, on the north. It was furnished with white bamboo furniture with cheerful color accents in reds and yellows in the cushions, lamp bases, and floor covering. A profusion of plants gave it a greenhouse effect.

In the middle of this charming setting was Mrs. Thayer. Even with no makeup and a few tearstains, she was very handsome, easily recognizable as the original of the picture in yesterday's *Herald-Star*. A very pretty young woman, an older edition of Jill, sat solicitously on one side of her, and a handsome young man in a polo shirt and checked trousers sat across from her, looking a little ill-at-ease.

"Please, Jill, I don't understand a word you or Lucy are saying, but don't shout, darling, my nerves absolutely won't stand it."

I moved past Lucy into the room and went over to Mrs. Thayer's couch. "Mrs. Thayer, I'm very sorry about your husband and your son," I said. "My name is V. I. Warshawski. I'm a private detective. Your daughter asked me to come up here this morning to see if I could help out."

The young man answered, sticking his jaw out. "I'm Mrs. Thayer's son-in-law, and I think I can safely say that if my father-in-law threw you out of the house on Saturday, that you're probably not wanted here."

"Jill, did you call her?" the young woman asked, shocked.

"Yes, I did," Jill answered, setting her jaw mulishly. "And you can't throw her out, Jack: it's not your house. I asked her to come up, and I've hired her to find out who killed Daddy and Pete. She thinks the same person did it both times."

"Really, Jill," the other woman said, "I think we can leave this to the police without upsetting Mother by bringing in hired detectives."

"Just what I tried telling her, Mrs. Thorndale, but of course she wouldn't listen." That was Lucy, triumphant.

Jill's face was screwed up again, as if she were going to cry. "Take it easy, honey," I said. "Let's not get everyone more worked up than they are already. Why don't you tell me who's who?"

"Sorry," she gulped. "This is my mother, my sister, Susan Thorndale, and her husband, Jack. And Jack thinks because he can boss Susan around he can do that to me, but—"

"Steady, Jill," I said, putting a hand on her shoulder.

Susan's face was pink. "Jill, if you hadn't been spoiled rotten all these years you would show a little respect to someone like Jack who has a lot more experience than you do. Do you have any idea what people are going to be saying about Daddy, the way he was killed and all? Why, why it looks like a gang killing, and it makes Daddy look as if he was involved with the gang." Her voice rose to a high pitch on the last sentence.

"Mob," I said. Susan looked at me blankly. "It looks like a mob killing.

Some gangs may go in for that style of execution, but usually they don't have the resources."

"Now look here," Jack said angrily. "We've already asked you to leave. Why don't you go, instead of showing off your smart mouth! Like Susan said, it's going to be hard enough explaining away the way Mr. Thayer died, without having to explain why we got a private detective involved as well."

"Is that all you care about?" Jill cried. "What people will say? With Pete dead, and Daddy dead?"

"No one is sorrier than me that Peter was shot," Jack said, "but if he had done what your father wanted and lived in a proper apartment, instead of that slummy dump with that slut of a girl, he would never have been shot in the first place."

"Oh!" Jill screamed. "How can you talk about Peter that way! He was trying to do something warm and real instead of— You're such a fake. All you and Susan care about is how much money you make and what the neighbors will say! I hate you!" She ended on another flood of tears and flung herself into my arms. I gave her a hug and wrapped my right arm around her while I fished in my bag for some tissues with the left.

"Jill," her mother said in a soft, complaining voice, "Jill, honey, please don't shout like that in here. My nerves just absolutely cannot take it. I'm just as sorry as you are that Petey is dead, but Jack is right, honey: if he'd listened to your father all this wouldn't have happened, and your father wouldn't be—be . . ." Her voice broke off and she started weeping quietly.

Susan put an arm around her mother and patted her shoulder. "Now, see what you've done," she said venomously, whether to me or to her sister I wasn't sure.

"Now you've caused enough disturbance, you polack detective, whatever your name is," Lucy began.

"Don't you dare talk to her like that," Jill cried, her voice partly muffled by my shoulder. "Her name is Miss Warshawski, and you should call her Miss Warshawski!"

"Well, Mother Thayer," Jack said with a rueful laugh, "sorry to drag you into this, but since Jill won't listen to her sister or me, will you tell her that she has to get this woman out of the house?"

"Oh, please, Jack," his mother-in-law said, leaning on Susan. She stretched out a hand to him without looking at him, and I was interested to note that her eyes didn't turn red with crying. "I just don't have the strength to deal with Jill in one of her moods." However, she pulled herself into a sitting position, still holding on to Jack's hand, and looked at Jill earnestly. "Jill, I just cannot stand for you to have one of your temper tantrums right now. You and Peter never listen to what anyone has to say to you. If Petey had, he wouldn't be dead now. With Petey dead, and John, I just can't take anything else. So don't talk to this private detective any longer. She's taking advantage of you to get her name in the paper, and I can't bear another scandal about this family."

Before I could say anything, Jill tore herself away from me, her little face crimson. "Don't talk like that to me!" she screamed. "I care about Pete and Daddy and you don't! You're the one who's bringing scandals into the house. Everybody knows you didn't love Daddy! Everybody knows what you and Dr. Mulgrave were up to! Daddy was probably—"

Susan leaped up from the couch and slapped her sister hard on the face. "You goddamn brat, be quiet!" Mrs. Thayer started weeping in earnest. Jill, overcome by assorted strong and uncontrollable feelings, began sobbing again.

At that moment a worried-looking man in a business suit came into the room, escorted by one of the patrolmen. He crossed to Mrs. Thayer and clasped her hands. "Margaret! I came as soon as I heard the news. How are you?"

Susan blushed. Jill's sobs died away. Jack looked as though he had been stuffed. Mrs. Thayer turned large tragic eyes to the newcomer's face. "Ted. How kind of you," she said in a brave voice, barely above a whisper.

"Dr. Mulgrave, I presume," I said.

He dropped Mrs. Thayer's wrists and stood up straight. "Yes, I'm Dr. Mulgrave." He looked at Jack. "Is this a policewoman?"

"No," I said. "I'm a private investigator. Miss Thayer has hired me to find out who killed her father and brother."

"Margaret?" he asked incredulously.

"No. *Miss* Thayer. Jill," I said.

Jack said, "Mrs. Thayer just ordered you to leave her house and leave her daughter alone. I'd think even an ambulance chaser like you would know how to take a hint like that."

"Oh, cool it, Thorndale," I said. "What's eating you? Jill asked me to come up here because she's scared silly—as any normal person would be with all this going on. But you guys are so defensive you make me wonder what you're hiding."

"What do you mean?" he scowled.

"Well, why don't you want me looking into your father-in-law's death? What are you afraid I'll find out—that he and Peter caught you with your fingers in the till and you had them shot to shut them up?"

I ignored his outraged gasp. "What about you, Doctor? Did Mr. Thayer learn about your relations with his wife and threaten divorce—but you decided a wealthy widow was a better bet than a woman who couldn't make a very good case for alimony?"

"Now look here, whatever your name is. I don't have to listen to that kind of crap," Mulgrave started.

"Then leave," I said. "Maybe Lucy is using this house as a center for burglarizing wealthy homes on the North Shore—after all, as a maid, she probably hears a lot about where jewelry, documents, and so on are kept. When Mr. Thayer and his son got too hot on her trail, she hired a murderer." I smiled enthusiastically at Susan, who was starting to babble—I was getting carried away by my own fantasies. "I could probably think of a motive for you too, Mrs. Thorndale. All I'm trying to say is, you people are so hostile that it starts me wondering. The less you want me to undertake a murder investigation, the more I start thinking there might be something to my ideas."

When I stopped talking, they were silent for a minute. Mulgrave was clasping Mrs. Thayer's hands again, sitting next to her now. Susan looked like a kitten getting ready to spit at a dog. My client was sitting on one of the bamboo side chairs, her hands clenched in her lap, her face intent. Then Mulgrave said, "Are you trying to threaten us—threaten the Thayer family?"

"If you mean, am I threatening to find out the truth, the answer is yes; if that means turning up a lot of sordid junk along the way, tough."

"Just a minute, Ted," Jack said, waving an arm at the older man. "I know how to deal with her." He nodded at me. "Come on, name your price," he said, pulling out his checkbook.

My fingers itched to bring out the Smith & Wesson and pistol-whip him. "Grow up, Thorndale," I snapped. "There are things in this life that money can't buy. Regardless of what you, or your mother-in-law, or the mayor of Winnetka says, I am investigating this murder—these murders." I laughed a little, mirthlessly. "Two days ago, John Thayer tried to give me $5,000 to buy me out of this case. You guys up here on the North Shore live in some kind of dream world. You think you can buy a cover-up for anything that goes wrong in your lives, just like you hire the garbagemen to take away your filth, or Lucy here to clean it up and carry it outside for you. It doesn't work that way. John Thayer is dead. He couldn't pay enough to get whatever filth he was involved in away from him, nor away from his son. Now whatever it was that caused their deaths isn't private anymore. It doesn't belong to you. Anyone who wants it can find out about it. I intend to."

Mrs. Thayer was moaning softly. Jack looked uncomfortable. With an effort to save his dignity he said, "Naturally, if you choose to poke around in something that's none of your business we can't stop you. It's just that we think matters are better off left to the police."

"Yeah, well, they're not batting a thousand right now," I said. "They thought they had a guy behind bars for the crime, but while he was eating his prison breakfast this morning John Thayer got killed."

Susan turned to Jill. "This is all your fault! You brought this person up here. Now we've been insulted and embarrassed—I've never been more ashamed in my life. Daddy's been killed and all you can think about is bringing in some outsider to call us names."

Mulgrave turned back to Mrs. Thayer, and Jack and Susan both started talking to him at once. While this was going on, I walked over to Jill and knelt down to look her in the face. She was looking as though she might collapse or go into shock. "Look, I think you need to get away from all this. Is there any friend or relative you can visit until the worst of the fuss is over?"

She thought for a minute, then shook her head. "Not really. I've got lots of friends, you know, but I don't think any of their mothers would like having me around right now." She gave a wobbly smile. "The scandal, you know, like Jack said. I wish Anita were here."

I hesitated a minute. "Would you like to come back to Chicago with me? My apartment's been torn up, and I'm staying with a friend, but she'll be glad to have you, too, for a few days." Lotty would never mind another stray. I needed Jill where I could ask her some questions, and I wanted her away from her family. She was tough and could fight back, but she didn't need to do that kind of fighting on top of the shock of her father's death.

Her face lightened. "Do you really mean that?"

I nodded. "Why don't you run upstairs now and pack an overnight bag while everyone is still arguing here."

When she had left the room, I explained what I was doing to Mrs. Thayer. This, predictably, started a fresh uproar from the family. Finally, though, Mulgrave said, "It's important that Margaret—Mrs. Thayer—be kept absolutely quiet. If Jill really is worrying her, perhaps it would be better if she did leave for a few days. I can make some inquiries about this person, and if she's not reliable, we can always bring Jill back home."

Mrs. Thayer gave a martyred smile. "Thank you, Ted. If you say it's all right, I'm sure it will be. As long as you live in a safe neighborhood, Miss—"

"Warshawski," I said dryly. "Well, no one's been machine-gunned there this week."

Mulgrave and Jack decided I ought to give them some references to call. I saw that as a face-saving effort and gave them the name of one of my old law professors. He would be startled but supportive if he got an inquiry into my character.

When Jill came back, she'd brushed her hair and washed her face. She went over to her mother, who was still sitting on the couch. "I'm sorry, Mother," she muttered. "I didn't mean to be rude to you."

Mrs. Thayer smiled wanly. "It's all right, dear. I don't expect you to understand how I feel." She looked at me. "Take good care of her for me."

"Sure," I answered.

"I don't want any trouble," Jack warned me.

"I'll keep that in mind, Mr. Thorndale." I picked up Jill's suitcase and she followed me out the door.

She stopped in the doorway to look at her family. "Well, good-bye," she said. They all looked at her but no one said anything.

When we got to the front door, I explained to the sergeant that Miss Thayer was coming home with me for a few days to get a little rest and attention; had the police taken all the statements they needed from her? After some talk with his lieutenant over the walkie-talkie, he agreed that she could leave, as long as I gave him my address. I gave it to him and we walked down the drive.

Jill didn't say anything on the way over to the Edens. She looked straight ahead and didn't pay much attention to the countryside. As we joined the stop-and-go traffic on the southbound Kennedy, though, she turned to look at me. "Do you think I was wrong, leaving my mother like that?"

I braked to let a fifty-ton semi merge in front of me. "Well, Jill, it seemed to me that everyone there was trying to play on your guilt feelings. Now you're feeling guilty, so maybe they got what they wanted out of you."

She digested that for a few minutes. "Is that a scandal, the way my father was killed?"

"People are probably talking about it, and that will make Jack and Susan very uncomfortable. The real question, though, is why he was killed—and even the answer to that question doesn't have to be a scandal to you." I threaded my way around a *Herald-Star* delivery van. "Thing is, you have to have your own sense of what's right built inside you. If your father ran afoul of the type of people who do machine-gun-style executions, it may be because they tried to violate his sense of what's right. No scandal to that. And even if he happened to be involved in some kind of shady activity, it doesn't have to affect you unless you want it to." I changed lanes. "I don't believe in the visitation of the sins of the fathers, and I don't believe in people brooding over vengeance for twenty years."

Jill turned a puzzled face toward me. "Oh, it can happen. It's just that you've got to want to make it happen. Like your mother—unhappy woman —right?" Jill nodded. "And probably unhappy because of things that happened thirty years ago. That's her choice. You've got the same choice. Suppose your father did something criminal and we find that out? It's going to be rough, but it only has to be a scandal and make your life miserable if you let it. Lots of things in this life happen to you no matter what you do, or through no fault of your own—like your father and brother getting killed. But how you make those events part of your life is under your control. You can get bitter, although I don't think you have that kind of character, or you can learn and grow from it."

I realized that I'd passed the Addison exit and turned onto the Belmont off-ramp. "Sorry—that answer turned into a sermon, and I got so carried away I missed my exit. Does it help any?"

Jill nodded and was quiet again as I drove north along Pulaski and then turned east on Addison. "It's lonely now, with Peter gone," she said finally. "He was the only one in the family who—who cared about me."

"Yeah, it's going to be rough, sweetie," I said gently, and squeezed her hand.

"Thank you for coming up, Miss Warshawski," she whispered.

I had to lean over to hear her. "My friends call me Vic," I said.

11
FRIENDLY PERSUASION

I stopped at the clinic before going to the apartment to let Lotty know I'd made free with her hospitality and to see if she thought Jill needed anything for shock. A small group of women, most of them with young children, were waiting in the little anteroom. Jill looked around her curiously. I poked my head into the inner door, where Lotty's nurse, a young Puerto Rican woman, saw me. "Hello, Vic," she said. "Lotty's with a patient. Do you need something?"

"Hi, Carol. Tell her that I'd like to bring my young friend back to her apartment—the one I went out this morning to see. She'll know whom you mean. And ask her if she can take a quick look at her—healthy kid, but she's had a lot of stress lately."

Carol went into the tiny examining room where she spoke for a few minutes. "Bring her into the office. Lotty will take a quick look at her after Mrs. Segi has left. And of course, take her to the apartment."

I took Jill into Lotty's office, among disapproving frowns from those who had been waiting longer. While we waited, I told her a little bit about Lotty, Austrian war refugee, brilliant London University medical student, maverick doctor, warm friend. Lotty herself came bustling in.

"So, this is Miss Thayer," she said briskly. "Vic has brought you down for a little rest? That's good." She lifted Jill's chin with her hand, looked at her pupils, made her do some simple tests, talking all the while.

"What was the trouble?" she asked.

"Her father was shot," I explained.

Lotty clicked her tongue and shook her head, then turned to Jill. "Now, open your mouth. No, I know you haven't got a sore throat, but it's free, I'm a doctor, and I have to look. Good. Nothing wrong with you, but you need some rest and something to eat. Vic, when you get her home, a little brandy. Don't talk too much, let her get some rest. Are you going out?"

"Yes, I've got a lot to do."

She pursed her lips and thought a minute. "I'll send Carol over in about an hour. She can stay with Jill until one of us gets home."

At that moment I realized how much I liked Lotty. I'd been a little uneasy about leaving Jill alone, in case Earl was close on my trail. Whether

Lotty knew that, or simply felt a scared young girl should not be left alone, it was a worry I now did not have to speak aloud.

"Great. I'll wait until she gets there."

We left the clinic among more baleful stares while Carol summoned the next patient. "She's nice, isn't she?" Jill said as we got into the car.

"Lotty or Carol?"

"Both, but Lotty, I meant. She really doesn't mind me showing up like this, does she?"

"No," I agreed. "All of Lotty's instincts are directed at helping people. She's just not sentimental about it."

When we got back to the apartment, I made Jill stay in the car while I checked the street and the entrance way. I didn't want to add to her fears, but I didn't want anyone getting a shot at her, either. The coast was still clear. Maybe Earl really did believe he'd scared me off. Or maybe with the police arresting poor Donald Mackenzie, he was resting easy.

When we got inside, I told Jill to take a hot bath. I was going to prepare some breakfast, and I would have to ask her a few questions, but then she was to sleep. "I can tell by your eyes that you haven't been doing that for a while," I said.

Jill agreed shyly. I helped her unpack her small suitcase in the room I'd been sleeping in; I could sleep on the daybed in the living room. I got out one of Lotty's enormous white bath sheets and showed her the bathroom.

I realized that I was quite hungry; it was ten and I hadn't eaten the toast Lotty had thrust at me. I foraged in the refrigerator: no juice—Lotty never drank anything out of cans. I found a drawer full of oranges and squeezed a small pitcher of juice, and then took some of Lotty's thick light Viennese bread and turned it into French toast, whistling under my breath. I realized I felt good, despite Thayer's death and all the unexplained dangling pieces to the case. Some instinct told me that things were finally starting to happen.

When Jill emerged pink and sleepy from the bath, I set her to eating, holding my questions and telling her a little bit about myself in answer to her inquiries. She wanted to know if I always caught the killer.

"This is the first time I've ever really dealt directly with a killer," I answered. "But generally, yes, I do get to the root of the problems I'm asked to look into."

"Are you scared?" Jill asked. "I mean, you've been beaten up and your apartment got torn up, and they—they shot Daddy and Pete."

"Yes, of course I'm scared," I said calmly. "Only a fool would look at a mess like this and not be. It's just that it doesn't panic me—it makes me careful, being scared does, but it doesn't override my judgment.

"Now, I want you to tell me everything you can remember about whom your father talked to in the last few days, and what they said. We'll go sit on the bed, and you'll drink some hot milk with brandy as Lotty ordered, so that when I'm done you'll go to sleep."

She followed me into the bedroom and got into bed, obediently sipping at the milk. I had put in brown sugar and nutmeg and laced it heavily. She made a face but continued sipping it while we talked.

"When I came out on Saturday, you said your father at first didn't believe this Mackenzie they've arrested killed your brother, but the neighbors talked him out of it. What neighbors?"

"Well, a lot of people came by, and they all more or less said the same thing. Do you want all their names?"

"If you can remember them and remember what they said."

We went through a list of about a dozen people, which included Yardley Masters and his wife, the only name I recognized. I got some long histories of relations among the families, and Jill contorted her face in the effort of trying to remember exactly what they'd all said.

"You said they 'all more or less said the same thing,'" I repeated after a while. "Was anyone more emphatic about it than the others?"

She nodded at that. "Mr. Masters. Daddy kept raving that he was sure that Anita's father had done it, and Mr. Masters said something like, 'Look, John, you don't want to keep going around saying things like that. A lot of things could come out that you don't want to hear.' Then Daddy got mad and started yelling, 'What do you mean? Are you threatening me?' And Mr. Masters said, 'No, of course not, John. We're friends. Just giving you some advice,' or something like that."

"I see," I said. Very illuminating. "Was that all?"

"Yes, but it was after Mr. and Mrs. Masters left that Daddy said he guessed he was wrong, which made me glad at the time, because of course Anita wouldn't try to kill Peter. But then he started saying terrible things about Peter."

"Yeah, let's not talk about that now. I want you to calm down so you can sleep. Did anything happen yesterday?"

"Well, he got into a fight with someone on the phone, but I don't know who, or what it was about. I think it was some deal going on at the bank, because he said, 'I won't be a party to it'—that's all I heard. He'd been so—strange." She gulped and swallowed some more milk. "At the funeral, you know, I sort of was staying out of his way. And when I heard him start yelling on the phone, I just went outside. Susan was after me anyway to put on a dress and sit in the living room entertaining all these gruesome people who came over after the funeral, so I just sort of left and went down to the beach."

I laughed a little. "Good for you. This fight on the telephone—did your father get a call or make a call?"

"I'm pretty sure he made it. At least, I don't remember hearing the phone ring."

"Okay, all that's a help. Now try to put it out of your mind. You finish your milk while I brush your hair, and then you sleep."

She was really very tired; between the hairbrushing and the brandy she relaxed and lay down. "Stay with me," she asked drowsily. I pulled the shades behind the burlap curtains and sat down beside Jill, holding her hand. Something about her pierced my heart, made me long for the child I'd never had, and I watched her carefully until she was in a deep sleep.

While I waited for Carol, I made some phone calls, first to Ralph. I had to wait a few minutes while a secretary hunted him down on the floor, but he was as cheerful as ever when he came on the line. "How's it going, Sherlock?" he asked breezily.

"Pretty well," I answered.

"You're not calling to cancel dinner tonight, are you?"

"No, no," I assured him. "I'd just like you to do something that you can find out more easily than I can."

"What's that?"

"Just find out if your boss has had any calls from a guy named Andrew McGraw. And do it without letting him know you're asking."

"Are you still flogging that dead horse?" he asked, a little exasperated.

"I haven't written anyone off, Ralph, not even you."

"But the police made an arrest."

"Well, in that case, your boss is innocent. Just look on it as a favor to a lady who's had a rough week."

"All right," he agreed, not too happily. "But I wish you could believe the police know as much about catching murderers as you do."

I laughed. "You're not the only one. . . . By the way, did you know young Peter's father was killed this morning?"

"What!" he exclaimed. "How did that happen?"

"Well, he was shot. Too bad Donald Mackenzie is already in jail, but there must be some dope dealers on the North Shore to take the blame for this one."

"You think Peter's death is connected to this?"

"Well, it staggers the imagination if two members of the same family are killed within a week of each other and those events are only randomly associated."

"All right, all right," Ralph said. "You've made your point—no need to be sarcastic. . . . I'll ask Yardley's secretary."

"Thanks, Ralph, see you tonight."

The claim draft, Masters's remarks to Thayer, which might or might not have been vague threats. It didn't add up to much, but it was worth pursuing. The other piece to the puzzle was McGraw and the fact that McGraw knew Smeissen. Now, if I could connect McGraw and Masters, or Masters and Smeissen. . . . I should have asked Ralph to check on Earl too. Well, I could do that tonight. Say McGraw and Masters were doing an unspecified something together. If they were smart, they wouldn't leave names when they called each other. Even McGraw's enchanting secretary might give him away to the police if the evidence was hot enough. But they might get together, meet for a drink. I might make a trip to bars in the Loop and near Knifegrinder headquarters to see if the two had ever been seen together. Or

Thayer with McGraw, for that matter. I needed some photographs, and I had an idea where to find them.

Carol arrived as I was looking a number up in the directory. "Jill's asleep," I told her. "I hope she'll sleep through the afternoon."

"Good," she answered. "I've brought all the old medical records over: we're always too busy at the clinic to get them updated, but this is a good opportunity."

We chatted for a few minutes about her mother, who had emphysema, and the prospects for finding the arsonists who were plaguing the neighborhood, before I went back to the phone.

Murray Ryerson was the crime reporter for the *Herald-Star* who interviewed me after the Transicon case broke. He'd had a by-line, and a lot of his stuff was good. It was getting close to lunch, and I wasn't sure he'd be in when I called the city desk, but my luck seemed to be turning.

"Ryerson," he rumbled into the phone.

"This is V. I. Warshawski."

"Oh, hi," he said, mind turning over competently and remembering me without trouble. "Got any good stories for me today?"

"Not today. But I might have later in the week. I need some help, though. A couple of pictures."

"Whose?"

"Look, if I tell you, will you promise not to put two and two together in the paper until I have some evidence?"

"Maybe. Depends on how close you're coming to a story that we know is happening anyway."

"Andrew McGraw on any of your hot lists?"

"Oh, he's a perennial favorite but we don't have anything breaking on him right now. Who's the other?"

"Guy named Yardley Masters. He's a vice-president over at Ajax, and you probably have something in your file from Crusade of Mercy publicity or something like that."

"You tying McGraw to Ajax?"

"Stop slobbering in the phone, Murray; Ajax doesn't do any business with the Knifegrinders."

"Well, are you tying McGraw to Masters?" he persisted.

"What is this, twenty questions?" I said irritably. "I need two pictures. If a story breaks, you can have it—you did all right from me on Transicon, didn't you?"

"Tell you what—you eaten yet? Good, I'll meet you at Fiorella's in an hour with the pictures, if any, and try to pick your brains over a beer."

"Great, Murray, thanks." I hung up and looked at my watch. An hour would give me time to stop and register the Smith & Wesson. I started humming *"Ch'io mi scordi di te"* again. "Tell Lotty I'll be back around six but I'll be eating dinner out," I called to Carol on my way out.

12

PUB CRAWL

The eager bureaucrats at City Hall took longer than I expected with forms, fees, incomprehensible directions, and anger at being asked to repeat them. I was already running late, but I decided to stop at my lawyer's office to drop off a Xerox of the claim draft I'd found in Peter Thayer's apartment. He was a dry, imperturbable man, and accepted without a blink my instructions to give the draft to Murray Ryerson should anything happen to me in the next few days.

By the time I got to Fiorella's, a pleasant restaurant whose outdoor tables overlooked the Chicago River, Murray was already finishing his second beer. He was a big man who looked like a red-haired Elliott Gould, and he waved a hand at me lazily when he saw me coming.

A high-masted sailboat was floating past. "You know, they're going to raise every drawbridge along here for that one boat. Hell of a system, isn't it," he said as I came up.

"Oh, there's something appealing about a little boat being able to stop all the traffic on Michigan Avenue. Unless, of course, the bridge gets stuck up just when you need to cross the river." This was an all-too-frequent happening: motorists had no choice but to sit and boil quietly while they waited. "Has there ever been a murder when one of these bridges is stuck—someone getting too angry and shooting the bridge tender or something?"

"Not yet," Murray said. "If it happens, I'll be on the spot to interview you. . . . What are you drinking?"

I don't like beer that well; I ordered a white wine.

"Got your pix for you." Murray tossed a folder over to me. "We had a lot of choice on McGraw, but only dug one up for Masters—he's receiving some civic award out in Winnetka—they never ran the shot but it's a pretty good three-quarter view. I got you a couple of copies."

"Thanks," I said, opening the folder. The one of Masters was good. He was shaking hands with the Illinois president of the Boy Scouts of America. At his right was a solemn-faced youth in uniform who apparently was his son. The picture was two years old.

Murray had brought me several of McGraw, one outside a federal courtroom where he was walking pugnaciously in front of a trio of Treasury men. Another, taken under happier circumstances, showed him at the gala celebration when he was first elected president of the Knifegrinders nine years ago. The best for my purposes, though, was a close-up, taken apparently without his knowledge. His face was relaxed, but concentrating.

I held it out toward Murray. "This is great. Where was it taken?"

Murray smiled. "Senate hearings on racketeering and the unions."

No wonder he looked so thoughtful.

A waiter came by for our order. I asked for mostaccioli; Murray chose spaghetti with meatballs. I was going to have to start running again, sore muscles or not, with all the starch I was eating lately.

"Now, V. I. Warshawski, most beautiful detective in Chicago, what gives with these pictures," Murray said, clasping his hands together on the table and leaning over them toward me. "I recall seeing that dead young Peter Thayer worked for Ajax, in fact for Mr. Masters, an old family friend. Also, somewhere in the thousands of lines that have been churned out since he died, I recall reading that his girl friend, the lovely and dedicated Anita McGraw, was the daughter of well-known union leader Andrew McGraw. Now you want pictures of both of them. Is it possible that you are suggesting they colluded in the death of young Thayer, and possibly his father as well?"

I looked at him seriously. "It was like this, Murray: McGraw has what amounts to a psychopathic hatred of capitalist bosses. When he realized that his pure young daughter, who had always been protected from any contact with management, was seriously considering marrying not just a boss, but the son of one of Chicago's wealthiest businessmen, he decided the only thing to do was to have the young man put six feet underground. His psychosis is such that he decided to have John Thayer eliminated as well, just for—"

"Spare me the rest," Murray said. "I can spell it out for myself. Is either McGraw or Masters your client?"

"You'd better be buying this lunch, Murray—it is definitely a business expense."

The waiter brought our food, slapping it down in the hurried, careless way that is the hallmark of business restaurants at lunch. I snatched the pictures back just in time to save them from spaghetti sauce and started sprinkling cheese on my pasta: I love it really cheesy.

"Do you have a client?" he asked, spearing a meatball.

"Yes, I do."

"But you won't tell me who it is?" I smiled and nodded agreement.

"You buy Mackenzie as Thayer Junior's murderer?" Murray asked.

"I haven't talked to the man. But one does have to wonder who killed Thayer Senior if Mackenzie killed the son. I don't like the thought of two people in the same family killed in the same week for totally unconnected reasons by unconnected people: laws of chance are against that," I answered. "What about you?"

He gave a big Elliott Gould smile. "You know, I talked to Lieutenant Mallory after the case first broke, and he didn't say anything about robbery, either of the boy or of the apartment. Now, you found the body, didn't you? Well, did the apartment look ransacked?"

"I couldn't really tell if anything had been taken—I didn't know what was supposed to be there."

"By the way, what took you down there in the first place?" he asked casually.

"Nostalgia, Murray—I used to go to school down there and I got an itch to see what the old place looked like."

Murray laughed. "Okay, Vic, you win—can't fault me for trying though, can you?"

I laughed too. I didn't mind. I finished my pasta—no child had ever died in India because of my inhumane failure to clean my plate.

"If I find out anything you might be interested in, I'll let you know," I said.

Murray asked me when I thought the Cubs would break this year. They were looking scrappy right now—two and a half games out.

"You know, Murray, I am a person with very few illusions about life. I like to have the Cubs as one of them." I stirred my coffee. "But I'd guess the second week in August. What about you?"

"Well, this is the third week in July. I give them ten more games. Martin and Buckner can't carry that team."

I agreed sadly. We finished lunch on baseball and split the check when it came.

"There is one thing, Murray."

He looked at me intently. I almost laughed, the change in his whole posture had been so complete—he really looked like a bloodhound on the trail, now.

"I have what I think is a clue. I don't know what it means, or why it is a clue. But I've left a copy of it with my attorney. If I should be bumped off, or put out of action for any length of time, he has instructions to give it to you."

"What is it?" Murray asked.

"You ought to be a detective, Murray—you ask as many questions and you're just as hot when you're on the trail. One thing I will say—Earl Smeissen's hovering around this case. He gave me this beautiful black eye which you've been too gentlemanly to mention. It wouldn't be totally out of the question for my body to come floating down the Chicago River—you might look out your office window every hour or so to see."

Murray didn't look surprised. "You already knew that?" I asked.

He grinned. "You know who arrested Donald Mackenzie?"

"Yes, Frank Carlson."

"And whose boy is Carlson?" he asked.

"Henry Vespucci."

"And do you know who's been covering Vespucci's back all these years?"

I thought about it. "Tim Sullivan?" I guessed.

"The lady wins a Kewpie doll," Murray said. "Since you know that much, I'll tell you who Sullivan spent Christmas in Florida with last year."

"Oh, Christ! Not Earl."

Murray laughed. "Yes. Earl Smeissen himself. If you're playing around with that crowd, you'd better be very, very careful."

I got up and stuck the folder in my shoulder bag. "Thanks, Murray, you're not the first one to tell me so. Thanks for the pictures. I'll let you know if anything turns up."

As I climbed over the barrier separating the restaurant from the sidewalk, I could hear Murray yelling a question behind me. He came pounding up to me just as I reached the top of the stairs leading from the river level to Michigan Avenue. "I want to know what it was you gave your lawyer," he panted.

I grinned. "So long, Murray," I said, and boarded a Michigan Avenue bus.

I had a plan that was really a stab in the dark more than anything else. I was assuming that McGraw and Masters worked together. And I was hoping they met at some point. They could handle everything over the phone or by mail. But McGraw might be wary of federal wiretaps and mail interception. He might prefer to do business in person. So say they met from time to time. Why not in a bar? And if in a bar, why not one near to one or the other of their offices? Of course, it was possible that they met as far from anyplace connected to either of them as they could. But my whole plan was based on a series of shots in the dark. I didn't have the resources to comb the whole city, so I'd just have to add one more assumption to my agenda, and hope that if they met, and if they met in a bar, they did so near where they worked. My plan might not net me anything, but it was all I could think of. I was pinning more hope on what I might learn about Anita from the radical women's group tomorrow night; in the meantime I needed to keep busy.

Ajax's glass-and-steel high-rise was on Michigan Avenue at Adams. In the Loop, Michigan is the easternmost street. The Art Institute is across the street, and then Grant Park goes down to the lake in a series of pleasant fountains and gardens. I decided to take the Fort Dearborn Trust on La Salle Street as my western border, and to work from Van Buren, two blocks south of Ajax, up to Washington, three blocks north. A purely arbitrary decision, but the bars in that area would keep me busy for some time; I could expand it in desperation if that was necessary.

I rode my bus south past the Art Institute to Van Buren and got off. I felt very small walking between the high-rises when I thought of the vast territory I had to cover. I wondered how much I might have to drink to get responses from the myriad bartenders. There probably is a better way to do this, I thought, but this was the only way that occurred to me. I had to work with what I could come up with—no Peter Wimsey at home thinking of the perfect logical answer for me.

I squared my shoulders and walked half a block along Van Buren and went into the Spot, the first bar I came to. I'd debated about an elaborate cover story, and finally decided that something approximating the truth was best.

The Spot was a dark, narrow bar built like a railway caboose. Booths lined the west wall and a long bar ran the length of the east, leaving just enough room for the stout, bleached waitress who had to tend to orders in the booths.

I sat up at the bar. The bartender was cleaning glasses. Most of the luncheon trade had left; only a few diehard drinkers were sitting farther down from me. A couple of women were finishing hamburgers and daiquiris in one of the booths. The bartender continued his work methodically until the last glass was rinsed before coming down to take my order. I stared ahead with the air of a woman in no particular hurry.

Beer is not my usual drink, but it was probably the best thing to order on an all-day pub crawl. It wouldn't make me drunk. Or at least not as quickly as wine or liquor.

"I'd like a draft," I said.

He went to his spigots and filled a glass with pale yellow and foam. When he brought it back to me, I pulled out my folder. "You ever see these two guys come in here?" I asked.

He gave me a sour look. "What are you, a cop or something?"

"Yes," I said. "Have you ever seen these two guys in here together?"

"I'd better get the boss on this one," he said. Raising his voice, he called "Herman!" and a heavy man in a polyester suit got up from the booth at the far end of the room. I hadn't noticed him when I came in, but now I saw that another waitress was sitting in the booth. The two were sharing a late lunch after the hectic noon-hour rush.

The heavy man joined the bartender behind the bar.

"What's up, Luke?"

Luke jerked his head toward me. "Lady's got a question." He went back to his glasses, stacking them in careful pyramids on either side of the cash register. Herman came down toward me. His heavyset face looked tough but not mean. "What do you want, ma'am?"

I pulled my photos out again. "I'm trying to find out if these two men have ever been in here together," I said in a neutral voice.

"You got a legal reason for asking?"

I pulled my P.I. license from my handbag. "I'm a private investigator. There's a grand jury investigation and there's some question of collusion between a witness and a juror." I showed him the ID.

He looked at the ID briefly, grunted, and tossed it back to me. "Yeah, I see you're a private investigator, all right. But I don't know about this grand jury story. I know this guy." He tapped Masters's picture. "He works up at Ajax. Doesn't come in here often, maybe three times a year, but he's been doing it as long as I've owned the place."

I didn't say anything, but took a swallow of beer. Anything tastes good when your throat is dry from embarrassment.

"Tell you for free, though, this other fellow's never been in here. At least not when I've been here." He gave a shout of laughter and reached across the bar to pat my cheek. "That's okay, cookie, I won't spoil your story for you."

"Thanks," I said dryly. "What do I owe you for the beer?"

"On the house." He gave another snort of laughter and rolled back down the aisle to his unfinished lunch. I took another swallow of the thin beer. Then I put a dollar on the counter for Luke and walked slowly out of the bar.

I walked on down Van Buren past Sears's main Chicago store. A lot of short-order food places were on the other side, but I had to go another block to find another bar. The bartender looked blankly at the photos and called the waitress over. She looked at both of them doubtfully, and then picked up McGraw's. "He looks kind of familiar," she said. "Is he on TV or something?" I said no, but had she ever seen him in the bar. She didn't think so, but she couldn't swear to it. What about Masters? She didn't think so, but a lot of businessmen came in there, and all men with gray hair and business suits ran together in her mind after a while. I put two singles on the counter, one for her and one for the bartender, and went on down the street.

Her TV question gave me an idea for a better cover story. The next place I went to I said I was a market researcher looking for viewer recognition. Did anyone remember ever seeing these two people together? This approach got more interest, but drew another blank.

The game was on TV in this bar, bottom of the fourth with Cincinnati leading 4-0. I watched Biittner hit a single and then die on second after a hair-raising steal before I moved on. In all, I went to thirty-two bars that afternoon, catching most of the game in between. The Cubs lost, 6-2. I'd covered my territory pretty thoroughly. A couple of places recognized McGraw vaguely, but I put that down to the number of times his picture had been in the paper over the years. Most people probably had a vague recognition of Jimmy Hoffa, too. One other bar knew Masters by sight as one of the men from Ajax, and Billy's knew him by name and title as well. But neither place remembered seeing McGraw with him. Some places were hostile and took a combination of bribes and threats to get an answer. Some were indifferent. Others, like the Spot, had to have the manager make the decision. But none of them had seen my pair together.

It was after six by the time I got to Washington and State, two blocks west of Michigan. After my fifth bar I'd stopped drinking any of the beer I ordered, but I was feeling slightly bloated, as well as sweaty and depressed. I'd agreed to meet Ralph at Ahab's at eight. I decided to call it an afternoon and go home to wash up first.

Marshall Field occupies the whole north side of the street between State and Wabash. It seemed to me there might be one other bar on Washington, close to Michigan, if my memory of the layout was correct. That could wait

until another day. I went down the stairs to the State Street subway and
boarded a B train to Addison.

Evening rush hour was still in full force. I couldn't get a seat and had to
stand all the way to Fullerton.

At Lotty's I headed straight for the bathroom and a cold shower. When I
came out, I looked into the guest room; Jill was up, so I dumped my clothes
in a drawer and put on a caftan. Jill was sitting on the living-room floor
playing with two rosy-cheeked, dark-haired children who looked to be three
or four.

"Hi, honey. You get a good rest?"

She looked up at me and smiled. A lot of color had returned to her face
and she seemed much more relaxed. "Hi," she said. "Yes, I only woke up an
hour ago. These are Carol's nieces. She was supposed to baby-sit tonight,
but Lotty talked her into coming over here and making homemade enchiladas, yum-yum."

"Yum-yum," the two little girls chorused.

"That sounds great. I'm afraid I have to go back out tonight, so I'll have
to give it a miss."

Jill nodded. "Lotty told me. Are you doing some more detecting?"

"Well, I hope so."

Lotty called out from the kitchen and I went in to say hi. Carol was
working busily at the stove and turned briefly to flash me a bright smile.
Lotty was sitting at the table reading the paper, drinking her ever-lasting
coffee. She looked at me through narrowed eyes. "The detective work wasn't
so agreeable this afternoon, eh?"

I laughed. "No. I learned nothing and had to drink too much beer doing
so. This stuff smells great; wish I could cancel this evening out."

"Then do so."

I shook my head. "I feel as though I don't have much time—maybe this
second murder. Even though I feel a little rocky—too long a day, too much
heat, I can't stop. I just hope I don't get sick at dinner—my date is getting
fed up with me as it is. Although maybe if I fainted or something it would
make him feel stronger, more protective." I shrugged. "Jill looks a lot better,
don't you think?"

"Oh, yes. The sleep did her good. That was well thought of, to get her
out of that house for a while. I talked to her a bit when I came in; she's very
well behaved, doesn't whine and complain, but it's obvious the mother has
no emotions to spare for her. As for the sister—" Lotty made an expressive
gesture.

"Yeah, I agree. We can't keep her down here forever, though. Besides,
what on earth can she do during the day? I've got to be gone again tomorrow, and not on the kind of errand that she can go along with."

"Well, I've been thinking about that. Carol and I had a bit of an idea,
watching her with Rosa and Tracy—the two nieces. Jill is good with these
children—took them on, we didn't ask her to look after them. Babies are

good when you're depressed—something soft and unquestioning to cuddle. What would you think of her coming over to the clinic and minding children there for a day? As you saw this morning, they're always tumbling around the place—mothers who are sick can't leave them alone; or if one baby is sick, who looks after the other when Mama brings him in?"

I thought it over for a minute, but couldn't see anything wrong with it. "Ask her," I said. "I'm sure the best thing for her right now would be to have something to do."

Lotty got up and went to the living room. I followed. We stood for a minute, watching the three girls on the floor. They were terribly busy about something, although it wasn't clear what. Lotty squatted down next to them, moving easily. I moved into the background. Lotty spoke perfect Spanish, and she talked to the little girls in that language for a minute. Jill watched her respectfully.

Then Lotty turned to Jill, still balancing easily on her haunches. "You're very good with these little ones. Have you worked with young children before?"

"I was a counselor at a little neighborhood day camp in June," Jill said, flushing a bit. "But that's all. I never baby-sit or anything like that."

"Well, I had a bit of a plan. See what you think. Vic must be gone all the time, trying to find out why your father and brother were killed. Now while you are visiting down here, you could be of great help to me at the clinic." She outlined her idea.

Jill's face lit up. "But you know," she said seriously, "I don't have any training. I might not know what to do if they all started to cry or something."

"Well, if that happens, that will be the test of your knack and patience," Lotty said. "I will provide you a little assistance by way of a drawerful of lollipops. Bad for the teeth, perhaps, but great for tears."

I went into the bedroom to change for dinner. Jill hadn't made the bed. The sheets were crumpled. I straightened them out, then thought I might just lie down for a minute to recover my equilibrium.

The next thing I knew Lotty was shaking me awake. "It's seven thirty, Vic: don't you have to be going?"

"Oh, hell!" I swore. My head was thick with sleep. "Thanks, Lotty." I swung out of bed and hurriedly put on a bright orange sundress. I stuck the Smith & Wesson in my handbag, grabbed a sweater, and ran out the door, calling good-bye to Jill as I went. Poor Ralph, I thought. I really am abusing him, keeping him waiting in restaurants just so that I can pick his brains about Ajax.

It was 7:50 when I turned south on Lake Shore Drive and just 8:00 when I got onto Rush Street, where the restaurant lay. One of my prejudices is against paying to park the car, but tonight I didn't waste time looking for street parking. I turned the car over to a parking attendant across from Ahab's. I looked at my watch as I went in the door: 8:08. Damned good, I thought. My head still felt woolly from my hour of sleep, but I was glad I'd gotten it.

Ralph was waiting by the entrance. He kissed me lightly in greeting, then stood back to examine my face. "Definitely improving," he agreed. "And I see you can walk again."

The headwaiter came over. Monday was a light night and he took us directly to our table. "Tim will be your waiter," he said. "Would you like a drink?"

Ralph ordered a gin-and-tonic; I settled for a glass of club soda—Scotch on top of beer didn't sound too appetizing.

"One of the things about being divorced and moving into the city is all the great restaurants," Ralph remarked. "I've come to this place a couple of times, but there are a lot in my neighborhood."

"Where do you live?" I asked.

"Over on Elm Street, not too far from here, actually. It's a furnished place with a housekeeping service."

"Convenient." That must cost a fair amount, I thought. I wondered what his income was. "That's quite a lot of money with your alimony, too."

"Don't tell me." He grinned. "I didn't know anything about the city when I moved in here, barring the area right around Ajax, and I didn't want to get into a long lease in a place I'd hate. Eventually I expect I'll buy a condominium."

"By the way, did you find out whether McGraw had ever called Masters?"

"Yes, I did you that little favor, Vic. And it's just what I told you. He's never had a call from the guy."

"You didn't ask him, did you?"

"No." Ralph's cheerful face clouded with resentment. "I kept your wishes in mind and only talked to his secretary. Of course, I don't have any guarantee that she won't mention the matter to him. Do you think you could let this drop now?"

I was feeling a little angry, too, but I kept it under control: I still wanted Ralph to look at the claim draft.

Tim arrived to take our orders. I asked for poached salmon and Ralph took the scampi. We both went to the salad bar while I cast about for a neutral topic to keep us going until after dinner. I didn't want to produce the draft until we'd eaten.

"I've talked so much about my divorce I've never asked whether you were ever married," Ralph remarked.

"Yes, I was."

"What happened?"

"It was a long time ago. I don't think either of us was ready for it. He's a successful attorney now living in Hinsdale with a wife and three young children."

"Do you still see him?" Ralph wanted to know.

"No, and I really don't think about him. But his name is in the papers a fair amount. He sent me a card at Christmas, that's how I know about the children and Hinsdale—one of those gooey things with the children smiling sentimentally in front of a fireplace. I'm not sure whether he sent it to prove his virility or to let me know what I'm missing."

"Do you miss it?"

I was getting angry. "Are you trying to ask in a subtle way about whether I wish I had a husband and a family? I certainly do not miss Dick, nor am I sorry that I don't have three kids getting under my feet."

Ralph looked astonished. "Take it easy, Vic. Can't you miss having a family without confusing that with Dick's family? I don't miss Dorothy—but that doesn't mean I'm giving up on marriage. And I wouldn't be much of a man if I didn't miss my children."

Tim brought our dinners. The salmon had a very good pimento sauce, but my emotions were still riding me and I couldn't enjoy it properly. I forced a smile. "Sorry. Guess I'm overreacting to people who think a woman without a child is like Welch's without grapes."

"Well, please don't take it out on me. Just because I've been acting like a protective man, trying to stop you from running after gangsters, doesn't mean I think you ought to be sitting home watching soaps and doing laundry."

I ate some salmon and thought about Dick and our short, unhappy marriage. Ralph was looking at me, and his mobile face showed concern and a little anxiety.

"The reason my first marriage fell apart was because I'm too independent. Also, I'm not into housekeeping, as you noticed the other night. But the real problem is my independence. I guess you could call it a strong sense of turf. It's—it's hard for me—" I smiled. "It's hard for me to talk about it." I swallowed and concentrated on my plate for a few minutes. I bit my lower lip and continued. "I have some close women friends, because I don't feel they're trying to take over my turf. But with men, it always seems, or often seems, as though I'm having to fight to maintain who I am."

Ralph nodded. I wasn't sure he understood, but he seemed interested. I ate a little more fish and swallowed some wine.

"With Dick, it was worse. I'm not sure why I married him—sometimes I think it's because he represented the white Anglo-Saxon establishment, and part of me wanted to belong to that. But Dick was a terrible husband for someone like me. He was an attorney with Crawford, Meade—they're a very big, high-prestige corporate firm, if you don't know them—and I was an eager young lawyer on the Public Defender's roster. We met at a bar association meeting. Dick thought he'd fallen in love with me because I'm so independent; afterwards it seemed to me that it was because he saw my independence as a challenge, and when he couldn't break it down, he got angry.

"Then I got disillusioned with working for the Public Defender. The setup is pretty corrupt—you're never arguing for justice, always on points of law. I wanted to get out of it, but I still wanted to do something that would make me feel that I was working on my concept of justice, not legal point-scoring. I resigned from the Public Defender's office, and was wondering what to do next, when a girl came to me and asked me to clear her brother of a robbery charge. He looked hopelessly guilty—it was a charge of stealing video equipment from a big corporate studio, and he had access, opportunity, and so on, but I took the case on and I discovered he was innocent by finding out who the guilty person really was."

I drank some more wine and poked at my salmon. Ralph's plate was clean, but he was waving off Tim—"Wait until the lady's finished."

"Well, all this time, Dick was waiting for me to settle down to being a housewife. He was very supportive when I was worrying through leaving the Public Defender, but it turned out that that was because he was hoping I'd quit to stay home on the sidelines applauding him while he clawed his way up the ladder in the legal world. When I took on that case—although it didn't seem like a case at the time, just a favor to the woman who had sent the girl to me—" (That had been Lotty.) It had been awhile since I'd thought about all this and I started to laugh. Ralph looked a question. "Well, I take my obligations very seriously, and I ended up spending a night on a loading dock, which was really the turning point in the case. It was the same night that Crawford, Meade were having a big cocktail party, wives invited. I had on a cocktail dress, because I thought I'd just slip down to the dock and then go to the party, but the time slipped away, and Dick couldn't forgive me for not showing up. So we split up. At the time it was horrible, but when I look back on it, the evening was so ludicrous it makes me laugh."

I pushed my plate away. I'd only eaten half the fish, but I didn't have much of an appetite. "The trouble is, I guess I'm a bit gun-shy now. There really are times when I wish I did have a couple of children and was doing the middle-class family thing. But that's a myth, you know: very few people live like an advertisement, with golden harmony, and enough money, and so on. And I know I'm feeling a longing for a myth, not the reality. It's just—I get scared that I've made the wrong choice, or—I don't quite know how to say it. Maybe I should be home watching the soaps, maybe I'm not doing the best thing with my life. So if people try to suggest it, I bite their heads off."

Ralph reached across the table and squeezed my hand. "I think you're remarkable, Vic. I like your style. Dick sounds like an ass. Don't give up on us men just because of him."

I smiled and squeezed his hand in return. "I know. But—I'm a good detective, and I've got an established name now. And it's not a job that's easy to combine with marriage. It's only intermittently demanding, but when I'm hot after something, I don't want to be distracted by the thought of someone at home stewing because he doesn't know what to do about dinner. Or fussing at me because Earl Smeissen beat me up."

Ralph looked down at his empty plate, nodding thoughtfully. "I see." He grinned. "Of course, you might find a guy who'd already done the children-

and-suburbia number who would stand on the sidelines cheering your successes."

Tim came back to take dessert orders. I chose Ahab's spectacular ice-cream-and-cordial dessert. I hadn't eaten all my fish, and I was sick of being virtuous anyway. Ralph decided to have some too.

"But I think this Earl Smeissen business would take a lot of getting used to," he added after Tim had disappeared again.

"Aren't there any dangers to claim handling?" I asked. "I would imagine you'd come across fraudulent claimants from time to time who aren't too happy to have their frauds uncovered."

"That's true," he agreed. "But it's harder to prove a fraudulent claim than you might think. Especially if it's an accident case. There are lots of corrupt doctors out there who will happily testify to nonprovable injuries—something like a strained back, which doesn't show up on an X ray—for a cut of the award.

"I've never been in any danger. Usually what happens if you know it's a blown-up claim, and they know you know, but no one can prove it either way, you give them a cash settlement considerably below what it would be if it came to court. That gets them off your back—litigation is very expensive for an insurance company, because juries almost always favor the claimant, so it's really not as shocking as it sounds."

"How much of there is that?" I asked.

"Well, everyone thinks the insurance company is there to give them a free ride—they don't understand that it all comes out in higher rates in the end. But how often do we really get taken to the cleaners? I couldn't say. When I was working in the field, my gut sense was that maybe one in every twenty or thirty cases was a phony. You handle so many, though, that it's hard to evaluate each one of them properly—you just concentrate on the big ones."

Tim had brought the ice cream, which was sinfully delicious. I scraped the last drops out of the bottom of my dish. "I found a claim draft lying around an apartment the other day. It was an Ajax draft, a carbon of one. I wondered if it was a real one."

"You did?" Ralph was surprised. "Where did you find it? In your apartment?"

"No. Actually, in young Thayer's place."

"Do you have it? I'd like to see it."

I picked my bag up from the floor and got the paper out of the zippered side compartment and handed it to Ralph. He studied it intently. Finally he said, "This looks like one of ours all right. I wonder what the boy was doing with that on him. No claim files are supposed to go home with you."

He folded it and put it in his wallet. "This should go back to the office."

I wasn't surprised, just pleased I'd had the forethought to make Xeroxes of it. "Do you know the claimant?" I asked.

He pulled out the paper again and looked at the name. "No, I can't even pronounce it. But it's the maximum indemnity payment for this state, so he must be on a total disability case—either temporary or permanent. That means there should be a pretty comprehensive file on him. How did it get so greasy?"

"Oh, it was lying on the floor," I said vaguely.

When Tim brought the check, I insisted on splitting it with Ralph. "Too many dinners like this and you'll have to give up either your alimony or your apartment."

He finally let me pay my part of the bill. "By the way, before they kick me out for not paying the rent, would you like to see my place?"

I laughed. "Sure, Ralph. I'd love to."

13

THE MARK OF ZAV

Ralph's alarm went off at 6:30; I cracked my eyes briefly to look at the clock and then buried my head under the pillows. Ralph tried burrowing in after me, but I kept the covers pulled around my ears and fought him off successfully. The skirmish woke me up more thoroughly. I sat up. "Why so early? Do you have to be at the office at seven thirty?"

"This isn't early to me, baby: when I lived in Downers Grove I had to get up at five forty-five every day—this is luxury. Besides, I like morning—best time of day."

I groaned and lay down again. "Yeah, I've often said God must have loved mornings, he made so many of them. How about bringing me some coffee?"

He got out of bed and flexed his muscles. "Sure thing, Miss Warshawski, ma'am. Service with a smile."

I had to laugh. "If you're going to be so full of pep this early in the day, I think I'll head back north for breakfast." I swung my legs out of bed. It was now the fourth morning since my encounter with Earl and his boys, and I scarcely felt a twinge. Clearly, exercising paid off. I'd better get at it again—it would be easy to get out of the habit on the excuse that I was an invalid.

"I can feed you," Ralph said. "Not lavishly, but I've got toast."

"Tell you the truth, I want to go running this morning before I eat. I haven't been out for five days, and it's easy to go downhill if you don't keep it up. Besides, I have a teen-age guest at Lotty's, and I ought to go see how she's doing."

"Just as long as you aren't importing teen-age boys for some weird orgy or other, I don't mind. How about coming back here tonight?"

"Mmm, maybe not. I've got to go to a meeting tonight, and I want to spend some time with Lotty and my friend." I was still bothered by Ralph's persistence. Did he want to keep tabs on me, or was he a lonely guy going after the first woman he'd met who turned him on? If Masters were involved in the deaths of John and Peter Thayer, it wasn't impossible that his assistant, who had worked for him for three years, was involved as well.

"You get to work early every morning?" I asked.

"Unless I'm sick."

"Last Monday morning too?" I asked.

He looked at me, puzzled. "I suppose. Why do you ask—oh. When Peter was shot. No, I forgot: I wasn't in early that morning. I went down to Thayer's apartment and held him down while Yardley shot him."

"Yardley get in on time that morning?" I persisted.

"I'm not his goddamn secretary!" Ralph snapped. "He doesn't always show up at the same time—he has breakfast meetings and crap—and I don't sit with a stopwatch waiting for him to arrive."

"Okay, okay. Take it easy. I know you think Masters is purity personified. But if he were doing something illegal, wouldn't he call on you, his trusty henchman, for help? You wouldn't want him relying on someone else, someone less able than you, would you?"

His face relaxed and he gave a snort of laughter. "You're outrageous. If you were a man, you couldn't get away with crap like that."

"If I were a man, I wouldn't be lying here," I pointed out. I held out an arm and pulled him back down into the bed, but I still wondered what he'd been doing Monday morning.

Ralph went off to shower, whistling slightly. I pulled the curtains back to look outside. The air had a faint yellow tinge. Even this early in the morning the city looked slightly baked. The break in the weather was over; we were in for another hot, polluted spell.

I showered and dressed and joined Ralph at the table for a cup of coffee. His apartment included one large room with a half wall making a partially private eating area. The kitchen must have once been a closet: stove, sink, and refrigerator were stacked neatly, allowing room to stand and work, but not enough space even for a chair. It wasn't a bad-looking place. A large couch faced the front entrance, and a heavy armchair stood pulled back from the windows at right angles to it. I'd read somewhere that people who lived in rooms with floor-to-ceiling windows keep the furniture pulled back away from them—some illusion of falling if you're right up against the glass. A good two feet lay between the chair back and the lightly curtained windows. All the upholstery and the curtains were in the same light floral pattern. Nice for a prefurnished place.

At 7:30 Ralph stood up. "I hear those claims calling me," he explained. "I'll get in touch with you tomorrow, Vic."

"Fine," I said. We rode down in the elevator in amiable silence. Ralph walked me to my car, which I'd had to park near Lake Shore Drive. "Want a ride downtown?" I asked. He declined, saying he got his exercise walking the mile and a half to Ajax each day.

As I drove off, I could see him moving down the street in my rearview mirror, a jaunty figure despite the close air.

It was only eight when I got back to Lotty's. She was having toast and coffee in the kitchen. Jill, her oval face alive and expressive, was talking animatedly, a half-drunk glass of milk in front of her. Her innocent good spirits made me feel old and decadent. I made a face at myself.

"Good morning, ladies. It's a stinker outside."

"Good morning, Vic," said Lotty, her face amused. "What a pity you had to work all night."

I gave her a playful punch on the shoulder. Jill asked, "Were you really working all night?" in a serious, worried voice.

"No, and Lotty knows it. I spent the night at a friend's place after doing a little work. You have a pleasant evening? How were the enchiladas?"

"Oh, they were great!" Jill said enthusiastically. "Did you know that Carol has been cooking since she was seven?" She giggled. "I don't know how to do one useful thing, like ironing or even making scrambled eggs. Carol says I'd better marry someone with lots of money."

"Oh, just marry someone who likes to cook and iron," I said.

"Well, maybe you can practice on some scrambled eggs tonight," Lotty suggested. "Are you going to be here tonight?" she asked me.

"Can you make it an early dinner? I've got a seven thirty meeting down at the University of Chicago—someone who may be able to help me find Anita."

"How about it, Jill?" Lotty asked.

Jill made a face. "I think I'll plan on marrying someone rich." Lotty and I laughed. "How about peanut butter sandwiches?" she suggested. "I already know how to make those."

"I'll make you a fritata, Lotty," I promised, "if you and Jill will pick up some spinach and onions on your way home."

Lotty made a face. "Vic is a good cook, but a messy one," she told Jill. "She'll make a simple dinner for four in half an hour, but you and I will spend the night cleaning the kitchen."

"Lotty!" I expostulated. "From a fritata? I promise you—" I thought a minute, then laughed. "No promises. I don't want to be late for my meeting. Jill, you can clean up."

Jill looked at me uncertainly: Was I angry because she didn't want to make dinner? "Look," I said, "you don't have to be perfect: Lotty and I will like you even if you have temper tantrums, don't make your bed, and refuse to cook dinner. Okay?"

"Certainly," Lotty agreed, amused. "I've been Vic's friend these last fifteen years, and I've yet to see her make a bed."

Jill smiled at that. "Are you going detecting today?"

"Yes, up to the North Side. Looking for a needle in a haystack. I'd like to have lunch with you, but I don't know what my timetable is going to be like. I'll call down to the clinic around noon, though."

I went into the guest room and changed into shorts, T-shirt, and running shoes. Jill came in as I was halfway through my warm-up stretches. My muscles had tightened up in response to their abuse, and I was having to go more slowly and carefully than normal. When Jill came in, I was sweating a little, not from exertion, but from the residual pain. She stood watching me for a minute. "Mind if I get dressed while you're in here?" she asked finally.

"No," I grunted. "Unless—you'd feel more—comfortable—alone." I pulled myself upright. "You thought about calling your mother?"

She made a face. "Lotty had the same idea. I've decided to be a runaway and stay down here." She put on her jeans and one of her man-sized shirts. "I like it here."

"It's just the novelty. You'll get lonesome for your private beach after a while." I gave her a quick hug. "But I invite you to stay at Lotty's for as long as you like."

She laughed at that. "Okay, I'll call my mom."

"Atta girl. 'Bye, Lotty," I called, and started out the door. Sheffield Avenue is about a mile from the lake. I figured if I ran over to the lake, eight blocks down to Diversey and back again, that would give me close to four miles. I went slowly, partly to ease my muscles and partly because of the stifling weather. I usually run seven-and-a-half-minute miles, but I tried to pace it at about nine minutes this morning. I was sweating freely by the time I got to Diversey, and my legs felt wobbly. I cut the pace going north, but I was so tired I wasn't paying too much attention to the traffic around me. As I left the lake path, a squad car pulled out in front of me. Sergeant McGonnigal was sitting in the passenger seat.

"Good morning, Miss Warshawski."

"Morning, Sergeant," I said, trying to breathe evenly.

"Lieutenant Mallory asked me to find you," he said, getting out of the car. "He got a call yesterday from the Winnetka police. Seems you fast-talked your way past them to get into the Thayer house."

"Oh, yeah?" I said. "Nice to see so much cooperation between the suburban and the city forces." I did a few toe touches to keep my leg muscles from stiffening.

"They're concerned about the Thayer girl. They think she should be home with her mother."

"That's thoughtful of them. They can call her at Dr. Herschel's and suggest that to her. Is that why you tracked me down?"

"Not entirely. The Winnetka police finally turned up a witness to the shooter's car, though not to the shooting." He paused.

"Oh, yeah? Enough of an ID to make an arrest?"

"Unfortunately the witness is only five years old. He's scared silly and his parents have roped him around with lawyers and guards. Seems he'd been playing in the ditch alongside Sheridan Road, which was a no-no, but his folks were asleep, so he sneaked out. That's apparently why he went—because it's off limits. He was playing some crazy game, you know how kids are, thought he was stalking Darth Vader or something, when he saw the car. Big, black car, he says, sitting outside the Thayer house. He decided to stalk it when he saw a guy in the passenger seat who scared the daylights out of him."

McGonnigal stopped again to make sure I was following. He emphasized his next words carefully. "He finally said—after hours of talk, and many promises to the parents that we wouldn't subpoena him or publish the news —that what scared him about the guy was that Zorro had got him. Why Zorro? It seems this guy had some kind of mark on his face. That's all he knows: He saw it, panicked, and ran for his life. Doesn't know if the guy saw him or not."

"Sounds like a good lead," I commented politely. "All you have to do is find a big black car and a man with a mark on his face, and ask him if he knows Zorro."

McGonnigal looked sharply at me. "We police are not total idiots, Miss Warshawski. It's not something we can take to court, because of promising the parents and the lawyers. Anyway, the testimony isn't very good. But Zorro—you know, Zorro's mark is a big Z, and the lieutenant and I wondered if you knew anyone with a big Z on his face?"

I felt my face twitch. Earl's gofer, Tony, had had such a scar. I shook my head. "Should I?"

"Not too many guys with that kind of mark. We thought it might be Tony Bronsky. He got cut like that by a guy named Zav who objected to Tony taking away his girl friend seven-eight years ago. He hangs around Earl Smeissen these days."

"Oh?" I said. "Earl and I aren't exactly social friends, Sergeant—I don't know all his companions."

"Well, the lieutenant thought you'd like to know about it. He said he knew you'd sure hate for anything to happen to the little Thayer girl while you were looking after her." He got back into his car.

"The lieutenant has a fine sense of drama," I called after him. "He's been watching too many *Kojak* reruns late at night. Tell him that from me."

McGonnigal drove off and I walked the rest of the way home. I'd completely lost interest in exercise. Lotty and Jill had already left. I took a long, hot shower, easing my leg muscles and thinking over McGonnigal's message. It didn't surprise me that Earl was involved in John Thayer's death. I wondered if Jill really was in any danger, though. And if she was, was she worse off with Lotty and me? I toweled dry and weighed myself. I was down two pounds, surprising with all the starch I'd been eating lately.

I went into the kitchen to squeeze some orange juice. There was one way in which Jill was worse off with me, I realized. If Earl decided I needed to be blown away completely, she'd make a perfect hostage for him. I suddenly felt very cold.

Nothing I was doing was getting me anyplace—unless Thayer's execution could be called a destination. I couldn't tie McGraw to Masters or Thayer. I didn't have a clue about Anita. The one person who might supply me with anything was McGraw, and he wouldn't. Why the hell had he come to me in the first place?

On impulse I looked up the Knifegrinders' number in the white pages and dialed. The receptionist transferred me to Mildred. I didn't identify myself but asked for McGraw. He was in a meeting and couldn't be disturbed.

"It's important," I said. "Tell him it concerns Earl Smeissen and John Thayer."

Mildred put me on hold. I studied my fingernails. They needed filing. At last the phone clicked and McGraw's husky voice came on the line.

"Yes? What is it?" he asked.

"This is V. I. Warshawski. Did you finger Thayer for Earl?"

"What the hell are you talking about? I told you to stay out of my business."

"You dragged me in in the first place, McGraw. You made it my business. Now I want to know, did you finger Thayer for Earl?"

He was quiet.

"One of Earl's men shot Thayer. You brought Thayer's name into this to begin with. You've hedged about why. Did you want to be sure he got dragged into the case from the beginning? You were afraid the police might jump on Anita, and you wanted to make sure his name got in the pot? Then what—he threatened to squeal, and you asked Earl to kill him just in case?"

"Warshawski, I got a tape running. You make any more accusations like this and I could see you in court."

"Don't try it, McGraw: They might subpoena the rest of your tapes."

He slammed the phone down. I didn't feel any better.

I dressed in a hurry, but checked the Smith & Wesson carefully before putting it in my shoulder holster. My continuing hope was that Earl thought he'd rendered me negligible, and that he'd continue thinking so until I'd unraveled enough of the truth to make it too late for any other action he might take. But I took no chances, leaving the apartment from the rear and circling the block to come to my car. The coast was still clear.

I decided to abandon Loop bars and go to the Knifegrinders' neighborhood. I could return to the Loop tomorrow if necessary. On my way north I stopped at the clinic. Although it was early in the day, the waiting room was already full. I again walked past the baleful glares from those who had been sitting for an hour.

"I need to talk to Lotty," I said abruptly to Carol. She took one look at my face and got Lotty out of the examining room. I quickly explained to her what had happened. "I don't want to get Jill upset," I said, "but I don't want to feel like we're sitting on a land mine here."

Lotty nodded. "Yes, but what's to stop them from taking her out of the Thayer house?" she asked. "If they decide she would be a good hostage, I'm afraid they could get her wherever she was. It is not your peace of mind, but Jill's we need to think of. And I think she's better down here for another couple of days. Until her father's funeral, anyway; she called the mother—the funeral won't be until Friday."

"Yes, but, Lotty, I'm running against the clock here. I've got to keep going, I can't sit guarding Jill."

"No." She frowned, then her face cleared. "Carol's brother. Big, bruising, good-natured guy. He's an architecture student at Circle—maybe he can come and watch out for thugs." She called to Carol, who listened eagerly to the problem, threw up her hands at the thought of Jill in danger, but agreed that Paul would be glad to come and help. "He looks mean and stupid," she said. "A perfect disguise, since he is really friendly and brilliant."

I had to be satisfied with that, but I wasn't happy: I'd have liked to ship Jill up to Wisconsin until everything was over.

I went on north and drove around the Knifegrinder territory, staking out my route for the day. There weren't nearly as many bars here as there were in the Loop. I picked a twenty-block square and decided to keep the car. This morning, no matter what sort of ill will it raised in the bars, I was not going to drink. I cannot face beer before noon. Or even Scotch.

I started at the west end of my territory, along the Howard el tracks. The first place, Clara's, looked so down-at-the-heels, I wasn't sure I wanted to go into it. Surely someone as fastidious as Masters looked would not go to a dump like that. On the other hand, maybe that's the kind of place he'd want —something that no one would associate with him. I braced my shoulders and pushed into the gloom out of the sticky air.

By noon I'd drawn nine blanks and was beginning to think I'd come up with a truly rotten idea, one that was wasting a lot of valuable time as well. I would finish my present stint, but not go back for a second crack at the Loop. I called the clinic. Carol's brother was in residence, enchanted by Jill and helping entertain some seven toddlers. I told Lotty I was going to stay where I was and to give my apologies to Jill.

By now the humid, polluted heat was stifling. I felt as though I were being pushed to the earth by it every time I walked back outside. The smell of stale beer in the bars began to nauseate me. Everyplace I went into had a few pathetic souls riveted to their stools, sipping down one drink after another, even though it was only morning. I was meeting with the same variety of hostility, indifference, and cooperation that I'd found downtown, and the same lack of recognition of my photos.

After calling Lotty, I decided to get lunch. I wasn't far from Sheridan Road; I walked over and found a decent-looking steak house at the end of the block. I opted against lunch in a bar, and walked in thankfully out of the heat. The High Corral, as the place called itself, was small, clean, and full of good food smells, a welcome contrast to sour beer. About two-thirds of the tables were filled. A plump, middle-aged woman came up with a menu and a cheerful smile and led me to a corner table. I began to feel better.

I ordered a small butt steak, an undressed salad, and a tall gin fizz and took my time over the food when it arrived. No one would ever write it up for *Chicago* magazine, but it was a simple, well-prepared meal and mellowed my spirits considerably. I ordered coffee, and lingered over that too. At 1:45 I realized I was procrastinating. "'When duty beckons, "Lo thou must," Youth replies to Age, "I can,"'" I muttered encouragingly to myself. I put two dollars on the table and carried my bill over to the cash register. The plump hostess bustled up from the back of the restaurant to take my money.

"Very pleasant lunch," I said.

"I'm glad you enjoyed it. Are you new to this neighborhood?"

I shook my head. "I was just passing by and your sign looked inviting." On impulse I pulled out my folder, now grimy and wilted around the edges. "I wonder if these two men have ever come in here together."

She picked up the pictures and looked at them. "Oh, yes."

I couldn't believe it. "Are you sure?"

"I couldn't be mistaken. Not unless it's something I'd have to go to court for." Her friendly face clouded a bit. "If it's a legal matter you're talking about—" She shoved the pictures back at me.

"Not at all," I said hastily. "Or at least, not one that you'll have to be involved in." I couldn't think of a plausible story on the spur of the moment.

"If anyone sends me a summons, I never saw either of them," she reiterated.

"But off the record, just for my ears, how long have they been coming here?" I said, in what I hoped was a sincere, persuasive voice.

"What's the problem?" She was still suspicious.

"Paternity suit," I said promptly, the first thing that came into my mind. It sounded ridiculous, even to me, but she relaxed.

"Well, that doesn't sound too dreadful. I guess it's been about five years. This is my husband's restaurant, and we've been working it together for eighteen years now. I remember most of my regular customers."

"Do they come in often?" I asked.

"Oh, maybe three times a year. But over a period of time, you get to recognize your regulars. Besides, this man"—she tapped McGraw's picture —"comes in a lot. I think he's with that big union down the road."

"Oh, really?" I said politely. I pulled Thayer's picture out. "What about him?" I asked.

She studied it. "It looks familiar," she said, "but he's never been in here."

"Well, I certainly won't spread your name any further. And thanks for a very nice lunch."

I felt dizzy walking out into the blinding heat. I couldn't believe my luck. Every now and then you get a break like that as a detective, and you start to think maybe you're on the side of right and good after all and a benevolent

Providence is guiding your steps. Hot damn! I thought. I've got Masters tied to McGraw. And McGraw knows Smeissen. And the twig is on the branch, the branch is on the tree, the tree is on the hill. Vic, you are a genius, I told myself. The only question is, what is tying these two guys together? It must be that beautiful claim draft I found in Peter Thayer's apartment, but how?

I found a pay phone and called Ralph to see if he had tracked down the Gielczowski file. He was in a meeting. No, I wouldn't leave a message, I'd call later.

There was another question too. What was the connection among Thayer, McGraw, and Masters? Still, that shouldn't be too difficult to find out. The whole thing probably revolved around some way to make money, maybe nontaxable money. If that were so, then Thayer came in naturally as Masters's neighbor and good friend and vice-president of a bank. He could probably launder money in a dozen different ways that I couldn't begin to imagine. Say he laundered the money and Peter found out. McGraw got Smeissen to kill Peter. Then Thayer was overcome with remorse. "I won't be a party to it," he said—to Masters? to McGraw? and they got Earl to blow him away too.

Steady, Vic, I told myself, getting into the car. So far you only have one fact: McGraw and Masters know each other. But what a beautiful, highly suggestive fact.

It was the bottom of the fifth inning at Wrigley Field, and the Cubs were rolling over Philadelphia. For some reason, smoggy, wilting air acted on them like a tonic; everyone else was dying, but the Cubs were leading 8-1. Kingman hit his thirty-fourth homer. I thought maybe I'd earned a trip to the park to see the rest of the game, but sternly squashed the idea.

I got back to the clinic at 2:30. The outer room was even more crowded than it had been in the morning. A small window air conditioner fought against the heat and the combined bodies and lost. As I walked into the room, the inner door opened and a face looked around. "Mean and stupid" summed it up exactly. I went on across the room. "You must be Paul," I said, holding out a hand. "I'm Vic."

He smiled. The transformation was incredible. I could see the bright intelligence in his eyes, and he looked handsome rather than brutish. I wondered fleetingly if Jill was old enough to fall in love.

"Everything's quiet here," he said. "Everything but the babies, of course. Do you want to come out and see how Jill is doing?"

I followed him to the back. Lotty had moved the steel table out of her second examining room. In this tiny space Jill sat playing with five children between the ages of two and seven. She had the self-important look of someone coping with a major crisis. I grinned to myself. A baby was asleep in a basket in the corner. She looked up when I came in, and said hello, but her smile was for Paul. Was that an unnecessary complication or a help? I wondered.

"How's it going?" I asked.

"Great. Whenever things get too hectic, Paul makes a quick trip to the Good Humor man. I'm just afraid they'll catch on and squawk all the time."

"Do you think you could leave them for a few minutes? I'd like to ask you a few questions."

She looked at the group doubtfully. "Go ahead," Paul said cheerfully. "I'll fill in for you—you've been at it too long, anyway."

She got up. One of the children, a little boy, protested. "You can't go," he said in a loud, bossy voice.

"Sure, she can," Paul said, squatting easily in her place. "Now where were you?"

I took Jill into Lotty's office. "Looks like you're a natural," I said. "Lotty will probably try to talk you into spending the rest of the summer down here."

She flushed. "I'd like to. I wonder if I really could."

"No reason not, once we get this other business cleared up. Have you ever met Anita's father?"

She shook her head. I pulled out my package of pictures and took out the ones of McGraw. "This is he. Have you ever seen him, either with your dad, or maybe in the neighborhood?"

She studied them for a while. "I don't think I've ever seen him before. He doesn't look at all like Anita."

I stopped for a minute, not sure of the least hurting way to say what I wanted. "I think Mr. McGraw and Mr. Masters are partners in some scheme or other—I don't know what. I believe your father must have been involved in some way, maybe without realizing what it was he was involved in." In fact, I suddenly thought, if Thayer had been obviously a party to it, wouldn't Peter have confronted him first? "Do you remember Peter and your father fighting in the last week or two before Peter's death?"

"No. In fact, Peter hadn't been home for seven weeks. If he and Daddy had a fight, it had to be over the telephone. Maybe at the office, but not out at the house."

"That's good. Now, going back to this other business, I've got to know what it is your father knew about their deal. Can you think of anything that might help me? Did he and Mr. Masters lock themselves up in the study for long talks?"

"Yes, but lots of men do that—did that. Daddy did business with lots of people, and they would often come over to the house to talk about it."

"Well, what about money?" I asked. "Did Mr. Masters ever give your father a lot of money? or the other way around?"

She laughed embarrassedly and shrugged her shoulders. "I just don't know about any of that kind of stuff. I know Daddy worked for the bank and was an officer and all, but I don't know what he did exactly, and I don't know anything about the money. I guess I should. I know my family is well off, we've all got these big trusts from my grandparents, but I don't know anything about Daddy's money."

That wasn't too surprising. "Suppose I asked you to go back to Winnetka and look through his study to see if he had any papers that mention McGraw or Masters or both. Would that make you feel dishonest and slimy?"

She shook her head. "If it would help I'll do it. But I don't want to leave here."

"That is a problem," I agreed. I looked at my watch and calculated times. "I don't think we could fit it in before dinner this evening, anyway. But how about first thing tomorrow morning? Then we could come back here to the clinic in time for the baby rush hour."

"Sure," she agreed. "Would you want to come along? I mean, I don't have a car or anything, and I would like to come back, and they might try to talk me into staying up there once I got there."

"I wouldn't miss it." By tomorrow morning the house probably wouldn't be filled with police anymore, either.

Jill got up and went back to the nursery. I could hear her saying in a maternal voice, "Well, whose turn is it?" I grinned, popped my head in Lotty's door, and told her I was going home to sleep.

14
IN THE HEAT
OF THE NIGHT

I set off for the University Women United meeting at seven. I'd slept for three hours and felt on top of the world. The fritata had turned out well—an old recipe of my mother's, accompanied by lots of toast, a salad constructed by Paul, and Paul's warm appreciation. He'd decided his bodyguarding included spending the night, and had brought a sleeping bag. The dining room was the only place with space for him, Lotty warned him. "And I want you to stay in it," she added. Jill was delighted. I could just imagine her sister's reaction if she came back with Paul as a boyfriend.

It was an easy drive south, a lazy evening with a lot of people out cooling off. This was my favorite time of day in the summer. There was something about the smell and feel of it that evoked the magic of childhood.

I didn't have any trouble parking on campus, and got into the meeting room just before things began. About a dozen women were there, wearing work pants and oversized T-shirts, or denim skirts made out of blue jeans with the legs cut apart and restitched, seams facing out. I was wearing jeans and a big loose shirt to cover the gun, but I was still dressed more elegantly than anyone else in the room.

Gail Sugarman was there. She recognized me when I came in, and said, "Hi, I'm glad you remembered the meeting." The others stopped to look at me. "This is—" Gail stopped, embarrassed. "I've forgotten your name—it's Italian, I remember you told me that. Anyway, I met her at the Swift coffee shop last week and told her about the meetings and here she is."

"You're not a reporter, are you?" one woman asked.

"No, I'm not," I said neutrally. "I have a B.A. from here, pretty old degree at this point. I was down here the other day talking to Harold Weinstein and ran into Gail."

"Weinstein," another one snorted. "Thinks he's a radical because he wears work shirts and curses capitalism."

"Yeah," another agreed. "I was in his class on 'Big Business and Big Labor.' He felt the major battle against oppression had been won when Ford lost the battle with the UAW in the forties. If you tried to talk about how women have been excluded not just from big business but from the unions as well, he said that didn't indicate oppression, merely a reflection of the current social mores."

"That argument justifies all oppression," a plump woman with short curling hair put in. "Hell, the Stalin labor camps reflected Soviet mores of the 1930s. Not to mention Shcharansky's exile with hard labor."

Thin, dark Mary, the older woman who'd been with Gail at the coffee shop on Friday, tried to call the group to order. "We don't have a program tonight," she said. "In the summer our attendance is too low to justify a speaker. But why don't we get in a circle on the floor so that we can have a group discussion." She was smoking, sucking in her cheeks with her intense inhaling. I had a feeling she was eyeing me suspiciously, but that may have just been my own nerves.

I obediently took a spot on the floor, drawing my legs up in front of me. My calf muscles were sensitive. The other women straggled over, getting cups of evil-looking coffee as they came. I'd taken one look at the overboiled brew on my way in and decided it wasn't necessary to drink it to prove I was one of the group.

When all but two were seated, Mary suggested we go around the circle and introduce ourselves. "There are a couple of new people here tonight," she said. "I'm Mary Annasdaughter." She turned to the woman on her right, the one who'd protested women's exclusion from big unions. When they got to me, I said, "I'm V. I. Warshawski. Most people call me Vic."

When they'd finished, one said curiously, "Do you go by your initials or is Vic your real name?"

"It's a nickname," I said. "I usually use my initials. I started out my working life as a lawyer, and I found it was harder for male colleagues and opponents to patronize me if they didn't know my first name."

"Good point," Mary said, taking the meeting back. "Tonight I'd like to see what we can do to support the ERA booth at the Illinois State Fair. The state NOW group usually has a booth where they distribute literature. This year they want to do something more elaborate, have a slide show, and they need more people. Someone who can go down to Springfield for one or more days the week of August fourth to tenth to staff the booth and the slide show."

"Are they sending a car down?" the plump, curly-haired one asked.

"I expect the transportation will depend on how many people volunteer. I thought I might go. If some of the rest of you want to, we could all take the bus together—it's not that long a ride."

"Where would we stay?" someone wanted to know.

"I plan to camp out," Mary said. "But you can probably find some NOW people to share a hotel room with. I can check back at the headquarters."

"I kind of hate doing anything with NOW," a rosy-cheeked woman with waist-long hair said. She was wearing a T-shirt and bib overalls; she had the face of a peaceful Victorian matron.

"Why, Annette?" Gail asked.

"They ignore the real issues—women's social position, inequities of marriage, divorce, child care—and go screwing around supporting establishment politicians. They'll support a candidate who does one measly little thing for child care, and overlook the fact that he doesn't have any women on his staff, and that his wife is a plastic mannequin sitting at home supporting his career."

"Well, you're never going to have social justice until you get some basic political and economic inequalities solved," a stocky woman, whose name I thought was Ruth, said. "And political problems can be grappled with. You can't go around trying to uproot the fundamental oppression between men and women without some tool to dig with: laws represent that tool."

This was an old argument; it went back to the start of radical feminism in the late sixties: Do you concentrate on equal pay and equal legal rights, or do you go off and try to convert the whole society to a new set of sexual values? Mary let the tide roll in for ten minutes. Then she rapped the floor with her knuckles.

"I'm not asking for a consensus on NOW, or even on the ERA," she said. "I just want a head count of those who'd like to go to Springfield."

Gail volunteered first, predictably, and Ruth. The two who'd been dissecting Weinstein's politics also agreed to go.

"What about you, Vic?" Mary said.

"Thanks, but no," I said.

"Why don't you tell us why you're really here," Mary said in a steely voice. "You may be an old UC student, but no one stops by a rap group on Tuesday night just to check out politics on the old campus."

"They don't change that much, but you're right: I came here because I'm trying to find Anita McGraw. I don't know anyone here well, but I know this is a group she was close to, and I'm hoping that someone here can tell me where she is."

"In that case, you can get out," Mary said angrily. The group silently closed against me; I could feel their hostility like a physical force. "We've all had the police on us—now I guess they thought a woman pig could infiltrate this meeting and worm Anita's address out of one of us—assuming we had it to worm. I don't know it myself—I don't know if anyone in here knows it—but you pigs just can't give up, can you?"

I didn't move. "I'm not with the police, and I'm not a reporter. Do you think the police want to find Anita so that they can lay Peter Thayer's death on her?"

"Of course," Mary snorted. "They've been poking around trying to find if Peter slept around and Anita was jealous or if he'd made a will leaving her money. Well, I'm sorry—you can go back and tell them that they just cannot get away with that."

"I'd like to present an alternative scenario," I said.

"Screw yourself," Mary said. "We're not interested. Now get out."

"Not until you've listened to me."

"Do you want me to throw her out, Mary?" Annette asked.

"You can try," I said. "But it'll just make you madder if I hurt one of you, and I'm still not going to leave until you've listened to what I have to say."

"All right," Mary said angrily. She took out her watch. "You can have five minutes. Then Annette throws you out."

"Thank you. My tale is short: I can embellish it later if you have questions.

"Yesterday morning, John Thayer, Peter's father, was gunned down in front of his home. The police presume, but cannot prove, that this was the work of a hired killer known to them. It is my belief, not shared by the police, that this same killer shot Peter Thayer last Monday.

"Now, why was Peter shot? The answer is that he knew something that was potentially damaging to a very powerful and very corrupt labor leader. I don't know what he knew, but I assume it had something to do with illegal financial transactions. It is further possible that his father was a party to these transactions, as was the man Peter worked for."

I stretched my legs out and leaned back on my hands. No one spoke. "These are all assumptions. I have no proof at the moment that could be used in court, but I have the proof that comes from watching human relationships and reactions. If I am correct in my assumptions, then I believe Anita McGraw's life is in serious danger. The overwhelming probability is that Peter Thayer shared with her the secret that got him killed, and that when she came home last Monday evening to find his dead body, she panicked and ran. But as long as she is alive, and in lonely possession of this secret—whatever it is—then the men who have killed twice to protect it will not care about killing her as well."

"You know a lot about it," Ruth said. "How do you happen to be involved if you're not a reporter and not a cop?"

"I'm a private investigator," I said levelly. "At the moment my client is a fourteen-year-old girl who saw her father murdered and is very frightened."

Mary was still angry. "You're still a cop, then. It doesn't make any difference who is paying your salary."

"You're wrong," I said. "It makes an enormous difference. I'm the only person I take orders from, not a hierarchy of officers, aldermen, and commissioners."

"What kind of proof do you have?" Ruth asked.

"I was beaten up last Friday night by the man who employs the killer who probably killed the two Thayers. He warned me away from the case. I have a presumption, not provable, of who hired him: a man who got his name from an associate on speaking terms with many prominent criminals. This man is the person Peter Thayer was working for this summer. And I know the other guy, the one with the criminal contacts, has been seen with Peter's boss. Ex-boss. I don't know about the money, that's just a guess. No one in that crowd would be hurt by sex scandals, and spying is very unlikely."

"What about dope?" Gail asked.

"I don't think so," I said. "But anyway, that is certainly an illegal source of income for which you might kill to cover up."

"Frankly, V.I., or Vic, or whatever your real name is, you haven't convinced me. I don't believe Anita's life could be in danger. But if anyone disagrees with me and knows where Anita is, go ahead and betray her."

"I have another question," Ruth said. "Assuming we did know where she is and told you, what good would that do her—if everything you're saying is true?"

"If I can find out what the transaction is, I can probably get some definite proof of who the murderer is," I said. "The more quickly that happens, the less likely it is that this hired killer can get to her."

No one said anything else. I waited a few minutes. I kind of hoped Annette would try to throw me out: I felt like breaking someone's arm. Radicals are so goddamn paranoid. And radical students combine that with isolation and pomposity. Maybe I'd break all their arms, just for fun. But Annette didn't move. And no one chirped up with Anita's address.

"Satisfied?" Mary asked triumphantly, her thin cheeks pulled back in a smirk.

"Thanks for the time, sisters," I said. "If any of you changes her mind, I'm leaving some business cards with my phone number by the coffee." I put them down and left.

I felt very depressed driving home. Peter Wimsey would have gone in and charmed all those uncouth radicals into slobbering all over him. He would never have revealed he was a private detective—he would have started some clever conversation that would have told him everything he wanted to know and then given two hundred pounds to the Lesbian Freedom Fund.

I turned left onto Lake Shore Drive, going much too fast and getting a reckless pleasure from feeling the car careening, almost out of control. I didn't even care at this point if someone stopped me. I did the four miles between Fifty-seventh Street and McCormick Place in three minutes. It was at that point that I realized someone was following me.

The speed limit in that area is forty-five and I was doing eighty, yet I was holding the same pair of headlights in my rearview mirror that had been behind me in the other lane when I got on the Drive. I braked quickly, and changed to the outside lane. The other car didn't change lanes, but slowed down also.

How long had I been carrying a tail, and why? If Earl wanted to blow me away, he had unlimited opportunities, no need to waste manpower and money on a tail. He might not know where I'd gone after leaving my apartment, but I didn't think so. My answering service had Lotty's phone number, and it's a simple matter to get an address from the phone company if you have the number.

Maybe they wanted Jill and didn't realize I'd taken her to Lotty's. I drove slowly and normally, not trying to change lanes or make an unexpected exit. My companion stayed with me, in the center lane, letting a few cars get between us. As we moved downtown, the lights got brighter and I could see the car better—a mid-sized gray sedan, it looked like.

If they got Jill, they would have a potent weapon to force me off the case. I couldn't believe that Earl thought I had a case. He'd given me the big scare, he'd torn my apartment apart, and he'd gotten the police to make an arrest. As far as I could tell, despite John Thayer's death, Donald Mackenzie was still in jail. Perhaps they thought I could lead them to the document they had overlooked at Peter Thayer's, and not found in my apartment.

The phrase "lead them to" clicked in my brain. Of course. They weren't interested in me, or in Jill, or even in that claim draft. They wanted Anita McGraw, just as I did, and they thought I could lead them to her. How had they known I was going to the campus tonight? They hadn't: they'd followed me there. I'd told McGraw I had a lead on a lead to Anita and he had told— Smeissen?—Masters? I didn't like the thought of McGraw fingering his daughter. He must have told someone he thought he could trust. Surely not Masters, though.

If my deduction was correct, I ought to keep them guessing. As long as they thought I knew something, my life was probably safe. I got off the Drive downtown, going past Buckingham Fountain as it shot up jets of colored water high into the night. A large crowd had gathered to see the nightly show. I wondered if I could lose myself in it, but didn't think much of my chances. I went on over to Michigan Avenue, and parked across the street from the Conrad Hilton Hotel. I locked the car door and leisurely crossed the street. I stopped inside the glass doors for a glance outside, and was pleased to see the gray sedan pull up next to my car. I didn't wait to see what the occupants would do, but moved quickly down the hotel's long corridor to the side entrance on Eighth Street.

This part of the hotel had airline ticket offices, and as I walked past them, a doorman was calling, "Last call for the airport bus. Nonstop to O'Hare Field." Without thinking or stopping to look behind me, I pushed in front of a small crew of laughing flight attendants and got on the bus. They followed me more slowly; the conductor checked his load and got off, and the bus started moving. As we turned the corner onto Michigan, I could see a man looking up and down the street. I thought it might be Freddie.

The bus moved ponderously across the Loop to Ontario Street, some twelve blocks north, and I kept an anxious lookout through the rear window, but it seemed as though Freddie's slow wits had not considered the possibility of my being on the bus.

It was 9:30 when we got to O'Hare. I moved from the bus to stand in the shadow of one of the giant pillars supporting the terminal, but saw no gray sedan. I was about to step out when I thought perhaps they had a second car, so I looked to see if any vehicle repeated its circuit more than once, and scanned the occupants to see if I recognized any of Smeissen's crew. By ten I decided I was clear and caught a cab back to Lotty's.

I had the driver drop me at the top of her street. Then I went down the alley behind her building, keeping a hand close to my gun. I didn't see anyone but a group of three teen-age boys, drinking beer and talking lazily.

I had to pound on the back door for several minutes before Lotty heard and came to let me in. Her thick black eyebrows went up in surprise. "Trouble?" she said.

"A little, downtown. I'm not sure whether anyone is watching the front."

"Jill?" she asked.

"I don't think so. I think they're hoping I'll lead them to Anita McGraw. Unless I do, or unless they find her first I think we're all pretty safe." I shook my head in dissatisfaction. "I don't like it, though. They could snatch Jill and hold her to ransom if they thought I knew where Anita was. I didn't find out tonight. I'm sure one of those goddamned radical women knows where she is, but they think they're being noble and winning a great war against the pigs, and they won't tell me. It's so frustrating."

"Yes, I see," Lotty said seriously. "Maybe it's not so good for the child to be here. She and Paul are watching the movie on television," she added, jerking her head toward the living room.

"I left my car downtown," I said. "Someone was following me back from the university and I shook them off in the Loop—took the bus out to O'Hare—long and expensive way to shake a tail, but it worked.

"Tomorrow, Jill's taking me out to Winnetka to go through her father's papers. Maybe she should just stay there."

"We'll sleep on it," Lotty suggested. "Paul is loving his guard duty, but he couldn't do much against men with machine guns. Besides, he is an architecture student and should not miss too many of his classes."

We went back into the living room. Jill was curled up on the daybed, watching the movie. Paul was lying on his stomach, looking up at her every few minutes. Jill didn't seem aware of the impression she was creating—this seemed to be her first conquest—but she glowed with contentment.

I went into the guest room to make some phone calls. Larry Anderson said they'd finished my apartment. "I didn't think you'd want that couch, so I let one of the guys take it home. And about the door—I've got a friend who does some carpentry. He has a beautiful oak door, out of some mansion or other. He could fix it up for you and put some dead bolts in it, if you'd like."

"Larry, I can't begin to thank you," I said, much moved. "That sounds like a beautiful idea. How did you close the place up today?"

"Oh, we nailed it shut," he said cheerfully. Larry and I had gone to school together years ago, but he'd dropped out earlier and further than I had. We chatted for a few minutes, then I hung up to call Ralph.

"It's me, Sherlock Holmes," I said. "How did your claim files go?"

"Oh, fine. Summer is a busy time for accidents with so many people on the road. They should stay home, but then they'd cut off their legs with lawnmowers or something and we'd be paying just the same."

"Did you refile that draft without any trouble?" I asked.

"Actually not, I couldn't find the file. I looked up the guy's account, though: he must have been in a doozy of an accident—we've been sending him weekly checks for four years now." He chuckled a little. "I was going to inspect Yardley's face today to see if he looked guilty of multiple homicide, but he's taking the rest of the week off—apparently cut up about Thayer's death."

"I see." I wasn't going to bother telling him about the link I'd found between Masters and McGraw; I was tired of arguing with him over whether I had a case or not.

"Dinner tomorrow night?" he asked.

"Make it Thursday," I suggested. "Tomorrow's going to be pretty open-ended."

As soon as I put the phone down, it rang. "Dr. Herschel's residence," I said. It was my favorite reporter, Murray Ryerson.

"Just got a squeal that Tony Bronsky may have killed John Thayer," he said.

"Oh, really? Are you going to publish that?"

"Oh, I think we'll paint a murky picture of gangland involvement. It's just a whiff, no proof, he wasn't caught at the scene, and our legal people have decided mentioning his name would be actionable."

"Thanks for sharing the news," I said politely.

"I wasn't calling out of charity," Murray responded. "But in my lumbering Swedish way it dawned on me that Bronsky works for Smeissen. We agreed yesterday that his name has been cropping up here and there around the place. What's his angle, Vic—why would he kill a respectable banker and his son?"

"Beats the hell out of me, Murray," I said, and hung up.

I went back and watched the rest of the movie, *The Guns of Navarone*, with Lotty, Jill, and Paul. I felt restless and on edge. Lotty didn't keep Scotch. She didn't have any liquor at all except brandy. I went into the kitchen and poured myself a healthy slug. Lotty looked questioningly at me, but said nothing.

Around midnight, as the movie was ending, the phone rang. Lotty answered it in her bedroom and came back, her face troubled. She gave me a quiet signal to follow her to the kitchen. "A man," she said in a low voice. "He asked if you were here; when I said yes, he hung up."

"Oh, hell," I muttered. "Well, nothing to be done about it now. . . . My apartment will be ready tomorrow night—I'll go back and remove this powder keg from your home."

Lotty shook her head and gave her twisted smile. "Not to worry, Vic— I'm counting on you fixing the AMA for me someday."

Lotty sent Jill unceremoniously off to bed. Paul got out his sleeping bag. I helped him move the heavy walnut dining-room table against the wall, and Lotty brought him a pillow from her bed, then went to sleep, herself.

The night was muggy; Lotty's brick, thick-walled building kept out the worst of the weather, and exhaust fans in the kitchen and dining rooms moved the air enough to make sleep possible. But the air felt close to me anyway. I lay on the daybed in a T-shirt, and sweated, dozed a bit, woke, tossed, and dozed again. At last I sat up angrily. I wanted to do something, but there was nothing for me to do. I turned on the light. It was 3:30.

I pulled on a pair of jeans and tiptoed out to the kitchen to make some coffee. While water dripped through the white porcelain filter, I looked through a bookcase in the living room for something to read. All books look equally boring in the middle of the night. I finally selected *Vienna in the Seventeenth Century* by Dorfman, fetched a cup of coffee, and flipped the pages, reading about the devastating plague following the Thirty Years War, and the street now called Graben—"the grave"—because so many dead had been buried there. The terrible story fit my jangled mood.

Above the hum of the fans I could hear the phone ring faintly in Lotty's room. We'd turned it off next to the spare bed where Jill was sleeping. I told myself it had to be for Lotty—some mother in labor, or some bleeding teenager—but I sat tensely anyway and was somehow not surprised when Lotty came out of her room, wrapped in a thin, striped cotton robe.

"For you: A Ruth Yonkers."

I shrugged my shoulders; the name meant nothing to me. "Sorry to get you up," I said, and went down the short hallway to Lotty's room. I felt as if all the night's tension had had its focus in waiting for this unexpected phone call from an unknown woman. The instrument was on a small Indonesian table next to Lotty's bed. I sat on the bed and spoke into it.

"This is Ruth Yonkers," a husky voice responded. "I talked to you at the UWU meeting tonight."

"Oh, yes," I said calmly. "I remember you." She'd been the stocky, square young woman who'd asked me all the questions at the end.

"I talked to Anita after the meeting. I didn't know how seriously to take you, but I thought she ought to know about it." I held my breath and said nothing. "She called me last week, told me about finding Peter's—finding Peter. She made me promise not to tell anyone where she was without checking with her first. Not even her father, or the police. It was all rather— bizarre."

"I see," I said.

"Do you?" she asked doubtfully.

"You thought she'd killed Peter, didn't you," I said in a comfortable tone. "And you felt caught by her choosing you to confide in. You didn't want to betray her, but you didn't want to be involved in a murder. So you were relieved to have a promise to fall back on."

Ruth gave a little sigh, half laugh, that came ghostily over the line. "Yes, that was it exactly. You're smarter than I thought you were. I hadn't realized Anita might be in danger herself—that was why she sounded so scared. Anyway, I called her. We've been talking for several hours. She's never heard of you and we've been debating whether we can trust you." She paused and I was quiet. "I think we have to. That's what it boils down to. If it's true, if there really are some mob people after her—it all sounds surreal, but she says you're right."

"Where is she?" I asked gently.

"Up in Wisconsin. I'll take you to her."

"No. Tell me where she is, and I'll find her. I'm being followed, and it'll just double the danger to try to meet up with you."

"Then I won't tell you where she is," Ruth said. "My agreement with her was that I would bring you to her."

"You've been a good friend, Ruth, and you've carried a heavy load. But if the people who are after Anita find out you know where she is, and suspect you're in her confidence, your own life is in danger. Let me run the risk—it's my job, after all."

We argued for several more minutes, but Ruth let herself be persuaded. She'd been under a tremendous strain for the five days since Anita had first called her, and she was glad to let someone else take it over. Anita was in Hartford, a little town northwest of Milwaukee. She was working as a waitress in a café. She'd cut her red hair short and dyed it black, and she was calling herself Jody Hill. If I left now, I could catch her just as the café opened for breakfast in the morning.

It was after four when I hung up. I felt refreshed and alert, as if I'd slept soundly for eight hours instead of tossing miserably for three.

Lotty was sitting in the kitchen, drinking coffee and reading. "Lotty, I do apologize. You get little enough sleep as it is. But I think this is the beginning of the end."

"Ah, good," she said, putting a marker in her book and shutting it. "The missing girl?"

"Yes. That was a friend who gave me the address. All I have to do now is get away from here without being seen."

"Where is she?" I hesitated. "My dear, I've been questioned by tougher experts than these Smeissen hoodlums. And perhaps someone else should know."

I grinned. "You're right." I told her, then added, "The question is, what about Jill? We were going to go up to Winnetka tomorrow—today, that is— to see if her father had any papers that might explain his connection with Masters and McGraw. Now maybe Anita can make that tie-in for me. But I'd still be happier to get Jill back up there. This whole arrangement—Paul under the dining-room table, Jill and the babies—makes me uncomfortable. If she wants to come back for the rest of the summer, sure—she can stay with me once this mess is cleared up. But for now—let's get her back home."

Lotty pursed her lips and stared into her coffee cup for several minutes. Finally she said, "Yes. I believe you're right. She's much better—two good nights of sleep, with calm people who like her—she can probably go back to her family. I agree. The whole thing with Paul is too volatile. Very sweet, but too volatile in such a cramped space."

"My car is across from the Conrad Hilton downtown. I can't take it—it's being watched. Maybe Paul can pick it up tomorrow, take Jill home. I'll be back here tomorrow night, say good-bye, and give you a little privacy."

"Do you want to take my car?" Lotty suggested.

I thought it over. "Where are you parked?"

"Out front. Across the street."

"Thanks, but I've got to get away from here without being seen. I don't know that your place is being watched—but these guys want Anita McGraw very badly. And they did call earlier to make sure I was here."

Lotty got up and turned out the kitchen light. She looked out the window, concealed partly by a hanging geranium and thin gauze curtains. "I don't see anyone. . . . Why not wake up Paul? He can take my car, drive it around the block a few times. Then, if no one follows him, he can pick you up in the alley. You drop him down the street."

"I don't like it. You'll be without a car, and when he comes back on foot, if there is someone out there, they'll be suspicious."

"Vic, my dear, it's not like you to be so full of quibbles. We won't be without a car—we'll have yours. As for the second—" She thought a minute. "Ah! Drop Paul at the clinic. He can finish his sleep there. We have a bed, for nights when Carol or I have to stay over."

I laughed. "Can't think of any more quibbles, Lotty. Let's wake up Paul and give it a try."

Paul woke up quickly and cheerfully. When the plan was explained to him, he accepted it enthusiastically. "Want me to beat up anyone hanging around outside?"

"Unnecessary, my dear," said Lotty, amused. "Let's try not to attract too much attention to ourselves. There's an all-night restaurant on Sheffield off Addison—give us a call from there."

We left Paul to dress in privacy. He came out to the kitchen a few minutes later, pushing his black hair back from his square face with his left hand and buttoning a blue workshirt with the right. Lotty gave him her car keys. We watched the street from Lotty's dark bedroom. No one attacked Paul as he got into the car and started it; we couldn't see anyone follow him down the street.

I went back to the living room and dressed properly. Lotty watched me without speaking while I loaded the Smith & Wesson and stuck it into the shoulder holster. I was wearing well-cut jeans and a blouson jacket over a ribbed knit shirt.

About ten minutes later Lotty's phone rang. "All clear," Paul said. "There is someone out front, though. I think I'd better not drive down the alley—it might bring him around to the rear. I'll be at the mouth of the alley at the north end of the street."

I relayed this to Lotty. She nodded. "Why don't you leave from the basement? You can go down there from inside, and outside the door is hidden by stairs and garbage cans." She led me downstairs. I felt very alert, very keyed up. Through a window on the stairwell we could see the night clearing into a predawn gray. It was 4:40 and the apartment was very quiet. A siren sounded in the distance, but no traffic was going down Lotty's street.

Lotty had brought a flashlight with her, rather than turn on a light that might show through the street-side window. She pointed it down the stairs so I could see the way, then turned it off. I padded down after her. At the bottom she seized my wrist, led me around bicycles and a washing machine, and very slowly and quietly drew back the dead bolts in the outside door. There was a little *click* as they snapped open. She waited several minutes before pulling the door open. It moved into the basement, quietly, on oiled hinges. I slipped out up the stairs in crepe-soled shoes.

From behind the screen of garbage cans I peered into the alley. Freddie sat propped against the back of the wall at the south end of the alley two buildings down. As far as I could tell, he was asleep.

I moved quietly back down the stairs. "Give me ten minutes," I mouthed into Lotty's ear. "I may need a quick escape route." Lotty nodded without speaking.

At the top of the stairs I checked Freddie again. Did he have the subtlety to fake sleep? I moved from behind the garbage cans into the shadow of the next building, my right hand on the revolver's handle. Freddie didn't stir. Keeping close to the walls, I moved quickly down the alley. As soon as I was halfway down, I broke into a quiet sprint.

15

THE UNION MAID

Paul was waiting as promised. He had a good head—the car was out of sight of the alley. I slid into the front seat and drew the door closed. "Any trouble?" he said, starting the engine and pulling away from the curb.

"No, but I recognized a guy asleep in the alley. You'd better call Lotty from the clinic. Tell her not to leave Jill alone in the apartment. Maybe she can get a police escort to the clinic. Tell her to call a Lieutenant Mallory to request it."

"Sure thing." He was very likable. We drove the short way to the clinic in silence. I handed him my car keys, and reiterated where the car was. "It's a dark blue Monza."

"Good luck," he said in his rich voice. "Don't worry about Jill and Lotty —I'll take care of them."

"I never worry about Lotty," I said, sliding into the driver's seat. "She's a force unto herself." I adjusted the side mirror and the rearview mirror, and let in the clutch: Lotty drove a small Datsun, as practical and unadorned as she was.

I kept checking the road behind me as I drove across Addison to the Kennedy, but it seemed to be clear. The air was clammy, the damp of a muggy night before the sun would rise and turn it into smog again. The eastern sky was light now, and I was moving quickly through the empty streets. Traffic was light on the expressway, and I cleared the suburbs to the northbound Milwaukee toll road in forty-five minutes.

Lotty's Datsun handled well, although I was out of practice with a standard shift and ground the gears a bit changing down. She had an FM radio, and I listened to WFMT well past the Illinois border. After that the reception grew fuzzy so I switched it off.

It was six in clear daylight when I reached the Milwaukee bypass. I'd never been to Hartford, but I'd been to Port Washington, thirty miles to the east of it on Lake Michigan, many times. As far as I could tell, the route was the same, except for turning west onto route 60 instead of east when you get twenty miles north of Milwaukee.

At 6:50 I eased the Datsun to a halt on Hartford's main street, across from Ronna's Café—Homemade Food, and in front of the First National Bank of Hartford. My heart was beating fast. I unbuckled the seat belt and got out, stretching my legs. The trip had been just under 140 miles; I'd done it in two hours and ten minutes. Not bad.

Hartford is in the beautiful moraine country, the heart of Wisconsin dairy farming. There's a small Chrysler plant there that makes outboard motors, and up the hill I could see a Libby's cannery. But most of the money in the town comes from farming, and people were up early. Ronna's opened at 5:30, according to the legend on the door, and at seven most of the tables were full. I bought the *Milwaukee Sentinel* from a coin box by the door, and sat down at an empty table near the back.

One waitress was taking care of the crowd at the counter. Another covered all the tables. She was rushing through the swinging doors at the back, her arms loaded up with plates. Her short, curly hair had been dyed black. It was Anita McGraw.

She unloaded pancakes, fried eggs, toast, hash browns, at a table where three heavyset men in bib overalls were drinking coffee, and brought a fried egg to a good-looking young guy in a dark blue boiler suit at the table next to me. She looked at me with the harrassment common to all overworked waitresses in coffee shops. "I'll be right with you. Coffee?"

I nodded. "Take your time," I said, opening the paper. The men in the bib overalls were kidding the good-looking guy—he was a veterinarian, apparently, and they were farmers who'd used his services. "You grow that beard to make everyone think you're grown up, Doc?" one of them said.

"Naw, just to hide from the FBI," the vet said. Anita was carrying a cup of coffee to me; her hand shook and she spilled it on the veterinarian. She flushed and started apologizing. I got up and took the cup from her before any more spilled, and the young man said good-naturedly, "Oh, it just wakes you up faster if you pour it all over yourself—especially if it's still hot. Believe me, Jody," he added as she dabbed ineffectually at the wet spot on his arm with a napkin, "this is the nicest stuff that's likely to spill on this outfit today."

The farmers laughed at that, and Anita came over to take my order. I asked for a Denver omelette, no potatoes, whole-wheat toast, and juice. When in farm country, eat like a farmer. The vet finished his egg and coffee. "Well, I hear those cows calling me," he said, put some money on the table, and left. Other people began drifting out too: It was 7:15—time for the day to be under way. For the farmers this was a short break between morning milking and some business in town. They lingered over a second cup of coffee. By the time Anita brought back my omelette, though, only three tables had people still eating, and just a handful were left at the counter.

I ate half the omelette, slowly, and read every word in the paper. People kept drifting in and out; I had a fourth cup of coffee. When Anita brought my bill, I put a five on it and, on top of that, one of my cards. I'd written on it: "Ruth sent me. I'm in the green Datsun across the street."

I went out and put some money in the meter, then got back in the car. I sat for another half hour, working the crossword puzzle, before Anita appeared. She opened the passenger door and sat down without speaking. I folded up the paper and put it in the backseat and looked at her gravely. The picture I'd found in her apartment had shown a laughing young woman, not precisely beautiful, but full of the vitality that is better than beauty in a young woman. Now her face was strained and gaunt. The police would never have found her from a photograph—she looked closer to thirty than twenty—lack of sleep, fear, and tension cutting unnatural lines in her young face. The black hair did not go with her skin, the delicate creamy skin of a true red-head.

"What made you choose Hartford?" I asked.

She looked surprised—possibly the last question she'd expected. "Peter and I came up here last summer to the Washington County Fair—just for fun. We had a sandwich in that café, and I remembered it." Her voice was husky with fatigue. She turned to look at me and said rapidly, "I hope I can trust you—I've got to trust someone. Ruth doesn't know—doesn't know the kind of people who—who might shoot someone. I don't either, really, but I think I have a better idea than she does." She gave a bleak smile. "I'm going to lose my mind if I stay here alone any longer. But I can't go back to Chicago. I need help. If you can't do it, if you blow it and I get shot—or if you're some clever female hit man who fooled Ruth into giving you my address—I don't know. I have to take the chance." She was holding her hands together so tightly that the knuckles were white.

"I'm a private investigator," I said. "Your father hired me last week to find you, and I found Peter Thayer's body instead. Over the weekend, he told me to stop looking. I have my own guesses as to what all that was about. That's how I got involved. I agree that you're in a pretty tough spot. And if I blow it, neither of us will be in very good shape. You can't hide here forever, though, and I think that I'm tough enough, quick enough, and smart enough to get things settled so that you can come out of hiding. I can't cure the pain, and there's more to come, but I can get you back to Chicago—or wherever else you want so that you can live openly and with dignity."

She thought about that, nodding her head. People were walking up and down the sidewalk; I felt as if we were in a fishbowl. "Is there somewhere we can go to talk—somewhere with a little more room?"

"There's a park."

"That'd be fine." It was back along route 60 toward Milwaukee. I parked the Datsun out of sight of the road and we walked down to sit on the bank of a little stream that ran through the park, dividing it from the back wall of the Chrysler plant on the other side. The day was hot, but here in the country the air was clear and sweet.

"You said something about living with dignity," she said, looking at the water, her mouth twisted in a harsh smile. "I don't think I'll ever do that again. I know what happened to Peter, you see. In a way, I guess you could say I killed him."

"Why do you say that?" I asked gently.

"You say you found his body. Well, so did I. I came home at four and found him. I knew then what had happened. I lost my head and ran. I didn't know where to go—I didn't come here until the next day. I spent the night at Mary's house, and then I came up here. I couldn't figure out why they weren't waiting for me, but I knew if I went back they'd get me." She was starting to sob, great dry sobs that heaved her shoulders and chest. "Dignity!" she said in a hoarse voice. "Oh, Christ! I'd settle for a night's sleep." I didn't say anything, but sat watching her. After a few minutes she calmed down a bit. "How much do you know?" she asked.

"I don't know much for certain—that I can prove, I mean. But I've got some guesses. What I know for certain is that your father and Yardley Masters have a deal going. I don't know what it is, but I found a claim draft from Ajax in your apartment. I presume that Peter brought it home, so one of my guesses is that the deal has to do with claim drafts. I know that your father knows Earl Smeissen, and I know that someone wanted something very badly that they thought was in your apartment and then thought that I had taken it and put in mine. They wanted it badly enough to ransack both places. My guess is that they were looking for the claim draft, and that it was Smeissen, or one of his people, who did the ransacking."

"Is Smeissen a killer?" she asked in her harsh, strained voice.

"Well, he's doing pretty well these days: he doesn't kill, himself, but he's got muscle to do it for him."

"So my father had him kill Peter, didn't he?" She stared at me challengingly, her eyes hard and dry, her mouth twisted. This was the nightmare she'd been lying down with every night. No wonder she wasn't sleeping.

"I don't know. This is one of my guesses. Your father loves you, you know, and he's going nuts right now. He would never knowingly have put your life in danger. And he would never knowingly have let Peter be shot. I think what happened was that Peter confronted Masters, and Masters panicked and called your dad." I stopped. "This isn't pretty and it's hard to say to you. But your dad knows the kind of people who will put someone away for a price. He's made it to the top of a rough union in a rough industry, and he's had to know those kinds of people."

She nodded wearily, not looking at me. "I know. I never wanted to know it in the past, but I know it now. So my—my father, gave him this Smeissen's name. Is that what you're getting at?"

"Yes. I'm sure Masters didn't tell him who it was who'd crossed his path —just that someone had tumbled to the secret, and had to be eliminated. It's the only thing that explains your father's behavior."

"What do you mean?" she asked, not very interested.

"Your father came to me last Wednesday, gave me a fake name and a phony story, but he wanted me to find you. He knew about Peter's death at that point, and he was upset because you'd run away. You called and accused him of killing Peter, didn't you?"

She nodded again. "It was too stupid for words. I was off my head, with anger, and fear, and—and grief. Not just for Peter, you know, but for my father, and the union, and everything I'd grown up thinking was fine and—and worth fighting for."

"Yes that was tough." She didn't say anything else, so I went on. "Your father didn't know at first what had happened. It was only a few days later that he connected Peter with Masters. Then he knew that Masters had had Peter killed. Then he knew that you were in trouble, too. And that's when he fired me. He didn't want me to find you because he didn't want anyone else to find you, either."

She looked at me again. "I hear you," she said in that same weary voice. "I hear you, but it doesn't make it any better. My father is the kind of man who gets people killed, and he got Peter killed."

We sat looking at the stream for a few minutes without talking. Then she said, "I grew up on the union. My mother died when I was three. I didn't have any brothers or sisters, and my dad and I—we were very close. He was a hero, I knew he was in a lot of fights, but he was a hero. I grew up knowing he had to fight because of the bosses, and that if he could lick them, America would be a better place for working men and women everywhere." She smiled mirthlessly again. "It sounds like a child's history book, doesn't it? It was child's history. As my dad moved up in the union, we had more money. The University of Chicago—that was something I'd always wanted. Seven thousand dollars a year? No problem. He bought it for me. My own car, you name it. Part of me knew that a working-class hero didn't have that kind of money, but I pushed it aside. 'He's entitled,' I'd say. And when I met Peter, I thought, why not? The Thayers have more money than my father ever dreamed of, and they never worked for it." She paused again. "That was my rationalization, you see. And guys like Smeissen. They're around the house—not much, but some. I just wouldn't believe any of it. You read about some mobster in the paper, and he's been over drinking with your father? No way." She shook her head.

"Peter came home from the office, you see. He'd been working for Masters as a favor to his dad. He was sick of the whole money thing—that was before we fell in love, even, although I know his father blamed me for it. He wanted to do something really fine with his life—he didn't know what. But just to be nice, he agreed to work at Ajax. I don't think my father knew. I didn't tell him. I didn't talk to him about Peter much—he didn't like me going around with the son of such an important banker. And he is kind of a Puritan—he hated my living with Peter like that. So like I said, I didn't talk to him about Peter.

"Anyway, Peter knew who some of the big shots in the union are. You know, when you're in love, you learn that kind of thing about each other. I knew who the chairman of the Fort Dearborn Trust is, and that's not the kind of thing I know as a rule."

The story was starting to come easily now. I didn't say anything, just made myself part of the landscape that Anita was talking to.

"Well, Peter did rather boring things for Masters. It was a kind of make-work job in the budget department. He worked for the budget director, a guy he liked, and one of the things they asked him to do was check records of claim drafts against claim files—see if they matched, you know. Did Joe Blow get fifteen thousand dollars when his file shows he should only have gotten twelve thousand dollars. That kind of thing. They had a computer program that did it, but they thought there was something wrong with the program, so they wanted Peter to do a manual check." She laughed, a laugh that was really a sob. "You know, if Ajax had a good computer system, Peter would still be alive. I think of that sometimes, too, and it makes me want to shoot all their programmers. Oh, well. He started with the biggest ones—there were thousands and thousands—they have three hundred thousand Workers Compensation claims every year, but he was only going to do a spot check. So he started with some of the really big ones—total disability claims that had been going on for a while. At first it was fun, you know, to see what kinds of things had happened to people. Then one day he found a claim set up for Carl O'Malley. Total disability, lost his right arm and been crippled by a freak accident with a conveyor belt. That happens, you know—someone gets caught on a belt and pulled into a machine. It's really terrible."

I nodded agreement.

She looked at me and started talking to me, rather than just in front of me. "Only it hadn't happened, you see. Carl is one of the senior vice-presidents, my dad's right-hand man—he's been part of my life since before I can remember. I call him Uncle Carl. Peter knew that, so he brought home the address, and it was Carl's address. Carl is as well as you or me—he's never been in an accident, and he's been away from the assembly line for twenty-three years."

"I see. You didn't know what to think, but you didn't ask your father about it?"

"No, I didn't know what to ask. I couldn't figure it out. I guess I thought Uncle Carl had put in for a fake accident, and we kind of treated it like a joke, Peter and I did. But he got to thinking about it; he was like that, you know, he really thought things through. And he looked up the other guys on the executive board. And they all had indemnity claims. Not all of them for total disability, and not all of them permanent, but all of them good-sized sums. And that was the terrible thing. You see, my dad had one, too. Then I got scared, and I didn't want to say anything to him."

"Is Joseph Gielczowski on the executive board?" I asked.

"Yes, he's one of the vice-presidents, and president of Local 3051, a very powerful local in Calumet City. Do you know him?"

"That was the name of the claim draft I found." I could see why they didn't want that innocent little stick of dynamite in my hands. No wonder they'd torn my place apart looking for it. "So Peter decided to talk to Masters? You didn't know Masters was involved, did you?"

"No, and Peter thought he owed it to him, to talk to him first, you know.

We weren't sure what we would do next—talk to my dad, we had to. But we thought Masters should know." Her blue eyes were dark pools of fear in her face. "What happened was, he told Masters, and Masters told him it sounded really serious, and that he'd like to talk it over with Peter in private, because it might have to go to the State Insurance Commission. So Peter said sure, and Masters said he would come down Monday morning before work." She looked at me. "That was strange, wasn't it? We should have known it was strange, we should have known a vice-president doesn't do that, he talks to you in his office. I guess we just assumed it was Peter being a friend of the family." She looked back at the stream. "I wanted to be there, but I had a job, you see, I was doing some research for one of the guys in the Political Science Department."

"Harold Weinstein?" I guessed.

"Yeah. You really have been detecting me, haven't you? Well, I had to be there at eight-thirty, and Masters was coming by around nine, so I left Peter to it. I really left him to it, didn't I? Oh, God, why did I think that job was so goddamn important? Why didn't I stay there with him?" Now she was crying, real tears, not the dry heaves. She hid her face in her hands and sobbed. She kept repeating that she'd left Peter alone to be killed, and she should have been the one that died; her father was the one with all the criminal friends, not his. I let her go on for several minutes.

"Listen, Anita," I said in a clear sharp voice, "you can blame yourself for this for the rest of your life. But you didn't kill Peter. You didn't abandon him. You didn't set him up. If you had been there, you'd be dead, too, and the truth of what happened might never come out."

"I don't care about the truth," she sobbed. "I know it. It doesn't matter whether the rest of the world knows it or not."

"If the rest of the world doesn't know it, then you're as good as dead," I said brutally. "And the next nice young boy or girl who goes through those files and learns what you and Peter learned is dead, too. I know this is rotten. I know you've been through hell and more besides, and you've got worse ahead. But the quicker we get going and finish off this business, the quicker you can get that part over with. It will only get more unbearable, the longer you have to anticipate it."

She sat with her head in her hands, but her sobs died down. After a while she sat up and looked at me again. Her face was tear-streaked and her eyes red, but some of the strain had gone out of it, and she looked younger, less like a death mask of herself. "You're right. I was brought up not to be afraid of dealing with people. But I don't want to go through this with my dad."

"I know," I said gently. "My father died ten years ago. I was his only child, and we were very close. I know what you must be feeling."

She was wearing a ridiculous waitress costume, black rayon with a white apron. She blew her nose into the apron.

"Who cashed the drafts?" I asked. "The people they were made out to?"

She shook her head. "There's no way of telling. You don't cash drafts, you see: you present them to the bank and the bank verifies you have an account there and tells the insurance company to send a check to that account. You'd have to know what bank the drafts were presented to, and that information wasn't in the files—only carbons of the drafts were there. I don't know if they kept the originals or if they went to the controller's department, or what. And Peter—Peter didn't like to probe too far without Masters knowing."

"How was Peter's father involved?" I asked.

Her eyes opened at that. "Peter's father? He wasn't."

"He had to be: he was killed the other day—Monday."

Her head started moving back and forth and she looked ill. "I'm sorry," I said. "That was thoughtless, to spring it on you like that." I put an arm around her shoulders. I didn't say anything more. But I bet Thayer had helped Masters and McGraw cash in on the drafts. Maybe some of the other Knifegrinders were involved, but they wouldn't share a kitty like that with the whole executive board. Besides, that was the kind of secret that everyone would know if that many people knew. Masters and McGraw, maybe a doctor, to put a bonafide report in the files. Thayer sets up an account for them. Doesn't know what it is, doesn't ask any questions. But they give him a present every year, maybe, and when he threatens to push the investigation into his son's death, they stick in the knife: he's been involved, and he can be prosecuted. It looked good to me. I wondered if Paul and Jill would find anything in Thayer's study. Or if Lucy would let either of them into the house. Meanwhile there was Anita to think of.

We sat quietly for a while. Anita was off in her own thoughts, sorting out our conversation. Presently she said, "It makes it better, telling someone else about it. Not quite so horrible."

I grunted agreement. She looked down at her absurd outfit. "Me, dressed up like this! If Peter could see me, he'd—" The sentence trailed off into a sniff. "I'd like to leave here, stop doing the Jody Hill thing. Do you think I can go back to Chicago?"

I considered this. "Where were you planning to go?"

She thought for a few minutes. "That's a problem, I guess. I can't involve Ruth and Mary any more."

"You're right. Not just because of Ruth and Mary, but also because I was followed to the UWU meeting last night, so chances are Earl will keep an eye on some of the members for a while. And you know you can't go home until this whole business is cleared up."

"Okay," she agreed. "It's just—it's so hard—it was smart in a way, coming up here, but I'm always looking over my shoulder, you know, and I can't talk to anyone about what's really going on in my mind. They're always teasing me about boyfriends, like that nice Dr. Dan, the one I spilled coffee on this morning, and I can't tell them about Peter, so they think I'm unfriendly."

"I could probably get you back to Chicago," I said slowly. "But you'd have to hole up for a few days—until I get matters straightened out. . . . We could publish an account of the insurance scheme, but that would get your dad in trouble without necessarily getting Masters. And I want him implicated in a way he can't slide out of before I let everything else out. Do you understand?" She nodded. "Okay, in that case, I can see that you get put up in a Chicago hotel. I think I can fix it so that no one will know you are there. You wouldn't be able to go out. But someone trustworthy would stop by every now and then to talk to you so you won't go completely stir crazy. That sound all right?"

She made a face. "I guess I don't have any choice, do I? At least I'd be back in Chicago, closer to the things I know. . . . Thanks," she added belatedly. "I didn't mean to sound so grudging—I really appreciate everything you're doing for me."

"Don't worry about your party manners right now; I'm not doing it for the thanks, anyway."

We walked slowly back to the Datsun together. Little insects hummed and jumped in the grass and birds kept up an unending medley. A woman with two young children had come into the park. The children were rooting industriously in the dirt. The woman was reading a book, looking up at them every few minutes. They had a picnic basket propped under a tree. As we walked by, the woman called, "Matt! Eve! How about a snack?" The children came running up. I felt a small stirring of envy. On a beautiful summer day it might be nice to be having a picnic with my children instead of hiding a fugitive from the police and the mob.

"Is there anything you want to collect in Hartford?" I asked.

She shook her head. "I should stop at Ronna's and tell them I'm leaving."

I parked in front of the restaurant and she went in while I used a phone on the corner to call the *Herald-Star*. It was almost ten and Ryerson was at his desk.

"Murray, I've got the story of a lifetime for you if you can keep a key witness on ice for a few days."

"Where are you?" he asked. "You sound like you're calling from the North Pole. Who's the witness? The McGraw girl?"

"Murray, your mind works like a steel trap. I want a promise and I need some help."

"I've already helped you," he protested. "Lots. First by giving you those photos, and then by not running a story that you were dead so I could collect your document from your lawyer."

"Murray, if there was another soul on earth I could turn to right now, I would. But you are absolutely incorruptible if faced with the promise of a good story."

"All right," he agreed. "I'll do what I can for you."

"Good. I'm in Hartford, Wisconsin, with Anita McGraw. I want to get her back to Chicago and keep her under close wraps until this case blows over. That means no one must have a whiff of where she is, because if they do, you'll be covering her obituary. I can't bring her down myself because I'm a hot property now. What I want to do is take her to Milwaukee and put her on a train and have you meet her at Union Station. When you do, get her into a hotel. Some place far enough from the Loop that some smart bellhop on Smeissen's payroll won't put two and two together when she comes in. Can do?"

"Jesus, Vic, you don't do anything in a small way, do you? Sure. What's the story? Why is she in danger? Smeissen knock off her boyfriend?"

"Murray, I'm telling you, you put any of this in print before the whole story is finished, and they're going to be fishing *your* body out of the Chicago River: I guarantee I'll put it there."

"You have my word of honor as a gent who is waiting to scoop the City of Chicago. What time is the train coming in?"

"I don't know. I'll call you again from Milwaukee."

When I hung up, Anita had come back out and was waiting by the car. "They weren't real happy about me quitting," she said.

I laughed. "Well, worry about that on the way down. It'll keep your mind off your troubles."

16
PRICE OF A CLAIM

We had to wait in Milwaukee until 1:30 for a Chicago train. I left Anita at the station and went out to buy her some jeans and a shirt. When she had washed up in the station rest room and changed, she looked younger and healthier. As soon as she got that terrible black dye out of her hair, she'd be in good shape. She thought her life was ruined, and it certainly didn't look great at the moment. But she was only twenty; she'd recover.

Murray agreed to meet the train and get her to a hotel. He'd decided on the Ritz. "If she's going to be holed up for a few days, it might as well be someplace where she'll be comfortable," he explained. "The *Star* will share the bill with you."

"Thanks, Murray," I said dryly. He was to call my answering service and leave a message: "yes" or "no"—no name. "No" meant something had gone wrong with pickup or delivery and I would get back to him. I wasn't going to go near the hotel. He'd stop by a couple of times a day with food and chat—we didn't want Anita calling room service.

As soon as the train pulled out, I headed back to the tollway and Chicago. I had almost all the threads in my hands now. The problem was, I couldn't prove that Masters had killed Peter Thayer. Caused him to be killed. Of course, Anita's story confirmed it: Master had had an appointment with Peter. But there was no proof, nothing that would make Bobby swear out a warrant and bring handcuffs to a senior vice-president of an influential Chicago corporation. Somehow I had to stir around in the nest enough to make the king hornet come out and get me.

As I left the toll road for the Edens Expressway, I made a detour to Winnetka to see if Jill had gone home, and if she had turned up anything among her father's papers. I stopped at a service station on Willow Road and called the Thayer house.

Jack answered the phone. Yes, Jill had come home, but she wasn't talking to reporters. "I'm not a reporter," I said. "This is V. I. Warshawski."

"She certainly isn't talking to you. You've caused Mother Thayer enough pain already."

"Thorndale, you are the stupidest SOB I have ever met. If you don't put Jill on the phone, I will be at the house in five minutes. I will make a lot of noise, and I will go and bother all the neighbors until I find one who will put a phone call through to Jill for me."

He banged the receiver down hard, on a tabletop I guessed, since the connection still held. A few minutes later Jill's clear, high voice came onto the line. "What did you say to Jack?" she giggled. "I've never seen him so angry."

"Oh, I just threatened to get all your neighbors involved in what's going on," I answered. "Not that they aren't anyway—the police have probably been visiting all of them, asking questions. . . . You get out to Winnetka all right?"

"Oh, yes. It was very exciting. Paul got a police escort for us to the clinic. Lotty didn't want to do it, but he insisted. Then he went and got your car and we got a blast-off with sirens from the clinic. Sergeant McGonnigal was really, really super."

"Sounds good. How are things on the home front?"

"Oh, they're okay. Mother has decided to forgive me, but Jack is acting like the stupid phony he is. He keeps telling me I've made Mother very, very unhappy. I asked Paul to stay to lunch, and Jack kept treating him as if he were the garbage collector or something. I got really mad, but Paul told me he was used to it. I hate Jack," she concluded.

I laughed at this outburst. "Good girl! Paul's a neat guy—worth standing up for. Did you have a chance to look through your father's papers?"

"Oh, yes. Of course, Lucy had a fit. But I just pretended I was Lotty and didn't pay any attention to her. I didn't really know what I was looking for," she said, "but I found some kind of document that had both Mr. Master's and Mr. McGraw's names on it."

I suddenly felt completely at peace, as though I'd been through a major crisis and come out whole on the other side. I found myself grinning into the telephone. "Did you now," I said. "What was it?"

"I don't know," Jill said doubtfully. "Do you want me to get it and read it to you?"

"That's probably the best thing," I agreed. She put the phone down. I started singing under my breath. What will you be, O document? What kind of laundry ticket?

"It's a Xerox," Jill announced, back at the phone. "My dad wrote the date in ink at the top—March eighteenth, 1974. Then it says: 'Agreement of Trust. The Undersigned, Yardley Leland Masters and Andrew Solomon McGraw, are herein granted fiduciary responsibility for any and all monies submitted to this account under their authority for the following.'" She stumbled over *fiduciary*. "Then it gives a list of names—Andrew McGraw, Carl O'Malley, Joseph Giel—I can't pronounce it. There are about—let's see—" I could hear her counting under her breath: "—twenty-three names. Then it adds, 'and any other names as shall be added at their discretion under my countersignature.' Then Daddy's name, and a place for him to sign it. Is that what you were looking for?"

"That's what I was looking for, Jill." My voice was as calm and steady as if I were announcing that the Cubs had won the World Series.

"What does it mean?" she asked. She was sobering up from her glee at triumphing over Jack and Lucy. "Does it mean Daddy killed Peter?"

"No, Jill, it does not. Your father did not kill your brother. What it means is that your father knew about a dirty scheme that your brother found out about. Your brother was killed because he found out about it."

"I see." She was quiet for a few minutes. "Do you know who killed him?" she asked presently.

"I think so. You hang loose, Jill. Stay close to the house and don't go out with anyone but Paul. I'll come up to see you tomorrow or the next day— everything should be over by then." I started to hang up, then thought I should warn her to hide the paper. "Oh, Jill," I said, but she had hung up. Oh, well, I thought. If anyone suspected it was there, they would have been around looking by now.

What that document meant was that Masters could set up fake claims for anyone; then he and McGraw could cash the drafts, or whatever one did with them. Put them into the trust account, which Thayer ostensibly oversaw. In fact, I wondered why they even bothered to use real names. Why not just made-up people—easier to disguise. If they'd done that, Peter Thayer and his father would still be alive. Maybe they'd gotten to that later. I'd have to see a complete list of the names on the account and check them against the Knifegrinders' roster.

It was almost four. Anita should have made it to Chicago by now. I called my answering service, but no one had rung up with the message of "yes" or "no." I got back in the car and returned to the Edens. Inbound traffic moved at a crawl. Repairs on two of the lanes turned rush hour into a nightmare. I oozed slowly onto the Kennedy, irate and impatient, although I didn't have an agenda. Just an impatience. I didn't know what to do next. I could certainly expose the fake claim drafts. But as I'd pointed out to Anita, Masters would certainly disclaim all knowledge: the Knifegrinders might well have set them up, with complete doctors' reports. Did claim handlers actually physically look at accident victims? I wondered. I'd better talk to Ralph, explain what I'd learned today, and see if there was some legal angle that would link Masters irretrievably with the fraud. Even that wasn't good enough, though. I had to link him with the killing. And I couldn't think of a way.

It was 5:30 by the time I exited at Addison, and then I had to fight my way across town. I finally swung off onto a small side street, full of potholes, but not much traffic. I was about to turn up Sheffield to Lotty's, when I thought that might mean walking open-armed into a setup. I found the all-night restaurant on the corner of Addison and gave her a call.

"My dear Vic," she greeted me. "Can you believe, those Gestapo actually had the effrontery to break into this apartment? Whether they were looking for you, Jill, or the McGraw girl, I couldn't say, but they have been here."

"Oh, my God, Lotty," I said, my stomach sinking. "I am so sorry. How bad is the damage?"

"Oh, it's nothing—just the locks, and Paul is here now replacing them; it's just the wantonness of it that makes me so angry."

"I know," I said remorsefully. "I'll certainly repair whatever damage has been done. I'll come by to get my stuff right now, and be gone."

I hung up and decided to take my chances on a trap. It would be just as well if Smeissen knew I had gone back home—I didn't want Lotty put in any more danger, or to suffer any more invasions. I raced up the street to her building, and only gave cursory attention to potential marksmen in the street. I didn't see anyone I knew, and no one opened fire as I dashed up the stairs.

Paul was in the doorway, screwing a dead-bolt lock into the door. His square face looked very mean. "This is pretty bad, Vic—you think Jill is in any danger?"

"Not too likely," I said.

"Well, I think I should go up there and see."

I grinned. "Sounds like a good idea to me. Be careful though, you hear?"

"Don't worry." His breathtaking smile came. "But I'm not sure whether I'm protecting her from that brother-in-law or from a gunman."

"Well, do both." I went on into the apartment. Lotty was at the back, trying to reattach a screen to the back door. For a woman with such skillful medical fingers she was remarkably inept. I took the hammer from her and quickly finished the job. Her thin face was set and hard, her mouth in a fine line.

"I am glad you gave the warning to Paul and had that Sergeant Mc-Whatever take us to the clinic. At the time, I was annoyed, with you and with

Paul, but clearly it saved the child's life." Her Viennese accent was very heavy in her anger. I thought she was exaggerating about the danger to Jill but didn't want to argue the point. I went through the apartment with her but had to agree that there really had been no damage. Not even the medical samples, some of which had great street value, had been removed.

Lotty kept up a stream of invective during the inspection which became heavily laden with German, a language I don't speak. I gave up trying to calm her down and merely nodded and grunted agreement. Paul finally brought it to a halt by coming in to say that the front door was now secure, and did she want him to do anything else?

"No, my dear, thank you. Go out and visit Jill, and take very good care of her. We don't want her harmed."

Paul agreed fervently. He gave me my car keys, and told me the Chevy was over on Seminary off Irving Park Road. I'd thought about leaving him the car, but felt I'd better hang on to it: I didn't know what the evening would bring in the way of action.

I called Larry to see if my apartment was ready for occupation. It was; he'd left the keys to the new locks with the first-floor tenants; they'd seemed a bit friendlier than Mrs. Alvarez on the second floor.

"Well, everything is all set, Lotty: I can go home. Sorry I didn't yesterday, and sleep with the place nailed shut—it would have spared you this invasion."

Her mouth twisted in her sardonic smile. "Ah, forget it, Vic, my anger storm has passed, blown over. Now I am feeling a little melancholy at being alone—I shall miss those two children. They are very sweet together. . . . I forgot to ask: Did you find Miss McGraw?"

"I forgot to tell you—I did. And I should check to see whether she is safely ensconced in her new hiding place." I put in a call to my answering service; yes, that long-suffering outfit reported, someone had called up and left a message "yes." They had not left a name, but said I would know what it meant. I told them they could switch my office calls to my own home number. In the activity of the last few days I'd forgotten to get a Kelly Girl to tidy my office, but at least it was boarded shut. I'd wait until tomorrow to go down there.

I tried Ralph, but there was no answer. He wasn't at the office, either. Out for dinner? Was I jealous? "Well, Lotty, this is it. Thanks for letting me disrupt your life for a few days. You've made a major impression on Jill—she told me the maid up there was trying to hassle her but she 'pretended she was Lotty' and didn't pay her any mind."

"I'm not sure that's such a good idea—to model herself on me, that is. A very attractive girl—amazing that she's avoided all that suburban insularity." She sat on the daybed to watch me pack. "What now? Can you expose the killer?"

"I've got to find a lever," I said. "I know who did it—not who fired the actual shot, that's probably a guy named Tony Bronsky, but it could have been any one of several of Smeissen's crew. But who desired that shot to be fired—that I know but can't prove. I know what the crime was, though, and I know how it was worked." I zipped the canvas bag shut. "What I need is a lever, or maybe a wedge." I was talking to myself more than to Lotty. "A wedge to pry this guy apart a bit. If I can find out that the fiddle couldn't be worked without his involvement, then maybe I can force him into the open."

I was standing with one foot on the bed, absentmindedly tapping the suitcase with my fingers while I thought. Lotty said, "If I were a sculptor, I would make a statue of you—Nemesis come to life. You will think of a way—I see it in your face." She stood on tiptoe and gave me a kiss. "I'll walk you to the street—if anyone shoots at you, then I can patch you up quickly, before too much blood is lost."

I laughed. "Lotty, you're wonderful. By all means, cover my back for me."

She walked me to the corner of Seminary, but the street was clear. "That's because of that Sergeant Mc-Something," she said. "I think he's been driving around here from time to time. Still, Vic, be careful: you have no mother, but you are a daughter of my spirit. I should not like anything to happen to you."

"Lotty, that's melodrama," I protested. "Don't start getting old, for God's sake." She shrugged her thin shoulders in a way wholly European and gave me a sardonic smile, but her eyes were serious as I walked up the street to my car.

17.
SHOOT-OUT ON ELM STREET

Larry and his friend the carpenter had done a beautiful job on my apartment. The door was a masterpiece, with carved flowers on the panels. The carpenter had installed two dead bolts, and the action on them was clean and quiet. Inside, the place shone as it had not for months. Not a trace of the weekend ravage remained. Although Larry had sent the shredded couch away, he had moved chairs and an occasional table around to fill the empty space. He had left a bill in the middle of the kitchen table. Two people for two days at $8.00 an hour, $256.00. The door, locks, and installation, $315.00. New supplies of flour, sugar, beans, and spices; new pillows for the bed: $97.00. It seemed like a pretty reasonable bill to me. I wondered who was going to pay me, though. Maybe Jill could borrow from her mother until her trust fund matured.

I went to look through my jewelry box. By some miracle the vandals had not taken my mother's few valuable pieces, but I thought I'd better lock them in a bank vault and not leave them around for the next invader. Larry seemed to have thrown out the shards of the broken Venetian glass. I should have told him to save them, but that couldn't be helped; it was beyond restoration, anyway. The other seven held pride of place in the built-in china cupboard, but I couldn't look at them without a thud in my stomach.

I tried Ralph again. This time he answered on the fourth ring. "What's up, Miss Marple?" he asked. "I thought you were out after Professor Moriarty until tomorrow."

"I found him earlier than I expected. In fact, I found out the secret that Peter Thayer died to protect. Only he didn't want to protect it. You know that claim draft I gave you? Did you ever find the file?"

"No. I told you I put it on the missing-file search, but it hasn't turned up."

"Well, it may never. Do you know who Joseph Gielczowski is?"

"What is this? Twenty questions? I've got someone coming over in twenty minutes, Vic."

"Joseph Gielczowski is a senior vice-president of the Knifegrinders union. He has not been on an assembly line for twenty-three years. If you went to visit him in his home, you would find he was as healthy as you are. Or you could go see him at Knifegrinders headquarters where he is able to work and draw a salary without needing any indemnity payments."

There was a pause. "Are you trying to tell me that that guy is fraudulently drawing Workers Compensation payments?"

"No," I said.

"Goddamnit, Vic, if he's healthy and is getting indemnity drafts, then he's drawing them fraudulently."

"No," I reiterated. "Sure, they're fraudulent, but he's not drawing them."

"Well, who is, then?"

"Your boss."

Ralph exploded into the phone. "You've got this damned bee in your bonnet about Masters, Vic, and I'm sick of it! He's one of the most respected members of a highly respected company in a very respectable industry. To suggest that he's involved in something like that—"

"I'm not suggesting it, I know it," I said coldly. "I know that he and Andrew McGraw, head of the Knifegrinders union, set up a fund with themselves as joint trustees, enabling them to cash drafts, or whatever it is you do to get payments on drafts, drawn to Gielczowski and at least twenty-two other healthy people."

"How can you possibly know something like that?" Ralph said, furious.

"Because, I just listened to someone read a copy of the agreement to me over the phone. I've also found someone who has seen Masters with McGraw on numerous occasions up near Knifegrinder headquarters. And I know that Masters had an appointment with Peter Thayer—at his apartment —at nine on the morning he was killed."

"I still don't believe it. I have worked for Yardley for three years, and been in his organization for ten years before that, and I'm sure there's a different explanation for everything you've found out—if you've found it out. You haven't seen this trust agreement. And Yardley may have eaten with McGraw, or drunk with him or something—maybe he was checking out some coverage or claims, or something. We do do that from time to time."

I felt like screaming with frustration. "Just let me know ten minutes before you go to Masters to check the story with him, will you? So I can get there in time to save your ass."

"If you think I'm going to jeopardize my career by telling my boss that I've been listening to that kind of rumor about him, you're nuts," Ralph roared. "As a matter of fact, he's coming over here in a few minutes, and I promise you, without any difficulty, that I am not such an ass as to tell him about it. Of course, if that Gielczowski claim is fraudulent, that explains a lot. I'll tell him that."

My hair seemed to stand straight up on my head. "What? Ralph, you are so goddamn naive it's unbelievable. Why the hell is he coming over?"

"You really don't have any right to ask me that," he snapped, "but I'll tell you anyway, since you started the whole uproar by finding that draft. Claims that big are handled out of the home office, not by a field adjustor. I went around to the guys today and asked who'd handled the file. No one remembered it. If anyone had been handling such a big file for so many years, there's no way they would forget it. This puzzled me, so when I called Yardley this afternoon—he hasn't been in the office this week—I call him at home once a day—I mentioned it to him."

"Oh, Christ! That is the absolute end. So he told you it sounded like a serious problem, didn't he? And that since he had to come down to the city tonight for some other reason, he'd just drop by and talk it over with you? Is that right?" I said savagely.

"Why, yes, it is," he shouted. "Now go find someone's missing poodle and stop screwing around in the Claim Department."

"Ralph, I'm coming over. Tell Yardley *that* when he walks in the door, as soon as he walks in, and maybe it will save your goddamn ass for a few minutes." I slammed down the phone without waiting for his answer.

I looked at my watch. 7:12. Masters was due there in twenty minutes. Roughly. Say he got there around 7:30, maybe a few minutes earlier. I put my driver's license, my gun permit, and my P.I. license in my hip pocket with some money—I didn't want a purse in my way at this point. Checked the gun. Put extra rounds in my jacket pocket. Wasted forty-five seconds changing to running shoes. Locked the new, oiled dead bolts behind me and sprinted down the stairs three at a time. Ran the half-block to my car in fifteen seconds. Put it in gear and headed for Lake Shore Drive.

Why was every goddamn person in Chicago out tonight, and why were so many of them on Belmont Avenue? I wondered savagely. And why were the lights timed so that every time you hit a corner they turned and some asshole grandfather wouldn't clear the intersection in front of you on the yellow? I pounded the steering wheel in impatience, but it didn't make the traffic flow faster. No point in sitting on the horn, either. I took some deep diaphragm breaths to steady myself. Ralph, you stupid jerk. Making a present of your life to a man who's had two people killed in the last two weeks. Because Masters wears the old-boy network tie and you're on his team he couldn't possibly do something criminal. Naturally not. I swooped around a bus and got a clear run to Sheridan Road and the mouth of the Drive. It was 7:24. I prayed to the patron saint who protects speeders from speed traps and floored the Monza. At 7:26 I slid off the Drive onto La Salle Street, and down the inner parallel road to Elm Street. At 7:29 I left the car at a fireplug next to Ralph's building and sprinted inside.

The building didn't have a doorman. I pushed twenty buttons in quick succession. Several people squawked "Who is it?" through the intercom, but someone buzzed me in. No matter how many break-ins are executed this way, there is always some stupid idiot who will buzz you into an apartment building without knowing who you are. The elevator took a century or two to arrive. Once it came, though, it carried me quickly to the seventeenth floor. I ran down the hall to Ralph's apartment and pounded on the door, my Smith & Wesson in my hand.

I flattened myself against the wall as the door opened, then dove into the apartment, gun out. Ralph was staring at me in amazement. "What the hell do you think you're doing?" he said. No one else was in the room.

"Good question," I said, standing up.

The bell rang and Ralph went to push the buzzer. "I wouldn't mind if you left," he remarked. I didn't move. "At least put that goddamn gun away." I put it in my jacket pocket but kept my hand on it.

"Do me one favor," I said. "When you open the door, stand behind it, don't frame yourself in the doorway."

"You are the craziest goddamn—"

"If you call me a crazy broad I will shoot you in the back. Block your damned body with the door when you open it."

Ralph glared at me. When the knocking came a few minutes later, he went straight to the door and deliberately opened it so that it would frame his body squarely. I moved to the side of the room parallel with the door and braced myself. No shots sounded.

"Hello, Yardley, what's all this?" Ralph was saying.

"This is my young neighbor, Jill Thayer, and these are some associates who've come along with me."

I was stunned and moved toward the door to look. "Jill?" I said.

"Are you here, Vic?" the clear little voice quavered a bit. "I'm sorry. Paul called to say he was coming up on the train and I started to walk into town to meet him at the station. And Mr.—Mr. Masters passed me in his car and stopped to give me a lift—and—and I asked him about that paper and he made me come along with him. I'm sorry, Vic, I know I shouldn't have said anything."

"That's okay, honey—" I started to say, but Masters interrupted with "Ah, you're here, are you? We thought we'd come visit you and that Viennese doctor Jill admires so much a little later, but you've saved us a trip." He looked at my gun, which I'd pulled out, and smiled offensively. "I would put that away if I were you. Tony here is pretty trigger-happy and I know you'd hate to watch anything happen to Jill."

Tony Bronsky had come into the room behind Masters. With him was Earl. Ralph was shaking his head, like a man trying to wake up from a dream. I put the gun back into my pocket.

"Don't blame the girl," Masters said to me. "But you really shouldn't have gotten her involved, you know. As soon as Margaret Thayer told me she had come back home, I tried finding a way of talking to her without anyone in the house knowing about it. Sheer luck, really, that she walked down Sheridan just at that time. But we got her to explain quite a bit, didn't we, Jill?"

I could see now that there was an ugly bruise on the side of her face. "Cute, Masters," I said. "You're at your best when you're beating up little girls. I'd like to see you with a grandmother." He was right: I'd been stupid to bring her down to Lotty's and get her involved in things that Masters and Smeissen didn't want anyone to know about. I'd save my self-reproach for later, though—I didn't have time for it now.

"Want me to put her away?" Tony breathed, his eyes glistening with happiness, his Z-shaped scar vivid as a wound.

"Not yet, Tony," Masters said. "We want to find out how much she knows and who she's told it to . . . You, too, Ralph. It's really a shame you got this Polish gal over here—we weren't going to shoot you unless it was absolutely necessary, but now I'm afraid we'll have to." He turned to Smeissen. "Earl, you've had more experience at this kind of thing than I have. What's the best way to set them up?"

"Get the Warchoski broad's gun away from her," Earl said in his squeaky voice. "Then have her and the guy sit together on the couch so that Tony can cover them both."

"You heard him," Masters said. He started toward me.

"No," Earl squeaked. "Don't go close to her. Make her drop it. Tony, cover the kid."

Tony pointed his Browning at Jill. I dropped the S&W on the floor. Earl came and kicked it into the corner. Jill's little face was white and pinched.

"Over to the couch," Masters said. Tony continued to cover Jill. I went and sat down. The couch was firm, one good thing—one didn't sink into it. I kept my weight distributed forward onto my legs and feet. "Move," Earl squeaked at Ralph. Ralph was looking dazed. Little drops of sweat covered his face. He stumbled a bit on the thick carpet as he came to sit next to me.

"You know, Masters, this cesspool you've built is stinking so high you're going to have to kill everyone in Chicago to cover it up," I said.

"You think so, do you? Who knows about it besides you?" He was still smiling unpleasantly. My hand itched to break his lower jaw.

"Oh, the *Star* has a pretty good idea. My attorney. A few others. Even little Earl over here isn't going to be able to buy off the cops if you shoot down an entire newspaper crew."

"Is this true, Yardley?" Ralph asked. His voice came out in a hoarse whisper and he cleared his throat. "I don't believe it. I wouldn't believe Vic when she tried to tell me. You didn't shoot Peter, did you?"

Masters gave a superior little laugh. "Of course not. Tony here shot him. I had to go along, though, just as I did tonight—to get Tony into the building. And Earl came along as an accessory. Earl doesn't usually get involved, do you, Earl? But we don't want any blackmail after this."

"That's good, Masters," I praised him. "The reason Earl's ass is so fat is because he's been protecting it all these years."

Earl turned red. "You two-cent bitch, just for that, I'm going to let Tony work you over again before he shoots you!" he squeaked.

"Attaboy, Earl." I looked at Masters. "Earl never beats anyone up himself," I explained. "I used to think it was because he didn't have any balls, but last week I found out that wasn't true, right, Earl?"

Earl started for me, as I hoped he would, but Masters held him back. "Calm down, Earl, she's just trying to ride you. You can do whatever you want to her—after I find out how much she knows and where Anita McGraw is."

"I don't know, Yardley," I said brightly.

"Don't give me that," he said, leaning forward to hit me on the mouth. "You disappeared early this morning. That heap of shit Smeissen had watching the back alley went to sleep and you got away. But we questioned some of the girls you talked to at the UWU meeting last night and Tony here— persuaded—one of them to tell him where Anita had gone. But when we got to Hartford, Wisconsin, at noon, she'd disappeared. And the woman at the restaurant described you pretty well. An older sister, she thought, who'd come to take Jody Hill away with her. Now where is she?"

I uttered a silent prayer of thanks for the urge that had prompted Anita to want to leave Hartford. "There's got to be more to this racket than just those twenty-three names on the original deed of trust Jill found," I said. "Even at two hundred fifty dollars a week apiece, that isn't paying for the services of a guy like Smeissen. Round-the-clock surveillance on me? That must have cost you a bundle, Masters."

"Tony," Masters said conversationally, "hit the girl. Hard."

Jill gave a gasp, a scream held back. Good girl. Lots of guts. "You kill the girl, Masters, you got nothing to stop me," I said. "You're in a little ol' jam. The minute Tony takes that gun off her, she's going to roll on the floor and get behind that big chair, and I'm going to jump Tony and break his neck. And if he kills her, the same thing will happen. So sure, I don't want to watch you rough up Jill, but you're using up your weapon doing it."

"Go ahead and kill Warchoski," Earl squeaked. "You're going to sooner or later anyway."

Masters shook his head. "Not until we know where the McGraw girl is."

"Tell you what, Yardley," I offered. "I'll trade you Jill for Anita. You send the kid outside, let her go home, and I'll tell you where Anita is."

Masters actually wasted a minute thinking about it. "You do think I'm dumb, don't you? If I let her go, all she'll do is call the police."

"Of course I think you're dumb. As Dick Tracy once put it so well, all crooks are dumb. How many fake claimants do you have pulling indemnity payments into that dummy account?"

He laughed, his fake-hearty laugh again. "Oh, close to three hundred now, set up in different parts of the country. That deed of trust is quite outdated, and I see John never bothered to go back and check the original to see how it was growing."

"What was his cut for overseeing the account?"

"I really didn't come here to answer a smart-mouthed broad's questions," Yardley said, still good-natured, still in control. "I want to know how much you know."

"Oh, I know quite a bit," I said. "I know that you called McGraw and got Earl's name from him when Peter Thayer came to you with those incriminating files. I know you didn't tell McGraw who you were having put away, and when he found out, he panicked. You've got him in a cleft stick, haven't you: he knows you're gunning for his kid, but he can't turn state's evidence, or he hasn't got the guts to, anyway, because then he'll be an accessory before the fact, sending a professional killer to you. Let's see. I also know that you talked Thayer out of continuing the investigation into his son's death by telling him he'd been a party to the crime for which Peter died. And that if he pushed the investigation, the Thayer name would be mud and he'd lose his position at the bank. And I know he wrestled with that grim news for two days, then decided he couldn't live with himself and called you and told you he wouldn't be a party to his son's death. So you got cute little Tony here to gun him down the next morning before he could get to the state's attorney." I turned to Tony. "You aren't as good as you used to be, Tony, my boy: someone saw you waiting outside the Thayer place. That witness is on ice now—you didn't get him when you had the opportunity."

Earl's face turned red again. "You had a witness and you didn't see him?" he screeched, as much of a shout as his high voice could manage. "God-damnit, what do I pay you for? I want amateurs, I pull one off the street. And what about Freddie? He's paid to watch—he doesn't see anyone? Goddamn dumb bastards, all of you!" He was pumping his fat little arms up and down in his rage. I glanced at Ralph; his face was gray. He was in shock. I couldn't do anything about that now. Jill gave me a little smile. She'd caught the message. As soon as Tony lifted the gun, she'd roll behind the chair.

"See," I said disgustedly, "you guys have made so many mistakes that piling up three more corpses isn't going to help you one bit. I told you before, Earl: Bobby Mallory's no dummy. You can't knock off four people in his territory and get away with it forever."

Earl smirked. "They never hung one on me yet, Warchoski, you know that."

"It's Warshawski, you goddamn kraut. You know why Polish jokes are so short?" I asked Masters. "So the Germans can remember them."

"This is enough, Warchoski or whatever your name is," Masters said. He used a stern voice, the kind that got him heard with his junior staff. "You tell me where the McGraw girl is. You're right—Jill is as good as dead. I hate to do it, I've known that girl since she was born, but I just can't take the risk. But you've got a choice. I can have Tony kill her, one clean shot and it's done, or I can have him rape her while you watch, and then kill her. You tell me where the McGraw girl is, and you'll save her a lot of grief."

Jill was very white; her gray eyes looked huge and black in her face. "Oh, jeez, Yardley," I said. "You big he-men really impress the shit out of me. Are you telling me Tony's going to rape that girl on your command? Why do you think the boy carries a gun? He can't get it up, never could, so he has a big old penis he carries around in his hand."

I braced my hands on the couch at my sides as I spoke. Tony turned crimson and gave a primitive shriek in the back of his throat. He turned to look at me.

"Now!" I yelled, and jumped. Jill dived behind the armchair. Tony's bullet went wide and I reached him in one spring and chopped his gun arm hard enough to break the bone. He screamed in pain and dropped the Browning. As I spun away, Masters lunged over for it. I made a diving slide, but he got there first, sitting down hard. He brandished the Browning at me while he got up and I backed away a few paces.

The report from Tony's shot had brought Ralph back to life. Out of the corner of my eye I saw him move over on the couch toward the phone and lift the receiver. Masters saw it, too, and turned and shot him. In the second he turned, I made a rolling fall into the corner of the room and got the Smith & Wesson. As Masters turned to fire at me, I shot him in the knee. He wasn't used to pain: he fell with a great cry of surprised agony and dropped the gun. Earl, who'd been dancing in the background, pretending he was part of the fight, moved forward to get it. I shot at his hand. I was out of practice and missed, but he jumped back anyway.

I pointed the Smith & Wesson at Tony. "Onto the couch. Move." Tears were running down his cheeks. His right arm hung in a funny way: I'd broken the ulna. "You guys are worse than trash and I'd love to shoot the three of you dead. Save the state a lot of money. If any of you goes for that gun, I'll kill you. Earl, get your fat little body over on the couch next to Tony." He looked like a two-year-old whose mother has unexpectedly spanked him; his whole face was squashed up as if he, too, were about to burst into tears. But he moved over next to Tony. I picked up the Browning, continuing to cover the two on the couch. Masters was bleeding into the carpet. He wasn't in any shape to move. "The police are going to love this gun," I said. "I bet it fired the bullet that shot Peter Thayer, didn't it, Tony?"

I called to Jill, "You still alive back there, honey?"

"Yes, Vic," she said in a little voice.

"Good. You come on out now and call the number I'm going to give you. We're going to call the police and have them collect this garbage. Then maybe you'd better call Lotty, get her over here to look at Ralph." I hoped there was something left of him for Lotty to work on. He wasn't moving, but I couldn't go to him—he'd fallen on the far side of the room, and the couch and phone table would block me if I went over to where he lay.

Jill came out from behind the big armchair where she'd been crouching. The little oval face was still very white, and she was shaking a bit. "Walk behind me, honey," I told her. "And take a couple of deep breaths. In a few minutes you can relax and let it all out, but right now you've got to keep on going."

She turned her head away from the floor where Masters lay bleeding and walked over to the phone. I gave her Mallory's office number and told her to ask for him. He'd gone home for the day, she reported. I gave her the home number. "Is Lieutenant Mallory there, please?" she asked in her clear, polite voice. When he came on the line, I told her to bring the phone over to me, but not to get in front of me at all.

"Bobby? Vic. I'm at two-oh-three East Elm with Earl Smeissen, Tony Bronsky, and a guy from Ajax named Yardley Masters. Masters has a shattered knee, and Bronsky a broken ulna. I also have the gun that was used to shoot Peter Thayer."

Mallory made an explosive noise into the phone. "Is this some kind of joke, Vicki?"

"Bobby, I'm a cop's daughter. I never make that kind of joke. Two-oh-three East Elm. Apartment seventeen-oh-eight. I'll try not to kill the three of them before you get here."

18
BLOOD IS THICKER
THAN GOLD

It was ten, and the short black nurse said, "You shouldn't be here at all, but he won't go to sleep until you stop by." I followed her into the room where Ralph lay, his face very white, but his gray eyes alive. Lotty had made a good job of bandaging him up and the surgeon at Passavant had only changed the dressing without disturbing her work. As Lotty said, she'd done a lot of bullet wounds.

Paul had come with Lotty to Ralph's apartment, frantic. He'd gotten to Winnetka and forced his way past Lucy about twenty minutes after Masters had picked up Jill. He went straight from there to Lotty's. The two of them had called me, called the police to report Jill missing, but fortunately had stayed at Lotty's close to the phone.

Jill ran sobbing into Paul's arms when they arrived and Lotty had given a characteristic shake of the head. "Good idea. Get her out of here, get her some brandy," then turned her attention to Ralph, who lay unconscious and bleeding in the corner. The bullet had gone through his right shoulder, tearing up a lot of bone and muscle, but coming out clean on the other side.

Now I looked down at him on the hospital bed. He took hold of my right hand with his left and squeezed it weakly; he was pretty drugged. I sat on the bed.

"Get off the bed," the little nurse said.

I was exhausted. I wanted to tell her to go to hell, but I didn't feel like fighting the hospital on top of everything else. I stood up.

"I'm sorry," Ralph said, his words slightly slurred.

"Don't worry about it. As it turned out, that was probably the best thing that could have happened. I couldn't figure out how to get Masters to show his hand."

"No, but I should have listened to you. I couldn't believe you knew what you were talking about. I guess deep down I didn't take your detecting seriously. I thought it was a hobby, like Dorothy's painting."

I didn't say anything.

"Yardley shot me. I worked for him for three years and didn't see that about him. You met him once and knew he was that kind of guy." His words were slurred but his eyes were hurt and angry.

"Don't keep hitting yourself with that," I said gently. "I know what it means to be a team player. You don't expect your teammates, your quarterback, to do that kind of thing. I came at it from the outside, so I was able to see things differently."

He was quiet again, but the hold on my fingers tightened, so I knew he wasn't sleeping. Presently he said, "I've been falling in love with you, Vic, but you don't need me." His mouth twisted and he turned his head to one side to hide some tears.

My throat was tight and I couldn't get any words out. "That's not true," I tried to say, but I didn't know if it was or not. I swallowed and cleared my throat. "I wasn't just using you to get Masters." My words came out in a harsh squawk. "I liked you, Ralph."

He shook his head slightly; the movement made him wince. "It's not the same thing. It just wouldn't work out."

I squeezed his hand painfully. "No. It would never work out." I wished I didn't feel so much like crying.

Gradually the hold on my fingers relaxed. He was asleep. The little nurse pulled me away from the bed; I didn't look around before leaving the room.

I wanted to go home and get drunk and go to bed or pass out or something but I owed Murray his story, and Anita should be let out of captivity. I called Murray from the Passavant lobby.

"I was beginning to wonder about you, Vic," he said. "The news about Smeissen's arrest just came in, and my gofer at the police station says Bronsky and an Ajax executive are both in the police ward at Cook County."

"Yeah." I was bone tired. "Things are mostly over. Anita can come out of hiding. I'd like to pick her up and take her down to see her dad. That's something that's got to be done sooner or later, and it might as well be now." Masters was sure to squeal on McGraw as soon as he started talking, and I wanted to see him before Mallory did.

"Tell you what," Murray said. "I'll meet you in the lobby at the Ritz, and you can tell me about it on the way down. Then I can get a few heartrending shots of the crusty old union guy being reunited with his daughter."

"Bad idea, Murray. I'll meet you in the lobby and fill you in on the broad outline. If Anita wants you to come along, you can, but don't bet on it. Don't worry about your story, though: you'll still scoop the town."

I hung up and walked out of the hospital. I was going to have to talk to Bobby myself. I'd gone with Lotty and Ralph when the ambulance came, and Mallory had been too busy to do more than shout, "I need to talk to you!" at me as I went out the door. I didn't feel like doing it tonight. Jill was going to be okay, that was one good thing. But poor Anita—Still, I owed it to her to get her down to her father before the police got to him.

It was only four blocks from the hospital to the Ritz. The night was clear and warm and caressing. I needed a mother just now, and mother night felt like a good companion, folding dark arms around me.

The lobby of the Ritz, plush and discreet, hovered twelve stories above the street. The rich atmosphere jarred on my mood. I didn't fit in too well with it, either. In the mirrored walls of the elevator riding up, I'd seen myself disheveled, with blood on my jacket and jeans, my hair uncombed. As I waited for Murray, I half expected the house detective. Murray and he arrived at the same time.

"Excuse me, madam," he said urbanely, "I wonder if you'd mind coming with me."

Murray laughed. "Sorry, Vic, but you earned that." He turned to the house detective. "I'm Murray Ryerson, with the *Star*. This is V. I. Warshawski, a private investigator. We've come to pick up a guest of yours, and then we'll be gone."

The detective frowned over Murray's press card, then nodded. "Very well, sir. Madam, I wonder if you would mind waiting near the desk."

"Not at all," I said politely. "I understand that most of your guests never see any more blood than is contained by the average steak tartare. . . . Actually, maybe I could wash up while Mr. Ryerson waits for Miss McGraw?"

The detective ushered me happily to a private washroom in the manager's office. I scrubbed off the worst of the mess and washed my face. I found a brush in the cabinet over the sink and got my hair shaped up. On the whole I looked a lot better. Maybe not material for the Ritz, but not someone to be thrown out on sight.

Anita was waiting with Murray in the lobby when I got back. She looked at me doubtfully. "Murray says I'm out of danger?"

"Yes. Smeissen, Masters, and Smeissen's gunman have been arrested. Do you want to talk to your dad before he's arrested, too?" Murray's mouth dropped open. I put a hand on his arm to keep him from talking.

Anita thought for a minute. "Yes," she finally said. "I've been thinking it over today. You're right—the longer I put it off the worse it will be."

"I'm coming along," Murray announced.

"No," Anita said. "No, I'm not showing all that to the newspapers. Vic will give you the story later. But I'm not having reporters hanging around for this."

"You got it, Murray," I said. "Catch up with me later on tonight. I'll be —I don't know. I'll be at my bar downtown."

Anita and I started for the elevator. "Where's that?" he demanded, catching up with us.

"The Golden Glow on Federal and Adams."

I called a cab to take us back to my car. A zealous officer, possibly one who'd been left guarding the lobby, had put a parking ticket on the windshield. Twenty dollars for blocking a fire hydrant. They serve and protect.

I was so tired I didn't think I could drive and talk at the same time. I realized that this was the same day that I'd made the three-hundred-mile round trip to Hartford, and that I hadn't slept the night before. It was all catching up with me now.

Anita was preoccupied with her private worries. After giving me directions on how to get to her father's Elmwood Park house, she sat quietly, staring out the window. I liked her, I felt a lot of empathy with her, but I was too drained to reach out and give her anything at the moment.

We were on the Eisenhower Expressway, the road that runs from the Loop to the western suburbs, and had gone about five miles before Anita spoke. "What happened to Masters?"

"He showed up with his hired help to try to blow me and Ralph Devereux away. They had Jill Thayer with them—they were using her as a hostage. I managed to jump the gunman and break his arm, and disable Masters. Jill is all right."

"Is she? She's such a good kid. I'd hate like hell for anything to happen to her. Have you met her at all?"

"Yes, she spent a few days with me. She's a great kid, you're right."

"She's a lot like Peter. The mother is very self-centered, into clothes and the body beautiful, and the sister is incredible, you'd think someone made her up for a book. But Jill and Peter both are—are . . ." She groped for words. ". . . Self-assured, but completely turned out on the world. Everything always is—was—so interesting to Peter—what makes it work, how to solve the problem. Every person was someone he might want to be best friends with. Jill's a lot the same."

"I think she's falling in love with a Puerto Rican boy. That should keep things stirred up in Winnetka."

Anita gave a little chuckle. "For sure. That'll be worse than me—I was a labor leader's daughter, but at least I wasn't black or Spanish." She was quiet for a while. Then she said, "You know, this week has changed my life. Or made it seem upside-down. My whole life was directed to the union. I was going to go to law school and be a union lawyer. Now—it doesn't seem worth a lifetime. But there's a big empty hole. I don't know what to put there instead. And with Peter gone—I lost the union and Peter all at the same time. I was so busy last week being terrified that I didn't notice it. Now I do."

"Oh, yes. That's going to take a while. All mourning takes a long time, and you can't rush it along. My dad's been dead ten years now, and every now and then, something comes up that lets me know that the mourning is still going on, and another piece of it is in place. The hard part doesn't last so long. While it is going on, though, don't fight it—the more you poke away the grief and anger, the longer it takes to sort it out."

She wanted to know more about my dad and our life together. The rest of the way out I spent telling her about Tony. Funny that he should have the same name as that stupid gunman of Earl's. My father, my Tony, had been a bit of a dreamer, an idealist, a man who had never shot another human being in all his years on the force—warning shots in the air, but no one killed because of Tony Warshawski. Mallory couldn't believe it—I remember that, as Tony was dying. They were talking one evening, Bobby came over a lot at night those days, and Bobby asked him how many people he'd killed in his years on the force. Tony replied he'd never even wounded a man.

After a few minutes of silence, I thought of a small point that had been bothering me. "What's with this fake-name business? When your father first came to me he called you Anita Hill. Up in Wisconsin you were Jody Hill. I can see he gave you a false name in a not-too-bright effort to keep you out of things—but why'd you both use Hill?"

"Oh, not collusion. But Joe Hill has always been a big hero of ours. Jody Hill just came to me subconsciously. He probably picked it for the same reason."

We had reached our exit, and Anita started giving me detailed directions. When we pulled up in front of the house, she sat for a bit without speaking. Finally she said, "I couldn't decide whether to ask you to come in with me or not. But I think you should. This whole thing got started—or your involvement got started—because he came to you. Now I don't know whether he'll believe it's over without your story."

"Okay." We walked up to the house together. A man was sitting outside the front door.

"Bodyguard," Anita murmured to me. "Daddy's had one as long as I can remember." Aloud she said, "Hi, Chuck. It's me, Anita—I've dyed my hair."

The man was taken aback. "I heard you ran off, that someone was gunning for you. You okay?"

"Oh, yes, I'm fine. My dad home?"

"Yup, he's in there alone."

We went into the house, a small ranch house on a large plot. Anita led me through the living room to a sunken family room. Andrew McGraw was watching television. He turned as he heard us coming. For a second he didn't recognize Anita with her short black hair. Then he jumped up.

"Annie?"

"Yes, it's me," she said quietly. "Miss Warshawski here found me, as you asked her to. She shot Yardley Masters, and broke the arm of Earl Smeissen's hired gunman. They're all three in jail now. So we can talk."

"Is that true?" he demanded. "You disabled Bronsky and shot Masters?"

"Yes," I said. "But your troubles aren't over, you know: as soon as Masters has recovered somewhat, he's going to talk."

He looked from me to Anita, the heavy square face uncertain. "How much do you know?" he finally said.

"I know a lot," Anita said. Her voice wasn't hostile, but it was cold, the voice of someone who didn't know the person she was talking to very well and wasn't sure she'd want to. "I know you've been using the union as a front for collecting money on illegal insurance claims. I know that Peter found that out and went to Yardley Masters about it. And Masters called you and got the name of a hit man."

"Listen, Annie," he said in a low urgent tone, much different from the angry bluster I'd heard before. "You've got to believe I didn't know it was Peter when Yardley called."

She stayed in the doorway to the room, looking down at him as he stood in his shirt-sleeves. I moved over to one side. "Don't you see," she said, her voice breaking a little, "it doesn't matter. It doesn't matter whether you knew who it was or not. What matters is that you were using the union for fraud, and that you knew a killer when Masters needed one. I know you wouldn't have had Peter shot in cold blood. But it's because you knew how to get people shot that it happened at all."

He was silent, thinking. "Yes, I see," he said finally, in that same low voice. "Do you think I haven't seen it, sitting here for ten days wondering if I'd see you dead, too, and know that I had killed you?" She said nothing. "Look, Annie. You and the union—that's been my whole life for twenty years. I thought for ten days that I'd lost both of you. Now you're back. I'm going to have to give up the union—are you going to make me do without you as well?"

Behind us an insanely grinning woman on TV was urging the room to buy some kind of shampoo. Anita stared at her father. "It can never be the same, you know. Our life, you know, the foundation's broken."

"Look at me, Annie," he said hoarsely. "I haven't slept for ten days, I haven't eaten. I keep watching television, expecting to hear that they've found your dead body someplace. . . . I asked Warshawski here to find you when I thought I could keep a step ahead of Masters. But when they made it clear you'd be dead if you showed up, I had to call her off."

He looked at me. "You were right—about almost everything. I used Thayer's card because I wanted to plant the idea of him in your mind. It was stupid. Everything I've done this last week's been stupid. Once I realized Annie was in trouble, I just lost my head and acted on crazy impulses. I wasn't mad at you, you know. I was just hoping to God you'd stop before you found Annie. I knew if Earl was watching you you'd lead him straight to her."

I nodded.

"Maybe I should never have known any gangsters," he said to Anita. "But that started so long ago. Before you were born. Once you get in bed with those boys, you don't get out again. The Knifegrinders were a pretty rough bunch in those days—you think we're tough now, you should have seen us then. And the big manufacturers, they all hired hooligans to kill us and keep the union out. We hired muscle to get the union in. Only once we were in, we couldn't get rid of the muscle. If I'd wanted to get away, the only way I could have done it was to leave the Knifegrinders. And I couldn't do that. I was a shop steward when I was fifteen. I met your mother when I was picketing Western Springs Cutlery and she was a kid herself screwing scissors together. The union was my life. And guys like Smeissen were the dirty part that came along with it."

"But you betrayed the union. You betrayed it when you started dealing with Masters on those phony claims." Anita was close to tears.

"Yeah, you're right." He ran a hand through his hair. "Probably the dumbest thing I ever did. He came up to me at Comiskey Park one day. Someone pointed me out to him. He'd been looking for years, I guess—he'd figured out the deal, you see, but he needed someone on the outside to send the claims into him.

"All I saw was the money. I just didn't want to look down that road. If I had . . . It's like some story I heard once. Some guy, Greek I think, was so greedy he begged the gods to give him a gift—everything he touched would turn to gold. Only thing is, these gods, they zap you: they always give you what you ask for but it turns out not to be what you want. Well, this guy was like me: he had a daughter that he loved more than life. But he forgot to look down the road. And when he touched her, she turned to gold, too. That's what I've done, haven't I?"

"King Midas," I said. "But he repented, and the gods forgave him and brought his daughter back to life."

Anita looked uncertainly at her father; he looked back, his harsh face stripped and pleading. Murray was waiting for his story. I didn't say good-bye.

BLOOD SHOT

For Dominick

ACKNOWLEDGMENTS

A writer working on a project that includes much technical material incurs many debts. As with the Bill of Rights, the enumeration of some does not mean that others are not considered equally important.

Judy Freeman and Rennie Heath, environmental specialists with the South Chicago Development Commission, gave freely of their time and expertise on both the geography and the economic issues facing South Chicago. Jeffrey S. Brown, Environmental Manager of Velsicol Corporation, and John Thompson, Executive Director of the Central States Education Center, both provided valuable insights into the corporate and technical problems that might arise in the situation I envisioned. Doctors Sarah Neely and Susan S. Riter were most helpful in diagnosing the problems besetting Louisa Djiak. And Sergeant Michael Black of the Matteson Police Department has been unfailingly helpful throughout V.I.'s career with advice on police procedure, handgun use, and other matters.

Because this is a work of fiction, all companies, persons, chemicals, manufacturing processes, medical side effects, and political or community organizations are totally the creation of my unaided—and unfettered—imagination. While some major corporations are mentioned by name, it is only where their plants form a well-known part of the Chicago landscape—to omit them would mean too much tampering with geography. For the same reason, existing ward boundaries were used, without in any way referring to real politicians who serve the citizens of those wards.

For those who are fanatics about geographical details, some minor ones have been deliberately altered to facilitate the story. However, South Chicago does contain some of Illinois's last wetlands for migratory birds, and a part of that marsh is really known as Dead Stick Pond.

CONTENTS

1 HIGHWAY 41 REVISITED

I had forgotten the smell. Even with the South Works on strike and Wisconsin Steel padlocked and rusting away, a pungent mix of chemicals streamed in through the engine vents. I turned off the car heater, but the stench—you couldn't call it air—slid through minute cracks in the Chevy's windows, burning my eyes and sinuses.

I followed Route 41 south. A couple of miles back it had been Lake Shore Drive, with Lake Michigan spewing foam against the rocks on my left, expensive high rises haughtily looking on from the right. At Seventy-ninth Street the lake disappeared abruptly. The weed-choked yards surrounding the giant USX South Works stretched away to the east, filling the mile or so of land between road and water. In the distance, pylons, gantries, and towers loomed through the smoke-hung February air. Not the land of high rises and beaches anymore, but landfill and worn-out factories.

Decaying bungalows looked on the South Works from the right side of the street. Some were missing pieces of siding, or shamefacedly showing stretches of peeling paint. In others the concrete in the front steps cracked and sagged. But the windows were all whole, tightly sealed, and not a scrap of debris lay in the yards. Poverty might have overtaken the area, but my old neighbors gallantly refused to give in to it.

I could remember when eighteen thousand men poured from those tidy little homes every day into the South Works, Wisconsin Steel, the Ford assembly plant, or the Xerxes solvent factory. I remembered when each piece of trim was painted fresh every second spring and new Buicks or Oldsmobiles were an autumn commonplace. But that was in a different life, for me as well as South Chicago.

At Eighty-ninth Street I turned west, flipping down the sun visor to shield my eyes from the waning winter sun. Beyond the tangle of deadwood, rusty cars, and collapsed houses on my left lay the Calumet River. My friends and I used to flout our parents by swimming there; my stomach turned now at the thought of sticking my face into the filthy water.

The high school stood across from the river. It was an enormous structure, sprawling over several acres, but its dark red brick somehow looked homey, like a nineteenth-century girls' college. Light pouring from the windows and streams of young people going through the vast double doors on the west end added to the effect of quaintness. I turned off the engine, reached for my gym bag, and joined the crowd.

The high, vaulted ceilings were built when heat was cheap and education respected enough for people to want schools to look like cathedrals. The cavernous hallways served as perfect echo chambers for the laughing, shouting crowd. Noise hurled from the ceiling, the walls, and the metal lockers. I wondered why I never noticed the din when I was a student.

They say you don't forget the things you learn young. I'd last been here twenty years ago, but at the gym entrance I turned left without thinking to follow the hall down to the women's locker room. Caroline Djiak was waiting at the door, clipboard in hand.

"Vic! I thought maybe you'd chickened out. Everyone else got here half an hour ago. They're suited up, at least the ones who can still get into their uniforms. You did bring yours, didn't you? Joan Lacey's here from the *Herald-Star* and she'd like to talk to you. After all, you were tournament MVP, weren't you?"

Caroline hadn't changed. The copper pigtails were cut into a curly halo around her freckled face, but that seemed to be the only difference. She was still short, energetic, and tactless.

I followed her into the locker room. The din there rivaled the noise level in the hall outside. Ten young women in various stages of undress were screaming at each other—for a nail file, a tampon, who stole my fucking deodorant. In bras and panties they looked muscular and trim, much fitter than my friends and I had been at that age. Certainly fitter than we were now.

In a corner of the locker room, making almost as much noise, were seven of the ten Lady Tigers with whom I'd won the state Class AA championship twenty years ago. Five of the seven had on their old black-and-gold uniforms. On some the T-shirts stretched tight across their breasts, and the shorts looked as though they might split if the wearer tried a fast breakaway.

The one packed tightest into her uniform might have been Lily Goldring, our leading free-throw shooter, but the permed hair and extra chin made it hard to be sure. I thought Alma Lowell was the black woman who had spread far beyond the capacity of her uniform and had her letter jacket perched uneasily on her massive shoulders.

The only two I recognized for certain were Diane Logan and Nancy Cleghorn. Diane's strong slender legs could still do for a *Vogue* cover. She'd been our star forward, co-captain, honors student. Caroline had told me Diane now ran a successful Loop PR agency, specializing in promoting black companies and personalities.

Nancy Cleghorn and I had stayed in touch through college; even so, her strong square face and frizzy blond hair were so unchanged, I would have known her anyplace. She was responsible for my being here tonight. She directed environmental affairs for SCRAP—the South Chicago Reawakening Project where Caroline Djiak was the deputy director. When the two of them realized the Lady Tigers were going into the regional championships for the first time in twenty years, they decided to get the old team together for a pregame ceremony. Publicity for the neighborhood, publicity for SCRAP, support for the team—good for everyone.

Nancy grinned when she saw me. "Yo, Warshawski—get your ass moving. We gotta be on the floor in ten minutes."

"Hi, Nancy. I ought to have my head examined for letting you get me down here. Don't you know you can't go home again?"

I found four square inches of bench to dump my gym bag on and quickly stripped, stuffing my jeans into the bag and putting on my faded uniform. I adjusted the socks and tied the high-lacing shoes.

Diane put an arm around me. "You're looking good, Whitey, like you still could move around if you had to."

We looked into the mirror. While some of the current Tigers topped six feet, at five-eight I'd been the tallest one on our team. Diane's afro was about level with my nose. Black and white, we'd both wanted to play basketball when race fights were a daily disruption in hall and locker room. We hadn't liked each other, but junior year we'd forced a truce on the rest of the team and the next February we'd taken them to the first statewide girls tournament.

She grinned, sharing the memory. "All that garbage we used to put ourselves through seems mighty trivial now, Warshawski. Come over and meet the reporter. Say something nice about the old neighborhood."

The *Herald-Star*'s Joan Lacey was the city's only woman sports columnist. When I said I read her stuff regularly she smiled with pleasure. "Tell my editor. Better still, write a letter. So how do you feel putting on your uniform after all these years?"

"Like an idiot. I haven't held a basketball since I left college." I'd gone to the University of Chicago on an athletic scholarship. The U of C offered them long before the rest of the country knew that women played sports.

We talked for a few minutes, about the past, about aging athletes, about the fifty percent unemployed in the neighborhood, about the current team's prospects.

"We're rooting for them, of course," I said. "I'm anxious to see them on the court. In here they look as though they take conditioning much more seriously than we did twenty years ago."

"Yeah, they keep hoping the women's pro league will revive. There're some top-notch women players in high school and college with no place to go."

Joan put her notebook away and told a photographer to get us out on the court for some shots. We eight old-timers straggled out to the gym floor, Caroline worrying around us like an overzealous terrier.

Diane picked up a ball and dribbled it behind her, under her legs, then bounced it to me. I turned and shot. The ball caromed from the backboard and I ran in to get it and dunk it. My old teammates gave me a ragged hand.

The photographer took some pictures of us together, then of Diane and me playing one-on-one under the net. The crowd got into it a little, but their real interest was on the current team. When the Lady Tigers took the floor in their warm-up suits, they got a big round. We worked out a little with them, but turned the floor over to them as soon as possible: this was their big night.

When the girls from visiting St. Sophia came out in their red-and-white sweats, I slid back to the locker room and started to change back to my civvies. Caroline found me as I finished tying my neck scarf.

"Vic! Where are you going? You know you promised to come over to see Ma after the game!"

"I said I'd try, if I could stay down here."

"She's counting on seeing you. She can hardly get out of bed she's in such bad shape. This really matters to her."

In the mirror I could see her face flush and her blue eyes darken with the same hurt look she used to give me when she was five and I wouldn't let her tag along with my friends. I felt my temper rise with twenty-year-old irritation.

"Did you arrange this basketball farce to manipulate me into visiting Louisa? Or did that only come to you later?"

The flush deepened to scarlet. "What do you mean, farce? I'm trying to do something for this community. I'm not a la-di-da snot going off to the North Side and abandoning people to their fate!"

"What, you think if I'd stayed down here I could've saved Wisconsin Steel? Or stopped the assholes at USX from striking one of the last operating plants around here?" I grabbed my peajacket from the bench and angrily thrust my arms into it.

"Vic! Where are you going?"

"Home. I have a dinner date. I want to change clothes."

"You can't. I need you," she wailed loudly. The big eyes were swimming with tears now, a prelude to a squawk to her mother or mine that I was being mean to her. It brought back all the times Gabriella had come to the door—saying "What difference can it make to you, Victoria? Take the child with you"—so forcibly it was all I could do not to slap Caroline's wide trembling mouth.

"What do you need me for? To make good on a promise you made without consulting me?"

"Ma isn't going to live much longer," she shouted. "Isn't that more important than some stupid-ass date?"

"Certainly. If this were a social occasion, I would call and say excuse me, the little brat next door committed me to something I can't get out of. But this is dinner with a client. He's temperamental but he pays on time and I like to keep him happy."

Tears were streaming across the freckles now. "Vic, you never take me seriously. I told you when we were discussing this how important it would be for Ma if you came to visit. And you completely forgot. You still think I'm five years old and nothing I say or think matters."

That shut me up. She had a point. And if Louisa was that sick, I really ought to see her.

"Oh, all right. I'll phone and change my plans. One last time."

The tears disappeared instantly. "Thanks, Vic. I won't forget it. I knew I could count on you."

"You mean you knew you could make another end run around me," I said disagreeably.

She laughed. "Let me show you where the phones are."

"I'm not senile yet—I can still find them. And no, I won't sneak off while you're not looking," I added, seeing her uneasy look.

She grinned. "As God is your witness?"

It was an old pledge, picked up from her mother's drunk Uncle Stan, who used it to prove he was sober.

"As God is my witness," I agreed solemnly. "I just hope Graham's feelings aren't so hurt, he decides not to pay his bill."

I found the pay phones near the front entrance and wasted several quarters before running Darrough Graham down at the Forty-Nine Club. He wasn't happy—he had made reservations at the Filagree—but I managed to end the conversation on a friendly note. Slinging my bag over my shoulder, I made my way back to the gym.

2

BRINGING UP BABY

St. Sophia gave the Lady Tigers a tough ride, leading through much of the second half. The play was intense, much faster paced than in my basketball years. Two starters for the Lady Tigers fouled out with seven minutes left, and things looked bad. Then the toughest Saint guard went out with three minutes left. The Tigers' star forward, who'd been penned in all evening, came to life, scoring eight unanswered points. The home team won 54–51.

I found myself cheering as eagerly as anyone. I even felt a nostalgic warmth for my own high school team, which surprised me: my adolescent memories are so dominated by my mother's illness and death, I guess I've forgotten having any good times.

Nancy Cleghorn had left to attend a meeting, but Diane Logan and I joined the rest of our old team in the locker room to congratulate our successors and wish them well in the regional semifinals. We didn't stay long: they clearly thought we were too old to understand basketball, let alone have played it.

Diane came over to say good-bye to me. "You couldn't pay me enough to relive my adolescence," she said, brushing my cheek with her own. "I'm going back to the Gold Coast. And I'm definitely staying there. Take it easy, Warshawski." She was gone in a shimmer of silver fox and Opium.

Caroline hovered anxiously around the locker-room door, worried I would leave without her. She was so tense I began to feel uneasy about what I was going to find at her house. She'd acted just this way when she'd dragged me home from college one weekend, ostensibly because Louisa had hurt her back and needed help replacing a broken window. After I got there I found she expected me to explain why she'd given Louisa's little pearl ring to the St. Wenceslaus Lenten fund drive.

"Is Louisa really sick?" I demanded as we finally left the locker room.

She looked at me soberly. "Very sick, Vic. You're not going to like seeing her."

"What's the rest of your agenda, then?"

The ready color flooded her cheeks. "I don't know what you're talking about."

She flounced out the school door. I followed slowly, in time to see her get into a battered car parked with its nose well into the street. She rolled down the window as I walked by to yell that she'd see me at the house and took off in a squeal of rubber. My shoulders were sagging a little as I unlocked the Chevy door and slid in.

My gloom increased when I made the turn onto Houston Street. I'd last been on the block in 1976 when my father died and I came back down to sell the house. I'd seen Louisa then, and Caroline, who was fourteen and following determinedly in my steps—she even tried playing basketball, but at five feet even her tireless energy couldn't get her onto the first squad.

That was the last time I had talked to any of the other neighbors who had known my parents. There was genuine grief for my gentle, good-humored father. Grudging respect for Gabriella, dead ten years at the time. After all, the other women on the block had shared her scraping, saving, cutting each penny five ways to feed and shelter their families.

Now she was dead, they glossed over the eccentricities that used to make them shake their heads—taking the girl to the opera with an extra ten dollars instead of buying her a new winter coat. Not baptizing her or giving her to the sisters at St. Wenceslaus for schooling. That disturbed them enough that they sent the principal, Mother Joseph Something, around one day for a memorable confrontation.

Maybe the biggest folly of all to them was her insisting on college for me, and demanding that it be the University of Chicago. Only the best did for Gabriella, and she'd decided that was Chicago's best when I was two. Not, perhaps, comparing in her mind with the University of Pisa. Just as the shoes she bought herself at Callabrano's on Morgan Street didn't compare to

Milan. But one did what one could. So two years after my mother's death I'd left on a scholarship for what my neighbors called Red University, half scared, half excited to meet the demons up there. And after that, I'd never really gone home again.

Louisa Djiak was the one woman on the block who always stood up for Gabriella, dead or alive. But then, she owed Gabriella. And me, too, I thought with a flash of bitterness that startled me. I realized I was still pissed at spending all those glorious summer days baby-sitting, at doing my home-work with Louisa's baby howling in the background.

Well, the baby was grown up now, but she was still howling exigently in my ear. I pulled up behind her Capri and turned off the engine.

The house was smaller than I remembered, and dingier. Louisa wasn't well enough to wash and starch the curtains every six months and Caroline belonged to a generation that emphatically avoided such tasks. I should know—I was part of it myself.

Caroline was waiting in the doorway for me, still edgy. She gave a brief, tense smile. "Ma's really excited you're here, Vic. She's waited all day to have her coffee so she could drink it with you."

She took me through the small, cluttered dining room to the kitchen, saying over her shoulder, "She's not supposed to drink coffee anymore. But it was too hard for her to give it up—along with everything else that's changed for her. So we compromise on one cup a day."

She busied herself at the stove, tackling the coffee with energetic ineffi-ciency. Despite a trail of spilled water and coffee grounds on the stove, she carefully arranged a TV tray with china, cloth napkins, and a geranium cut from a coffee can in the window. Finally she set out a little dish of ice cream with a geranium leaf in it. When she picked up the tray I stood up from my perch on the kitchen stool to follow her.

Louisa's bedroom lay to the right of the dining room. As soon as Caroline opened the door the smell of sickness hit me like a physical force, bringing back the odor of medicine and decaying flesh that had hung around Gabriella the last year of her life. I dug the nails into the palm of my right hand and willed myself into the room.

My first reaction was shock, even though I thought I'd prepared myself. Louisa sat propped in bed, her face gaunt and tinged a queer greenish gray under her wispy hair. Her twisted hands emerged from the loose sleeves of a worn pink cardigan. When she held them out to me with a smile, though, I caught a glimpse of the beautiful young woman who'd rented the house next to ours when she was pregnant with Caroline.

"Good to see you, Victoria. Knew you'd come by. You're like your ma that way. Look like her, too, even though you have your daddy's gray eyes."

I knelt by the bed and hugged her. Underneath the cardigan her bones felt tiny and brittle.

She gave a racking cough that shook her frame. "Excuse me. Too many damned cigarettes for too many years. Little missy here hides 'em from me—as if they could hurt me any worse now.''

Caroline bit her lips and moved over next to the bed. "I brought you your coffee, Ma. Maybe it'll take your mind off your cigs.''

"Yeah, my one cup. Damned doctors. First they pump you so full of shit you don't know whether you're coming or going. Then when they got you tied by the hind legs they take away anything that'd make the time pass easier. I'm telling you, girl, don't ever get yourself in this spot.''

I took the thick china mug from Caroline and handed it to Louisa. Her hands shook slightly and she pressed the mug against her breast to steady it. I slid off my heels into a straight-backed chair near the bed.

"You want to spend some time alone with Vic, Ma?" Caroline asked.

"Yeah, sure. You go on, girl. I know you got work to do.''

When the door shut behind Caroline I said, "I'm really sorry to see you like this.''

She made a throwaway gesture. "Ah—what the hell. I'm sick of thinking about it, and I talk about it to the damned docs often enough. I want to hear about you. I follow all your cases when they make it to the papers. Your ma'd be real proud of you.''

I laughed. "I'm not so sure. She hoped I'd be a concert singer. Or maybe a high-priced lawyer. I can just imagine her if she saw the way I live.''

Louisa laid a bony hand on my arm. "Don't you think so, Victoria. Don't you think so for one minute. You know Gabriella—she'd of gave her last shirt to a beggar. Look how she stood up for me when people came by and threw eggs and shit at my windows. No. Maybe she'd of liked to see you living better than you do. Heck—I feel that way about Caroline. Her brains, her education and all, she could do better than hanging around this dump. But I'm real proud of her. She's honest and hardworking and she sticks up for what she believes in. And you're just the same. No, sir. Gabriella could see you now she'd be as proud as can be.''

"Well, we couldn't have managed without your help when she was so sick," I muttered, uncomfortable.

"Oh, shit, girl. My one chance to pay her back for everything she did? I can still see her when the righteous ladies from St. Wenceslaus were out parading around my front door. Gabriella come out with a head of steam that damn near drove 'em into the Calumet.''

She gave a shout of hoarse laughter that changed to a coughing fit which left her breathless and slightly purple. She lay quietly for a few minutes, panting in short, gasping breaths.

"Hard to believe folks cared so much about one pregnant unmarried teenager, ain't it," she said finally. "Here we got half the people outa work in the community—that's life and death, girl. But back then I guess it seemed like the end of the world to folks. I mean, my own ma and pa, even, throwing me out like they did." Her face worked for a minute. "Like it was all my fault or something. Your ma was the only one stood up for me. Even when my folks come around and decided to admit Caroline was alive, they never really forgave her for being born or me for doing it."

Gabriella never did anything by half measures: I helped her look after the baby so Louisa could work the night shift at Xerxes. The days when I had to take Caroline to her grandparents' were my worst torment. Rigid, humorless, they wouldn't let me into the house unless I took my shoes off. A couple of times they even bathed Caroline outside before they'd admit her to their pristine portals.

Louisa's parents were only in their sixties—same age as Gabriella and Tony would be if they were still alive. Because Louisa had a baby and lived by herself, I'd always thought of her as part of my parents' generation, but she was only five or six years older than me.

"When did you stop working?" I asked. I called Louisa occasionally, when my guilty imagination conjured up Gabriella's image, but it had been awhile. South Chicago hovered too uneasily at the base of my mind for me to willingly court its return to my life, and it had been over two years since I'd spoken to Louisa. She hadn't said anything then about feeling bad.

"Oh, it got so I couldn't stand anymore about—must be just over a year. So they put me on disability then. It's only been the last six months or so I couldn't get around at all."

She flicked the covers back from her legs. They were twigs, thin bones a bird might use but mottled greeny-gray like her face. Livid patches on her feet and ankles showed where her veins had given up carting blood around.

"It's my kidneys," she said. "Darned things don't want me to pee properly. Caroline takes me over two, three times a week and they stick me on that damned machine, supposed to clean me out, but between you and me, girl, I'd just as soon they'd let me go in peace." She held up a thin hand. "Don't you go telling Caroline that, now—she's doing everything to see I get the best. And the company pays for it, so it's not like I feel she's digging into her own savings. I don't want her to think I ain't grateful."

"No, no," I said soothingly, pulling the cover up gently.

She reverted to the old days on the block, to the days when her legs were slim and muscular, when she used to go dancing after getting off work at midnight. To Steve Ferraro, who wanted to marry her, and Joey Pankowski, who didn't, and how if she had to do it over, she'd do it the same, because she had Caroline, but for Caroline she wanted something different, something better than staying on in South Chicago working herself to an early old age.

At last I took the bony fingers and squeezed them gently. "I've got to go, Louisa—it's twenty miles to my place. But I'll come back."

"Well, it's been real good to see you again, girl." She cocked her head on one side and gave a naughty smile. "Don't suppose you could find a way to slip me a pack of cigarettes, do you?"

I laughed. "I'm not touching that with a barge pole, Louisa—you work it out with Caroline."

I shook out her pillows and turned on the TV for her before going off to find Caroline. Louisa had never been much given to kissing, but she squeezed my hand tightly for a few seconds.

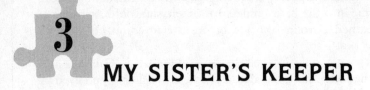

3

MY SISTER'S KEEPER

Caroline was sitting at the dining-room table, eating fried chicken and making notes on a colored graph. Chaotic stacks of paper—reports, magazines, flyers—covered all of the small surface. A large pile near her left elbow teetered uncertainly on the table edge. She put down her pencil when she heard me come into the room.

"I went out for some Kentucky Fried while you were in with Ma. Want some? What did you think—kind of a shock, huh?"

I shook my head in dismay. "It's terrible to see her like this. How are you holding up?"

She grimaced. "It wasn't so bad until her legs wouldn't support her anymore. She show 'em to you? I knew she would. It's really tough on her not being able to get around. The hard part for me was realizing how long she'd been sick before I noticed anything. You know Ma—she'd never complain in a million years, especially about anything as private as her kidneys."

She rubbed a greasy hand through her unruly curls. "It was only three years ago, when I suddenly noticed how much weight she'd been losing, that I even knew anything was wrong. Then it came out she'd been feeling off for a long time—dizzy and stuff, her feet numb—but she didn't want to say anything that might jeopardize her job."

The story sounded depressingly familiar. People on the hip North Side went to the doctor every time they stubbed their toes, but in South Chicago you expected life to be tough. Dizziness and weight loss happened to lots of people; it was the kind of thing grown-ups kept to themselves.

"You satisfied with the doctors she's seeing?"

Caroline finished gnawing on the chicken thigh and licked her fingers. "They're okay. We go to Help of Christians because that's where Xerxes has their medical plan, and they do as much as anyone could. I mean, her kidneys just aren't working at all—they call it acute renal failure—and it looks like she may have some bone marrow problems and maybe starting with emphysema. That's our only real problem—she keeps going on about her damned cigarettes. Hell, they may have helped get her into this fix to begin with."

I said awkwardly, "If she's in that bad shape, the cigarettes aren't going to make her any worse, you know."

"Vic! You didn't say that to her, did you? I have to fight her about them ten times a day as it is. If she thinks you're backing her up, I might as well quit on the spot." She slapped the table emphatically; the teetering pile of papers flew across the floor. "I was sure you of all people would support me on this."

"You know how I feel about smoking," I said, annoyed. "I expect Tony would be alive today if he hadn't had a two-pack-a-day habit—I still hear him wheezing and coughing in my nightmares. But how much time is smoking going to shave from Louisa's life at this point? She's in there by herself, got nothing but the tube to keep her company. I'm just saying it'd make her feel better mentally and won't make her any worse physically."

Caroline set her mouth in an uncompromising line. "No. I don't even want to talk about it."

I sighed and got down on the floor to help her with the loose papers. When we had them all collated again I looked at her suspiciously: she had reverted to her tense abstracted mood.

"Well, I think it's time for me to push off. I hope the Lady Tigers go all the way again."

"I—Vic. I need to talk to you. I need your help."

"Caroline, I came down and pranced around in my basketball uniform for you. I saw Louisa. Not that I grudge the time with her, but how many items you got on your agenda tonight?"

"I want to hire you. Professionally. I need your help as a detective," she said defiantly.

"What for? You give SCRAP's money to the church Lenten fund and now you want me to find it for you again?"

"Goddamn you, Vic! Could you stop acting like I'm still five years old and treat me seriously for a minute?"

"If you wanted to hire me, why couldn't you have said something about it on the phone?" I asked. "Your step-by-step approach to me isn't exactly designed to make me feel serious about you."

"I wanted you to see Ma before I talked to you about it," she muttered, looking at her graph. "I thought if you saw how bad off she is, you'd think it was more important."

I sat at the end of the table. "Caroline, lay it out for me. I promise I'll listen as seriously to you as to any other potential client. But tell me the whole story, front, middle, and end. Then we can decide if you really need a detective, if it should be me, and so on."

She took a breath and said quickly, "I want you to find my father for me."

I was quiet for a minute.

"Isn't that a job for a detective?" she demanded.

"Do you know who he is?" I asked gently.

"No, that's partly what I need you to find out for me. You see how bad Ma is, Vic. She's going to die soon." She tried to keep her voice matter-of-fact, but it quavered a little. "Her folks always treated me like—I don't know —not the same way they are to my cousins. Second-class, I guess. When she dies I'd like to have some kind of family. I mean, maybe my old man will turn out to be an asshole jerk. The kind of guy who lets a girl go through what Ma did when she was pregnant might be. But maybe he'd have folks who'd like me. And if he didn't, at least I'd know."

"What does Louisa say? Have you asked her?"

"She practically killed me. Practically killed herself—she got so upset she almost choked to death. Screaming how I was ungrateful, she'd worked herself to the bone for me, I never wanted for anything, why'd I have to go nosing around in something that wasn't any of my damned business. So I knew I couldn't go on about it with her. But I have to find out. I know you could do it for me."

"Caroline, maybe you're better off not knowing. Even if I knew how to go about it—missing persons aren't a big part of my business—if it's that painful to Louisa, you might prefer not to find out."

"You know who he is, don't you!" she cried.

I shook my head. "I have no idea, honestly. Why did you think I do?"

She looked down. "I'm sure she told Gabriella. I thought maybe Gabriella told you."

I moved over to sit down next to her. "Maybe Louisa told my mother, but if so, it wasn't the kind of thing Gabriella thought I ought to know about. As God is my witness, I don't know."

She gave a little smile at that. "So will you find him for me?"

If I hadn't known her all her life, it would have been easier to say no. I specialize in financial crime. Missing persons takes a certain kind of skill, and certain kinds of contacts I've never bothered cultivating. And this guy'd been gone more than a quarter of a century.

But in addition to whining and teasing and tagging along when I didn't want her, Caroline used to adore me. When I went off to college she'd race to meet my train if I came home for the weekend, copper pigtails flying around her head, plump legs pumping as hard as they could. She even went out for basketball because I did. She almost drowned following me into Lake Michigan when she was four. The memories were endless. Her blue eyes still looked at me with total trust. I didn't want to, but I couldn't keep from responding.

"You got any idea where to start this search?"

"Well, you know. It had to be someone who lived in East Side. She never went anyplace else. I mean, she'd never even been to the Loop until your mother took us there to look at the Christmas decorations when I was three."

East Side was an all-white neighborhood to the east of South Chicago. It was cut off from the city by the Calumet River, and its residents tended to lead parochial, inbred lives. Louisa's parents still lived there in the house she'd grown up in.

"That's helpful," I said encouragingly. "What do you figure the population was in 1960? Twenty thousand? And only half of them were men. And many of those were children. You got any other ideas?"

"No," she said doggedly. "That's why I need a detective."

Before I could say anything else the doorbell rang. Caroline looked at her watch. "That might be Aunt Connie. She sometimes comes this late. Be back in a minute."

She trotted out to the entryway. While she dealt with the caller I flipped through a magazine devoted to the solid-waste-disposal industry, wondering if I was really insane enough to look for Caroline's father. I was staring at a picture of a giant incinerator when she came back into the room. Nancy Cleghorn, my old basketball pal who now worked for SCRAP, was trailing behind her.

"Hi, Vic. Sorry to barge in, but I wanted to fill Caroline in on a problem."

Caroline looked at me apologetically and asked if I'd mind waiting a few minutes to finish up.

"Not at all," I said politely, wondering if I was doomed to spend the night in South Chicago. "Want me to go to the other room?"

Nancy shook her head. "It's not private. Just annoying."

She sat down and unbuttoned her coat. She'd changed from her basketball uniform to a tan dress with a red scarf, and she'd put on makeup, but she still managed to appear disheveled.

"I got to the meeting in plenty of time. Ron was waiting for me—Ron Kappelman, our lawyer"—she put in an aside to me—"and we found we weren't on the agenda. So Ron went up to talk to that fat moron Martin O'Gara, saying we'd filed our material in plenty of time and talked to the secretary this morning to make sure she included us. So O'Gara makes this big show of not knowing what the hell is going on, and calls the board secretary and disappears for a while. Then he comes back and says there were so many legal problems with our submission, they'd decided not to consider it this evening."

"We want to build a solvent recycling plant here," Caroline explained to me. "We've got funding, we have a site, we have specs that have passed every EPA test we can think of, and we have some customers right on our doorstep —Xerxes and Glow-Rite. It means a good hundred jobs down here, and a chance to make a dent in the crap going into the ground."

She turned back to Nancy. "So what can the problem be? What did Ron say?"

"I was so mad I couldn't speak. He was so mad I was afraid he'd break O'Gara's neck—if he could find it underneath the fat rolls. But he called Dan Zimring, the EPA lawyer, you know. Dan said we could come by his place, so we went over there and he looked through everything and said it couldn't be in better shape."

Nancy fluffed out her frizzy hair so that it stood up wildly around her head. She helped herself absently to a piece of chicken.

"I'll tell you what I think the problem is," Caroline snapped, cheeks flushed. "They probably showed the submission to Art Jurshak—you know, professional courtesy or some shit. I think he blocked it."

"Art Jurshak," I echoed. "Is he still alderman down here? He must be a hundred and fifty by now."

"No, no," Caroline said impatiently. "He's only in his sixties somewhere. Don't you agree, Nancy?"

"I think he's sixty-two," she answered through a mouthful of chicken.

"Not about his age," Caroline said impatiently. "That Jurshak must be trying to block the plant."

Nancy licked her fingers. She looked around for a place to put the bone and finally laid it back on the plate with the rest of the chicken. "I don't see how you figure that, Caroline. There could be a lot of people who don't want to see a recycling center down here."

Caroline looked at her through narrowed eyes. "What did O'Gara say? I mean, he must have given some reason for not giving us a hearing."

Nancy frowned. "He said we shouldn't try to make proposals like this without community backing. I told him the community was a hundred percent behind us, and got ready to show him copies of petitions and crap, when he gave this jolly laugh and said, not a hundred percent. He'd heard from people who weren't behind it at all."

"But why Jurshak?" I asked, interested in spite of myself. "Why not Xerxes, or the Mob, or some rival solvent recycler?"

"Just the political tie-in," Caroline answered. "O'Gara's chairman of the zoning board because he's good buddies with all the old hack Dems."

"But, Caroline—Art's got no reason to oppose us. Our last meeting he even acted like he would support us."

"He never put it in so many words," Caroline said grimly. "And all it would take is someone willing to wave a big enough campaign contribution in front of him for him to change his mind."

"I suppose," Nancy agreed reluctantly. "I just don't like to think it."

"Why are you so pally with Jurshak all of a sudden?" Caroline demanded.

It was Nancy's turn to flush. "I'm not. But if he's against us, it'll be damned near impossible to get O'Gara to give us a hearing. Unless we could come up with a bribe big enough to make Jurshak respond to us. So how do I find who's against the plant, Vic? Aren't you a detective or something these days?"

I frowned at her and said hurriedly, "Or something. Trouble is, you've got too many possibilities in a political mess like this. The Mob. They're into a lot of waste-disposal projects in Chicago. Maybe they figure you'd be cutting into their turf. Or Return to Eden. I know they're supposed to be foursquare for the environment, but they've been raising a lot of money lately based on dramatic gestures they're making here in South Chicago. Maybe they don't want something that cuts off their fund-raising tactics. Or the Sanitary District—maybe they're taking kickbacks to look the other way on local pollution and they don't want to lose the revenues. Or Xerxes doesn't—"

"Enough!" she protested. "You're right, of course. It could be all of them or any of them. But in my place, where would you look first?"

"I don't know," I said thoughtfully. "Probably nuzzle up to someone on Jurshak's staff. See if the pressure came from there to begin with. And if it did, why. It'd save you the trouble of making the rounds of an infinite number of possibilities. Plus you wouldn't rub against someone who might want to put you in cement booties just for asking."

"You know some of the people who work for Art, don't you?" Caroline asked Nancy.

"Yes, yes I do." She fiddled with another piece of chicken. "It's just I haven't wanted . . . Oh, well. Anything for the cause of right and justice, I guess."

She picked up her coat and headed for the door. She stood looking at us for a moment, then set her lips firmly and left.

"I thought you might want to help her find out who's against the plant," Caroline said.

"I know you did, sweet pea. And even though it would be lots of fun, working for one poor customer in South Chicago is about all my budget can take at a time."

"You mean you'll help me? You'll find my father?" The blue eyes turned dark with excitement. "I can pay you, Vic. Really. I'm not asking you to do it for nothing. I've got a thousand dollars saved."

My usual rate is two-fifty a day, plus expenses. Even with a twenty percent family discount, I had a feeling she was going to run out of money before I ran out of detecting. But no one had forced me to agree. I was a free agent, governed only by my own whims, and guilt.

"I'll send you a contract to sign tomorrow," I told her. "And you can't be on the phone to me every half hour demanding results. This is going to take a long time."

"No, Vic. I won't." She smiled tremulously. "I can't tell you how much it means to me to know you're helping me out."

4

THE OLD FOLKS AT HOME

In my sleep that night I saw Caroline again as a baby, her face pink and blotchy from crying. My mother stood behind me telling me to look after the child. When I woke at nine the dream lay heavy in my head, cloaking me in lethargy. The job I'd agreed to do filled me with distaste.

Find Caroline's father for a thousand dollars. Find Caroline's father against Louisa's strongly voiced opposition. If she felt that violently about the guy after all this time, he was probably better left unfound. Assuming he was still alive. Assuming he'd lived in Chicago and hadn't been an itinerant journeyman amusing himself on his way through town.

At last I stuck a leaden foot out from under the bedclothes. The room was cold. We'd had such a mild winter I'd turned off the radiator to keep the place from becoming stuffy, but the temperature had apparently dropped during the night. I pulled my leg back under the blanket for a minute, but moving cracked my shell of indolence. I swung the covers back and got up.

Grabbing a sweatshirt from a pile on a chair, I trotted into the kitchen to start coffee. Maybe it was too cold out to go running. I parted the curtain overlooking the backyard. The sky was gray and an east wind was blowing debris against the back fence. I was dropping the curtain when a black nose and two paws appeared against the window, followed by a sharp bark. It was Peppy, the golden retriever I shared with my downstairs neighbor.

I opened the door, but she wouldn't come in. Instead she danced around on the little porch, indicating that the weather was perfect for running and would I please get a move on?

"Oh, all right," I grumbled. I turned off the water and went into the living room to do my stretches. Peppy didn't understand why I wasn't limber and ready to go as soon as I got out of bed. Every few minutes she'd give a minatory bark from the back. When I finally appeared in my sweats and running shoes, she raced down the stairs, turning at every half landing to make sure I was still coming. She gave little grunts of ecstasy when I opened the gate to the alley, even though we make the trip together three or four times a week.

I like to run about five miles. Since that's beyond Peppy's range, she stops at the lagoon when we get to the lake. She spends the time nosing out ducks and muskrats, rolling in mud or rotted fish when she can find them, and bounds out at me with her tongue hanging out in a self-satisfied grin when I make my way back west. We do the last mile home at a mild jog and I hand her over to my downstairs neighbor. Mr. Contreras shakes his head, chews us both out for letting her get dirty, then spends a pleasurable half hour grooming her coat back to its gleaming golden-red.

He was waiting as usual this morning when we got back. "You two have a good run, doll? You keep the dog out of the water, I hope? This cold weather it isn't good for her to get wet, you know."

He hung in the doorway prepared to talk indefinitely. He's a retired machinist, and the dog, his cooking, and I make up the bulk of his entertainment. I extricated myself as quickly as I could, but it was still close to eleven by the time I'd showered. I ate breakfast in my bedroom while I dressed, knowing if I sat down with coffee and the paper I would keep making excuses for lingering. Leaving the dishes on the dresser, I wrapped a wool scarf around my neck, picked up my bag and car coat from the hall where I'd dumped them the night before, and headed south.

The wind was whipping up the lake. Ten-foot waves crashed against the rocky barrier and spewed fingers of water onto the road. The display of nature, angry, contemptuous, made me feel small.

Every detail of decay struck me as the road wound southward. The white paint was peeling and the gates sagging at the old South Shore Country Club, once a symbol of that area's wealth and exclusivity. As a child I used to imagine I would grow up to ride a horse along its private bridle paths. The memory of such fantasies embarrasses me slightly now—the trappings of caste don't sit well on my adult conscience. But I would have wished a better fate for the club than to rot slowly under the hands of the Park District, its indifferent current masters.

South Chicago itself looked moribund, its life frozen somewhere around the time of World War II. When I drove past the main business area I saw that most of the stores had Spanish names now. Other than that they looked much as they had when I was a little girl. Their grimy concrete walls still framed tawdry window displays of white nylon communion dresses, vinyl shoes, plastic furniture. Women wrapped in threadbare wool coats still wore cotton babushkas as they bent their heads into the wind. On the corners, near the ubiquitous storefront taverns, stood vacant-eyed, shabbily clad men. They had always been a presence, but the massive unemployment in the mills swelled their numbers now.

I had forgotten the trick to getting into East Side and had to double back to Ninety-fifth Street, where an old-fashioned drawbridge crosses the Calumet River. If South Chicago hadn't changed since 1945, East Side stuck itself in formaldehyde when Woodrow Wilson was President. Five bridges form the neighborhood's only link to the rest of the city. Its members live in a stubborn isolation, trying to recreate the Eastern European villages of their grandparents. They don't like people from across the river, and anyone north of Seventy-first Street might as well have rolled in on a Soviet tank for the reception they get.

I drove under the massive concrete legs of the interstate to 106th Street. Louisa's parents lived south of 106th on Ewing. I thought her mother would be home and hoped her father wouldn't be. He'd retired some years ago from the little printshop he'd managed, but he was active in the Knights of Columbus and his VFW lodge and he might be out having lunch with the boys.

The street was crammed with well-kept bungalows set on obsessively tidy lots. Not a scrap of paper lay on the street. Art Jurshak tended this part of his ward with loving hands. Street-cleaning and repair crews came through regularly. All along the southeast side, sidewalks had been built three or four feet above the original ground level. South Chicago held numerous gaping pits where the newer paving had collapsed, but in East Side not a crack showed between sidewalk and house. As I got out of my car I felt as though I should have undergone a surgical scrubdown before visiting the neighborhood.

The Djiak house lay halfway down the block. Its curtained front windows gleamed in the dull air, and the stoop shone from much scouring. I rang the bell, trying to build up enough mental energy to talk to Louisa's parents.

Martha Djiak came to the door. Her square, lined face was set in a frown suitable for dismissing door-to-door salesmen. After a moment she recognized me and the frown lightened a little. She opened the inner door. I could see she had an apron covering the crisply ironed front of her dress: I'd never seen her at home without an apron on.

"Well, Victoria. It's been a long time since you brought little Caroline over for a visit, hasn't it?"

"Yeah, it has," I agreed unenthusiastically.

Louisa would not let Caroline go to her grandparents' alone. If she or Gabriella couldn't take her, they gave me two quarters for the bus and careful instructions to stay with Caroline until it was time to return home again. I never understood why Mrs. Djiak couldn't come and fetch Caroline herself. Maybe Louisa was afraid her mother would try to keep the baby so she wouldn't grow up with an unwed single parent.

"Since you're down here, maybe you'd like a cup of coffee."

It wasn't effusive, but she'd never been demonstrative. I accepted with as much good cheer as I could muster and she opened the storm door for me. She was careful not to touch the glass panel with her hands. I slid through as unobtrusively as I could, remembering to take my shoes off in the tiny entryway before following her to the kitchen.

As I'd hoped, she was alone. The ironing board stood open in front of the stove, a shirt draped across it. She folded the shirt, laid it on the clothes basket, and collapsed the ironing board with quick silent motions. When everything was stowed in the tiny pantry behind the refrigerator, she put on water to boil.

"I talked to Louisa this morning. She said you'd been down there yesterday."

"Yes," I acknowledged. "It's tough to see someone that lively laid up the way she is."

Mrs. Djiak spooned coffee into the pot. "Lots of people suffer more with less cause."

"And lots of people carry on like Attila the Hun and never get a pimple. It just goes to show, doesn't it?"

She took two cups from a shelf and stood them primly on the table. "I hear you're a detective now. Doesn't really seem like a woman's job, does it? Kind of like Caroline, working on community development, or whatever she calls it. I don't know why you two girls couldn't get married, settle down, raise a family."

"I guess we're waiting for men as good as Mr. Djiak to come along," I said.

She looked at me seriously. "That's the trouble with you girls. You think life is romantic, like they show in the movies. A good steady man who brings his pay home every Friday is worth a lot more than fancy dinners and flowers."

"Was that Louisa's problem too?" I asked gently.

She set her lips in a thin line and turned back to the coffee. "Louisa had other problems," she said shortly.

"Like what?"

She carefully took a covered sugar bowl down from the cupboard over the stove and placed it with a little pitcher of cream in the middle of the table. She didn't say anything until she'd finished pouring the coffee.

"Louisa's problems are old now. And they never were any of your business."

"And what about Caroline? Are they any concern of hers?" I sipped the rich coffee, which Louisa still infused in the old European style.

"They don't have anything to do with her. She'd be a good deal better off if she learned not to poke around in other people's closets."

"Louisa's past matters a lot to Caroline. Louisa is dying and Caroline is feeling very lonely. She'd like to know who her father was."

"And that's why you came down here? To help her dig up all that trash? She should be ashamed she doesn't have any father, instead of talking about it with everyone she knows."

"What's she supposed to do?" I asked impatiently. "Kill herself because Louisa never married the man who got her pregnant? You act like it was all Louisa and Caroline's fault. Louisa was sixteen years old—fifteen when she got pregnant. Don't you think the man had any responsibility in this?"

She clenched the coffee cup so tightly, I was afraid the ceramic might shatter. "Men—have difficulty controlling themselves. We all know that," she said thickly. "Louisa must have led him on. But she would never admit it."

"All I want to know is his name," I said as quietly as I could. "I think Caroline has a right to know if she really wants to. And a right to see if her father's family would give her a little warmth."

"Rights!" she said bitterly. "Caroline's rights. Louisa's! What about my right to a life of peace and decency? You're as bad as your mother was."

"Yeah," I said. "In my book that's a compliment."

Behind me someone turned a key in the back door. Martha paled slightly and set down her coffee cup.

"You must not mention any of this in front of him," she said urgently. "Tell him you were just visiting Louisa and stopped by. Promise, Victoria."

I made a sour face. "Yeah, sure, I suppose."

As Ed Djiak came into the room Martha said brightly, "See who's come to visit us? You'll never recognize her from the little Victoria she used to be!"

Ed Djiak was tall. All the lines in his face and body were elongated, like a Modigliani painting, from his long, cavernous face to his long, dangling fingers. Caroline and Louisa inherited their short, square good looks from Martha. Who knows where their lively tempers came from.

"So, Victoria. You went off to the University of Chicago and got too good for the old neighborhood, huh?" He grunted and shifted a sack of groceries onto the table. "I got the apples and pork chops, but the beans didn't look right so I didn't buy any."

Martha quickly unpacked the groceries and stowed them and the bag in their appointed cells. "Victoria and I were just having some coffee, Ed. You want a cup?"

"You think I'm some old lady to drink coffee in the middle of the day? Get me a beer."

He sat down at the end of the small table. Martha moved to the refrigerator, which stood immediately to his side, and took a Pabst from the bottom shelf. She poured it carefully into a glass mug and put the can in the trash.

"I've been visiting Louisa," I said to him. "I'm sorry she's in such bad shape. But her spirits are impressive."

"We suffered for her for twenty-five years. Now it's her turn to suffer a little, huh?" He stared at me with sneering, angry eyes.

"Spell it out for me, Mr. Djiak," I said offensively. "What'd she do to make you suffer so?"

Martha made a little noise in her throat. "Victoria is working as a detective now, Ed. Isn't that nice?"

He ignored her. "You're just like your mother, you know. She used to carry on like Louisa was some kind of saint, instead of the whore she really was. You're just as bad. What did she do to me? Got herself pregnant. Used my name. Stayed in the neighborhood flaunting her baby instead of going off to the sisters the way we arranged for her to do."

"Louisa got herself pregnant?" I echoed. "With a turkey baster in the basement, you mean? There wasn't a man involved?"

Martha sucked in a nervous breath. "Victoria. We don't like to talk about these things."

"No, we don't," Ed agreed nastily, turning to her. "Your daughter. You couldn't control her. For twenty-five years the neighbors whispered behind my back, and now I have to be insulted in my own house by that Italian bitch's daughter."

My face turned hot. "You're disgusting, Djiak. You're terrified of women. You hate your own wife and daughter. No wonder Louisa turned to someone else for a little affection. Who was it to get you so exercised? Your local priest?"

He sprang up from the table, knocking over his beer stein, and hit me in the mouth. "Get out of my house, you mongrel bitch! Don't ever come back with your filthy mind, your vile tongue!"

I got up slowly and went over to stand in front of him, my face close enough to smell the beer on his breath. "You may *not* insult my mother, Djiak. Any other garbage from the cesspool you call a mind I'll tolerate. But you ever insult my mother again in my hearing I will break your neck."

I stared at him fiercely until he turned his head uneasily away.

"Good-bye, Mrs. Djiak. Thanks for the coffee."

She was on her knees mopping the floor by the time I got to the kitchen door. The beer had soaked through my socks. In the entryway I paused to take them off, slipping my bare feet into my running shoes. Mrs. Djiak came up behind me, cleaning my beery footprints.

"I begged you not to talk to him about it, Victoria."

"Mrs. Djiak, all I want is Caroline's father's name. Tell me and I won't bother you anymore."

"You mustn't come back. He will call the police. Or perhaps even shoot you himself."

"Yeah, well, I'll bring my gun the next time I come." I fished a card from my handbag. "Call me if you change your mind."

She didn't say anything, but she took the card and tucked it into her apron pocket. I pulled the gleaming door open and left her frowning in the entryway.

5

THE SIMPLE JOYS
OF CHILDHOOD

I sat in the car for a long time before my anger cooled and my breathing returned to normal. "How she made us suffer!" I mimicked savagely. Poor scared, spunky teenager. What courage it must have taken even to tell the Djiaks she was pregnant, let alone not to go to the home for unwed mothers they'd picked out for her. Girls in my high school class who hadn't been as resilient returned with horrifying tales of backbreaking work, spartan rooms, poor nourishment as a nine-month punishment meted out by the nuns.

I felt fiercely proud of my mother for standing up to her righteous neighbors. I remembered the night they marched in front of Louisa's house, throwing eggs and yelling insults. Gabriella came out on the front stoop and stared them down. "Yes, you are Christians, aren't you?" she told them in her heavily accented English. "Your Christ will be very proud of you tonight."

My bare feet were beginning to freeze inside my shoes. The cold slowly brought me back to myself. I started the car and turned on the heater. When my toes were warm again I drove down to 112th Street and turned west to Avenue L. Louisa's sister Connie lived there with her husband, Mike, and their five children. While I was churning up the South Side I might as well include her.

Connie was five years older than Louisa, but she'd still been living at home when her sister got pregnant. On the South Side you lived with your parents until you got married yourself. In Connie's case, she lived with her parents even after she married while she and her husband saved money for a house of their own. When they finally bought their three-bedroom place she quit her job to become a mother—another South Side tradition.

Compared to her mother, Connie was quite a slattern. A basketball lay on the tiny front lawn, and even my untutored eye could tell that no one had washed the front stoop in recent memory. The glass in the storm door and front windows gleamed without a streak, however, and no fingerprints marred the wood on the frame.

Connie came to the door when I rang the bell. She smiled when she saw me, but nervously, as if her parents had called to warn her I would be stopping by.

"Oh. Oh, it's you, Vic. I—I was just going to the store, actually."

Her long, bony face wasn't suited to lying. The skin, pink and freckled like her niece's, turned crimson as she spoke.

"What a pity," I said dryly. "It's been over ten years since we last saw each other. I was hoping to catch up on the kids and Mike and so on."

She stood with the door open. "Oh. You've been to see Louisa, haven't you? Ma—Ma told me. She's not very well."

"Louisa's in terrible shape. I gather from Caroline there's nothing they can do for her except try to keep her comfortable. I wish someone had told me sooner—I'd have been down months ago."

"I'm sorry—we didn't think—Louisa didn't want to bother you, and Ma didn't want—didn't think—" She broke off, blushing more furiously than ever.

"Your mother didn't want me coming down here and stirring the pot. I understand. But here I am, and I'm doing it anyway, so why don't you put off your trip to the store for five minutes and talk to me."

I pulled the storm door toward me as I spoke and moved closer to her in what I hoped was a nonthreatening, persuasive manner. She backed away uncertainly. I followed her into the house.

"I—uh, would you like a cup of coffee?" She stood twisting her hands like a schoolgirl in front of a hostile teacher, not a woman pushing fifty with a life of her own.

"Coffee would be great," I said bravely, hoping my kidneys could handle another cup.

"The house is really a mess," Connie said apologetically, picking up a pair of gym shoes that stood in the little entryway.

I never say that to visitors—it's obvious that I haven't hung up my clothes or carried out the papers or vacuumed in two weeks. In Connie's case, it was hard to see anything she might be talking about, other than the gym shoes. The floors were scoured, chairs stood at right angles to each other, and not a book or paper marred the shelves or tables as we went through the living room into the back of the house.

I sat at the green Formica table while she filled an electric coffee maker. This small deviation from her mother cheered me slightly: if she could make the switch from boiling water to percolator, who knows how far she might go.

"You and Louisa were never much alike, were you?" I asked abruptly.

She blushed again. "She was always the pretty one. People don't expect so much of you if you're pretty."

The poignant gaucherie of her reply seemed almost unbearable. "What, didn't your mother expect her to help out around the house?"

"Well, she was younger, you know—she didn't have to do as much as I did. But you know Ma. Everything got cleaned every day whether you'd used it or not. When she got mad at us we had to scrub the underside of the sinks and the toilets. I swore my girls would never do any of that kind of thing." Her mouth set in the hard line of remembered grievance.

"It sounds rough," I said, appalled. "Do you feel Louisa left you holding the bag too often?"

She shook her head. "It wasn't really her fault as much as the way they treated her. I can see that now. You know, Louisa could talk back and Pa'd think it was kind of cute. At least when she was little. He wouldn't take it even from her when she got older.

"And Ma's brother liked Louisa to sing and dance for him when he came over. She was so little and pretty, you know, it was like having a doll around. Then when she got older it was too late, of course. Too late to discipline her, I mean."

"Seems like they did a pretty good job," I commented. "Throwing her out of the house and all. That must have been scary for you too."

"Oh, it was." She was rubbing her hands over and over in the towel she'd taken out to wipe up a little spot of water left from filling the coffeepot. "They didn't even tell me what was going on at first."

"You mean you didn't know she was pregnant?" I asked, incredulous.

She turned so red I thought blood might actually start oozing through her skin. "I know you won't understand," she said in a voice that was little more than a whisper. "You led such a different life. You had boyfriends before you got married. I know. Ma—Ma kind of follows your life.

"But when Mike and I were married, I didn't even know—I didn't know —I—the nuns never talked about things like that at school. Ma, of course, she couldn't—couldn't begin to say anything. If Louisa was missing her—her period—she wouldn't have said anything to me. She probably didn't know what it meant, anyway."

Tears spurted from her eyes against her will. Her shoulders shook as she tried controlling her sobbing. She wound the towel so tightly around her hands that the veins in her arms stood out. I got up from my chair to put a hand on one heaving shoulder. She didn't move or say anything, but after a few minutes the spasms calmed down and her breathing grew more normal.

"So Louisa got pregnant because she didn't know what she was doing, or that she might start a baby?"

She nodded mutely, her eyes on the floor.

"Do you know who the father might have been?" I asked gently, keeping my hand on her shoulder.

She shook her head. "Pa—Pa wouldn't let us date. He said he hadn't paid all that money to send us to Catholic school to see—see us chasing after boys. Of course lots of boys liked Louisa, but she—she wouldn't have been going out with any of them."

"Can you remember any of their names?"

She shook her head again. "Not after all this time. I know the boy at the grocery store used to buy her pop when she'd go in. I think his name was Ralph. Ralph Sow-something. Sower or Sowling or something."

She turned to the coffeepot. "Vic, the terrible thing is—I was so jealous of her, at first I was glad to see her in trouble."

"God, Connie, I hope so. If I had a sister who everyone said was prettier than me, and was petted and fussed over while they sent me off to Mass, I'd put an ax through her head instead of waiting for her to get pregnant and be kicked out of the house."

She turned to look up at me, astonished. "But, Vic! You're so—so cool. Nothing ever bothered you. Not even when you were fifteen years old. When your mother died Ma said God gave you a stone instead of a heart, you were so cool." She put her hand over her mouth, mortified, and started to protest.

"Well, I was fucked if I was going to sob in public in front of all those women like your mother, who never had a good word to say about Gabriella," I said, stung. "But you'd better believe I cried plenty in private. And anyway, Connie, that's the whole point. My parents loved me. They thought I could succeed at anything I wanted to do. So even though I lose my temper a hundred times a week or so, it's not like I had to spend my life listening to my folks tell me how my baby sister was wonderful and I was garbage. Loosen up, Connie. Give yourself a break."

She looked at me doubtfully. "Do you really mean it? After what I said and everything?"

I took her shoulders between my hands and turned her to face me. "I really mean it, Connie. Now how about some coffee?"

After that we talked about Mike and his job at the waste-management plant, and young Mike and his football playing, and her three daughters, and her youngest, who was eight and so bright she really thought they'd have to try to get him to go to college, although Mike was nervous, he thought it gave people ideas that they were better than their parents or their neighborhood. The last comment made me grin to myself—I could hear Ed Djiak warning Connie: You don't want the kid turning out like Victoria, do you?—but I listened patiently for forty-five minutes before moving my chair back and getting to my feet.

"It was really good to see you again, Vic. I—I'm glad you came by," she said at the door.

"Thanks, Connie. Take it easy. And say hi to Mike for me."

I walked slowly back to my car. The heel of my left shoe was rubbing on the back of my foot. I savored the pain the way you do when you're feeling like crap. A little pain: the gods letting you expiate the damage you caused.

How had I learned the facts of life? A little in the locker room, a little from Gabriella, a little from our basketball coach, a relaxed, sensible woman except on the court. How could Connie have made it through junior high without one of her friends tipping her off? I pictured her at fourteen, tall, gawky, timid. Maybe she hadn't had any friends.

It was only two o'clock. I felt as though I had spent a whole day loading bales on the levee instead of a few hours drinking coffee with the old folks at home. I felt as though I'd already earned a thousand dollars, and I didn't even know where to start looking. I put the car into gear and headed back to the mainland.

My socks were still damp. They filled the car with the smell of beer and sweat, but when I opened a window the cold air was too much for my bare toes. My irritation rose with my discomfort: I wanted to stop at a service station and call Caroline at SCRAP to tell her the deal was off. Whatever her mother had done a quarter century ago should decently be left to rest there. Unfortunately, I found myself making the turn to Houston Street when I should have been heading north to Lake Shore Drive and freedom.

The block looked worse in daylight than it had at night. Cars were parked at all angles. One was abandoned in the street, black showing around the hood and windshield where a fire had burned the engine block. I left the Chevy in front of a hydrant. If the traffic patrols were as assiduous down here as the street cleaners, I could probably stay until Labor Day without getting a ticket.

I went around to the back, where Louisa always used to leave a spare key on the ledge above the little porch. It was still there. As I let myself in a curtain twitched in the house next door. Within minutes everyone on the block would know a strange woman was going into the Djiaks'.

I heard voices inside the house and called out to let people know I was there. When I got to Louisa's bedroom I realized she had the television on at top volume—what I thought were visitors was only *General Hospital*. I knocked as hard as I could. The volume went down and her scratchy voice called out, "That you, Connie?"

I opened the door. "Me, Louisa. How're you doing?"

Her thin face lighted in a smile. "Well, well, girl. Come right in. Make yourself at home. How's it going?"

I pulled the straight-backed chair next to the bed. "I just went down to see Connie and your folks."

"Did you now?" She looked at me warily. "Ma never was one of your biggest fans. What're you up to, young Warshawski?"

"Spreading joy and truth. Why did your mother hate Gabriella so much, Louisa?"

She shrugged bony shoulders under her cardigan. "Gabriella never went in much for hypocrisy. She didn't keep to herself how she felt about Ma and Pa kicking me out."

"Why did they?" I asked. "Were they mad at you just for getting pregnant, or did they have something special against the boy—the father?"

She didn't say anything for a few minutes, but lay with her eyes on the television. Finally she turned back to me.

"I could kick your ass right out the back door for poking around in this." Her voice was calm. "But I know what happened. I know Caroline and how she always twisted you around her little finger. She called you down here, didn't she—wants to know who her old man was. Spoiled stubborn little bitch. When I blew up at her she called you in. Isn't that right?"

My face was hot with embarrassment, but I said gently, "Don't you think she has a right to know?"

Her mouth set in a tight line. "Twenty-six years ago a goddamn bastard tried to ruin my life. I don't want Caroline anywhere near him. And if you're your ma's daughter, Victoria, you'll do your best to keep Caroline from prying into it instead of helping her out."

Tears smarted in her eyes. "I love that girl. You'd think I was trying to beat her, or kick *her* out on the street instead of protecting her. I did my best to see she got a different shot at life than I did and I'm not watching that go down a sewer now."

"You did a great job, Louisa. But she's grown up now. She doesn't need protecting. Can't you let her make her own decision on this?"

"Goddamn you, no, Victoria! And if you're going to keep on about it, get your ass out of here and don't come back!"

Her face turned red under its greenish sheen and she started coughing. I was batting a thousand with the Djiak women today, getting them furious in descending order of age. All I needed to do was tell Caroline I was quitting and I could make it four for four.

I waited for the paroxysm to subside, then led the conversation gently back to topics Louisa enjoyed, to her young days after Caroline was born. After talking to Connie I could see why Louisa had relished that time as one of freedom and gaiety.

I finally left around four. All during the long drive home through the evening rush hour I listened to Caroline's and Louisa's voices debating in my head. I could understand Louisa's strong wish to protect her privacy. She was dying, too, which gave her desires more weight.

At the same time I could empathize with Caroline's fear of isolation and loneliness. And after seeing the Djiaks close up, I understood why she'd like to find other relatives. Even if her father turned out to be a real jerk, he couldn't have a crazier family than the one she already knew about.

In the end I decided to look for the two men Louisa had talked about last night and this afternoon—Steve Ferraro and Joey Pankowski. They'd worked together at the Xerxes plant, and it was possible she'd gotten the job through her lover. I'd also try to track down the grocery clerk Connie had mentioned —Ron Sowling or whoever. East Side was such a stable, unchanging neighborhood, it was possible that the same people still owned the store and that they would remember Ron and Louisa. If Ed Djiak had come around playing the heavy father, it might have made an indelible memory.

Making a decision, even one to compromise, brings a certain amount of relief. I called up an old friend and spent a pleasant evening on Lincoln Avenue. The blister on my left heel didn't stop my dancing until past midnight.

6

THE MILL ON THE CALUMET

In the morning I was ready early, at least early for me. By nine I had done my exercises. Skipping a run, I dressed for the corporate world in a tailored navy suit that was supposed to make me look imposing and competent. I steeled my heart against Peppy's importunate cries and headed for the South Side for the third day in a row. Instead of following the lake down, this morning I went west to an expressway that would spew me into the heart of the Calumet Industrial District.

It's been over a century since the Army Corps of Engineers and George Pullman decided to turn the sprawling marshes between Lake Calumet and Lake Michigan into an industrial center. It wasn't just Pullman, of course—Andrew Carnegie, Judge Gary, and a host of lesser barons all played a part, working on it for sixty or seventy years. They took an area about four miles square and filled it with dirt, with clay dredged from Lake Calumet, with phenols, oils, ferrous sulfide, and thousands of other substances you not only never heard of, you never want to.

When I got off the expressway at 103rd Street, I had the familiar sensation of landing on the moon, or returning to earth after a nuclear decimation. Life probably exists in the oily mud around Lake Calumet. It's just not anything you'd recognize outside a microscope or a Steven Spielberg movie. You don't see trees or grass or birds. Only the occasional feral dog, ribs protruding, eyes red with madness and hunger.

The Xerxes plant lay in the heart of the ex-swamp, at 110th Street east of Torrence. The building was an old one, put up in the early fifties. From the road I could see their sign, "Xerxes, King of Solvents." The royal purple had faded to an indeterminate pink, while the logo, a crown with double X's in it, had almost disappeared.

Made of concrete blocks, the plant was shaped like a giant U whose arms backed onto the Calumet River. That way the solvents manufactured there could flow easily onto barges and the waste products into the river. They don't dump into the river anymore, of course—when the Clean Water Act was passed Xerxes built giant lagoons to hold their wastes, with clay walls providing a precarious barrier between the river and the toxins.

I parked my car in the gravel yard and gingerly picked my way through the oily ruts to a side entrance. The strong smell, reminiscent of a darkroom, hadn't changed from the times I used to drive down with my dad to drop off Louisa if she'd missed her bus.

I had never been inside the plant. Instead of the crowded noisy cauldron of my imagination, I found myself in an empty hall. It was long and dimly lit, with a concrete floor and cinder-block walls that went the height of the building, making me feel as though I were at the bottom of a mine shaft.

Following the arm of the U in the direction of the river, I came at length to a series of cubbyholes cut into the interior wall. Their walls were made of that grainy glass used for shower doors; I could see light and movement through them but couldn't distinguish shapes. I knocked at the middle door. When no one answered I turned the knob and went in.

I entered a time warp, a long narrow room whose furnishings apparently hadn't changed since the building had gone up thirty-five years ago. Olive-drab filing cabinets and gunmetal desks lined the wall across from the doors. Fluorescent lights hung from an old acoustic-tile ceiling. The outer doors all opened into the room, but two had been blocked shut by filing cabinets.

Four middle-aged women in purple smocks sat at the row of desks. They were working on vast bales of paper with Sisyphus-like doggedness, making entries, shifting invoices, using old-fashioned adding machines with experienced stubby fingers. Two were smoking. The smell of cigarettes mingled with the darkroom chemical scent in acrid harmony.

"Sorry to interrupt," I said. "I was trying to find the personnel office."

The woman nearest the door turned heavy, uninterested eyes to me. "They're not hiring." She went back to her papers.

"I'm not looking for a job," I said patiently. "I just want to talk to the personnel manager."

All four of them looked up at that, weighing my suit, my relative youth, trying to decide if I was OSHA or EPA, state or federal. The woman who'd spoken jerked her faded brown hair toward a door facing the one I'd entered by.

"Across the plant," she said laconically.

"Can I get there from inside or should I go around?"

One of the smokers reluctantly put down her cigarette and got up. "I'll take her," she said hoarsely.

The others looked at the old-fashioned electric clock over their desks. "You going on break then?" a flabby woman in the back asked.

My guide shrugged. "Might as well."

The others looked chagrined: she'd been faster than they to think how to squeeze five extra minutes from the system. One of them pushed her chair back in a hopeful way, but the first speaker said sternly, "One's enough to go," and the would-be rebel scooted back to her station.

My guide took me out the far door. Beyond it lay the inferno I'd been expecting when I first entered the plant. We were in a dimly lit room that stretched the length of the building. Stainless-steel pipes ran along the ceiling and at intervals below, so that you felt suspended in a steel maze that had flipped up on its side. Steam hissed from the overhead pipes in little puffs, filling the maze with vapor. Large red "No Smoking" signs hung every thirty feet along the walls. Enormous cauldrons were hooked to the pipes at intervals, huge vats designed for a coven of giant witches. The white-suited figures tending the place might have been their familiars.

Although the air in here actually smelled better than it did outside, a number of the workers wore respirators. I wondered about the majority who didn't, as well as how smart it was for my guide and me to be taking the shortcut through the plant. I tried asking her over the hissing and clatter of the pipes, but she apparently had decided I must be an OSHA spy or something and refused to answer. When an overhead valve let out a belch so loud that I jumped, she gave a small smile but said nothing.

Skirting the maze expertly, she led me to a door diagonally across the plant from the one we'd entered by. We were in another narrow, cinder-block hallway, this one forming the base of the U. She took me down it, turning left to follow the second arm toward the river. Halfway along, she stopped at a door labeled "Canteen—Employees Only."

"Mr. Joiner's on down there—third door on your right. Door marked 'Administration.' "

"Well, thanks for your help," I said, but she had already disappeared into the canteen.

The door marked "Administration" was also made of grainy glass but the rooms beyond it looked a little classier than the Tartarus where I'd visited the four clerks. Carpeting, not linoleum, covered the concrete floor. Wallboard ceiling and wall covering created an illusion of an intimate space within the cinder-block tunnel.

A woman in street clothes sat behind a desk with a modern phone bank and a not-so-modern electric typewriter. Like the clerks I'd stumbled on, she was middle-aged. But her skin was firm under a generous layer of makeup, and she'd dressed with care, if not style, in a crisp pink shirtwaist with large plastic pearls at her neck and clipped to her ears.

"You need something, honey?" she asked.

"I'd like to see Mr. Joiner. I don't have an appointment, but it shouldn't take more than five minutes." I dug in my handbag for a business card and handed it to her.

She gave a little laugh. "Ooh, honey, don't expect me to pronounce that one."

This wasn't a Loop office where receptionists give you a KGB-style interrogation before grudgingly agreeing to find out if Mr. So-and-so can see you. She picked up a phone and told Mr. Joiner there was a girl out here asking for him. She gave another little laugh and said she didn't know and hung up.

"He's back there," she said brightly, pointing over her shoulder. "Middle door."

Three little offices were carved into the wall behind her, each about eight feet square. The door to the first one was open and I glanced in curiously. No one was there, but an array of papers and a wall covered with production charts showed it was a working office. A little sign next to the open middle door announced it was home to "Gary Joiner, Accounting, Safety, and Personnel." I knocked briefly and went in.

Joiner was a young man, maybe thirty years old, with sandy hair cut so short it merged with his pink skin. He was frowning over a stack of ledger printouts but looked up when I came in. His face was blotchy and he smiled at me with worried, innocent eyes.

"Thanks for taking the time to see me," I said briskly, shaking his hand. I explained who I was. "For personal reasons—nothing to do with Xerxes—I'm trying to find two men who worked here in the early sixties."

I pulled a slip of paper with Joey Pankowski and Steve Ferraro's names on it from my purse and handed it to him. I had a story about why I wanted to find them, something dull about being witnesses to an accident, but I didn't want to volunteer a reason unless he asked for it. Unlike Goebbels's belief in the big lie, I believe in the dull lie—make your story boring enough and no one will question it.

Joiner studied the paper. "I don't think those guys work here. We only employ a hundred and twenty people, so I'd know their names. But I've only been here two years, so if they go back to the sixties. . . ."

He turned to a filing cabinet and riffled through some files. I was struck suddenly by the absence of any computer terminals, either here or elsewhere in the plant. Most personnel or accounting officers would be able to look up employees on a screen.

"Nope. Of course, you can see we barely have room for current files." He swept an arm in an arc that knocked part of the ledger sheets to the floor. He blushed vividly as he bent to pick them up. "If someone leaves or retires or whatever and we don't have activity on them—you know, like an ongoing comp claim—we ship the files out to our warehouse in Stickney. Want me to check for you?"

"That'd be great." I got up. "When can I call back? Monday too soon?"

He assured me Monday would be fine—he lived out west and could stop off at the warehouse on his way home tonight. He conscientiously scribbled a note in his pocket diary, inserting the scrap of paper with the names on it. By the time I left the room he had already returned to his printouts.

7

THE BOYS IN THE BACK ROOM

I'd had enough of the city, of pollution and cramped, painful lives. When I got home I changed into jeans, packed an overnight bag, and took off with the dog to spend the weekend in Michigan. Although the water was too cold and wild for swimming, we spent two invigorating days on the beach, running, chasing sticks, or reading, depending on individual temperament. When I got back to Chicago late Sunday I felt as though my head had been thoroughly aired out. I turned the dog over to a jealous Mr. Contreras and headed upstairs to bed.

I'd told the personnel guy at Xerxes I'd call him in the morning, but when I woke up I decided to go visit him in person. If he had addresses for Pankowski and Ferraro, I could go see them and maybe get the whole mess cleared up in one morning. And if he'd forgotten to stop at the Stickney warehouse, a personal visit would make him more responsive than a phone call.

It had rained overnight, turning Xerxes's gravel yard into an oily mud puddle. I parked as close to the side entrance as I could and picked my way through the sludge. Inside, the cavernous hallway was cold; I was shivering slightly by the time I reached the pebbly glass entrance to the administrative suite.

Joiner wasn't in his office, but the incurious secretary cheerfully directed me to a loading bay where he was managing a shipment. I followed the hall down to the river end of the long building. Heavy steel doors, difficult to open, led to the bay. Beyond lay a world of dirt and clamor.

Sliding steel doors enclosing the loading bay had been rolled open on two sides. At the far end, facing me, the Calumet lapped against the walls, its brackish waters green and roiling from the downpour. A cement barge lay motionless in the turbulent water. A gang of dockhands was removing large barrels from it, rolling them along the concrete floor with a clatter echoed and intensified by the steel walls.

The other door opened on a truck bay. A phalanx of silver tankers was lined up there, looking like menacing cows attached to a high-tech milking machine as they received solvents from an overhead pipe rack. Their diesels vibrated, filling the air with an urgent racket, making it impossible to understand the shouts of the men who were moving around them.

I spied a group in conference around a man with a clipboard. The light was too dim to make out faces but I assumed the man was Joiner and headed toward him. Someone darted from behind a vat and seized my arm.

"Hard-hat area," he bellowed in my ear. "What are you doing here?"

"Gary Joiner!" I bawled back at him. "I need to talk to him."

He escorted me back to the entrance to wait. I watched him go over to the confabbing group and tap one of the figures on the arm. He jerked his head to where I was standing. Joiner stuck his clipboard on a barrel and trotted over to me.

"Oh," he said. "It's you."

"Yeah," I agreed. "I was in the neighborhood and thought I'd stop by instead of phoning. I can tell this is a bad time to talk to you—want me to wait in your office?"

"No, no. I—uh, I couldn't find anything about those men. I don't think they ever worked here."

Even in the dim light I could tell his splotchy skin was flushing.

"I bet that warehouse is a mess," I said sympathetically. "No one has time to look after records when you're running a manufacturing plant."

"Yes," he agreed eagerly. "Yes, that's for sure."

"I'm a trained investigator. If you gave me some kind of authorization, I could have a look through there. You know, see if their records were misplaced or something."

He flickered his eyes nervously around the room. "No. No. Things aren't that big a mess. The guys never worked here. I gotta go now."

He hurried away before I could say anything else. I started after him, but even if I could get past the foreman, I couldn't think of a way to get Joiner to tell me the truth. I didn't know him, didn't know the plant, didn't have a clue as to why he would lie to me.

I walked slowly back down the long hall to my car, absentmindedly stepping in an oozy patch that plastered sludge firmly to my right shoe. I cursed loudly—I'd paid over a hundred dollars for those pumps. As I sat in the car trying to scrape it clean, I got oily sludge on my skirt. Feeling outraged with the world, I threw the shoe petulantly into the backseat and changed back into my running gear. Even though Caroline hadn't sent me to the plant, I blamed my problems on her.

As I drove up Torrence, passing rusted-out factories that looked dingier than ever from the rain, I wondered if Louisa had called Joiner, asking him not to help me if I turned up. I didn't think her mind worked that way, though: she'd told me to mind my own business, and as far as she was concerned, I was doing just that. Maybe the Djiaks had fumed self-righteously to Xerxes, but I thought they were too myopic to analyze how I might conduct an investigation. They could only see how Louisa had hurt them.

On the other hand, if Joiner didn't want to talk to me about the men because of some problem the company was having with them—say a lawsuit

—he would have known when I came in on Friday. But the first time I spoke to him he'd obviously never heard of them.

I couldn't figure it out, but the thought of lawsuits made me realize another place to look for the men. Neither Pankowski nor Ferraro was in the phone book, but the old ward voter registration records might still be around. I turned right on Ninety-fifth Street and headed into East Side.

The ward offices were still in the tidy brick two-flat on Avenue M. A variety of errands may take you to your committeeman's office, from help with parking tickets to ways of getting on the city payroll. The local cops are in and out a lot what with one thing and another, and even though my dad's beat had been North Milwaukee Avenue, I'd come here with him more than once. The sign proclaiming Art Jurshak alderman and Freddy Parma ward committeeman, which covered all of the building's exposed north wall, hadn't changed. And the storefront next door still housed the insurance agency that had given Art his toehold in the community.

I knocked most of the sludge from my right shoe and put my pumps back on. Brushing my skirt as best I could with a Kleenex, I went into the building. I didn't recognize any of the men lounging in the first-floor office, but judging from their age and their air of being as one with the furnishings, I thought they probably went back to my childhood.

There were three of them. One, a graying man smoking the fat little cigar that used to be a Democratic pol's badge of office, was huddled in the sports pages. The other two, one bald-headed, the other with a white Tip O'Neill-style mop, were talking earnestly. Despite their differing hairdos, they looked remarkably alike, their shaved faces red and jowly, their forty extra pounds hanging casually over the belts of their shiny pants.

They glanced sidelong at me when I came in but didn't say anything: I was a woman and a stranger. If I was from the mayor's office, it would do me good to cool my heels. If I was anyone else, I couldn't do anything for them.

The two speakers were going over the rival merits of their pickup trucks, Chevy versus Ford. No one down here buys foreign—bad form with three quarters of the steel industry unemployed.

"Hi," I said loudly.

They looked up reluctantly. The newspaper reader didn't stir, but I saw him move the pages expectantly.

I pulled up a rollaway chair. "I'm a lawyer," I said, taking a business card from my purse. "I'm looking for two men who used to live down here, maybe twenty years ago."

"You oughta try the police, cookie—this isn't the lost-and-found," the bald-headed one said.

The newspaper rattled appreciatively.

I slapped my forehead. "Damn! You're so right. When I lived down here Art used to like to help out the community. Shows you how times have changed, I guess."

"Yeah, ain't nothing like it used to be." Baldy seemed to be the designated spokesman.

"Except the money it takes to run a campaign," I said mournfully. "That's still pretty expensive, what I hear."

Baldy and Whitey exchanged wary glances: Was I trying to do the honorable thing and slip them a little cash, or was I part of the latest round of federal entrapment artists hoping to catch Jurshak putting the squeeze on the citizenry? Whitey nodded fractionally.

Baldy spoke. "Why you looking for these guys?"

I shrugged. "The usual. Old car accident they were in in '80. Finally settled. It's not a lot of money, twenty-five hundred each is all. Not worth a lot of effort to hunt them down, and if they're retired, they've got pensions anyway."

I stood up, but I could see the little calculators moving in their brains; the newspaper reader had let Michael Jordan's exploits drop to his knees to join in the telepathic exercise. If they arranged a meeting, how much could they reasonably skim? Make it six hundred and that'd be two apiece.

The other two nodded and Baldy spoke again. "What did you say their names were?"

"I didn't. And you're probably right—I should have taken this to the cops to begin with." I started slowly for the door.

"Hey, just a minute, sister. Can't you take a little kidding?"

I turned around and looked uncertain. "Well, if you're sure . . . It's Joey Pankowski and Steve Ferraro."

Whitey got up and ambled over to a row of filing cabinets. He asked me to spell the names, letter by painful letter. Moving his lips as he read the names on old voter registration forms, he finally brightened.

"Here we are—1985 was the last year Pankowski was registered, '83 for Ferraro. Why don't you bring their drafts in here? We can get them cashed through Art's agency and see that the boys get their money. We should get 'em to reregister and it'd save you another trip down here."

"Gee, thanks," I said earnestly. "Trouble is, I have to get them to personally sign a release." I thought for a minute and smiled. "Tell you what—give me their addresses and I'll go see them this afternoon, make sure they still live down here. Then next month when the claim drafts are issued I can just mail them both to you here."

They thought it over slowly. They finally agreed, again silently, that there was nothing wrong with the idea. Whitey wrote Pankowski's and Ferraro's addresses down in a large, round hand. I thanked him graciously and headed for the door again.

Just as I was opening it a young man came in, hesitantly, as if unsure of his welcome. He had curly auburn hair and wore a navy wool suit that enhanced the staggering beauty of his pale face. I couldn't remember ever seeing a man with such perfect good looks—he might have posed for

Michelangelo's *David*. When he gave a diffident smile it made him look vaguely familiar.

"Hiya, Art," Baldy said. "Your old man's downtown."

Young Art Jurshak. Big Art had never looked this good, but the smile must have made the kid resemble his old man's campaign posters.

He flushed. "That's okay. I just wanted to look at some ward files. You don't mind, do you?"

Baldy hunched an impatient shoulder. "You're a partner in the old man's firm. You do what you want, Art. Think I'm going for a bite, anyway. Coming, Fred?"

The white-haired man and the newspaper reader both got up. Food sounded like a swell idea to me. Even a detective looking at a meager fee has to eat some of the time. The four of us left young Art alone in the middle of the room.

Fratesi's Restaurant was still where I remembered it, on the corner of Ninety-seventh and Ewing. Gabriella had disapproved of them because they cooked southern Italian instead of her familiar dishes of the Piedmont, but the food was good and it used to be a place to go for special occasions.

Today there wasn't much of a lunchtime crowd. The decorations around the fountain in the middle of the floor, which used to enchant me as a child, had been allowed to decay. I recognized old Mrs. Fratesi behind the counter, but felt the place had grown too sad for me to identify myself to her. I ate a salad made of iceberg lettuce and an old tomato and a frittata that was surprisingly light and carefully seasoned.

In the little ladies' room at the back I got the most noticeable chunks of dirt off my skirt. I didn't look fabulous, but maybe that suited the neighborhood better. I paid the tab, a modest four dollars, and left. I didn't know you could get bread and butter in Chicago for under four dollars anymore.

All during lunch I'd turned over various approaches to Pankowski and Ferraro in my mind. If they were married, wives at home, children, they wouldn't want to hear about Louisa Djiak. Or maybe they would. Maybe it would bring back the happy days of yore. I finally decided I'd have to play it by ear.

Steve Ferraro's home was nearer to the restaurant, so I went there first. It was another of the endless array of East Side bungalows, but a little seedier than most of its neighbors. The porch hadn't been swept recently, my critical housekeeping eye noted, and the glass on the storm door could have done with a washing.

A long interval passed after I rang the bell. I pushed it again and was about to leave when I heard the inner door being unlocked. An old woman stood there, short, wispy-haired, and menacing.

"Yes," she said in one harsh, heavily accented syllable.

"Scusi," I said. *"Cerco il signor Ferraro."*

Her face lightened marginally and she answered in Italian. What did I want him for? An old lawsuit that might finally be going to pay out? To him only, or to his heirs?

"To him only," I said firmly in Italian, but my heart sank. Her next words confirmed my misgivings: *il signor Ferraro* was her son, her only child, and he had died in 1984. No, he had never married. He had talked once about a girl in the place where he worked, but *madre de dio*, the girl already had a baby; she was relieved when nothing came of it.

I gave her my card, with a request to call me if she thought of anything else, and set out for Green Bay Avenue without any high expectations.

Again a woman answered the door, a younger one this time, perhaps even my age, but too heavy and worn out for me to be certain. She gave me the cold fish eye reserved for life insurance salesmen and Jehovah's Witnesses and prepared to shut the door on me.

"I'm a lawyer," I said quickly. "I'm looking for Joey Pankowski."

"Some lawyer," she said contemptuously. "You'd better ask in Queen of Angels Cemetery—that's where he's spent the last two years. At least, that's his story. Knowing that bastard, he probably pretended to die so he could go off with his latest little chickadee."

I blinked a little under her fire. "I'm sorry, Mrs. Pankowski. It's an old case that's been settled rather slowly. A matter of some twenty-five hundred dollars, not really worth bothering you about."

Her blue eyes almost disappeared into her cheeks. "Not so fast, lady. You got twenty-five hundred, I deserve that money. I suffered enough with that bastard, God knows. And then when he died there wasn't even any insurance."

"I don't know," I said fussily. "His oldest child—"

"Little Joey," she said promptly. "Born August 1963. In the Army now. I could hold it for him till he gets home next January."

"I was told there was another child. A girl born in 1962. Know anything about her?"

"That bastard!" she screamed. "That lying, cheating bastard. He screwed me when he was alive and now he's dead he's screwing me still!"

"So you know about the girl?" I asked, startled at the thought that my search might be over so easily.

She shook her head. "I know Joey, though. He could of had a dozen kids before he got me pregnant with little Joey. If this girl thinks she's the first, all I can say is you better run an ad in the *Little Calumet Times.*"

I took a twenty from my purse and held it casually. "We could probably advance something from the settlement. Do you know anyone who could tell me for certain if he had any children before little Joey? A brother, maybe? Or his priest?"

"Priest?" she cackled. "I had to pay extra just to get his bones into Queen of Angels."

She was thinking hard, though, trying not to look directly at the money. At last she said, "You know who might know? Doc at the plant. He talked to them every spring, took their blood, their histories. Knew more about them than God, Joey once said."

She couldn't tell me his name; if Joey ever mentioned it, she couldn't be expected to remember it after all this time, could she? But she took the money with dignity and told me to come back if I was in the neighborhood.

"I don't expect to see any more of it," she added with unexpected cheerfulness. "Not from what I know of that bastard. If my old man hadn't made him, he wouldn't of married me. And between you and me, I'd of been better off."

8
THE GOOD DOCTOR

Louisa and Caroline were returning from the dialysis center when I stopped by. I helped Caroline maneuver Louisa into a wheelchair for the short ride up the front walk. Getting her up the five steep steps took ten minutes of patient labor while she leaned heavily on my shoulder to hoist herself up each rise, then rested until she had enough wind for the next one.

By the time we had her settled in her bed, her breathing had turned to shallow, stertorous gasps. I panicked a little at the sound and at the purplish tinge beneath her waxy green skin, but Caroline treated her with cheerful efficiency, giving her oxygen and massaging her bony shoulders until she could breathe on her own again. However much Caroline might irritate me, I could only admire her unflagging goodwill in looking after her mother.

She left me alone with Louisa while she went off to make herself a snack. Louisa was drifting into sleep, but she remembered the Xerxes doctor with a hoarse little chuckle: Chigwell. They called him Chigwell the Chigger because he was always sucking their blood. I waited until she was sleeping soundly before releasing my hand from the grasp of her bony fingers.

Caroline was hovering in the dining room, her little body vibrating with anxiety. "I've wanted to call you every day, but I've forced myself not to. Especially last week when Ma told me you'd been by and she'd ordered you not to look for him." She was eating a peanut-butter sandwich and the words came through thickly. "Have you found out anything?"

I shook my head. "I tracked down the two guys she remembers best, but they're both dead. It's possible one of them might have been your father, but I don't have any real way of knowing. My only hope is the company doctor. He apparently used to compile copious records on the employees, and people tell their doctor things they might not say to anyone else. There's also a clerk who worked at the corner grocery twenty-five years ago, but Connie couldn't remember his name."

She caught my doubtful tone. "You don't think any of these guys might have been the one?"

I pursed my lips, trying to put my doubts into words. Steve Ferraro had wanted to marry Louisa, baby and all. That sounded as though he knew her after Caroline's birth, not before. Joey Pankowski did seem like the kind of person who could have gotten Louisa pregnant and gone off unconcerned. Which would fit. That repressive household, Connie's and her total ignorance of sex—she might well have turned to some happy-go-lucky type. But in that case why be so upset about it now? Unless she'd absorbed so much of the Djiak's fundamental fear of sex that the very memory of it terrified her. But that didn't fit my memories of Louisa as a young woman.

"I don't know," I finally said helplessly. "It just has the wrong kind of feel to it."

I debated with myself a minute, then added, "I think you need to prepare yourself for failure. My failure, I mean. If I can't learn anything from the doctor or track down this clerk, I'm going to have to throw it in."

She scowled fiercely. "I'm *counting* on you, Vic."

"Let's not play that record again right now, Caroline. I'm beat. I'll call you in a day or two and we'll take it from there."

It was almost four, time for the evening rush hour to congeal the traffic. It was close to five-thirty before I'd oozed the twenty-some miles home. When I got there Mr. Contreras stopped me to ask about the burrs I'd allowed the sacred dog to collect in her golden tail. The dog herself came out and expressed herself ready for a run. I listened to both with such patience as I could muster, but after five minutes of his nonstop flow I left abruptly in mid-sentence and headed for my place on the third floor.

I took off my suit and left it on the entryway floor where I'd be sure to remember it for the cleaners in the morning. I didn't know what to do about the shoe, so I left it with the suit—maybe the cleaners would know a place that could resurrect it.

While I ran a bath I pulled my stack of city and suburban directories from the floor under the piano. No Chigwell was listed in the metropolitan area. Naturally. He'd probably died himself. Or retired to Majorca.

I poured an inch of whiskey and stomped into the bathroom. While lying half submerged in the old-fashioned tub, it occurred to me that he might be in the medical directories. I hoisted myself out of the tub and went into the bedroom to call Lotty Herschel. She was just getting ready to leave the clinic she runs near the corner of Irving Park and Damen.

"Can't it wait until the morning, Victoria?"

"Yeah, it can wait. I just want to get this monster out of my life as fast as possible." I sketched Caroline and Louisa's story as quickly as I could. "If I can run this Chigwell down, I only have one other lead I need to look into and then I can get back to the real world."

"Wherever that is," she said dryly. "You don't know this man's first name or his speciality, do you? Of course not. Industrial medicine probably, hmm?"

I could hear her rustling through the pages of a book. "Chan, Chessick, Childress. No Chigwell. I don't have a complete directory, though. Max probably does—why don't you give him a call? And why do you let this Caroline run you through hoops? You are manipulated by people only when you allow yourself to be, my dear."

On that cheering note she hung up. I tried Max Loewenthal, who was executive director of Beth Israel Hospital, but he had gone home for the day. As any rational person would have. Only Lotty stayed at her clinic until six, and of course a detective's work is never done. Even if you're only willingly responding to the manipulations of an old neighbor.

I poured the rest of the whiskey down the sink and changed into my sweats. When I'm in a febrile mood the best thing to do is exercise. I picked up Peppy from Mr. Contreras—neither he nor the dog was capable of harboring a grievance. By the time Peppy and I returned home, panting, I'd run the discontent out of my system. The old man fried some pork chops for me and we sat drinking his foul grappa and talking until eleven.

I reached Max easily in the morning. He listened with his usual courteous urbanity to my saga, put me on hold for five minutes, and came back with the news that Chigwell was retired but living in suburban Hinsdale. Max even had his address and his first name, which was Curtis.

"He's seventy-nine, V.I. If he doesn't talk willingly, go easy on him," he finished, only half joking.

"Thanks a whole bunch, Max. I'll try to restrain my more animal impulses, but old men and children generally bring out the worst in me."

He laughed and hung up.

Hinsdale is an old town about twenty miles west of the Loop whose tall oaks and gracious homes were gradually being accreted by urban sprawl. It's not Chicagoland's trendiest address, but there's an aura of established self-assurance about the place. Hoping to fit into its genteel atmosphere, I put on a black dress with a full skirt and gold buttons. A leather portfolio completed the ensemble. I looked at my navy suit on the entryway floor as I left, but decided it would keep another day.

When you go from the city to the north or west suburbs, the first thing you notice is the quiet cleanness. After a day in South Chicago I felt I'd stepped into paradise. Even though the trees were barren of leaves and the grass matted and brown, everything was raked and tidied for spring. I had total faith that the brown mats would turn to green, but couldn't imagine what it would take to create life in the sludge around the Xerxes plant.

Chigwell lived on an older street near the center of town. The house was a two-story, neo-Georgian structure whose wood siding gleamed white in the dull day. Its well-kept yellow shutters and a sprinkling of old trees and bushes created an air of stately harmony. A screened porch faced the street. I followed flagstones through the shrubs around the side to the entrance and rang the bell.

After a few minutes the door opened. That's the second thing you notice in the burbs—when you ring the bell people open the doors, they don't peer through peepholes and undo bolts.

An old woman in a severe navy dress stood frowning in the doorway. The scowl seemed to be a habitual expression, not aimed at me personally. I gave a brisk, no-nonsense smile.

"Mrs. Chigwell?"

"*Miss* Chigwell. Do I know you?"

"No, ma'am. I'm a professional investigator and I'd like to speak with Dr. Chigwell."

"He didn't tell me he was expecting anyone."

"Well, ma'am, we like to make our inquiries unannounced. If people have too much time to think about them, their answers often seem forced."

I took a card from my bag and handed it to her, moving forward a few steps. "V. I. Warshawski. Financial investigative services. Just tell the doctor I'm here. I won't keep him more than half an hour."

She didn't invite me in, but grudgingly took the card and moved off into the interior of the house. I looked around at the blank-windowed houses next door and across the street. The third thing you notice in the suburbs is, you might as well be on the moon. In a city or small-town neighborhood, curtains would flutter as the neighbors tried to see what strange woman was visiting the Chigwells. Then telephone calls or exchanges in the Laundromat. Yes, their niece. You know, the one whose mother moved to Arizona all those years ago. Here, not a curtain stirred. No shrill voices betokened preschoolers recreating war and peace. I had an uneasy feeling that with all its noise and grime, I preferred city life.

Miss Chigwell rematerialized in the doorway. "Dr. Chigwell has gone out."

"That's very sudden, isn't it? When do you expect him back?"

"I—he didn't say. It will be a long while."

"Then I'll wait a long while," I said peaceably. "Would you like to invite me inside, or would you prefer me to wait in my car?"

"You should leave," she said, her frown deepening. "He doesn't want to talk to you."

"How can you know that, ma'am? If he's away, you haven't spoken to him about me."

"I know who my brother does and does not wish to see. And he would have told me if he wanted to see you." She shut the door as forcefully as she could, given both their ages and the thick carpeting underneath.

I returned to my car and moved it to where it was clearly visible from the front door. WNIV was playing a cycle of Hugo Wolf songs. I leaned back in the seat, my eyes half closed, listening to Kathleen Battle's golden voice, wondering what there was about talking to an investigator that would fluster Curtis Chigwell.

In the half hour I waited I saw one person go down the street. I began feeling as though I were on a movie set, not part of a human community at all, when Miss Chigwell appeared on the flagstone walk. She moved determinedly to the car, her thin body as rigid as an umbrella frame, and as bony. I courteously got out.

"I must ask you to leave, young woman."

I shook my head. "Public property, ma'am. There's no law against my being here. I'm not playing loud music or selling dope or doing anything else that the law might construe as a nuisance."

"If you don't drive away now, I'm going to call the police as soon as I'm back inside."

I admired her courage: to be seventy-something and confront a young stranger takes a lot of guts. I could see the fear mingling with the determination in her pale eyes.

"I'm an officer of the court, ma'am. I would be happy to explain to the police why I want to speak to your—brother, is it?"

That was only partially true. Any licensed attorney is an officer of the court, but I much prefer never talking to the police, especially suburban cops, who hate urban detectives on principle. Fortunately, Miss Chigwell, impressed (I hoped) by my professional demeanor, didn't demand a badge or a certificate. She compressed her lips until they almost disappeared into her angular face and went back to the house.

I had barely settled back in my car when she returned to the walk and beckoned me vigorously. When I joined her at the side of the house she said abruptly:

"He'll see you. He was here all along, of course. I don't like telling his lies for him, but after all these years it's hard to start saying no. He's my brother. My twin, so I got into too many bad habits too long ago. But you don't want to hear all that."

My admiration for her increased, but I didn't know how to express it without sounding patronizing. I followed her silently into the house. We went through a passageway that looked onto the garage. A dinghy was leaned neatly on its side next to the open door. Beyond it was a tidy array of gardening tools.

Ms. Chigwell whisked me along to the living room. It was not large, but gracefully proportioned, with chintz furniture facing a rose-marble fireplace. While she went for her brother I prowled around a bit.

A handsome old clock stood in the center of the mantel, the kind that has an enamel face and brass pendulum. On either side of it were porcelain figures, shepherd girls, lute players. A few old family photos stood in the recessed shelves in the corner, one showing a little girl in a starched sailor dress standing proudly with her father in front of a sailboat.

When Ms. Chigwell returned with her brother, it was obvious they'd been arguing. His cheeks, softer than her angular face, were flushed and his lips were compressed. She started to introduce me, but he cut her off sharply.

"I don't need you to oversee my affairs, Clio. I'm perfectly able to look after myself."

"I'd like to see you do so, then," she said bitterly. "If you're in some kind of trouble with the law, I want to hear what it is now, not next month or whenever you feel brave enough to tell me about it."

"I'm sorry," I said. "I seem to have caused a problem, most inadvertently. There's no trouble with the law that I know of, Miss Chigwell. Merely, I need some information on some people who used to work at the Xerxes plant in South Chicago."

I turned to her brother. "My name is V. I. Warshawski, Dr. Chigwell. I'm a lawyer and a private investigator. And I've been retained as the result of a lawsuit whose settlement leaves some money to the estate of Joey Pankowski."

When he ignored my outstretched hand I looked around and chose a comfortable armchair to sit in. Dr. Chigwell remained standing. In his ramrod posture he resembled his sister.

"Joey Pankowski used to work at the Xerxes plant," I continued, "but he died in 1985. Now there's some question that Louisa Djiak, who also worked there, has a child whose father he may have been. That child is also entitled to a share of the settlement, but Ms. Djiak is very ill and her mind wanders—we can't get a clear answer from her as to who the father is."

"I can't help you, young lady. I have no recollection of any of these names."

"Well, I understand you took blood and medical histories from all the employees every spring for a number of years. If you would just go back and look at your records, you might find that—"

He cut me off with a violence that surprised me. "I don't know who you've been talking to, but that's an absolute lie. I won't stand to be harassed and harangued in my own house. Now you get out right now, or I'll call the police. And if you're an officer of the court, you can explain that to them in jail." He turned without waiting for a reply and marched from the room.

Clio Chigwell watched him leave, her scowl deeper than ever. "You'll have to go."

"He did the tests," I said. "Why is he so upset?"

"I don't know anything about it. But you can't ask him to violate his patients' confidentiality. Now you'd better leave, unless you do want to speak with the police."

I got up as nonchalantly as I could under the circumstances. "You have my card," I said to her at the door. "If something occurs to you, give me a call."

9

LIFESTYLES OF THE RICH AND FAMOUS

A light drizzle had started to fall. I sat in the car staring at the windshield, watching the rain break up on the greasy glass. After a while I turned on the engine, hoping to coax a little heat from the noisy motor.

Was it the Pankowski name that had rattled Chigwell so? Or was it me? Had Joiner phoned him telling him to beware Polish detectives and the questions they bring? No, that couldn't be right. If that was the case, Chigwell would never have agreed to see me at all. And anyway, Joiner wouldn't know Chigwell. The doctor was almost eighty; he must have been long retired when Joiner started at the plant two years ago. So it had to have been the mention either of Pankowski or Louisa. But why?

I wondered with growing uneasiness what Caroline knew that she hadn't bothered to tell me. I remembered in vivid detail the winter she had asked me to fight an eviction notice served on Louisa. After a week of running between courts and landlord, I saw an article in the *Sun-Times* on "Teens Who Make a Difference." It featured a glowing sixteen-year-old Caroline and the soup kitchen she'd used the rent money to set up. That was the last cry for help I'd answered from her for ten years, and I was beginning to think I should have let it go for twenty.

I fished around on the backseat for a Kleenex and found a towel I'd used at the beach last summer. After wiping a peephole in the windshield I finally put the car into gear and headed for the expressway. I was torn between calling Caroline to tell her the deal was off and the elephant child's 'satiable curiosity to find out what had rattled Chigwell so badly.

In the end I did nothing. When I had fought my way through the noon-time Loop traffic to my office, messages from several clients awaited me—inquiries I'd let slide while I mucked around in Caroline's problem. One was from an old customer who wanted help with computer security. I referred him to a friend of mine who's a computer expert and tackled the other two. These were routine financial investigations, my bread and butter. It felt good to work on something where I could identify both problem and solution, and I spent the afternoon burrowing through files in the State of Illinois Building.

I returned to my office around seven to type the reports. They were worth five hundred dollars to me; since both clients paid promptly, I wanted to get the invoices into the mail.

I was rattling along on my old standard Olympia when the phone rang. I looked at my watch. Almost eight. Wrong number. Caroline. Maybe Lotty. I picked up the phone on the third ring, right before the answering service kicked in.

"Ms. Warshawski?" It was an old man's voice, fragile and quavering.

"Yes," I said.

"I want to speak to Ms. Warshawski, please." For all its quavering, the voice was confident, used to managing people on the phone.

"Speaking," I said as patiently as I could. I had missed lunch and was dreaming of a steak and whiskey.

"Mr. Gustav Humboldt would like to see you. When would it be convenient to schedule an appointment?"

"Can you tell me what he wants to see me about?" I backspaced and used white-out to cover a typo. It's getting harder to find correction fluid and typewriter ribbons in these days of word processors, so I capped the bottle carefully to save it.

"I understand it's a confidential matter, miss. If you're free this evening, he could see you now. Or tomorrow afternoon at three."

"Just a minute while I check my schedule." I put the phone down and got *Who's Who in Chicago Commerce* from the top of my filing cabinet. Gustav Humboldt's listing covered a column and a half of six-point type. Born in Bremerhaven in 1904. Emigrated in 1930. Chairman and chief stockholder of Humboldt Chemical, founded in 1937, with plants in forty countries, 1986 sales of $8 billion, assets of $10 billion, director of this, member of that. Headquarters in Chicago. Of course. I'd passed the Humboldt Building a million times walking down Madison Street, an old no-nonsense structure without the attention-getting lobbies of the modern giants.

I picked up the phone. "I could make it around nine-thirty tonight," I offered.

"That will be fine, Ms. Warshawski. The address is the Roanoke Building, twelfth floor. I'll tell the doorman to look out for your car."

The Roanoke was an old dowager on Oak Street, one of six or seven buildings bordering the strip between the lake and Michigan Avenue. All had gone up in the early decades of this century, providing housing for the McCormicks and Swifts and other riffraff. Nowadays if you had a million dollars to invest in housing and were related to the British royal family, they might let you in after a year or two of intensive checking.

I set a speed record for two-finger typing and got reports and invoices into their envelopes by eight-thirty. I'd have to forgo whiskey and steak—I didn't want to be logy for an encounter with someone who could set me up for life—but there was time for soup and a salad at the little Italian restaurant up Wabash from my office. Especially if I didn't have to worry about parking at the other end.

In the restaurant bathroom I saw that my hair was frizzing around my head from this morning's drizzle, but at least the black dress still looked tidy and professional. I put on a little light makeup and retrieved my car from the underground garage.

It was just nine-thirty when I pulled into the semicircle under the Roanoke's green awning. The doorman, resplendent in matching green livery, bent his head courteously while I gave him my name.

"Ah, yes, Ms. Warshawski." His voice was fruity, his tone avuncular. "Mr. Humboldt is expecting you. If you'll just give me your keys?"

He led me into the lobby. Most modern buildings going up for the rich these days feature glass and chrome lobbies with monstrous plants and hangings, but the Roanoke had been built when labor was cheaper and more skillful. The floor was an intricate mosaic of geometric shapes and the wood-paneled walls were festooned with Egyptian figurines.

An old man, also in green livery, was sitting on a chair next to some wooden double doors. He got up when the doorman and I came in.

"Young lady for Mr. Humboldt, Fred. I'll let them know she's here if you'll take her on up."

Fred unlocked the door—no remote-control clicks here—and took me to the elevator at a stately tread. I followed him into a roomy cage with a floral carpet on the floor and a plush-upholstered bench against the back wall. I sat casually on the bench, crossing my legs, as though personal elevator service were an everyday occurrence with me.

The elevator opened onto what might have been the foyer of a mansion. Gray-white marble tiles showing streaks of pink were covered here and there by throw rugs that had probably been made in Persia when the Ayatollah's grandfather was a baby. The hall seemed to form an atrium, with the elevator at its center, but before I could tiptoe down to a marble statue in the left corner to explore, the carved wooden door in front of me opened.

An old man stood there in morning dress. His scalp showed pink through wisps of fine white hair. He inclined his head briefly, a token bow, but his blue eyes were frosty and remote. Rising to the solemnity of the occasion, I fished in my bag and handed him a card without speaking.

"Very good, miss. Mr. Humboldt will see you now. If you'll follow me. . . ."

He walked slowly, either from age or from some concept of a butler's proper gait, giving me time to gawk in what I trusted was a discreet fashion. About halfway along the length of the building he opened a door on the left and held it for me to enter. Looking at the books lining three walls and the opulent red-leather furniture in front of a fireplace in the fourth, my keen intuition told me we were in the library. A florid man, heavy without being corpulent, sat in front of the fire with a newspaper. As the door opened he put the paper down and got to his feet.

"Ms. Warshawski. How good of you to come on such short notice." He held out a firm hand.

"Not at all, Mr. Humboldt."

He motioned me to a leather armchair on the other side of the fire from him. I knew from the *Who's Who* entry that he was eighty-four, but he could have said sixty without anyone raising an eyebrow. His thick hair still showed a touch of pale yellow, and his blue eyes were sharp and clear in a face almost free of wrinkles.

"Anton, bring us some cognac—you drink cognac, Ms. Warshawski?— and then we'll be fine on our own."

The butler disappeared for perhaps two minutes, during which my host courteously made sure the fire wasn't too hot for me. Anton returned with a decanter and snifters, poured, carefully placed the decanter in the center of a small table at Humboldt's right hand, fiddled with the fire tongs. I realized he was as curious as I about what Humboldt wanted and was trying to think of ways to linger, but Humboldt dismissed him briskly.

"Ms. Warshawski, I have an awkward matter to discuss, and I beg your indulgence if I don't do so with maximum grace. I'm an industrialist, after all, an engineer more at home with chemicals than beautiful young women." He had come to America as a grown man; even after close to sixty years a mild accent remained.

I smiled sardonically. When the owner of a ten-billion-dollar empire starts apologizing for his style, it's time to hold tightly to your purse and count all your fingers.

"I'm sure you underestimate yourself, sir."

He gave me a quick, sidelong glance and decided that warranted a barking laugh. "I see you are a careful woman, Ms. Warshawski."

I sipped the cognac. It was staggeringly smooth. Please let him call me for frequent consultations, I begged the golden liquid. "I can be reckless when I have to, Mr. Humboldt."

"Good. That's very good. So you're a private investigator. And do you find it a job that allows you to be both careful and reckless?"

"I like being my own boss. And I don't have the desire to do it on the scale you've achieved."

"Your clients speak very highly of you. I was talking to Gordon Firth just today and he mentioned how grateful the Ajax board was for your efforts there."

"I'm delighted to hear it," I said, sinking back in the chair and sipping some more.

"Gordon does a lot of my insurance, of course."

Of course. Gustav calls Gordon and tells him he needs a thousand tons of insurance and Gordon says sure and thirty young men and women work eighty-hour weeks for a month putting it all together and then the two shake hands genially at the Standard Club and thank each other for their trouble.

"So I thought I might be able to help you out with one of your inquiries.

After listening to Gordon's glowing report I knew you were intelligent and discreet and not likely to abuse information given you in confidence."

With enormous effort I kept myself from bolting up in the chair and spilling cognac all over my skirt. "It's hard for me to imagine where our spheres of activity intersect, sir. By the way, this is most excellent cognac. It's like drinking a fine single malt."

At that Humboldt roared with genuine laughter. "Beautiful, my dear Ms. Warshawski. Beautiful. To take my news so calmly and then praise my liquor with the most subtle of insults! I wish I could persuade you to cease being your own boss."

I smiled and put the snifter down. "I love compliments as much as the next person, and it's been a tough day—I can use them. But I'm beginning to wonder who is meant to be helping whom. Not that it wouldn't be a privilege to be of service to you."

He nodded. "I think we can be of service to each other. You asked where our spheres of activity intersect—a fine expression. And the answer lies in South Chicago."

I thought for a minute. Of course. I should have known. Xerxes had to be part of Humboldt Chemical. It was just being so used to thinking of it as part of my childhood's landscape that I hadn't made the connection when Anton phoned.

I casually mentioned it and Humboldt nodded again. "Very good, Ms. Warshawski. The chemical industry made a great contribution to the war effort. The Second World War I'm talking about, of course. And the war effort in turn prompted research and development on a grand scale. Many of the products that all of us—I mean Dow, Ciba, Imperial Chemical, all of us —make our bread and butter on today can be traced to research we did then. Xerxine was one of Humboldt's great discoveries, one of the 1, 2 dichlorethanes. The last one I was able to devote time to myself."

He stopped himself with a turned-up hand. "You're not a chemist. That won't be of interest to you. But we called the product Xerxes, because of the Xerxine, of course, and opened the South Chicago plant in 1949. My wife was an artist. She designed the logo, the crown on the purple background."

He stopped to offer me the decanter. I didn't want to appear greedy. On the other hand, to refuse might have seemed rude.

"Well, that South Chicago plant was the start of Humboldt's international expansion, and it's always meant a great deal to me. So even though I no longer concern myself with the day-to-day running of the company—I have grandchildren, Ms. Warshawski, and an old man fancies himself reliving his youth with young children. But my people know I care about that plant. So when a beautiful young detective begins poking around, asking questions, they naturally tell me."

I shook my head. "I'm sorry if they needlessly alarmed you, sir. I'm not poking around in the plant. Merely trying to trace some men as part of a personal inquiry. For some reason your Mr. Joiner—the personnel manager —wanted me to believe they never worked for you."

"So you found Dr. Chigwell." His deep voice had sunk to a rumbling murmur, difficult to make out.

"Who was even more electrified by my questions than young Joiner. I couldn't help wondering if he had a personal agenda of his own. Some transactions of his youth that weigh on his old-age conscience."

Humboldt held his snifter so that he could look through it toward the fire. "How people rush to protect you when you are old and they want you to know they care about your interests." He spoke to the glass. "And what problems they needlessly cause. It's a constant issue with my daughter, one of nature's worriers."

He turned back to me. "We had a problem with these men, with Pankowski and Ferraro. Enough of a problem that I even know their names, you see, out of fifty-some thousand employees worldwide. They engaged in an attempted sabotage of the plant. Of the product, actually. Changing the balance in the mixture so that we had highly unstable vapor and a residue that stopped up the flow pipes. We had to shut the plant down three times in 1979 to clean everything. It took a year of investigation to find out who lay behind it. They and two other men were fired, and they then sued us for wrongful dismissal. The whole thing was a nightmare. A terrible nightmare."

He grimaced and drained his glass. "So when you came around my people naturally assumed you were egged on by some unscrupulous lawyer trying to open these old wounds. But I knew from my friend Gordon Firth that that could not be so. So I have taken a risk. Invited you here. Explained the whole story to you. And I hope I am right, that you are not going to run back to some lawyer saying I tried to suborn you or whatever the expression is."

"Suborn will do admirably," I said, finishing my own glass and shaking my head at the proffered decanter. "And I can safely assure you that my inquiries have nothing to do with any suit these men might have been involved in. It is a purely personal matter."

"Well, if it involves Xerxes employees, I can see that you get whatever assistance you need."

I don't like revealing my clients' business. Especially not to strangers. But in the end I decided to tell him—it was the easiest way to get help. Not the whole story, of course. Not Gabriella and the baby-sitting and Caroline's insistent manipulativeness and the angry Djiaks. But Louisa dying and Caroline wanting to find out who her father was and Louisa not wanting to tell.

"I'm European and old-fashioned," he said when I finished. "I don't like the girl not wanting to respect her mother's wishes. But if you are committed, you are committed. And you think she might have said something to Chigwell because he was the plant doctor? I'll call and ask him. He probably won't want to talk to you himself. But my secretary will phone you in a few days with the information."

That was a dismissal. I slid forward to the edge of the chair so that I could stand without bracing my arms on the sides and was pleased to find that I moved smoothly, without the brandy affecting me. If I could make it out the front door without bumping into a priceless art object, I could easily handle the drive home.

I thanked Humboldt for the brandy and his help. He turned it aside with another chuckle.

"It's a pleasure for me, Ms. Warshawski, to talk to an attractive young woman, and one who is brave enough to stand her ground with an old lion. You must come again when you are in the neighborhood."

Anton was hovering outside the library to escort me to the door.

"I'm sorry," I said when we reached the entryway. "I promised not to tell."

He stiffly pretended not to hear me and summoned the elevator with frigid aloofness. I wasn't sure what to do about the doorman and my car, but when I tentatively displayed a five-dollar bill he caused it to vanish while tenderly helping me into the Chevy.

I devoted the drive home to thinking of reasons why I was better off as a PI than a billionaire chemist. The list was much shorter than the drive.

10

FIRE WHEN READY

I was drowning in a sea of thick gray Xerxine. I was choking while Gustav Humboldt and Caroline stood talking earnestly on the shore, ignoring my cries for help. I woke up at four-thirty, sweaty and panting, too roused by the dream to go back to sleep.

I finally got out of bed when it started to get light. It wasn't cold in the bedroom, but I was shivering. I pulled a sweatshirt from the pile next to my bed and wandered around the apartment, trying to find something to turn my mind to. I picked out a scale on the piano, but stopped after one: it would be unfair to the neighbors to work on my rusty voice at this hour of the morning. I moved to the kitchen to make coffee, but lost interest after washing out the pot.

My four rooms normally seem open and spacious to me, but now they were making me feel cramped. The jumble of books, papers, and clothes, which usually looks homelike, began to appear shameful and squalid.

Don't tell me you've been infected by Djiakism, I scolded myself crossly.

Next thing you'll be on your hands and knees in the lobby scrubbing the floor every morning.

Finally I pulled on jeans and my running shoes and went out. The dog recognized my step behind the locked first-floor door and let out a little yelping bark. I would have liked her company, but I didn't have a key to Mr. Contreras's place. I walked over to the lake alone, unable to work up energy for running.

It was another gray day. I could tell the sun was rising only by a change in the intensity behind the clouds on the eastern horizon. Under the sullen sky the lake resembled the thick gray liquid of my nightmare. I stared at it, trying to reason away my lingering unease, trying to lose myself in the changing patterns and colors of the water.

Early as it was, joggers were already on the lake path, getting in their miles before putting on pinstripe and panty hose for the day. They looked like the hollow men, each wrapped in a cocoon of sound from his private radio, their faces blank, their isolation chilling. I dug my hands deep into my pockets, shivering, and turned toward home.

I stopped on the way for breakfast at the Chesterton Hotel. It's a residential hotel for well-heeled widows. The little Hungarian restaurant where you can get cappuccino and croissants caters to their slower pace and better manners.

As I stirred the foam in my second cappuccino I kept wondering why Gustav Humboldt had summoned me to his presence. Yes, he didn't want me nosing around in his plant. No executive likes that. And yes, he had the inside dope on Pankowski and Ferraro. But the chairman of the board calling in the lowly detective to tell her in person? Despite all his talk of Gordon Firth, I'd never even seen the Ajax chairman in the course of three investigations involving the insurance company. Heads of multinational corporations, even if they're eighty-four and dote on their grandchildren, have layers and layers of underlings to do that kind of job for them.

Last night my vanity had been tickled. The invitation alone was exciting, let alone the rarefied surroundings and incredible brandy. I hadn't stopped to wonder about his comradely flow of information, but maybe I should.

And what of little Caroline? What did she know that she hadn't been telling me? That Louisa's two pals had been fired? Perhaps that Louisa herself had been involved in the efforts to sabotage the plant? Maybe Gustav Humboldt had been her lover long ago and had stepped in to protect her now. It would explain his personal involvement. Maybe he was Caroline's father and she was due a gigantic inheritance, out of which a modest fee to me would be eminently feasible.

As my speculations grew more ludicrous, my mood lightened. I headed home much faster than I'd left, passing the second-floor tenants on their way to work with a "good morning" almost cheery enough for a flight attendant.

I was getting really sick of panty hose and pumps, but I put them on again so as to make a favorable impression at the Department of Labor. A friend of mine from law school worked for their Chicago office; he might be able to tell me about the sabotage and if the men really had been suing Humboldt for wrongful dismissal. My red shoes were still in the front hallway with my navy suit. If eventually, why not eventually? I scooped them up and took off.

By the time I found a place to park near the Federal Building it was after ten. The Loop has been attacked by a development fervor the last few years that has turned the business district into a jammed, honking copy of New York. Many of the public garages have been scrapped to make way for skyscrapers taller than city code permits, so we have four times the traffic we used to vying for half as much parking.

My temper wasn't the best by the time I made it to the sixteenth floor of the Dirksen Building. It wasn't helped by the attitude of the receptionist, who looked briefly my way before returning to her typing with the curt announcement that Jonathan Michaels wasn't available.

"Is he dead?" I snapped. "Out of town? Under indictment?"

She looked at me coldly. "I said he's not available and that's all you need to know."

The door leading to the offices was kept locked. The receptionist or someone on the other side could buzz you in, but this woman clearly wasn't going to let me wander back among the cubicles to find Jonathan. I sat in one of the plastic straight-backed chairs and told her I'd wait.

"Suit yourself," she snapped, typing furiously.

When a business-suited black man came in she made a big play of friendliness with him, cooing over him and flirting a little. She flashed him a sugary smile and a wish for a nice day while releasing the lock. When I went in behind him she was too taken aback even to squawk.

My escort raised his brows at me. "You belong in here?"

"Yeah," I said. "I pay your salary. And I'm here to talk to Jonathan Michaels about it."

He looked momentarily startled, trying to figure out which Washington bureaucrat I might be. Then my meaning dawned on him and he said, "Well, maybe you'd better wait outside until Gloria tells you to go in."

"Since she never bothered to find out my name or my business, I can't imagine her interest in serving the taxpaying public is enormous."

I knew where Jonathan's office was and quickened my pace to move ahead of my attendant. I could hear him speeding up on the carpet behind me calling, "Miss—uh, miss," as I opened the corner door.

Jonathan was standing in the outer office next to his secretary's desk. When he saw me his rosy face lightened into a smile. "Oh, it's you, Vic."

I grinned at him. "Gloria call to tell you the Weather Underground was heading in to smash up your office and tear your golden hair out by the roots?"

"What's left of it," he said plaintively. He had gone partly bald, which made him look like a youthful Father William.

Jonathan Michaels had been a quiet idealist in my law school class. While students like me—locked in our liberal straitjackets, as one conservative JD put it—rushed off to become public defenders, Jonathan had surveyed social issues quietly. He had clerked in a federal circuit court for two years and then moved to the Department of Labor. He was now senior counsel for the Chicago district.

He took me into his office and shut the door. "I've got a dozen attorneys from St. Louis in the conference room. Can you do your business in thirty seconds?"

I explained fast. "I want to know if there's any trail—through OSHA, the NLRB, the Contract Compliance people, or maybe Justice—of Ferraro and Pankowski. The sabotage and the suit."

I wrote their names on one of his yellow pads and added Louisa Djiak. "She might have been a party. I don't want to tell you the whole story now —there isn't time—but I had the news personally from Gustav Humboldt. He's not anxious to have it made public."

Jonathan picked up his phone while I was still talking. "Myra, get Dutton over here, will you? I've got a research job." He spelled it out in a few words and hung up. "Vic, next time, do me a big favor and do what the ad says— phone first."

I kissed his cheek. "I will, Jonathan. But only if I can afford to spend two days playing phone tag before I talk to you. *Ciao, ciao, bambino.*"

He was back in the conference room before I had made it out the outer door. When Gloria saw me return to the reception area, she started typing furiously again. In a spirit of malice I waited outside for a minute, then peered around the door. She had picked up the *Herald-Star*.

"Get busy," I said sternly. "The taxpayers expect value for their money."

She gave me a glance of loathing. I went to the elevator laughing lightly to myself. I hope someday to outgrow such juvenile pleasures.

I walked the four blocks to my office. When I checked in with my answering service I learned that Nancy Cleghorn had been trying to reach me. Once early this morning, when I was out feeling sorry for myself along the lakefront, and again ten minutes ago. In the tiresome way that people have, she hadn't bothered to leave a phone number.

I sighed aggrievedly and pulled my city directory from under a stack of papers on the windowsill. The Wabash el runs under my windows and the directory had a fine layer of soot on it, which I smeared on the front of my green wool dress.

Nancy was the environmental affairs director for Caroline's community development group. I looked up SCRAP, which was a waste of time, since of course it was under South Chicago Reawakening Project. And that was a waste of time because Nancy wasn't in, she hadn't been in all day, and they didn't know when to expect her. And no, they wouldn't give me her home phone number, especially if I said I was her sister, because everyone knew she had four brothers, and if I didn't stop harassing them, they'd get the police.

"Can you at least take a message? Without bringing the police into it, I mean?" I spelled my name slowly, twice, not that it would make any difference—it would still probably come out as Watchski or some other hideous mutation. The secretary said she'd see Nancy got the message in that tone that tells you they're trashing the paper as soon as you hang up.

I turned back to the directory. Nancy wasn't listed, but Ellen Cleghorn was still living on Muskegon. Talking to Nancy's mother made a welcome change to the way I'd been greeted today. She remembered me perfectly, loved reading about me when my cases made the papers, wished I'd come down and have dinner with them sometime when I was in the neighborhood.

"Nancy bought herself a place in South Shore. One of those huge old mansions that's falling to bits. She's fixing it up on her own. Kind of a big place for a single woman, but she likes it." She gave me the number and hung up with repeated dinner invitations.

Nancy wasn't home. I gave it up. If she wanted me that badly, she'd call again.

I looked at the dirt on the front of my dress. My suit was still in the car. If I drove home now, I could change into jeans, dump the lot at the cleaners, and spend the rest of the afternoon on myself.

It was close to five—as I was happily working my way through the syncope of *"In dem Schatten meiner Locken,"* without Kathleen Battle's voice— that the phone rang. I left the piano unwillingly, and was even sorrier as soon as I picked up the receiver: it was Caroline.

"Vic, I need to talk to you."

"Talk away," I said resignedly.

"In person, I mean." Her husky voice was urgent, but it always was.

"You want to drive up to Lake View, be my guest. But I ain't trekking down to South Chicago this afternoon."

"Oh, fuck you, Vic. Can you ever talk to me without being a total snot?"

"Can it, Caroline. You want to talk to me, speak. Otherwise I'm going back to what I was doing when you interrupted."

There was a pause during which I could picture her gentian eyes smoldering. Then she said, so quickly I almost didn't understand, "I want you to stop."

I was confused for a minute. "Caroline, if you ever realized how upsetting I find it to have you spin me around in circles, you might understand why I sound like a snot to you."

"Not that," she said impatiently. "Stop trying to find my father, I mean."

"What!" I shouted. "Two days ago you were batting your baby blues and telling me pathetically you *counted* on me."

"That was then. I didn't see then—I didn't know—anyway, that's why I need to see you in person. You can't possibly understand over the phone if you're going to get so honked off. Just don't do any more looking until I can talk to you in person, for God's sake."

There was no denying the thread of panic in her voice. I pulled a string from the fringe where my left knee was poking through the denim. She knew about Pankowski and the plant sabotage. I pulled another. She didn't know.

"You're too late, babe," I finally said.

"You mean you've found him?"

"Nope. I mean the investigation is beyond your power to stop."

"Vic, I hired you. I can fire you," she said with terrifying ferocity.

"Nope," I repeated steadily. "You could have last week. But the investigation has moved into a new phase. You can't fire me. I don't mean that. You *can* fire me, of course. You just have. What I mean is, you may choose not to pay me but you can't stop my inquiries now. And the top one, first on the list, is why you didn't tell me about Ferraro and Pankowski."

"I don't even know who they are!" she shouted. "Ma never talks about her old lovers to me. She's like you—she thinks I'm a fucking baby."

"Not about their being her lovers. About the sabotage and their getting fired. And the lawsuit."

"I don't know what in hell you're talking about, V. I. Know-it-all Warshawski, and I don't have to listen to it. As far as I'm concerned, V.I. stands for vicious insect, which I would use Raid on if I had any." She slammed the phone in my ear.

It was the childish insult she ended on that convinced me she really didn't know about the two men. I also realized suddenly that I had no idea why she was firing me. I scowled and rang up SCRAP, but she refused to come to the phone.

"Ah, screw you, you little brat," I muttered, slamming down the phone myself.

I tried returning to Hugo Wolf, but my enthusiasm was gone. I wandered to the living-room window and watched the nine-to-fivers returning home. Suppose my speculations this morning hadn't been so far out after all. Suppose Louisa Djiak had been involved in the plant sabotage and Humboldt was protecting her. Maybe he'd called Caroline and pushed her into firing me. Although Caroline was not the kind that pushed easily. If someone Humboldt's size came for her, she'd be more inclined to sink her teeth into his calf and hang on until he got sick of the pain.

It occurred to me that whatever Nancy wanted to talk to me about might shed some light on the general problem. I tried her number again, but she still didn't answer.

"Come on, Cleghorn," I muttered. "You wanted me bad enough to leave two messages. You get run over by a train or something?"

I finally got fed up with my futile churning and called Lotty Herschel. She was free for dinner and glad to have company. We went to the Gypsy and shared a roast duck, then back to her place, where she beat me five times in a row at gin.

11
THE BRAT'S TALE

I was skimming the paper while I made coffee the next morning when Nancy Cleghorn's name leapt out at me. The story was on the front page of *ChicagoBeat*. It explained why she hadn't been around to answer her phone yesterday. Her body had been found around eight last evening by two young boys who'd ignored both the government and their parents and gone into the posted area around Dead Stick Pond.

A small section of the original marsh remained as Illinois's last wetland for migratory birds. Dead Stick Pond had once been a great feeding and resting ground, but was now so full of PCBs that little could survive there. Even so, in the middle of the dead mills you could find herons and other unusual birds, and the occasional beaver or muskrat.

The two boys had come on a muskrat there once and hoped to see it again. At the water's edge they stumbled over a discarded boot. Since there were fifty of those for every animal—and it was dark—it had taken them a few minutes to realize it still had a body connected to it.

Nancy had been hit on the back of the head. The internal injury would have killed her eventually, but she apparently drowned when her body was dumped in the pond. The police knew of no one with a reason to kill her. She was well respected, her work at SCRAP had earned her a lot of kudos in the environmentally troubled community, and so on. She was survived by her mother and four brothers.

I slowly finished making the coffee and took the paper out to the living room, where I reread the story six or seven times. I didn't learn anything new. Nancy. My snappish thought last night, maybe she'd fallen under a train, made the little hairs prickle on the sides of my face. My thinking hadn't caused her death. My mind knew that, but my body didn't.

If only I hadn't taken that hike to the lake yesterday morning—I broke off the thought when I realized how stupid it was. If I stayed chained to my phone twenty-four hours a day, I'd be at home to needy friends or telemarketers and would have no other life. But Nancy. I'd known her since I was six years old. In my mind I thought we were still young together—that because we'd been young together we would protect each other from ever getting old.

I wandered to the window and stared out. It was raining hard again in thick sheets that made it impossible to see the street. I squinted at the water, moving my head to make patterns with it, wondering what to do. It was only eight-thirty—too early to call my friends at the papers to see if they had news that hadn't made it to the morning edition. People who go to bed at three or four in the morning are more cooperative if you let them sleep in.

She'd been found in the Fourth Police District. I didn't know anyone there—my dad had worked the Loop and northwest sides, not his own neighborhood. Besides, that's been over ten years ago.

I was chewing on my fingertip, trying to decide whom to call, when the doorbell rang. I figured it was Mr. Contreras, trying to get me to come down to take the dog out in the downpour, and scowled at the foggy window without moving. The third time the bell clamored I reluctantly left my hideout. Cup in hand, I unbolted the outer door and padded barefoot down the three flights.

Two bulky figures stood in the outer hallway. Rain glistened on their shaved faces and dripped from their navy slickers to form dirty pools on the tiled floor.

When I opened the door the older one said with heavy sarcasm, "Good morning, sunshine. I hope we didn't interrupt your beauty sleep."

"Not at all, Bobby," I said heartily. "I've been up for an hour at least. I just hoped it was a wrong number. Hi, Sergeant," I added to the younger man. "You guys want some coffee?"

As they came past me into the stairwell cold water from their slickers dripped onto my bare toes. If it had just been Bobby Mallory, I would have thought it deliberate. But Sergeant McGonnigal was always scrupulously polite to me, never participating in his lieutenant's hostility.

The truth of the matter was that Bobby had been my father's closest friend, both on and off the force. His feelings toward me were compounded of guilt at flourishing when my father had stayed in beat patrol, at living while Tony had died—and frustration at my being grown up and a professional investigator instead of a little girl he could dandle on his knee.

He looked around in the little entryway of my apartment for a place to put his dripping raincoat, finally sticking it on the floor outside the door. His wife was a meticulous housekeeper and he had been well trained. Sergeant McGonnigal followed suit, running his fingers through his thick curly hair to squeeze some of the excess water out.

I solemnly took them into the living room and brought coffee in mugs, remembering extra sugar for Bobby.

"It's good to see you," I said politely when they were seated on the couch. "Especially on such a rotten day. How are you?"

Bobby looked at me sternly, quickly glancing away when he saw I didn't have a bra on under my T-shirt. "I didn't want to come here. The captain thought someone should talk to you and since I know you he thought it should be me. I didn't agree, but he's the captain. If you'll answer my questions seriously and try not to be a wisenheimer, the whole thing'll go faster and we'll both be happy."

"And I thought you were being social," I said mournfully. "No, no, sorry, bad start. I'm serious as—as a traffic court judge. Ask me anything."

"Nancy Cleghorn," Bobby said flatly.

"That's not a question, and I don't have an answer. I just read in this morning's paper that she was killed yesterday. I expect you know a lot more about it than I do."

"Oh, yes," he agreed heavily. "We know a great deal—that she died around six P.M. From the amount of internal bleeding, the M.E. says she was probably hit around four. We know she was thirty-six years old and had been pregnant at least once, that she ate too much high-fat food and broke her right leg as an adult. I know that a man, or a woman with size thirteen shoes and a forty-inch stride, dragged her in a green blanket to the south end of Dead Stick Pond. The blanket was sold at a Sears store somewhere in the United States sometime between 1978 when they started making them and 1984 when they discontinued that brand. Someone else, presumably also a man, came along for the stroll but didn't help with the dragging or dumping."

"The lab worked overtime last night. I didn't think they did that for your average dead citizen."

Bobby refused to let me ride him. "There's also a little bit I don't know, but it's the part that counts. I don't have any idea who wanted her to die. But I understand you two grew up together and used to be pretty good friends."

"And you want me to find her murderer? I would have thought you guys had the machinery to do that easier than me."

His look would have made an academy recruit faint. "I want you to *tell* me."

"I don't know."

"That's not what I hear." He glared at a point somewhere over my head.

I couldn't imagine what he was talking about, then the messages I'd left for Nancy at SCRAP and with her mother came back to me. Those seemed like mighty small straws to build a house from.

"Let me guess," I said brightly. "It's not even business hours and you've already rounded up everyone at SCRAP and talked to them."

McGonnigal shifted uneasily and looked at Mallory. The lieutenant nodded briefly. McGonnigal said, "I talked with a Ms. Caroline Djiak late last night. She said you advised Cleghorn on how to investigate a problem they were having with a zoning permit for a recycling plant. She said you would know who the deceased spoke to about it."

I stared at him speechlessly. Finally I choked out, "Are those her exact words?"

McGonnigal fished in his breast pocket for a notebook. He flipped through the pages, squinting at his notes. "I didn't take it down word for word, but that's pretty much it," he said at last.

"I wouldn't call Caroline Djiak a pathological liar," I remarked conversationally. "Just a manipulative little squirt. But even though I'm mad enough at her to go down and personally break in the back of *her* head, it doesn't cheer me any you coming at me this way. I mean, we go through this every time you think I'm involved in a crime, don't we, Lieutenant? You make a frontal assault that takes my guilty knowledge for granted.

"You could've started by telling me about Caroline's never-never-land remarks and asking me if they were true. Then I would've told you everything that happened, which was about five minutes of conversation in Caroline's dining room, and you could have taken off with one loose end tied up."

I got up from the floor and headed for the kitchen. Bobby came in as I was poking around the refrigerator to see if there was anything edible I might use for breakfast. The yogurt had changed to mold and sour milk. There wasn't any fruit, and the only bread I had left was hard enough to use for ammo.

Bobby unconsciously wrinkled his nose at the dirty dishes, but heroically refrained from commenting on them. Instead he said, "Seeing you near a murder always gets me in the gut. You know that."

It was as close as he was going to get to an apology. "I'm not near this one," I said impatiently. "I don't know why Caroline wants me there. She dragged me down to South Chicago last week to a basketball-team reunion. Then she manipulated me into helping her with a personal problem. Then she called to tell me to bug out of her life. Now she wants me back. Or maybe she's just trying to punish me."

I dug some crackers out of a cupboard and spread them with peanut butter. "While we were eating fried chicken Nancy Cleghorn came by to talk about a zoning problem. This would have been just a week ago. Caroline thought Jurshak—the alderman down there—was blocking the permit. She asked me what I'd do if I were investigating. I said the easiest thing to do was talk to a friend on Jurshak's staff if she or Nancy had one. Nancy left. The total of my involvement."

I poured some more coffee, angry enough that my hand shook and I spilled it across the stove. "Despite your little dig, we hadn't seen each other for more than ten years. I didn't know who her friends or enemies were. Now Caroline makes it sound as though Jurshak killed Nancy, for which there isn't an atom of evidence. And she wants to make out that I egged him on to do it. Hell!"

Bobby flinched. "Don't talk dirty, Vicki. It doesn't help anything. What are you working on for the Djiak girl?"

"Woman," I said automatically through a mouthful of peanut butter. "Or maybe brat. I'll tell you for nothing, even though it's none of your business. Her mother was one of Gabriella's charities. Now she's dying. Very unpleasantly. Caroline wanted me to find some people her mother used to work with in the hopes they'd come see her. But as she probably told you, she fired me two days ago."

Bobby's blue eyes narrowed to slits in his ruddy face. "There's some truth there. I just wish I knew how much."

"I should have known better than to speak frankly with you," I said bitterly. "Especially when you opened the conversation with an accusation."

"Oh, keep your shirt on, Vicki," Bobby said. He blushed suddenly as the image hit home with him. "And clean up your kitchen more than once a year. Place looks like the projects."

When he had stomped away with McGonnigal I went to my bedroom to change. As I scrambled back into the black dress I looked out the window—the water was forming little rivers on the walk below. I put on running shoes and carried a pair of black pumps in my bag.

Even with an extra-wide umbrella my legs and feet got soaked on my dash to the car. Most Februaries, though, this would be snow a foot or two deep, so I tried not to complain too bitterly.

The little Chevy's defroster couldn't make much headway on the fogged windshield, but at least the car hadn't died, the fate of a number of others I passed. The storm and the stalls made for a slow trek south; it was close to ten by the time I turned from Route 41 onto Ninety-second Street. By the time I found a parking space near the corner of Commercial, the rain was finally lifting—it was clear enough for me to change into my pumps.

SCRAP's offices were in the second story of a block of little shops. I trotted around the corner to the business entrance—my dentist used to have his office here and the opening on Commercial remained an indelible memory.

I stopped at the top of the uncarpeted stairs, reading the wall directory while combing my hair and straightening my skirt. Dr. Zdunek wasn't there anymore. Neither were a lot of the other tenants; I passed half a dozen or so empty offices on my way down the hall.

At the far end I walked into a room that had the unmistakable air of a poor not-for-profit agency. The scarred metal furniture and newspaper articles taped to the walls wavered under a badly winking fluorescent bulb. Papers and phone books were stacked on the floor and the electric typewriters were models IBM had abandoned when I was still in college.

A young black woman was typing while talking on the phone. She smiled at me, but held up a finger to ask me to wait. I could hear voices from an open conference room; ignoring the receptionist's urgent hissing, I went to the door to look in.

A group of five, four women and a man, sat at a rickety deal table. Caroline was in the middle, talking heatedly. When she saw me at the door she broke off and flushed to the roots of her coppery hair.

"Vic! I'm in a meeting. Can't you wait?"

"All day, if it's for you, my sweet. We need a tête-à-tête about John McGonnigal—he visited me first thing this morning."

"John McGonnigal?" Her little nose wrinkled questioningly.

"*Sergeant* McGonnigal. Chicago Police," I said helpfully.

She turned even redder. "Oh. Him. Maybe we'd better talk now. Will you all excuse me?"

She got up and took me to a cubbyhole next to the conference room. The chaos there, compounded of books, papers, graphs, old newspapers, and candy wrappers, made my office look like a convent cell. Caroline dumped a phone directory from a folding chair for me and seated herself in the rickety swivel chair behind her desk. She gripped her hands together in front of her, but stared at me defiantly.

"Caroline, I've known you twenty-six years, and you've pulled tricks that would shame Oliver North, but this one has got to head the list. After whining and snuffling you got me to agree to look for your old man. Then you called me off without any reason. Now, to top it all off, you lied to the police about my involvement with Nancy. You want to explain why? Without resorting to Hans Christian Andersen?" I was having trouble keeping my voice below a shout.

"What are you on your high horse about?" she said belligerently. "You did give Nancy advice about—"

"Shut up!" I snapped. "You're not talking to the cops, sweetie pie. I can just picture you blushing and winking away your tears with Sergeant McGonnigal. But I know what I told Nancy that night as well as you do. So cut the crap and tell me why you lied about me to the police."

"I didn't! You try and prove it! Nancy did come by that night. You did tell her to talk to someone in Jurshak's office. And she's dead now."

I shook my head like a wet dog, trying to clear my brain. "Could we start this at the beginning? Why did you tell me to stop hunting for your old man?"

She looked at the desktop. "I decided it wasn't fair to Ma. Going behind her back when it upset her so much."

"Whew boy," I said. "Hold it there. Let me get onto Cardinal Bernardin and the Pope to start beatification proceedings. When did you ever put Louisa, or anyone else, ahead of what you wanted?"

"Stop it!" she shouted, bursting into tears. "Believe me or not, I don't care. I love my mother and I don't want anyone hurting her no matter what you may think."

I looked at her warily. Caroline might bat a few tears around as part of her tragic orphan routine, but she wasn't prone to sobbing fits.

"Okay," I said slowly. "I take it back. That was cruel. Is that why you sicced the cops on me? To punish me for saying I was continuing the investigation?"

She blew her nose noisily. "It wasn't like that!"

"What was it like then?"

She caught her lower lip in her teeth. "Nancy called me Tuesday morning. She said she'd gotten threatening phone calls and she thought someone was following her."

"What were they threatening her about?"

"The plant, of course."

"Caroline, I want you to be absolutely clear on this. Did she specifically say the calls were about the plant?"

She opened her mouth, then took a breath. "No," she finally muttered. "I just assumed they were. Because it was the last thing she and I had been talking about."

"But you went ahead and told the police that she was killed because of the recycling plant. And that I told her who to talk to. Do you understand how outrageous that is?"

"But, Vic. It's not just a wild guess. I mean—"

"You mean shit!" My anger returned, making my voice husky. "Can't you tell the difference between your head games and reality? Nancy was killed. Murdered. Instead of helping the police find the murderer, you slandered me and got them on my butt."

"They don't care about Nancy, anyway. They don't care about any of us down here." She got to her feet, her eyes flashing. "They respond to political pressure, and as far as Jurshak is concerned, South Chicago might as well be the South Pole. You know that as well as I do. You know the last time he got a street repaired down here—it sure as hell was before you left the neighborhood."

"Bobby Mallory is a good, honest, thorough cop," I said doggedly. "Just because Jurshak is twenty kinds of asshole doesn't change that."

"Yeah, you don't care, either. You proved that pretty good when you moved away from here and never came back until I pushed you into it."

The pulse beside my right temple started throbbing. I pounded the desk hard enough to knock some of the papers to the floor. "I busted my ass for a week trying to find your old man for you. Your grandparents insulted me, Louisa blew up at me, and you! You couldn't be content with manipulating me into going to look for the guy and then spinning me around a few times. You had to lie to the police about me."

"And I thought you'd give a fuck," she yelled. "I thought if you didn't care about me, you'd at least do something for Nancy because you played on the same team together. I guess that proves how wrong I was."

She started for the door. I caught her arm and forced her to face me.

"Caroline, I'm mad enough to beat the shit out of you. But I'm not so mad I can't think. You fingered me to the cops because there's something you know that you're scared to talk about. I want to know what that is."

She looked at me fiercely. "I don't know anything. Just that someone had started following Nancy around over the weekend."

"And she called the police and reported it. Or you did."

"No. She talked to the state's attorney and they said they'd open a file. I guess they have something to put in it now."

She gave the smile of a triumphant martyr. I forced myself to speak calmly to her. After a few minutes she reluctantly agreed to sit back down and tell me what she knew. If she was telling the truth—a big if—it wasn't much. She didn't know whom Nancy had seen at the state's attorney's office, but she thought it could have been Hugh McInerney; he was the person they dealt with on other issues. Under further probing she admitted that McInerney had taken statements from them eighteen months ago about their problems with Steve Dresberg, a local Mob figure involved in garbage disposal.

I vaguely remembered the trial over Dresberg's PCB incinerator and his alleged sweetheart deal with the Sanitary District but didn't realize she and Nancy had been involved. When I demanded to know what role the two had played, she scowled but said she and Nancy had testified to receiving death threats for their opposition to the incinerator.

"Obviously Dresberg knew who to pay off at the Sanitary District. It didn't matter what we said. I guess he figured SCRAP was too puny to listen to so he didn't have to make good his threats."

"And you didn't tell the cops that." I rubbed my hands tiredly across my face. "Caroline, you need to call McGonnigal and make an amended statement. You need to get them looking at people you *know* threatened Nancy in the past. I'm going to phone the sergeant myself as soon as I get home to tell him about this conversation. And if you're thinking of lying to him a second time, think again—he's known me professionally for years. He may not like me, but he knows he can believe what I tell him."

She looked at me furiously. "I'm not five years old anymore. I don't have to do what you say."

I went to the door. "Just do me a favor, Caroline—the next time you're in trouble, dial 911 like the rest of the citizenry. Or talk to a shrink. Don't come hounding me."

12 COMMON SENSE

I dragged my feet back to the Chevy, feeling as though I were a hundred years old. I was disgusted with Caroline, with myself for being stupid enough to get caught in her net once again, with Gabriella for ever befriending Louisa Djiak. If my mother had known what Louisa's damned baby would get me into . . . I could hear Gabriella's golden voice in response to the same plaint twenty-two years ago. "Of her I expect nothing but trouble, *cara*. But of you I expect rationality. Not because you are older, but because it is your nature."

I made a bitter face at the memory and started the car. Sometimes the burden of being rational and responsible while everyone around me was howling was more than I liked. Even so, instead of washing my hands of Caroline's problems and heading north toward home, I found myself driving west. Toward Nancy's childhood house on Muskegon.

But it wasn't to help out Caroline that I was making the trek. I didn't care that I'd told Nancy to talk to someone at Jurshak's office, or even that we'd shared the old school towel. I was hoping to assuage my own feeling of guilt for not having been there when Nancy called me.

Of course she might have been phoning to condole about the Lady Tigers —our successors had been eliminated in the state quarterfinals. But I didn't think so. Despite my bravura performance with Caroline, I sort of thought she was right: Nancy had learned something about the recycling plant that she needed my help to deal with.

I didn't have any trouble finding Nancy's mother's place, which didn't exactly cheer me up. I thought I'd left the South Side behind, but it seemed my unconscious had perfect recall of every house I used to spend time in down here.

Three cars were crowded into the short driveway. The curb in front was filled, too, and I had to go some way down the street before I found a parking space. I fiddled with my car keys for a moment before starting up the walk—perhaps I should postpone my visit until her mourning callers had gone. But even if it were my nature to be rational, patience isn't my leading virtue. I stuck the keys in my skirt pocket and headed up the walk.

The door was opened by a strange young woman of thirty or so, wearing jeans and a sweatshirt. She looked at me questioningly without saying anything. When a minute had stretched by without her speaking, I finally gave her my name.

"I'm an old friend of Nancy's. I'd like to talk to Mrs. Cleghorn for a few minutes if she's up to seeing me."

"I'll go ask," she muttered.

She came back again, hunched a shoulder, told me I could go on in, and returned to whatever she'd been doing when I rang the bell. I was startled by the clamor when I got into the little foyer—it was more like the noisy house of Nancy's and my childhood than a place of mourning.

As I followed the sound toward the living room, two small boys erupted from it, chasing each other with sweet rolls they were using as guns. The lead one caromed into me and bounced off without apology. I sidestepped the other and looked cautiously around the doorway before entering.

The long, homey room was packed with people. I didn't recognize any of them, but assumed the men were Nancy's four brothers grown to adulthood. The three young women were presumably their wives. What looked like a nursery school in full session was crammed around the edges, with children jabbing each other, scuffling, giggling, ignoring adult admonitions for silence.

No one paid any attention to me, but I finally spied Ellen Cleghorn at the far end of the room, holding a howling baby without much enthusiasm. When she saw me she struggled to her feet and gave the baby to one of the young women. She picked her way through her swarming grandchildren to me.

"I'm so sorry about Nancy," I said, squeezing her hand. "And I'm sorry to bother you at a time like this."

"I'm glad you came, dear," she said, giving a warm smile and kissing my cheek. "The boys mean well—they all took the day off and thought it would cheer up Grandma to see the kiddies—but the chaos is too much for me. Let's go into the dining room. There's cake in there and one of the girls is making coffee."

Ellen Cleghorn had aged well. She was a plumper edition of Nancy, with the same frizzy blond hair. It had darkened with time rather than graying and her skin was still soft and clear. She had been divorced for many years, ever since her husband ran off with another woman. She'd never gotten child support or alimony and had raised her large family on her meager earnings as a librarian, always making room for me at the dinner table after basketball practice.

Ellen had been unique on the South Side in her indifference to housekeeping. The disarray in the dining room was much as I remembered it, with dust balls in the corners and books and papers shoved to one side to make room for the food. Even so, the house had always seemed romantic to me when I was young. It was one of a handful of big homes in the neighborhood —Mr. Cleghorn had been a grade school principal before he decamped—and all five children had their own bedrooms. Unheard-of luxury on the South

Side. Nancy's even had a little turreted window where we acted out *Bluebeard*.

Mrs. Cleghorn sat down behind a stack of newspapers at the head of the table and gestured me to the chair catty-corner to her.

I fiddled with the pages of the book in front of me, then said abruptly, "Nancy was trying to get in touch with me yesterday. I guess I told you that when you gave me her number. Do you know what she wanted?"

She shook her head. "I hadn't talked to her for several weeks."

"I know it's rotten of me to bug you about it today. But—I keep thinking it had something to do with—with what happened to her. I mean, we hadn't seen each other for so long. And when we did talk it was about my being a detective and what I would do in her situation. So she would have thought of me in that context, you know—something came up that she thought my special experience might help her with."

"I just don't know, dear." Her voice trembled and she struggled to control it. "Don't let it worry you. You couldn't have done anything to help her, I'm sure."

"I wish I could agree with you. Look, I'm not trying to be a ghoul, or pressure you when you're so upset. But I feel responsible. I'm an experienced investigator. I might have been able to help her if I'd been home when she called. The only thing I can do to assuage my conscience is try to find who killed her."

"Vic, I know you and Nancy were friends, and I'm sure you think you're helping by getting involved. But can't you just leave it to the police? I don't want to have to talk about it or think about it anymore. It's bad enough having to get ready for her funeral with all these children screaming through the house. If I have to worry about—about why someone wanted to kill her —I keep thinking of her in that marsh. We used to go bird-watching there when she was in Girl Scouts and she was always so scared of the water. I keep thinking of her in there being alone and afraid—" She broke off and struggled against her tears.

I knew Nancy was afraid of water. She had never joined our surreptitious swims in the Calumet and she had to get a written statement from a doctor to excuse her from the swimming requirement in college. I didn't want to think of her last minutes in the marsh. Maybe she'd never regained consciousness. It was the best I could hope for.

"That's why it matters to me to find out who put her through such torment. It makes me feel that she was a little less helpless if I can go to bat for her now. Can you understand that and tell me who Nancy might've talked to? If not to you, I mean?"

She and Nancy had always had a kind of careless camaraderie, which I'd envied. Even though I loved my mother, she was too intense for an easy relationship. If Nancy hadn't told Ellen Cleghorn what was going on with the recycling center, she'd certainly have talked to her about friends and lovers. And after a few more minutes of coaxing Mrs. Cleghorn started speaking about them.

Nancy had been in love, been pregnant, had an abortion. Since she and Charles broke up five years ago there hadn't been any special men in her life. And no close women friends down here, either.

"It wasn't really a good place for her to meet people. I hoped maybe after she bought that house—South Shore is a little livelier neighborhood and lots of university people live down there now. But there wasn't anyone in this area she would've been close enough to talk to. Except maybe Caroline Djiak, and Nancy thought she was such a hothead, she wouldn't have told her anything she wasn't dead certain about." The unconscious phrase made her wince.

I rubbed my eyes. "She talked to one of the state's attorneys. If it had something to do with SCRAP, she might've talked to their lawyer too. What's his name? She mentioned it that night she came by Caroline's and I can't remember it."

"I guess that would be Ron Kappelman, Vic. She went out with him a few times but they didn't really click together."

"When was that?" I asked, suddenly alert. Maybe it was a crime of passion after all.

"It must have been two years ago, I guess. When he first started working with SCRAP."

Maybe not. Who waits two years to revenge himself on love gone sour? Outside Agatha Christie, that is.

Mrs. Cleghorn couldn't tell me anything else. Other than the date of the funeral, set for Monday at Mount of Olives Methodist Church. I told her I'd be there and left her to the ministrations of her grandchildren.

Back at the car, I slumped dejectedly against the steering wheel. Except for the financial searches I'd done on Tuesday, I hadn't had a paying customer for three weeks. And now, if I was really going to look into Nancy's death, I'd have to talk to the state's attorney. See if Nancy had revealed anything when she told him she was being followed. Talk to Ron Kappelman. See whether he might've felt like a man scorned or, failing that, if he knew what she'd been up to the last few days.

I rubbed my head tiredly. Maybe I was getting too old for gestures of bravado. Maybe I should just call John McGonnigal, tell him about my conversation with Caroline, and go back to what I know how to do—investigate industrial fraud.

On that sensible, even rational, note, I started the car and took off. Not toward Lake Shore Drive and common sense, but to the south, where Nancy Cleghorn had died.

13 DEAD STICK POND

Dead Stick Pond lay deep in the labyrinth of marsh, landfill, and factories. I'd been there only once, as part of the Girl Scout bird-watching expedition, and wasn't sure I could find it again. At 103rd Street I headed west to Stony Island, the street that threads the maze. North of 103rd it's a major thoroughfare, but down here it turns into a gravel track of indeterminate width, worn to potholes by the giant semis chewing their way in and out of the factories.

The heavy rain had turned the track to a muddy glaze. The Chevy bounced and slid uneasily in the ruts between the high marsh grasses. Passing trucks splattered the windshield with mud. When I swerved to miss them the Chevy bucked dangerously and headed for the drainage ditches lining the road.

My arms were sore from wrestling with the steering when I finally saw the pond to my left. Parking on a patch of high ground next to the road, I donned my running shoes for my expedition. I followed the road to a posted track on the east rim of the pond, then picked my way gingerly through the marshy ground and dead grasses. Mud squelched up under my feet and slid inside my running shoes.

The pond was part of an overflow of the Calumet River. It wasn't very deep, but its murky waters covered a vast expanse of the marsh. Close up I read conflicting signs tacked to the trees, one proclaiming the area a federal clean-water project, the other warning trespassers of hazardous wastes. Some oversight agency had made a haphazard attempt to enclose the pond, but the low wire fence had fallen down in a number of places, making it easy to breach. Gathering my skirt in one hand, I stepped over one of these collapsed sections to the water's edge.

Dead Stick Pond used to be a great feeding area for migrating birds. Now the water was a dull black, with stark tree stumps poking surreal fingers through its surface. Fish have been returning to the Calumet River and its tributaries since the passage of the Clean Water Act, but the ones that make their way into the pond show up with massive tumors and rotted fins. Even so I passed a fishing couple trying to find dinner in the dirty water. The two were shapeless, ageless, sexless in their layers of worn garments. I could feel them watching me until I disappeared around a curve in the marsh grasses.

I followed a track to the south end of the pond, where the papers said Nancy had died. I found the spot easily enough—it was still marked with yellow police tape and the big yellow signs declaring the area off limits as the site of a police investigation. They hadn't bothered to leave a patrolman—who would have agreed to such a posting? Anyway, the rain had doubtless washed away anything the evidence team hadn't picked up last night. I ducked under the yellow tape.

The killers had parked where I left my car. Or near there. They had dragged her along the path I had just traversed. In broad daylight. They'd gone past the fishing couple, or past the place where the two stood. Just lucky that no one had seen them? Or relying on the furtive lives of those who frequent the swamps to protect them from idle curiosity?

The rain had washed away any signs of Nancy's body, but the police had marked an outline with stones. I squatted next to them. She had been dumped from the blanket and landed on her right side, head partly in the water. And had lain there in the oily water until she drowned.

I shivered in the damp air and finally pushed myself back to my feet. There was nothing to be seen here, no trace of life or death. I headed slowly back down the path, stopping every few feet to inspect the bushes and grasses. It was a futile gesture. Sherlock Holmes would no doubt have spotted the telltale cigarette butt, the gravel from another county that didn't belong here, the fragment of a missing envelope. All I saw was the endless array of bottles, potato-chip bags, old shoes, coats, proving that Nancy was only one of many discarded bundles in the swamp.

The fishing couple were standing exactly as they had on my way in. On impulse I started toward them to see if they'd been here yesterday, if they'd noticed anything. But when I stepped off the path a gaunt German shepherd got to its feet, glaring at me with wild red eyes. It braced its forelegs and bared its teeth. I muttered, "Nice doggie," and returned to the trail. Let the police interrogate the couple—they were being paid for the work and I wasn't.

Back at the road, I hunted around for the place where the killers had carried her over the fence. I finally found a few green threads snagged on the wire about twenty feet from where I'd left the car. I could see where last year's grasses still lay broken under the weight of her assailants' feet. The area was relatively untrampled, though, so I didn't think the police had bothered with a search at this end.

I moved carefully through the undergrowth, inspecting every piece of litter. I cut my hands parting the dead grasses. The skirt of my black dress grew stiff with mud and my fingers and toes were frozen when I finally decided there was nothing I could accomplish here. I turned the Chevy around and headed north to try to find Nancy's man in the state's attorney's office.

With my bedraggled dress and mud-streaked legs, I wasn't dressed for success, or even for making a good impression on public servants. It was getting close to three, though; if I went home to change, I'd never get back to Twenty-sixth and California before the end of the business day.

I'd spent my years on the county payroll as a public defender. Not only did that put me on the other side of the bench from the state's attorneys, it left me with a permanent suspicion of them. We all worked for the Cook County Board, but they earned fifty percent more than we did. And if a hot case made it to the papers, the prosecutors always got mentioned by name. We never did, even if our brilliant defense made them look like dog food. Of course I'd cultivated my share of prosecutors working out plea bargains and other deals. But there wasn't anyone on Richie Daley's staff who'd be glad to give me information for old times' sake. I'd have to do my Dick Butkus imitation and bull my way through the middle of the line.

The bailiff who searched me at the entrance remembered me. She was inclined to chaff me about my bedraggled appearance, but at least she didn't try to stop me as a dangerous abettor of criminals. I stopped in the ladies' room to wash the mud from my legs. Nothing could be done about the dress at this point, other than burning it, but with a little makeup and my hair combed, I at least didn't look like someone who'd broken out of custody.

I went up to the third floor and looked sternly at the receptionist. "My name's Warshawski; I'm a detective," I said harshly. "I want to talk to Hugh McInerney about the Cleghorn case."

Police and sheriff's deputies are a dime a dozen at the criminal courts. I figured they didn't flash a badge every time they wanted to see someone, so why should I? The receptionist responded to my bullying tone by quickly punching numbers on the house phone. Even though she was a patronage employee, like everyone else in the building, it didn't help to get a black mark with a detective.

State's attorneys are young men and women en route to big law firms or good political appointments. You never see any old people on the left side of the bench—I don't know where they ship the ones who don't move on naturally. Hugh McInerney looked to be in his late twenties. He was tall, with thick blond hair and the kind of trim muscularity that comes from a lot of racquetball.

"What can I do for you, Detective?" His deep voice, matching his build, was tailor-made for the courtroom.

"Nancy Cleghorn," I said briskly. "Can we talk in private?"

He led me through the inner door to a conference room, with the bare walls and scuffed furniture I remembered from my own county days. He left me alone for a minute to get his file on Nancy.

"You know she's dead," I said when he got back.

"I saw it in the morning paper. I've been kind of waiting for you guys to get here."

"You didn't think of using some initiative and calling us yourself?" I raised my eyebrows haughtily.

He hunched a shoulder. "I didn't have anything concrete to tell you. She came to see me Tuesday because she thought someone was following her."

"She have any idea who?"

He shook his head. "Believe me, Detective, if I'd had a name in here, I'd have been on the phone first thing this morning."

"You didn't think about Steve Dresberg?"

He shifted uncomfortably. "I—uh, I talked to Dresberg's attorney, Leon Haas. He—uh, he thought Dresberg was pretty happy with the situation down there these days."

"Yeah, he should be," I said nastily. "He made you guys look like cole slaw in court, didn't he, on that incinerator deal. You ask Haas how Dresberg felt about the recycling plant Cleghorn was working on? If he issued death threats over an incinerator, I'm not sure he'd jump for joy over a recycling center. Or did you decide that Cleghorn was imagining things, Mr. McInerney?"

"Hey, Detective—lay off. We're on the same side on this. You find who killed the Cleghorn woman and I'll prosecute hell out of him. I promise you that. I don't think it was Steve Dresberg, but hey, I'll call Haas and feel him out."

I grinned savagely and stood up. "Better leave that for the police, Mr. McInerney. Let them investigate and find someone for you to prosecute hell out of."

I strode arrogantly from the office, but once I got on the elevator my shoulders sagged. I didn't want to mess with Steve Dresberg. If half the things they said about him were true, he could get you into the Chicago River faster than you could change your socks. But he hadn't done anything to Nancy or Caroline over the incinerator. Or maybe he figured the first time around you got a warning; the second time meant sudden death. I soberly merged the Chevy with the rush-hour jam on the Kennedy and headed for home.

14

MUDDY WATERS

When I got home Mr. Contreras was in front of the building with the dog. She was gnawing on a large stick while he cleaned debris from the little patch of front yard. Peppy jumped up when she saw me, but sank back down when she realized I didn't have my running clothes on.

Mr. Contreras sketched a wave. "Hiya, doll. You get caught in the rain this morning?" He straightened and looked at me. "My, my, you're certainly a sight. Look like you've been wading through a mud puddle that came up to your waist."

"Yeah. I've been down in the South Chicago swamp. It kind of stays with you."

"Oh yeah? Didn't even know there was a South Chicago swamp."

"Well, there is," I said shortly, pushing the dog away impatiently.

He looked at me closely. "You need a bath. Hot bath and a drink, doll. You go on up and rest. I'll look after her royal highness here. She don't need to go to the lake every day of her life, you know."

"Yeah, right." I collected my mail and moved slowly up the stairs to the third floor. When I saw myself in the full-length mirror on the bathroom door, I couldn't believe I'd gotten McInerney to talk to me without a struggle. I looked as though I belonged with the fishing couple out at Dead Stick Pond. My panty hose were in shreds and my legs were streaked with black where I'd tried washing the mud off down at the county building. The hem of my dress was heavy with caked dirt. Even my black pumps had gotten dusty from the dirt on my legs.

I kicked the shoes off outside the bathroom door and threw out the panty hose while turning on the bath water. I hoped the cleaners could rescue the dress—I didn't want to sacrifice my entire wardrobe to the old neighborhood.

I took the portable phone from the bedroom into the bath with me. Once I was in the tub with whiskey at close reach I checked in with the answering service. Jonathan Michaels had tried to reach me. He'd left his office number, but the switchboard was closed for the day and I didn't have his unlisted home number. I stuck the phone up on the sink and leaned back in the tub with my eyes closed.

Steve Dresberg. Also known as the Garbage King. Not because of his character, but because if you wanted to bury, burn, or ship refuse in the Chicago area, you had to cut him in on the action. Some people say that two independent haulers who disappeared after refusing to deal with him are rotting in the CID landfill. Others think the arson in a waste storage shed that caused the evacuation of six square blocks on the South Side last summer could be traced to his door—if you had enough people with paid-up life insurance to do the tracing.

Dresberg was definitely police business, if not FBI. And since the odds were against Caroline phoning McGonnigal with an amended statement, that meant I should play Cindy Citizen and tell him myself.

Holding my breath, I slid down so that the water covered my head. Suppose Dresberg wasn't involved at all, though. If I pointed the cops toward him, it would only divert their attention from more promising lines of inquiry.

I sat up and started rubbing shampoo into my hair. The water around me was turning black; I opened the drain and turned on the hot-water tap. All I had to do was find someone on Jurshak's staff who would talk to me with the same frankness he'd used with Nancy. Then, when sinister figures began following me, I would take out my trusty Smith & Wesson and blow them away. Preferably, before they could bonk me on the head and dump me in the swamp.

I wrapped myself in a terry-cloth robe and went into the kitchen to forage. The maid hadn't been shopping for some time and pickings were slim. I took the jar of peanut butter and the bottle of Black Label and went back into the living room with them.

I was on my second whiskey and my fourth spoonful of peanut butter when I heard a tentative knock on the door. I groaned in resignation; it was Mr. Contreras with a laden TV tray. The dog was at his heels.

"Hope you don't mind me barging up like this, doll, but I could see you was all in and I thought you might like some supper. Did me a little barbecue chicken in the kitchen, and even without the charcoal it tastes pretty good, if I say so. I know you try to eat healthy so I made you a big salad. Now you want to be alone, you just say the word and Peppy and me'll head back down. Won't hurt my feelings any. But you can't live on that stuff you're drinking. And peanut butter? Scotch and peanut butter? No way, doll. You're too busy to buy food, you just let me know. No trouble for me to pick up something extra when I'm buying for myself, you know that."

I thanked him lamely and invited him in. "Just let me put on some clothes."

I guess I should have sent him back downstairs—I didn't want it to become a habit with him, thinking he could come up whenever he felt like it. But the chicken smelled good and the salad looked healthy and the peanut butter was lying kind of heavily on my stomach.

I ended up telling him about Nancy's death and my trek to Dead Stick Pond. He'd never been below the Field Museum and had no inkling of life on the South Side. I got out my city map and showed him Houston Street, where I'd grown up, and then the route down to the Cal Industrial District and the wetlands, where Nancy had been found.

He shook his head. "Dead Stick Pond, huh? Guess the name says it all. It's rough losing a friend that way, one you played basketball with and all. I never even knew you was on a team, but I mighta guessed it, the way you run. But you want to be careful, doll. If this Dresburg guy is the one behind all this, he's an awful lot bigger than you. You know me, I've never backed away from a fight, but I know better than to go in single-handed against a tank division too."

He was going into an elaborate illustration based on his experiences at Anzio when Jonathan Michaels phoned. I excused myself and took the call on the bedroom extension.

"I wanted to get you before I leave town in the morning." Jonathan spoke without preamble. "I had one of my staff people look up your two guys—Pankowski and Ferraro. They did sue Humboldt. Apparently not over wrongful dismissal, but whether they could get worker's comp. It looks as though they quit due to illness and were trying to prove it was job related. They didn't get anywhere with the suit—the thing came to trial here and Humboldt didn't have any trouble winning, and then the two died and the lawyer didn't seem to want to follow up on appeal. I don't know how far you want to follow this, but the lawyer who handled it was a Frederick Manheim."

He cut short my thanks with a crisp "Gotta run."

I was hanging up when he came back on the line. "You still there? Good. I almost forgot—we didn't see anything about sabotage, but Humboldt could have kept that quiet—not wanting the idea to get popular, you know."

After he hung up I sat on the bed looking at the phone. I felt so overloaded with unconnected information that I couldn't think at all. My professional curiosity had been piqued by the reaction I'd gotten first from the Xerxes personnel manager and then the doctor. I'd wanted to find out what lay behind their jumpy behavior. Then Humboldt seemed to have a glib explanation and Nancy's death had made me shift my priorities anyway; I couldn't untangle the whole universe, and finding her killers seemed more urgent than scratching the Xerxes itch.

Now the wheel seemed to turn the other way up again. Why had Humboldt gone out of his way to lie to me? Or had he? Maybe they'd sued for worker's comp but had lost because they'd been fired for sabotage. Nancy. Humboldt. Caroline. Louisa. Chigwell. The images spun uselessly through my mind.

"You all right in there, doll?" It was Mr. Contreras hovering anxiously in the hall.

"Yeah, I'm okay. I guess." I got to my feet and went back out to him with what I hoped was a reassuring smile. "I just need to spend some time alone. Okay?"

"Yeah, sure. Fine." He was a little hurt but worked valiantly to keep it from showing. He collected the dirty dishes, waving off my offers of help, and took the tray and the dog back downstairs.

Once he'd gone I wandered moodily around the apartment. Caroline had asked me to stop looking for her father; there wasn't any reason to push matters with Humboldt. But when a ten-billion-dollar man undertakes to run me through hoops it gets my hackles up.

I hunted around for the phone book. It had somehow gotten buried under a stack of music on the piano. Naturally enough, Humboldt's number wasn't listed. Frederick Manheim, Attorney, had an office at Ninety-fifth and Halsted and a home in neighboring Beverly. Lawyers with large incomes or criminal practices don't give their home numbers. Nor do they usually hide out on the southwest side, away from the courts and the major action.

I was restless enough to want to move now, call Manheim, get the story from him, and gallop down to Oak Street to confront Humboldt. *"Festina lente,"* I muttered to myself. Get the facts, then shoot. It would be better to wait until morning and make the trek down south to see the guy in person. Which meant yet another day in nylons. Which meant I'd better get my black pumps clean.

I foraged in the hall closet for shoe polish and finally found a tin of black under a sleeping bag. I was carefully cleaning the shoes when Bobby Mallory called.

I cradled the phone under my ear and started buffing the left shoe. "Evening, Lieutenant. What can I do for you?"

"You can give me a good reason for not running you in." He spoke in the pleasant conversational tone that meant his temper was on a tight rein.

"For what?" I asked.

"It's considered a crime to impersonate a police officer. By everyone but you, I believe."

"Not guilty." I looked at the shoe. It was never going to recover the smooth finish it had when it left Florence, but it wasn't too bad.

"You aren't the woman—tall, thirtyish, short curly hair—who told Hugh McInerney you were with the police?"

"I told him I was a detective. And when I spoke of the police, I carefully used third- not first-person pronouns. As far as I know that is not a crime, but maybe the City Council blew one by me." I picked up the right shoe.

"You don't think you could leave the investigation of the Cleghorn woman's death to the police, do you?"

"Oh, I don't know. You think Steve Dresberg killed her?"

"If I told you yes, would you drop out of sight and go do the stuff you're qualified to work on?"

"If you have a warrant with the guy's name on it, I might. Without arguing over what I'm qualified to do." I capped the polish tin and laid it and the rag on a newspaper.

"Vicki, look. You're a cop's daughter. You should know better than to go stirring around in a police investigation. When you talk to someone like McInerney without telling us, it just makes our job a hundred times harder. Okay?''

"Yeah, okay, I guess," I said grudgingly. "I won't talk to the state's attorney again without clearing it with you or McGonnigal."

"Or anyone else?"

"Give me a break, Bobby. If it says POLICE BUSINESS in all caps, I'll leave it to you. That's the best you're going to get from me."

We hung up in mutual irritation. I spent the rest of the evening in front of the tube watching a badly cut version of *Rebel Without a Cause*. It did nothing to abate my ill humor.

15

CHEMISTRY LESSON

Manheim's office lay between a beauty parlor and a florist among the little storefronts crowding Ninety-fifth Street. He had put his name on the plate glass in those black-and-gold transfers that are supposed to look old-fashioned and discreet—Frederick Manheim, Attorney-at-Law.

The front of the place, the part the little shops used as their sales floors, had been turned into a reception area. It held a couple of vinyl chairs and a desk with a typewriter and an African violet set on it. A few old copies of *Sports Illustrated* sat on a pressed-wood table in front of the vinyl chairs. I flipped through one for a few minutes to give the help a chance to make an appearance. When no one showed up I tapped on the door at the back of the room and turned the knob.

The door opened on a tiny hallway. A few pieces of wallboard had been stuck in the area where the stores held their excess inventory to create an office and a little bathroom.

I knocked on the door that had Manheim's name on it—this time in solid black Gothic—and got a thick "Just a minute." Paper rustled, a drawer slammed, and Manheim opened the door still chewing, wiping his mouth on the back of his hand. He was a young man with rosy cheeks and thick fair hair that hung over the tops of heavy glasses.

"Oh, hi. Annie didn't tell me I had an appointment this morning. Come on in."

I shook his proffered hand and told him my name. "I don't have an appointment. I'm sorry to just come barging in, but I was in the area and hoped you might have a minute or two."

He waved me in. "Sure, sure. No problem. Sorry I can't offer you any coffee—I get mine from the Dunkin' Donuts on the way over."

He'd crammed a couple of visitors' chairs in between his desk and the door. If you leaned back in the one on the left, you ran into the filing cabinet. The one on the right was jammed against the wall; a line of gray scuff marks showed where people had rubbed too hard against the paste-board. I felt kind of bad about not being able to infuse a little cash into the operation.

He'd taken out a pad of legal paper, carefully setting the Dunkin' Donuts coffee to one side.

"Can you spell your name for me, please?"

I spelled it out. "I'm a lawyer, Mr. Manheim, but these days I work primarily as a private investigator. A case I'm involved in has brought me to two clients of yours. Former clients, I guess. Joey Pankowski and Steve Fer-raro."

He'd been looking at me courteously through his thick lenses, his hands clasped loosely around his pen. At the mention of Pankowski and Ferraro he let the pen drop and looked as troubled as a man with rosy cherub's cheeks could.

"Pankowski and Ferraro? I'm not sure—"

"Employees at Humboldt Chemical's Xerxes plant in South Chicago. Died two or three years ago."

"Oh, yes. I remember now. They needed some legal advice, but I'm afraid I couldn't do much for them." He blinked unhappily behind his glasses.

"I know you don't want to talk about your clients. I don't like talking about mine, either. But if I explain what's gotten me interested in Pankowski and Ferraro, will you answer a couple of questions about them for me?"

He looked down at the desktop and fiddled with his pen. "I—I really can't—"

"What is going on with these two guys? Every time I mention their names grown men tremble in their shoes."

He looked up at me. "Who are you working for?"

"Myself." Myself, myself, it is enough, or so Medea said.

"You're not working for a company?"

"You mean like Humboldt Chemical? No. I was hired originally by the young woman who used to live next door to me to find out who her father was. It seemed remotely possible that one of those two—most likely Pankow-ski—could have been the guy and I started poking around trying to find someone at Xerxes who knew him. This woman fired me on Wednesday, but I've gotten piqued by the way people are reacting to me. Lying to me, basically, about what went on between Pankowski and Ferraro and Xerxes.

And then a guy I know at the Department of Labor told me you used to represent them. So here I am."

He smiled unhappily. "I don't suppose there's any reason the company would send someone around after all this time. But it's kind of hard for me to believe you're on your own. Too many people got too excited over that case, and now you come in out of the blue? It's too—too strange. Too pat."

I rubbed my forehead, trying to coax some ideas into my brain. Finally I said, "I'm going to do something I've never done in my whole history as an investigator. I'm going to tell you exactly what happened. If after that you still feel you can't trust me, so be it."

I started at the very beginning, with Louisa showing up pregnant in the house next door a few months before my eleventh birthday. With Gabriella and her quixotic impulses. With Caroline's exuberant philanthropy at other people's expense and the nagging feeling I still had of being her older sister and somehow responsible for her. I didn't tell him about Nancy ending up in Dead Stick Pond, but I described everything that had happened at Xerxes, my conversation with Dr. Chigwell, and finally Humboldt's intervention. That was the only episode I muted. I couldn't bring myself to tell him the owner of the company had had me in for brandy—I felt embarrassed because I'd let myself be gulled by the trappings of wealth. So I mumbled that I'd had a call from one of the company's senior officers.

After I finished Manheim took off his glasses and went through an elaborate cleaning ritual involving his necktie. It was clearly a habitual gesture of nervousness, but his eyes looked so naked without their protective lenses that I glanced away.

At last he put the glasses back on and picked up his pen again. "I'm not a bad lawyer. I'm really a pretty decent lawyer. Just not very ambitious. I grew up on the South Side and I like it down here. I help a lot of the businesses on the street with leasing problems, employment issues, that kind of thing. So when those two guys came to me maybe I should have sent them someplace else, but I thought I could handle the case—I've done some comp claims— and it made a nice change. Pankowski's sister owns the flower shop next door —that's why they picked me—she told them I'd done a good job for her."

He started for the filing cabinet and changed his mind. "I don't know why I want the folder—nervous habit, I guess. I mean, I know the whole damned case by heart, even after all this time."

He stopped, but I didn't prompt him. Whatever he said now would be to himself more than to me and I didn't want to intrude on the flow. After a few minutes he went on.

"It's Xerxine, you know. The way they used to make it, it left these toxic residues in the air. Do you know any chemistry? I don't either, but I made quite a study of this at the time. Xerxine is a chlorinated hydrocarbon—they add chlorine to ethylene gas usually and get a solvent. You know, the kind of thing you might clean oil from sheet metal with, or paint, or anything.

"Well, if you breathe the vapors while they're manufacturing it, it doesn't do you a whole lot of good. Affects the liver and kidneys and central nervous system and all those good things. When Humboldt first started making Xerxine back in the fifties, no one knew anything about that stuff. You know, they didn't run the plants to kill the employees, but they weren't very careful about controlling how much of the chlorinated vapors got into the air."

Now that he was into his story his manner had changed. He seemed self-confident and knowledgeable; his claim to being a good lawyer didn't seem at all farfetched.

"Then in the sixties and seventies, when people started thinking seriously about the environment, guys like Irving Selikoff began looking at industrial pollution and worker health. And they started finding that chemicals like Xerxine could be toxic at pretty low concentrations—you know, a hundred molecules per million molecules of air. What they call parts per million. So Xerxes put in air scrubbers and closed up their pipes better, and got their ppm down to federal standards. That would have been in the late seventies, when the EPA issued a standard on Xerxine. Fifty parts per million."

He smiled apologetically. "Sorry to be so technical. I can't think about this case in simple terms anymore. Anyway, Pankowski and Ferraro came to me early in 1983. They were both sick as hell, one with liver cancer, the other with aplastic anemia. They'd worked at Humboldt for a long time—since '59 for Ferraro and '61 for Pankowski—but they'd quit when they got too sick to work. That would have been two years earlier. So they couldn't collect disability. I don't think they were told it was an option."

I nodded in agreement. Companies don't willingly offer information on benefits that will add to their insurance premiums. Especially looking at a case like Louisa's, where she was getting major medical payments besides her disability check.

"But what about their union?" I asked. "Wouldn't the shop steward have notified them?"

He shook his head. "It's a single-shop union and it's pretty much a mouthpiece for the company. Especially now—there's so much unemployment in the neighborhood they don't want to rock the boat."

"Unlike the Steelworkers," I interjected dryly.

He grinned for the first time, looking even younger than before. "Well, you can't blame them. The Xerxes union, I mean. But anyway, the two guys had read someplace that Xerxine could cause these health problems, and since they were both up against it financially, they thought maybe they could at least collect workers' comp for not being able to work. You know, job-related condition and all that."

"I see. So you went to Humboldt and tried to work something out? Or you went directly to litigation?"

"I had to work fast—it wasn't clear how long either of them would live. I went to the company first, but when they didn't want to play ball I didn't fool around—I filed a suit. Of course if we'd won after they died, their families would have been entitled to an indemnity payment. And that would make quite a difference to them financially. But you like your clients to be alive to see their victories."

I nodded. It would have made a big difference, especially to Mrs. Pankowski with all her children. Illinois insurers pay a quarter of a million to families of workers who die on the job, so it was worth the effort.

"So what happened?"

"Well, I saw right away the company was going to stonewall, so we sued. Then we got an early docket. Even being stuck down on the South Side, I've got a few connections." He smiled to himself, but declined to share the joke.

"Trouble was, both guys smoked, Pankowski was a heavy drinker, and they'd both lived all their lives in South Chicago. I guess if you grew up there, I don't have to tell you what the air was like. So Humboldt socked us. They said on the one hand that there wasn't any way to prove Xerxine had made these guys sick instead of their cigarettes or the general shit in the air. And they also pointed out that both of them had been working there before anyone knew how toxic the stuff was. So even if Xerxine did make them sick, it didn't count—you know, they operated the plant based on current medical knowledge. So we lost handily. I talked to a really good appellate lawyer and he felt there just wasn't anything to go on with. End of story."

I thought about it for a minute. "Yeah, but if that's all that happened, why is Xerxes jumping like a nervous rabbit when it hears those guys' names?"

He shrugged. "Probably same reason I didn't want to talk to you to begin with. They don't believe you're on your own. They don't think you're looking for a long-lost father. They think you're trying to stir the pot up again. You've got to admit your story looks pretty farfetched."

Reluctantly, I looked at it from his point of view. Given all this history I hadn't known about, I could understand, sort of. I still couldn't figure out why Humboldt felt he had to intervene. If his company had won the case fair and square, what difference did it make if his subordinates talked to me about Pankowski and Ferraro?

"And also," I added aloud, "why are you so upset? Do you think they were wrong? I mean, do you think the trial was rigged somehow?"

He shook his head unhappily. "No. Based on the evidence, I don't think we could have won. I think we should have. I mean, I think these guys deserved something for putting twenty years of their lives into the company, especially since it's probable that working there killed them. I mean, look at your friend's mother. She's dying too. Kidney failure did you say? But the law spells it out, or the precedents do—you can't fault the company for operating under the best knowledge they had available at the time."

"So that's it? You just don't like to talk about it because you feel bad that you couldn't win for them?"

He communed again with his glasses and his tie. "Oh, that would get me down. No one likes losing, and God, you couldn't help wanting these guys to win. But then, you know, the company could see that plant go belly-up if we set a successful precedent. Everyone who'd ever been sick or died there coming back for these big settlements."

He stopped. I made myself sit very quietly.

At last he said, "No. It's just that I got a threatening phone call. After the case. When we were considering the appeal."

"That would be grounds for overturning the verdict," I burst out. "Didn't you go to the state's attorney?"

He shook his head. "I just got the one phone call. And whoever called didn't mention the case by name—just a generic reference to the dangers of using the appellate system. I'm not very tough physically, but I'm not a coward either. The call made me angry, angrier than I've ever been, and I pushed and prodded every way after that to build an appeal. There just wasn't any way to."

"They didn't call you later to congratulate you for following their advice?"

"I never heard from the guy again. But when you showed up out of nowhere. . . ."

I laughed. "Glad to know I could be mistaken for muscle. I may need it before the day is over."

He blushed. "No, no. You don't look—I don't mean—I mean, you're a very attractive lady. But you never know these days. . . . I wish I could tell you something about your friend's father, but we never talked about anything like that. My clients and I."

"No, I can see you wouldn't have." I thanked him for his frankness and got up.

"If you come across anything else you think I could help you with, let me know," he said, shaking my hand. "Especially if it might give me some grounds for a writ of certiorari."

I assured him I would and left. I was wiser than I'd been when I came in, but no less confused.

16
HOUSE CALL

It was well past noon by the time Manheim and I finished talking. I headed for the Loop and picked up a Diet Coke and a sandwich—corned beef, which I reserve for occasions when I need special nourishment—and took them to my office.

I could see Manheim's point. Sort of. If Humboldt lost a suit like that, it could spell disaster, the kind of problem that drove Johns-Manville to seek bankruptcy protection. But Manville's situation had been different: they had known asbestos was toxic and covered up their knowledge. So when the ugly truth came out workers sued for punitive damages.

All Humboldt would have faced was a series of comp claims. Even so, that might be sticky. Say they'd had a thousand workers at the plant over a ten-year period and they all died: at a quarter of a million a pop, even if Ajax was paying for it, that was a lot of balloons.

I licked mustard from my fingers. Maybe I was looking at it wrong—maybe it was Ajax not wanting to make the payout—Gordon Firth telling his good buddy Gustav Humboldt to cool out any attempts to reopen the case. But Firth couldn't have known I was involved—the word wouldn't have run around Chicago that fast. Or maybe it would. You've never seen gossip and rumor mills until you've spent a week in a large corporation.

And then, why had someone threatened Manheim about the appeal? If Humboldt was dead to rights on the legal issues, there wasn't any percentage in going after Manheim—it would just cause a judge to vacate the decree. So it couldn't have been the company trying to brush him back.

Or maybe it was some very junior person. Someone who thought he could make a name for himself in the company by putting a little muscle on the plaintiffs. That wasn't a totally improbable scenario. You get a corporate atmosphere where ethics are a little loose and subordinates think that the way to management's heart is across their opponents' bodies.

But that still didn't explain why Humboldt had lied about the suit. Why dump a charge of sabotage on the poor bastards when all they wanted was some workers' comp money? I wondered if it would be worthwhile to try to speak to Humboldt again. I visualized his full, jovial face with the cold blue eyes. You have to swim carefully when your waters are shared by a great shark. I wasn't sure I wanted to go to the big man just yet.

I groaned to myself. The problem was spreading out in front of me like ripples in a pond. I was the stone dropped in the middle and the lines were moving farther and farther away from me. I just couldn't handle so many intangible waves on my own.

I tried to turn my attention to some problems that had come in the mail, including a notice of insufficient funds to cover the check of a small hardware store whose pilfering problems I'd solved a few weeks ago. I made a call that brought me no satisfaction and decided to pack it in for the day. I'd just slung my mail into the wastebasket when the phone rang.

An efficient alto told me she was Clarissa Hollingsworth, Mr. Humboldt's personal secretary.

I sat up in my chair. Time to be alert. I wasn't ready to go to him, but the shark wanted to swim to me. "Yes, Ms. Hollingsworth. What can I do for Mr. Humboldt?"

"I don't believe he wants you to do anything," she said coolly. "He just asked me to pass on some information to you. About someone named—uh—Louisa Djiak."

She stumbled over the name—she should have practiced pronouncing it before phoning.

I repeated Louisa's name correctly. "Yes?"

"Mr. Humboldt says he talked to Dr. Chigwell about her and that it is probable that Joey Pankowski was the child's father." She had trouble with Pankowski too. I expected better from Humboldt's private secretary.

I took the receiver away from my ear and looked at it, as though I could see Ms. Hollingsworth's face in it. Or Humboldt's. At last I held it back to my mouth and asked, "Do you know who did the investigation for Mr. Humboldt?"

"I believe he interested himself directly in the matter," she said primly.

I said slowly, "I think Dr. Chigwell may have misled Mr. Humboldt. It's important that I see him to discuss the matter with him."

"I doubt that very much, Ms. Warshawski. Mr. Humboldt and the doctor have worked together a long time. If he gave Mr. Humboldt the information, you may certainly depend on it."

"Perhaps so." I tried to make my tone conciliatory. "But Mr. Humboldt told me himself that his staff sometimes try to protect him from unfortunate events. I suspect something like that may have been going on in this case."

"Really," she said huffily. "*You* may work in an environment where people can't trust each other. But Dr. Chigwell has been a most reliable associate of Mr. Humboldt's for fifty years. Maybe someone like you can't appreciate it, but the idea of Dr. Chigwell lying to Mr. Humboldt is totally ludicrous."

"Just one thing before you hang up in righteous indignation. Someone misled Mr. Humboldt terribly about the true nature of the suit Pankowski and Ferraro brought against Xerxes. That's why I'm not too confident about this last bit of news."

There was a pause, then she said grudgingly, "I'll mention the matter to Mr. Humboldt. But I doubt very much that he'll want to talk to you."

That was the best I could get from her. I frowned at the phone some more, wondering what I would say to Humboldt if I saw him. Fruitless. I locked up the office and drove up to the little hardware store on Diversey. They hadn't wanted to talk to me on the phone, but when they saw I was prepared to be vocal in front of their customers they took me into the back and reluctantly wrote out another check. Plus the ten dollars handling for the bad one. I paid it directly into my bank and went home.

Slipping in through the back entrance, I managed to sidestep Mr. Contreras and the dog. I stopped in the kitchen to inspect the food supply. Still grim. I fixed a bowl of popcorn and took it into the living room with me. Popcorn and corned beef—um-um good.

Four-thirty is a terrible time to find anything on TV—I flipped through game shows, *Sesame Street,* and the beaming face of *The Frugal Gourmet.* I finally turned off the set in disgust and reached for the phone.

The Chigwells were listed under Clio's name. She answered on the third ring, her voice distant, unyielding. Yes, she remembered who I was. She didn't think her brother would want to speak to me, but she went to see, anyway. He didn't.

"Look, Ms. Chigwell. I hate having to be such a pest, but there's something I want to know. Has Gustav Humboldt called him in the last few days?"

She was surprised. "How did you know?"

"I didn't. His secretary passed on some information that Humboldt supposedly got from your brother. I wondered if Humboldt made it up."

"What did he say Curtis told him?"

"That Joey Pankowski was Caroline Djiak's father."

She asked me to explain who they were, then went off to confront her brother. She was gone for a quarter of an hour. I finished the popcorn and did some leg raises, lying with the phone near my ear so I could hear her return.

She came back on the line abruptly. "He says he knew about the man, that the girl's mother had told him all about it back when they hired her."

"I see," I said weakly.

"The trouble is, you can't spend your whole life with someone without knowing when they're lying. I don't know what part of it Curtis is making up, but one thing I can tell you—he'd say anything Gustav Humboldt told him to."

While I struggled to add this news to my pickled brain, something else struck me. "Why are you telling me this, Ms. Chigwell?"

"I don't know," she said, surprised. "Maybe after seventy-nine years, I'm tired of having Curtis hide behind me. Good-bye." She hung up with an abrupt click.

I spent Saturday stewing about Humboldt and Chigwell, unable to think of any reason why they would concoct a story about Louisa and Joey, unable to think of a way to get a handle on them. When Murray Ryerson, head of the *Herald-Star's* crime bureau, called me on Sunday because one of his gofers had dug up the news that Nancy Cleghorn and I went to high school together, I even agreed to talk to him.

Murray follows De Paul basketball. Or slobbers over it. Although I live—and die—with the Cubs every year, and maintain a wistful love for the Bears' Otis Wilson, I don't really care whether the Blue Demons ever score another basket. In Chicago that's extreme heresy—equivalent to saying you hate St. Patrick's Day parades. So I agreed to truck out to the Horizon and watch them scrap around with Indiana or Loyola or whoever.

"Anyway," Murray said, "you can sit there remembering how you and Nancy handled the same shots, only better. It will give a more intense flavor to your memories."

De Paul lost a squeaker, with Murray commenting libelously on young Joey Meyer and the entire offense during the hour wait to move from the parking lot back to the tollway. It was only when we were in Ethel's, a Lithuanian restaurant on the northwest side, filling Murray's six-four frame with a few dozen sweet-and-sour cabbage rolls, that he got down to the real business of the afternoon.

"So what's your interest in Cleghorn's death?" he asked casually. "Family call you in to investigate?"

"The cops got a tip that I sent her to her death." I calmly ate another fluffy dumpling. I'd have to run ten miles in the morning to work off all this.

"Come on. I must've heard a dozen people say you've been nosing around down there. What's going on?"

I shook my head. "I told you. I'm clearing my name."

"Yeah, and I'm the Ayatollah of Detroit."

I love it when I'm telling Murray the truth and he's convinced it's a big cover-up—it gives me terrific leverage. Unfortunately, there wasn't much to pry out of him. The police had called on Steve Dresberg, on Dresberg's mouthpiece, Leon Haas, on a few dozen other upstanding South Chicagoans —including some old lovers of Nancy's—and didn't have anything they considered a real lead.

Murray finally got tired of the game. "I guess there's enough that we could do a little human-interest story of Nancy and you in college, living on table scraps and studying the classics in between creaming the best women's teams in the region. I hate giving you print space when you're not earning it, but it'll help keep her name in front of the state's attorney."

"Thanks a whole bunch, Murray."

When he dropped me at my place on Racine, I got in my car and headed for Hinsdale. Seeing him had given me a nasty little idea on a way to pressure Chigwell.

It was close to seven when I rang the bell at the side door, not the ideal time for paying house calls. When Ms. Chigwell answered my ring I tried to make myself look earnest and trustworthy. Her stern features didn't give me any clue as to whether I was succeeding.

"Curtis won't talk to you," she said in her abrupt way, showing no surprise at my appearance.

"Try this on him," I suggested in an earnest, trustworthy manner. "His picture on the front page of the *Herald-Star* and some heartwarming stories on his medical career."

She looked at me grimly. Why she didn't just shut the door in my face I didn't understand. And why she went off to deliver the message puzzled me still further. It reminded me of some elderly cousins of my beloved ex-husband Dick, two brothers and a sister who lived together. The brothers had quarreled some thirteen years previously and refused to speak, so they would ask the sister to pass them salt, marmalade, and tea, and she obligingly did so.

However, Dr. Chigwell came to the door in person this time, not trusting his sister with the marmalade. With his thin neck bobbing forward, he looked like a harassed turkey.

"Listen here, young lady. I don't have to take these threats. If you're not away from this door in thirty seconds, I'm calling the police and you can explain to them why you've started a persecution campaign."

He had me. I could just imagine trying to tell a suburban cop—or even Bobby Mallory—that one of Chicago's ten wealthiest men was lying to me and getting his old plant doctor to collude. I bowed my head in resignation.

"Consider me gone. The reporter who'll be calling you in the morning is named Murray Ryerson. I'll explain to him about your old medical cases and so on."

"Get out of here!" His voice had turned to a hiss that chilled my blood. I left.

17

TOMBSTONE BLUES

Nancy's funeral was scheduled for eleven Monday morning in the Methodist church she had attended as a child. I seem to spend too much time at the funerals of friends—I have a navy suit associated so strongly with them that I can't bring myself to wear it anywhere else. I dawdled around in panty hose and a blouse, unable to shake a superstitious dread that putting on the suit would make Nancy's death final.

I couldn't set my mind to anything, to Chigwell or Humboldt, to organizing a plan to beat the police to Nancy's killer, or even to organizing the spreading papers in my living room. That was where I had started the morning, thinking with a few hours on my hands I could get things put away. I was too fragmented to create order.

Suddenly at ten of ten, still in my underwear, I looked up the number for Humboldt's corporate offices and phoned. An indifferent operator switched me through to his office, where I reached not Clarissa Hollingsworth but her assistant. When I asked for Mr. Humboldt, after a certain amount of dickering I got Ms. Hollingsworth.

The cool alto greeted me patronizingly. "I haven't had a chance to speak to Mr. Humboldt about seeing you, Ms. Warshawski. I'll make sure that he gets the message, but he doesn't come in every day anymore."

"Yeah, I don't suppose you call him at home for consultations, either. In case you do, you might add to my other message that I saw Dr. Chigwell last night."

She finished the conversation with a condescending speed that left me shouting into a dead phone. I finished dressing as easily as I could with my hands shaking and headed south once more.

Mount of Olives Methodist dated to the turn of the century, its high-backed dark pews and giant rose window evoking a time when it was filled with women in long dresses and children in high-buttoned shoes. Today's congregation couldn't afford to keep up the stained-glass windows showing Jesus in Calvary. Places where Jesus's brooding ascetic face had been broken were filled in with wired burglar glass, making him look like a sufferer from an acute skin disease.

While Nancy's four brothers served as ushers their children sat in the front pews, shoving and poking at each other despite the near presence of their aunt's draped casket. Their harshly whispered insults could be heard throughout the nave until drowned by some melancholy bars from the organ.

I went up to the front to let Mrs. Cleghorn know I was there. She smiled at me with tremulous warmth.

"Come over to the house after the service," she whispered. "We'll have coffee and a chance to talk."

She invited me to sit with her, glancing distastefully at her grandchildren. I disengaged myself gently—I didn't want to be a buffer between her and the wrestling monsters. Besides, I wanted to go to the back so I could see who showed up—it's a cliché, but murderers often can't resist going to their victims' funerals. Maybe part of a primitive superstition, trying to make sure the person is really dead, that she gets truly buried so her ghost doesn't walk.

After I'd settled myself near the entrance Diane Logan swept in, resplendent in her silver fox. She brushed my cheek and squeezed my hand before moving up the aisle.

"Who was that?" a voice muttered in my ear.

I gave a start and turned around. It was Sergeant McGonnigal, trying to look mournful in a dark suit. So the police were also hopeful.

"She used to play basketball with Nancy and me; she owns a Gold Coast PR firm nowadays," I muttered back. "I don't think she slugged Nancy—she could outplay her twenty years ago. Today, too, come to think of it. I don't know everyone's name—tell me which one the killer is."

He smiled a little. "When I saw you sitting here I thought my worries were over—little Polish detective is going to nab the murderer in front of the altar."

"Methodist church," I muttered. "I don't think they call it an altar."

Caroline clattered in with the group of people I'd seen in the SCRAP office with her. They had the preternatural earnestness of those who don't often find themselves at solemn functions. Caroline's copper curls were brushed into a semblance of tidiness. She wore a black suit designed for a much taller woman—the bunched clumps of material at the bottom showed where she'd hemmed it with her usual impatient inefficiency. If she saw me, she gave no sign, moving with the SCRAP contingent to a pew about half-way up the aisle.

Behind them came a handful of older women, perhaps Mrs. Cleghorn's pals at the local branch of the library. When they'd passed I saw a thin young man standing in their wake. The dim light picked out his angular silhouette. He looked around uncertainly, saw me staring at him, and looked away.

The self-deprecating embarrassment with which he turned his head brought back to me who he was: young Art Jurshak. He'd made just such an effacing move in talking to the old ward heelers at his father's office.

In the half-light from the windows I couldn't make out his beautifully chiseled features. He sidled into a seat toward the back.

McGonnigal tapped me on the shoulder. "Who's that alfalfa sprout?" he growled.

I smiled seraphically and put a finger to my lips—the organ had begun to play loudly, signaling the arrival of the minister. We went through "Abide with Me" at such a slow pace that I kept bracing myself for each succeeding chord.

The minister was a short, plump man whose remaining black hair was combed in two neat rows on either side of a wrinkled dome. He looked like the kind of TV preacher who makes your stomach turn, but as he spoke I realized I'd made the dread mistake of judging by appearances. He clearly had known Nancy well and spoke of her with eloquent forcefulness. I felt my throat tighten again and leaned back in the pew to inspect the ceiling beams. The wood had been painted in the blue and orange stencils popular in Victorian churches. By focusing on the intricate lacy patterns I was able to relax enough to join in the final hymn.

I kept glancing at young Art. He spent the service perched on the edge of his pew, gripping the back of the bench in front of him. When the last chords of "In Heavenly Love Abiding" had finally been wrenched painfully from the organ, he slid out of his seat and headed for the exit.

I caught up with him on the porch, where he was moving nervously from foot to foot, unable to free himself from a drunk panhandler. When I touched Art's arm he jumped.

"I didn't know you and Nancy were friends," I said. "She never mentioned you to me."

He mumbled something that sounded like "knew her slightly."

"I'm V. I. Warshawski. Nancy and I played high school and college basketball together. I saw you at the Tenth Ward office last week. You're Art Jurshak's son, aren't you?"

At that his chiseled-marble face turned even whiter; I was afraid he might faint. Even though he was a slender young man, I wasn't sure I could break his fall.

The drunk, who'd been listening interestedly, sidled closer. "Your friend looks pretty sick, lady. How about fifty cents for coffee—cup for him, cup for me."

I turned my back on him firmly and took Art's elbow. "I'm a private detective and I'm trying to look into Nancy's death. If you were friends with her, I'd like to talk to you. About her connections with your father's office."

He shook his head dumbly, his blue eyes dark with fear. After a long internal debate he seemed to be on the brink of forcing himself to speak. Unfortunately as he opened his mouth the other mourners began emerging from the church. As soon as people started passing us Art wrenched himself from my grip and bolted down the street.

I tried to follow, but tripped over the drunk. I cursed him roundly as I pulled myself back to my feet. He was reviling me in return, but broke off suddenly as McGonnigal appeared—years of living around the police gave him a sixth sense about them even in plainclothes.

"What's the redhead so scared of, Warshawski?" the sergeant demanded, ignoring the panhandler. We watched Art get into his car, a late-model Chrysler parked at the end of the street, and tear off.

"I have that effect on men," I said shortly. "Drives them mad. You find your murderer?"

"I don't know. Your male model here was the only person acting suspiciously. Why don't you show what a helpful citizen you are and give me his name?"

I turned to face him. "It's no secret—the name is real well known down in these parts. Art Jurshak."

McGonnigal's lips tightened. "Just because Mallory's my boss doesn't mean you have to jerk me around the way you do him. Tell me the kid's name."

I held up my right hand. "Scout's honor, Sergeant. Jurshak's his old man. Young Art just joined his agency or his office or something. If you catch up with him, don't use a rubber hose—I don't think he's got too much stamina."

McGonnigal grinned savagely. "Don't worry, Warshawski. He's got stronger protection than a thick skin. I won't mess up his curly locks. . . . You going over to the Cleghorn place for coffee? I heard some of the ladies talking about what they were bringing. Mind if I slide in with you?"

"We little Polish detectives live to help the cops. Come along."

He grinned and held the car door open for me. "That get under your skin, Warshawski? My apologies—you're not all that little."

A handful of mourners was already at the house on Muskegon when we got there. Mrs. Cleghorn, her makeup streaked with dried tears, greeted me warmly and accepted McGonnigal politely. I stood in the little entryway talking with her for a minute while the sergeant wandered into the back of the house.

"Kerry took the children to her house, so things will be a little calmer today," she said. "Maybe when I retire I'll move to Oregon."

I hugged her. "Go across the country to avoid being a grandmother? Maybe you could just change the locks—it'd be less drastic."

"I guess it proves how upset I am, Victoria, talking like that—I've never wanted anyone to know how I felt about my sons' children." She paused a moment, then added awkwardly, "If you want to talk to Ron Kappelman about—about Nancy or anything, he's in the living room."

The doorbell rang. While she moved to answer it I crossed the little hall to the living room. I'd never seen Ron Kappelman, but I didn't have any trouble recognizing him—he was the only man in the room. He was about my age, perhaps a bit older, stocky, with dark brown hair cut close to his head. He wore a gray tweed jacket, which was frayed at the lapels and cuffs, and corduroy pants. He was sitting by himself on a round Naugahyde hassock, flipping idly through the pages of an old *National Geographic.*

The four women in the room, the ones from church I'd assumed were Mrs. Cleghorn's co-workers, were murmuring together in the other corner. They glanced over at me, saw they didn't know me, and went back to their gentle buzzing.

I pulled up a straight-backed chair next to Kappelman. He glanced at me, made a bit of a face, then tossed the magazine back to the coffee table.

"I know," I said sympathetically. "It's a pain to talk to strangers at an affair like this. I wouldn't do it if I didn't think you could help me."

He raised his eyebrows. "I doubt it, but you can try me."

"My name's V. I. Warshawski. I'm an old friend of Nancy's. We played basketball together a while back. A long while back." I can't get over how fast the years started zipping by after my thirtieth birthday. It just didn't seem that long since Nancy and I had been in college.

"Sure. I know who you are. Nance talked about you a number of times— said you kept her from going mad when the two of you were in high school. I'm Ron Kappelman, but you seemed to know that when you came in."

"Nancy tell you I'm a private investigator these days? Well, I hadn't seen her for quite some time, but we got together for a basketball reunion a week or so ago."

"Yeah, I know," he cut in. "We went to a meeting together right after. She talked about it."

A swarm of people buzzed into the room. Even though they were keeping their voices subdued, there wasn't enough space to absorb the bodies or the sound. Someone standing over me lighted a cigarette and I felt hot ash land on the round neck of my bolero jacket.

"Could we go somewhere to talk?" I asked. "Nancy's old bedroom or a bar or something? I'm trying to look into her death, but I can't seem to get a thread to pull on. I was hoping you could tell me something."

He shook his head. "Believe me, if I thought I had any hot dope, I'd've been to the cops like a rocket. But I'd be glad to get out of here."

We pushed our way through the crowd, paying affectionate respects to Mrs. Cleghorn as we left. The warmth with which she spoke to Kappelman seemed to indicate that he and Nancy had remained on good terms. I wondered vaguely what had happened to McGonnigal, but he was a big cop, he could look after himself.

Outside, Kappelman said, "Why don't you follow me down to my place in Pullman? There isn't any coffee shop nearby that's clean and quiet. As you surely know."

I trailed his decrepit Rabbit down side streets to 113th and Langley. He stopped in front of one of the tidy brick row houses that line Pullman's streets, houses with sheer fronts and stoops that make you think of pictures of Philadelphia when the Constitution was signed.

The neat, well-kept exterior didn't really prepare me for the meticulous restoration inside. The walls were papered in bright Victorian floral designs, the paneling refinished to a glow of dark walnut, the furniture and rugs beautifully maintained period pieces set on well-finished hardwood floors.

"This is gorgeous," I said, overwhelmed. "Did you fix it up yourself?"

He nodded. "Carpentry is kind of my hobby—makes a good switch from mucking about with the stunads I spend my days with. The furniture is all stuff I picked up at area flea markets."

He led me into a little kitchen with Italian tile on the floor and countertops and gleaming copper-bottomed pots on the walls. I perched on a high stool at one side of a tiled island while he made coffee at the burners on the other.

"So who asked you to investigate Nancy's death? Her mother? Not sure the cops will buck the politicos down here and see that justice runs its inexorable course?" He cocked an eye at me while deftly assembling an infusion pot.

"Nope. If you know Mrs. Cleghorn at all, you must realize her mind doesn't run to vengeance."

"So who's your client?" He turned to the refrigerator and laid out cream and a plate of muffins.

I absentmindedly watched the seat of his trousers tighten across his rear while he bent over. The seam was fraying; a few more deep bends could create an interesting situation. I nobly refrained from dropping a plate at his feet, but waited to answer until he was facing me again.

"Part of what my clients buy when they hire me is confidentiality. If I blabbed their secrets to you, I could hardly expect you to blab yours to me, could I?"

He shook his head. "I haven't got any secrets. At least not relating to Nancy Cleghorn. I'm the counsel for SCRAP. I work for a number of community groups—public interest law's my specialty. Nancy was great to work with. She was organized, clearheaded, knew when to fight and when to drop back. Unlike her boss."

"Caroline?" It was hard to picture Caroline Djiak as anyone's boss. "So all your dealings with Nancy were purely professional?"

He pointed a coffee spoon at me. "Don't try to trip me up, Warshawski. I play ball with the big boys. Cream? You ought to, you know—binds with the caffeine and keeps you from getting stomach cancer."

He set a heavy porcelain mug in front of me and stuck the plate of muffins into the microwave. "No. Nance and I had a brief fling a couple of years back. When I started at SCRAP. She was getting over a heavy thing and I'd been divorced about ten months. We cheered each other up, but we didn't have anything special to offer each other. Besides friendship, which is special enough that you don't screw it up. Certainly not by banging your friends on the head and dropping them in a swamp."

He took the muffins out of the oven and climbed onto a stool at the end of the counter on my left. I drank some of the rich coffee and took a blueberry muffin.

"I'll let the cops take you through your paces. Where were you Thursday afternoon at two P.M. and so on. What I really want to know, though, is who Nancy thought was following her. Did she think she'd got Dresberg's back up? Or did it really have anything to do with the recycling plant?"

He grimaced. "Little Caroline's theory—which makes me want to trash it. Not a good attitude for her outfit's counsel to take. Truth is, I don't know. We were both pissed as hell after the hearing two weeks ago. When we talked on Tuesday, Nance said she'd cover the political angle, see if she could find out if and why Jurshak was blocking it. I was working on the legal stuff, wondering if we could finesse the MSD—Metropolitan Sanitary District—to get the permit. Maybe get the state and U.S. EPA departments involved."

He absentmindedly ate a second muffin and buttered a third. His bulging waistline made me shake my head when he offered me the plate.

"So you don't know who she talked to in Jurshak's office?"

He shook his head. "I had the impression, nothing concrete to go on, but I think she had a lover there. Someone she was a little ashamed of seeing and didn't want her pals to know about, or someone she thought she had to protect." He stared into the distance, trying to put his feelings into words. "Canceling dinner plans, not wanting to go to the Hawks games, which we shared season tickets to. Stuff like that. So she could've been getting information from him and not wanting me to know about it. The last time we spoke—a week ago today it must have been—she said she thought she was onto something but she needed more evidence. I never talked to her again." He stopped abruptly and busied himself with his coffee.

"Well, what about Dresberg? Based on what you know of the situation down there, would you think he might've been against this recycling center?"

"God, I wouldn't think so. Although with a guy like that you never know. Look."

He set down his coffee cup and leaned intently across the counter, sketching Dresberg's operations with sweeping gestures. The garbage empire included hauling, incinerating, storage-container and landfill operations. Within his domain Dresberg was protective of any perceived encroachments —even any questioning. Hence the threats a year before when Caroline and Nancy had tried to oppose a new PCB incinerator that didn't meet code standards.

"But the recycling center didn't have anything to do with any of his operations," he finished. "Xerxes and Glow-Rite are just dumping into their own lagoons right now. All SCRAP would do is take the wastes and recycle them."

I thought about it. "He could see expansion potential cutting into his business down the road. Or maybe he wants SCRAP to use his trucks to do the hauling."

He shook his head. "If that was the case, he'd just be putting an arm on them to use his trucks, not offing Nancy. I'm not saying it's impossible he was involved. The plant's certainly in his sphere. But it doesn't leap out at me on the surface."

We let the talk drift after that, to friends we had in common at the Illinois bar, to my cousin Boom-Boom, whom Kappelman used to watch at the Stadium when he was with the Hawks.

"There's never been another player like him," Kappelman said regretfully.

"You're telling me." I got up and put on my coat. "So if you come across something strange—anything, whether it seems to have a direct bearing on Nancy's death or not—give me a call, okay?"

"Yeah, sure." His gaze seemed a little unfocused. He seemed about to say something, then changed his mind, shook my hand, and escorted me to the door.

18 IN HIS FATHER'S SHADOW

I didn't disbelieve Kappelman. I didn't believe him, either. I mean the guy made a living persuading judges and commissioners to support community groups instead of the industrial or political heavyweights they usually favored. Despite his frayed trousers and jacket, I suspected he was pretty convincing. And if Nancy and he were the good buddies he claimed they'd been, was it really credible that she hadn't given him the ghost of an idea about what she'd learned from the alderman's office?

Of course it was a little pat on my part looking for Dresberg to be the fall guy. Just because he had made threats in the past and had a lot of muscle and was interested in waste disposal.

I meandered across side streets and headed into East Side, to the ward offices on Avenue M. It was a little after three and the place was hopping. I passed a couple of patrol cops coming out. When I got into the main office my old pals with the paunches were hard at it with a half dozen or so favor-seekers. Another couple, maybe patronage workers through with street cleaning for the day, were playing checkers in the window.

Nobody really looked at me, but the conversations quieted down. "I'm looking for young Art," I said amiably in the direction of the bald man who'd been the spokesman on my first visit.

"Not here," he said briefly, without looking up.

"When do you expect him?"

The three office workers exchanged the silent communication I'd observed earlier and agreed that my question warranted a slight chuckle.

"We don't," Baldy said, going back to his client.

"Do you know where else I could find him?"

"We don't keep tabs on the kid," Baldy expanded, thinking perhaps of the claim drafts they were expecting from me. "Sometimes he shows up in the afternoon, sometimes he don't. He hasn't been in today so he might turn up. You never know."

"I see." I picked up the *Sun-Times* from his desk and sat in one of the chairs lining the wall. It was an old wooden one, yellow and scuffed, extremely uncomfortable. I read "Sylvia," skimmed the sports pages, and tried interesting myself in the latest Greylord trial, shifting my pelvis around on the hard surface in an unsuccessful search for a spot that wouldn't rub against my bones. After about half an hour I gave it up and put one of my cards on Baldy's desk.

"V. I. Warshawski. I'll try back in a bit. Tell him to call me if I miss him."

Except for the blueberry muffin Ron Kappelman had given me, I hadn't really eaten today. I went down to the corner of Ewing where a neighborhood bar advertised submarines and Italian beef and had a meatball sub with a draft. I'm not much of a beer drinker, but it seemed more suited to the neighborhood than diet soda.

When I got back to the ward office the visitors had pretty well cleared out except for the checker players in the corner. Baldy shook his head at me to indicate—I think—that young Art hadn't been in. I felt proud of myself—I was beginning to seem like a regular.

I pulled a little spiral notebook from my bag. To entertain myself while I waited I tried calculating the expenses I'd incurred since starting to look for Caroline Djiak's old man. I've always been a little jealous of Kinsey Milhone's immaculate record-keeping; I didn't even have receipts for meals or gas. Certainly not for cleaning up the Magli pumps, which was going to run close to thirty dollars.

I'd gotten up to two hundred and fifty when young Art came in with his usual diffident step. There was something in his face, a naked desire for acceptance from the tired old pols in the room, that made me flinch. They looked at him unblinkingly, waiting for him to speak. And finally he obliged.

"Any—anything for me from my dad?" He licked his lips reflexively.

Baldy shook his head and returned to his paper. "Lady wants to talk to you," he said from the depths of the *Sun-Times*.

Art hadn't seen me until then—he'd been too intent on the disappointment he felt bound to suffer from the men. He looked around the room then and located me. He didn't recognize me at first: his perfect forehead furrowed in a momentary question. It wasn't until he'd come over to shake my hand that he remembered where he'd seen me, and then he didn't think he could flee without achieving total humiliation.

"Where can we go to talk?" I asked briskly, taking his hand in a firm grasp in case he decided to chance the indignity.

He smiled unhappily. "Upstairs, I guess. I—I have an office. A small office."

I followed him up the linoleum-covered stairs to a suite with his father's name on it. A middle-aged woman, her brown hair neatly coiffed above a well-cut dress, was sitting in the outer office. Her desk was a little jungle of potted plants twined around family photographs. Behind her were doors to the inner offices, one with Art, Sr.'s, name repeated on it, the other blank.

"Your dad isn't here, Art," she said in a motherly way. "He's been at a Council meeting all day. I really don't expect him until Wednesday."

He flushed miserably. "Thanks, Mrs. May. I just need to use my office for a few minutes."

"Of course, Art. You don't need my permission to do that." She continued to stare at me, hoping to force me to introduce myself. It seemed to me it would be a small but important victory for Art if she didn't know whom he was seeing. I smiled at her without speaking, but I'd underestimated her tenacity.

"I'm Ida Maiercyk, but everyone calls me Mrs. May," she said as I passed her desk.

"How do you do?" I continued to smile and went on by to where Art was standing miserably in front of his office. I hoped she was scowling impotently, but didn't turn around to check.

Art flipped on a wall switch and illuminated one of the most barren cubicles I'd seen outside a monastery. It held a plain pressed-wood desk and two metal folding chairs. Nothing else. Not even a filing cabinet to give the pretense of work. A wise alderman knows better than to live above the community that's supporting him, especially when half that community is out of work, but this was downright insulting. Even the secretary had more lavish appointments.

"Why do you put up with this?" I demanded.

"With what?" he said, flushing again.

"You know—with that loathsome woman out there treating you like a submoronic two-year-old. With those ward heelers waiting to bait you like a carp. Why don't you go get a position in someone else's agency?"

He shook his head. "These things aren't as easy as they look to you. I just graduated two years ago. If—if I can prove to my dad that I can handle some of his workload . . ." His voice trailed away.

"If you're hanging around hoping for his approval, you'll be here the rest of your life," I said brutally. "If he doesn't want to give it to you, there's nothing you can do to make him. You're better off stopping the effort, because you're only making yourself miserable and you're not impressing him."

He gave an unhappy little smile that made me want to take him by the scruff of the neck and shake him. "You don't know him and you don't know me, so you don't know what you're talking about. I'm just—I've always been —just too big a disappointment. But it's nothing to do with you. If you've come around to talk to me about Nancy Cleghorn, I can't help you any more than I could this morning."

"You and she were lovers, weren't you?" I wondered if his chiseled good looks could possibly have compensated Nancy for his youth and insecurity.

He shook his head without speaking.

"Nancy had a lover here that she didn't want any of her friends to know about. It doesn't seem too likely that it was Moe, Curly, or Larry downstairs. Or even Mrs. May—Nancy had better taste than that. And anyway, why else would you go to her funeral?"

"Maybe I just respected the work she was doing here in the community," he muttered.

Mrs. May opened the door without knocking. "You two need anything?

If you don't, I'm going to take off now. You want to leave any message for your father about your meeting, Art?"

He looked helplessly at me for a second, then just shook his head again without speaking.

"Thanks, Mrs. May," I said genially. "It was good to meet you."

She shot me a look of venom and snapped the door to. I could see her shadow outlined against the glass upper half of the door as she hesitated over a possible retaliatory strike, then her silhouette faded as she marched off toward home.

"If you don't want to talk about your relations with Nancy, maybe you can just give me the same information you gave her about Big Art's interest in SCRAP's recycling plant."

He gripped the front of the pressed-wood desk and looked at me imploringly. "I didn't tell her anything. I hardly knew her. And I don't know what my dad is doing about their recycling plant. Now can you please go away? I'd be as happy as—as anybody if you found her killer, but you must see I don't know anything about her."

I scowled in frustration. He was upset, but it sure wasn't because of me. He had to have been Nancy's lover. Had to. Otherwise he wouldn't have been in church this morning. But I couldn't think of any way to get him to trust me enough to talk about it.

"Yeah, I guess I'll go. One last question. How well do you know Leon Haas?"

He looked at me blankly. "I never heard of him."

"Steve Dresberg?"

His face went totally white and he fainted on me.

19

YOU CAN'T GO HOME AGAIN

By the time I got home it was past dark. I had stayed in South Chicago long enough to make sure young Art was fit to drive. It seemed unnecessarily cruel to turn him over to the ward heelers for comfort, but my display of charity didn't make him any more willing to talk. Frustrated, I finally left him at the door of the ward office.

The drive north brought me no solace. I walked wearily up the front walk, dropped my keys as I fumbled with the inner lobby door, then dropped them again as I was going upstairs. Bone-tired, I turned back down the stairs to retrieve them. Behind Mr. Contreras's door, Peppy gave a welcoming bark. As I headed back up I heard his locks scraping back behind me. I stiffened, waiting for the flow.

"That you, doll? You just getting back? Your friend's funeral was today, huh? You haven't been out drinking, have you? People think it's a way to drown their sorrows, but believe me, it only causes you more grief than you started with. I should know—I tried it more than once. But then when Clara died I took one drink and remembered how it used to get her down, me coming home from a funeral with a good one tied on. I said I wouldn't do it, not for her, not after all the times she told me how stupid I was, crying over some friend when I was too drunk to get his name out straight."

"No," I said, forcing a smile, holding my hand out for the dog to lick. "I haven't been drinking. I had to see a whole bunch of people. Not a lot of fun."

"Well, you go on upstairs and take a hot bath, doll. By the time you've done that and had a chance to rest, I'll have some dinner ready. I have me a nice steak I've been saving for sometime special, and that's what you need when you're feeling this low. A little red meat, get your blood flowing again, and life'll look a whole lot better to you."

"Thanks," I said. "It's very good of you, but I really don't—"

"Nope. You think you want to be alone, but believe me, cookie, that's the worst thing for you when you're feeling like this. Her royal highness and I'll get you fed, and then if you're ready to be on your own again, you say the word and we'll be back down here on the double."

I just couldn't bring myself to bring the cloud of hurt to his faded brown eyes by insisting on being alone. Cursing myself for my soft heart, I trudged up the stairs to my apartment. Despite my neighbor's dire words, I headed straight for the Black Label bottle, kicking off my pumps and pulling off my panty hose while I unscrewed the cap. I drank from the bottle, a long swallow that sent a glow of warmth to my weary shoulders.

Filling a glass, I took it into the bathroom with me. I dumped my funeral suit on the floor and climbed into the tub. By the time Mr. Contreras showed up with the steak, I was a little drunk and much more relaxed than I'd have thought possible a half hour before.

He had already had dinner; he brought his grappa bottle to keep me company while I ate. After a few bites I grudgingly admitted—only to myself —that he'd been right about the food: life did start to look better. The steak was done to a turn, crisply brown on the outside, red within. He'd cooked up some pan fries with garlic and brought his conscientious nod to my diet, a plate of lettuce. He was a good plain cook, self-taught as a hobby during his widowerhood—he'd never done more in the kitchen than fetch beer when his wife was still alive.

I was finishing off the fries with the rest of the meat juice when the phone rang. I handed Peppy the bone she'd been eyeing—not begging for, just keeping an eye on in case someone broke in and tried to steal it—and went over to the piano, where I'd left the living-room extension.

"Warshawski?" It was a man's voice, cold and harsh. Not one I knew.

"Yes."

"Maybe it's time you butted out of South Chicago, Warshawski. You don't live there anymore, you don't have any business there."

I wished I hadn't had the third whiskey and desperately tried assembling my scrambled brain. "And you do?" I asked insolently.

He ignored me. "I hear you can swim pretty good, Warshawski. But the swimmer hasn't been born that can float through a swamp."

"You calling on Art Jurshak's behalf? Or Steve Dresberg's?"

"It doesn't matter to you, Warshawski. Because if you're smart, you're butting out, and if you're not, you won't be around to worry about it."

He hung up. My knees felt slightly weak. I sat on the piano bench to steady myself.

"Bad news, cookie?"

Mr. Contreras's weather-beaten face showed kindly concern. On second thought, it wasn't such a bad idea to have him with me tonight.

"Just an old-style thug. Reminding me that Chicago's the world float-fish capital." I tried keeping my tone airy, but the words came out heavier than I wanted.

"He threaten you?"

"Sort of." I tried to grin, but to my annoyance my lips were trembling. The image of the rank marsh grasses, the mud, the shapeless fishing couple and their wild red-eyed dog made me shiver uncontrollably.

Mr. Contreras hovered over me solicitously: Shouldn't I get out my Smith & Wesson? Call the police? Barricade the doors? Check into a hotel under an assumed name? When I turned down those offers he suggested I call Murray Ryerson at the *Herald-Star*—an act of true nobility because he had a fierce jealousy of Murray. Peppy, sensing his tension, dropped her bone and came over with a little bark.

"It's okay, guys," I assured them. "It's just talk. No one's going to shoot me. At least not tonight."

Mr. Contreras, unable to do anything else, offered me his grappa bottle. I waved it aside. The threat had cleared out my brain; I didn't see any point in fogging it up again with my neighbor's repellent booze.

On the other hand, I wasn't quite ready to be on my own again. Amid the stack of old notebooks and school papers in the back closet I dug out a worn checker set my dad and Bobby Mallory used to linger over.

We played four or five games, the dog contentedly returning to her bone in the corner behind the piano. Mr. Contreras was just getting reluctantly to his feet when the doorbell rang. The dog let out a deep bark. The old man became extremely excited, urging me to get out my gun, to let him go downstairs, telling me to go down the back way and summon help.

"Oh, nonsense," I said. "No one's going to shoot me in my own home two hours after a phone call—they'll at least wait until morning to see if I've listened to them."

I went to the intercom by the front door.

"Vic! Let me in! I need to see you." It was Caroline Djiak.

I pressed the button releasing the lobby door and went out to wait in the upper hallway for her. Peppy stood next to me, her golden tail lowered and moving gently to show she was on the alert. Caroline ran up the stairs, her feet clattering on the uncarpeted risers like an ancient el rounding the curve at Thirty-fifth Street.

"Vic!" she shrieked when she saw me. "What are you doing? I thought I told you to stop looking for my father. Why can't you just once do what I ask you to!"

Peppy, taking exception to her ferocity, began to bark. One of the second-floor tenants came to his door and yelled up at us to shut up. "Some people have to work, you know!"

Before Mr. Contreras could leap to my defense, I took Caroline firmly by the arm and dragged her into my apartment. Mr. Contreras looked at her critically. Deciding she wasn't dangerous—at least not an immediate physical threat—he stuck a calloused hand at her and introduced himself.

Caroline was in no mood for ordinary civility. "Vic, I'm begging you. I came all this way since you wouldn't listen to me on the phone. You've got to leave my affairs alone."

"Caroline Djiak," I informed Mr. Contreras. "She's pretty upset. Maybe you should leave me to talk to her."

He started getting the dinner dishes together. I pulled Caroline to the couch.

"What is going on with you, Caroline? What is frightening you so much?"

"I'm not frightened," she yelled. "I'm angry. Angry with you for not leaving me alone when I asked you to."

"Look, kiddo, I'm not a television you turn on and off. I could overlook my conversation with your grandparents—they're so sick nothing I could do would make any difference to them anyway. But everyone at Humboldt Chemical is lying to me about the men your mother used to work with, the ones who had the best chance of being your father. I just can't let that go. And it's not trivial, what they're saying—they're completely reinventing the last years of these guys' lives."

"Vic, you don't understand." She grabbed my right hand in her intensity, squeezing it hard. "You can't keep crossing these people. They're totally ruthless. You don't know what they might do."

"Such as what?"

She looked wildly around the room, seeking inspiration. "They might kill you, Vic. They might see you end up in the swamp the way Nancy did, or in the river!"

Mr. Contreras had stopped all pretense of getting ready to leave. I removed my hand from Caroline's grasp and stared at her coldly.

"Okay. I want the truth now. Not your embellished version. What do you know about the people who killed Nancy?"

"Nothing, Vic. Nothing. Honestly. You have to believe me. It's just . . . just . . ."

"Just what?" I grabbed her shoulders and shook her. "Who threatened Nancy? You've been saying for the last week that it was Art Jurshak because he didn't want her starting the recycling plant. Now you want it to be the people down at Xerxes because I'm hunting for your old man there? Goddamnit, Caroline, can't you see how important this is? Can't you see that this is life and death?"

"That's what I've been telling you, Vic!" She shouted so loudly that the dog started barking again. "That's why I'm telling you to mind your own business!"

"Caroline!" I felt my voice go into an upper register and tried to get a grip on myself before I broke her neck. I moved to the easy chair next to the sofa.

"Caroline. Who called you? Dr. Chigwell? Art Jurshak? Steve Dresberg? Gustav Humboldt himself?"

"No one, Vic." The gentian eyes were awash with tears. "No one. You just don't understand anything about life in South Chicago anymore, you've been away so long. Can't you just take my word for it, take my word that you should quit already?"

I ignored her. "Ron Kappelman? Did he call you this afternoon?"

"People talk to me," she said. "You know how it is down there. At least you would if—"

"If I hadn't been a chicken shit and run away," I finished for her. "You've been hearing little rumblings around the office that someone—you don't know who—has it in for me, and you're here to save my butt. Thanks a bundle. You're scared out of your little mind, Caroline. I want to know who's been frightening you, and don't tell me it's some street snitch with tales of drowning me because I just won't buy it. You wouldn't be beside yourself if it was just that. Lay it out for me. Now."

Caroline jerked herself to her feet. "What do I have to do to get you to listen to me?" she screamed. "Someone called me today from the Xerxes plant and said they were sorry I'd gone to all the expense of hiring you. They said that they had proof that Joey Pankowski was my father. They told me to get you to believe me and get off the case."

"And did they offer to show you this remarkable evidence?"

"I didn't need to see it! I'm not as untrusting as you are."

I put a restraining hand on Peppy, who was starting to growl. "And did they threaten you with mayhem if you didn't force me to withdraw?"

"I wouldn't care what anyone threatened me with. Can't you believe that?"

I looked at her as calmly as I could. She was wild, manipulative, unscrupulous in getting her own way. But I would never in my remotest imagination think of her as a coward.

"I can believe it," I said slowly. "But I want to hear the truth. Did they really tell you they'd hurt me if I didn't stop looking?"

The gentian eyes turned away. "Yes," she muttered.

"Not good enough, Caroline."

"Believe what you want to. If they kill you, don't expect me to show up at your funeral because I won't care." She burst into tears and stormed out of the apartment.

20

WHITE ELEPHANT

Mr. Contreras finally left around one. I slept fitfully, my mind thrashing over Caroline's visit. Caroline didn't fear anything. That's why she confidently followed me into Lake Michigan's pounding surf when she was four years old. Even a near-drowning hadn't scared her—she'd been ready to go right back again when I'd gotten her lungs cleaned out. If someone had told her my life was on the line, it might've made her mad, but it wouldn't terrify her.

Someone had called to tell her Joey Pankowski was her father. She couldn't have pulled that out of the blue. But had they added a rider about hurting me, or was that an inspired guess? I hadn't seen her for a decade, but you don't forget the mannerisms of the people you grow up with: that sidelong glance when I asked her directly made me think she was lying.

The only reason I believed her at all—about the threat, that is—was because I'd gotten my own call. Until Caroline showed up I'd been assuming my threat came from Art Jurshak because I'd accosted his son. Or because I'd talked to Ron Kappelman. But what if it came from Humboldt?

When the orange clock readout glowed three-fifteen I turned on the light and sat up in bed to use the phone. Murray Ryerson had left the paper forty-five minutes earlier. He wasn't home yet. On the chance, I tried the Golden Glow—Sal shuts down at four. Third time lucky.

"Vic! I'm overwhelmed. You had insomnia and you thought of me. I can see the headline now—'Girl Detective Can't Sleep for Love.'"

"And I thought it was the onions I had for dinner. Must've been what was wrong with me the day I agreed to marry Dick. You know our little conversation yesterday?"

"What little conversation?" he snorted. "I told you stuff about Nancy Cleghorn and you sat with Velcro on your mouth."

"Something came back to me," I said limpidly.

"Better make it good, Warshawski."

"Curtis Chigwell," I said. "He's a doctor who lives in Hinsdale. Used to work at a plant down in South Chicago."

"He killed Nancy Cleghorn?"

"As far as I know he never met Nancy Cleghorn."

I felt rather than heard Murray sputter. "It's been a tough day, V.I. Don't make me play Twenty Questions with you."

I reached down next to the bed for a T-shirt. Somehow the night was making me feel too exposed in my nakedness. As I leaned over the lamplight highlighted dust in the corner of the bedroom. If I lived past next week, I'd vacuum.

"That's what I've got for you," I said slowly. "Twenty questions. No answers. Curtis Chigwell knows something that he doesn't want to tell. Twenty-four hours ago I didn't think it had the remotest possible connection to Nancy. But I got a threatening phone call tonight telling me to bug out of South Chicago."

"From Chigwell?" I could almost feel Murray's breath through the phone line.

"No. I thought it had to come from Jurshak or Dresberg. Only thing, a couple of hours later I heard the same thing from someone who knows me only through the Xerxes side—the plant that Chigwell used to work for."

I explained the discrepancies I'd gotten between Manheim and Humboldt's version of Pankowski and Ferraro's suit—without telling him about hearing it from Gustav Humboldt himself. "Chigwell knows what the truth is and why. He just doesn't want to say. And if the Xerxes people are threatening me, he'll know why."

Murray tried a thousand different ways to get me to tell him more about it. I just couldn't give him Caroline and Louisa—Louisa didn't deserve to have her unhappy past spinning around the streets of Chicago. And I didn't know anything else. Anything about what possible connection there could be between Nancy's death and Joey Pankowski.

Murray finally said, "You're not trying to help me, you're getting me to do your legwork. I can feel it. But it's not a bad story—I'll send someone out to talk to the guy."

When he hung up I managed to sleep a little, but I woke again for good around six-thirty. It was another gray February day. Sharp cold with snow would have been preferable to this unending misty chill. I pulled on my sweats, did my stretches, and ruthlessly roused Mr. Contreras by knocking on his door until the dog barked him awake. I took her to the lake and back, stopping now and then to tie my shoes, to blow my nose, to throw her a stick —gestures that let me subtly check my rear. I didn't think anyone was on it.

After depositing the dog I went to the corner diner for pancakes. Back home to change, I'd just about made up my mind to visit Louisa, see if she could shed any light on Caroline's panic, when Ellen Cleghorn called. She was most upset: she'd gone over to Nancy's house in South Chicago to collect her financial records and found the place ransacked.

"Ransacked?" I repeated foolishly. "How do you know?"

"The way you always do, Victoria—the place had been ripped to shreds. Nancy didn't have much and she'd only been able to fix up a couple of rooms. The furniture was pulled apart and her papers strewn all over the place."

I shuddered involuntarily. "Sounds like housebreakers gone mad. Could you tell if anything was missing?"

"I didn't try to see." Her voice caught a little on a nervous sob. "I looked at her bedroom and ran out of there as fast as I could. I—I was hoping you might come down and go through the house with me. I can't bear to be alone there with this—this ravaging of Nancy."

I promised to meet her in front of her house within the hour. I'd wanted to go directly to Nancy's, but Mrs. Cleghorn was too nervous about the intruders to hang around her daughter's house, even outside. I finished pulling on jeans and a sweatshirt, and then, not too happily, went to the little wall safe I'd built into the bedroom closet and took out the Smith & Wesson.

I don't make a habit of carrying a gun—if you do, you get dependent on them and your wits slow down. But I'd been jumpy enough already between Nancy's murder and the threat to send me into the swamp after her. Now this housebreaking. I supposed it could have been local punks casing the place and seeing that no one was home. But tearing the furniture apart. It could have been a druggie coked so far out of his mind that he'd torn the furniture apart looking for money. But it could also have been her killers looking for something she had that might incriminate them. So I stuck a second clip into my handbag and pushed the loaded gun into my jeans waistband; my wits were not fast enough to stop a speeding bullet.

The Cleghorn house looked remote and bedraggled in the gray mist. Even the turret that had been Nancy's bedroom seemed to be drooping a little. Mrs. Cleghorn was waiting for me on the front walk, her normally pleasant, round face gaunt and strained. She gave a tremulous smile and climbed into my car.

"I'll ride with you if you don't mind. I'm shaking so badly I don't even know how I got home."

"You can just give me her house keys," I said. "You don't need to come along if you'd be happier staying here."

She shook her head. "If you went by yourself, I'd only spend the time worrying that someone was waiting in ambush for you."

While I followed her directions for the quickest way up, along South Chicago to Yates, I asked if she'd called the police.

"I thought I'd wait. Wait until you saw what happened. Then"—she gave a twisted little smile—"maybe you could do it for me. I think I've done all the talking to police that I can stand. Not just for now, but forever."

I reached across the gearshift to pat her hand. "It's okay. Happy to be of service."

Nancy's house was up on Crandon, near Seventy-third Street. I could see why Mrs. Cleghorn called it a white elephant—a big wooden monster, its three full stories filled an outsize lot. But I could also see why Nancy had bought it—the little cupolas at the corners, the stained-glass windows, the carved wooden banister on the stairwell inside, all evoked the comfort and order of Alcott or Thackeray.

It wasn't immediately obvious that someone had been in the house. Nancy had apparently put everything she had into buying it, so the front hallway had no furniture. It wasn't until I went up the oak stairs and found the main bedroom that I saw the damage. I sympathized fully with Mrs. Cleghorn's decision to wait for me in the entryway.

Nancy had apparently made the main bedroom her first rehab project. The floor was finished, the walls plastered and painted, and a working fireplace, with a tiled mantel and gleaming brass fittings, was set in the wall opposite the bed. The effect would have been charming, except that the furniture and bedding had been thrown about the room.

I tiptoed gingerly through the rubble. I was violating all possible police rules—not calling to report the destruction, walking through it and disturbing the evidence, adding my detritus to that of the vandals. But it's only in rule books that every crime gets detailed lab inspection. In real life I didn't think they'd pay too close attention, even though the homeowner had been murdered.

Whatever the vandals had been looking for didn't take up much space. Not only had they ripped the mattress cover away and slashed through the stuffing, but they had taken up the grate in the fireplace and removed several bricks. Either money, if I stayed with the coked-out-addict theory. Or papers. Some kind of evidence Nancy had of something so hideous, people were willing to kill to keep it a secret.

I went back downstairs, my own hands shaking a little. The destruction of a house is such a personal violation. If you can't be safe within your home base, you feel you have no security anywhere.

Mrs. Cleghorn was waiting at the bottom. She put a motherly arm around my waist—seeing me upset helped her gain some composure.

"The dining room is the only other room Nancy really had fixed up. She was using the built-in cupboards as a little home office until she had the time and the money to fix up the study."

I suggested that Mrs. Cleghorn continue to stay in the hall. If the marauders hadn't found what they were looking for upstairs, I had an unwilling vision of what the cupboards might look like.

The reality was far worse than anything I had brought myself to imagine. Plates and tableware lay scattered on the floor. The seats had been ripped from the chairs. All the shelves in the walnut cupboards that formed the far wall of the room were splintered. And the papers that made up Nancy's personal life were strewn about like ticker tape the day after a big parade.

I compressed my lips tightly, trying to hold my feelings in while I picked through the rubble. By and by Mrs. Cleghorn called to me from the doorway: I'd been away so long she'd gotten worried and braced herself to face the destruction. Together we culled bank statements, picked an address book from the heap, and took anything relating to mortgage or insurance for Mrs. Cleghorn to go through later.

Before leaving I poked around in the other rooms. Here and there a loose floorboard had been pried up. The fireplaces—there were six altogether—were missing their grates. The old-fashioned kitchen had come in for its share of damage. It probably hadn't looked too good to begin with, its fixtures dating from the twenties, old sink, old icebox, and badly peeling walls. In typical vandal style the intruders had dumped flour and sugar on the floor and pulled all the food from the refrigerator. If the police ever caught up with them, I'd recommend a year spent fixing up the house as the first part of their sentence.

They'd come in through the back door. The lock had been jimmied and they hadn't bothered to shut it properly behind them. The backyard was so overgrown, no one passing in the alley would be able to see that the place was open. Mrs. Cleghorn dug a hammer and nails out of the workshop Nancy had set up next to the pantry; I hammered a board across the back door to keep it shut. There seemed to be nothing further we could do to restore wholeness to the place. We left wordlessly.

Back at the house on Muskegon, I called Bobby to tell him what happened. He grunted and said he'd refer the matter to the Third District, but for me to stand by in case they wanted to ask me anything.

"Yeah, sure," I muttered. "I'll stick by the phone for the rest of the week if it'll keep the police happy." Perhaps it was just as well that Bobby had already hung up.

Mrs. Cleghorn busied herself with coffee. She brought it to me in the dining room, with leftover cake and salad.

"What were they looking for, Victoria?" she finally asked after her second cup.

I picked moodily at some spice cake. "Something small. Flat. Papers of some kind, I suppose. I don't think they can have found them, or they wouldn't have been prying up the bricks in the other fireplaces. so where else would Nancy have left something? You're sure she didn't drop anything off here?"

Mrs. Cleghorn shook her head. "She might have come in while I was at work. But—I don't know. Do you want to look at her old bedroom?"

She sent me alone up the attic stairs to the old turret where Nancy and I had waited for Sister Anne or battled pirates. It was an unbearably sad room, the remains of childhood sitting forlornly on the worn furniture. I turned over teddy bears and trophies and a worn poster of the early Beatles with studied indifference, but found nothing.

The police arrived when I got back downstairs and we spent an hour or so talking to them. We told them I'd gone over with Mrs. Cleghorn to help her find Nancy's papers—that she didn't want to go alone and I was an old friend and that we'd found the chaos and called them. We talked to a couple of junior grade detectives who wrote everything down in slow longhand but didn't seem any more concerned about this break-in than that of any other South Side householder. They left eventually without giving us any special instructions or admonitions.

I got up to leave shortly after they did. "I don't want to alarm you, but it's possible that the people who were looking at Nancy's place will come here. You should consider going to stay with one of your sons, however much you may dislike it."

Mrs. Cleghorn nodded reluctantly; the only one of her sons who didn't have children lived in a trailer with his girlfriend. Not the ideal guesthouse.

"I suppose I should get Nancy's car put away safely too. Who knows where these insane creatures will strike next?"

"Her car?" I stopped in my tracks. "Where is her car?"

"Out front. She'd left it by the SCRAP offices and one of the women who works there brought it over for me after the funeral. I had a spare set of car keys, so they must . . ." Her voice trailed off as she caught my expression. "Of course. We ought to look in the car, oughtn't we? If Nancy really did have something a—a killer wanted. Although I can't imagine what it could be."

She'd said the same thing earlier and I repeated my own meaningless reassurances: that Nancy probably didn't know she had something someone else wanted so badly. I went out to Nancy's sky-blue Honda with Mrs. Cleghorn and pulled the heap of papers from the backseat. Nancy had dumped her briefcase there along with a stack of files too big to fit into the case.

"Why don't you just take them, dear?" Mrs. Cleghorn smiled tremulously. "If you can look after them, get her work papers back to SCRAP, it would be a big help to me."

I hoisted the heap under my left arm and put my right arm around her shoulders. "Yeah, sure. Call me if anything else happens, or if you need help with the cops." It was more work than I wanted, but it seemed the least I could do under the circumstances.

21
MAMA'S BOY

I sat in my car with the heater on, flipping through Nancy's files. Anything that had to do with routine SCRAP business I put to one side. I wanted to drop the lot at the office on Commercial before leaving South Chicago.

I was looking for something that would tell me why Alderman Jurshak was opposing the SCRAP recycling plant. That was what Nancy had been trying to find the last time I talked to her. If she'd been killed because of something hot she knew on the South Side, I assumed it was in connection with the plant.

In the end I did find a document with the Jurshak name on it, but it had nothing to do with the recycling proposal—or any other environmental issue. It was a photocopy of a letter, dated back in 1963, to the Mariners Rest Life Assurance Company, explaining that Jurshak & Parma were now fiduciaries for Humboldt Chemical's Xerxes plant. Attached to it was an actuarial study showing that Xerxes losses were in line with those of other comparable companies in the area and asking for the same rate consideration.

I read the report through three times. It made no sense to me. That is, it made no sense as being the document that could have gotten Nancy killed. Life and health insurance are not my specialty, but this looked like perfectly ordinary, straightforward insurance stuff. It wouldn't even have seemed out of place to me except that it was so old and so unconnected to anything Nancy worked on.

There was one person who could explain the significance to me. Well, more than one, but I didn't feel like going to Big Art with it. Where did you find this, young lady? Oh, blowing around the street, you know how these things happen.

But young Art might tell me. Even though he was clearly on the periphery of his father's life, he might know enough about the insurance side to explain the document. Or, if Nancy had found it and it had meant something to her, she might have told him. In fact, she must have: that was why he was so nervous. He knew why she'd been killed and he didn't want to let on.

That seemed like a good theory. How to get Art to reveal what he knew was another question altogether. I contorted my face in an effort to concentrate. When that didn't produce results I tried relaxing all my muscles and hoped that an idea would float to the top of my mind. Instead I found myself thinking about Nancy and our childhood together. The first time I'd gone to her house for dinner, in fourth grade, when her mother had served canned spaghetti. I'd been afraid to tell Gabriella what we'd eaten—I thought she wouldn't let me go back to a house where they didn't make their own pasta.

It was Nancy who got me to try out for the junior high basketball team. I'd always been good at sports, but softball was my game. When I made the team my dad tacked a hoop to the side of the house and played with Nancy and me. He used to come to all our games in high school, and after our last game in college, the one against Lake Forest, he'd taken us to the Empire Room for drinks and dancing. He'd taught us how to fade, how to fake the pass then turn and dunk, and I'd won the game in the last seconds with just that move. The fake and the dunk.

I sat up. Nancy and I had worked it so many times in the past, why not now? I didn't have any proof, but let young Art think I did.

I pulled Nancy's most recent diary from the stack on the seat next to me. She had entered three phone numbers for him in her crabbed handwriting. I made my best guess at deciphering them and went to the public phone outside the beach house.

The first number turned out to be the ward office, where Mrs. May's syrupy tones denied knowledge of young Art's whereabouts while trying to probe me for who I was and what I wanted. She even offered me to Art, Sr., before I could end the conversation.

I dialed the second number and got the Jurshak, Parma insurance offices. There a nasal-toned receptionist told me at length that she hadn't seen young Art since Friday and she'd like to know since when she'd been hired to baby-sit for him. The cops had been around this morning looking for him and she was supposed to get a contract typed by noon and how could she possibly do it if—

"Don't let me keep you," I said shortly, and hung up on her.

I dug in my pockets for change but I'd used my last two quarters. Nancy had penciled an address next to the third number, down on Avenue G. That had to be Art's home. Anyway, if I got the kid on the phone, he'd probably hang up. Better to confront him in person.

I got back in the car and drove back down to East Side, to 115th and Avenue G. The house was halfway up the block, a new brick place with a high fence around it and an electronic lock on the gate. I rang the bell and waited. I was just about to ring again when a woman's voice came uncertainly through the squawk box.

"I'm here to see young Art," I bellowed. "My name is Warshawski."

There was a long silence and then the lock clicked. I pushed the gate open and moved into the estate. At least it looked more like an estate than it did your typical East Side bungalow. If this really was Art's home, I presumed it was because he still lived with his parents.

However modestly Big Art kept his office, he hadn't stinted on his home

comforts. The lot to the right had been annexed and converted into a beautifully landscaped yard. At one end stood a glass building that might have
housed an indoor swimming pool. Since a forest preserve ran along the back
of the property, one had the sensation of being out in the country while only
half a mile from some of the world's busiest manufacturing sites.

I trotted up the flagstone walk to the entrance, a porticoed porch whose
columns looked a little incongruous against the modern brick. A faded blond
woman stood in the doorway. The setting had some claim to grandeur but
she was pure South Side in her crisply ironed print dress and the starched
apron covering it.

She greeted me nervously, without trying to invite me in. "Who—who
did you say you were?"

I pulled a card from my bag and handed it to her. "I'm a friend of young
Art's. I wouldn't be bothering him at home but they haven't seen him at the
ward offices and it's pretty important that I get in touch with him."

She shook her head blindly, a movement that gave her a fleeting resemblance to her son. "He—he's not home."

"I don't think he'd mind talking to me. Honestly, Mrs. Jurshak. I know
the police are trying to get in touch with him, but I'm on his side, not theirs.
Or his father's," I added with a flash of inspiration.

"He really isn't home." She looked at me wretchedly. "When Sergeant
McGonnigal came around asking for him Mr. Jurshak got really angry, but I
don't know where he is, Miss—uh. I haven't seen him since breakfast yesterday morning."

I tried to digest that. Maybe young Art hadn't been fit to drive last night
after all. But if he'd been in an accident, his mother would have been the first
to know. I shook away an unwelcome vision of Dead Stick Pond.

"Can you give me the names of any of his friends? Anyone he trusts
enough to spend the night with uninvited?"

"Sergeant McGonnigal asked me the same thing. But—but he never had
any friends. I mean, I liked him to stay here at night. I didn't want him
running around the way so many boys do these days, getting involved in
drugs and gangs, and he's my only child, it's not like there are others if you
lose one. That's why I'm so worried now. He knows how upset I get if I
don't hear from him and yet here he is, gone all night."

I didn't know what to say, since none of the comments I wanted to make
would have kept her speaking to me. I finally asked if it was the first time he'd
ever stayed away from home.

"Oh, no," she said simply. "Sometimes he has to work all night. On
important presentations to clients or something. He's been doing a lot of
those in the last few months. But never without calling me."

I grinned a little to myself: the kid was more enterprising than I would
have suspected. I thought a minute, then said carefully, "I'm involved in one
of those important cases, Mrs. Jurshak. The client's name is Nancy Cleghorn.
Art is looking for some papers from her. Will you tell him that I have them?"

The name didn't seem to mean anything to her. At least she didn't turn pale and faint or cower back in alarm. Instead she asked me if I could write it down since she had a terrible memory, and she was so worried about Art she didn't think she'd get the names straight if she had to. I scribbled Nancy's name and a brief message about having her files on the back of my card.

"If something comes up, Mrs. Jurshak, you can leave a message for me at that number. Anytime, day or night."

When I got to the gate she was still standing in the doorway, her hands wrapped in her apron.

I wished I'd been more persistent with young Art last night. He was scared. He knew whatever it was that Nancy knew. So either my coming had been the last turn of the screw—he'd fled to avoid her fate. Or he'd met her fate. I should go to McGonnigal, tell him what I knew, or rather what I suspected. But. But. I really didn't have anything concrete. Maybe I'd give the kid twenty-four hours to show up. If he was already dead, it wouldn't matter. But if he was still alive, I should tell McGonnigal so he could help keep him that way. Round and round I went with it.

In the end I postponed a decision by driving back down to South Chicago, first to drop Nancy's files at SCRAP, then to visit Louisa. She was delighted to see me, using the remote-control button to turn off the tube, then gripping my hand with her brittle fingers.

When I edged the conversation around to Pankowski and Ferraro and their unsuccessful suit, she seemed genuinely surprised.

"I didn't know them two was so sick," she said in her raspy voice. "I saw 'em both off and on before they died and they never said word one about it. Didn't know they was suing Xerxes. Company's been real good to me— maybe the boys got themselves in some kind of trouble. Could see it with Joey—he was always a problem for someone. Usually a girl who didn't have her head screwed on right. But old Steve, he was your original straight arrow, if you know what I mean. Hard to see why he wouldn't get his benefits."

I told her what I knew about their illnesses and death and about the harried life that Mrs. Pankowski led. That brought her cough-racked laugh.

"Yeah, I could've told her a thing or two about Joey. We girls on the night shift all could of, come to that. I didn't even know he was married the first year I was working there. When I found that out you'd better believe I gave him his walking papers. None of that being the other woman for me. Course there was others who wasn't as picky, and he could make you laugh. Awful to think of him going through what I'm doing these days."

We talked until Louisa fell into her gasping sleep. She clearly knew nothing of Caroline's worries. I had to hand it to the little brat—she did protect her mother.

22

THE DOCTOR'S DILEMMA

Mr. Contreras was waiting anxiously on the front walk when I came home. The dog, picking up his worried state, yawned nervously at his feet. When they saw me each expressed his joy: the dog leapt around me in little circles while the old man scolded me for not leaving him my day's route.

I put an arm around him. "You aren't going to start breathing down my neck are you? Repeat twenty times a day—she's a big girl, she can fall on her butt if she wants to."

"Don't joke about it, cookie. You know I shouldn't say this, I shouldn't even think it, but you're more family to me than my own family. Every time I look at Ruthie it beats me how Clara and I coulda had a kid like that. When I see you it's like looking at my own flesh and blood. I mean that, doll. You gotta look after yourself. For me and her royal highness here."

I gave a wry smile. "I guess I take after you, then—I'm real hardheaded and stubborn."

He thought it over a minute. "Okay, doll," he agreed reluctantly. "You gotta do things your way. I don't like it but I understand."

When I went in the front door I heard him saying to the dog, "Takes after me. You hear that, princess? She gets it from me."

Despite my bravado with him, I'd been watching my back off and on all day. I also checked my apartment carefully before sitting down with my mail, but no one had tried getting past the reinforced steel in the front door or the sliding bars on the back.

I couldn't face another evening of whiskey and peanut butter. Nor did I want my downstairs neighbor feeling he had the right to hover over me. Carefully locking up once more, I headed over to the Treasure Island on Broadway to stock up.

I was sautéeing chicken thighs with garlic and olives when Max Loewenthal phoned. My first thought on hearing from him out of the blue was that something had happened to Lotty.

"No, no, she's fine, Victoria. But this doctor you asked me about two weeks ago, this Curtis Chigwell—he tried to kill himself. You didn't know that?"

"No." I smelled burning olive oil and reached my left hand the length of the cord to turn off the stove. "What happened? How do you know?"

It had been on the six o'clock news. Chigwell's sister had found him when she went to the garage for some gardening tools at four.

"Victoria, I feel most uncomfortable about this. Most uncomfortable. Two weeks ago you ask for his address and today he tries to commit suicide. What was your role in this?"

I stiffened immediately. "Thanks, Max. I appreciate the compliment. Most days I don't feel that powerful."

"Please don't turn this off with your flippancy. You involved me. I want to know if I contributed to a man's despair."

I tried to control my anger. "You mean did I go throw his ugly past in his face to the point where he couldn't stand it and turned on the monoxide?"

"Something like that, yes." Max was very grave, his strong Viennese accent heavier than usual. "You know, Victoria, in your search for the truth you often force people to face things about themselves they are better off not knowing. I can forgive you for doing it with Lotty—she's tough, she can take it. And you don't spare yourself. But because you are very strong you don't see that other people cannot deal with these truths."

"Look, Max—I don't know why Chigwell tried to kill himself. I haven't seen a medical report so I don't even know that he did—maybe he had a stroke as he was turning on the car engine. But if it was because of the questions I was asking, I don't feel one minute of remorse. He's involved in a cover-up for Humboldt Chemical. What or why or how serious I don't know. But that has nothing to do with his personal strengths and weaknesses —it has to do with the lives of a lot of other people. If—and it's a mighty big if—if I'd known two weeks ago that my seeing him would make him turn on the gas, you'd better believe I'd do it again." By the time I finished speaking I was breathing hard, my mouth very tight.

"I do believe you, Victoria. And I have no wish to talk to you in such a mood. But I do have one request—that you not think of me the next time you need help in one of your chases." He hung up before I could say anything.

"Well, damn you anyway, you righteous bastard," I shouted at the dead phone. "You think you're my mother? Or just the scales of justice?"

Despite my rage I felt uneasy—I'd sicced Murray Ryerson on the guy in the middle of the night. Maybe they'd hounded him and his imagination had converted a minor peccadillo to murder. Hoping to ease my conscience, I tracked the crime editor down at the *Herald-Star*'s city desk. He was indignant—he'd sent reporters out to question the doctor about Pankowski and Ferraro, but they'd never been allowed in.

"Don't give me hounding, Miss Wise-ass. You're the one who talked to the guy. There's something you're not telling me, but I'm not even going to speculate on what it is. We've got some gofers down at that Xerxes plant and we'll get on it faster without mixed signals from you. We're running a lovely human-interest story on Mrs. Pankowski tomorrow, and I expect to have something from that lawyer Manheim who represented them."

Murray did finally part grudgingly with more details about Chigwell's attempted suicide. He had disappeared after lunch, but his sister didn't miss him since she was busy around the house. At four she decided to go to the garage to check over her gardening gear so she'd be ready for spring. Her comments to the press did not include any mention of me or Xerxes, just that her brother had been troubled the last several days. He was prone to depression and she hadn't thought much about it at the time.

"Is there any doubt he did it himself?"

"You mean did someone come into the garage, bind and gag him, strap him into the car, then undo the ropes when he was unconscious, assuming he'd die and it'd look like suicide? Give me a break, Warshawski."

When I finally finished the conversation I was in a worse mood than I'd been at the start. I'd made the cardinal sin of giving Murray far more information than I'd received in exchange. As a result he knew as much about Pankowski and Ferraro as I did. Since he had a staff who could follow a range of inquiries, he might well untangle what lay behind Humboldt's and Chigwell's lies before I did.

I'm as competitive as the next person—more than many of them—but it wasn't just fear of finishing behind Murray that upset me. It was Louisa's right to privacy—she didn't deserve the press pawing through her past. And it kept bugging me—irrationally, I agree—that I'd never been home when Nancy tried calling the day she died.

I looked balefully at the partly cooked chicken. The only scrap I hadn't given Murray was the letter to Mariners Rest I'd found in Nancy's car. And now that young Art had gone missing I wasn't sure who I could talk to about it. I poured myself a drink (one of the ten warning signs—do you turn to alcohol when you're upset or frustrated?) and went into the living room.

Mariners Rest was a large life and health insurer based in Boston, but they had a big branch office in Chicago. I'd seen their TV ads a million times, with a confident-looking sailor leaning against a hammock—rest with the mariners and sleep with their peace of mind.

It would be tricky explaining to a corporate actuary where I'd gotten the data. Almost as hard as trying to explain it to Big Art. Insurance companies guard their actuarial data with the care usually associated with the Holy Grail. So even if they'd accept my word on having a right to the documents, it would be hard to get them to tell me if they meant anything—like were the data accurate. They'd have to get clearance from their home office in Boston and that could take a month or more.

Caroline might know what the document meant, but she wasn't speaking to me. The only other person I could think of to ask was Ron Kappelman. The insurance information didn't look as though it had anything to do with the SCRAP recycling plant, but Nancy had liked Ron, she worked closely with him. Maybe he'd see the same exciting possibilities in the letter that she had.

By a mercy his home number was listed, and—greater miracle still—he was in. When I told him what I had he seemed most interested, asking a lot of sharp questions about how I'd come to have it. I responded vaguely that Nancy had bequeathed me responsibility for some of her private affairs, and I got him to agree to stop by at nine the next morning before he went to work.

I looked again at the mess in the living room. There was no way putting away back issues of *The Wall Street Journal* would make my place look as good as his gleaming house on Langley. I stuck the skillet with the chicken into refrigerator—I'd lost interest in cooking, let alone eating. I called an old friend of mine, Velma Riter, and went to see *The Witches of Eastwick* with her. By the time I got home I'd gotten enough of Chigwell and Max out of my brain to be able to sleep.

23
END RUN

I was in the Chigwells' garage. Max had his hand around my wrist in a fierce grip. He forced me to go with him to the black sedan where the doctor sat. "You will kill him now, Victoria," Max said. I tried fighting him, but his grip on my hand was so fierce that he forced my arm up, forced me to pull the trigger. When I fired Chigwell's face dissolved, turning into the red-eyed dog at Dead Stick Pond. I was thrashing through the swamp grasses, trying to escape, but the feral dog hunted me remorselessly.

I woke up at six drenched with sweat, panting, fighting an impulse to dissolve into tears. The swamp dog in my dream had looked just like Peppy.

Despite the early hour, I didn't want to stay in bed any longer—I would only lie there sweating, my head filled with grit. I took the sheets off, bundled them together with my dirty sweats, put on jeans and a T-shirt, and padded down to the washing machine in the basement. If I could find something to run in, I'd be able to take the dog out. A run and a cold shower would get my head cleared for Ron Kappelman.

After a long search I found my old college warm-up pants stuffed in the bottom of a box in the hall closet. The elastic was loose—the drawstring would barely keep them on—and the maroon had faded to a washed-out pink, but they'd do for one morning. I weighed the gun, but my dream was too much with me—I couldn't bear to carry it just now. No one was going to attack me in front of all the joggers crowding the lakefront. Especially if a large dog accompanied me. I hoped.

Mr. Contreras had already let Peppy out by the time I finished my stretches. I met her on the stairs outside my kitchen door and the two of us set off.

It was another misty morning, about forty degrees, the skies leaden. No matter what the weather, the dog was ecstatic to be out in it. I left her at the lagoon, her tail waving like a golden pennant, and headed on to the lake.

A handful of fishermen stood along the rocks, hopeful even in this dreary weather. I nodded at a trio of black slickers who were seated on the seawall in front of me and headed out to the harbor entrance. I stood at the end of the promontory for a moment, watching the sullen water break against the rocks, but in the chilly mist my sweaty clothes started clinging to me uncomfortably. I retied the loose drawstring on the sweats and turned back.

The fierce storms earlier in the winter had washed boulders across the seawall all along the edge of the harbor; I had to leave the path more than once to keep from tripping on the loose rocks. By the time I got back to the land end of the harbor my legs were sore from broken field running; I slowed to a jog.

The trio of slickered fishermen had been watching my approach. They didn't seem to be doing much fishing. In fact, they didn't seem to have any gear. As I came to the end of the seawall they got up and formed a casual barrier between me and the road. A lone jogger passed behind the men.

"Hey!" I called.

The runner was deep in his Sony earphones. He paid no heed to us.

"Give it up, girlie," one of the men said. "We're just fishermen stopping a pretty girl for the time."

I was moving away from them, trying frantically to think. I could head back up the seawall to the lake. And get trapped between boulder and water trying to get past someone's Walkman for attention. Maybe if I went sideways—

A shiny black arm swung out and grabbed my left wrist. "The time, girlie. We'll just look at your watch here."

I swung quickly in the circle of his arm, bringing myself in and chopping hard, upward on his elbow. He was well padded with slicker and sweater, but I got enough on the bone that he grunted and loosed his grip. As his fingers slackened slightly I wrenched myself free and tore off across the park, yelling for help. None of the few people who'd ventured out in the mist were close enough to hear me over their earphones.

I usually just follow the seawall in and out. I didn't know this stretch of the park, what hiding places it might hold, where it would take me. I hoped to land at Lake Shore Drive, but I might be dead-ending on a driving range.

My assailants were weighed down by their heavy clothes. Despite my fatigue, I put some distance between us. I could see one of them working his way across to my left. The other two were presumably coming around the top, trying to set up a pincer. It all depended on how fast I could reach the road.

I put out a burst of energy, cutting at an angle to the direction I'd been going. I'd surprised the man I could see—he gave a shout of warning to the two I couldn't. It gave me confidence and I started running all out. I was going at top speed when I saw water in front of me.

The lake. It stuck a finger into the park here. The end of the inlet lay about thirty yards to my left. The man I'd hit had moved down there, blocking my exit. On my right I could see the other two slickers, moving behind me at a casual jog.

I waited until they were within fifteen yards, getting my breath, getting my courage. When they were close enough that they could start calling to me —"It's no use running—Give it up, girlie—No point in fighting"—I jumped.

The water was nearly ice. I took in a frozen filthy mouthful and spat. My lungs and heart banged in protest. My bones and head began to ache. My ears rang and light spots danced in my eyes. Yards. It's only yards. You can do it. One arm after the other. One foot up, one down, don't worry about the weight of the shoes, you're almost across, you're almost out, there's a boulder, slide across it, now you can walk, now you can climb up this bank.

The drawstring on my warm-up pants gave up completely. I wrestled myself free of them and lumbered toward the road. The wet cold was making me dizzy; inky shapes floated in front of me. I couldn't focus, couldn't see if the man at the bottom of the inlet had been able to move across the end before I'd swum over, couldn't see the size or shape of my pursuit. In my wet shoes, with my teeth chattering, I could hardly move, but help lay ahead. I pushed myself doggedly.

I would have made it if it hadn't been for the goddamn boulders. I was just too tired, too disoriented to see. I tripped over a giant rock and fell heavily. I was taking great gasps of air, trying to get to my feet, and then I was writhing in black-slickered arms, kicking, flailing, even biting, when all the floating inky spots gathered to a giant ball and fire exploded in my brain.

After a time I knew I was very sick. I couldn't breathe. Pneumonia. I'd waited outside in the rain for my daddy. He promised to pick me up during a break on his shift and the break didn't come—he never thought I'd wait that long. Lie under this tent, breathe slowly, watch for Mama, she says everything will be all right and you know she never lies. I tried opening my eyes. The movement stabbed great fingers of pain into my brain, forcing me back into darkness.

I woke again, rocking helplessly back and forth, my arms tied, a boulder pushing into my side. I was wrapped in something heavy, something that pushed into my mouth. If I threw up, I'd suffocate myself. Lie as still as possible. Not the time to struggle.

I knew who I was this time. V. I. Warshawski. Girl detective. Idiot *extra-*

ordinaire. The heavy stuff was a blanket. I couldn't see, but I imagined it—green, standard Sears issue. I was wedged against the backseat of a car. Not a boulder, but the drive shaft. When I got out of here I'd get City Council to make front-wheel drive mandatory for all Chicago criminals. Get stopped with a drive shaft in your car and you'd do time, like the IRS getting Al Capone. When I got out of here.

My slickered friends were talking but I couldn't make out their words through the buzzing in my ears and the thickness of the blanket. I thought at first the buzzing was left over from my cold-water bath, but by and by my tired brain sorted it into the sound of wheels on the road coming through the floorboard. The rocking and the warmth of my cocoon sent me back to sleep.

I woke up to feel cold air on my head. My arms were numb where they'd been tied behind me, my tongue thick with suppressed nausea.

"Is she still out?"

I didn't know the voice. Cold, indifferent. The voice of the man who'd called in the threat? Only two days ago? Was that all? I couldn't tell, either of time or the voice.

"She isn't moving. Want me to open her up and check?" A black man's thicker tones.

"Leave her as she is." The cold voice again. "An old carpet we're dumping. You never know who may see you, even down here. Who might remember seeing a face."

I kept myself as limp as possible. I didn't need another blow to the skull. I was pulled roughly from the car, banging my poor head, my aching arms, my sore back on the door, clenching my numb fingers to keep from crying out. Someone slung me over his back like an old roll of carpet, as though a hundred and forty pounds was nothing to him, as though I was nothing more than a light and careless load. I could hear twigs snapping underfoot, the swishing of the dead grasses. What I hadn't noticed on my previous trip here was the smell. The rank stench of putrifying grasses, mixed with the chemicals that drained into the marsh. I tried not to choke, tried not to think of the fish with their rotting fins, tried to suppress the well of nausea that grew with the pounding in my head as it bounced against my bearer's back.

"Okay, Troy. X marks the spot."

Troy grunted, slid me from his shoulder, and dropped me. "Far enough in?"

"She isn't going anyplace. Let's split."

The rank grasses and soft mud broke my fall. I lay against the chill earth. The cool mud soaking through the blanket brought a moment's relief to my sick head, but as I lay there my body's weight caused water to ooze up through the mud. I felt the dampness in my ears and panicked, thrashing uselessly. Alone in this dark cocoon, I was going to drown, black swamp water in my lungs, my heart, my brain. The blood roared in my head and I cried tears of utter helplessness.

24

IN GRIMPEN MIRE

I had passed out again. When I slowly came to I was wet all through. Water had oozed into my hair and was tickling my ears. My shoulders felt as though someone had stuck iron bars into them to separate them from my breastbone. Somehow, though, the sleep and the cold muddy water had healed my head a little. I didn't want to think—it was too scary. But minute by minute I could still make it if I used a little sense.

I rolled to one side, the blanket heavy with mud. Using every ounce of strength, I pushed myself to a sitting position. My ankles were bound together and my hands were tied behind me at the wrist—there was no way I could work them to the front of my body. But by pushing them down at my tailbone I could brace myself enough to inch forward with my legs.

I had to assume they'd taken me down the same track where they'd dumped Nancy—it was the farthest from the road, anyway. After some time of trial and error, which left me gasping for breath inside my muddy cocoon, I reckoned that the water lay to my right. I carefully made a one-hundred-eighty-degree turn so that my inching motion would take me back toward the road. I tried not to think of the distance, tried not to compute my probable speed. Forced thoughts of food, baths, bed away and imagined myself on a sunny beach. Maybe Hawaii. Maybe Magnum would appear suddenly and cut me out of my prison.

My legs and arms were shaking. Too much exertion, too little glucose. I had to stop every few pushes and rest. The second time I stopped I fell asleep again, waking only as I fell over into the grasses. After that I forced myself to a counting pattern. Five shoves, count fifteen, five shoves, count fifteen, five shoves, count fifteen. Legs wobbling, brain turning, fifteen. My fifteenth birthday. Gabriella had died two days before. The last breath in Tony's arms while I was at the beach. Maybe there really was a heaven, Gabriella with her pure voice in the angelic choir waiting for me with wings outstretched, her arms opened in boundless love, waiting for my contralto to blend with her soprano.

A dog's bark brought me back to myself. The red-eyed hound. This time I couldn't help it: I was sick, a little trickle of bile down my front. I could hear the dog coming closer, breath heaving, short, sharp barks, then a nose pushing into the side of the blanket, knocking me over. I lay on my side in a helpless tangle of mud and blanket, kicking uselessly in the air, and felt paws press heavily into my arm.

I kicked helplessly at the blanket, trying to force the hound away. Little tears of fear slid into my nose. All the while on the other side fangs pulled at my head, my arms. When it had bit through the blanket how would I protect my throat? My arms were behind me. It wasn't minding my feeble thrashing.

Panic roared in my ears, turned my useless legs to water. Over the roaring I heard a voice. With the tiny energy left in me, I tried to cry out.

"You got her? You found her? Is that you, doll? Are you in there? Can you hear me?"

Not the hound of hell after all, but Peppy. With Mr. Contreras. My euphoria was so great that my sore muscles felt momentarily healed. I grunted feebly. The old man wrestled feverishly with the knots, talking to himself all the while.

"I mighta known to bring a knife instead of this wrench. Should have guessed that, you stupid old man, why do you want to go carrying pipe wrenches when a knife is what you need? Steady in there, doll, we almost got it, don't give up the ship now, not when we're this close."

He finally managed to rip the blanket away from my head. "Oh my, this is bad. Let's get you out of here."

He worked frantically, clumsily on the knots behind my back. The dog looked at me anxiously, then started to lick my face—I was her long-lost puppy found in the nick of time. All the while that Mr. Contreras freed my hands, rubbing some semblance of circulation back into my arms, she kept washing my face.

He was shocked to see me in my underwear, afraid I'd been raped, could hardly take in my assurances that it was just drowning my assailants had been after. Leaning heavily on his shoulder, I let him guide me, half carrying me, back to the road.

"I got some young hotshot here. Some lawyer, he says. Didn't believe you could really be down here, so he waited at the car. When her royal highness came back from the lake without you, I got kinda worried. Then this snot-nose shows up, says you was going to meet with him at nine and where was you, he can't wait all day. I know you don't want me breathing down your neck, doll, but I was there when the guy called, I heard that little friend of yours say they was going to dump you in the marsh, so I made him drive us down here. Me and her highness, you know, I figured we could find the place after you showed it to me on the map and all."

He went over and over it on the way to the road. Ron Kappelman stood there, leaning on his beat-up Rabbit, whistling lightly, looking at nothing. When he saw the three of us coming he leapt upright and sprinted across the road. He helped Mr. Contraras lift me over the fence and into the backseat of the car. Peppy gave a little bark and shoved past them to push her heavy body next to mine.

"Damn, Warshawski. You miss an appointment, you do it in a big way. What the hell happened to you?"

"You leave her alone, young man, and don't go talking dirty like that. There's plenty other words in the English language without going around swearing all the time. I don't know what your mother would think if she could hear you, but what we gotta do is get this lady to a doctor, get her patched up, then you want to butt your nose in and find out how she got where she was, maybe she'll feel like talking to you."

Kappelman stiffened as if to fight back, then realized the futility of it and got into the driver's seat. I was unconscious before he had the car turned around.

I don't remember anything of the rest of the day. How Kappelman flagged down a state patrol car and got us an eighty-mile-an-hour escort to Lotty's clinic, Mr. Contreras stubbornly insisting he wouldn't let them take me to a hospital without her say-so. Or how Lotty, taking one look at me in the back of the car, summoned an ambulance to take me to Beth Israel at top speed. Or even how Peppy wouldn't relinquish me to the paramedics. She apparently seized a wrist in her strong jaw and refused to let go. They tell me they woke me up long enough to make her drop the guy's arm, but I don't have any memory of it, not even as a dream fragment.

I finally resurfaced around six Thursday morning. After a few puzzled minutes I realized I was in a hospital bed, but I couldn't imagine what I was doing there or how I'd come to be there. As soon as I tried sitting up, though, my shoulders sent out so severe a message of pain that memory came flooding back.

Dead Stick Pond. That horrible cocoon of death. I held my arms out in front of me, despite the agony moving them brought. My wrists and hands were wrapped in gauze; my fingers looked like bright red sausages emerging from the white bandages. An IV needle was taped to my left forearm above the gauze. I followed it to a series of bags overhead and squinted at the labels. D5.45NS. That told me a lot.

I touched my fingertips gently together. They were swollen, but I could feel. I lay back again, filled with a peaceful satisfaction. I had survived. My hands were all right. They had tried to kill me, tried to humiliate me at the moment of my death, but I was alive. I fell back into sleep.

When I woke again it was to the full bustle of morning hospital routine—blood pressure, temperature, rounds—and no questions answered: doctor will tell you. After the nurses came a brisk intern who looked at my eyes and stuck pins into my feet. The pin seems to be neuroscience's most advanced piece of technology. Another intern was busy with my roommate, a woman my age who'd just had cosmetic surgery. After they'd finished Lotty herself swept in, dark eyes bright with nonclinical feeling. My intern hovered at her elbow, anxious to tell her his findings on my body. She listened for a minute, then dismissed him with an imperious wave.

"I'm sure your reflexes are all in perfect order, but let me see for myself.

First let's have your chest. Breathe. Hold it. Exhale. Yes." She listened to me fore and aft, then had me shut my eyes and touch my hands together, get out of bed—a slow, lurching process—and walk on my heels, then my toes. It wasn't much compared to my usual workout, but it left me panting.

"You really should have children, Victoria—you could produce a whole new breed of superheroes. Why you are even alive at this point is a medical miracle, let alone that you can walk."

"Thank you, Lotty. I'm pretty pleased myself. Tell me how I got here and when I can leave."

She gave me the details of Peppy and the ambulance men. "And your friend Mr. Contreras is waiting anxiously down the hall. He stayed here all night, with the dog, totally against hospital policy, but the two of you are well matched—stubborn, pigheaded, with only one allowable way to do things—your own."

"Pot calling the kettle black, Lotty," I said unrepentantly, lying down. "And don't tell me the dog didn't stay here with your connivance. Or at least Max's."

I frowned and bit off my words, remembering my last conversation with the hospital's executive director. Lotty looked at me sympathetically.

"Yes, Max also wants to talk to you. He is feeling a bit remorseful. And that is no doubt why the dog spent the night in the hospital. But she must go home now, so if you will tell your tiresome neighbor you're going to live to tilt at more windmills, we'll get them to leave. Meanwhile, since your brain is no worse than usual, I'll get someone to take that needle out of you."

She whirled off at her usual forty knots. Mr. Contreras came in a minute or two later, his eyes filled with tears, his hands shaking a little. I swung my feet over the side of the bed and held out my arms to him.

"Oh, cookie, I'm never gonna forget the way we found you yesterday. More dead than alive, you was. And that young snot not believing you could be down there and me having to practically knock him out before he'd drive us. And then I couldn't get the nurses here to tell me anything about how you was doing, I kept asking and asking and they wouldn't say because I wasn't family. Me, not your family. Who has more right, I'd like to know, I says to them, some cousin in Melrose Park who don't even send her a Christmas card, or me who saved her life. But Dr. Lotty showed up and straightened it all out, her and Mr. Loewenthal between them, and put me and the dog in an empty room down the hall from you, but we had to promise not to disturb you."

He pulled a giant red handkerchief from a back pocket and blew his nose loudly. "Well, all's well that ends well, and I gotta take her highness home and feed her, but don't go telling me to mind my own business anymore, cookie, not when you got guys like this on your case."

I thanked him as best I could, giving him a tight hug and a kiss. After he left I lay back down again, cursing my lack of stamina. Lotty wanted me to stay here another day—she said I wouldn't rest if I went off on my own. She was right: I was already in a pretty fretful state, made more irritable by my sore shoulder muscles. But she'd thrown out all my clothes and wasn't going to bring me any more until Friday morning.

As it turned out most of the people I would have tried to see came to visit me, along with a few I could just as well have done without, such as the police. Lieutenant Mallory arrived in person, a sign not of my importance but of his angry concern—angry because I should have stayed clear of police business, concern because he'd been close to both my parents.

"Vicki, put yourself in my place for a change. One of your oldest friends dies and every time you turn around his only kid is thumbing her nose at you. How do you think I feel?"

"I know how you feel; you've told me six billion times," I said churlishly. I hate having to talk to people in a hospital gown—it's like you're a kid in bed and they're tucking you in for the night.

"If you'd been killed, I would have carried that responsibility to my grave. Can't you understand that? Can't you see when I give you orders it's out of concern for your safety, because of what I owe Tony and Gabriella? What will it take to pound some sense into you?"

I glowered at the bedclothes. "I'm self-employed just so I don't have to take orders from anyone. Anyway, Bobby, I did agree not to go to the state's attorney about Nancy Cleghorn. And I agreed to tell you if I ran into anything that looked like a lead into her death. I didn't."

"You obviously did!" he shouted, pounding the bedside table so hard that the water pitcher fell over. That put the cap to his anger—he yelled out the door for an orderly, then shouted at the man until the floor was cleaned to his satisfaction. My roommate turned off *The Dating Game* and scurried out to the lounge.

When the place was dry again Bobby made an effort to smother his anger. He took me through the details of the episode, waiting patiently at the spots that were hard for me to talk about, prompting me professionally when I couldn't remember something. The fact that I had a name, even just a first name, cheered him slightly—if Troy was a pro tied to any known organization, the police would have a file on him.

"Now, Vicki"—Bobby was genial—"let's get to the heart of the matter. If you didn't know anything about Cleghorn's death, why did someone try to kill you in the same manner, and in the same place that they murdered her?"

"Gee, Bobby, the way you put it, I guess I must know who killed her. Or at least why."

"Exactly. Now let's have it."

I shook my head, gingerly, since the back was still on the sore side. "It's just the way *you* put it. The way I look at it, I must've talked to someone who thinks I know more than I really do. The trouble is, I've talked to so many people the last few days and all of them have been so unpleasant that I don't know which I'd choose as my grade-A suspect."

"Okay." Bobby was determinedly patient. "Let's have who you've talked to."

I looked at the water stains on the ceiling. "There's young Art Jurshak. You know, the alderman's son. And Curtis Chigwell, the doctor who tried killing himself in Hinsdale the other day. And Ron Kappelman—SCRAP's counsel. Gustav Humboldt, of course. Murray Ryerson—"

"Gustav Humboldt?" Bobby's voice went up a register.

"You know, the chairman of Humboldt Chemical."

"I know who you mean," he said bitingly. "You want to share with me why you were talking to him? In reference to the Cleghorn woman?"

"I wasn't really talking to him about the Cleghorn woman at all," I said earnestly, turning to look at Bobby's clenched jaw. "That's what I meant—I didn't talk to any of these people about Nancy. But since they were all more or less unpleasant, any of them might have wanted to dump me in the swamp."

"For two cents I'd get someone to put you back there. It'd save a lot of time. You know something and you think you're going to be a hotshot again, go looking without saying squat to me about it. They almost got you this time. Next time they will, but until they do I have to waste city money by having someone keep an eye on you."

His blue eyes glittered. "Eileen's all upset about you being in here. She wanted to send over flowers, she wanted to take you home with her and fuss over you. I told her you just ain't worth it."

25

VISITING HOURS

After Bobby left I lay back down. I tried to sleep, but the pain in my shoulders had moved to the foreground of my mind. Angry tears prickled under my eyes. I had almost gotten killed, and all he could do was insult me. I wasn't worth the bother of looking after, just because I wasn't a blabber-mouth who would tell him everything I knew. I'd tried mentioning Gustav Humboldt's name, and all I'd gotten for my pains was an incredulous shout.

I twitched uncomfortably. The knot in the hospital gown was digging into my sore neck muscles. Of course I could have given him chapter and verse on all my activities for the last week. But Bobby just wouldn't have believed that a bigshot like Gustav Humboldt could be involved in bonking young women on the head. Although maybe if I'd tried giving it to him straight . . . Was he right? Was I just hotdogging, hoping to thumb my nose at him one more time?

As I lay still, letting images flow through my mind, I realized that this time, at least, wanting to give the powers-that-be a Bronx cheer wasn't what had kept me quiet. I was well and truly scared. Every time I tried sending my mind back to the three black-slickered men I shied away from the memory like a horse frightened by fire. There were a lot of parts of the assault I hadn't told Bobby, not because I was trying to hold back on him but because I couldn't bear to touch the memories. The hope that some forgotten phrase or cadence would give me a lead to who they worked for wasn't enough to force the memory of that terrifying near-suffocation.

If I spilled everything I knew to Bobby, turning the whole tangled mess over to him, it was a way of saying it out loud. Hey, guys, whoever you are, you got me. You didn't kill me but you got me so scared that I'm abdicating responsibility for my life.

Once I'd let that little piece of self-knowledge float to the top of my mind, a terrible rage began to seize hold of me. I would not be turned into a eunuch, be driven to living my life in the margins designed by someone else's will. I didn't know what was going on in South Chicago, but no one, be it Steve Dresberg, Gustav Humboldt, or even Caroline Djiak, was going to keep me from finding out.

When Murray Ryerson showed up a little after eleven, I was pacing the room in my bare feet, my hospital gown flapping around my legs. I'd vaguely seen my roommate stand uncertainly in the door and move away again, and I mistook Murray's presence for her return until he spoke.

"They told me you were fifteen minutes from death, but I knew better than to believe that."

I jumped. "Murray! Didn't your mother teach you to knock before barging in on people?"

"I tried, but you weren't anywhere near planet earth." He straddled the chair next to my bed. "You look like that Siberian tiger in that great open area at Lincoln Park Zoo, V.I. You're making me nervous. Sit down and let me have an exclusive on your brush with death. Who tried to do you in? Dr. Chigwell's sister? The folks down at the Xerxes plant? Or your pal Caroline Djiak?"

That stopped me. I pulled up my roommate's chair to face Murray. I had hoped to keep Louisa's affairs out of the papers, but once Murray started digging he'd find out pretty much anything.

"What'd little Caroline tell you—that I'd come by my ill deserts honestly?"

"Caroline's a bit confusing to talk to. She says you were looking into Nancy Cleghorn's death for SCRAP, although no one else down there seems to know anything about it. She claims she knows nothing about Pankowski or Ferraro, although I'm not sure I believe her."

Murray poured himself a glass of water from the pitcher the orderly had replaced. "The people at Xerxes keep referring us to counsel if we want to hear about those two. Or about their suicidal doctor. And it does always kind of make you wonder when people only talk to you through their lawyers. We're working on the plant secretary, the gal who works for the accountant-cum-personnel administrator. And one of my assistants is hanging out at the bar where the shift goes after work, so we'll get something. But you could sure make it easier, Miss Marple."

I slid from the chair back to bed and pulled the covers up to my chin. Caroline was protecting Louisa. Of course. That was what lay behind her song and dance. A threat to her mother was the only thing that would scare her, the only explanation consistent with her fierce terrier personality. She didn't care anything for her own safety—and certainly not enough for mine to grow hysterical over my failure to drop the investigation.

It was hard to imagine how they could menace a woman in Louisa's condition. Maybe blasting the private affairs she so ardently desired to keep secret out into the open—perhaps her most important concern in the last months of her life. Although Louisa hadn't seemed worried when I saw her on Tuesday. . . .

"Come on, Vic. Give." Murray's voice had an edge that brought me back to the room.

"Murray, it wasn't two days ago you were looking haughtily down that elephant-child snout of yours telling me you didn't need anything from me and wouldn't do anything for me. So give me a reason why I should suddenly help you out."

Murray waved his hand around the hospital room. "This, baby doll. Someone wants you dead awful bad. The more people who know what you know, the less likely they'll be to try to take you out a second time."

I smiled sweetly—at least that was the goal. "I talked to the police."

"And told them everything you know."

"That would take more time than Lieutenant Mallory has. I told him who I spoke with the day before the—the assault. That included you—you weren't very pleasant, and he wanted to know about anyone who seemed hostile."

Murray's eyes narrowed above his red beard. "I came here prepared to be sympathetic, maybe even to rub ointment into the sore spots. You have a way of destroying people's tender feelings, kiddo."

I made a sour face. "Funny—Bobby Mallory said much the same thing."

"Any reasonable man would. . . . Okay. Let's have the assault story. All I have is the sketch the hospital reported to the cops. You made all four TV news spots last night, if that makes you feel more important."

It didn't. It made me feel more exposed. Whoever had tried to dump me into the South Chicago swamp had plenty of access to the news that I'd managed to crawl away. There wasn't any point to asking Murray to keep a lid on it: I gave him as much as I could bear to reveal about the experience.

"I take it back, V.I.," he said when I finished. "That's a harrowing story even with most of the details missing. You're entitled to thrash your tail awhile."

Even so he tried wheedling more information from me, stopping only when the lunches were brought in, chicken and overcooked peas, followed nervously by the woman recovering from plastic surgery. I was chewed out rather sternly by the floor head for having visitors who frightened my room-mate out of her own bed. Since Murray takes up about as much space as a full-grown grizzly, she devoted enough of her remarks to him that he fled in some embarrassment.

After lunch a petite Asian underling came to inform me that Dr. Herschel had ordered deep heat for me down in physical therapy. She found a hospital robe for me. Even though I was twice her size, she helped me solicitously into a wheelchair and pushed me down to the PT unit, deep in the bowels of the hospital. I spent a pleasant hour getting wet packs, deep heat, and a massage, finishing with ten minutes in the whirlpool.

By the time my attendant had brought me back to my room, I was drowsy and ready for sleep. It was not meant to be, however: I found Ron Kappelman sitting in the visitor's chair. He put away a folder of papers when he saw me and offered me a pot of geraniums.

"You sure seem better today than I would've believed twenty-four hours ago," he said soberly. "I'm most sorry I didn't take your neighbor seriously —I just assumed something important had come up and you'd taken off. I still can't figure out how he bullied me into driving him all the way down there."

I slid back into bed and lay down. "Mr. Contreras is a little excitable, at least about my well-being, but I'm not exactly in the mood to fight it today. You find anything out about that insurance report? Or why Jurshak was appointed the fiduciary?"

"You look as though you should be convalescing, not worrying about a bunch of old files," he said disapprovingly.

"Has their status changed? Tuesday you were pretty excited about them. What turned them into old files?" Lying down wasn't a good idea—I kept drifting. I cranked the bed so I could sit up.

"The way you looked when that old man dragged you up to the fence. They didn't seem worth that much trouble."

I scanned his face for signs of menace or lies or something. All he showed was manly concern. What did that prove?

"Is that why I was dumped into the marsh? Because of the report to Mariners Rest?"

He looked startled. "I guess I assumed—because we'd talked about them and then you didn't show up for our meeting."

"You tell anyone about my having that letter, Kappelman?"

He leaned forward in his chair, his mouth set in a thin line. "I'm begin-ning to dislike the turn this conversation is taking, Warshawski. Are you trying to imply that I had anything to do with what happened to you yester-day?"

This made the third well-wisher whose mind I'd changed within minutes of entering the room. "I'm trying to make sure that you didn't. Look, Ron, all I know about you is that you had a brief fling with an old friend of mine. That doesn't tell me anything—I mean, I was once married to a guy I wouldn't trust with a kid's piggy bank. All it proves is that hormones are stronger than brains.

"I talked to you and to one other person about those documents. If they're the reason I was dumped into that swamp yesterday—and that's a big question mark—because I just don't know—it had to be because of one of you guys."

He made a sour face. "Okay. I guess I can buy that—just. I don't know how to convince you I didn't hire those thugs—other than on my honor as a Boy Scout. I was one once, thirty years ago or so. Will you take that as evidence of probity?"

"I'll take it into account." I lowered the bed again—I was too tired to try to push him any further. "They're springing me tomorrow. Want to try again on these papers?"

He frowned. "You really are a cold-blooded bitch, aren't you? Near death one day and hot on the trail the next. Sherlock Holmes didn't have anything on you. I guess I still want to see those damned documents—I'll stop by around six if they've let you go home."

He got up and pointed at the geraniums. "Don't eat those—they're just for the spirit. Try to enjoy them."

"Very funny," I muttered to his back. Before he'd disappeared I was deep in sleep.

When I woke again around six Max was sitting in the visitor's chair. He was reading a magazine with peaceful absorption, but when he realized I was awake he folded it neatly and stuck it in his attaché case.

"I would have been here much sooner, but my day was spent in meetings, I fear. Lotty tells me you are fine, that you need nothing but rest to be completely healed."

I ran a hand through my hair. It felt matted and sticky, which made me feel at a disadvantage. I eyed Max warily.

"Victoria." He took my left hand and held it between his two. "I hope you can forgive my cold words of a few days ago. When Lotty told me what had happened to you, I felt truly remorseful."

"Don't," I said awkwardly. "You weren't responsible for anything that happened to me."

His soft brown eyes looked at me shrewdly. "Nothing is without connec-tion in our lives. If I hadn't goaded you about Dr. Chigwell, you might not have acted so fiercely as to get yourself into trouble."

I started to answer him, then stopped. If he hadn't goaded me, I might not have felt so reluctant to take my gun with me on my run yesterday. Maybe I even exposed myself unconsciously to danger to assuage my guilt.

"But I did have something to feel guilty about," I said aloud. "You weren't that far off the mark, you know—I only pressured Chigwell because he made me angry. So maybe I gave the final turn to his screw."

"So maybe we can both learn a little from this, to look before we leap." Max stood up to reveal a magnificent array of flowers in a Chinese porcelain bowl. "I know you leave tomorrow, but take these with you for some cheer while your poor muscles heal."

Max was an expert on oriental porcelain. The pot looked as though it had come from his personal collection. I tried to let him know how much the gesture pleased me; he accepted my thanks with his usual cheerful courtesy and left.

26

BACK TO HOME BASE

I had a new roommate in the morning, a twenty-year-old named Jean Fishbeck whose lover had shot at her and hit a shoulder before she got him in the stomach. The cosmetic surgery patient had moved three rooms down the hall.

I got the whole shooting story, with loud-pitched expletives, at midnight when Ms. Fishbeck came in from postop. At seven, when the morning shift came in to see if we'd expired in the night, she vented her rage at being awakened in the clarion nasal of the northwest side. By the time Lotty showed up at eight-thirty I was ready to go anywhere, even the psychiatric wing, just to get away from the obscenities and cigarettes.

"I don't care what shape I'm in," I told Lotty irritably. "Just sign my discharge and let me out of here. I'll leave in my nightgown if I have to."

Lotty cocked an eye at the crumpled chewing-gum wrappers and cigarette pack on the floor. She raised both eyebrows as a stream of profanity poured from behind the closed curtain while an intern tried to conduct an exam.

"The floor head told me you'd been rough on your roommate yesterday and that they were giving you someone more suited to your personality. Did you vent your anger by handing her a few punches?" She started probing my shoulder muscles.

"Ow, damn you, that hurts. And the word you want is *throw*, not *hand*. Or *land*, maybe."

Lotty used her ophthalmoscope on my eyes. "We gave you X rays and a CT scan after we stabilized you on Wednesday. By some miracle you don't have any cracks or breaks. Some more physical therapy over the next few days should help your sore muscles, but don't expect them to recover overnight—tissue tears can take as long as a year to heal if you don't rest the muscles properly. And yes, you can go home—you can do the therapy as an outpatient. If you give me your keys, I'll have Carol bring you some clothes at lunchtime."

I'd tied the keys through the laces of my running shoes before setting out on Wednesday. Lotty had rescued them before giving orders to trash what clothes I'd still been wearing on arrival at Beth Israel.

She stood up and looked at me gravely. When she spoke again her Viennese accent was pronounced. "I would ask that you not be reckless, Victoria. I would ask it except that you seem to be in love with danger and death. You make life very hard for those who love you."

I couldn't think of anything to say. She stared at me for a long moment, her eyes very dark in her angular face, then gave her head a little shake and left.

My twenty-four-hour character summary wasn't too appealing: a coldhearted bitch in love with death and danger who drove timid cosmetic surgery patients to the nursing staff for refuge. When an orderly came by an hour or so later to take me down for physical therapy, I went along morosely. The normal hospital routine, which depersonalizes patients at its expense, usually drives me into a frenzy of uncooperative sarcasm. Today I took it like a good little lump.

After my physical therapy I myself took refuge from my vituperous roommate, waiting in the lounge for my clothes with a stack of old *Glamour*s and *Sports Illustrated*. Carol Alvarez, the nurse and chief backup at Lotty's clinic, arrived a little before two. She greeted me warmly, with a hug, a kiss, and little exclamations of horror over my ordeal.

"Even Mama has been praying to the Blessed Mother for your safety, Vic." That was something, indeed—Mrs. Alvarez usually looked on me with silent contempt.

Carol had brought jeans, a sweatshirt, and a pair of boots. The clothes and underwear seemed unnaturally clean. I'd forgotten leaving them in the laundry on Wednesday. Apparently one of my downstairs neighbors had dumped them in a wet heap outside my apartment door with an angry note—Carol had generously taken the time to run them back through the machine.

She helped me quickly with the discharge routine. Since she knew a lot of the nurses on the floor, their hostility toward me cooled a little when they saw me with her. With me carrying Max's oriental bowl and Carol the geraniums, we made our way through the long corridors to the staff parking lot behind the hospital.

My head seemed stuffed with cotton, remote not just from my body but from the day around me. It had been only two days since my ill-fated run, but I felt as though I'd been away from the world for months. My boots felt new and strange and I couldn't get used to the sensation of the jeans zipped close to my body. At that they weren't as close as they used to be—the last few days seemed to have taken a good five pounds off me.

Mr. Contreras was waiting for me when we got to my apartment on Racine. He had tied a big red ribbon around Peppy's neck and groomed her auburn hair until it shone in the dull gray day. Carol turned me over to them with another kiss and left us at the door.

I would have much preferred to be alone to order my thoughts, but he had earned the right to fuss. I submitted to his ushering me into the arm-chair, pulling off my boots and tucking a blanket tenderly around my legs and feet.

He'd fixed an elaborate tray of fruit and cheese, which he set next to me along with a pot of tea. "Now, cookie, I'm leaving her highness here to keep you company. You want anything, you just call me. I printed my number next to the phone so you don't have to look it up. And before you go off sticking your head into trouble, you let me know. I ain't gotta hover over you—I know you hate that—but someone's gotta know where to come looking for you. You promise me that or I'm going to have to hire me a detective just to follow you around."

I held out a hand. "It's a deal, Uncle."

The honorary title moved him so much that he spoke sternly to the dog, outlining her duties to me, before slapping me on my sore shoulder and moving off down the stairs.

I'm not much of a tea drinker, but it was pleasant to stay where I'd been planted. I poured myself a cup, mixed it with a lot of heavy cream, and alternately fed grapes to myself and the dog. She sat on her haunches watching me with unwavering eyes, panting slightly, taking her guard duties seriously, assuring herself that I wasn't going to disappear again without her.

I forced my weary mind back to the time before my assault. Only three days earlier, but the neurons moved as though they'd been rusted over for years. When every muscle aches it's hard to remember feeling whole.

I'd been warned out of South Chicago Monday night. On Wednesday I'd been dispatched most efficiently. That meant something I'd done Tuesday had brought an immediate reaction. I frowned, trying to remember what all happened that day.

I'd found Jurshak's insurance report and talked to Ron Kappelman about it. I'd also left a message for young Art implying I had the material. These were tangible documents and it was tempting to think they showed something so damaging that people would kill to keep them secure. It might be difficult to pry the truth from Kappelman if he was concealing something, but Jurshak was such a fragile young man, I ought to be able to pound the facts from him. If only I could find him. If he was still alive.

Still, I shouldn't concentrate on those two at the expense of the other people involved. Curtis Chigwell, for example. Early Tuesday I'd sicced Murray Ryerson on him and twelve hours later he'd tried to kill himself. And then there was the big shark, Gustav Humboldt himself. Whatever Chigwell knew, whatever they were concealing about Joey Pankowski and Steve Ferraro, Gustav Humboldt had full knowledge of. Otherwise he would never have sought me out to try to get me to swallow lies about two insignificant workers in his worldwide empire. And the insurance report Nancy had found dealt with his company. That must mean something—I just didn't yet know what.

Finally, of course, there was little Caroline. Now that I'd worked out that she was protecting Louisa, I figured I could get her to talk. She might even know what Nancy had seen in the insurance report. She was my best starting point.

I took the blanket from my legs and got up. The dog immediately sprang to her feet, waving her tail—if I stood up, it was clearly time to go running. When she saw me just move to the phone, she flopped down in depression.

Caroline was in a meeting, the SCRAP receptionist told me. She was not to be disturbed.

"Just write the following on a note and take in into her—'Louisa's life story on the front page of the *Herald-Star?*' And add my name. I guarantee she'll be on the phone within nanoseconds."

I had to cajole a little more, but the woman finally agreed. I carried the phone back over to the easy chair. Peppy eyed me in disgust, but I wanted to be sitting down for the coming blast.

Caroline came on the line without preamble. I let her rant at me unchecked for some minutes, shredding my character, expressing remorse that I'd risen unchastened from the swamp, even lamenting that I didn't now lie buried in the mud.

At that I decided to interrupt. "Caroline, that was vile and offensive. If you had any imagination or sensitivity, you would never have thought such a thing, let alone said it."

She was silent for a minute, then said gruffly. "I'm sorry, Vic. But you shouldn't have sent me messages threatening Ma."

"Right, kiddo. I understand. I understand that the only reason you've been behaving more like a horse's rear end than usual is because someone was gunning for Louisa. I need to know who and why."

"How do you know?" she blurted.

"It's your character, sweetie. It just took me awhile to remember it. You're manipulative, you'll bend the rules any old way to get what you want, but you're no chicken. You'd run scared for only one reason."

She was silent for another long moment. "I'm not going to say if you're right or wrong," she finally said. "I just can't talk about it. If you're right, you can understand why. If you're wrong—I guess it's because I'm a horse's rear end."

I tried to will my personality into the phone. "Caroline, this is important.

If someone told you they'd hurt Louisa unless you got me to stop hunting for your father, I need to know it. Because it means there's a tie-in between Nancy's death and my looking at Joey Pankowski and Steve Ferraro."

"You'd have to sell me and I don't think you can." She was serious, more mature than I was used to hearing her.

"At least let me give it a shot, babe. Come up here some time tomorrow? As you can imagine, I'm not too fit right now or I'd zip down to see you tonight."

She finally, reluctantly, agreed to come by in the afternoon. We hung up in greater amity than I'd have thought possible ten minutes earlier.

27

THE GAME'S AFOOT

An annoying lassitude gripped my body. Even the short conversation with Caroline had tired me out. I poured some more tea and flicked on the tube. With spring training still two weeks away, there wasn't much doing during the day. I moved from soap to soap to a tearful prayer meeting —Tammy Faye's sobbing successor—to *Sesame Street* and turned the set off in disgust. It was too much to expect me to sort papers or pay bills in my enfeebled state; I wrapped myself in my blanket and lay down on the sofa for a nap.

I woke up about twenty minutes before Kappelman was due and stumbled into the bathroom to rinse my face with cold water. Someone had stolen all the dirty towels, scrubbed the sink and bathtub, and tidied up odds and ends of toiletries and makeup. Peeping into my bedroom, I was staggered to see the bed made and clothes and shoes put away. I hated to admit it, but the tidy rooms were cheering to my sore spirits.

I'd hidden Nancy's documents in the stacks of music on the piano. The elves had carefully put the music inside the piano bench, but the insurance material lay undisturbed between the *Italienisches Liederbuch* and Mozart's *Concert Arias*.

I was picking my way through *"Che no sei capace"*—whose title line seemed admirably apt, in that I understood nothing—when Kappelman rang the bell. Before I could get to the intercom Mr. Contreras had bounded out to the lobby to inspect him. When I opened my door I could hear their voices in the stairwell as they came up together—Mr. Contreras trying to tamp down the suspicions he felt toward any man who visited me, Kappelman trying to suppress his impatience with the escort.

My neighbor started talking to me as soon as his head cleared the last turn and he caught sight of me. "Oh, hi there, cookie. You have a good rest? I'm just coming to pick up her highness here, get her some air, a little food. You weren't feeding her cheese, were you? I meant to tell you—she can't tolerate it."

He came into the room and started inspecting Peppy for signs of illness. "You don't want to go walking her alone, now, nor going off by yourself on one of your runs. And don't let this young guy here keep you going past when you've got yourself worn out. And you want any help with anything, me and the dog'll be at the ready; you just give us a holler."

With this thinly veiled warning, he collected Peppy. He hovered at the door with more admonitions until I finally thrust him gently onto the landing.

Kappelman looked at me sourly. "If I'd known the old man was going to investigate my character, I'd've brought my own attorney along. I'd say you were safe if you kept him with you—anyone attacks you he'll talk them to death."

"He just likes to imagine I'm sixteen and he's both my parents," I said with more indulgence than I felt. Owing my life to Mr. Contreras didn't keep me from finding him a little wearing.

I offered Kappelman a drink. His first choice was beer, which I rarely have in the house, followed by bourbon. I finally unearthed a bottle of that from the back of my liquor cupboard.

"An old South Sider like you ought to be ready with a shot and a beer," he grumbled.

"I guess it's just one more sign of how much I've abandoned my roots." I took him into the living room, folding up the blanket I'd left on the couch so he could sit there. My place was never going to be the equal of his Pullman showcase, but at least it was neat. I didn't get any compliments, but then he couldn't be expected to know how it usually looked.

After a few polite nothings about my health and his day, I handed Nancy's packet to him. He pulled a pair of glasses from the breast pocket of his shabby jacket and carefully went through the document a page at a time. I sipped my whiskey and read the day's papers, trying not to fidget.

When he'd finished he put his glasses away with a little gesture of puzzled helplessness. "I don't know why Nance had these. Or why she thought they might have been important."

I gritted my teeth. "Don't tell me they're completely meaningless."

"I don't know." He hunched a shoulder. "You can see what they are as easily as I can. I don't know that much about insurance, but it looks as though Xerxes might have been paying more than these other guys and Jurshak was trying to persuade the company"—he looked at the document searching for the name—"Mariners Rest to lower their rates. It obviously meant something to Nancy, but it sure doesn't to me. Sorry."

I scowled horribly, causing the kind of wrinkles they warn starlets against. "Maybe the point isn't the data but the fact that Jurshak handled the insurance. Maybe still does. He wouldn't be my first choice as either an agent or a fiduciary."

Ron smiled a little. "You can afford to be superior—you aren't trying to do business in South Chicago. Maybe Humboldt felt it was easier to go with the flow on Jurshak than use an independent agent. Or maybe it was genuine altruism, trying to give business to the community where he set up his plant. Jurshak wasn't very big in South Chicago, let alone the city, back in '63."

"Maybe." I swirled my glass, watching the golden liquid change to amber as it picked up the lamplight. Art and Gustav doing good for the good of the community as a whole. I could see it on a billboard, but not so easily in real life. But I'd grown up around Art so I followed revelations about him—deals that made him or his partner, Freddy Parma, a director—and insurance provider—for a local trucking company, a steel firm, a rail freight hauler, and other outfits. Campaign contributions flowed from these companies in a most gratifying stream. Mariners Rest Assurance Company might not know these things, but Ron Kappelman ought to.

"You're looking awfully sinister." Kappelman interrupted my reverie. "Like you think I'm an ax murderer."

"Just my coldhearted bitch expression. I was wondering how much you know about Art Jurshak's insurance business."

"You mean stuff like Mid-States Rail? Of course I do. Why do you—" He broke off mid-sentence, his eyes widening slightly. "Yes. In that light going to Jurshak for fiduciary assistance doesn't make much sense. You think Jurshak has something on Humboldt?"

"Could be the other way around. Could be Humboldt has something to cover up and he figures Jurshak is the man to do it for him."

I wished I knew if I could trust Kappelman—he shouldn't have needed me to spell that out for him. I took the documents back and looked at them broodingly.

After a pause Kappelman smiled at me quizzically. "How about dinner before I head south? You fit enough to go out?"

Real food. I thought I could make the effort. Just in case Kappelman was leading me back to my pals in the black raincoats, I went into the bedroom to get my gun. And make a call on the extension by my bed.

Young Art's mother answered the phone; her son still hadn't shown up, she told me in a worried whisper. Mr. Jurshak didn't know yet that he had disappeared, so she'd appreciate my keeping it quiet.

"If he shows up, or if you hear from him, make sure he gets in touch with me. I can't tell you how important it is that he do so." I hesitated, not sure whether melodrama would make her totally nonfunctional or guarantee her giving my message to her son. "His life may be in danger, but if I can talk to him, I think I can keep anything from happening to him."

She was starting to hiss questions at me in a strained whisper, but Big Art cut in behind her, wanting to know who she was talking to. She hung up hurriedly.

The longer young Art stayed away, the less I liked it. The kid didn't have any friends and he didn't have any street sense. I shook my head uselessly and stuck the Smith & Wesson into the waist of my jeans.

Kappelman was calmly reading *The Wall Street Journal* when I came back to the living room. He didn't look as though he'd been monitoring me on the phone, but if he was truly an evil creep, he'd be able to appear innocent. I gave up chewing on it.

"I have to tell Mr. Contreras I'm going out—otherwise, when he realizes I'm not up here he's going to call the cops and have you arrested for murdering me."

He made a fatalistic gesture. "I thought I'd left that kind of crap behind when I moved out of my mother's house. That's why I'm in Pullman—it was as far as I could reasonably get from Highland Park."

As I locked the dead bolt the phone started to ring. Thinking it might be young Art, I excused myself to Ron and went back into the apartment. Much to my astonishment it was Ms. Chigwell, in extreme distress. I braced myself, thinking she had called to upbraid me for driving her brother to attempt suicide. I tried a few awkward apologies.

"Yes, yes, it was very sad. But Curtis was never a strong character—it didn't surprise me. Nor that he wasn't able to do it successfully. I suspect he meant to be found—he left all the lights on in the garage, and he knew I would come in to see why. After all, he believes I drove him to it."

I blinked a little at the indulgent contempt in her voice. She surely wasn't phoning to assuage any putative guilt on my part. I asked an exploratory question.

"Well, really, it's just something—something very strange happened this afternoon." She was suddenly stumbling, losing her usual gruff assurance.

"Yes?" I said encouragingly.

"I know it's inconsiderate of me to bother you, when you just had such a terrible ordeal yourself, but you are an investigator, and it seemed to me you were a more proper person to go to than the police."

Another long pause. I lay down on the couch to ease the soreness between my shoulders.

"It's—well, it's Curtis. I'm sure he broke in here this afternoon."

That was sufficiently startling that I sat up again. "Broke in? I thought he lived with you!"

"He does, of course. But, well, I rushed him to the hospital when I found him on Tuesday. He wasn't very sick and they released him on Wednesday. He was terribly embarrassed, didn't want to face me over the breakfast table, and said he was going to stay with friends. And to be frank with you, Miss Warshawski, I was just as happy to be rid of him for a few days."

Kappelman came over to where I was sitting. He waved a note under my nose—he would be down with Mr. Contreras getting permission for my outing. I nodded abstractedly and asked Ms. Chigwell to continue.

She took a breath, audible across the lines. "Fridays are my day at the hospital, you know. I do volunteer work with elderly ladies who no longer— well, you don't want to hear about that now. But when I got back I knew the house had been broken into."

"And you called the police and stayed with a friend until they arrived?"

"No. No, I didn't. Because I realized almost immediately it had to be Curtis. Or that he had let someone in who wouldn't have known the house well enough not to create a disturbance."

Confusion was making me impatient. I interrupted to ask if any valuables were gone.

"Nothing like that. But you see, Curtis's medical notebooks are missing. I'd hidden them from him after he tried burning them, and that's why—" She broke off. "I'm explaining this so badly. It's why I hoped you would come, even though it's a great distance and you are most tired yourself. I feel sure that whatever Curtis was involved with down at the Xerxes plant that he didn't want to tell you is in those notebooks."

"Which are missing," I interjected shortly.

She gave the ghost of a laugh. "Only his copies. I kept the originals. I typed his notes up for him over the years. That's all that's missing. I never told him I kept all the original notebooks.

"You see—he had put the data in Father's old leather diaries, the ones he had custom-bound for himself in London. It seemed—a kind of desecration to throw them out, but I knew Curtis would be horribly angry to think I was keeping them out of memory for Father. So I never told him."

I felt a little prickling along the base of my neck, that primitive adrenaline jolt that lets you know you're getting close to the saber-toothed tiger. I told her I'd be at her house within the hour.

28
THE GOLDEN NOTEBOOKS

Kappelman and Mr. Contreras had struck an uneasy truce over the grappa bottle. Ron got quickly to his feet when I came in, putting a stop to a long anecdote about how Mr. Contreras knew when he first saw him what a lightweight one of my old lovers had been. I explained glibly that I'd had an urgent SOS from an aunt of mine in the suburbs, one I couldn't ignore.

"Your aunt, doll? I thought you and her—" Mr. Contreras caught the look of steel in my eyes. "Oh, your aunt. Is she in some kind of trouble?"

"More just panicking over me," I said firmly. "But she's my mother's only surviving relative. She's old and I can't leave her hanging." It seemed wrong somehow to confuse the redoubtable Ms. Chigwell with my mother's mad Aunt Rosa, but you have to work with what's at hand.

Kappelman agreed with me politely—whether he believed me was another matter. He finished his grappa in a long swallow, winced as the raw alcohol hit his esophagus, and said he'd see me to my car. "Relatives are a trial, aren't they?" he added sardonically.

He waited patiently while I looked around the car for any obvious signs of bombs, then shut the door for me with an old-fashioned courtesy at variance with his bedraggled clothes.

The temperature had dropped some ten degrees, just below freezing. After the dull fog of the last few weeks, the sharper air braced me. A few snowflakes drifted into the windshield, but the roads were clear and I had a quick run out the Eisenhower to York Road.

Ms. Chigwell was waiting for me at the door, her gaunt fierce face unchanged for the trying events of the last few days. She thanked me unsmilingly for making the trip, but I was beginning to know her and could tell her rough manner wasn't meant to be as unfriendly as it appeared.

"I'm having a cup of tea. My brother keeps telling me it's a sign of weakness, turning to stimulants when one feels troubled, but I think I've proved to be tougher than him. Would you like a cup?"

One serving of tea a day was all the stimulus I could handle. Declining as politely as I could, I followed her into the living room. It presented a scene of cozy domesticity worthy of Harriet Beecher Stowe. A fire burning cleanly in the grate refracted rich colors in the silver tea service on a low table nearby. Ms. Chigwell gestured me to one of the chintz armchairs facing the fireplace.

"In my day young ladies did not have lives of their own outside the household," she said abruptly, pouring tea into a translucent china cup. "We were supposed to marry. My father was a doctor out here, when it was really a separate little town, not part of the city at all. I used to help him out. By the time I was sixteen I could've set a simple fracture, treated a lot of the fevers he saw. But when it came time for college and medical training, that was Curtis's role. After Father died in 1939, Curtis tried keeping up the practice. He wasn't much good at it, though; patients kept going elsewhere until finally he had to take a position at that plant."

She looked at me fiercely. "I see you're an active young woman, you do what you want, you don't take no for an answer. I wish I'd had your backbone at your age, that's all."

"Yes," I said gently. "But I had help. My mother ended up on her own in a strange country—she couldn't speak the language; the only thing she could do was sing. She almost died as a result, so she swore I would never be as helpless and scared as she was. Believe me, that makes a big difference. You're asking too much of yourself to think you should have done it all on your own."

Ms. Chigwell swallowed her tea in large gulps, her throat muscles working, her left hand clenching and unclenching. Finally she felt enough in command of herself to speak again.

"Well, as you can tell, I never married. My mother died when we were seventeen. I kept house for my father and then for Curtis. I even learned to type so I could help them with their work."

She smiled mirthlessly. "I didn't try to follow what Curtis did at that company he worked for. My father had been a great country doctor, a master diagnostician. I suspect all Curtis did was take people's temperatures when they felt ill to see if they had a legitimate excuse to leave work early. By 1955, when he started in with these detailed records of his, I no longer knew anything of what went on in the medical world—the changes were too vast from my childhood days. But I still knew how to type, so I typed whatever he brought home for me."

Her story made me shiver a little. And mutter a little word of thanks to my mother's spirit. Fierce, intense, prickly, she'd been difficult to live with, but my earliest memories included her strong belief in me and what I could achieve with my life.

Ms. Chigwell must have seen some of the thought in my face. "Don't pity me. I've had many fine moments in this life of mine. And I never indulge in self-pity—a far greater weakness than tea, and one Curtis is most subject to."

We sat quietly for a while. She poured herself a second cup and drank it in slow, measured sips, staring sightlessly into the fire. When she had finished she put the cup down with a decisive snap and moved the tray to one side.

"Well, I mustn't keep you with my maundering. You've come a great distance and I can tell you're in a fair amount of pain, even though you're trying to hide it."

She stood upright with only a slight effort. I copied her slowly and stiffly and followed her up the carpeted stairs to the second floor. The upper landing was lined with bookshelves. Clearly a great many of Ms. Chigwell's fine moments had come from books—there were easily a thousand of them, all neatly dusted and carefully aligned on their shelves. How she'd ever known something was amiss among this orderly infantry was amazing. It took someone axing my front door to bits for me to know I'd suffered a home invasion.

Ms. Chigwell nodded toward an open door on my right. "Curtis's study. I came in here last Monday evening because I smelled fire. He was trying to burn his notebooks in his waste can. An appalling idea, since the waste can was leather, and it, too, began to burn with a terrible odor. I knew then that whatever was bothering him had to do with those records. But I thought it would be most wrong of him to back away from the facts by destroying them."

I felt an uneasy sympathy for Curtis Chigwell, living with this battalion of rectitude. It would drive me to stronger stimulants than tea.

"Anyway, I took them, and hid them behind my boating books. Obviously a foolish mistake, since boating has always been my great love. It is the first place Curtis would have thought to look. But I believe he felt so humiliated by my catching him in the act, or perhaps so frightened about not being able to get rid of his guilty secret, that the next afternoon he tried killing himself."

I shook my head. So Max had been right in a way. By stirring up the Xerxes pot I'd put so much pressure on Chigwell that he'd felt he had no options left. It made me feel a little seasick. I followed Ms. Chigwell quietly down the hall, my feet sinking in the soft gray pile.

A room at the end held a profusion of flowering plants that absorbed the eye. This was Ms. Chigwell's sitting room, with a rocking chair, her knitting basket, and a serviceable old Remington on a small table. The books continued in here, in shelves that were built only to waist level, serving as platforms for the red and yellow and purple flowers.

She knelt in front of the shelf next to the typewriter and started pulling leather-bound volumes from it. They were old-fashioned diaries, bound in rich green, with Horace Chigwell, M.D., tooled in gold on each cover.

"I hated Curtis using Father's personal diaries, but there seemed no good reason for him not to. Of course the war—Hitler's war—put a stop to things like personally bound diaries, and Curtis never had his own. He coveted these terribly."

There were twelve altogether, covering a period of twenty-eight years. I flipped through them curiously. Dr. Chigwell had written in a prim, spidery hand. It looked neat on the page, all the letters carefully aligned, but it proved tough to read. The books seemed to be an inventory of the medical history of the Xerxes employees. At least I presumed the names spelled out in the difficult script were the employees'.

Sitting in a wicker straight-backed chair, I rummaged among the volumes until I found 1962—the year Louisa had started at Humboldt. I thumbed slowly through the names—they weren't presented in alphabetical order—but didn't see hers. In 1963, after she'd been there a year, she showed up near the end of the list as a white female, age seventeen, address on Houston. My mother's name leapt out at me—Gabriella Warshawski was the person to be notified in case of an emergency. Nothing about the baby, nothing about its father. Of course that didn't prove Chigwell hadn't known about Caroline —just that he hadn't put the information in his notebooks.

The rest of the entry seemed to be a series of notes in medical shorthand: "BP 110/72, Hgb 13, BUN 10, Bili 0.6, CR 0.7." I assumed "BP" was blood pressure but couldn't even begin to guess what the other letters meant. I asked Ms. Chigwell, but she shook her head.

"All this technical medicine is long after my time. My father never did any blood work—they didn't even know about typing blood in his day, let alone what they can do with it now. I suppose I was too bitter about not becoming a doctor to want to know anything."

I puzzled over the entries a few more minutes, but this was work for Lotty. I stacked the books. Time for me to do something I could understand: I asked her how the intruders had gotten into the house.

"I presume Curtis let them in," she said stiffly.

I leaned back in the chair and looked at her thoughtfully. Maybe no one had been in the house this afternoon. Maybe she was seizing the opportunity offered by her brother's disappearance to avenge herself for his bungling their father's practice all these years. Or perhaps in the confusion of the last few days she'd forgotten where she'd hidden the typed notes. She was, after all, nearly eighty.

I tried probing, but not very skillfully. She frowned ferociously.

"Young lady, please do not treat me like a senile old woman. I am in full possession of my faculties. I saw Curtis trying to burn his notes five days ago. I can even show you the spot where the wastebasket burned through to the carpet.

"Why he wanted to destroy them I have no idea. Nor why he should sneak in here to steal them. But both of these things occurred."

My face felt a little hot. I got up and told her I'd check out the premises. She was still a little frosty, but she took me on a tour of the house. Although she said she'd tidied any disarray among her books and silver, she hadn't vacuumed or dusted. After a painstaking search worthy of Sherlock Holmes, I did find traces of dried mud on the stairwell carpeting. I wasn't sure what that proved, but I could easily believe it wouldn't have come from Ms. Chigwell. None of the locks showed any sign of forcing.

I didn't think she should stay the night here alone—anyone who came in once in such a way could easily return, with or without her brother. And if they had seen me arrive, they might easily come back to demand why in ways that an old lady—however tough she might be—would be unable to withstand.

"No one is forcing me from my home. I grew up in this house and I am not leaving it now." She scowled at me fiercely.

I tried my best to dissuade her, but she was adamant. Either she was scared and didn't want to admit it, or she knew why her brother was so desperate to get his hands on the notebooks. But then she wouldn't have given the originals to me.

I shook my head in irritation. I was exhausted, my shoulders ached, my head was throbbing slightly where I'd been hit. If Ms. Chigwell wasn't telling the truth, tonight wasn't the night for me to figure it out—I needed to go to bed. As I was leaving, though, something else occurred to me.

"Who did your brother go to stay with?"

At that she looked a little embarrassed—she didn't know. "I was surprised when he said he was going to stay with friends, because he doesn't have any. He did get a call Wednesday afternoon about two hours after he got out of the hospital, and it was a little after that that he announced he was going away for a few days. But he left when I was doing my volunteer stint at the hospital, so I don't have any idea who might have come by for him."

Ms. Chigwell also had no idea who had called her brother. It had been a man, because she had picked up an extension at the same time Curtis had. Hearing a man say her brother's name, she'd immediately hung up. It was a pity, really, that her sense of moral rectitude had been too great for her to eavesdrop on her brother, but you can't have everything in an imperfect world.

It was close to eleven when I finally left. Looking back, I could see her gaunt frame silhouetted in the doorway. She lifted a hand in a formal gesture and shut the door.

29

NIGHT CRAWLERS

I hadn't realized how tired I was until I got into my car. The pain in my shoulders returned in a wave that swept me back limply in the front seat. Little tears of hurt and self-pity pricked my eyelids. Quitters never win and winners never quit, I quoted my old basketball coach grimly. Play through the pain, not against it.

I rolled the car window down, my sore arm moving slowly to the commands of my brain. I sat for a while, watching the Chigwell house and the surrounding street, dozing a bit, finally deciding the indomitable old lady wasn't under surveillance before putting the car into gear and heading for home.

The Eisenhower is never really clear of traffic—trucks thunder into the city throughout the night, some people are getting off late-night shifts, others heading for the action that begins only after dark. I joined the sweep of anonymous vehicles at Hillside. The steady stream of lights, red from the cars, orange on the sides of the trucks, the rows of streetlamps stretching into the distance as far as the eye could see, made me feel isolated and alone. A little speck in the great universe of lights, an atom of dust who could merge with the mud of Dead Stick Pond without leaving a trace behind.

My fragmented mood stayed with me as I drove slowly along Belmont to my apartment on Racine. I was hoping with the bottom half of my mind that Mr. Contreras and Peppy would be up to greet me—the top half sternly said I didn't want the old man breathing down my neck all the time.

That secret yearning may have saved my life. I had paused outside Mr. Contreras's ground-floor apartment, putting down the diaries to tie my shoes, seeing if my presence might rouse the dog so that I'd have a little companionship before going to bed.

The silence on the other side of the door told me the apartment was empty. Peppy certainly would have made herself known when she heard me, and the old man would never leave her outside alone this late at night. I looked up the stairs, foolishly wondering if they might be waiting for me at the top.

My unconscious mind realized something was wrong. I forced myself to stand motionless, pushed my tired brain to thought. The upper stairwell lay in darkness. One landing light might burn out, but both in the same evening stretched coincidence too far. Since the well of the lobby was lighted, anyone coming up the steps to the second or third floor would stand well framed in a pool of light.

From the topmost landing came a faint murmuring, not the sound of Mr. Contreras talking to Peppy. Picking up the notebooks, I eased my way to the lobby floor. I tucked the stack under one arm, pulled the gun out, flipped the safety off. Turned to face the street. Crouching low, I opened the outer door and slid into the night.

No one shot at me. The only person on the street was a moody-looking young man who lived down the block. He didn't even glance at me as I hurried by him toward Belmont. I didn't want to take my car—if someone was waiting for me outside the apartment, they might be keeping an eye on my Chevy: let them think I was still hanging around. If someone was waiting. Maybe fear and fatigue were making me jump at fantastic interpretations of light and street sounds.

At Belmont I tucked the Smith & Wesson back into my jeans and flagged a cab to Lotty's apartment. It was only a mile or so away, but I was in no condition to walk that far tonight. I asked the cabby to wait until I knew whether anyone was going to let me in. In the helpful style of today's drivers, he snarled at me.

"You don't own me. I give you ride, not my service for life."

"Splendid." I pulled back the five I'd been about to hand him. "Then I'll pay you after I know whether I'm spending the night here."

He started shouting at me, but I ignored him and opened the passenger door. That prompted him to get physical; he turned full around in the seat and swung at me. I slammed the stack of journals down on his arm with all the force of the pent-up frustrations from the last few days.

"Bitch!" he snarled. "You leave. You get from my cab. I don't need your money."

I slid from the backseat, keeping a wary eye on him until he drove off with a great squealing of rubber. All I needed now was for Lotty to be away at an emergency or sleeping too soundly to hear the bell. But the gods had not ordained me to have a total season of disaster this evening. After a few minutes, while my nervous irritation grew, her voice twanged at me through the intercom.

"It's me, Vic. Can I come up?"

She met me at the door to her apartment wrapped in a bright red dressing gown, looking like a little Mandarin with her dark eyes blinking away sleep.

"I'm sorry, Lotty—sorry to wake you. I had to go out this evening. When I got home I thought there might be a reception committee waiting for me."

"If you want me to come with you to blaze away at a few muggers, the answer is emphatically no," she said sardonically. "But I am glad to see you had a little more care for your skin than to go after them by yourself."

I couldn't respond to her breezy mood. "I want to call the police. And I don't want to go back over to Racine until they've had a chance to check the place out."

"Very good indeed," Lotty said, amazed. "I begin even to think you might live to be forty."

"Thanks a bunch," I muttered at her, going to the phone. I didn't like turning tail, handing my problems over to someone else to solve. But refusing to get help just because Lotty was being sarcastic seemed stupid.

Bobby Mallory was home. Like Lotty, he was inclined to taunt me a little over going to him for help, but once he'd absorbed the facts his professional persona took over. He asked me a few crisp questions, then assured me he'd have a squad car there without lights before he left his house. Before hanging up, though, he couldn't keep from rubbing my nose in it.

"You just stay put now, Vicki. I can't believe you're letting the police handle police business, but remember—the last thing we want is for you to come bounding up and get in between us and a couple of hoods."

"Right," I said sourly. "I'll look at the morning papers to see how things turn out."

The line went dead in my ear. I spent the next hour or so moving restlessly around Lotty's sitting room. She tried at first to talk me into going to sleep in her spare bed, preparing hot milk with brandy for me, but she finally left me to myself.

"I need my sleep even if you don't, Victoria. I'm not going to lecture you on rest after your physical ordeal—if by now you don't know you should, no words of mine will have any effect. Just remember—your body is an aging organism. It will repair itself more and more slowly as time goes by, and the less help you give it, the less you will be able to rely on it."

I knew by the tone as much as the words that Lotty was truly angry, but I was too fragmented still to make any kind of response. She loves me; she was afraid I would put myself at such risk I would die and abandon her. I understood that; I just couldn't fix it tonight.

It was only when she'd shut her door with an angry snap that I remembered the Chigwell notebooks. Not the time to knock at her bedroom and ask for help in deciphering his medical shorthand. I drank some of the milk and lay down on the daybed with my boots off, but I couldn't relax. All I could think was that I had run scared from my problems, had turned to the police, and now I was waiting like some good old-fashioned damsel in distress for rescue.

It was too much. A little after midnight I pulled my boots back on. Leaving a note on the kitchen table for Lotty, I crept out of the apartment, quietly closing the door behind me. I started walking south, keeping to the main streets, hoping to find a cab. My restless energy held my fatigue at bay; when I got to Belmont I stopped looking for taxis and covered the last half mile at a brisk walk.

I'd been imagining the street filled with flashing blue-and-whites and uniformed men racing around. By the time I got home, however, any police activity had disappeared without a trace. I went cautiously into the lobby, crouching a little, hugging the walls out of range of the stairwell.

The upper-landing lights were on again. As I climbed the first half flight, going sideways with my back sliding along the wall, Mr. Contreras's apartment door opened. Peppy bounded out, followed by the old man.

When he saw me tears started streaming down his cheeks. "Oh, doll, thank God you're all right. The cops was here, they wouldn't tell me nothing, wouldn't let me into your place or tell me if they knew where you was. What happened to you? Where you been?"

After a few disjointed minutes we got our stories out. Around ten-thirty someone had called him, telling him I was down in my office and in bad shape. It didn't occur to him to summon help or ask himself who the strange phone caller was. Instead he bundled Peppy up, bullied a passing cab into taking both of them, and hurled himself downtown. He'd never been to my office, so he'd wasted some time finding the place. When he saw that the door was locked and the lights out, he'd been too impatient to find the night watchman: he'd used his trusty pipe wrench to break the lock.

"I'm sorry, doll," he said dolefully. "I'll fix it for you in the morning. If I'd been using my head, I guess I would've known it was someone trying to get me and the dog out of the way."

I nodded abstractedly. Someone was keeping close enough tabs on me to know that my downstairs neighbor would be watching if they set up an ambush. Ron Kappelman. Who else had seen Mr. Contreras at such close quarters?

"Did the police find anyone here?" I asked abruptly.

"They took a couple of guys away in a paddy wagon, but I didn't get any kind of look at them. I couldn't even do that for you. They came gunning for you and they got me out of the way with a cheap trick that wouldn't of fooled a six-year-old. And then me not knowing where'd you'd gone off to or nothing. I knew it couldn't be your aunt, not after what you told me about her and your ma, but I just didn't have any idea where you could be."

It took me awhile to get him calmed down enough that he would let me spend the night alone. After a few more rehearsals of worry and self-reproach, he finally saw me up the stairs to my apartment. Someone had tried breaking into my apartment, but the steel-lined door I'd had installed after my last home invasion had held. They couldn't cut through it, and they hadn't been able to get by my third dead bolt. Even so I made a thorough tour of the premises with Mr. Contreras and the dog. He left her with me, waiting outside until he heard the last bolt slide home before going downstairs to his own bed.

I tried calling Bobby at the Central District, but he'd disappeared—or didn't want to take my call. None of the other officers I knew were in and the ones I didn't know wouldn't tell me anything about the men they'd picked up at my place. I had to give it a rest until morning.

30

FENCE MENDING

I was being buried alive. An executioner wearing a black plastic hood poured dirt on me. "Just tell us the time, girlie," he said. Lotty and Max Loewenthal sat nearby eating asparagus and drinking cognac, ignoring my helpless screams. I woke from the dream sweating and panting, but every time I went back to sleep the nightmare returned.

When I finally got up for good it was late morning. I was stiff and sore, my head filled with the cotton wool an uneasy night always leaves behind. I moved on thick, ungainly legs to the bathroom. With Peppy watching anxiously from the doorway, I soaked in the tub for a long while.

It had to be Kappelman who'd arranged for last night's ambush. He was the only one who knew I was leaving my apartment, the only one who knew the anxious care Mr. Contreras lavished on me. But try as I might, I couldn't think why he'd do it.

It wasn't beyond belief to think he might have murdered Nancy. Love affairs gone awry bring at least one person a day to Twenty-sixth and California. But a crime of passion had nothing to do with me. All my machinations about Humboldt, about why Pankowski and Ferraro had sued the company, about Chigwell didn't seem to connect with Ron Kappelman. Unless he knew something he was desperate to keep hidden about Jurshak's insurance file. But what could his involvement have been with them?

It was easier to think that Art Jurshak had staged last night's aborted attack. After all, he could have drawn the old man off without knowing I wasn't at home, then decided to lie in wait until I got back. My mind churned fruitlessly. The water grew cold, but I didn't stir until the telephone began to ring. It was Bobby, brighter and more alert than I could tolerate in my febrile state.

"Dr. Herschel says you left her in the middle of the night. I thought I told you to stay away from your apartment until we gave you the all-clear."

"I didn't want to wait for the Second Coming of Christ. Who did you find at my place last night?"

"Watch your language around me, young lady," Bobby said automatically —he doesn't think nice girls should talk like hard-boiled dicks. And even though he knows half the reason I do it is to ride him, he can't resist rising to the bait. Before I could put in my two cents about not being a subaltern he could order about—there are baits I also can't resist—he hurried on.

"We picked up two guys hanging around your door. They say they'd just come upstairs for a smoke, but they both had picklocks and guns. The state's attorney got us twenty-four hours with them on concealed and unregistered felony weapons. We want you to come down to a lineup—see if you can identify either of these gents as being involved in Wednesday's attack on you."

"Yeah, I guess," I said unenthusiastically. "They had black slickers on, the kind with hoods that cover a lot of the face. I'm not sure I'd ever recognize them again."

"Great." Bobby ignored my lack of ardor. "I'll have a uniformed man pick you up in half an hour—unless that's too early for you."

"Like Justice, I never sleep," I said politely, and hung up.

Murray phoned next. They'd put the morning edition to bed before word of an arrest outside my place had come in from one of his police snitches. His boss, knowing of our relationship, had woken him with the news. Murray pumped away with tireless energy for several minutes. Finally I cut him off crossly:

"I'm going down to look at a lineup. If either Art Jurshak or Dr. Chigwell's sister is there, I'll give you a call back. Which reminds me—the good doctor has gone off with the kind of guys who like to break into other people's houses."

I hung up on his squawk. The phone rang again as I was stomping into the bedroom to get dressed. I chose to ignore it—let Murray get his news from public radio or something. As I was brushing my hair with surly ill will, Mr. Contreras brought breakfast to the door. My last night's desire for his companionship had worn off. I drank a cup of coffee ungraciously and told him I didn't have time to eat. When he started fussing over me I lost my temper and snapped at him.

A hurt look came into his faded brown eyes. He collected the dog with quiet dignity and left. I immediately felt ashamed of myself and ran after him. He'd already reached the lobby, though, and I didn't have my keys with me. I headed back up the stairs.

While I was gathering my keys and my handbag, sticking the Smith & Wesson into my jeans, the uniformed man arrived to take me down to the lineup. I carefully locked the dead bolt behind me—some days I don't bother with it—and ran down the stairs. Soonest started, soonest ended, or whatever it was Lady Macbeth said.

The uniformed man turned out to be a woman, Patrol Officer Mary Louise Neely. She was quiet and serious, holding herself ramrod straight in her fiercely pressed navy serge, calling me "ma'am" in a way that made me acutely aware of the twelve or more years between us. She opened the door for me with military crispness and ushered me down the walk to the waiting patrol car.

Mr. Contreras was out in front with Peppy. I wanted to make some gesture of reconciliation, but Officer Neely's stern presence robbed me of any words. I held out a hand, but he nodded stiffly to me, calling the dog sharply as she headed down the walk behind me.

I tried asking the patrolwoman insightful questions about her work and whether the Cubs or the Sox could worsen their abysmal performance of last season. She snubbed me completely, though, keeping her stern gaze on malefactors on Lake Shore Drive, murmuring periodically into her lapel transmitter.

We covered the six miles to the Central District at a good clip. She pulled smartly into the police lot about fifteen minutes after leaving my apartment. Okay, it was Saturday, not much traffic, but it was still an impressive performance.

Neely whisked me through the labyrinth of the old building, exchanging unsmiling greetings with fellow officers, and brought me to an observation room. Bobby was there, with Sergeant McGonnigal and Detective Finchley. Neely saluted them so sharply, I thought she might keel over backward.

"Thanks, Officer." Bobby dismissed her genially. "We'll carry on from here."

I found my palms sweating slightly, my heart beating a little faster. I didn't want to see the men who'd bundled me into that blanket on Wednesday. That was why I'd fled my place last night. They had me well and truly spooked. And now I was to perform like an obedient dog under the watchful eyes of the police?

"You got names on the two you picked up?" I asked, keeping my tone cool, trying to shade it with a little arrogance.

"Yeah," Bobby grunted. "Joe Jones and Fred Smith. They're almost as funny to deal with as you are. And yes, we've requested a print check, but these things never happen as fast as you hope they will. We can make a case on the loitering in a private building and carrying concealed unregistered weapons. But you know and I know they'll be on the street Monday unless we can back it up with attempted murder. So you're to tell me if they're your pals who sent you swimming on Wednesday."

He nodded to Finchley, a black plainclothesman I'd known when he started on patrol. The detective went to a door across the room and gave orders to unseen people beyond to start the lineup.

Eyewitness identification is not the great revelation they make of it in courtroom dramas. Under stress the memory plays tricks on you—you're sure you saw a tall black man in blue jeans and it was really a fat white man in a business suit. Stuff like that. Probably a third of my presentations as a public defender had been based on reciting remarkable instances of mistaken identity. On the other hand, stress can burn some indelible memories—a gesture, a birthmark—that come back when you see the person again. It never hurts to try.

Keeping my hands in my pockets so as to hide their tremor, I walked with

Bobby to the one-way observation window. McGonnigal turned out the lights on our side and the little room beyond sprang into relief.

"We've got two sets for you," Bobby murmured in my ear. "You know the routine—take your time, ask for any of them to turn around or whatever."

Six men walked in with self-conscious pugnacity. They all looked alike to me—white, burly, somewhere around forty. I tried to imagine them with black hoods, the executioner of my nightmare this morning.

"Ask them to talk," I said abruptly. "Ask them to say 'Just tell us the time, girlie' and then 'Dump her here, Troy. X marks the spot.' "

Finchley conveyed the request to the unseen officers running the show. One by one the men obediently mumbled their lines. I kept watching the second guy from the left. He had a kind of secretive smile—he knew they'd never make a serious charge stick. His eyes. Could I remember the eyes of the man who'd come up to me at the edge of the lagoon? Cold, flat, calculating his words to find my weaknesses.

But when this man spoke I didn't recognize the voice. It was husky, with the twang of the South Side, not the emotionless tones I remembered.

I shook my head. "I think it's the second guy from the left. But I don't recognize the voice and I can't be absolutely certain."

Bobby nodded fractionally and Finchley gave orders to dismiss the lineup. "Well?" I demanded. "Is he the one?"

The lieutenant smiled reluctantly. "I thought it was a long shot, but he's the guy we picked up outside your front door last night. I don't know if your ID is strong enough for the state's attorney. But maybe we can find out who puts up bond for him."

They brought in the second lineup, a parade of black men. I'd seen only one of my attackers close up. Even though I presumed Troy was one of the men in front of me, I couldn't pick him out, even with a voice check.

Bobby was in high good humor with my ID of the first man. He ran me genially through the paperwork and got Officer Neely to take me home, sending me off with a pat on the arm and a promise of telling me when the first court date would be.

My own mood wasn't nearly as pleasant. When Neely had dropped me at my apartment I went up to change into running shoes. I wasn't up for a run yet, but I needed a long walk to clear my brain before seeing little Caroline this afternoon.

First, though, I had to mend a few fences. Mr. Contreras received me coolly, trying to mask his hurt feelings under a veneer of formality. But subtlety wasn't really part of his makeup. He unbent after a few minutes, told me he would never come up to my apartment again without phoning first, and fried up some eggs and bacon for lunch. I sat talking with him afterward, curbing my impatience at the long flow of irrelevant reminiscence. Anyway, the longer he talked the longer I could put off facing a tougher conversation.

At two, though, I figured I'd avoided Lotty long enough and set off for Sheffield.

Lotty wasn't as easy to kiss and make up with. She was home in between her morning clinic hours and an afternoon concert with Max. We talked in the kitchen while she whipped tiny stitches into the hem of a black skirt. At least she didn't slam the door on me.

"I don't know how many times I have patched you up in the last ten years, Victoria. Many. And almost every time a life-threatening situation. Why do you value yourself so little?"

I stared at the floor. "I don't want anyone solving my problems for me."

"But you came here last night. You involved me in your problems, and then you disappeared without a word. That isn't independence—that is thoughtless cruelty. You must make up your mind about what you want with me. If it is just to be your doctor—the person who patches you up when you've decided to run your head in front of a bullet—fine. We will go to such cold encounters. But if you want to be friends, you cannot behave with such careless disregard for my feelings for you. Can you understand that?"

I rubbed my head tiredly. Finally I looked at her. "Lotty, I'm scared. I've never been this frightened, not since the day my dad told me Gabriella was dying and nothing could be done for her. I knew then that it was a terrible mistake to depend on someone else to solve my problems for me. Now I seem to be too terrorized to solve them for myself and I'm thrashing around. But when I ask for help it just drives me wild. I know it's hard on you. I'm sorry for that. But I can't get enough distance right now to do anything about it."

Lotty finished pulling the thread through her hem and put the skirt down. She gave a wry little smile. "Yes. It is not an easy thing to lose one's mother, is it? Could we make a little compromise, my dear? I won't demand of you responses you can't make. But when you find yourself in this state, will you tell me, so that I am not making myself so angry with you?"

I nodded a few times, my throat too tight for me to speak. She came over to me and held me close to her. "You are the daughter of my heart, Victoria. I know it's not the same as having Gabriella, but the love is there."

I smiled shakily. "In your fierceness you're two of a kind."

After that I told her about the notebooks I'd left behind. She promised to look at them on Sunday, to see if she could make anything of them.

"And now I must dress, my dear. But why not come spend the night here? Maybe we'll both feel a little better."

31
OLD FIREBALL

When I got back to my apartment I stopped to tell Mr. Contreras I was home and let him know Caroline would be arriving soon. My conversation with Lotty had done something to restore my equilibrium. I felt calm enough to abandon my plan for a walk in favor of a little housekeeping.

The partially cooked chicken I'd stashed in the refrigerator Tuesday night had become pretty rank. I carried it down to the garbage can in the alley, scrubbed the refrigerator with soda to deaden the smell, and bundled my newspapers out front for the recycling team to pick up. By the time Caroline arrived a little after four, I'd paid all my December bills and had organized the receipts for my tax returns. I was also feeling all my sore muscles.

Caroline came quietly up the stairs, smiling a little nervously. She followed me into the living room, turning down my offer of refreshments in a soft, breathy voice. I couldn't remember ever seeing her so ill at ease.

"How's Louisa doing?" I asked.

She made a throwaway gesture. "She seems stable right now. But kidney failure leaves you pretty depressed—it seems dialysis only gets a fraction of impurities out of the system, so you're always feeling nightmarish."

"Did you tell her about the call you got—about Joey Pankowski being your father?"

She shook her head. "I haven't told her anything. About your looking for him or—or, well, about anything. I had to let her know Nancy was dead, of course—she would have seen it on TV or heard it from her sister. But she can't take any more upsets like that."

She played nervously with the fringe on one of the sofa cushions, then burst out, "I wish I'd never asked you to find my father for me. I don't know what magic I thought you could work. And I don't know why I thought finding him would alter my life in any way." She gave a harsh little laugh. "What am I saying? Just having you look for him has changed my life."

"Could we talk about that a little?" I asked gently. "Someone called you two weeks ago and told you to chase me away, didn't they? That was when you phoned me with that incredible rigmarole about not wanting me to look for your father."

Her head was bent down so far all I could see was her wild copper curls. I waited patiently. She would not have made the trek up to Lakeview if she hadn't decided to tell me the truth—it was just taking her some time to give her courage the last screw.

"It's the mortgage," she finally whispered to her feet. "We rented for years and years. Then when I started working we could finally save enough to make a down payment. I got a call. A man—I don't know who he was. He said—he said—he'd been looking into our loan. He thought—he told me—they would cancel it if I didn't make you stop looking for my father—stop you from asking all those questions about Ferraro and Pankowski."

At last she looked up at me, her freckles standing out sharply from the pallor of her face. She held out her hands beseechingly and I moved from my chair to put my arms around her. For a few minutes she nestled against me, trembling, as though she were still little Caroline and I was the big kid who could save her from any danger.

"Did you call the bank?" I asked her presently. "See if they knew anything about it?"

"I was afraid if they heard me asking questions, they might do it, you know." Her voice was muffled against my armpit.

"What bank is it?"

She sat up at that and looked at me in alarm. "You're not going to go talk to them about it, Vic! You mustn't!"

"I may know someone who works there, or someone on the board," I said patiently. "If I find I can't ask a few questions very discreetly, I promise not to paw up the dirt. Okay? Anyway, it's a pretty good bet that it's Iron-workers Savings & Loan—that's where everyone in the neighborhood has always gone."

Her big eyes searched my face anxiously. "It is, Vic. But you have to promise, really promise, you won't do anything that will jeopardize our mortgage. It would kill Ma if something like that happened now. You know it would."

I nodded solemnly and gave my word. I didn't think she was exaggerating the effect on Louisa of any kind of major disturbance. As I thought about Caroline's frantic response to the threat on her mother, something else occurred to me.

"When Nancy was murdered you told the police I knew why she'd been killed. Why did you do that? Was it because you really wanted me to keep an eye on you and Louisa?"

She blushed violently. "Yes. But it didn't do me any good." Her voice was barely a squeak.

"You mean they did it? Cut off your mortgage?"

"Worse. They—they somehow figured out—I'd gone to you about her murder. They called me again. At least it was the same man. And said if I didn't want to see Ma's medical benefits cut off, I'd better get you away from South Chicago. So I was really scared then. I tried my best, and when this man called me back I told him—told him I couldn't—couldn't stop you, that you were on your own."

"So they decided to stop me themselves." My throat was dry; my own voice came out harshly.

She looked at me fearfully. "Can you forgive me, Vic? When I saw the news, saw what happened to you, it shattered me. But if I had to do it again, I'd have to do it the same way. I couldn't let them hurt Ma. Not after everything she went through for me. Not with all her suffering now."

I got up and paced angrily to the window. "Didn't it occur to you, if you told me I could do something about it? Protect her and you? Instead of running blind, so that I almost got killed myself?"

"I didn't think you could," she said simply. "When I asked you to find my father I was still imagining you were my big sister, that you could solve all my problems for me. Then I saw you weren't as powerful as I'd imagined you to be. It was just, with Ma so sick and everything, I needed someone so badly to look after me, and I thought maybe you'd still be that person."

Her statement dissipated my anger. I came back to the couch and smiled wryly at her. "I think you've finally grown up, Caroline. That's what it is all right—no big people to clean up all the mess around us. But even if I'm not still the kid who could whip the neighborhood to save your butt, I'm not totally ineffective. I think it's possible to tidy some of the garbage floating around on this one."

She gave a shaky smile. "Okay, Vic. I'll see if I can help you."

I went to the dining room and pulled a bottle of Barolo from the liquor cupboard. Caroline rarely drank, but the heavy wine helped steady her. We talked for a while, not about our current problems, but general things— whether Caroline really wanted a law degree if she didn't have to play catch-up with me. After a glass or two we both felt able to return to the discussion at hand.

I told her about Pankowski and Ferraro and the conflicting reports on their suit against Humboldt Chemical. "I don't know what that has to do with Nancy's death. Or with the attack on me. But it was when I found out about it and started questioning people about them that someone threatened me."

She listened to a detailed report on my encounters with Dr. Chigwell and his sister, but she couldn't shed any light on the blood work he'd kept on Xerxes employees.

"This is the first I ever heard about it. You know the kind of person Ma is —if they sent her in for a medical exam every year, she did it without think-ing about it. A lot of things people told her to do on the job didn't make any sense to her, and this would be one of them. I can't believe it has anything to do with Nancy's death."

"Okay. Let's try another one. Why did Xerxes buy their insurance through Art? Is Jurshak still the fiduciary on their life-health stuff? Why was it important enough to Nancy that she was carrying it around?"

Caroline shrugged. "Art keeps a pretty tight grip on a number of the businesses down there. He might have gotten their insurance in exchange for a tax break or something. Of course when Washington was elected Art didn't have as many favors to hand out, but he still can do a lot for a company if they do something for him."

I pulled Jurshak's report to Mariners Rest from Mozart's *Concert Arias* and handed it to Caroline. She frowned over it for several minutes.

"I don't know anything about insurance," she finally said. "All I can tell you is that Ma's benefits have been first-class. I don't know about any of these other companies."

Her words triggered an elusive memory. Something someone had said to me in the last few weeks about Xerxes and insurance. I frowned, trying to drag it to the surface, but I couldn't get hold of it.

"It meant something to Nancy," I said impatiently. "What? Did she collect data on health and mortality rates for any of these companies? Maybe she had some way of checking the accuracy of this report." Maybe the report didn't mean anything. But then why had Nancy been carrying it around?

"Yes. She did track all these health statistics—she was the director of Health and Environmental Services."

"So let's go down to SCRAP and check her files." I got up and started hunting for my boots.

Caroline shook her head. "Nancy's files are gone. The police impounded what she had in her desk, but someone had cleaned out her health files before the cops got them. We just assumed she'd taken them home with her."

My anger returned in a rush, fueled by disappointment: I was sure we'd reached a break in the case. "Why the hell didn't you tell the police that two weeks ago? Or me! Don't you see, Caroline? Whoever killed her took her papers. We could have been looking exclusively at people involved in these companies, instead of trailing around after vengeful lovers and all that crap!"

She heated up just as fast. "I told you at the time she was killed because of her work! You just were on your usual fucking arrogant head trip and wouldn't pay any attention to me!"

"You said it was because of the recycling plant, which this has nothing to do with. And anyway, why didn't you tell me that her files had disappeared?"

We went at it like a couple of six-year-olds, both venting our fury over the threats and humiliations of the past few weeks. I don't know how we would have extricated ourselves from the escalating insults if we hadn't been interrupted by the buzzer outside my front door. I left Caroline in the living room and stormed to the entrance.

Mr. Contreras was standing there. "I don't mean to be butting in, cookie," he said apologetically, "but this young fella's been ringing the lobby bell for the last couple of minutes and you two was so wrapped up, I thought maybe you couldn't hear him."

Young Art trailed in behind Mr. Contreras. His square, chiseled face was flushed and his auburn hair disheveled. He was biting his lips, clenching and unclenching his hands, in so much turmoil that his usual beauty was obscured. The family resemblance I saw in his distraught face staggered me so much that it muffled my surprise at seeing him.

I finally said weakly, "What are you doing here? Where have you been? Did your mother send you?"

He cleared his throat, trying to speak, but he couldn't seem to get any words out.

Mr. Contreras, his promise not to breathe down my neck still present in his mind, didn't linger to issue his usual unsubtle threats against my male visitors. Or maybe he'd summed up Art and figured he didn't need to worry.

When the old man had left Art finally spoke. "I need to talk to you. It—things are worse than I thought." His voice came out in a squawky little whisper.

Caroline came to the living-room door to see what the uproar was about. I turned to her and said as gently as I could, "This is young Art Jurshak, Caroline. I don't know if you've ever met, but he's the alderman's son. He's got something confidential he needs to tell me. Can you call some of your pals at SCRAP, see if any of them know anything about this report Nancy was carrying around with her?"

I was afraid she was going to argue with me, but my stunned mood got across to her. She asked if I was all right, if it was okay to leave me with young Art. When I reassured her she went back to the living room for her coat.

She stopped briefly at the door on her way out and said in a small voice, "I didn't mean all those things I was saying. I came here to get back on good terms with you, not to shout like that."

I rubbed her shoulders gently. "It's okay, fireball—it goes with the territory. I said some stupid things myself. Let's forget it."

She gave me a quick hug and took off.

32

FLUSHED OUT OF THE POCKET

I took Art into the living room and poured him a glass of the Barolo. He gulped it down. Water would probably have been just as good under the circumstances.

"Where have you been hiding? Do you know every beat cop in Chicago is carrying your description? Or that your mother's going crazy?" They weren't the questions I really wanted to ask, but I couldn't figure out how to frame those.

His lips stretched in a nervous parody of his usual beautiful smile. "I was at Nancy's. I figured no one would look there."

"Hn-unh." I shook my head. "You've been gone since Monday night and I was at Nancy's on Tuesday with Mrs. Cleghorn."

"I spent Monday night in my car. Then I figured no one would be bothering with Nancy's house. I—I could see it had been torn up pretty good. It's been kind of spooky, but I knew I'd be safe there since they'd already searched it."

"Who's 'they'?"

"The people who killed Nancy."

"And who are they?" I felt as though I was interrogating a jug of molasses.

"I don't know," he muttered, looking away.

"But you can guess," I prodded. "Tell me about the insurance your father manages for Xerxes. What was Nancy's interest in it?"

"How did you get those papers?" he whispered. "I called my mother this morning, I knew she'd be worried, and she said you had been by. My—my old man—Big Art had found the card you left and really blown sky high, she said. He was screaming that—that if he got his hands on me, he'd see I remembered never to betray him again. That's why I came here. To see what you know. See if you can help me."

I looked at him sourly. "I've been trying to get you to tell me a few things for the last two weeks and you've been acting as though English was your second language and you weren't too fluent in it."

He scrunched up his face in misery. "I know. But when Nancy died I was so afraid. Afraid my old man had something to do with it."

"Why didn't you run away then? Why wait until I talked to you?"

He flushed an even deeper red. "I thought maybe no one would know—know the connection. But if you saw it, anyone could."

"Like the police, you mean? Or Big Art?" When he didn't answer I said with what patience I could muster, "Okay. Why did you come here today?"

"I called my mother this morning. I knew my old man would be at a meeting, that I could count on him not being home. The slate-makers, you know." He smiled unhappily. "With Washington dead, they were all getting together this morning to plan for the election. Dad—Art—might miss a Council meeting, but he wouldn't stay away from that.

"Anyway, Mother told me about you. About how you'd been around but then you'd almost ended up the same—the same way as Nancy. I couldn't stay in her place forever, there was hardly any food anyway and I was scared to turn on the lights at night in case someone saw and came in to inspect. And if they were going to go after anyone who knew about Nancy and the insurance, I figured I'd better get help or I'd be dead."

I curbed my impatience as best I could. It was going to be a long afternoon, getting information from him. The questions that were really burning my tongue—about his family—would have to wait until I could pry his story from him.

The first thing I wanted to clear up was his relationship with Nancy. Since he had let himself into her house he couldn't very well keep denying they'd been lovers. And the story came out, sweet, sad, and stupid.

He and Nancy had met a year before on a community project. She was representing SCRAP, he the alderman's office. She'd attracted him immediately—he'd always liked older women who had her kind of looks and warmth and he'd wanted to go out with her right away. But she'd put him off with one excuse or another until a few months ago. Then they'd started dating and had rapidly moved to a full-blown affair. He'd been deliriously happy. She was warm, loving—on and on.

"So why didn't anyone know about it if you were both so happy?" I asked. I could just see it, barely. When he wasn't shredding himself with misery his incredible beauty made you want to touch him. Maybe it was enough for Nancy, maybe she thought the aesthetics of it compensated for his immaturity. She might have been cold-blooded enough to want him as a conduit to the alderman's office, but I didn't think so.

He shifted uncomfortably. "My dad always raved on so much against SCRAP, I knew he'd hate it if I was dating someone who worked there. He felt they were trying to take over the ward from him, you know, always criticizing things like the broken sidewalks in South Chicago and the unemployment and stuff. It's not his fault, you know, but when Washington got in charge, you didn't see a penny going to the white ethnic neighborhoods."

I opened my mouth to argue the point, then shut it again. South Chicago had begun its demise under the late great Mayor Daley and had been assiduously ignored by Bilandic and Byrne alike. And Art, Sr., had been alderman all that time. But fighting such a war wasn't going to do me any good this afternoon.

"So you didn't want him to know. And Nancy didn't want her friends to know about you, either. Same reason?"

He squirmed again. "I don't think so. I think—she was a little bit older than me, you know. Only ten years. Well, almost eleven. But I think she was afraid people would laugh at her if they knew she was seeing someone so young."

"Okay. So it was a big secret. Then she came to you three weeks ago to see if Art was opposed to the recycling plant. What happened then?"

He reached nervously for the wine bottle and poured the last of the Barolo into his glass. When he'd gulped most of it down he started spitting out the story, a bit at a time. He knew Art was against the recycling plant. His dad was working hard to bring new industry to South Chicago, and he was afraid a recycling plant would put some companies off—that they wouldn't want to operate in a community where they had to go to the extra trouble of putting their wastes in drums for recycling instead of just dumping them into lagoons.

He'd told Nancy that and she had insisted on seeing any files about the project. Apparently, like me, she'd figured it wasn't worth arguing whether Art, Sr.'s, professed reasons were the real ones.

Young Art hadn't wanted to do it, but she'd pushed hard. They went back to the insurance office late one night and she went through Art's desk. It was horrible, the most horrible night he'd ever spent, worrying about his father or his father's secretary coming in on them, or one of the beat cops seeing a light and surprising them.

"I understand. The first time you break and enter is always the hardest. But why did Nancy choose this insurance file over something about recycling?"

He shook his head. "I don't know. She was looking for anything with the names of any of the companies involved in the recycling plant on it. And then she saw these papers and said she didn't know we—my dad's agency—handled Xerxes's insurance, and then she read through them and said this was hot stuff, she'd better copy it and take it along. So she went down the hall to use the machine. And Big Art came in."

"Your father saw her?" I gasped.

He nodded miserably. "He had Steve Dresberg with him. Nancy ran, but she scattered the originals all over the floor. So they knew she was copying them."

"And what did you do?"

His face disappeared into a little ball of such abject shame that I felt almost sorry for him. "They never knew I was there. I hid in my own office with the lights off."

I didn't know what to say. That he could have abandoned Nancy to her fate. That he knew Dresberg had been there with his old man. And at the same time the logical part of my mind began worrying about the problem: Was it the insurance papers or was it the fact that Nancy had seen Art with Dresberg? It wasn't surprising that the alderman had ties to the Garbage King. But it was understandable that he kept them quiet.

"Don't you understand?" I finally cried out, my voice close to a howl. "If you'd said something about your father and Dresberg last week, we might have gotten somewhere in investigating Nancy's death. Don't you care anything about finding her killers?"

He stared at me through tragic blue eyes. "If it was your father, would you want to know—really know—he was doing that kind of thing? Anyway, he already thinks I'm such a failure. What would he think if I turned him in to the cops? He'd say I was siding with SCRAP and the Washington faction against him."

I shook my head to see if that would clear my brain, but it didn't seem to help any. I tried speaking, but every sentence I started ended in a few sputtered words. Finally I asked weakly what he wanted me to do.

"I need help," he muttered.

"You ain't kidding, boy. But I don't know if even a Michigan Avenue analyst could do anything for you, and I'm damned sure I can't."

"I know I'm not very tough. Not like you or—or Nancy. But I'm not an imbecile, either. I don't need you making fun of me. I can't fix this myself. I need help and I thought since you'd been a friend of hers you might . . ." His voice trailed off.

"Rescue you?" I finished sardonically. "Okay. I'll help you. In exchange for which I want some information about your family."

He looked wildly at me. "My family? What's that got to do with anything?"

"Just tell me. It's got nothing to do with you. What was your mother's maiden name?"

"My mother's maiden name?" he repeated stupidly. "Kludka. Why do you want to know?"

"It wasn't Djiak? You never heard of that?"

"Djiak? Of course I know the name. My father's sister married some guy named Ed Djiak. But they moved to Canada before I was born. I've never met them—I wouldn't even have heard of Dad's sister if I hadn't seen the name on a letter when I joined the agency—when I asked my father he told me about it—said they'd never gotten along and she'd cut the connection. Why do you want to know about them?"

I didn't answer him. I felt so nauseated that I leaned my head over onto my knees. When Art had come in with his face all flushed, his auburn hair wildly standing around his head, his resemblance to Caroline had been so strong that they might have been twins. He'd gotten his red hair from his father. Caroline took after Louisa. Of course. How simple. How simple and how horrifying. All the same genes. All in the same family. I just hadn't wanted to begin thinking such a thing when I saw them side by side. Instead

I'd been trying to work out some way Art's wife could be related to Caroline.

My conversation with Ed and Martha Djiak three weeks earlier came back to me in full force. And with Connie. How her uncle liked to come around and have Louisa dance for him. Mrs. Djiak knew. What had she said? "Men have difficulty controlling themselves." But that it was Louisa's fault—that she'd led him on.

My gorge rose so violently, I thought I would choke. Blame her. Blame their fifteen-year-old daughter when it was her own brother who got her pregnant? My one thought was to get out of here, to get down to East Side with my gun and beat the Djiaks until they admitted the truth.

I got up, but the room swam darkly in front of me. I sat back down again, steadying myself, becoming aware of young Art talking frightenedly in the chair across from me.

"I told you what you asked. Now you've got to help me."

"Yeah, right. I'll help you. Come along with me."

He started to protest, to demand to know what I was going to do, but I cut him off sharply. "Just come with me. I don't have any more time right now."

My tone more than my words stopped him. He watched silently while I got my coat. I tucked my driver's license and money into my jeans pocket so I wouldn't be hampered by a purse. He started to stammer some more questions—was I going to shoot his old man?—when he saw me take out the Smith & Wesson and check the clip.

"Shoe's on the other foot," I said curtly. "Your father's buddies have been gunning for me all week."

He blushed again with shame and lapsed back into silence.

I took him down to Mr. Contreras. "This is Art Jurshak. His papa may have had something to do with Nancy's death and he isn't feeling too kindly toward his kid right now. Can you keep him here until I can make some other arrangement for him? Maybe Murray will want to take him."

The old man preened himself importantly. "Sure thing, doll. I won't say a word to anybody, and you can count on her highness here to do the same. No need to go asking that Ryerson guy to do anything—I'm perfectly happy to keep him as long as you want."

I smiled faintly. "After a couple of hours with him you may change your mind—he's not a lot of fun. Just don't tell anyone about him. That lawyer—Ron Kappelman—may come around. Say you don't know where I've gone or when I'll be back. And not a word about your guest."

"Where are you going, doll?"

I pressed my lips together in a reflex of annoyance, then remembered our truce. I beckoned him into the hall so I could tell him without Art's hearing. Mr. Contreras came quickly, the dog at his ankles, and nodded gravely to show he remembered both name and address.

"I'll be here when you come back. I won't let anyone lure me away tonight. But if you're not back by midnight, I'm calling Lieutenant Mallory, doll."

The dog padded after me to the door, but gave a little sigh of resignation when Mr. Contreras called her back. She knew I had my boots on, not my running shoes—she'd just been hoping.

33

A FAMILY AFFAIR

I could hear Mrs. Djiak's hurried footsteps after I rang the bell. She opened the door, drying her hands on her apron.

"Victoria!" She was horrified. "What are you doing here this late at night? I begged you not to come back again. Mr. Djiak will be furious if he knows you're here."

Ed Djiak's nasal baritone wafted down the hallway, demanding of his wife who was at the door.

"Just—just one of the neighbor children, Ed," she called back breathlessly. To me she said in a hurried undervoice, "Now go quickly, before he sees you."

I shook my head. "I'm coming in, Mrs. Djiak. We're going to talk, all three of us, about the man who got Louisa pregnant."

Her eyes dilated in her strained face. She grabbed beseechingly at my arm, but I was too angry to feel any compassion for her. I shook her hand from me. Ignoring her piteous cries, I brushed past her into the house and down the hall. I didn't take my boots off—not to add a deliberate insult to her distress, but because I wanted to be able to leave quickly if I had to.

Ed Djiak was sitting at the table in the immaculate kitchen, a little black-and-white TV in front of him, a beer mug in his hand. He didn't look up immediately, assuming it was just his wife, but when he saw me his long dark face turned a deep umber.

"You have no business in this house, young woman."

"I wish I could agree with you," I said, pulling a chair back from the table to face him. "It nauseates me to be here and I won't prolong the visit. I just want to talk about Mrs. Djiak's brother."

"She doesn't have a brother," he said harshly.

"Don't pretend Art Jurshak isn't her brother. I don't think we'd have too much trouble finding Mrs. Djiak's maiden name—I'd have to wait until Monday, when I could go down to City Hall and check your marriage license, but I expect it'll say Martha Jurshak. Then I could get copies of Art's and her birth certificates and that'd probably clinch the matter."

The umber in his face deepened to mahogany. He turned to his wife. "You damned talkative bitch! Who have you been telling our private affairs to?"

"No one, Ed. Really. I haven't said a word to anyone. Not once in all these years. Not even to Father Stepanek, when I begged you—"

He cut her off with a slice of his hand. "Who's been talking to you, Victoria? Who's been spreading slander about my family?"

"Slander implies false report," I responded insolently. "Everything you've said since I came into this house confirms that it's true."

"That what's true?" he demanded, recovering himself with a strong effort. "That my wife's maiden name was Jurshak? What if it was?"

"Just this. That her brother Art got your daughter Louisa pregnant. You told me he wasn't very strong, Martha. Did he have a history of liking little girls?"

She was wiping her hands over and over in her apron. "He—he promised he would never do it again."

"Damn you, don't say anything to her," Djiak roared, springing from his chair. He shoved past me roughly to where Mrs. Djiak stood and slapped her.

I was on my feet smashing my fist into his face before I realized what I was doing. He was thirty years older than me, but still very strong. It was only because I took him completely by surprise that I managed to hit him full force. He recoiled against the refrigerator and stood for a moment, shaking his head to recover from the blow. Then the ugly anger returned and he came for me.

I was ready. As he charged I slid a chair in his path. He crashed against it, his momentum forcing him and the chair into the table. His fall brought down the TV set and the beer in a jumbled mess of glass and fluid. He lay sprawled under the table, the chair on top of him.

Martha Djiak gave a little moan of horror, whether over the sight of her husband or the mess on the floor I couldn't know. I stood over him, panting from fury, my gun in my hand barrel-first, ready to smash it into him if he started to get up. His face was glazed—none of his womenfolk had ever fought back against him.

Mrs. Djiak screamed suddenly. I turned to look at her. She couldn't speak, only point, but I saw a little fire sparkling along the back of the television where something had mixed with the exposed wires. Maybe a jar of solvent that was kept at the ready for oil stains menacing the kitchen. I stuffed the gun back into my jeans waistband and snatched the dish towel from her apron pocket. Carefully skirting the pool of beer, I crawled under the table and unplugged the set.

"Baking soda," I called sharply to Mrs. Djiak.

The demand for a commonplace household item helped her regain some balance. I watched her feet move to a cupboard. She crouched down and handed me the box across her husband's body. I dumped the contents on the blue flames flickering around the set and watched the fire go out.

Mr. Djiak slowly untangled himself from the mess of chair and broken glass. He stood for a moment looking at the wreck on the floor, at the wet stains on his pants. Then, without saying anything, he left the room. I could hear his heavy footsteps pass down the hall. Martha Djiak and I listened to the front door slam.

She was shaking. I seated her in one of the plastic-covered chairs and heated water in the teakettle. She watched me dumbly while I rummaged through her cupboards looking for tea. When I found the Lipton bags tucked neatly into a canister, I made her a cup, mixing it well with sugar and milk. She drank it obediently in scalding gulps.

"Do you think you can tell me about Louisa now?" I asked when she'd turned down a second cup.

"How did you find out?" Her eyes were lifeless, her voice little more than a tired thread.

"Your brother's son came to visit me this afternoon. Each time I've seen him I thought he looked familiar, but I put it down to years of looking at Art on posters or TV. But today Caroline was with me. She and I were in the middle of an argument. Young Art walked in with his face flushed, all agitated, and suddenly I realized how much he resembled Caroline. They might almost be twins, you know—I just hadn't connected them before because I wasn't expecting it. Of course he's got that unearthly beauty and she's always so disheveled, it wasn't until they were both upset at the same time that you could really see it."

She listened to my explanation with her face screwed up painfully, as if I were lecturing in Latin and she was trying to make me think she could follow me. When she didn't say anything I prodded her a little.

"Why did you throw Louisa out of the house when she got pregnant?"

She looked at me directly then, some mix of fear and disgust on her face. "Keep her in the house? With that shame for all the world to know about?"

"It wasn't her shame. It was Art's, your brother's. How can you even compare the two?"

"She wouldn't have gotten—gotten in trouble if she hadn't led him on. She saw how much he liked her to dance for him and kiss him. He—he had a weakness. She should have kept away from him."

My nausea was so acute, it took all my will not to jump on her physically, to slam her body into the debris under the table. "If you knew he had a weakness for little girls, why the *hell* did you let him near your daughters?"

"He—he said he wouldn't do it again. After I saw him—playing with—with Connie when she was five, I told him I would tell Ed about it if he ever did it again. He promised. He was afraid of Ed. But Louisa was too much for him, she was too evil-minded, she led him on against his own strength. When we saw she was going to have a baby, she told us how it happened and Art explained it to us, how she led him on against his own strength."

"So you threw her out into the world. If it hadn't been for Gabriella, who knows what would have happened to her? The two of you—what a couple of sanctimonious righteous bastards you are."

She took my insults unflinchingly. She couldn't understand why I would be angry over such logical parental behavior, but she'd seen me beat up her husband. She wasn't going to risk exciting me.

"Was Art already married then?" I asked abruptly.

"No. We told him he was going to have to find a wife, start a family, or we'd have to tell Father Stepanek, tell the priest, about Louisa. We promised we wouldn't say anything if she moved away and he started a family."

I didn't know what to say. All I could think of was Louisa at sixteen, pregnant, out on her own, the holy ladies of St. Wenceslaus parading in front of her door. And Gabriella riding in on her white horse to the rescue. All the old insults from the Djiaks about Gabriella's being a Jew came back to me.

"How can you pretend to call yourselves Christians? My mother was a thousand times the Christian you ever were. She didn't go around blathering a lot of sanctimonious bullshit; she lived charity. But you and Ed, you let your brother seduce your child and you call her wicked. If there really was a god he would annihilate you for daring to come to his altar, babbling about your righteousness. If there is a god, my only prayer is that I never have to be within a mile of you again."

I lurched to my feet, my eyes hot with furious tears. She shrank back in her chair.

"I won't hit you," I said. "What good would it do either of us?"

Before I'd reached the hall she was already on her hands and knees cleaning up the broken glass.

34
BANK SHOT

I staggered from the house to the car, my stomach heaving, my throat tight and tainted with bile. All I could think of was to get to Lotty, not to stop for anything, for a toothbrush or a change of underwear. Just go straight to sanity.

I made it there on luck. A blaring horn at Seventy-first Street brought me briefly to myself. I skirted my way carefully through Jackson Park, but I almost hit a bicyclist darting across the Drive at Fifty-ninth. Even after that I kept finding the speedometer needle around seventy.

Max was drinking cognac in Lotty's sitting room when I got there. I smiled jerkily at him. With a great effort, I remembered the two had gone to a recital together and asked how they'd enjoyed the music.

"Superb. The Cellini Quintet. We knew them in London when they were just getting started after the war." He reminded Lotty of an evening in Wigmore Hall when the power had gone off, and how the two of them had stood holding flashlights over the music so their friends could continue the concert.

Lotty laughed and was adding a memoir of her own when she broke off. "Vic! I hadn't seen your face in the light when you came up. What is the matter?"

I forced my lips to the form of a smile. "Nothing life-threatening. Just a strange conversation that I'll tell you about sometime."

"I must be off anyway, my dear," Max said, rising. "I've stayed far too long drinking your excellent cognac."

Lotty saw him to the door, then hurried back to me. "What is it, *Liebchen?* You look like death."

I tried smiling again. To my dismay, I found myself sobbing instead. "Lotty, I thought I'd seen every horrible thing people could do to each other in this town. Men killing each other for a bottle of wine. Women pouring lye on their lovers. Why this should upset me so much I don't know."

"Here." Lotty put some brandy to my mouth. "Drink this and settle yourself a bit. Try to tell me what happened."

I swallowed some of the cognac. It washed the taste of bile from my throat. With Lotty holding my hand, I blurted out the story. How I'd seen the resemblance between young Art and Caroline, and thought his mother must have been related to Caroline's father. Only to learn that it was his father who was related to Caroline's grandmother.

"That part wasn't so awful," I gulped. "I mean, of course it's awful. But what made me so sick is their horrible scrubbed piety and the way they insist Louisa was to blame. Do you know how they raised her? How strictly those two sisters were watched? No dates, no boys, no talk about sex. And then her mother's brother. He molested the one girl and they let him stay around to molest the other. And then they punish her."

My voice was rising; I couldn't seem to control it. "It can't be, Lotty. It shouldn't be. I should be able to stop something that vile from going on, but I don't have any power."

Lotty took me in her arms and held me without speaking. After a time my sobbing dried up, but I continued to lie against her shoulder.

"You can't heal the world, *Liebchen.* I know you know that. You can only work with one person at a time, in a very small way. And over the individuals you help you have much effect. It's only the megalomaniacs, the Hitlers and their ilk, who think they have the answer for everyone's life. You are in the world of the sane, Victoria, the world of the limited."

She took me into the kitchen and fed me the remains of the chicken she'd cooked for Max. She continued to pour brandy into me until I was ready for sleep. After that she took me to her spare room and undressed me.

"Mr. Contreras," I said thickly. "I forgot to tell him I was spending the night here. Can you call him for me? Otherwise he'll have Bobby Mallory dragging the lake for me."

"Certainly, my dear. I'll do it as soon as I see you're sleeping. Just rest and don't worry."

When I woke Sunday morning I felt light-headed, the result of too much brandy and tears. But I'd had my first thorough sleep since my attack; the soreness in my shoulders had diminished to the point where I no longer noticed it every time I moved.

Lotty brought in *The New York Times* with a plate of crisp rolls and jam. We spent a leisurely morning over papers and coffee. At noon, when I wanted to start talking about Art Jurshak—about some way to get past his ubiquitous bodyguards to speak to him—Lotty silenced me.

"This will be a day of rest for you, Victoria. We're going to the country, get fresh air, turn the mind off completely from all worries. It will make everything seem more possible tomorrow."

I gave in with as good grace as I could muster, but she was right. We drove into Michigan, spent the day walking at the sand dunes, letting the cold lake air whip our hair. We dawdled around in the little wineries, buying a bottle of cherry-cranberry wine as a souvenir for Max, who prided himself on his palate. When we finally returned home around ten that night, I felt clean throughout.

It was a good thing I'd had that day of rest. Monday turned into a long, frustrating day. Lotty was gone when I woke up—she makes rounds at Beth Israel before opening her clinic at eight-thirty. She left me a note saying she'd looked at Dr. Chigwell's notebooks after I went to bed, but didn't feel confident in interpreting the blood values he'd been recording. She was taking them to a friend who specialized in nephrology for a reading.

I called Mr. Contreras. He reported a quiet night, but said that young Art was getting restless. He'd loaned him a razor and a change of underwear, but he wasn't sure how long he could keep the boy at the apartment.

"If he wants to leave, let him," I said. "He's the one who wanted protection. I don't really care too much if he doesn't want to accept it."

I told him I'd be by to pack a small suitcase, but that I was going to stay with Lotty until I felt more secure against midnight marauders. He agreed, wistfully—he'd much rather I sent young Art to Lotty and stayed with him and Peppy.

After stopping at my place for a shower and a change of clothes, I went downstairs to spend a few minutes with Peppy and Mr. Contreras. The strain of the last few weeks was starting to etch hollow lines in young Art's face. Or maybe it was just thirty-six hours spent with Mr. Contreras.

"Do you—have you done anything?" His uncertain voice had faded to a pathetic whisper.

"I can't do anything until I've talked to your old man. You can help make that happen. I don't see how I can get past his security guards to see him alone."

That alarmed him—he didn't want Art, Sr., to know he'd come to me; that would really get him in hot water. I reasoned and cajoled to no avail. Finally, getting a little testy, I headed for the door.

"I'll just have to call your mother and tell her I know where you are. I'm sure she'd be glad to set up a meeting between me and your old man in exchange for knowing her precious baby was safe and sound."

"Goddamn you, Warshawski," he squeaked. "You know I don't want you talking to her."

Mr. Contreras took umbrage at the young man's swearing at me and started to interrupt. I held up a hand, which mercifully stopped him.

"Then help me get in touch with your dad."

At last, fulminating, he agreed to call his father, to say he needed to talk to him alone and to set up a meeting in front of Buckingham Fountain.

I told Art to try to set the appointment for two today—that I'd call back at eleven to check on the time. As I left I could hear Mr. Contreras upbraiding him for talking so rudely to me. It sent me southward with my only laugh of the day.

My parents had banked at Ironworkers Savings & Loan. My mother had opened my first savings account for me there when I was ten so I could stash stray quarters and baby-sitting earnings against the college education she long had promised me. In my memory it remained an imposing, gilt-covered palace.

When I walked up to the grimy stone building at Ninety-third and Commercial, it seemed to have shrunk so with the years that I checked the name over the entrance to make sure I was at the right place. The vaulted ceiling, which had awed me as a child, now seemed merely grubby. Instead of having to stand on tiptoe to peer into the teller's cage, I towered over the acned young woman behind the counter.

She didn't know anything about the bank's annual report, but she directed me indifferently to an officer in the back. The glib story I'd prepared to explain why I wanted it proved unnecessary. The middle-aged man who spoke to me was only too glad to find someone interested in a decaying savings and loan. He talked to me at length about the strong ethical values of the community, where people did everything to keep their little homes in order, and how the bank itself renegotiated loans for its longtime customers when hard times hit them.

"We don't have an annual report of the kind you're used to examining, since we're privately owned," he concluded. "But you can look at our year-end statements if you want."

"It's really the names of your board I'd like to see," I told him.

"Of course." He rummaged in a drawer and pulled out a stack of papers. "You're sure you don't want to inspect the statements? If you were thinking of investing, I can assure you we are in extremely sound condition despite the death of the mills down here."

If I'd had a few thousand to spare, I would have felt obligated to give it to the bank to cover my embarrassment. As it was I muttered something non-committal and took the directors list from him. It held thirteen names, but I knew only one of them: Gustav Humboldt.

Oh, yes, my informant told me proudly, Mr. Humboldt had agreed to become a director back in the forties when he first started doing business down here. Even now that his company had become one of the largest in the world and he was a director of a dozen Fortune 500 companies, he still stayed on the Ironworkers board.

"Mr. Humboldt has missed only eight meetings in the last fifteen years," he finished.

I murmured something that could be taken for extravagant awe at the great man's dedication. The picture was becoming tolerably clear to me. There was some problem with the insurance on the work force at the Xerxes plant that Humboldt was determined not come to light. I couldn't see what that had to do with the lawsuit or the deaths of Ferraro and Pankowski. But maybe Chigwell knew what the actuarial data I'd found meant—perhaps that was what his medical notebooks would reveal. That part didn't bother me too much. It was Humboldt's personal role that both scared and angered me. I was tired of being jerked around by him. It was time to beard him directly. I extricated myself from the Ironworkers' hopeful officer and headed for the Loop.

I wasn't in the mood to waste time hunting out cheap parking. I pulled into the lot next to the Humboldt Building on Madison. Stopping just long enough to comb my hair in the rearview mirror, I headed into the shark's cove.

The Humboldt Building housed the company's corporate offices. Like most manufacturing conglomerates, the real business went on in the plants spread across the globe, so I wasn't surprised that their headquarters could be squeezed into twenty-five stories. It was a strictly functional building, with no trees or sculptures in the lobby. The floor was covered with the utilitarian tile you used to see in all skyscrapers before Helmut Jahn and his pals started filling them with marble-lined atria.

The old-fashioned black notice board in the hallway didn't list Gustav Humboldt, but it told me the corporate offices were on twenty-two. I summoned one of the bronze-doored elevators and made my slow way up.

The hall that I entered from the elevator was austere, but the tone had changed subtly. The lower half of the walls was paneled in a dark wood that also showed on either side of the pale green carpet. Framed prints of medieval alchemists with retorts, toads, and bats hung above the paneling.

I headed down the green pile to an open door on my right. The green carpeting continued past the door, where it spread into a large pool. The dark wood was picked up in a polished desk. Behind it sat a woman with a phone bank and a word processor. She was impeccably polished herself, her dark hair pulled back in a smooth chignon to show the large pearls in her shell-shaped ears. She turned from the word processor to greet me with practiced courtesy.

"I'm here to see Gustav Humboldt," I said, trying to sound authoritative.

"I see. May I have your name please?"

I handed her a card and she turned with it to the phones. When she'd finished she smiled apologetically.

"You don't seem to be in the appointment calendar, Ms. Warshawski. Is Mr. Humboldt expecting you?"

"Yes. He's been leaving messages for me all over town. This is just my first opportunity to get back to him."

She returned to the phones. This time when she finished she asked me to take a seat. I lowered myself into an overstuffed armchair and flipped through a copy of the annual report thoughtfully placed next to it. Humboldt's Brazil operations had shown a staggering growth last year, accounting for sixty percent of overseas profits. Their capital investment of $500 million in the Amazon River Project was now paying handsome dividends. I couldn't help wondering how much capital development it would take before the Amazon looked like the Calumet.

I was studying the breakdown of profits by product line, feeling a proprietary pleasure in the good performance of Xerxine, when the polished receptionist summoned me—Mr. Redwick would see me. I followed her to the third in a series of doors in a little hallway behind her desk. She knocked and opened the door, then returned to her station.

Mr. Redwick got up from his desk to hold out a hand to me. He was a tall, well-groomed man about my own age, with remote gray eyes. He studied me unsmilingly while we shook hands and uttered conventional greetings, then gestured me to a small sofa set against one wall.

"I understand you think Mr. Humboldt wishes to see you."

"I *know* Mr. Humboldt wishes to see me," I corrected him. "You wouldn't be talking to me if that weren't the case."

"What is it you think he wants to see you about?" He pressed his fingertips together.

"He's left a couple of messages for me. One at the insurance offices of Art Jurshak, the other at the Ironworkers bank in South Chicago. Both messages were most urgent. That's why I came here in person."

"Why don't you tell me what he said, and then I can evaluate whether he needs to talk to you himself or whether I can handle the matter."

I smiled. "Either you are totally in Mr. Humboldt's confidence, in which case you know what he said, or you're not—in which case he would much prefer that you not find it out."

The remote eyes grew colder. "You can safely assume that I'm in Mr. Humboldt's confidence—I'm his executive assistant."

I yawned and got up to study a print on the wall across from the sofa. It was a Nast cartoon of the Oil Trust, and as nearly as my inexpert eye could tell, it seemed to be an original.

"If you aren't willing to talk to me, you're going to have to leave," Redwick said sharply.

I didn't turn around. "Why don't you just check with the big guy—let him know I'm here and getting restless."

"He knows you're here and he asked me to meet with you."

"How hard it is when strong-willed people disagree so vehemently," I said mournfully, and left the room.

I walked fast, trying each of the doors I came to, surprising a succession of hardworking assistants. The door on the end opened to the great man's cove. A secretary, presumably Ms. Hollingsworth, looked up in surprise at my entrance. Before she could utter a protest, I'd gone into the inner chamber. Redwick was on my heels, grabbing at my arms.

Behind the mahogany door, in the midst of a collection of antique office furnishings, sat Gustav Humboldt, a document unopened on his knees. He looked beyond me to his executive assistant.

"Redwick. I thought I made it clear this woman was not to disturb me. Have you come to think that my decisions no longer carry authority?"

With a considerable diminution in his cool poise, Redwick tried explaining what had happened.

"He really did do his best," I chimed in helpfully. "But I knew that deep down you would be sorry forever if you didn't talk to me. You see, I just came from the Ironworkers Savings and Loan, so I know you're the person who pressured Caroline Djiak into firing me. And then there's the matter of the life and health insurance that Art Jurshak's been handling for you. Not my idea of a proper fiduciary, a man who pals around with guys like Steve Dresberg, and the state insurance commissioner would probably agree with me."

I was on thin ice there, since I wasn't sure what the report meant. Obviously it had rung a thousand bells with Nancy, but I could only guess at why. I danced my way through possibilities, throwing in references to Joey Pankowski and Steve Ferraro, but Humboldt refused to rise to the bait. He strode to his desk and picked up the phone.

"Why did you lie to me about that lawsuit?" I continued conversationally when he had hung up. "I know a big ego is a sine qua non for success on the scale you've achieved, but you must really be myopic if you thought I'd take your unsupported word on that suit. Too many things had been happening in South Chicago for me not to be suspicious of a high-powered CEO who—"

I was interrupted by some new arrivals—three security guards. I couldn't help being flattered that Humboldt thought it would take so many men to get me out of his building—one of that size and apparent conditioning would have done the trick given the shape I was in. I didn't feel up to a bravado display but went along without a fuss.

As they ushered me from the room—with more force than was really necessary—I called over my shoulder, "You gotta get better help, Gustav. The guys who dumped me in Dead Stick Pond are in custody and it's only a matter of time before they cop a plea by telling the police who hired them."

He didn't answer me. As Redwick shut the door behind us, though, I heard Humboldt say, "Someone has got to shut that meddlesome bitch up for me."

Alas, this seemed to put paid to the idea of my ever drinking his remarkable brandy again.

35
CHANGING WORDS AT BUCKINGHAM FOUNTAIN

It was a little after eleven when the great apes finished escorting me from the zoo, time for me to check in with young Art. I was within walking distance of my office, but I wanted to get clean away from the Humboldt Building. I paid my eight dollars for the privilege of parking next to it for an hour and moved the car to the underground garage.

I'd forgotten Mr. Contreras's forcible entry to my office Friday night. He'd done a thorough job on the door. First he'd smashed in the glass in the hopes of being able to reach in and turn the lock. When he'd found it was a key-operated dead bolt, he'd methodically broken all the wood around it and pulled it from the frame. I ground my teeth at the sight, but didn't see any point in mentioning it when I called the old man. It would be easier to arrange for someone else to repair it than to go through his long string of remorse—and far easier to get outside help than to go through the agony of watching Mr. Contreras fix it.

Art came uneasily to the phone. He had spoken with his dad, but he wanted me to know that I really owed him. It had been pure hell having to negotiate with Big Art. Oh, yes, he'd gotten the old man to agree to come to the fountain, although he said he couldn't make it before two-thirty. It had taken a lot of cajoling; his father had pressured him unbelievably to be told where he was staying. If I had any idea how hard it was to stand up to Big Art, I might treat him with a little more respect.

"And can't you think of some place better for me than here? This old man can't leave me alone. He treats me like I'm some kind of child."

I replied more soothingly than I felt, "And if you really want to go someplace else, I don't have any objection. I'll see if I can arrange something with Murray Ryerson at the *Herald-Star* when I talk to him this afternoon. Of course he'll want some kind of story in exchange."

I hung up on his shrieking that I had to promise not to go to the papers about him, but I did forbear to mention his name to Murray when I called.

"You know, Warshawski, you're a fucking pain in the ass," he greeted me. "Don't you ever check in with your answering service? I left about ten messages for you over the weekend. What did you do to the Chigwell woman? Hypnotize her? She won't talk to the press—she says you can handle any queries we have about her brother."

"It's a course I took by mail," I said, surprised and pleased. "You send in all these matchbooks and they ship you a set of lessons on how to make yourself invisible, how to enter the thoughts of another person—all that kind of stuff. I just never had a chance to try it before."

"Right, wise-ass," he said resignedly. "Are you now prepared to reveal all to the people of Chicago?"

"You told me you didn't need me—that you were getting all your info direct from the people at Xerxes. I want to talk to you about something much more exciting—my life. Or its possible termination."

"That's old news. We already covered it last week. You'll have to go all the way this time for us to get excited about it."

"Well, stay tuned—you may get your wish. I've got some heavy guys gunning for me." I watched a handful of pigeons vying for space on the windowsill. Tough dirty urban birds—better decor for my office than original prints by Nast or Daumier.

"Why are you telling me this now?" he demanded suspiciously.

A train rattled by on the Wabash el tracks. The pigeons fluttered momentarily as the vibrations shook the window, then settled back on the sill.

"In case I don't live through the night I want someone who'll follow my trail to know where it's been taking me. I'd like that person to be you, since you're better able to think ill of the gods than the cops are, but the hitch is, I need to talk to you before one-thirty."

"What happens at one-thirty?"

"I strap on my six-guns and walk alone down Main Street."

After some more poking, to see if matters were as urgent as I claimed, Murray agreed to meet me near the newspaper for a sandwich at noon. Before leaving the Pulteney I sorted my mail, tossed everything but a check from one of the clients I'd done a financial search for, then called a friend to replace my office door. He said he'd get to it by Wednesday afternoon.

Since it was close to twelve already, I headed north to the river. The air had thickened to a light drizzle. Despite Lotty's dire words, my shoulders felt pretty good. Another couple of days—If I stayed a jump ahead of Gustav Humboldt—and I could start running again.

The *Herald-Star* faces the *Sun-Times* from the south side of the Chicago River. A lot of that area is getting trendy, with racquet courts and chichi little restaurants springing up, but Carl's still serves a no-nonsense sandwich to the newspaper people. Its scarred booths and deal tables are packed into a dingy stone building on Wacker where it runs under the main road next to the river.

Murray swept into the tavern a few minutes after me, raindrops making his red hair glint under the dim lights. Lucy Moynihan, Carl's daughter, who took over the place when he died, likes Murray. She let us jump the crowd to take a booth at the back and stayed for a few minutes to kid with Murray about the money he'd lost to her in last week's basketball pool.

Over a hamburger I told him much of what I'd been doing the last three weeks. For all his flamboyance and conceit, Murray is an intent listener, absorbing information through every pore. They say you remember only thirty percent of what anyone tells you, but I've never had to repeat a story to Murray.

When I'd finished he said, "Okay. You got a mess. You have your old childhood brat wanting you to find who croaked your teammate, an indigestible young Jurshak, and a strangely behaving chemical company. And maybe the Garbage King. You be careful if Steve Dresberg is really involved. That boy plays very much for keeps. I can see him being tied in with Jurshak, but what's Humboldt got to do with it?"

"I wish I knew. Jurshak handles his insurance, which isn't a crime as much as a misdemeanor, but I can't help wondering what Jurshak's doing for Humboldt in return." The elusive memory I'd been trying to force since Saturday swam across the surface of my mind again and disappeared.

"What?" Murray demanded suspiciously.

"Nothing. I thought I remembered something but I can't quite get it. But I wish I knew why Humboldt is lying about Joey Pankowski and Steve Ferraro. It's got to be something really important because when I went to his office today to ask him about it, I got hefted out by some enormous security apes."

"Maybe he just doesn't like you buzzing around him," Murray said maliciously. "There are times when I wish I had security apes to kick you out too."

I faked a punch at him but he took hold of my hand and held it for a minute. "Give, Warshawski. There's no story here yet. Just speculations that I can't put in print. Why are we having lunch together?"

I pulled my hand away. "I'm doing some research. When I have some results I may have a better idea of why Humboldt's lying, but right now I'm off to meet with Art Jurshak. I've got a major club to use on him, so I hope he'll cough up what he knows. So that's what I want from you. If I somehow die, talk to Lotty, to Caroline Djiak, and to Jurshak. Those three are the key."

"How serious are you about being in danger?"

I watched Murray drain his stein and signal for a third. He weighs two-forty, maybe two-fifty—he can absorb it. I stuck with coffee—I wanted my head as clear as possible for Jurshak.

"More than I like. Someone left me for dead five days ago. Two of the same hoods were waiting outside my apartment on Friday. And today Gustav Humboldt sounded strangely like Peter O'Toole trying to get his barons to do in Becket. It's pretty real."

Of course Murray wanted to know the club I had on Jurshak, but I was absolutely determined not to let that get public. We fought about it until one-fifteen, when I got up and laid a five on the table and headed out. Murray hollered after me, but I hoped to be on a southbound bus before he could extricate himself and follow.

A 147 bus was just closing its doors as I reached the top of the stairs. The driver, a rare humanitarian, opened them again when he saw me running for the curb. Art had said two-thirty instead of two—I just wanted to make sure he didn't show up early with some kind of armed escort. I hardly knew young Art and I sure didn't trust him—he might have lied to me about fooling his father. Or maybe Big Art didn't trust his kid, either, and discounted the story. Just in case, I wanted to get there ahead of a trap.

I rode down to Jackson and walked the three blocks east to the fountain. In the summer Buckingham Fountain is the showpiece of the lakefront. Then it's shrouded by trees and crowded with tourists. In the winter, with the foliage dead and the water turned off, it makes a good spot to talk. Few people visit it, and those who do can be seen a good way off.

Today Grant Park was desolate under the dull winter sky. Empty potato-chip bags and whiskey bottles mixed in with the dead leaves provided the only signs of human presence in the area. I retreated to the rose garden on the fountain's south side and perched on the base of one of the statues at its corners. I stuck the Smith & Wesson in my jacket pocket with my thumb resting on the safety.

A light drizzle kept up intermittently during the afternoon. Despite the relative warmth of the winter air, I was chilled through from sitting still in the damp. I hadn't worn gloves so that I could handle the gun more readily, but by the time Jurshak showed up my fingers were so numb, I'm not sure I could have fired.

Around a quarter to three a limo stopped on Lake Shore Drive to deposit the alderman and a companion. The limo moved on up the drive to Monroe, where it circled and came to a halt about a quarter mile from the fountain. When I was sure no one was getting out to take a bead, I scrambled down from my perch and made my way back to the park.

Jurshak was looking around, trying to find his son. He paid only passing attention to me until he realized I was planning to talk to him.

"Art won't be able to make it, Mr. Jurshak—he sent me instead. I'm V. I. Warshawski. I think you've heard my name from your wife. Or from Gustav Humboldt."

Jurshak was wearing a black cashmere coat that buttoned up to his chin. With his face set off by the black collar, I could see an overwhelming resemblance to Caroline—the same high round cheeks, short nose, long upper lip. Even his eyes were the same gentian, a bit faded with age, but that true blue that you rarely see. In fact, he looked more obviously like her than he did young Art.

"What have you done with my son? Where are you holding him?" he demanded in a forceful, husky voice.

I shook my head. "He came to me on Saturday afraid for his life—said you'd told his mother he was as good as dead for letting me get that report you filed for Xerxes with Mariners Rest. He's someplace safe. I don't want to talk to you about your son, but your daughter. You may want to ask your friend to step aside while we speak."

"What are you talking about? Art's my only child! I demand that you take me to him at once, or I'll get the police along quicker than you can blink." His mouth set in the angry stubborn line I'd seen on Caroline's face a thousand times.

Art had been a power in Chicago since before I'd started college. Even without his clique controlling the City Council, there were plenty of police who owed Jurshak favors and would be happy to run me in if he wanted them to.

"Think back a quarter century," I said softly, trying not to let anger turn my voice ragged. "Your sister's daughters. Those luxurious afternoons when your niece danced for you while your brother-in-law was away at work. You can't have forgotten how important you were in the lives of those two girls."

His expression, as mobile as Caroline's, changed from rage to fear. The wind had whipped color into his cheeks, but beneath the red his face looked gray.

"Take a walk, Manny," he said to the stocky man at his side. "Go wait in the car. I'll be over in a couple of minutes."

"If she's threatening you, Art, I oughta stay."

Jurshak shook his head. "Just some old family problems. I thought this was going to be business when I asked you and the boys to come along. Go ahead—one of us oughta stay warm."

The stocky man looked at me narrowly. He apparently decided the bulge in my pocket must be gloves or a notebook and headed back to the limo.

"Okay, Warshawski, what do you want?" Jurshak hissed.

"A whole bunch of answers. In exchange for answers I will not let the fact that you are a child molester with a daughter who is also your great-niece get into the papers."

"You can't prove anything." He sounded mean, but he didn't try moving away.

"Screw that," I said impatiently. "Ed and Martha told me the whole story the other night. And your daughter looks so much like you, it'd be an easy make. Murray Ryerson at the *Herald-Star* would be on it in a minute if I asked him, or Edie Gibson at the *Trib*."

I moved to one of the metal benches at the edge of the paving around the fountain. "We've got a lot to say. So you might as well make yourself comfortable."

I saw him looking over at the limo. "Don't even think it. I've got a gun, I know how to use it, and even if your boys finished me off, Murray Ryerson knows I'm meeting with you. Come sit down and get it over with."

He came over, his head down, his hands jammed into his pockets. "I'm not admitting anything. I think you're full of hot air, but once the press got their teeth into a story like that, they'd ruin me just with the innuendoes."

I gave what was meant to be an engaging smile. "All you'd have to do is say I'm blackmailing you. Of course I'd run Caroline's photo, and they'd interview her mother and all that stuff, but you could give it a shot. Now let's see—we've got so much old family business to talk about, I don't even know where to begin. With Louisa Djiak's mortgage, or me in the mud at Dead Stick Pond, or Nancy Cleghorn."

I spoke musingly, watching him out of the corner of my eye. He seemed a little jumpier at Nancy's name than Louisa's.

"I know! That report you sent to Mariners Rest for Xerxes. You're running a fiddle on the insurance, aren't you? What are they doing—paying a higher rate than they're charged so you can pocket the difference? And what difference does it make if someone finds out? It ain't exactly going to ruin you in the neighborhood. You've been charged with worse and been re-elected."

Suddenly the memory that had been eluding me since I talked to Caroline on Saturday popped to the surface. Mrs. Pankowski standing in her doorway, telling me her financial woes, saying Joey didn't leave her any insurance. Maybe he hadn't signed up for the group plan. But that was a Xerxes benefit, I thought, noncontributory life insurance. Only maybe it was term; since he hadn't been with the company when he died, he wouldn't be covered. Still, it was worth asking.

"When Joey Pankowski died, why didn't he get any life insurance?"

"I don't know what the hell you're talking about."

"Joey Pankowski. He used to work at Xerxes. You're the fiduciary on their LHP business, so you must know why an employee doesn't collect life insurance when he dies."

He looked suddenly as though he'd collapsed through the middle. I thought frantically, trying to follow up my advantage with piercing questions. But he was an old hand at taking the heat and he could tell I didn't really have anything. He recovered enough poise to keep up a front of stubborn denial.

"Okay. Let it go. I can figure it out fast enough when I talk to the carrier. Or some other employees. Let's go back to Nancy Cleghorn. She saw you and Dresberg together at your office, and you know as well as I do that no insurance commissioner will let you keep your license if you hang around with the mob."

"Oh, knock it off, Warshawski. I don't know who this Cleghorn girl is, other than reading in the papers that she got herself killed. I may talk to Dresberg from time to time—he does a lot of business in my ward and I'm the alderman for the whole ward. I can't afford to be a dainty lady holding her nose when she smells garbage. The insurance commissioner isn't going to think once about it, let alone twice."

"So it wouldn't bother you to let it be known that you and Dresberg met in your office late at night?"

"Prove it."

I yawned. "How do you think I even heard about it? There was a witness, of course. One who's still alive."

Even that didn't shake him enough for me to be able to pry anything from him. When the conversation ended I not only felt frustrated but too young for the job. Art just had too much more experience than I. I felt like grinding my teeth and saying "Just you wait, Black Jack, I'll get you in the end." Instead I told him I'd be in touch.

I walked away from him toward Lake Shore Drive. Sprinting across in front of the traffic, I watched him from the far side. He stood for a long moment looking at nothing, then shook himself and headed back toward his limo.

36

BAD BLOOD

I retrieved my car and headed back to Lotty's. All I'd really gotten from seeing Jurshak was information that he'd been working some kind of fraud with the Xerxes insurance. And something major, based on his expression. But I didn't know what it was. And I needed to find out quickly, before all the people who were mad at me converged once and for all and sent me to my permanent rest. The urgency tightened my stomach and congealed my brain.

Rush-hour traffic was already thickening the main streets downtown. The menace in Humboldt's voice this morning lingered in my ears. I drove cautiously through the February twilight, trying to make sure no one was tailing me. I drove all the way up to Montrose and exited at the park, doubling around twice before figuring I was in the clear and heading back to Lotty's.

It didn't surprise me that I got there before she did—to accommodate working mothers Lotty keeps the clinic open until six most evenings. I went out for some food—the least I could do in thanks for her hospitality was to have dinner ready. I started again on the chicken with garlic and olives I'd been trying to make the night before my attack, hoping that if I kept the front of my mind occupied, the back would begin to sprout ideas. This time I prepared the whole dish without interruption and set it to simmer over a low flame.

By then it was close to seven-thirty and Lotty still hadn't returned. I began to get worried, wondering whether I should check the clinic or with Max. A late emergency might have detained her, either at the clinic or hospital. But she'd also be an easy target for anyone bent on getting revenge on me.

At eight-thirty, when I'd tried both clinic and hospital without results, I headed out to search for her. Her car pulled up in front of the building just as I was locking the lobby door.

"Lotty! I was getting worried," I cried, dashing over to meet her.

She followed me back into the building, her pace lagging, most unlike her usual brisk trot. "Were you, my dear?" she asked tiredly. "I should have remembered how nervous you've been the last few days. It's not like you to be in such a fret over a few hours."

She was right. Another sign that I had moved beyond any semblance of rationality in dealing with the issues at hand. She moved slowly into her apartment, taking off her coat with careful movements and stowing it methodically inside a carved walnut wardrobe standing in the hallway. I led her to an armchair in her sitting room. She let me pour her a small brandy—the only alcohol she drinks, and then only when under severe strain.

"Thank you, my dear. That's most helpful." She slipped her shoes off; I found her slippers laid neatly next to her bed and brought them out for her.

"I spent the last two hours with Dr. Christophersen. She's the nephrologist I mentioned showing your chemical company notebooks to."

She finished the brandy but shook her head when I offered her the bottle. "I suspected something when I looked at the records, but I wanted a specialist to do a thorough interpretation." She opened her briefcase and pulled out a few pages of photocopies. "I left the notebooks locked in Max's safe at Beth Israel. They are too—too frightening to be floating around the city streets where anyone could lay hands on them. This is a summary of Ann's— Dr. Christophersen's—notes. She says she can do a thorough analysis if it's needed."

I took the pages from her and looked at Dr. Christophersen's square, tiny writing. She was citing the blood work reported in the pages of Chigwell's notebooks, using Louisa Djiak's and Steve Ferraro's records as an example. The blood chemistry details made no sense to me, but the summary at the bottom of the page was in plain English and appallingly clear:

These records show blood history for Ms. Louisa Djiak (white unmarried female, one parturition) from 1963 to 1982, the last year for which data were taken; and for Mr. Steve Ferraro (white unmarried male) from 1957 to 1982. Records also exist for approximately five hundred other employees at Humboldt Chemical's Xerxes plant covering the period 1955 to 1982. These records show changes in the values of creatine, blood urea nitrogen, bilirubin, hematocrit, and hemoglobin, and white blood count consistent with the development of renal, liver, and bone marrow dysfunction. Conversation with Dr. Daniel Peters, Ms. Djiak's attending physician, confirm that the patient first came to him in 1984, only at her daughter's insistence. At that time he diagnosed chronic renal failure, which has now progressed to an acute stage. Other complications kept Ms. Djiak from being a good candidate for transplant.

The blood work indicates that noticeable renal damage occurred as early as 1967 (CR = 1.9; BUN = 28) and severe damage by 1969 (CR = 2.4; BUN = 30). The patient herself began experiencing typical diffuse symptoms—itching, fatigue, headaches—around 1979 but thought perhaps she was experiencing "change of life" and did not deem it necessary to consult a physician.

The report went on to give a similar summary of Steve Ferraro, ending with his death from aplastic anemia in 1983. The rest of the precise script detailed the toxic properties of Xerxine, and showed that the changes in blood chemistry were consistent with exposure to Xerxine. I read the document through twice before putting it down to stare, appalled, at Lotty.

"Dr. Christophersen did a lot of work, calling Louisa's and Steve Ferraro's doctors and doing all that checking," was the only comment I could get out at first.

"She was horrified—most horrified—at what she was seeing. I gave her the names of two patients I knew could be checked on and she did the follow-up this afternoon. At least in the case of your friend and Mr. Ferraro, it seems abundantly clear that they had no idea what was happening to them."

I nodded. "It makes a hideous kind of sense. Louisa starts having vague symptoms that she thinks are menopause—at thirty-four?—but then she never had any sex education to speak of, maybe it's not so incredible. Anyway, she wouldn't blab it around the plant. A lot of them come from the kind of background she did—where anything having to do with private body functions was shameful and never to be discussed."

"But, Victoria," Lotty burst out, "what is the sense of all this? Who besides a Mengele is so cold, so calculating in keeping these kinds of records, and saying nothing, not one word, to the people involved?"

I rubbed my head. The spot where I'd been hit was pretty well healed, but now that my brain was so stressed out, the injury was throbbing in a dull way, the pounding drum in the jungle of my mind.

"I don't know." Lotty's enervated state had infected me. "I can see why they don't want any of it coming out now."

Lotty shook her head impatiently. "Not so I. Explain, Victoria."

"Damages. Pankowski and Ferraro sued for indemnity payments they believed were rightfully theirs—they tried to build a case saying their illnesses were the result of exposure to Xerxine. Humboldt defended himself successfully. According to the lawyer who handled their suit, the company had two workable defenses—the first was that these guys both smoked and drank heavily, so no one could prove that Xerxine had poisoned them. And the second, which seemed to do the trick, was that their exposure had taken place before Xerxine's toxicity was known. So that . . ."

My voice trailed off. The problem with Jurshak's report to Mariners Rest became staggeringly clear to me. He was helping Humboldt hide the high mortality and illness rates at Xerxes to get favorable rate consideration from the insurance carrier. I could imagine a couple of different ways they could work it, but the likeliest seemed to be that they'd buy a better package from Mariners Rest than they offered the employees. Employees would be told that they didn't have coverage for certain tests or certain amounts of hospital stay. Then when the bills came in they'd go through the fiduciary and he'd fix them before sending them to the insurance company. I thought about it from several different angles and it still looked good. I got up and headed for the phone extension in the kitchen.

"So that what, Vic?" Lotty called impatiently behind me. "What are you doing?"

Turning off the chicken for starters: I'd forgotten the dinner I'd left simmering happily on the back of the stove. The olives were little charred lumps while the chicken seemed to have welded itself to the bottom of the pan. Definitely not the most successful recipe in my repertoire. I tried scraping the mess into the garbage can.

"Oh, never mind the dinner," Lotty said irritably. "Just put it in the sink and tell me the rest of your thinking. The company argued that they couldn't be responsible for the illness of anyone who worked for them if it took place before 1975 when Xerxine's toxicity was established by Ciba-Geigy. Is that it?"

"Yeah, except I didn't know about Ciba-Geigy or that 1975 was the critical year. And my bet is that they claimed to have lowered their ppm of Xerxine to whatever the decreed standard was, and that that's what their reports to Washington show. The ones that Jurshak sent out for Humboldt. But that the analysis SCRAP did at the plant shows much higher levels. I need to call Caroline Djiak and find out."

"But, Vic," Lotty said, absently scraping charred chicken from the skillet, "you still don't explain why they wouldn't tell their workers their bodies were being damaged. If the standard wasn't set until 1975, what difference did it make *before* then?"

"Insurance," I said shortly, trying to find Louisa's number in the directory. She wasn't listed. Snarling, I went back to the spare room to dig my address book out of my suitcase.

I returned to the kitchen and started dialing. "The only person who might tell us definitely is Dr. Chigwell, and he's missing right now. I'm not sure I could make him talk even if I could find him—Humboldt scares him much more than I do."

Caroline answered the phone on the fifth ring. "Vic. Hi. I was just putting Ma to bed. Can you hold? Or should I call back?"

I told her I'd wait. "But you see," I added to Lotty, "those notebooks mean bankruptcy now. Not for the whole company necessarily, but certainly for the Xerxes operation. A good lawyer gets hold of that stuff, contacts the employees or their families, and really goes to town. They've got all those Manville settlements to use by way of precedent."

No wonder Humboldt had been desperate enough to seek me out personally. His little empire was being threatened by the Turks. Frederick Manheim had been right—it must have seemed incredible to all of them that a detective could start nosing around Pankowski and Ferraro and not be looking for evidence of the blood work.

Why had Chigwell tried to kill himself? Overcome by remorse? Or did someone threaten him with a fate worse than death if he told Murray or me anything? The people he'd pranced off to on Friday might well have killed him by now if they thought he was going to crack on them.

I didn't think I'd ever find out exactly what happened. Nor did I see a way of bringing Nancy's death back to the great shark. The only hope would be if the two thugs Bobby had in custody spilled their guts and somehow managed to implicate Humboldt. But I didn't pin much hope on that. Even if they did talk, someone like Humboldt knew too many ways of insulating himself from the direct consequences of his actions. Just like Henry II. I shivered.

When Caroline came back on the line I asked her if Louisa had a brochure describing her Xerxes benefits.

"Christ, Vic, I don't know," she said impatiently. "What difference does it make?"

"A lot," I answered shortly. "It could explain why Nancy was killed and a whole lot of other unpleasant stuff."

Caroline gave an exaggerated sigh. She said she'd ask Louisa and put the phone down.

Nancy would have known about Xerxes's real loss experience because she was monitoring that as SCRAP's environment and health director. So when she'd seen the letter to Mariners Rest and found the company's rate structure, she'd seen at once that Jurshak was handling some kind of fiddle for them. But who had taken her files out of her office at SCRAP? Or maybe she'd had them on her, preparing for a confrontation with Jurshak, and he'd seen they were found and destroyed. But she'd left the other stuff in her car and he hadn't looked there.

When Caroline came back on the line she told me that Louisa thought she'd brought a flyer home with her but it would be buried in her papers. Did I want to wait while she looked? I asked her just to find it and leave it out for me to pick up in the morning. She began a barrage of questions. I couldn't deal with the insistent pressure in her voice.

"Give my love to Louisa," I interrupted tiredly, and hung up on her indignant squawks.

Lotty and I went out for a sober supper at the Dortmunder. Both of us felt too overwhelmed by the enormity revealed by the Chigwell notebooks to have much appetite, or to want to talk.

When we got home I checked in with Mr. Contreras. Young Arthur had taken off. The old man had locked front and back doors when he took Peppy out for her evening walk, but Art had opened a window and jumped out. Mr. Contreras was miserable—he felt he'd let me down the one time I'd actively sought his help.

"Don't worry about it," I said earnestly. "You couldn't possibly watch him twenty-four hours a day. He came to us for protection—if he doesn't want it, it's his neck, after all. You and I can't spend our lives looking around for scissors if he wants to keep sticking his head into nooses."

That cheered him slightly. Although he apologized several times more, he was able to talk about something else—like how lonely Peppy was with me away.

"Yeah, I miss both of you," I said. "Even your hot breath down my neck when I want to be alone."

He laughed delightedly at that and hung up much happier than I was. Although I really didn't give a damn what happened to young Art, I wasn't sure how much he'd learned of what I was figuring out. I didn't relish the thought of his taking any of it back to his father.

My answering service told me Murray had been trying to reach me. I tracked him down and told him nothing had jelled yet. He didn't really believe me, but he didn't have any way to prove I was wrong.

37

THE SHARK PUTS OUT BAIT

My brain was in that numbed, feverish state where you sleep as though you are drugged—heavily but without getting any rest. The tragedy of Louisa's life kept playing itself out in my dreams, with Gabriella scolding me harshly in Italian for not having taken better care of our neighbor.

I woke for good at five and paced restlessly around Lotty's kitchen, wishing I had the dog with me, wishing I could get some exercise, wishing I could think of a way to force Gustav Humboldt to listen to me. Lotty joined me in the kitchen a little before six. Her drawn face told the tale of her own sleepless night. She put a strong hand on my shoulder and squeezed it gently, then went wordlessly to make coffee.

After Lotty had taken off for her early morning rounds at Beth Israel, I headed south once more to see Louisa. She was glad to see me, as always, but seemed tireder than the previous times I'd been there. I questioned her as gently and subtly as I knew how about the onset of her illness, when she'd first started feeling bad.

"You know those blood tests they used to take—old Chigwell the Chigger?"

She gave a scratchy laugh. "Oh my, yes. I saw where the old chigger tried to kill himself. It was on all the TV stations last week. He always was a weak little man, scared of his own shadow. Didn't surprise me he wasn't married. No woman wants a little shrimp like that who can't stand up for himself."

"What did he tell you when he took your blood?"

"One of our benefits, they called it, getting a physical every year like that with the blood work and everything. Not the kind of thing I would of thought of doing. Didn't know people went in for that sort of thing. But it was okay with the head of the union and the rest of us didn't care. Got us off the floor with pay one morning every year, you know."

"They never gave you any results? Or sent them to a doctor for you?"

"Go on, girl." Louisa flapped her hand and coughed loudly. "If they'd a gave us results, we wouldn't of known what they meant anyway. Dr. Chigwell showed me my chart once and I'm telling you, it was like Arab scrawl as far as I was concerned—you know those wiggly lines they put on their banners and all? That's about what medical tests look like to me."

I forced myself to laugh a little with her and sat talking awhile. She wore out quickly, though, and fell asleep in the middle of a sentence. I stayed with her while she slept, haunted by Gabriella's accusations in my dreams.

What a life. Growing up in that soul-killing house, raped by her own uncle, poisoned by her employer, and dying slowly and painfully. Yet she wasn't an unhappy person. When she'd moved next door she was frightened but not angry. She'd raised Caroline with joy and had taken pleasure in the freedom to lead her own life away from her parents. So maybe my pity was not only misplaced but condescending.

While I watched Louisa's chest rise and fall with her stertorous breath, I wondered what I should tell Caroline about her father. Not telling her was a form of control, a seizing of power in her life I had no right to. But telling her seemed unreasonably cruel. Did she deserve so heavy a knowledge?

I was still chewing it over in my mind when she dashed in at noon to fix Louisa's lunch, a light little meal with no salt and precious little food. Caroline was glad to see me but in a hurry, racing between meetings.

"Did you find the flyer? I left it by the coffeepot. I wish you'd tell me why you're so excited about it—if it concerns Ma I have a right to know."

"If I knew exactly how it concerned her, I'd tell you in a flash—I'm just picking my way through the forest right now."

I found the flyer and studied it while she took Louisa's lunch in to her. It left me more baffled than I'd been originally: all kinds of benefits Louisa got regularly were excluded. Outpatient care, dialysis, home oxygen. When Caroline came in I asked her who paid for all those things, wondering if she was somehow scraping the money together.

She shook her head. "Xerxes has been real good to Ma. They pay all these bills without asking. If you can't tell me what's going on with my own mother, I'm heading back to the office. And maybe I can find someone there who'll tell me. Maybe I'll hire my own investigator." She stuck out her tongue at me.

"Try it, brat—all the PI's in town have been informed that you're a bad risk."

She laughed and left. I stayed until Louisa had eaten her meager lunch and fallen asleep once more. Leaving the television on as white noise, I tiptoed out and returned the spare key to the ledge over the back porch.

I wished I understood the point of doing all that blood work years before anyone was interested in suing the company. Presumably it tied in with the insurance fiddle, but I couldn't see the exact connection. I didn't know anyone at Xerxes who might talk to me. Ms. Chigwell might, but her connection had been tenuous and not exactly sympathetic. She was all I had, though, so I made the long drive to Hinsdale.

Ms. Chigwell was in the garage painting her dinghy. She greeted me with her usual abrupt gruffness, but since she invited me in for tea I presumed she was glad to see me.

She had no idea why they had started doing the blood work down at the Xerxes plant. "I just remember that Curtis was in a flurry about it because they had to send all those specimens to some lab and then keep separate records of them, giving the employees numbers and so on. That's why he kept his own notebooks, so he could follow them by name and not have to worry about the numbering scheme."

I sat in the chintz armchair for over an hour, eating a large pile of cookies, while she discussed what she would do if she couldn't find her brother.

"I always wanted to go to Florence," she said. "But I'm too old now, I guess. I've never been able to get Curtis to agree to travel outside the country. He always suspects he'll get some terrible disease from the food or the water, or that foreigners will cheat him."

"I've always wanted to go to Florence, too—my mother came from a little town in southeastern Tuscany. My excuse is, I never have enough money together to pay for the airfare." I leaned forward and added persuasively, "You gave your brother most of your life. You don't have to spend the rest of it waiting at the window with a candle burning. If I was seventy-nine and in good health and had some money, I'd be at O'Hare with a suitcase and a passport in time for tonight's flight."

"You probably would," she agreed. "You're a brave girl."

I left soon after and headed back to Chicago, my shoulders aching again. Talking to Ms. Chigwell had been a long shot. I could've done it by phone if I didn't enjoy seeing her, but the fruitless errand at the end of a long week left me worn out. Maybe it was time to give the police what I had. I tried imagining how I'd tell Bobby my story:

"You see, they'd been doing all these blood tests on their employees and now they're afraid someone will find out and sue them for suppressing evidence of how toxic Xerxine really was."

And Bobby smiling indulgently and saying, "I know you took a liking to the old lady, but it's obvious she had a grudge against her brother all these years. I wouldn't take her reports at face value. How do you even know those notebooks were his? She has some medical training—she might have faked them just to get him in hot water. Then he disappears and she wants to unload them. Hell"—no, Bobby wouldn't use bad language in front of me— "Heck, Vicki, maybe they had one fight too many and she popped him on the head and then panicked and buried his body in Salt Creek. Then she calls you to say he's disappeared. You're high on the lady; you'll believe the story the way she wants to tell it."

And who was to say it hadn't happened that way? At any rate I was pretty sure that Bobby would look at it like that before he'd go after someone as important in Chicago as Gustav Humboldt. I could give Murray the whole story, but far from sharing Bobby's reluctance to go after Humboldt, Murray would leave a swath like General Sherman's through the lives of the people involved. I just didn't want to give him anything that would make him go after Louisa.

I stopped at my own apartment to cheer Mr. Contreras up over the loss of young Art and to see the dog. It was too dark for me to feel comfortable about going out with her, but she was clearly developing the restlessness an active animal feels when she doesn't get enough exercise. Another reason to get Humboldt off my back—so I could run the dog.

Once more I checked the roads around me, but my tail still seemed clear. In a way this made me less cheerful rather than more. Maybe my pals were just waiting for Troy and Wally to make bail. But maybe they'd decided that an ordinary hit wouldn't do and were looking for something more decisively spectacular, like a bomb in my car or at Lotty's apartment. Just in case, I parked some distance from her building and rode the bus back down Irving Park.

I made a frittata for dinner, a greater success than the chicken, since it wasn't scorched, but whether it had any taste I couldn't have said. I told Lotty my various dilemmas, about how to bring matters home to Jurshak and Humboldt, and about whether to tell Caroline I'd found her father.

She pursed her lips. "I can't advise you about Mr. Humboldt. You will have to think of a plan. But about Caroline's father, I must tell you that in my experience it is always better for people to know. You say it is horrible news, and it is. But she is not a weakling. And you cannot decide for her what she can know, what she is better off not learning. For one thing, she may discover it in a more terrible way from someone else. And for another, she can easily imagine things that seem more hideous to her. So in your place I would tell her."

It was a more articulate way of stating my own thoughts. I nodded. "Thanks, Lotty."

We spent the rest of the evening silently. Lotty was going through the morning's papers, the light making little prisms on the half-glasses she wore for reading. I did nothing. I felt as though my mind were encased in lead shielding—protective covering to keep any ideas from entering. The residue of my fear. I kept nipping at the big shark but I was afraid to find a harpoon and attack him directly. I hated knowing he'd been able to intimidate me, but knowing it didn't make a stream of ideas gush forth.

The phone startled me from my somber reverie around nine. One of the house staff at Beth Israel wasn't sure what to do with a patient of Lotty's. She talked to him for a while, then decided she'd better handle the delivery herself and left.

I'd bought a bottle of whiskey yesterday along with the groceries. After Lotty had been gone half an hour or so, I poured myself a drink and tried to get interested in John Wayne's televised antics. When the phone rang again around ten I turned off the set, thinking the caller might be one of Lotty's patients.

"Dr. Herschel's residence."

"I'm looking for a woman named Warshawski." It was a man's voice, cold, uninterested. The last time I'd heard it it had told me that the person hadn't been born who could swim in a swamp.

"If I see her, I'll be glad to give her a message," I said with what coolness I could muster.

"You can ask her if she knows Louisa Djiak," the cold voice went on flatly.

"And if she does?" My voice wobbled despite every effort I put into controlling it.

"Louisa Djiak doesn't have much longer to live. She could die at home in her bed. Or she could disappear in the lagoons behind the Xerxes plant. Your friend Warshawski can make the choice. Louisa is down at Xerxes now. She's well sedated. All you have to do—all you have to tell your friend Warshawski to do is go down and take a look at her. If she does, the Djiak woman will wake up in her bed tomorrow without knowing she ever left it. But if any police come along with Warshawski, they'll have to find some frogmen who like diving in Xerxine before they can give the Djiak woman a Christian burial." The line went dead.

I wasted a few minutes on useless self-recrimination. I'd been so focused on myself, on my closeness to Lotty, I'd never imagined Louisa's being in danger. Despite the fact that I'd told Jurshak I knew her secret. If she and I were gone, no one would remain to speak about it and he would be safe.

I forced myself to think calmly—cursing myself not only wasted time, it would cloud my judgment. The first thing to do was get moving—I could wait for the long drive south to develop some brilliant strategy. I loaded a second clip and stuck it in my jacket pocket, then scribbled a note for Lotty. I was amazed to see my handwriting flow in the same large dark strokes as always.

I was just locking Lotty's door when I remembered the ruse that had gotten Mr. Contreras away from our building a few nights ago. I didn't want to walk into a trap here. I went back inside to make sure that Louisa really was missing from the bungalow on Houston. No one answered the phone. After a few frantic calls—first to Mrs. Cleghorn to get the names and numbers of some other people at SCRAP—I learned Caroline had come back to the office around four. She was closeted now with some EPA lawyers downtown in what was likely to be an all-night session.

The woman I talked to had the number of the people living in my parents' old house, a couple named Santiago. Caroline had given their home phone number to everyone she worked with in case of some emergency. When I called Mrs. Santiago she obligingly told me that Louisa had been taken away in an ambulance around eight-thirty. I thanked her mechanically and hung up.

It had been almost half an hour since I'd gotten the call. It was time to move. I wanted company for the trip but it would be wanton to bring Mr. Contreras along—for him and Louisa both. I thought of friends, of police, of Murray, but of no one whom I could ask to go with me into such extreme danger.

I looked carefully around the hallway when I left Lotty's. Someone had known to phone me here—they might take the easy route and just shoot me as I walked down the stairs. I kept my back pressed against the stairwell wall, crouching low. Instead of going out the front door, I went on down to the basement. Carefully picked my way across the dark floor, fumbling cautiously with Lotty's keys for the one that undid the double lock on the basement door. Made my way down the alley to Irving Park Road.

A bus pulled up just as I got to the main road. I dug in my pocket to find a token under the spare clip and finally pried one out without having to flash my ammunition to the world at large. I rode the eight blocks down Irving Park standing, seeing nothing either of passengers or the night. At Ashland I hopped down and found my car.

The bus's grinding diesel had somehow provided the background I needed to relax my mind completely, for ideas to flow. If an ambulance had come for Louisa, if she was completely sedated, they must have found a doctor. And there could be only one guess as to what doctor would be involved in such an infamous scheme. So there was one person who shared my involvement whom it would not be criminal to ask to share my risk. For the second time today I headed out the Eisenhower to Hinsdale.

38

TOXIC SHOCK

Veils of fog rose from the drainage ditches lining the tollway, covering the road in patches so that other cars appeared only as shrouded pricks of red. I kept the speedometer pointed at eighty, even when the thick mist drowned the road in front of us. The Chevy vibrated noisily, prohibiting conversation. Every now and then I rolled the window down and put up a hand to feel the ropes. They'd loosened a bit but the dinghy stayed on top.

We exited at 127th Street for the trek eastward. We were about eight miles west of the Xerxes plant, but no expressway connects the east and west sides of Chicago this far south.

It was getting close to midnight. Fear and impatience gripped me so strongly, I could scarcely breathe. All my will went into the car, maneuvering around other vehicles, squeaking through lights as they turned, keeping a weather eye cocked for passing patrol cars as I managed to do fifty in the thirty-five-mile zones. Fourteen minutes after leaving the tollway we were turning north on the little track that Stony Island becomes that far south.

We were on private industrial property now, but I couldn't cut the headlights on the rutted, glass-filled track. I'd chosen a run-down looking plant in the hopes that they wouldn't run to a night watchman. Or dog. We pulled to a stop in front of a large cement barge. I looked at Ms. Chigwell. She nodded grimly.

We opened the car doors, trying to move quietly but more concerned with speed. Ms. Chigwell held a strong pencil flash for me while I cut the ropes. She folded a blanket across the hood so that I could slide the dinghy down as noiselessly as possible. We then laid the blanket on the ground to make a little cradle for the dinghy. I pulled it over to the cement barge while she followed, holding the flash and carrying the oars.

The barge was tied up next to a set of iron rungs built into the wall. We lowered the dinghy over the side, then I held its painter while Ms. Chigwell climbed briskly down the ladder. I followed her quickly.

We each took an oar. Despite her age, Ms. Chigwell had a strong, firm stroke. I matched mine to hers, forcing my mind from the incipient throb in my healing shoulders. She had to use both hands to row, so I held the pencil flash. We hugged the left bank; I periodically shone the light so we could avoid barges and keep track of the names on the slips as we rowed past. The bank had long since been cemented over; company names were painted in large letters next to the steel ladders that led to their loading bays.

The night was silent except for the soft clop of our oars breaking water. But the thick mist carrying the river's miasmas was a pungent reminder of the industrial maze we were floating through. Every now and then a spot-light broke the fog, pinpointing a giant steel tube, a barge, a girder. We were the only humans on the river, Eve and her mother in a grotesque mockery of Eden.

We rowed north past the Glow-Rite landing, beyond steel and wire com-panies, plants that did printing, made tools or saw blades, glided by the heavy barges tied up next to a rebar mill. Finally Ms. Chigwell's penetrating little flash picked up the double X's and the giant crown gleaming black in the fog.

We banked the oars. I looked at my watch. Twelve minutes to cover the half mile or so. It had seemed much longer. I grabbed a steel rung as we slid by and carefully pulled the dinghy up next to it. Ms. Chigwell tied the painter with practiced hands. My heart was beating hard enough to suffocate me, but she seemed utterly calm.

We pulled dark caps down low on our foreheads. We clasped hands for a moment, her compulsive squeeze showing what her impassive face hid. I pointed at my watch in an exaggerated movement and she nodded calmly.

Pulling my gun out and releasing the safety, I scrambled up the ladder, my right hand bare so that I could feel the trigger of the Smith & Wesson. I slowed down at the top, cautiously raising my dark-hatted head so that just my eyes came above the bank. If I cried out, Ms. Chigwell would row as fast as she could back to the car and raise an alarm.

I was at the back of the plant, at the concrete platform where the barge had been tied the last time I'd visited the place. Tonight the steel doors surrounding the loading bay were rolled shut and padlocked. Two spotlights at the corners of the building cut the haze around me. As nearly as I could tell no one was anticipating a river approach.

I slid my gun hand over the top of the bank and kept the Smith & Wesson in front of me as I hoisted myself onto land. I rolled over and lay still for a count of sixty. That was Ms. Chigwell's signal to start the climb herself. I could just make out the change in the darkness as her head popped over the edge of the bank—anyone farther away wouldn't be able to see her. She waited another count of twenty, then joined me on the loading platform.

The steel doors lay in a shadow cast by the projecting roof. We moved close to them, trying not to touch them—the sound of arms or gun brushing on steel would vibrate like a reggae band in the still night.

In front of us the spotlights turned the fog into a heavy curtain. Using its draperies as a shield, we moved slowly around to the north end of the plant where the clay-banked lagoons lay. Ms. Chigwell moved with the practiced silence of a lifelong second-story woman.

As soon as we rounded the corner we moved into thicker fog and danker smells. No lights shone on the lagoons. We sensed their pungent presence to our right but didn't dare use the flash. Ms. Chigwell stayed close to me, holding my muffler, feeling her way cat-footed behind me in the dark. After an eternity of careful steps, moving slowly through ruts, sidestepping metal scraps, we reached the front end of the plant.

The fog was thinner here. We crouched behind some steel drums and peered cautiously around them. A single light burned at the gate leading into the yard. After looking for a long moment I could make out a man standing near the entrance. A sentry or lookout. An ambulance was in the center of the drive. I wished I knew if Louisa was still in it.

"Is she going to show up or not?"

The unexpected voice near my left startled me so much, I almost knocked myself against the steel drum. I recovered, trembling, trying to control my breathing. Next to me, Ms. Chigwell remained as impassive as ever.

"It's been a little over two hours. We'll give her until one. Then we'll have to decide what to do with the Djiak woman." The second voice belonged to my anonymous phone caller.

"She'll have to go into the lagoon. We can't afford any more traces."

Now that my heart had settled to a less tumultuous pace, I recognized the first speaker. Art Jurshak, showing a strong family feeling for his niece.

"*You* can't." The second man spoke with his usual uninterested coldness. "The woman's going to die soon anyway. We'll just get the doctor to give her a little shot and return her to her bed. Her daughter will find she died in the night."

At the mention of the doctor it was Ms. Chigwell's turn to tremble a little.

"You're losing it," Art said angrily. "How're you going to get her back into the house without the daughter seeing you? Anyway, she'll know her mother's gone—she's probably roused the neighborhood by now as it is. Better just dispose of Louisa here and set a trap for Warshawski someplace else. It'd be best if they were both gone."

"I'll do it for you," the cold voice said flatly. "I'll get rid of them both and the daughter, too, if you want. But I can't if I don't know why you're so desperate to see them put away. It wouldn't be ethical." He used the last word without any hint of irony.

"Damn you, I'll take care of things myself," Art muttered furiously.

"Fine," the voice said irritatingly. "Either way it's fine. You tell me what they know and I'll have that, or you kill them yourself and I'll have that. It's a matter of complete indifference to me."

Jurshak was silent for a minute. "I'd better see how the doc is making out."

His footsteps echoed and disappeared. He'd gone inside. So Louisa wasn't in the ambulance. Presumably one of the flat-voiced man's sidekicks was waiting in its interior instead of Louisa—they'd left it temptingly in the middle of the yard so I'd head straight to it.

How to get past the cold-voiced man standing at the entrance was a tougher question. If I sent Ms. Chigwell out as a diversion, she'd be a dead diversion. I was wondering if we could jimmy a door or a window around the side when the man solved the problem for us. He strolled out to the center of the yard, where he stopped to knock on the back of the ambulance. The rear door opened a crack. He stood talking through the opening.

I tapped Ms. Chigwell on the shoulder. She stood up with me and we sidled slowly to the shadow of the wall. While we watched, the ambulance door shut again and the cold-voiced man wandered on out to the gate. As soon as he was on the far side of the vehicle, I crouched low and sprinted around the corner to the plant entrance. Ms. Chigwell's footsteps sounded softly behind me. The ambulance shielded us from the view of the gate sentry and we made it inside without hearing any outcry.

We were on a concrete apron outside the plant floor. The sliding steel curtain that separated the manufacturing area from the main entrance was shut, but a normal-sized door next to it stood ajar. We quickly darted through it, shutting it softly behind us, and found ourselves immediately in the plant.

We walked on tiptoe, although the noises around us would have drowned any sounds we made. The pipes let out their intermittent belches of steam and the cauldrons bubbled ominously under the dull green safety lights. Fritz Lang had invented this room. Presently we would come to the end and find only cameramen and laughing actors. A drop of liquid fell on me and I jumped, convinced I'd been poisoned with a toxic dose of Xerxine.

I glanced at Ms. Chigwell. She was looking straight ahead, ignoring the spitting from above as assiduously as she avoided the obscene graffiti crawled on the huge "No Smoking" signs. Suddenly, though, she bit back a cry. I followed her eyes to the far corner of the room. Louisa lay there on a stretcher. Dr. Chigwell stood on one side of her, Art Jurshak on the other. The two of them stared at us, slack-jawed.

Dr. Chigwell found his voice first. "Clio! What are you doing here?"

She marched forward fiercely. I held her arm to keep her from getting within Jurshak's grabbing range.

"I came to find you, Curtis." Her voice was sharp and carried authoritatively over the hissing pipes. "You've gotten yourself involved with some very nasty people. I presume you've spent the last week or so with them. I don't know what Mother would say if she were alive to see you, but I think it's time you came back home again. We'll help Miss Warshawski get this poor sick woman back into the ambulance and then you and I will return to Hinsdale."

I had my gun leveled at Art. Sweat stood out on his round face, but he said pugnaciously, "You can't shoot. Chigwell here has a needle ready to inject Louisa. If you shoot me, it's her death warrant."

"I'm overcome, Art, by your family feeling. If this is the first time you've seen your niece in twenty-seven years or so, your reaction would move even Klaus Barbie to tears."

Art made a violent gesture. He tried shouting at me, but the messages—guilt over his long-forgotten incest, fear of others finding it out, rage at seeing me alive—kept him from getting out anything coherent.

"Is this woman his niece?" Ms. Chigwell demanded of me.

"Yes, indeed," I said loudly. "And she has closer ties to you than that, doesn't she, Art?"

"Curtis, I will not tolerate your killing this unfortunate young woman. And if she is your friend's niece, it is absolutely unthinkable that you do so. It would be unethical and totally unworthy of you as the inheritor of Father's practice."

Chigwell looked at his sister dejectedly. He shrank a little inside his overcoat and his hands hung loosely at his sides. If I acted now, he wouldn't do anything to Louisa.

I was bracing myself to take a flying leap at Art when I saw malice replace the frustration in his face—he was watching someone come up behind us.

Without glancing around, I seized Ms. Chigwell and rolled with her behind the nearest vat. When I looked up I saw a man in a dark overcoat stroll into the area where we'd been standing. I knew his face—I'd seen it on TV or the papers or in court when I'd been a public defender—I just couldn't place it.

"You took your fucking time, Dresberg," Jurshak snapped. "Why'd you let that Warshawski bitch in here to begin with?"

Of course. Steve Dresberg. The Garbage King. Majestic slayer of little flies buzzing around his trash empire.

He spoke in the cold flat voice that made the hairs prickle along my spine. "She must've cut her way under the fence and come in when I was out talking to the boys. I'll get them to go take care of her car when we're done here."

"We're not done here yet, Dresberg," I announced from my nook. "Too much success has gone to your head, made you careless. You should never have tried to kill me the same way you did Nancy. You're getting soft, Dresberg. You're a loser now."

My taunts didn't move him. He was a pro, after all. He lifted his left hand from his coat pocket and pointed a large gun—maybe a Colt .358—at Louisa. "Come out now, girlie, or your sick friend here will be dead a few months before her time." He didn't look at me—a message that I was too trivial for direct attention.

"I listened to you and Art out front," I called. "The two of you agreed she's as good as dead already. But you'd better get me first, because if you shoot at her, you're dead meat."

He swung so fast, I didn't have time to drop before he fired. The bullet went wide as the shot boomed in the cavernous room. Ms. Chigwell crouched, white but stern, on the floor next to me. Unbidden, she took her keys from her sweater pocket. While she moved to one side of our protective vat, I slid to the other. When I nodded she darted around the end of the vat and hurled her keys at Dresberg's face.

He fired at the movement. From the corner of my eye I saw Ms. Chigwell drop. I couldn't go to her now. I got behind Dresberg and fired at him. The first shot went by him, but as he turned to face me I got him twice in the chest. Even then he fired two more rounds before collapsing.

I ran to him and jumped on his gun arm with all my force. His fingers loosened on the revolver. Jurshak was moving up on me, hoping to wrestle Dresberg's gun away before I could get to it. Fury was riding me, though, choking the breath from me, covering my eyes with a hazy film. I shot Jurshak in the chest. He gave an enraged cry and fell in front of me.

Chigwell had stood next to Louisa's stretcher throughout the fracas, his hands flaccidly at his side, his head hunched into his coat. I went over to him and slapped his face. I meant at first just to rouse him from his stupor, but my rage was consuming me so that I found myself pounding him over and over, screaming at him that he was a traitor to his oath, a miserable worm of a man, on and on, over and over. I might have kept at him until his body joined Jurshak and Dresberg on the floor, but through the haze I felt a tug on my arm.

Ms. Chigwell had staggered over, trailing blood on the dirty concrete. "He's all of that, Miss Warshawski. All that and more. But let him be. He's an old man and not likely to change at this time of life."

I shook my head, exhausted and sick. Sick of the stench in the plant, of the foulness of the three men, of my own destructive rage. My gorge rose; I skipped behind a vat to throw up. Wiping my face with a Kleenex, I returned to Ms. Chigwell. The bullet had grazed her upper arm, leaving a bloody furrow of singed flesh but no deep wound. I felt a small measure of relief.

"We've got to get into an office, someplace we can secure, and call the police. There're at least three more men outside and you and I are not taking on any more thugs tonight. We've got to move fast before they start worrying about Dresberg and come looking for him. Can you hold out awhile longer?"

She nodded gamely and helped me bully her brother into showing us the way to his old office. I pushed Louisa's stretcher behind them. She was still alive, her breath coming in short shallow gasps.

When we were inside with the door locked I moved Louisa into the tiny examining room to one side of the office. With the remaining shreds of my strength, I pushed the heavy metal desk athwart the door. I sank to the floor and pulled the phone down next to me.

"Bobby? It's me. Sorry to wake you, but I need your help. Lots of help and fast." I explained what had happened as clearly as I could. It took a few tries to get him to understand me and even then he was skeptical.

"Bobby!" My voice cracked. "You've got to come. I have an old woman with a bullet wound and Louisa Djiak with some awful drug in her and three thugs prowling outside. I need you." The anguish got through to him. He took directions to the plant and hung up before I could say anything else.

I sat for a moment with my head in my hands, wanting nothing more than to lie down on the floor and cry. Instead I forced myself to stand up, to release the half-empty clip and slip in a full one.

Chigwell had taken his sister into the little examining room to patch up her arm. I wandered in to look at Louisa. While I stood there her eyelids fluttered open.

"Gabriella?" she said scratchily. "Gabriella, I might've known you wouldn't forget me in my troubles."

39
PLANT CLEAN-UP

Louisa went back to sleep while I held her hand. When her weak grasp had relaxed I turned to Chigwell and demanded fiercely what he had given her.

"Just—just a sedative," he said, licking his lips nervously. "Just morphine. She'll sleep a lot for the next day, that's all."

From her seat at the desk Ms. Chigwell gave him a look of scalding contempt, but seemed too exhausted to put her feelings into words. I fixed a pallet for her in the examining room, but she came from a generation too modest to lie down in public. Instead she sat upright in the old office chair, her eyelids drooping in her white face.

Fatigue was combining with the tension of waiting to drive me into a frenzy of nervous irritation. I kept checking my barricades, moving into the examining room to listen to Louisa's shallow, gasping breaths, back to the office to look at Ms. Chigwell.

Finally I turned on the doctor, putting all my feverish energy into prying his story from him. It made a short, unedifying tale. He had worked so many years with the Xerxes blood tests that he'd managed to forget one niggling little detail: He wasn't letting people know he thought they might be getting sick. When I showed up asking questions about Pankowski and Ferraro, he'd gotten scared. And when Murray's reporters had shown up he'd become downright terrified. What if the truth came out? It would mean not just malpractice suits but terrible humiliation at Clio's hands—she'd never let him forget that he hadn't lived up to their father's standard. That comment brought him the only fleeting sympathy he had from me—his sister's fierce ethics must be hell to live with.

When the doctor's suicide attempt failed he didn't know what to do. Then Jurshak had called—Chigwell knew him from his workdays in South Chicago. If Chigwell would give them a little simple help, they would arrange for any evidence against him to be suppressed.

He'd had no choice, he muttered—to me, not his sister. When he learned all they wanted was for him to give Louisa Djiak a strong sedative and look after her down at the plant for a few hours, he was happy to comply. I didn't ask him how he felt about going one step further and giving her a fatal injection.

"But why?" I demanded. "Why go through that charade to begin with if you weren't going to give employees their results?"

"Humboldt told me to," he mumbled, looking at his hands.

"I could have guessed that part!" I snapped. "But why in God's name did he tell you to?"

"It—uh—it had to do with the insurance," he muttered in the back of his throat.

"Spit it out, Curtis. You're not leaving until I know, so say it and get it over with."

He stole a look at his sister, but she sat white and still, lost in her own cloud of exhaustion.

"The insurance," I prompted.

"We could see—Humboldt knew—we had too many health claims, too many people were losing work time. First our health insurance began going up, way up, then we were dropped by Ajax Assurance and had to find another company. They'd done a study, they told us our claims were too high."

My jaw dropped. "So you got Jurshak to act as your fiduciary and screw up the data so you could prove you were insurable to another carrier?"

"It was just a way of buying time until we could figure out what the problem was and fix it. That was when we started doing the blood studies."

"What was happening on the worker's comp side?"

"Nothing. None of the illnesses were compensable."

"Because they weren't work related?" My temples ached with the effort of following his convoluted tale. "But they were. You were proving they were with all that blood data."

"Not at all, young lady." For a moment his pompous side reasserted itself. "That data did not establish causality. It merely enabled us to project medical expenses and the probable turnover of the work force."

I was too appalled to speak. His words came out so glibly that they must have been spoken hundreds of times at committee meetings or before the board of directors. Let's just see what our work-force costs will be if we know that X percent of our employees will be sick Y fraction of the time. Run different cost projections tediously by hand in the days before computers. Then someone has the bright idea—get hard data and we'll know for sure.

The enormity of the whole scheme made me murderous with rage. Louisa's harsh breath in the background added fuel to my fury. I wanted to shoot Chigwell where he sat, then ride off to the Gold Coast and plug Humboldt. That bastard. That cynical, inhuman murderer. Anger swept through me in waves, making me weep.

"So no one got their proper life or health coverage just to save you guys a few miserable stupid dollars."

"Some of them did," Chigwell muttered. "Enough to keep the wrong people from asking questions. This woman here did. Jurshak said he knew her family so he was obligated to look after her."

At that I thought I really would commit murder, but a movement from Ms. Chigwell caught my attention. Her gaunt face was unchanged, but she'd apparently been listening despite her seeming remoteness. She tried holding out a hand to me, but her strength wasn't up to the task. Instead she said in the thread of a voice:

"What you're describing is too heinous to discuss, Curtis. We'll talk tomorrow about our arrangements. We can't go on living together after this."

He deflated again, shrinking inside himself without speaking. He probably couldn't think beyond tonight, with its threat of arrest and prison. Perhaps other horrors were adding to the gray pallor around his mouth, but I didn't think so—I didn't think he had enough imagination to picture what he'd really been doing as the Xerxes doctor. Maybe being booted into the cold by the sister who had always protected him was punishment enough—maybe it would hurt him worse than anything I could do.

Exhausted, I returned to the examining room to look at Louisa again. Her shallow breathing seemed unchanged. She muttered in her sleep—something about Caroline, I couldn't make out what.

It was then that the shots started. I looked at my watch: thirty-eight minutes since I'd called Bobby. It had to be the police. Had to be. I forced my weary shoulders into action, moving the desk back from the door. Telling my charges to stay put, I turned out the room lights and crept back to the plant. Another five minutes passed, and then the place was filled with boys in blue. I moved out from the cover of one of the vats to talk to them.

It took awhile to get things sorted out—who I was, why an alderman was lying in his own blood next to Steve Dresberg on a factory floor, what Louisa Djiak and the Chigwells were doing there. You know—all the usual stuff.

When Bobby Mallory showed up at three we started moving faster. He listened to my worries about Louisa for about thirty seconds, then had one of the men send for a fire department ambulance to take her to Help of Christians. Another ambulance had already carted Dresberg and Jurshak to County Hospital. Both were still alive, their futures uncertain.

I snatched a minute in the confusion to call Lotty, let her know the bare bones of what had happened and that I was unhurt. I told her not to wait up, but in my secret heart I begged her to.

When the state police arrived they assigned a car to ferry the Chigwells home. They'd wanted to send Ms. Chigwell to a hospital for observation, but she was adamant about returning to her own home.

Before Mallory came I'd been telling everyone that Jurshak had lured Chigwell down to the plant with a tale about finding a half-dead employee on the premises. Ms. Chigwell hadn't let him go alone this late at night and the two found themselves caught in the cross fire. Bobby looked narrowly at me, but finally agreed to my version when it was clear he wasn't going to get anything else from the doctor or his sister.

Bobby left me squatting wearily against a pillar on the plant floor while he conferred with the Fifth District commander. The light winking from uniform jackets and hardware made me dizzy; I shut my eyes, but I couldn't keep out the clamor, or the murky Xerxine smell. What would my creatine level be after tonight? I pictured my kidneys filled with lesions—blood-red with black holes in them, oozing Xerxine. Someone shook me roughly. I opened my eyes. Sergeant McGonnigal was standing over me, his square face displaying unusual concern.

"Let's get you outside—you need some fresh air, Vic."

I let him help me to my feet and stumbled after him to the loading bay, where the police had rolled back the steel doors leading to the river. The fog had lifted; stars showed little yellow pricks in the polluted heavens. The air was still pungent with the scent of many chemicals but the cold made it fresher than it was inside the plant. I looked down at the water glinting black in the moonlight and shivered.

"You've had a pretty rough night."

McGonnigal's voice held just the right level of concern. I tried not to imagine him learning how to talk to difficult witnesses like that at a seminar in Springfield—I tried to think he really cared about the horrors I'd been through. After all, we'd known each other six or seven years.

"A little exhausting," I admitted.

"You want to tell me about it, or do you want to wait to talk to the lieutenant?"

So it was role-playing from a seminar. My shoulders sagged a bit farther. "If I tell you, will I have to repeat it to Mallory? It's not a story I feel like going over more than once."

"You know the cops, Warshawski—we never take any story just once. But if you'll give me the outline tonight, I'll make sure that does for now—get you home while there's still a little left of the night to sleep in."

Maybe there was a little personal concern mixed in. Not enough to make me tell the whole truth and nothing but—I mean, I wasn't going to explain about the doctor's medical texts. And certainly not Jurshak's relations with Louisa. But after I'd pulled a crate over to the water's edge and sat on it, I gave him more details than I'd originally planned to.

I started with the call from Dresberg. "He knew Louisa was important to me—my mother had looked after her when she was pregnant and they'd been pretty good friends. So they must have realized she was one person I'd come out here to help."

"Why didn't you call us then?" McGonnigal asked impatiently.

"I didn't know how you'd manage a quiet assault. They had her in the back of the plant here—they'd simply have murdered her if they figured they were under attack. I wanted to sneak in here myself."

"And just how did you manage that? They had a lookout where the road turns off to here and another guy at the gates. Don't tell me you sprayed some amnesiac in the air and slid by them."

I shook my head and pointed at the dinghy floating below us. The floodlights overhead picked up the incredulity in McGonnigal's face.

"You rowed up the river in that? Come on, Warshawski. Get real."

"It's the truth," I said stubbornly. "Believe it or not. Ms. Chigwell was with me—it's her boat."

"I thought you said they'd come here together."

I nodded. "I knew if I told you the truth, you'd keep her and her brother here all night and they're too old for that. Besides, she got shot in the arm, even if it did just graze her—she should have been in bed hours ago."

McGonnigal pounded the crate with the flat of his hand. "You don't have an armlock on empathy, Warshawski. Even the police are capable of showing concern for a couple as old as the Chigwells. Can't you drop your sixties 'Off the Pigs' mentality for five minutes and let us do our job? You could have been killed and gotten the Djiak woman and your elderly friends knocked off in the bargain."

"For your information," I said coldly, "my father was a beat cop and I never in my life referred to the police as pigs. Anyway, no one got killed, not even those two pieces of shit who deserved it. Do you want to hear the rest of my story or would you rather get up in your pulpit and preach at me some more?"

He sat stiffly for a moment. "I guess I can see why Bobby Mallory shows up at his worst around you. I was bragging to myself that I was going to show the lieutenant what a younger officer with sensitivity training could do with a witness like you, and I blew it in five minutes. Finish your story—I won't criticize your methods."

I finished my story. I told him I didn't know how Chigwell had gotten hooked up with Jurshak and Dresberg, but that they'd forced him to come along tonight to look after Louisa. And that Ms. Chigwell was worried about him, so when I showed up with my crazy suggestion that we row up the Calumet and sneak up on the plant from the rear, she jumped at the chance.

"I know she's seventy-nine, but sailing's been her hobby since she was a kid and she sure handled her oar splendidly. So then we got here, and we had a lucky break—Jurshak went into the plant and Dresberg walked off to check on the people in the ambulance. Who was in it? Is that who shot at you guys when you showed up?"

"No, that was the sentry," McGonnigal explained. "He tried making a run for it. Someone got him in the abdomen."

I suddenly realized that Caroline Djiak didn't know where her own mother was. I explained the problem to McGonnigal. "She's probably roused the mayor by now. I should call her if I can get back into one of the offices."

He shook his head. "I think you've done enough running around for one evening. I'll send a uniformed man over to her house—then she can get an escort down to the hospital if she wants. I'll run you home."

I thought it over. Maybe I'd just as soon not include a close encounter with Caroline in the night's strains.

"Could we go pick up my car? It's down on Stony a half mile or so."

He pulled out his walkie-talkie and summoned a uniformed officer—my pal Mary Louise Neely. She saluted him smartly, but I could see she was eyeing me curiously. So maybe she was human after all.

"Neely, I want you to drive Ms. Warshawski and me down the road to pick up her car. Then go to the address she gives you on Houston." He sketched the situation with Caroline and Louisa.

Officer Neely nodded enthusiastically—it's a break to be signaled out for a special assignment from among so many. Even though it was just chauffeuring duty, it gave her a chance to make an impression on a senior man. She trailed behind us as McGonnigal went to tell Bobby what we were doing.

Bobby agreed reluctantly—he wasn't going to contradict his sergeant in front of me or a uniformed officer. "But you're talking to me tomorrow, Vicki, whether you like it or not. You hear?"

"Yeah, Bobby. I hear. Just wait until the afternoon—I'll be a lot more cooperative if I get some sleep."

"Yeah, princess. You private operators work when you feel like it and leave the garbage for the cops to sweep up. You'll talk to me when I'm ready for you."

The light was dancing in my eyes again. I had moved beyond fatigue to a state where I'd start hallucinating if I wasn't careful. I followed McGonnigal and Neely into the night without trying to respond.

40
NIGHT SHAKES

When Officer Neely had dropped us at my car, I dug the keys from my jeans pocket and handed them wordlessly to McGonnigal. He turned the car in the rutted yard while I leaned back in the passenger seat, releasing it so it was almost horizontal.

I was sure I'd fall asleep as soon as I lay back, but images from the night kept exploding in my head. Not the silent trip up the Calumet—that had already faded to the surreal world of half-remembered dreams. Louisa lying on the cart at the end of the plant, Dresberg's cold indifference, waiting for the police in Chigwell's office. I hadn't been afraid at the time, but the recurring pictures gave me the shakes now. I tried clenching my arms against the sides of the seat to control the shaking.

"It's aftershock." McGonnigal's voice came clinically in the dark. "Don't be ashamed of it."

I pulled the seat back to its upright position. "It's the ugliness," I said. "The horrible reasons Jurshak had for doing it, and the fact that Dresberg isn't a man anymore, he's an unfeeling death machine. If they'd just been a couple of punks jumping me in an alley, I wouldn't feel this way."

McGonnigal reached out an arm and groped for my left hand. He squeezed it reassuringly but didn't speak. After a minute his fingers stiffened; he withdrew them and concentrated on turning onto the Calumet Expressway.

"A good investigator would take advantage of your fatigue and get you to explain what Jurshak's horrible reasons were."

I braced myself in the dark, trying to prepare my wits. Never speak without thinking. A cardinal rule to my clients in my public defender days. First the cops wear you out, then they show you some sympathy, then they get you to spill your guts.

McGonnigal tried taking the Chevy up to eighty, but slowed to seventy when it started vibrating. Police privilege.

"I expect you have some cover story ready," he went on, "and it'd really be police brutality to force you to keep it up when you're this tired."

After that the temptation to tell him everything I knew became nearly irresistible. I forced myself to watch what aspect of landscape one could see from the expressway canyons, to push away the picture of Louisa's disoriented gaze confusing me with Gabriella.

McGonnigal didn't speak again until we were passing the Loop exits and then it was only to ask for Lotty's address.

"Would you like to come back to Jefferson Park with me instead?" he asked unexpectedly. "Have a brandy, unwind?"

"Spill all my secrets in bed after the second drink? No—don't get upset, that was supposed to be a joke. You just couldn't tell in the dark." It sounded appealing, but Lotty would be anxiously awaiting me—I couldn't leave her hanging. I tried explaining this to McGonnigal.

"She's the one person I never lie to. She's—not my conscience—the person who helps me see who I really am, I guess."

He didn't answer until he'd pulled off the Kennedy at Irving Park. "Yeah, I understand. My grandfather was like that. I was trying to picture myself in your situation with him waiting up for me; I'd have to go back too."

They didn't teach that in any seminar in Springfield. I asked about his grandfather. He'd died five years ago.

"The week before my promotion came through. I was so mad I almost resigned—why couldn't they have given it to me when he was still alive to see it? But then I could hear him saying, 'What do you think, Johnnie—God runs the universe with you in mind?' " He laughed a little to himself. "You know, Warshawski, I've never told that to another soul?"

He pulled up in front of Lotty's place.

"How're you going to get home?" I asked.

"Umm, I'll summon a squad car. They'll be glad to have an excuse to leave the mayhem in Uptown for a chance to drive me."

He held the keys out to me. Under the sodium light I could see his eyebrows lift in inquiry. I leaned across the seat divider and put my arms around him and kissed him. He smelled of leather and sweat, human smells that made me wriggle closer to him. We sat like that for several minutes, but the ashtray in the divider was digging into my side.

I pulled away. "Thanks for the ride, Sergeant."

"A pleasure, Warshawski. We serve and protect, you know."

I invited him to come up and call a squad car from Lotty's but he said he'd do it from the street, that he needed the night air. He watched while I undid the lobby locks, then sketched a wave and walked off.

Lotty was in her sitting room, still in the dark skirt and sweater she'd put on for the hospital seven hours earlier. She was flicking the pages of *The Guardian,* making only a pretext of interest in Scottish economic woes. She put the paper down as soon as she saw me.

It felt like home to nestle in her arms; I was glad I'd decided to come back here instead of going off with McGonnigal. While she bathed my face and fed me hot milk, I told her the night's tale, the strange ride up the river, my fears, Ms. Chigwell's indomitable courage. She frowned deeply over Chigwell's betrayal of his medical vows. Lotty knows there are unethical doctors but she never likes to hear about them.

"The worst part in a way was when Louisa woke up and thought I was Gabriella," I said as Lotty led me into the spare room. "I don't want to be back there, you know, back in South Chicago cleaning up behind the Djiaks the way my mother did."

Lotty slid my clothes off with practiced medical fingers. "A little late to be worrying about that, my dear—it's all you've been doing this last month."

I made a face—maybe I would have been better off with the sergeant after all.

Lotty pulled the covers over me. I was asleep before she'd turned out the light, falling deep into dreams of mad boat journeys, of scaling cliffs while being attacked by eagles, of Lotty waiting at the top for me saying, "A little late to be worrying, isn't it, Vic?"

When I woke at one the next afternoon I was unrefreshed. I lay for a bit in a drowsy lethargy, stiff both mentally and physically. I wanted to lie there indefinitely, to drift to sleep until Lotty came home and took care of me. The last few weeks had taken from me any ability to find pleasure in what I did for a living. Or indeed any reason for continuing it.

If I had been able to follow my mother's dreams, I'd be my generation's Geraldine Ferrar, sharing intimate moments across a concert stage with James Levine. I tried imagining what it would be like, to be talented and pampered and wealthy. If someone like Gustav Humboldt came after me, I'd have my press agent whip up a few paragraphs for the *Times* and call the police superintendent—who would be my lover—to knock him down a few pegs.

And when I was worn out some other person would stagger to the bathroom on badly swollen feet to try to clear her head under a cold-water tap. She would make my phone calls, run my errands, suffer hideous hardships for me. If I had time, I would thank her graciously.

In the absence of this selfless bunter, I called my answering service myself. Mr. Contreras had phoned once. Murray Ryerson had left seven messages, each progressively more emphatic. I didn't want to talk to him. Not ever. But since I'd have to eventually, I might as well get it over with. I found him steaming at the city desk.

"I've had it with you, Warshawski. You cannot get help from the press without delivering your side of the bargain. This fight in South Chicago is old news. The electronic guys already have it. I helped you out on the understanding you'd give me an exclusive."

"Stick it in your ear," I said nastily. "You did sweet nothing for me on this case. You took my leads and gave me back zero. I beat you to the finish line and now you're pissed. The only reason I'm calling at all is to keep the communications lines open for the future, because believe me, I'm not too interested in talking to you in the present."

Murray started to roar back, but his newspaper instincts won out. He put on the brakes and began asking questions. I thought about describing my midnight boat ride up the misty, acrid Calumet, or the utter fatigue of soul I felt after talking to Curtis Chigwell. But I didn't want to justify myself to Murray Ryerson. Instead I gave him everything I'd told the police, along with a vivid description of the fight around the solvent vats. He wanted me to join a photographer down at the Xerxes plant to show where I'd stood and got indignant at my refusal.

"You're a fucking ghoul, Ryerson," I said. "The kind of guy who asks disaster victims how they felt when they saw their husbands or children go up in smoke. I am not going into that plant again, not even if they gave me the Nobel Peace Prize for doing it. The faster I forget the place the happier I'll be."

"Well, Saint Victoria, you go feed the hungry and tend to the sick." He slammed the receiver in my ear.

My head still felt leaden. I went out to the kitchen and made myself a pot of coffee. Lotty had left a note in her thick black script next to the pot—she'd turned off the phone before she left, but both Murray and Mallory had called. I knew about Murray, of course, but Bobby had mercifully not hounded me after the one message. I suspected McGonnigal had intervened and was grateful.

I poked around the refrigerator but couldn't get interested in any of Lotty's healthy food. Finally I settled at the kitchen table with the coffee. Using the extension on the counter, I called Frederick Manheim.

"Mr. Manheim. It's V. I. Warshawski. The detective who came to see you a few weeks ago about Joey Pankowski and Steve Ferraro."

"I remember you, Ms. Warshawski—I remember everything connected with those men. I was sorry to read about the attack on you last week. That didn't have anything to do with Xerxes, did it?"

I leaned back in the chair, trying to find a comfortable spot for my sore shoulder muscles. "By a strange set of coincidences, yes. How would you feel about getting a cartload of material implying that Humboldt Chemical knew the toxic effects of Xerxine as early as 1955?"

He was silent for a long moment, then he said cautiously, "This isn't your idea of a joke is it, Ms. Warshawski? I don't know you well enough to figure out what you think is funny."

"I never felt less like laughing. I'm looking at such an incredible display of cynicism that every time I think of it I get consumed by rage. My old neighbor in South Chicago is dying right now. At the age of forty-two she looks like a war-ravaged grandmother." I checked myself.

"What I really want to know, Mr. Manheim, is whether you're prepared to organize and manage action on behalf of hundreds of former Xerxes employees. Maybe present ones as well. You should think about it carefully. It would be your entire life for the next decade. You couldn't handle it alone in your storefront—you'd have to take on researchers and associates and paralegals, and you'd have to fight off the big guns who'd want to cut you out because they smelled the contingency fees."

"You make it sound real attractive." He laughed quietly. "I told you about the threat I got when I was preparing to appeal. I don't think I have much choice. I mean, I don't see how I could live with myself if I had a chance now to win that case and passed it up just so I wouldn't have to give up my quiet practice. When can I get your cartload?"

"Tonight, if you can drive up to the North Side. Seven-thirty okay?" I gave him Lotty's address.

When he'd hung up I phoned Max at the hospital. After a few minutes on my late-night adventure—which had made the morning papers in skeleton form—he agreed to get the Chigwell documents copied. When I said I'd come by at the end of the day for the originals, he protested graciously: it would be his pleasure to bring them to Lotty's for me.

After that I really couldn't delay a heart-to-heart with Bobby. I tracked him down by phone at the Central District and agreed to meet him there in an hour. That gave me time for a soak in Lotty's tub to limber up my sore shoulders and a call to Mr. Contreras assuring him I was alive, moderately well, and would return home in the morning. He started a long, anxious dump about how he'd felt when he saw the news this morning; I cut him off gently.

"I've got a date with the police. I'll be pretty well tied up today, but we'll have a late breakfast tomorrow and catch up."

"Sounds good, doll. French toast or pancakes?"

"French toast." I couldn't help laughing. It got me down to police head-quarters in a light enough mood to deal with Bobby.

His pride was badly wounded by my nailing the Emperor of Trash. Dresberg had been dancing rings around Chicago's finest for years. For any private investigator to have caught him dead to rights would have hurt Mallory. But that it had to be me so upset him that he kept me downtown for four hours.

He interrogated me himself, while Officer Neely took notes, then sent in relays of people from the Organized Crime Division, followed by the Special Functions Unit, finishing with an escorted interview with a couple of feds. By then my fatigue had come back full force. I kept dropping off between questions and it was getting hard for me to remember what I was revealing and what I'd decided belonged to me alone. The third time the feds had to poke me awake they decided they'd had enough of a good time and urged Bobby to send me home.

"Yeah, I guess we've got everything we're going to get." He waited until his office was empty, then said edgily, "What'd you do to McGonnigal last night, Vicki? He made it real clear he wasn't going to be present while I talked to you."

"I didn't do anything," I said, raising my eyebrows. "He turn into a boar or something?"

Bobby frowned at me. "If you're trying to level any charges against John McGonnigal, who is one of the finest—"

"Circe," I cut in hastily. "That's what she did to Odysseus's crew. I assumed you were thinking of that. Or something like it."

Bobby narrowed his eyes but all he said was, "Go on home, Vicki. I don't have the energy for your sense of humor right now."

I was at the door when he lighted his last squib. "How well do you know Ron Kappelman?" His voice had a studied casualness that warned me to be careful.

I turned to look at him, my hand still on the doorknob. "I've talked to him three or four times. We're not lovers, if that's what you're asking."

Bobby's gray eyes measured me steadily. "You know Jurshak did a few favors for him when he signed on as SCRAP's counsel?"

I felt the bottom fall out of my stomach. "Like what?"

"Oh, cleared the way for him to do all the renovation work on his house. That kind of thing."

"And in exchange?"

"Information. Nothing unethical. He wouldn't jeopardize his clients' standing. Just let the alderman's office know what moves they might make. Or what moves a smart PI like you might be making."

"I see." It was an effort to get words out, let alone keep my voice steady. I braced myself against the door. "How do you know all this?"

"Jurshak talked a lot this morning. Nothing like the fear of death to get someone babbling. Of course the courts will throw it all out, information obtained under duress. But watch who you talk to, Vicki. You're a smart girl —smart young lady. I'll even agree you've done some good work. But you're one person alone. You just can't do the job the cops are paid to do."

I was too tired and soul-sick to argue. I felt too bad even to think he was wrong. My shoulders slumped, I slogged my way down the long corridors to the parking lot and headed back to Lotty.

41

A WISE CHILD

When I got to Lotty's, Max was already there. I felt so down after my talk with Mallory that I would have preferred canceling my meeting with Manheim: What could one person do alone, anyway? As it was I only had time to explain to Lotty who Frederick Manheim was and why I'd invited him when he showed up. His round solemn face was flushed with excitement, but he shook hands politely with Max and Lotty and offered Lotty a bottle of wine. It was a '78 Gruaud-Larose. Max raised his brows appreciatively, so I assumed it was a good bottle.

As we talked in the kitchen my drooping self-confidence began to revive. After all, I had been worried about Kappelman's role all along. It wasn't a failure on my part. Bobby just was trying to skewer me because I'd stopped Steve Dresberg when he and his thousands of backups hadn't been able to touch him.

I whipped up omelets while Max opened the wine, reverentially letting it breathe. While we ate at Lotty's kitchen table we talked about general topics —the wine was too splendid to pollute with Xerxine.

Afterward, though, we moved into Lotty's sitting room. I spelled out the story for Max and Manheim. Lounging on the daybed, I explained what I'd learned from Chigwell—that they'd done the tests because they could see their high rates of illness as early as 1955.

"You should see if you can talk to Ajax. They were handling Xerxes's life and health insurance at the time. I know they went to Mariners Rest in 1963 with evidence of how good and pure they were, but if you find out why Ajax dropped them back in the fifties you may get some inside dope on why they decided to look at blood instead of—I don't know, some other choice."

Manheim, propped on his elbows on the floor, was naturally most interested in what lay in Chigwell's notebooks. Lotty sketched the data for him, but warned him he would have to get an array of specialists.

"I am only a perinatologist, you know. So what I'm telling you is only what I've learned from Dr. Christophersen. You will need many people— blood specialists, a good renal pathologist. And above all, you will need a team in occupational health."

Manheim nodded soberly at all their advice. His rosy cherub's cheeks glowed deeper red as he filled legal pads with notes. Every now and then he asked me a question about the plant and the employees.

Lotty finally put a halt to the discussion—she had to get up early, I was her patient and wasn't fit for another all-night session, and so on. Manheim stood up reluctantly.

"I'm not going to do anything in a hurry," he warned me. "I want to double-check the data, find the lab that did the blood work for them, all that kind of stuff. And I'm going to have to consult with a specialist in environmental law."

I held up my hands. "It's your baby now. You do what you want with it. You just need to keep in mind that Gustav Humboldt isn't going to lie down with his legs up in the air while you're gathering facts—for all I know he's already figured out a way to put the clamps on the lab. You want one last chance to back out?"

He thought for a short minute, then grinned reluctantly. "I've spent enough time on my tush in Beverly—I can't turn down this one. As long as you agree to provide moral support every now and then."

"Yeah, sure, why not," I agreed as positively as I could—I didn't want tentacles from South Chicago to keep reaching out to strangle me.

When Manheim had gone I headed off to bed, leaving Max in the sitting room with a bottle of Lotty's cognac. Lotty came in for a minute after I'd brushed my teeth to tell me Caroline had phoned while I was with the police.

"She wants you to call her. But as she was angry and became rather rude, I thought it wouldn't hurt her to wait."

I grinned. "That's my Caroline. She say anything about Louisa?"

"I gather since she slept through her ordeal she's none the worse for it. Sleep well, my dear."

She was gone when I got up in the morning. I puttered aimlessly around the kitchen, drinking coffee. I started to make toast, then remembered my promise to eat breakfast with Mr. Contreras. I slowly packed my overnight bag. The longer I stayed at Lotty's the less interested I seemed to be in looking after myself. It was time to go before I slipped into unconquerable lassitude.

In deference to Lotty's tidy spirit, I took the sheets from the guest bed and bundled them up with the towels I'd used. I wrote a note telling her I'd taken them home with me to launder. I straightened up the other signs of my presence as best I could and headed over to Racine.

Mr. Contreras's delight at seeing me was equaled only by the dog's. Peppy jumped up to lick my face, her golden tail thumping the door hard enough to swing it shut. My neighbor took the laundry from me.

"These Dr. Lotty's things? I'll wash 'em for you, doll. After breakfast you'll want to unwind, look at your mail, do whatever. So the case is over? Everything locked up with those two villains in the hospital? I mighta known you'd take care of those guys, doll. I shouldn't of worried so much about you. No wonder you got teed off."

I put an arm around him. "Yeah, it all looks swell now that the battle's nearly over. But shooting someone in that kind of situation is just luck—you can't aim. I could be in intensive care instead of Dresberg if the luck had gone the other way."

"*Nearly* over?" His faded brown eyes showed concern. "You mean those guys still have someone gunning for you?"

"Other way around. There's a big old white shark thrashing around in the water. Dresberg and Jurshak were his allies. Who knows what else he's got stashed in his cove." I tried to keep my tone light. "Anyway, I came back here for French toast. Got any?"

"Sure, doll, sure. Everything's ready—just waiting for you before I turn on the griddle." He rubbed his hands together and bustled me inside.

Somewhere from the recesses of his life he'd dug up a white linen table-cloth. He'd cleared the dining-room table of the magazines and bric-a-brac that usually cluttered it and covered it with the cloth. A vase in the middle held red carnations. I was touched.

He swelled with pride at my compliments. "These were Clara's things. They never meant so much to me but I couldn't bring myself to give them to Ruthie when she died; Clara kind of treasured them and I just couldn't quite see Ruthie prizing them like she should."

He hurried off to the kitchen and came back with a glass of fresh orange juice. "Now you sit here, doll, and I'll have breakfast out to you in two shakes."

He fried up tall mounds of bacon and gargantuan stacks of French toast. I ate what I could and repaid him by telling the tale of my midnight trip up the Calumet. He was caught between awe at the exploit and jealousy that I hadn't picked him to go with me, pipe wrench and all.

I gallantly suppressed a shudder at the idea. "I didn't think it would be fair to Peppy," I explained. "If we both got killed or laid up, who would look after her?"

He accepted that grudgingly—and a bit suspiciously—and asked me to tell him again how I'd shot Dresberg. Finally, around noon, I felt I'd stayed long enough and made my escape upstairs. The old man had stacked my mail neatly inside my apartment door, letters in one pile, newspapers in another. I flipped through the letters quickly—nothing personal. Not one thing. Just bills and solicitations. In irritation I tossed the lot, including my home phone bill. The papers would keep—I'd go through them later and see how they'd covered Xerxes.

My rooms had that strange appearance of a place you haven't visited for a while—they seemed somehow unfamiliar, as though I'd heard them described but hadn't ever actually seen them. I moved around restlessly, trying to reestablish myself in my own existence. And trying not to wonder what Humboldt might next attempt. I wasn't entirely successful. At two when the doorbell rang I jumped a little. This has got to stop, Victoria, I admonished myself. I walked purposefully to the intercom and pressed it.

Caroline's voice came tinnily through. If anything were needed to restore my self-confidence, it would be a little roughhousing with her. I prepared myself for battle and buzzed her in.

I could hear her moving up the stairs with a slow, heavy tread most unlike her usual canter. When she made the last turning and came into view, I could see that she looked somber. My heart contracted. Louisa. Tuesday night's escapade had been too much for her weak system and she'd died.

"Hello, Caroline. Come on in."

She stood in the doorway. "Do you hate me, Vic?"

My eyebrows went up in surprise. "Why on earth do you ask that? I thought you'd shown up to chew me out for exposing Louisa to so much abuse two nights ago."

"It wasn't your fault. It was mine. If I'd told you what was going on . . . You almost got killed because of me. Twice. But all I could do was scream at you like the spoiled little brat you kept telling me I was."

I put an arm around her and dragged her into the apartment—the last thing I wanted was for Mr. Contreras to hear us and come bounding up. Caroline leaned against me and let me take her over to the couch.

"How's Louisa?"

"She's back home." Caroline hunched her shoulders. "She actually seems a little better today. She doesn't remember anything that happened, and whatever they shot her full of gave her a better sleep than she usually gets."

She picked up a copy of *Fortune* and started twisting it around. "The police came by right after I'd gotten home and found her missing. I'd been at a marathon meeting downtown, you know, going over the recycling stuff with some of the local EPA attorneys. I thought Ma'd had a bad turn, that the neighbors or Aunt Connie had taken her to the hospital. Then when the cops came for me I went a little crazy."

I nodded. "Lotty told me you'd called yesterday with an angry message. I just didn't have the strength to get back to you."

She looked at me directly for the first time since she'd arrived. "I don't blame you—I was mad enough to spit blood and then some. I was screaming my head off at you while I drove to Help of Christians. But when I got there all I could think of was you and your mother looking after Ma and me all those years. And then I thought of what you'd been through for the two of us just these last three weeks. And I felt terribly ashamed. It never would have happened if I hadn't pushed you into looking for my father when you didn't want to do it."

I took her hand and squeezed it. "I've been plenty mad at you—probably cursed you worse than you did me. And I'm not exactly wearing a halo—if I'd bugged out when you asked me to I'd never have been left for dead in the swamp and Louisa wouldn't have been kidnapped."

"But I don't think the police would ever have found out the truth," she objected. "They never would have found Nancy's killer, and Jurshak and Dresberg would still be ruling South Chicago. I shouldn't have been such a chicken—I should have told you about the threats to Louisa to begin with, so you wouldn't get blindsided."

I knew I needed to tell her about discovering who had gotten Louisa pregnant, but I couldn't seem to find the words. Or maybe it was just the courage. While I was fishing around for it Caroline said abruptly:

"I bought Ma some cigarettes. I remembered what you said that first night you came by, how they wouldn't make her any worse and they might cheer her up. And I could see all I was trying to do was have power over her, keeping her from having one thing that might bring her a little pleasure."

Her last words brought back Lotty's advice most strongly. I took a breath and said, "Caroline, I have to tell you—I did find out who your father was."

Her blue eyes turned very dark. "Not Joey Pankowski, right?"

I shook my head. "I'm afraid not. There isn't any easy way to say this, or to hear it, but it would be really wrong for me not to tell you—a most noxious way of controlling your life."

She looked at me solemnly. "Go ahead, Vic. I—I think I'm more grown up than I used to be. I can take it."

I took both her hands and said gently, "It was Art Jurshak. He was your—"

"Art Jurshak!" she burst out. "I don't believe you. Ma never would have come across him in a million years! You're making this up, aren't you?"

I shook my head. "I wish I were. Art—he—uh—your Grandmother Djiak is his sister. He used to spend a lot of time with Connie and Louisa when they were little, and the Djiaks chose not to notice that he was abusing them. Your grandparents are both terrified of sex, and your grandfather especially is frightened of women, so they made up a vile fairy tale for themselves that it was your mother's fault when she got pregnant. Although they did stop seeing Art, it was Louisa they punished. They're a pretty loathsome couple, Ed and Martha Djiak."

Her freckles stood out like polka dots against the pallor of her face. "Art Jurshak. He's my father? I'm related to him?"

"He gave you some chromosomes, babe, but you're not related to him, not by any manner of means. You're your own person, you know, not his. Not the Djiaks', either. You've got guts, you've got integrity, and, above all, you have valor. None of that has any relationship to Art Jurshak."

"I—Art Jurshak—" She gave a little bark of hysterical laughter. "All these years I thought your father had got Ma pregnant. I thought that was why your mother did so much for us. I thought I was really your sister. Now I see I don't have anyone at all."

She got up and ran for the door. I ran after her and caught her arm, but she wrenched herself free and jerked the door open.

"Caroline!" I tore down the stairs after her. "This doesn't change that. You will always be my sister, Caroline!"

I stood on the sidewalk in my shirt sleeves, watching helplessly as she drove recklessly down the street toward Belmont.

42

HUMBOLDT'S GIFT

I think the last time I felt this bad was the day after my mother's funeral, when her death suddenly became real to me. I tried calling Caroline, both at her house and at SCRAP. Both Louisa and a secretary agreed to take messages, but wherever Caroline was she didn't want to talk to me. A thousand times or so I thought of calling McGonnigal, asking the police to keep an eye out for her—but what could they do about one distraught citizen?

Around four I borrowed Peppy from Mr. Contreras and drove her over to the lake. I wasn't up to running, although she certainly was, but I needed her silent love and the expanse of sky and water to soothe my spirit. It wasn't out of the question that Humboldt, a sore loser if ever there was one, had some kind of backup to Dresberg, so I kept a hand on the Smith & Wesson in my jacket pocket.

I threw sticks left-handed for the dog. She didn't think much of the distance they went, but fetched them anyway to show she was a good sport. When she'd worked off some of her excess energy, we sat looking at the water while I kept my right hand on the gun.

In some remote part of my mind I knew I should think of a way to take the initiative with Humboldt, so that I didn't have to walk around with one hand in my pocket for the rest of my life. I could go to Ron Kappelman and force the issue with him, see how much he'd been feeding Jurshak about my investigation. Maybe he'd even know how to reach Humboldt.

The whole prospect of action seemed so impossible that just thinking about it made my eyelids feel leaden, my brain fogged over. Even the idea of getting up and walking to the car would take more effort than I could manage. I might have sat staring at the waves until spring if Peppy hadn't gotten fed up and started pushing me with her nose.

"You don't get it, do you?" I said to her. "Golden retrievers don't feel guilty about their neighbors' puppies. They don't feel obligated to look after them till death."

She agreed happily, tongue lolling. Whatever I said was fine as long as action accompanied it. We walked back to the car—or I walked and Peppy danced in a spiral around me to make sure I didn't stray or go back into catatonia.

When we got home Mr. Contreras came bustling out with Lotty's clean sheets and towels. I thanked him as best I could, but told him I wanted to be alone.

"I'd like to keep the dog awhile too. Okay?"

"Yeah, sure, doll, sure. Whatever you say. She misses your runs, that's for certain, so she'd probably be glad to stay with you, make sure you haven't forgotten her."

Back in my own place, I tried Caroline again, but she was still either gone or refusing to talk to me. Disheartened, I sat at the piano and picked my way through *"Ch'io scordi di te."* It had been Gabriella's favorite aria and it suited my mood of melancholy self-pity to play it through, then work at singing it. I felt tears of bathetic sorrow pricking my eyelids and went back to the middle, where the soprano line is most melodic.

When the phone rang I jumped up eagerly, sure it was Caroline willing finally to talk to me.

"Miss Warshawski?" It was the quavering voice of Humboldt's butler.

"Yes, Anton?" My voice was calm but an adrenaline surge cleared my lethargy like sunlight on fog.

"Mr. Humboldt would like to speak with you. Please hold." The voice held frosty disapproval. Perhaps he thought Humboldt wanted to make me his mistress and he feared I was too low class for the tone of the Roanoke.

A minute or so went by. I tried to get Peppy to come to the phone and act as my secretary but she wasn't interested. Finally Humboldt's rich baritone vibrated the earpiece.

"Ms. Warshawski. I would be most grateful if you would pay me a visit this evening. I have someone with me whom you would be sorry not to meet."

"Let's see," I said. "Dresberg and Jurshak are in the hospital. Troy is under arrest. Ron Kappelman isn't of much interest to me anymore. Who you got left?"

He gave his hearty chuckle to show that Monday's contretemps was just an unhappy memory. "You're always so direct, Ms. Warshawski. I assure you there will be no gunplay if you will pay me the courtesy of a visit."

"Knives? Hypodermics? Vats of chemicals?"

He laughed again. "Let us just say you would regret it forever if you did not meet my visitor. I'll send my car for you at six."

"You're very kind," I said formally, "but I prefer to drive myself. And I will bring a friend with me."

My heart was pounding when I hung up, and wild surmises flashed through my mind. He had Caroline hostage, or Lotty. I couldn't check on Caroline, but I did phone Lotty at the clinic. When she came to the phone, surprised at my urgency, I explained where I was going.

"If you don't hear from me by seven, call the police." I gave her Bobby's home and office numbers.

"You're not going alone, are you?" Lotty asked anxiously.

"No, no, I'm taking a friend."

"Vic! Not that meddlesome old man! He'll cause more trouble than he'll save you."

I laughed a little. "No, I agree with you totally. I'm taking someone who's silent and reliable."

Only after I promised to call her as soon as I got away from the Roanoke would she agree to my going without a police escort. When she'd hung up I turned to Peppy. "Come on, babe. You're going to the haunts of the rich and powerful."

The dog expressed herself interested as always in any expedition. She watched, her head cocked, while I checked the Smith & Wesson one last time to make sure a bullet was chambered, then bounded down the stairs ahead of me. We managed to make it outside without a checkup by Mr. Contreras— he must have been in the kitchen making supper.

I looked around cautiously to make sure I wasn't walking into an ambush, but no one was lying in wait. Peppy jumped into the backseat of the Chevy and we headed south.

The doorman at the Roanoke greeted me with the same avuncular courtesy I'd had on my first visit. Apparently Anton hadn't told him I was a menace to society. Or the memory of my five-dollar tip outweighed any nasty messages from the twelfth floor.

"The dog is accompanying you, ma'am?"

I smiled. "Mr. Humboldt is expecting her."

"Very good, ma'am." He turned us over to Fred at the elevator.

I moved with practiced grace to the little bench at the rear. Peppy sat alertly at my feet, her tongue hanging out, panting a little. She wasn't used to elevators, but she took the uncertain flooring with the cool poise of a champion. When we'd been decanted she sniffed around the marble floor of Humboldt's lobby, but came to attention at my side when Anton opened the ornate wooden door.

He looked coldly at Peppy. "We prefer not having dogs up here, as their habits are difficult to predict or control. I'll ask Marcus to keep her in the lobby until you're ready to leave."

I grinned a little savagely. "Uncontrollable habits sound as though they should mesh perfectly with your boss's style. I'm not coming in without her, so make up your mind how bad Humboldt wants to see me."

"Very good, madam." The frost in his voice had moved into the low Kelvin range. "If you will follow me?"

Humboldt was seated in front of his library fire. He was drinking out of a heavily cut glass—whiskey and soda as nearly as I could tell. My stomach twisted as I watched him, my anger returning and jolting my system.

Humboldt looked severely at Anton when Peppy came in at my left heel, but the majordomo said aloofly that I refused to see him without her. Humboldt immediately switched personae, genially asking the dog's name and trying to make much of her beauty. She'd picked up his antagonism, though, and didn't respond. I ostentatiously walked around the room with her, inviting her to sniff in corners. I flicked back the heavy brocade curtains, but the view was of the lake—there was no place for a sniper to hide.

I dropped the curtain. "I was kind of expecting a burst of machine-gun fire. Don't tell me my life is going to settle into monotony."

Humboldt gave his rich little chuckle. "Nothing affects you, does it, Ms. Warshawski? You really are a most remarkable young woman."

I sat in the armchair facing Humboldt; Peppy stood in front of me, looking from him to me with concern, her tail down. I patted her head and she went down on her haunches without relaxing.

"Your mystery guest hasn't arrived yet?"

"My guest will keep." He chuckled gently to himself. "I thought you and I could have a little chat first. It might not be necessary to produce my visitor. Whiskey?"

I shook my head. "Your rarefied cellars are giving me ideas above my income, I can't afford to get used to them."

"But you could, Ms. Warshawski. You could, you know, if you would stop going around with that outsize chip on your shoulder."

I leaned back in the chair and crossed my legs. "Now that is really unworthy of you. I expected a much grander, or at least more subtle, approach."

"Now, now, Ms. Warshawski. You're too hasty to react much of the time. You could do worse than listen to me."

"Yeah, I guess I could follow the Cubs on a road trip. But you might as well spit it out now so I'll know if I have to dodge your minions' bullets for the rest of my life."

He refused to let himself get ruffled. "You've paid a great deal of attention to my affairs recently, Ms. Warshawski. So I've returned the compliment and paid much attention to yours."

"I bet my researches were a lot more exciting than yours." I kept my hand on Peppy's head.

"Perhaps we have different ideas of what might prove exciting. For instance, I was most intrigued to learn that you owe a balance of fifty thousand dollars on your apartment and that your mortgage payments are not easy for you to meet."

"Oh, God, Gustav. You aren't going to pull the old I'll-get-the-bank-to-cut-off-your-mortgage routine, are you? That's getting pretty boring."

He continued as though I hadn't spoken. "Your parents are both dead, I understand. But you have a good friend who stands toward you as sort of a mother, I believe—this Dr. Charlotte Herschel. Yes?"

I tightened my fingers so strongly in Peppy's hair that she gave a little yelp. "If anything happens to Dr. Herschel—*anything*—from a flat tire to a bloody nose—you will be dead within twenty-four hours. That's a cast-iron prophecy."

He gave his hearty chuckle. "You're so active, Ms. Warshawski, that you imagine everyone must be as energetic as yourself. No, I was more concerned about Dr. Herschel's medical practice. Whether she would be able to keep her license."

He waited for me to react again, but I'd managed to regain enough self-control to keep quiet. I picked up *The New York Times* from the little table that lay between us and flipped to the sports section. The Islanders were on a roll—how disappointing.

"You're not curious, Ms. Warshawski?" he finally asked.

"Not especially." I turned to a discussion of the Mets' prospects going into training camp. "I mean, there're so many creepy things you might do it'd be a waste of energy wondering which particular one you've lighted on this time."

He put his whiskey glass down with a snap and leaned forward. Peppy growled a little in the back of her throat. I put what looked like a restraining hand on her—it's hard to imagine a golden retriever attacking someone, but if you don't like dogs, you might not know that.

He kept an eye on Peppy. "So you are prepared to sacrifice your home and Dr. Herschel's career to your stubborn pride?"

"What do you want me to do?" I said irritably. "Lie on the floor and kick and scream? I'm prepared to believe you have much more in the way of power, money, whatever than I do. You want to rub my nose in it, be my guest. Just don't expect me to act real excited about it."

"Don't jump so quickly to conclusions, Ms. Warshawski," he said plaintively. "You're not without options. You just don't want to hear what they are."

"Okay." I smiled brightly. "Tell me."

"Get your dog to lie down first."

I gave Peppy a hand signal and she obediently dropped to the floor, but she kept her back haunches tensed, ready to jump.

"I'm only offering possibilities. You mustn't be so quick to react to the first one. It's just one scenario, you see, your mortgage, Dr. Herschel's license. There are others. You might be able to pay off that debt with enough money left to get yourself a car more suited to your personality than that old Chevy—you see, I have been doing my research. What would you drive if you had the opportunity?"

"Gosh, I don't know, Mr. Humboldt. I haven't thought a lot about it. Maybe I'd move up to a Buick."

He sighed like a disappointed father. "You should listen to me seriously, young lady, or you will soon find yourself out of options."

"Okay, okay," I said. "I'd like to drive a Ferrari, but Magnum's already doing that. Maybe an Alfa . . . So you'll give me my co-op and a sports car and Dr. Herschel's license. What would you like from me as a show of gratitude for such generosity?"

He smiled: everyone can be pressured or bought. "Dr. Chigwell. A willing, hardworking man, but not, alas, of great ability. Unfortunately, to have a doctor at an industrial location does not give one access to physicians of Dr. Herschel's caliber."

I put the paper down and stopped petting the dog to prove I was all attention.

"He kept some notes over the years on our employees at Xerxes. Without my knowledge, of course—I can't keep on top of all the details of an operation the size of Humboldt."

"You and Ronald Reagan," I murmured sympathetically.

He looked at me suspiciously, but I kept an expression of intent interest on my face.

"I only recently learned about these notes. The information in them is useless because it's totally inaccurate. But in the wrong hands it might look most damaging to Xerxes. It could be difficult for me to prove that all the data he collected were wrong."

"Especially over a twenty-year period," I said. "But if you could get those notebooks, you would give me my mortgage? And withdraw any threat to Dr. Herschel?"

"There would also be a bonus for you because of the amount of trouble you've been subjected to by some of my overly zealous friends."

He reached inside his jacket pocket and held out a piece of parchment for me to look at. After glancing at it casually I dropped it on the little table between us. My coolness took an effort—the document represented two thousand preferred shares of Humboldt Chemical. I picked up the *Times* again and looked at the stock summaries.

"Closed at 101 3/8 yesterday. A two-hundred-thousand-dollar bonus with no brokerage fees. I'm impressed." I leaned back in the chair and looked at him squarely. "Trouble is, I could double that just by shorting Humboldt. If money was that important to me. It just isn't. And you're shit out of luck on the notebooks, anyway—they've already gone both to an attorney and to a team of medical specialists. You're dead. I don't know what the value of the coming lawsuits is, but half a billion probably isn't too far off the mark."

"You'd rather put your friend, the woman who has stood as a mother to you, out of practice, for the sake of some people you never met and who aren't worth your consideration anyway?"

"If you've been doing research on me, you know that Louisa Djiak isn't a casual acquaintance," I snapped. "And I defy you to think of any threat to Dr. Herschel that her reputation for probity wouldn't be equal to."

He gave a smile that made him look very like a shark. "Really, Ms. Warshawski. You must learn not to be so hasty. I would not make any threat I didn't feel competent to execute."

He rang a bell tucked into the mantel. Anton appeared so quickly, he must have been hovering in the hallway.

"Bring our other visitor, Anton."

The butler inclined his head and left. He returned a moment or two later with a woman of about twenty-five. Her brown hair was permed around her head in tight little corkscrews that exposed too much of her blotchy neck. She had obviously made an effort over her appearance; I supposed the ruffled acetate dress was her best, since the boxy high heels had been dyed a matching aqua. Under the thick pancake covering her acne she looked belligerent and a little frightened.

"This is Mrs. Portis, Ms. Warshawski. Her daughter was a patient of Dr. Herschel's. Isn't that right, Mrs. Portis?"

She nodded vigorously. "My Mandy. And Dr. Herschel did what she should have known better than to do, a grown woman with a little girl. Mandy was crying and screaming when she came out of the examining room, it took me days to get her settled down again and find out what went on. But when I found out—"

"You went to the state's attorney and made a full report," I finished smoothly, despite a rage that was making my cheeks flame.

"She was naturally too disturbed to know what do to," Humboldt said with an unctuousness that made me want to shoot him. "It's very difficult to bring charges against a family doctor, especially one who can summon the support that Dr. Herschel can. That's why I feel grateful for my own position, which enables me to help out a woman like this."

I stared incredulously at him. "You really think you can take someone with Dr. Herschel's reputation to court with a woman like this as your witness? An expert lawyer will shred her. You're not just an egomaniac, Humboldt—you're stupid with it."

"Be careful whom you call stupid, young lady—an expert lawyer can make anyone break down. Nothing turns a jury hostile faster. And besides, what would the publicity do to Dr. Herschel's practice? Not to mention the state licensing board? Especially if Mrs. Portis is joined by other worried mothers whose daughters Dr. Herschel has treated. After all, Dr. Herschel is almost sixty and has never married—a jury would be bound to suspect her sexual preferences."

The pulse in my neck was throbbing so violently, I could hardly breathe, let alone think. The dog was whimpering a little at my feet. I forced myself to stroke her gently; it helped slow my heartbeat a little. I got up and moved to a phone on a corner table, Peppy close on my heels.

Lotty was still at the clinic. "Vic! You're all right? It's nearly seven now."

"I'm okay physically, Dr. Herschel. But mentally I'm slightly deranged. I need to explain something to you and get your reaction. Do you have a patient named Mrs. Portis?"

Lotty was puzzled but didn't ask any questions. She came back to the phone quickly. "A woman who saw me once two years ago. Her daughter Amanda was eight at the time and throwing up a lot. I suggested psychological problems and it drove her away in a huff."

"Well, Humboldt has dug her up out of some ditch. And gotten her to agree to claim you abused her daughter. Sexually, you understand. Unless we turn Chigwell's notebooks over to him."

Lotty was silent a moment. "My license for the notebooks in other words?" she finally said. "And you thought you had to call to get my answer?"

"I didn't feel able to speak for you on such a matter. He's also offering me two hundred K in stock shares, just so you know the size of the bribe. And my mortgage."

"Is he with you? I will speak to him myself. But you should know I will tell him that I did not see my parents killed by Fascists only to bow down to them in my old age."

I turned to Humboldt. "Dr. Herschel would like to talk to you."

He pushed himself out of his armchair. Almost the only sign of his age was the effort it took when he got up. I stood next to him as he spoke to Lotty, my breath coming in short noisy pants. I could hear her concise alto going on at length, lecturing him as she might a failing student, although I couldn't make out the exact words.

"You are making a mistake, Doctor, a most serious error," Humboldt said heavily. "No, no, I will not be insulted further on my own phone, madam."

He hung up and glared at me. "You will be very sorry. Both of you. I don't think you appreciate how very much power I have in this town, young lady."

The pulse in my neck was still throbbing. "There are so many things you don't appreciate, Gustav, that I hardly know where to start. You're dead. You're through in this town. The *Herald-Star* is working on your connection to Steve Dresberg and believe me, they'll find it. You may think you have it buried fifty layers deep, but Murray Ryerson is a good archaeologist and he's burning right now.

"But more than that, your company is through. Your little chemical emporium just ain't big enough to absorb the shock when those Xerxine suits start pouring in. It may be six months, it may take two years, but you're looking at half a billion in claims, easy. And it's going to be like shooting rats in a barrel to prove malicious intent on your part—Humboldt's part. That company you built up—it's going to be like Jonah's gourd—grew in a night and withered in a night. You're dead meat, Humboldt, and you're so crazy you can't even smell the rot."

"You're wrong, you little Polish bitch! I'll show you how wrong you are!" He hurled his whiskey glass across the room where it smashed into one of the bookcases. "I'll break you just as easily as that glass. Gordon Firth will never hire you again. You'll lose your license. You'll never get another client again. I'll see you on West Madison with the other drunks and has-beens and I'll laugh at you. I'll roar with laughter."

"You do that," I said fiercely. "I'm sure your grandchildren will be much entertained by the spectacle. In fact, I bet they'd like to hear the whole story of how you poisoned people to maximize your goddamned bottom line."

"My grandchildren!" he roared. "If you dare come near them, neither you nor your friends will ever know another night's sleep in this city!"

He kept shouting, his threats escalating to include not just Lotty but other friends whose names his researchers had dredged up. Peppy's hackles rose and she growled menacingly. I kept one hand on her collar and pressed the buzzer in the mantel with the other. When Anton came I pointed at the shattered glass.

"You may want to clean that up. And I think Mrs. Portis would be more comfortable if you'd send her down to Marcus to get a cab. Come, Peppy." We left as quickly as we could, but it seemed I could hear that maniacal bellow all the way to the lobby.

43
BRINGING IT ALL BACK HOME

Lotty and I spent the next few days with my lawyer. I don't know if it was Carter Freeman's efforts, or Anton's, or just that the scene at the Roanoke had terrified her, but Mrs. Portis lost interest in bringing charges against Lotty. We had a tougher time over my mortgage—for a few weeks it looked as though I might have to find a place to rent. But Freeman managed to settle that somehow, too. I've always suspected that he put up a guarantee himself, but he only raises his brows and feigns ignorance and changes the conversation when I try asking him.

After a bit my life regained its normal flow—running Peppy, spending time with friends, breaking my heart over Chicago's sports teams—the Black Hawks at that particular season. I returned, too, to my normal workload, looking at industrial fraud, doing background searches on candidates for sensitive financial positions, that kind of thing.

I worked hard to keep thoughts of Humboldt and South Chicago at bay. In the normal course of things I wouldn't let loose ends drift away at the end of a case, but I just couldn't take any more involvement in the old neighborhood. So I decided to leave Ron Kappelman's role in the mess as an unanswered question. If Bobby's accusation was true, that he'd been feeding Jurshak news of my whereabouts, I should by rights go down to Pullman and confront him. I just didn't have the mental energy to pursue it any further, though. Let the state's attorney figure it all out when Jurshak and Dresberg came to trial.

Sergeant McGonnigal was another loose end that never got tied up. I saw him with Bobby a couple of times while going over endless statements and interrogations. He acted pretty cold until he realized I wasn't going to blow the whistle on his late-night lapse from policeman decorum. Over time I knew I was better off not getting too cozy with a cop, however empathic, but we never talked about it.

By May, with the Cubs already vying for last place, Humboldt Chemical was trading in the high fifties. Frederick Manheim had consulted enough experts in law and medicine that whispers of possible trouble had followed the trade winds east to Wall Street. Manheim came to consult with me a couple of times, but I was weary to the depths of my spirit of Humboldt.

I told Manheim I'd testify at any trials about my role in learning of the cover-up, but not to count on me for any other support. So I didn't know what Humboldt was doing to prepare a counterattack. A blurb in the papers a few days after our final encounter said he was being treated for stress at Passavant, but since the *Herald-Star* ran a photo of him throwing out the first pitch for the Sox on opening day, I guess he'd gotten over it.

Round about that time, as the Cubs moved north from Tempe, I got a postcard from Florence. "Don't wait until you're seventy-nine to see it," ran the brief message in Ms. Chigwell's spidery hand. When she returned home a few weeks later she called me.

"I just wanted to let you know that I'm not living with Curtis anymore. I bought his share in the house from him. He's gone to a retirement home in Clarendon Hills."

"How do you like living alone?"

"Very much. I just wish I'd done it sixty years ago, but I didn't have the courage to do it then. I wanted to tell you, because you're the one who made it possible, showing me how a woman can live an independent life. That's all."

She hung up on my incoherent protest. I smiled a little—gruff to the end. I hoped I was that tough forty years ahead.

The only thing that really troubled me was Caroline Djiak; I couldn't get her to talk to me. She'd resurfaced after a day's absence, but she wouldn't come to the phone, and when I drove down to Houston Street she shut the door on me, not even letting me in to see Louisa. I kept thinking I'd made a terrible mistake—not just in telling her about Jurshak, but in keeping up my dogged search when she'd been trying to call me off.

Lotty shook her head sternly when I fretted about it. "You're not God, Victoria. You can't pick and choose what's best for people's lives. And if you're going to spend hours in lachrymose self-pity, please do it someplace else—it's not an appetizing spectacle. Or find another line of work. Your dogged searches, as you call them, spring from a fundamental clarity of vision. If you no longer have that sight, you no longer are suited to your job."

Her bracing words didn't kill my self-doubts, but in time even my worries over Caroline receded. When she called in early June to tell me Louisa had died, I could accept her abrupt conversation with relative equanimity.

I went to the funeral at St. Wenceslaus, but not to the house on Houston for food afterward. Louisa's parents were running the event, and whether they aped pious grief or murmured sly animadversions on divine providence I would be hard put to control my desire to decimate them.

Caroline made no effort to speak to me at the service; by the time I got home my lachrymose self-pity over her had been replaced by an older, more familiar feeling—irritation at her brattiness. So when I found her waiting on my doorstep a month or so later, I didn't exactly welcome her with open arms.

"I've been here since three," she said without introduction. "I was afraid you'd gone out of town."

"Sorry I didn't leave my schedule with your secretary," I replied sardonically. "But then, of course, I wasn't anticipating the pleasure."

"Don't be mean, Vic," she begged. "I know I deserve it—I've been a horse's rear end the last four months. But I need to apologize or explain or— well, anyway, I don't want you only to be mad when you think about me."

I unlocked the lobby door. "You know, Caroline, I'm reminded irresistibly of Lucy and Charlie Brown and the football. You know how she always promises *this* time she won't pull it away just as he's kicking—and she always does, and he always lands smack on his butt? I have a feeling I'm about to end on my ass one last time, but come on up."

Her ready color came. "Vic, please—I know I deserve anything you want to say to me, but I've come here to apologize. Don't make it harder on me than it already is."

That shut me up, but it didn't quiet my suspicions. I led her silently to my apartment, fixed her a Coke while I had a rum and tonic, and took her to the little ledge that serves as my back porch. Mr. Contreras waved at us from his tomatoes, but stayed below. The dog came up to join the party.

After she'd fondled Peppy's ears and drunk her soda, Caroline took a deep breath and said, "Vic, I really am sorry I ran out on you last winter, and —and avoided you afterward. Somehow—somehow it's only since Louisa died that I could see it from your viewpoint. See that you weren't making fun of me."

"Making fun of you!" I was astonished.

She turned crimson again. "I thought, you see, you had such a wonderful father. I loved your dad so much, I wanted him to be my father too. I used to lie in bed and imagine it, imagine how much fun we'd have when we were all together as a family, him and me and Ma and Gabriella. And you'd be my real sister, so you wouldn't feel pissed off at having to look after me."

It was my turn to be embarrassed. I tried muttering something and finally said, "No eleven-year-old wants to be saddled with looking after a baby. I expect if you'd really been my sister, I would have been more annoyed instead of less. But I wasn't laughing at you for having a—a different father than mine. It never once crossed my mind."

"I know that now," she said. "It just took me a long time to figure it out. It was me that felt humiliated at the idea of Art Jurshak being—well, doing that to Ma. You know. Then when she died I suddenly saw what it must have been like for her. And it made me realize what a remarkable woman she was, because she was such a good mother, she was so lively, and really loved life and everything. And it would have been so easy for her to be angry and bitter and take it out on me."

She looked at me earnestly. "Then last week I went—went to see young Art. My brother, I guess he is. He was pretty good about it, even though I could see it was just hell for him. Having to talk to me, I mean. It was awful for him growing up. Art wasn't any kind of father. He only got married to keep the Djiaks from spoiling his political career, and after young Art was born he moved into the spare bedroom. He never wanted to have anything to do with his own son. So in a crazy kind of way I can see I was better off. You know, just with Ma. Even if—even if he hadn't been her uncle, it would have been so much worse living with him than it was growing up without a father."

My throat was a little tight. "I've been full of self-recriminations these last four months, thinking I made the colossal mistake of an egomaniac in keeping on the case when you asked me to quit. And then in telling you about him."

"Don't," she said. "I'm glad to know. It's better to find out for sure, rather than imagine it in my head, even if what I made up was a hell of a lot nicer than what reality turned out to be. Besides, if Tony Warshawski had really been my father, he'd seem like a pretty big sleaze moving Ma and me next door to you and Gabriella."

She laughed, but I took her hand and held it. After a bit she said hesitantly, "I—this next part is hard to tell you, after all the insults I shouted at you about leaving the neighborhood. But I'm leaving, too. I'm moving away from Chicago, actually. I always wanted to live out in the country, the real country, so I'm going to Montana to study forestry. I never admitted it to anyone, because I thought if I wasn't like you, doing social activism stuff, you know, that you would despise me."

I gave an inarticulate squawk that made Peppy jump.

"No, really, Vic. But all these things I've been thinking about, well, I see you never wanted me to be like you. It was just part of my head trip, how I thought if I did the same things you did, you would like me well enough to let me really be part of your family."

"No way, babe—I want you doing what's good for you, not what's right for me."

She nodded. "So I applied out there and rushed everything through and I'm leaving in two weeks. I'm making Ma's folks buy the house on Houston and that's giving me the money to go. But I wanted to tell you in person, and I hope you meant it, that you'll always be my sister, because, well, anyway, I hope you meant it."

I knelt next to her chair and put my arms around her. "Till death do us part, kid."

BURN MARKS

For Patti Shepherd, Jayanne Angell,
and Bill Mullins,
who believed in my writing before I did

THANKS

Angelo Polvere of the Mayfair Construction Company in Chicago provided me an overview of how a general contractor builds a major project and how a contractor's office works. Jay Meyer took me to the top of a sixty-story high rise going up in Chicago and walked me back down, explaining the different stages of construction. I experienced the terrors of an unenclosed concrete deck firsthand. Ed Keane made these connections for me. My ignorance of big projects greatly exceeds my knowledge—any errors of fact should be credited to my poor understanding rather than to these excellent teachers.

Ray Gibson shared different research tools for covering the kinds of things V.I. looks into in this book. Dr. Robert Kirschner, Chief Deputy Medical Examiner for Cook County, gave me a grand tour of the county morgue. It was not pleasant but it was enlightening.

As is always the case in V.I.'s adventures, no reference is made to any real public figures currently serving time or in office. Boots Meagher, Ralph MacDonald, Roz Fuentes, Alma Mejicana, and Wunsch and Grasso are products of my perfervid imagination. Nor is the construction at Rapelec Towers based on any building now standing or under construction in Chicago.

Courtenay, Cardhu, and other friends supported me through the various trials that beset me in writing this book.

CONTENTS

1 WAKE-UP CALL

My mother and I were trapped in her bedroom, the tiny upstairs room of our old house on Houston. Down below the dogs barked and snapped as they hunted us. Gabriella had fled the fascists of her native Italy but they tracked her all the way to South Chicago. The dogs' barking grew to an ear-splitting roar, drowning my mother's screams.

I sat up. It was three in the morning and someone was leaning on the doorbell. I was sweaty and trembling from the dream's insistent realism.

The urgent ringing recalled all the times in my childhood the phone or doorbell had roused my father to some police emergency. My mother and I would wait up for his return. She refused to admit her fear, although it stared at me through her fierce dark eyes, but would make sweet children's coffee for me in the kitchen—a tablespoon of coffee mixed with milk and chocolate —and tell me wild Italian folktales that made my heart race.

I pulled on a sweatshirt and shorts and fumbled with the locks to my door. The ringing echoed through the stairwell behind me as I stumbled down the three flights to the front entryway.

My aunt Elena stood on the other side of the glass door, her finger pressed determinedly to the bell. A faded quilt made an ungainly cloak around her shoulders. She had propped a vinyl duffel bag against the wall; a violet nightgown trailed from its top. I don't believe in prescience or ESP, but I couldn't help feeling that my dream—a familiar childhood nightmare— had been caused by some murky vibrations emanating from Elena to my bedroom.

My father's younger sister, Elena had always been the family Problem. "She drinks a little, you know," my grandmother Warshawski would tell people in a worried whisper after Elena had passed out at Thanksgiving dinner. More than once an embarrassed patrolman roused my dad at two in the morning to tell him Elena had been busted for soliciting on Clark Street. On those nights there were no fairy tales in the kitchen. My mother would send me back to my own bed with a tiny shake of the head, saying, "It's her nature, *cara*, we mustn't judge her."

When my grandmother died seven years ago, my father's surviving brother, Peter, gave his share of the Norwood Park bungalow to Elena on condition that she never ask him for anything else. She blithely signed the papers, but lost the bungalow four years later—without talking to me or Peter she had put it up as collateral in a wild development venture. When the fly-by-night company evaporated, she was the only partner the courts could find—they confiscated the house and sold it to meet the limited partnership's bills.

Three thousand remained after paying the debts. With that and her social security, Elena had been living in an SRO at Cermak and Indiana, playing a little twenty-one and still turning the occasional trick on the day the pension checks arrived. Despite years of drinking that had carved narrow furrows in her chin and forehead, she had remarkably good legs.

She caught sight of me through the glass and took her finger from the bell. When I opened the door she put her arms around me and gave me an enthusiastic kiss.

"Victoria, sweetie, you look terrific!"

The sour yeasty smell of stale beer poured over me. "Elena—what the hell are you doing here?"

The generous mouth pouted. "Baby, I need a place to stay. I'm desperate. The cops were going to take me to a shelter but of course I remembered you and they brought me here instead. A *very* nice young man with an absolutely gorgeous smile. I told him all about your daddy but he was just a boy, of course he'd never met him."

I ground my teeth together. "What happened to your hotel? They kick you out for screwing the old-age pensioners?"

"Vicki, baby—Victoria," she amended hastily. "Don't talk dirty—it doesn't sound right coming from a sweet girl like you."

"Elena, cut the crap." As she started a second reproach I corrected myself hastily. "I mean stop talking nonsense and tell me why you're out on the streets at three in the morning."

She pouted some more. "I'm trying to tell you, baby, but you keep interrupting. There was a fire. Our lovely little home was burned to the ground. Burned to an absolute crisp."

Tears welled in her faded blue eyes and coursed through deep furrows to her neck. "I hadn't gone to sleep yet and I just had time to stuff my things into a suitcase and get down the fire escape. Some people couldn't even do that much. Poor Marty Holman had to leave his false teeth behind." The tears stopped as abruptly as they began, to be replaced by a high-pitched giggle. "You should have seen him, Vicki, my God, you should have seen what the old geezer looked like with his cheeks all sunk in and his eyes popping out and him shouting in this mumbly kind of way, 'My teeth, I've lost my teeth.' "

"It must have been hilarious," I said dryly. "You cannot live with me, Elena. It would drive me to homicide within forty-eight hours. Maybe less."

Her lower lip started to tremble again and she said in a terrible parody of baby talk, "Don't be mean to me, Vicki, don't be mean to poor old Elena, who got burned out of her house in the middle of the night. You're my own goddamn flesh and blood, my favorite brother's little girl. You can't toss poor old Elena out on the street like some worn-out mattress."

A door slammed sharply behind us. The banker who had just moved into the first-floor-north apartment erupted into the stairwell, his hands on his hips, his jaw sticking out pugnaciously. He was wearing navy-striped cotton pajamas; despite the bleary sleep in his face, his hair was perfectly combed.

"What the hell is going on out here? You may not have to work for a living—God knows what you do all day long up there—but I do. If you have to conduct your business in the middle of the night, show *some* consideration for your neighbors and don't do it out in the hall. If you don't shut up and get the hell out of here, I'm calling the cops."

I stared at him coldly. "I run a crack house upstairs. This is my supplier. You could be arrested for complicity if you're found hanging around out here when the police arrive."

Elena giggled, but said, "Don't be rude to him, Victoria—you never know when you may want a boy with fabulous eyes like that to do something for you." She added to the banker, "Don't worry, sweetie, I'm just coming in. We'll let you get your beauty sleep."

Behind the closed door to one-south a dog began to bark. I ground my teeth some more and hustled Elena inside, snatching her duffel bag from her when she began wobbling under its weight.

The banker watched us through narrowed eyes. When Elena lurched against him he made a face of pure horror and retreated hastily to his apartment, fumbling with the lock. I tried moving Elena upstairs, but she wanted to stop and talk about the banker, demanding to know why I hadn't asked him to carry her bag.

"It would have been a perfect way for you two to get acquainted, make things up a little."

I was close to screaming with frustration when the door to one-south opened. Mr. Contreras came out, a staggering sight in a crimson dressing gown. The golden retriever I share with him was straining against her collar, but when she saw me her low-throated growls changed to whimpers of excitement.

"Oh, it's you, doll," the old man said with relief. "The princess here woke me up and then I heard all the noise and thought, Oh my God, the worst is happening, someone's breaking in in the middle of the night. You oughta be more considerate, doll—it's hard for people who have to work to get up in the middle of the night like this."

"Yes, it is," I agreed brightly. "And contrary to public opinion, I am one of those working people. And believe me, I had no more desire to get out of bed at three A.M. than you did."

Elena put on her warmest smile and stuck out her hand to Mr. Contreras like Princess Diana greeting a soldier. "Elena Warshawski," she said. "Charmed to meet you. This little girl is my niece, and she's the prettiest, sweetest niece anybody could hope for."

Mr. Contreras shook her hand, blinking at her like an owl with a flashlight in its face. "Pleased to meet you," he said automatically if unenthusiastically.

"Look, doll, you oughta get this lady—your aunt, you say?—you oughta get her up to bed. She ain't doing too great."

The sour yeasty smell had swept over him too. "Yep, that's just what I'll do. Come on, Elena. Let's get upstairs. Beddy-bye time."

Mr. Contreras headed back into his apartment. The dog was annoyed—if we were all having a party she wanted to join in.

"That wasn't very polite of him," Elena sniffed as Mr. Contreras's door closed behind us. "Didn't even tell me his own name when I went out of my way to introduce myself."

She grumbled all the way up the stairs. I didn't say anything, just kept a hand in the small of her back to propel her in the right direction, urging her on when she tried to stop for a breather at the second-floor landing.

Back in my apartment she wanted to ooh and aah over all my possessions. I ignored her and moved the coffee table so I could pull the bed out of the couch. I made it up and showed her where the bathroom was.

"Now listen, Elena. You are not staying here more than one night. Don't even think I'm going to waffle on this because I won't."

"Sure, baby, sure. What happened to your ma's piano? You sell it or something to buy this sweet little grand?"

"No," I said shortly. My mother's piano had been destroyed in the fire that gutted my own apartment three years earlier. "And don't think you can make me forget what I'm saying by raving over the piano. I'm going back to bed. You can sleep or not as you please, but in the morning you're going someplace else."

"Oh, don't look so ugly, Vicki. Victoria, I mean. It'll ruin your complexion if you frown like that. And where else am I supposed to turn in the middle of the night if not to my own flesh and blood?"

"Knock it off," I said wearily. "I'm too tired for it."

I shut the hall door without saying good night. I didn't bother to warn her not to rummage around for my liquor—if she wanted it badly enough, she'd find it, then apologize to me a hundred times the next day for breaking her promise not to drink it.

I lay in bed unable to sleep, feeling the pressure of Elena's presence from the next room. I could hear her scrabbling around for a while, then the hum of the TV turned conscientiously to low volume. I cursed my uncle Peter for moving to Kansas City and wished I'd had the foresight to hightail it to Quebec or Seattle or some other place equally remote from Chicago. Around five, as the birds began their predawn twittering, I finally dropped into an uneasy sleep.

2

THE LOWER DEPTHS

The doorbell jerked me awake again at eight. I pulled my sweat-shirt and shorts back on and stumbled into the living room. Nobody answered my query through the intercom. When I looked out the living-room window at the street, I could see the banker heading toward Diversey, his shoulders bobbing smugly. I flicked my thumb at his back.

Elena had slept through the episode, including my loud calls through the intercom. For a moment I felt possessed by the banker's angry impulse—I wanted to wake her and make her as uncomfortable as I was.

I stared down at her in disgust. She was lying on her back, mouth open, ragged snores jerking out as she inhaled, puffy short breaths as she exhaled. Her face was flushed. The broken veins on her nose stood out clearly. In the morning light I could see that the violet nightgown was long overdue for the laundry. The sight was appalling. But it was also unbearably pathetic. No one should be exposed to an outsider's view while she's sleeping, let alone someone as vulnerable as my aunt.

With a shudder I moved hastily to the back of the apartment. Unfortunately her pathos couldn't quell my anger at having her with me. Thanks to her, my head felt as though someone had dumped a load of gravel in it. Even worse, I was making a presentation to a potential client tomorrow. I wanted to finish my charts and get them turned into transparencies. Instead, it looked as though I'd be spending the day hunting for housing. Depending on how long that took, I could end up paying as much as quadruple overtime for the transparencies.

I sat on the dining-room floor and did some breathing exercises, trying to ease my knotted stomach. Finally I managed to relax enough to do my prerun stretches.

Not wanting to see Elena's flushed face again, I went down the back way, picking up Peppy outside Mr. Contreras's kitchen door. The old man stuck his head out and called to me as I closed the gate; I pretended not to hear him. I wasn't able to be similarly deaf when I got back—he was waiting for me, sitting on the back stairs with the *Sun-Times,* checking out his day's picks for Hawthorne. I tried leaving the dog and escaping up the stairs but he grabbed my hand.

"Hang on a second there, cookie. Who was that lady you was letting in last night?" Mr. Contreras is a retired machinist, a widower with a married daughter whom he doesn't particularly like. During the three years we've been living in the same building he's attached himself to my life like an adoptive uncle—or maybe a barnacle.

I jerked my hand free. "My aunt. My father's younger sister. She has a penchant for old men with good retirement benefits, so make sure you have all your clothes on if she stops by to chat this afternoon."

That kind of comment always makes him huffy. I'm sure he heard—and said—plenty worse on the floor in his machinist days—but he can't take even oblique references to sex from me. He turns red and gets as close to being angry as someone with his relentlessly cheerful disposition can manage.

"There's no need to talk dirty to me," he snapped. "I'm just concerned. And I gotta say, cookie, you shouldn't let people come see you at all hours like that. Least, if you do, you shouldn't keep them down in the hall talking loud enough to wake every soul in the building."

I felt like wrenching one of the loose slats from the stairwell railing and beating him with it. "I didn't invite her," I shrieked. "I didn't know she was coming. I didn't want her here. I didn't want to wake up at three in the morning."

"There's no need to shout," he said severely. "And even if you wasn't expecting her, you could'a gone up to your apartment to talk."

I opened and shut my mouth several times but couldn't construct a coherent response. Anyway, I'd kept Elena in the hall in the hopes she'd feel hurt enough to just pick up the duffel bag and go. But even as I'd done it I'd known in my heart of hearts that I couldn't turn her away at that hour. So the old man was right. Agreeing with him didn't make me any happier.

"Okay, okay," I snapped. "It won't happen again. Now get off my back —I've got a lot to do today." I stomped up the stairs to my kitchen.

Muted snores still seeped through the closed door from the living room. I made a pot of coffee and took a cup into the bathroom with me while I showered. Bent on leaving the apartment as fast as possible, I pulled on jeans and a white shirt and stopped in the kitchen to scratch together a breakfast.

Elena was sitting at the breakfast table. She'd put a soiled quilted dressing gown over the violet nightie. Her hands shook slightly; she used both of them to lift a cup of coffee to her mouth.

She produced an eager smile. "Wonderful coffee you make, baby. Just as good as your ma's."

"Thank you, Elena." I opened the refrigerator door and took stock of the meager contents. "I'm sorry I can't stay to chat, but I want to try to find you someplace to sleep tonight."

"Aw, Vicki—Victoria, I mean. Don't rush around like that. It ain't good for the heart. Let me stay here, just for a few days, anyway. Get over the shock of living through that inferno last night. I promise I won't bother you any. And I could get the place cleaned up a little while you're at work."

I shook my head implacably. "No way, Elena. I will not have you living here. Not one night longer."

Her face puckered. "Why do you hate me, baby? I'm your own daddy's sister. Family has to stick by family."

"I don't hate you. I don't want to live with anyone, but you and I lead especially incompatible lives. You know as well as I that Tony would say the same if he were still around."

There'd been a painful episode when Elena announced her independence from my grandmother and moved into her own apartment. Finding solitude not to her liking, she'd shown up at our house in South Chicago one weekend. She'd stayed three days. It wasn't my fierce mother who'd asked her to leave—Gabriella's love of the underdog somehow could encompass even Elena. But my easygoing father came home from the graveyard shift on Monday to find Elena passed out at the kitchen table. He put her into the detox unit at County and refused to talk to her for six months after she got out.

Elena apparently also remembered this episode. The pouty puckering disappeared from her face. She looked stricken, and somehow more real.

I squeezed her shoulder gently and offered to make her some eggs. She shook her head without speaking, watching me silently while I spread anchovy paste on toast. I ate it quickly and left before pity could overcome my judgment.

It was well past nine now. The morning rush was ending and I had an easy run across Belmont to the expressway. When I neared the Loop, though, the traffic congealed as we moved through a construction maze. The four miles on the Ryan between the Eisenhower and Thirty-first, supposedly the busiest eight lanes of traffic anywhere in the known universe, had finally crumbled under the stress of the semi's. The southbound lanes were closed while the feds performed reconstructive surgery.

My little Cavalier bounced between a couple of sixty-tonners as the slow lines of traffic snaked around the construction barricades. To my right the surface of the old roadbed had been completely removed; lattices of the reinforcing bars were exposed. They looked like tightly packed nests of vipers —here and there a rusty head stood up prepared to strike.

The turnoff to Lake Shore Drive had been so cleverly disguised that I was parallel with the barrel blocking one of the exit lanes before I realized it. With my sixty-ton pal close on my tail, I couldn't stand on the brakes and swerve around the barrel. I gnashed my teeth and rode down to Thirty-fifth, then took side streets up to Cermak.

Elena's SRO had stood a few doors north of the intersection with Indiana. A niggling doubt I'd had in her story vanished when I pulled up across the street from it. The Indiana Arms Hotel—transients welcome, rates by the day or by the month—had joined the other derelicts on the street in retirement. I parked and went over to look at the skeleton.

When I walked around to the north side of the building, I discovered a man in a sport jacket and hard hat poking around in the rubble. Every now and then he'd pick up some piece of debris with a pair of tongs and stick it into a plastic bag. He'd mark the bag and mutter into a pocket Dictaphone before continuing his exploration. He spotted me when he turned east to poke through a promising tell. He finished picking up an object and marking its container before coming over to me.

"You lose something here?" His tone was pleasant but his brown eyes were wary.

"Just sleep. Someone I know lived here until last night—she showed up at my place early this morning."

He pursed his lips, weighing my story. "In that case, what are you doing here now?"

I hunched a shoulder. "I guess I wanted to see it for myself. See if the place was really gone before I put all my energy into finding her a new home. Come to that, what are you doing here? A suspicious person might think you were making off with valuables."

He laughed and some of the wariness left his face. "They'd be right—in a way I am."

"Are you with the fire department?"

He shook his head. "Insurance company."

"Was it arson?" I'd been so bogged down in the sludge of family relations, I hadn't even wondered how the fire started.

His caution returned. "I'm just collecting things. The lab will give me a diagnosis."

I smiled. "You're right to be careful—you don't know who might come round in the aftermath of a blaze like this. My name's V. I. Warshawski. I'm a private investigator when I'm not looking for emergency housing. And I do projects for Ajax Insurance from time to time." I pulled a card from my bag and handed it to him.

He wiped a sooty hand on a Kleenex and shook mine. "Robin Bessinger. I'm with Ajax's arson and fraud division. I'm surprised I haven't heard your name."

It didn't surprise me. Ajax employed sixty thousand people around the world—no one could possibly keep track of all of them. I explained that my work for them had been in claims or reinsurance and gave him a few names he'd be likely to recognize. He thawed further and confided that the signs of arson were quite clear.

"I'd show you the places where they poured accelerant but I don't want you in the building if you don't have a hard hat. Chunks of plaster keep falling down."

I showed suitable regret at being denied this treat. "The owner buy a lot of extra insurance lately?"

He shook his head. "I don't know—I haven't seen the policies. They just asked me to get on over before the vandals took too much of the evidence. I hope your friend got all her stuff out—not too much survived this blast."

I'd forgotten to ask Elena if anyone had been badly hurt. Robin told me the police Violent Crimes Unit would have joined the Bomb and Arson Squad in force if anyone had died.

"You wouldn't have been allowed to park without showing good reason for being near the premises—it's a fact of life that torchers like to come back to see if the job got done right. No one was killed, but a good half dozen were ferried to Michael Reese with burns and respiratory problems. Torchers usually like to make sure a building can be cleared—they know an investigation into an old dump like this won't get too much attention if there aren't any murder charges to excite the cops." He looked at his wrist. "I'd better get back to work. Hope your friend finds a new place okay."

I agreed fervently and went off to start my hunt with an easy optimism bred of ignorance. I began at the Emergency Housing Bureau on south Michigan where I joined a long line. There were women with children of all ages, old men muttering to themselves, rolling their eyes wildly, women anxiously clutching suitcases or small appliances—a seemingly endless sea of people left on the streets from some crisis or other yesterday.

The high counters and bare walls made us feel as though we were suppliants at the gates of a Soviet labor camp. There weren't any chairs; I took a number and leaned against the wall to wait my turn.

Next to me a very pregnant woman of about twenty holding a large infant was struggling with a toddler. I offered to hold the baby or amuse the two-year-old.

"It's all right," she said in a soft slow voice. "Todd just be tired after staying up all night. We couldn't get into the shelter 'cause the one they sent us to don't allow babies. I couldn't get me no bus fare to come back here and get them to find us a different place."

"So what did you do?" I didn't know which was more horrible—her plight or the resigned gentle way she talked about it.

"Oh, we found us a park bench up at Edgewater by the shelter. The baby sleep but Todd just couldn't get comfortable."

"Don't you have any friends or relatives to help you out? What about the baby's father?"

"Oh, he be trying to find us a place," she said listlessly. "But he can't get no job. And my mother, we used to stay with her, but she had to go in the hospital, now it look like she going to be sick a long time and she can't keep up on her rent."

I looked around the room. Dozens of people were waiting ahead of me. Most of them had my neighbor's dragged-out look, bodies stooped over from too much shame. Those who didn't were pugnacious, waiting to take on a system they couldn't possibly beat. Elena's needs—my needs—could certainly take a far backseat to their demands for emergency shelter. Before I took off I asked if Todd and she would like some breakfast—I was going over to the Burger King to get something.

"They don't let you eat in here, but Todd could maybe go with you and get something."

Todd showed a great disinclination to be separated from his mother, even to get some food. Finally I left him whimpering at her side, went to the Burger King, got a dozen breakfast buns with eggs and wrapped the lot in a plastic bag to conceal the fact that it was food. I handed it to the woman and left as fast as I could. My skin was still trembling.

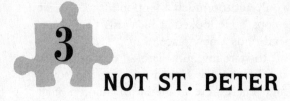

3
NOT ST. PETER

The kinds of places Elena could afford didn't seem to advertise in the papers. The only residential hotels listed in the classifieds were in Lincoln Park and started at a hundred a week. Elena had paid seventy-five a month for her little room at the Indiana Arms.

I spent four hours futilely pounding the pavements. I combed the Near South Side, covering Cermak Road between Indiana and Halsted. A century ago it housed the Fields, the Searses, and the Armours. When they moved to the North Shore the area collapsed rapidly. Today it consists of vacant lots, auto dealers, public housing, and the occasional SRO. A few years ago someone decided to restore a blockful of the original mansions. They stand like a macabre ghost town, empty opulent shells in the midst of the decay that permeates the neighborhood.

The stilts of the Dan Ryan L running overhead made me feel tiny and useless as I went door to door, asking drunk or indifferent supers about a room for my aunt. I vaguely remembered reading about all the SRO's that came down when Presidential Towers went up, but somehow the impact this had on the street hadn't hit me before. There just wasn't housing available for people with Elena's limited means. The hotels I did find were all full— and victims of last night's fire, savvier than me, had been there at dawn renting the few rooms available. I realized that the fourth time a blowsy manager said, "Sorry, if you'd gotten here first thing this morning when we had something . . ."

At three I called off the search. Panicked at the prospect of housing Elena for some indefinite future, I drove into my Loop office to call my uncle Peter. It was a decision I could make only while panicked.

Peter was the first member of my family to make something substantial of his life. Maybe the only member besides my cousin Boom-Boom. Nine years younger than Elena, Peter had gone to work in the stockyards when he returned from Korea. He quickly realized that the people getting rich in meat packing weren't the Poles hitting cows over the head with hammers. Scraping together a few bucks from friends and relations, he started his own sausage manufacturing firm. The rest was the classic story of the American dream.

He followed the yards to Kansas City when they moved there in the early seventies. Now he lived in a huge house in the tony Mission Hills district, sent his wife to Paris to buy her spring clothes, shipped my cousins off to expensive private schools and summer camps, and drove late-model Nissans. Only in America. Peter also distanced himself as much as possible from the low-budget end of the family.

My office in the Pulteney Building was definitely down market. Most of the Loop expansion in recent years has been to the west. The Pulteney is at the southeast fringe where peep shows and pawnshops push the rents down. The Wabash L rattles the fourth-floor windows, disturbing the pigeons and dirt that normally roost there.

My furnishings are Spartan gleanings from police auctions and resale shops. I used to hang an engraved sketch of the Uffizi over the filing cabinet, but last year I'd decided its intricate black detail looked too drab with all the olive furniture. In its place I'd put up some splashy posters of paintings by Nell Blaine and Georgia O'Keeffe. They gave the room a little color, but no one would mistake it for the hub of an international business.

Peter had been there once, when he brought his three children to Chicago for a tour several years ago. I had watched him swell visibly as he calculated the gap between our net present values.

Getting hold of him this afternoon took all my powers of persuasion, mixed in with a little bullying. My first worry, that he might be out of the country, or equally inaccessible on some golf course, proved groundless. But he had a phalanx of assistants convinced it was better to handle my business themselves than to disturb the great man. The most difficult skirmish came when I finally reached his personal secretary.

"I'm sorry, Miss Warshawski, but Mr. Warshawski has given me a list of family members who he'll let interrupt him and your name isn't on it." The Kansas twang was polite but unyielding.

I watched the pigeons check themselves for lice. "Could you get a message to him? While I hold? That his sister Elena will be arriving in Kansas City on the six o'clock flight and has cab fare to his house?"

"Does he know she's coming?"

"Nope. That's why I'm trying to get hold of him. To let him know."

Five minutes later—while I paid prime daytime rates to hold—Peter's deep voice was booming in my ear. What the hell did I mean, sending Elena to him unannounced like this. He wasn't having his children exposed to a lush like that, they didn't have guest space, he thought he'd made it clear four years ago that he was never—

"Yes, yes." I finally stanched the flow. "I know. A woman like Elena would just not fit into Mission Hills. The drunks there get manicures every week. I understand."

It wasn't the best opening to a plea for financial aid. After he'd finished shouting his outrage I explained the problem. The news that Elena was still in Chicago did not, as I'd hoped, bring him enough relief to agree to bail her out.

"Absolutely not. I made this totally clear to her the last time I helped her. That was when she foolishly squandered Mother's house in that cockamamie investment scheme. You may remember that I retained a lawyer for her who saw that she was able to salvage something from the sale. That was it—my last involvement in her affairs. It's time you learned the same lesson, Vic. An alkie like Elena will just milk you dry. The sooner you realize it, the easier your life will be."

Hearing some of my own negative thoughts echoed on his pompous lips made me squirm in my chair. "She paid for that lawyer though, Peter, if I remember rightly. She hasn't ever asked you for cash, has she? Anyway, I live in four rooms. I can't have her staying with me. All I want is enough money to make the rent on a decent apartment for a month while I help her find a place she can afford."

He gave a nasty laugh. "That's what your mother said that time Elena showed up at your place in South Chicago. Remember? Not even Tony could stomach having her around. Tony! He could tolerate anything."

"Unlike you," I commented dryly.

"I know you mean that as an insult but I take it as a compliment. What did Tony leave you when he died? That squalid house on Houston and the remains of his pension."

"And a name I'm proud to use," I snapped, thoroughly roused. "And come to that, you wouldn't have gotten your little meatball machine off the ground without his help. So do something for Elena in exchange. I'm sure wherever Tony is now he'd consider it a just quid pro quo."

"I paid Tony back to the nickel," Peter huffed. "And I don't owe him or you shit. And you know damned well it's sausages, not meatballs."

"Yeah, you paid back the nickel. But a share of the profits, even a little interest, wouldn't have killed you, would it?"

"Don't try that sentimental crap on me, Vic. I've been around the block too many times to fall for it."

"Just like a used car," I said bitterly.

The line went dead in my ear. The pleasure of having the exit line didn't compensate for losing the fight. Why in hell were the survivors in my father's family Peter and Elena? Why couldn't Peter have died and Tony been the one to hang around? Although not in the shape he was the last few years of his life. I swallowed bile and tried to shut out the image of my father the last year of his life, his face puffy, his body wrenched by uncontrollable coughing.

Pressing my lips together bitterly, I looked at the stack of unanswered mail and unfiled papers on my desk. Maybe it was time I got into the twentieth century while I still had a decade left to do it in. Make a big enough success of my work that I could at least afford a secretary to do some of the paperwork for me. An assistant who could take on some of the legwork.

I shuffled through the papers impatiently until I finally found the numbers I needed for my upcoming presentation. I called Visible Treasures to see how late I could bring them in for overnight processing. They told me if I got them there by eight, they would typeset them and create transparencies for me at only double overtime. When I got the price quote I felt a little better—it wasn't going to be quite as bad as I'd feared.

I typed up my drafts on my mother's old Olivetti. If I couldn't afford an assistant, maybe at least I should blow a few thousand on a desktop publishing system. On the other hand, the force it took to use the Olivetti's keyboard kept my wrists strong.

It was a little after six when I finished typing. I dug through my drawers looking for a manila folder to put the charts in. When I didn't find a fresh one I dumped the contents of an insurance file onto the desk and stuck my documents into it. Now the desktop looked like the city landfill right after the trucks drop off their loads. I could see Peter looking at it, his face creasing into little rivulets of suppressed smugness. Maybe being committed to truth, justice, and the American Way didn't have to include working in slum conditions.

I put the insurance material back into its folder and took it over to the filing cabinets, where I found a section on business expenses that seemed close enough. With a glow of virtue I stuck "insurance" in between "Illinois Bell" and "lease." Having gotten that far, I went through the two weeks of mail sitting on the desk, writing a few checks, filing documents, and trashing the circulars. Near the bottom of the stack I found a thick white letter the size of a wedding invitation with "Cook County Women for Open Government" in engraved script on the top left.

I was about to pitch it when I suddenly realized what it was—in a fit of insanity I had agreed to be a sponsor for a political fund-raiser. Marissa Duncan and I had worked together in the public defender's office an aeon or two ago. She was one of those people who live and die for politics, whether in the office or on the street, and she chose her issues carefully. She'd been active in our drive to unionize the PD's office, for example, but she'd steered clear of involvement in the politics of abortion—she didn't want anything to drag her down if she decided to run for office.

She'd left the PD a number of years ago to work in Jane Byrne's disastrous second mayoral campaign; she now had a cushy job with a big public relations firm that specialized in selling candidates. She phones me only when she's masterminding some great campaign. When she called four weeks ago I'd just finished a tricky job for a ball-bearing manufacturer in Kankakee. She'd caught me basking in the glow that comes from a display of competence combined with a large check.

"Great news," she'd said enthusiastically, riding over my tepid hello. "Boots Meagher is going to sponsor a fund-raiser for Rosalyn Fuentes."

"I appreciate your letting me know," I said politely. "I won't have to buy the *Star* in the morning."

"You always did have a great sense of humor, Vic." Politicians can't afford to tell you they think you're a pain in the butt. "But this is *really* exciting. It's the first time Boots has ever endorsed a woman in such a public way. He's going to hold a party at his place in Streamwood. It'll be a terrific chance to meet the candidate, get to know some of the people on the County Board. Everyone's going to be there. Rostenkowski and Dixon may even stop by."

"My heart is turning over just at the thought. How much you selling tickets for?"

"Five hundred to sponsor."

"Too rich for my blood. Anyway, I thought you said Meagher was sponsoring her," I objected, just to be obnoxious.

A thread of impatience finally hit her voice. "Vic, you know the drill. Five hundred to be listed in the program as a sponsor. Two-fifty to be a patron. A hundred to get in the front door."

"Sorry, Marissa. Way out of my league. And I ain't that big a fan of Boots anyway." His real name was Donnel—he'd gotten the nickname when the '72 reformers thought they could get Daley's men off the county slate. They'd run some poor earnest wimp whose name I couldn't even remember on the slogan of "Give Meagher the Boot." When Daley muscle got the big guy reelected by a landslide, his supporters at the Bismarck celebration party had screamed "Boots, Boots" when he appeared and he'd never been called anything else since.

Marissa said earnestly, "Vic, we need more women out there. Otherwise it's going to look as though Roz has sold out to Boots and we'll lose a lot of our grass-roots support. And even though you're not with the PD anymore, your name still commands a lot of respect with local women."

Anyway, to make a long story short, she'd used flattery, Fuentes's pro-choice record, and my guilt for having dropped out of political action for so long to get me to agree to be a patron. And I did have a two-thousand-dollar check beaming at me from the desk.

The thick white envelope held the invitation, a copy of the program, and a return envelope for my two hundred and fifty dollars. Marissa had scrawled on the program in her giant, schoolgirl hand, *"Really* looking forward to seeing you again."

I flipped through the booklet, looking at the list of sponsors and patrons. Having agreed to hold the fund-raiser, Boots had gone all out putting the arm on the regular Dems. Or maybe that was Marissa's work. The pages glittered with judges, state reps, state senators, and directors of large corporations. Near the end of the list of patrons was my name. From some ancient yearbook or birth certificate Marissa had dug up my middle name. When I saw the "Iphigenia" jumping out at me, I was tempted to call her and withdraw my support—I try to keep my mother's lunacy in naming me a secret known only to family.

The function was this coming Sunday. I looked at my watch—seven-fifteen. I could call Marissa and still make it to Visible Treasures in time.

Late though it was, she was still in her office. She tried to sound pleased at hearing from me, but couldn't quite carry it off—Marissa likes me better when I'm doing favors for her.

"You all set for Sunday, Vic?"

"You bet," I said enthusiastically. "What are we wearing? Jeans or evening gowns?"

She relaxed. "Oh, it's casual—barbecue, you know. I'll probably wear a dress, but jeans will be fine."

"Rosty coming? You said he might."

"No. But the head of his Chicago office will be there. Cindy Mathiessen."

"Great." I made myself sound like a cheerleader. "I want to talk to her about Presidential Towers."

Caution returned to Marissa's voice at once as she demanded to know why I wanted to discuss the complex.

"The SRO's," I said earnestly. "You know, about eight thousand rooms were lost when they cleared that area to put up the Towers. I've got this aunt, see." I explained about Elena and the fire. "So I'm not feeling too crazy about Boots, or Rosty, or any of the other local Dems since I can't find her a room. But I'm sure if I bring it to—what did you say her name was?—Cindy? If I talk to Cindy about it, she's bound to be able to help me out."

It seemed to me the phone vibrated with the sound of wheels turning in Marissa's brain. Finally she said, "What can your aunt afford?"

"She was paying seventy-five at the Indiana Arms. A month, I mean." It was past sundown now and the room was dark beyond the pool of light my desk lamp shed. I walked over to the wall with the phone to switch on the overheads.

"If I can get her a place, will you promise not to talk about Presidential Towers on Sunday? With anyone? It's a little touchy for people."

For the Dems, she meant. With the spotlight already on the Speaker of the House for ethics questions, they didn't want anything embarrassing said to one of his buddies.

I made a show of reluctance. "Can you do it by tomorrow night?"

"If that's what it'll take, Vic, I'll do it by tomorrow night." She didn't try to keep the snarl from her voice.

I had just twenty minutes to get to Visible Treasures before paying quadruple overtime, but I took the extra minute to write out a check to Cook County Women for Open Government. As I locked the office door behind me I started whistling for the first time all day. Who says blackmailers don't have fun?

4
AUNTIE DOES
A BUNK

It was almost nine by the time I got off the Kennedy at California and headed over to Racine. I hadn't had dinner, hadn't had anything since grabbing a Polish at a hole-in-the-wall on Canal at two. I wanted peace and quiet, a hot bath, a drink and a pleasant dinner—I had a veal chop in the freezer I'd been saving for just such a tired evening. Instead I braced myself for a night with Elena.

When I parked across the street and looked up at the third floor, the windows were dark. As I trudged up the stairs I imagined my aunt passed out at the kitchen table. Or on the unmade sofa bed in the living room. Or downstairs seducing Mr. Contreras.

I hadn't given Elena keys or instructions on the two dead bolts. I undid the bottom lock—the one that locks automatically when you shut the door— and switched on the light in the little entryway. It shed a dim glow into the living room. I could see the sofa was restored to its normal upright position.

I went through the dining room to the kitchen and turned on the light there. The kitchen was sparkling. The three days' accumulation of dishes in the sink had been washed and put away. The newspapers were gone, the floor washed, and the tabletop clean and tidy. In the middle sat a sheet torn from one of my yellow pads covered with Elena's sprawling, unsteady writing. She'd written "Vicki," then crossed it out and changed it to "Victoria, Baby."

Thanks a lot for the loan of a bed last night when I needed it. I knew I could count on you in a pinch, you always were a good girl, but I don't mean to hang around and be a burden on you, which I can see I would be, so here's good luck to you kid and I'll be seeing you in the sweet by and by, like they say.

She'd drawn eight big X's and signed her name.

Since three this morning I'd been cursing my aunt for coming to me and wishing I'd return home to find that I'd dreamed the whole episode. I'd gotten my wish, but instead of being elated I felt a little hollow under the diaphragm. Despite her easy camaraderie, Elena didn't have friends. Of course the streets and alleys of Chicago were strewn with her former lovers, but I didn't think any of them would remember Elena if she showed up at their doors. Come to think of it, I'm not sure Elena would remember any of them well enough to know which doors to knock on.

The other unpleasant notion hovering in my mind's back cupboard was prompted by Elena's final sentence. In a high school dramatization of *Tom Sawyer* we'd sung "In the sweet bye-and-bye." It was supposed to be typical of late Victorian hymnology. As I recalled, the sweet bye-and-bye was a syrupy euphemism for life beyond the grave. I had never spent enough time with Elena to know if it was just some catch phrase she used or if she'd gone off to throw herself over the Wacker Drive bridge.

I went carefully through the apartment to see if she'd left any clue to her intentions. The duffel bag was gone, along with the violet nightdress. When I looked in the liquor cabinet I saw nothing was missing except five inches from the open bottle of Johnnie Walker. But from the way she'd been sleeping this morning I kind of thought she'd drunk that before going to bed.

In a way I wished she'd taken the bottle—it would have made me more certain she hadn't any immediate intention of suicide. On the other hand, did someone really spend her whole life drinking and mooching off people and then suddenly have such a strong sense of remorse that at age sixty-six she couldn't take it anymore? On the surface it didn't sound too likely. Lack of sleep and my day among the burned-out buildings of the Near South Side were making me unnaturally morbid.

I debated phoning Lotty Herschel to discuss the matter with her. She's a doctor who sees a fair number of drunks in her storefront clinic on Damen. On the other hand, her day starts at seven with hospital rounds. This was a bit late for a call whose main function was to allay my uneasy conscience.

I put the Black Label back into the cupboard without pouring any. The drink part of my program had lost its appeal when I thought about Elena swallowing five inches and falling into a red-faced stupor. I went into the kitchen, pulled the veal chop from the freezer, and stuck it in my little toaster oven to thaw while I took a bath. Unless I wanted to rouse the police, there was nothing I could do about my aunt tonight.

Somehow soaking in the tub didn't relax me the way it usually did. The image of Elena, her gallant smile a bit lopsided, sitting on a park bench with the family I'd encountered at the Emergency Housing Bureau kept coming between me and rest. I lumbered out of the tub, turned off the little oven, and got dressed again.

Mr. Contreras's living-room light had been on when I came in. I went down the front stairs and knocked on his door. The dog whimpered impatiently as he scrabbled with the locks. When he finally opened the door she leapt up to lick my face. I asked the old man if he'd seen Elena leave.

Of course he had—when he wasn't gardening or checking the races, he was keeping a close eye on the building. We didn't really need a watchdog with him on the premises. Elena had left around two-thirty. No, he couldn't tell me what she was wearing, or if she had any makeup on, what kind of person did I think he was, staring at people and snooping into their private lives. What he could tell me was she'd caught a bus on Diversey on account of he'd gone down to the corner for some milk and seen her climb on. Eastbound, that was right.

"You wasn't expecting her to leave?"

I hunched my shoulders impatiently. "She doesn't have any place to go. Not that I know of."

He clicked his tongue sympathetically and started on a detailed interrogation. My thin stack of patience was about gone when the banker once more opened his door. He was wearing form-fitting Ralph Lauren jeans and a polo shirt.

"Jesus Christ! If I'd known you stood around yelling in the stairwell at all hours, I'd never have bought into this place." His round face puckered up in a scowl.

"And if I'd known what a tight-assed crybaby you were, I'd have blocked your purchase," I responded nastily.

The dog growled deep in her throat.

"You go on up, cookie," Mr. Contreras urged me hastily. "I'll call you if I remember anything else." He pulled the dog into the apartment with him and shut the door. I could hear Peppy whining and snuffling behind it, eager to join in the fight.

"Just what is it you *do* do?" the banker demanded.

I smiled. "Nothing I need a zoning permit for, sugar, so don't wear out your brain worrying about it."

"Well, if you don't stop doing it in the stairwells, I really will call the cops." He slammed his door shut on me.

I stomped back up the stairs. Now he'd have something substantial to tell his girlfriend or his mother or whoever he phoned at night. I live to serve others.

Back in my apartment I turned the little oven on again and started cooking mushrooms and onions in some red wine. Getting the picture of Elena heading east on the Diversey bus made me feel a bit easier. That sounded as though she had a specific destination in mind. In the morning, as a sop to my conscience, I'd talk to one of my police department pals. Maybe they wouldn't mind tracking down the bus driver, find out if he remembered her and where she'd headed when she'd left the bus. Maybe I'd be the first woman on the moon—stranger things have happened.

It was well after ten when I finally sat down with my dinner. The chop was cooked to a turn, just pink inside, and the glazed mushrooms complemented it perfectly. I'd eaten about half of it when the phone rang. I debated letting it go, then thought of Elena. If she'd been trying to sell her ass on Clark Street it could be the cops wanting me to bail her out.

It was a police officer, but he didn't know Elena and he was calling for purely personal reasons. At least partly personal reasons. I'd met Michael Furey when I went to the Mallorys' last New Year's Day for dinner. His father and Bobby had grown up together in Norwood Park. When Michael joined the police fresh out of junior college, Bobby kept an avuncular eye on him. In Chicago people look after their own, but Bobby is a scrupulously honorable cop—he wouldn't use personal influence to promote a friend's son's career. The boy proved himself on his own, though; after fifteen years Bobby was glad to welcome him into the Violent Crimes Unit at the Central District.

For a while following the transfer Eileen invited the two of us up to dinner on a regular basis. She longed not so much for my second marriage as for my children—she kept trotting the brightest and best of the Chicago police by me in the hopes that one of them would look like good father material to me.

Eileen belonged to the generation that believes a guy with a good set of wheels is more appealing than one who can afford only a Honda. Furey had a little money—his father's life insurance, he said, which he'd been able to invest—and he drove a silver Corvette. He was attractive and cheerful, and I did like driving the Corvette, but we didn't have much except the Mallorys and a love of sports in common. Our relationship settled into an occasional trip to the Stadium or a ball game together. Eileen masked her disappointment but stopped the dinner invitations.

"Vic! Glad I caught you in," Michael boomed cheerfully into my ear.

I finished chewing. "Hiya, Michael. What's up?"

"Just got off shift. Thought I'd check in and see how you're doing."

"Why, Michael," I said with mock sincerity, "how thoughtful of you. How long has it been—a month or so?—and you check in with me at ten P.M.?"

He laughed a little consciously. "Aw, heck, Vic. You know how it is. I got something to ask and I don't want you taking it the wrong way."

"Try me."

"It's—uh, well, just I didn't know you were interested in county politics."

"I'm not especially." I was surprised.

"Ernie told me you're listed as a sponsor for the Fuentes fund-raiser out at Boots's farm on Sunday."

"News sure do travel fast," I said lightly, but I felt myself tensing in reflexive annoyance—I hate having my activities monitored. "How does Ernie know and why does he care?"

Ernie Wunsch and Ron Grasso had grown up with Michael on the northwest side. The odd political jobs they'd done as teenagers and young adults hadn't hurt them any when they decided to join Ernie's dad's general contracting firm after college. Their company wasn't one of the giants, but more and more often you saw cement trucks with Wunsch & Grasso's red and green stripes at construction sites. Their biggest coup had been getting the bid on the Rapelec complex, an office-condo center under construction near the Gold Coast.

"I was afraid you'd take this the wrong way," Michael said plaintively. "Ernie doesn't care. He knows because he and his old man have done a certain amount of work for the county over the years. So of course he gets asked to all the fund-raisers. You know how it is in Chicago, Vic—if you do business with the city or the county, you gotta engage in a little reciprocity."

I knew how it was.

"So of course they got an advance look at the program. And Ernie knows you and I are—well, friends. So he mentioned it. Not something you really need to get hot about."

"No," I agreed meekly. "It just takes me by surprise when two unconnected parts of my life suddenly hook up."

"Know the feeling," he agreed. "I just was wondering if I could go with you. I might attend anyway, since the boys are roping in as many victims as they can. If you're going to be there . . ."

"Let me think about it," I said, after a pause too long to be really polite. "Although—look, I wonder if you could do something for me." I told him about Elena. "I don't know much about her—what her hangouts are. And even though I don't want her living with me, I'm a little worried. I'd kind of like to know she's okay, wherever she is."

"Christ, Vic, you don't want much, do you? You know damned well there's no way I can go to the CTA without a good reason. If I start checking routes and talking to drivers, their union'll be at Uncle Bobby's door within the hour screaming for my butt."

"Maybe I should call Bobby in the morning, talk it over with him." Besides being Michael's godfather, Bobby Mallory had been my own father's protégé and his best friend on the force. He might check up on Elena for Tony's sake—I wouldn't expect him to do it for mine.

"No, don't do that," Michael said hastily. "Tell you what—I'll pass it on to the uniforms on Madison and the Near South Side, ask them to keep an eye out for her and call me if they see her."

"I don't want her being hassled," I warned him.

"Cool your jets, Vic. Discretion is my middle name."

"Yeah, right, and I'm the Queen of Sheba."

He laughed. "So if I look into it, you'll go to Boots's with me on Sunday?"

"Something like that," I admitted, blushing in spite of myself.

"I ought to run you in for trying to bribe a cop." It was a grumble, but the tone was good-natured; he promised to call me tomorrow if he turned anything up. He arranged to meet me at three on Sunday; since he knew the way he offered to drive. I said I'd follow him in my own car—I didn't want to hang around Boots Meagher's farm until midnight while Michael caught up with his old precinct pals.

By the time we hung up my chop had gotten cold and the glazed wine sauce was congealed. I was too tired to heat it up again tonight. Sticking the plate in the refrigerator, I fell into bed and spent the night in uneasy dreams in which I chased Elena across Chicago, always just missing her as she boarded the eastbound Diversey bus.

5

ROYAL SUITE

I worked for the county for five years after passing the bar. During my summers in law school I interned at the Loop's giant firms, and I'd held a lot of weird jobs to finance my college education. The worst was selling books by phone for *Time-Life* from five to nine in the evening. You call people at dinner and they scream at you. Eight or nine times I phoned homes of dead people—once the woman had died only the day before. I extricated myself from her sobbing daughter swiftly and gracelessly.

So I know working for myself beats a whole roster of other employers I can list. Still, being a private investigator is not the romance of the loner knight that Marlowe and Spenser like to pretend—half the time you're doing some kind of tedious surveillance or spending your day in the Daley Center checking backgrounds. And a good chunk of the rest of the time goes to selling people on hiring your services. Often not successfully.

Cartwright & Wheeler, insurance brokers, listened closely to my presentation on the perils and possibilities of filing false claims. They asked a lot of questions, but the nine people in the room didn't feel able to make a decision on hiring me without consulting senior staff. I exuded warmth, professionalism, and a positive mental attitude while trying to force a commitment, but the best I could get was a promise to discuss it at Monday's management meeting.

I went back to my office to stow my five hundred dollars' worth of transparencies in a filing cabinet. Usually I don't get too upset by a lukewarm response, but I was feeling edgy enough about Elena that I slammed drawers and tore up mail to vent my irritation. Larry Bowa liked to destroy toilets after a bad game. We all have our little immature quirks.

When I'd calmed down some I checked in with my answering service. Marissa Duncan had left a message. I called back and spoke with her secretary. Marissa had found a room for Elena in a residential hotel on Kenmore between Wilson and Lawrence. They wanted ninety a month for it. I hesitated a moment. I hated to turn it down—Marissa would be peeved and she had enough connections that I was better off with her feeling good about me. Even worse, what if Elena showed up again at three in the morning?

"She can't move in right away," I said at last. "But I'll stop by and pay for the room on my way home."

"Cash," the secretary said briefly. "And no pets or children."

"Fine." I double-checked the address and hung up. For the first time in my life I found myself wondering what Elena had done for birth control all those years. And I suddenly realized why Gabriella had been so accepting the time she showed up at our house thirty years ago. I couldn't put my finger on exactly what had been said, but Elena had been pregnant. Gabriella helped her find some kind of underground abortion and Elena got drunk.

I sat at my desk, my shoulders slumped, watching the pigeons fight for space on the windowsill. Finally I stretched out a hand to switch on the desk lamp and called Michael Furey at the Central District. He didn't sound enthusiastic at hearing from me, but he said he'd checked the morgue and some of the area hospitals—no gray-haired drunk women had been hauled in since yesterday afternoon.

"Gotta go, Vic, we're hard at it. See you Sunday. . . ."

Normally I would have chafed him about being hard at a poker game, but I hung up without saying anything—I wasn't in the mood for jokes.

I'd noticed too late that one of the pieces of mail I was shredding was from an old client. I rummaged through the scraps on the floor and reconstructed enough of it to see that it was a request for a simple background check. It would keep until Monday—I wasn't in the humor to do that tonight, either. The rest of the paper I scooped up and put into the trash.

Embarrassed by my earlier outburst, I soberly filed the papers remaining on my desk, then went to the ladies' room on the seventh floor for some water to scrub down the surface. That looked so good that I finished by washing the windowsills and filing cabinets too. Clean now in thought, word, and deed, I locked up the office.

En route to the garage I stopped at a cash machine to get the ninety dollars, then joined the slow procession out of the Loop. Everyone leaves work early on Friday in order to maximize the amount of time spent sitting in traffic before starting the weekend.

It was a little before five when I reached the Windsor Arms on Kenmore. The building had gone up when the Duke was in his heyday, enjoying Goering's hospitality and lending his name to residential hotels that hoped to reflect his royal splendor. The Duke of Windsor was dead now, but the hotel hadn't been so lucky. If the facade had been washed since George VI's ascension, it didn't show. Not much more attention had been paid to basic repairs —a number of windows had pieces of cardboard filling in for missing panes.

The inside smelled faintly of boiled cabbage, despite a large poster over the desk that stated emphatically, *"Absolutely* No Cooking in Rooms." Next to the sign Alderman Helen Schiller's face smiled beatifically out at her voters.

No one was behind the desk, but a handful of residents sat in a small lounge watching Vanna White on a tiny TV chained high on the wall. I walked over and asked if anyone knew where the manager was. A middle-aged woman in a sleeveless housedress looked at me suspiciously—people in business suits and nylons who come to residential hotels are usually city inspectors or lawyers threatening action on behalf of the family of a dead resident.

I gave my most trustworthy smile. "I understand you have a room here. For Elena Warshawski."

"What about it?" The woman had the heavy flat drawl of the Irish South Side.

"I'm her niece. She'll be by in a couple of days to move in, but I wanted to pay for a month in advance to hold the room for her."

The woman looked me up and down, her watery gray eyes tight and ungiving. At last she decided my sanctimonious honesty was the real thing. She turned back to the set, waited for a commercial, then heaved herself ponderously out of the vinyl-coated armchair. I followed her out to the desk and behind it into a cubbyhole whose outstanding feature was a large lock-box.

The chatelaine counted my tens twice, wrote out a receipt in a labored hand, then put the money in a sealed envelope and slid it through a slot in the side of the box.

"I don't know how to get into that sucker, so don't think your boyfriend can come around and hold a gun on me to get your money back for you. They come and empty it out twice a week."

"No, ma'am," I agreed helplessly.

"Now I'll show you the room. When your aunt's ready to move in she can come on over. Make sure she brings the receipt with her."

We walked up three flights of stairs, slowly, to accommodate my guide's short, panting breaths, and down an uncarpeted corridor. Empty glass fixtures over the doors were a reminder of the Windsor Arms's grander days—the hall was lighted now by two naked bulbs. The desk clerk stopped at the second door from the end of the left side and unlocked it.

Whoever owned the building apparently owed Marissa Duncan a favor. Either that or hoped Marissa would provide a friendly push up the local political ladder. The window held all four panes, the floor was clean, and the narrow bed made up tidily. A white plastic chest of drawers stood in the corner. A deal table under the window completed the furnishings.

"Bathroom's down the hall. She can lock her stuff in a chest under the bed if she's afraid of junkies. Key comes to me when she's not in the room. And absolutely no cooking in here. The wiring's old. Don't want the place going up in smoke around us."

I agreed soberly and followed her back down the stairs. She returned to *Wheel of Fortune* without another look at me. Once outside I gulped in the air in great mouthfuls.

I never seem to make enough money to put more than a thousand or so into a Keogh plan every year. What was I going to live on when I got too old to hustle clients any longer? The thought of being sixty-six, alone, living in a little room with three plastic drawers to hold my clothes—a shudder swept through me, almost knocking me off balance. A woman with three children in tow yanked them past me—I was just a falling-down drunk for her children to stare at on their way home. I climbed heavily into the Chevy and headed south.

The mixture of guilt and fear the Windsor Arms stirred in me took the edge off my pleasure in the weekend. I went to the grocery Saturday morning and got fruit and yogurt for the week ahead. But when I picked out supplies for a pasta salad I was taking to an impromptu picnic that afternoon I bypassed my usual olive oil for a cheap brand—how could I spend eleven dollars on a pint of olive oil when I couldn't scrape together enough for a third-quarter deposit into my Keogh? I even bought domestic Parmesan. Gabriella would have upbraided me sharply—but then she wouldn't have approved of my buying pasta in a store to begin with.

I got all three morning papers and read them carefully before going over to the park. So far nobody had found any unidentified older women in the river or roaming dementedly about the streets. I had to trust that Furey, or Bobby Mallory himself, would call me if Elena had been arrested. There didn't seem to be anything else for me to do except join my pals at Montrose Harbor and take my aggressions out on a softball.

I couldn't quite shake off my depression, but a game-saving catch I made in the sixth inning cheered me—I hadn't known I could still dive for a ball and come up with it the way I did at twenty. Over Soave and grilled chicken afterwards, I couldn't quite get into the ribald spirits of my friends. I left while the party was still in progress so as to catch the ten o'clock news.

Elena still hadn't surfaced in a dramatic way. I finally decided she was hanging out someplace with Annie Greensleeves and went to bed, torn between disgust with her and irritation with myself.

I'd half been hoping that the gods would blight Boots's party with violent thundershowers, but Sunday dawned with more of the bright, merciless sunshine we'd suffered from all summer. With September drawing to a close, the days were merely warm instead of sweltering, but the Midwest was still suffering from its worst drought in fifty years.

All around the city sidewalks and roadbeds had buckled and collapsed. During the height of the heat wave sparks from the trains had ignited beams holding up the L platforms so that various stations were now closed more or less permanently. Given Chicago's perennial cash shortfall, I didn't expect to see those stops reopen in my lifetime.

I ran Peppy to Belmont Harbor and back, then made my way through the Sunday papers. The *Sun-Times* was the hardest—I've never figured out their organizational scheme and I had to read a lot more than I wanted about home decorating and fall festivals in Wisconsin before stumbling on the metropolitan news.

When I'd finished the *Herald-Star* without finding any word on Elena, it was time to shower and dress for my two-hundred-and-fifty-dollar barbecue. I knew Marissa would probably show up in silk lounging pajamas or something equally exotic, but unless Rosalyn Fuentes had changed dramatically, she would probably wear jeans. It seemed to me good fund-raising etiquette dictated not to upstage the guest of honor. Besides, I didn't want to worry about dry-clean-only clothes at a giant picnic. I put on khaki slacks and a loose-fitting olive shirt. Neat—would camouflage food spills and above all be comfortable for an afternoon in the sun.

Michael arrived a little before three, his black hair and dark eyes set off vividly by a navy blazer and pale blue polo shirt. His normal good spirits had spilled over into exuberance—he liked big parties, he liked getting together with his pals, and he had enough old-fashioned Dem in him to look forward to an afternoon hobnobbing with party bigwigs.

I made a great show of salaams at his elegance. "You sure you want to arrive at Boots's with me? It's really going to tone down your image."

He gave me a mock tap to the nose. "You make me look good, Warshawski. That's why I want you to stay close this afternoon."

"The slum next to the suburb? That's kind of how I feel about the whole affair." Somehow his effervescence made me feel like being disagreeable.

"Aw, come on, Warshawski. Do you really like living in the trash and graffiti? Secretly, down deep, wouldn't you live in the clean open spaces if you could afford it?"

"You stay in Norwood Park," I reminded him.

"Only because those of us who serve and protect you from the graffiti artists have to live in the city. And Chicago crime is more interesting to be around than the stuff in Streamwood."

"Well, that's what I think too. That's why I can't see myself out there." I took my billfold from my handbag and stuffed it in a pants pocket along with my invitation to the party—I didn't want to lug a purse around the picnic all afternoon.

"But you do a lot of investigations in the suburbs," Michael objected as we left my apartment.

"That's why I like city crime better." I turned the double locks. "Someone bonks you on the head and steals your purse. They don't sit in board rooms raving on about the niggers in Chicago while they're sliding a million or two off the top from the company."

"I could introduce you to some muggers," Michael offered when we reached the street. "They need some PR—maybe you're just the gal for them." He sketched a billboard with his hands. "I can kind of see it—clean, honest crime like your granddaddy used to commit."

I laughed in spite of myself. "Okay, okay. Muggers are scum. I just have a chip on my shoulder about the suburbs, that's all. Anyway, I can't afford them. I wouldn't mind knowing what Boots did to finance a move from Division and Central to Streamwood."

Michael framed my face with his hands and kissed me. "Do me a favor, Vic—just don't ask him this afternoon."

I disengaged myself and got into the Chevy. "Don't worry—my mama brought me up to know how to act in public. See you at the ball."

He hopped into the Corvette, flashed his lights at me a few times, and took off toward Belmont with a great screeching of rubber.

6
COUNTY PICNIC

Once we were on the Kennedy I lost track of Michael. He could afford to do eighty—the highway patrol would give him a professional wink they wouldn't extend to me. He was waiting for me at the exit to the Northwest Tollway; I had him more or less in view as we started winding our way through the hills that swell to the northwest as you leave Chicago.

I'm not sure I would have found Boots's spread if I hadn't been following Michael, at least not on the first go-round. The entrance, which lay on a twisting unlabeled street, was a discreet opening in the hedge separating the road from the gaze of the vulgar. Michael had been going close to sixty around the curves. He braked the Corvette and turned without warning, so that I had to screech to a halt beyond the entrance and find a long enough flat stretch to make a U in. Boys will be boys.

He was waiting for me beside a gate that lay ten feet or so from the hole in the hedge I had turned through. The shrubbery lining the drive partly concealed a ten-foot-high fence connected to the gate. If you tried to breach the ramparts anyway there were a couple of sheriff's deputies to shoot you down.

"Sorry, Vic," Furey said penitently, "I thought the turnoff was up the road another half mile. Shouldn't have been showing off on such a dangerous stretch." When one of the deputies asked me for my invitation, Furey added, "Oh, don't bother her—she's with me."

"Not so's you'd notice it." I fished in my bag for the invitation and held it out, but the guard waved me on without looking at it. This assumption of my relationship to Michael added to my ill humor. I got back into my Chevy while Michael joked with the other men, maneuvered around the Corvette, and drove away with a little spit of gravel. Before the road twisted I could see

Furey get back into the Corvette, but I turned a bend and found myself alone on a tree-lined drive.

Whatever damage the summer had done to the corn crop, it hadn't hurt Boots particularly. The trees here showed full, graceful leaves and the grass beyond them was thick and green. In the distance I could make out a stand of corn. I guess if you're chairman of the County Board there are ways to get water to your farm.

I turned another bend and found myself at the party. I'd been hearing music blaring in the distance ever since leaving the front gate. Now I could see a big bandstand beyond the main house with a band in straw boaters and navy blazers going full bore. On the other side of the house smoke hovered lazily over what was presumably the barbecue pit. Boots was sacrificing one of his own cows to Roz's campaign.

A sheriff's deputy, swinging an outsize flashlight, directed me to a crowd of cars in a big yard northeast of the house. Maybe it was a pasture—I remembered seeing one on a Girl Scout outing when I was eleven. Despite the presence of the deputies—or because of them—I carefully locked the Chevy.

Furey caught up with me as I headed toward the bandstand where most of the party was gathered. "Goddamnit, Vic, what's making you so shirty?"

I stopped to look at him. "Michael, I paid two hundred and fifty dollars for the doubtful pleasure of coming to this shindig. I'm not your date, nor yet 'the little woman' whom you can tuck under your arm and hustle past the guards."

His good-humored face tightened into a scowl. "What the hell are you talking about?"

"You treated me like a cipher out there—leaving me standing in the road and then telling the deputies to ignore me because I was your appendage. I don't like it."

He flung up his hands in exasperation. "I was trying to do you a favor, save you a little hassle with the boys at the gate. If I'd known you were going to treat it like a mortal insult I'd of saved my breath."

He strode off toward the crowd. I followed him slowly, irritated as much with myself as with Furey. I didn't like the little trick stunt he'd pulled at the turnoff, but that didn't justify my retaliating in kind. Maybe frustration over Elena's disappearance was making me testy. Or my innate bad humor. Or just being at a Cook County political fund-raiser.

The last time I remembered seeing Boots in the news one of his bodyguards had beaten in the face of a man who had come too close to the boss after a County Board meeting. The man claimed Boots had murdered his daughter—heavy accusations, although he had a long history at Elgin—but breaking someone's nose seemed like an excessive response to insanity. In fairness to Boots, he'd picked up the guy's hospital tab later on—but why did he need bodyguards at all?

That was only the most recent public episode Meagher had been involved in. He also had fingers in dozens of business ventures in the state, the kinds of deals where everybody gets rich if they know which way the tax breaks are going to land. Meagher was a you-scratch-my-back kind of guy—he wouldn't be hosting Rosalyn's fund-raiser if she hadn't made some significant concessions to him.

It wasn't as though Roz were a close pal. She'd been a community organizer in Logan Square when I was with the PD. I'd worked with her on some seminars on law and the community—some ABC's to teach the residents their rights in arenas ranging from housing to immigration officers. Roz was bright, energetic, and a skillful politician. And ambitious. And that meant getting into bed with Boots if she was going to rule a wider sphere than Logan Square. I understood that and I knew it wasn't any of my business, anyway. So why was I getting my tail in a knot?

I skirted my way through the crowd at the bandstand to a bright canopy covering the refreshment arena. Young women in thigh-high minis were threading their way cheerfully through the throng with canapé-laden trays. Just the costume for a feminist activist like Rosalyn, I snarled to myself. I went up to the bar and got a rum and tonic.

Drink in hand, I jostled aimlessly through the crowd. Behind the refreshment tent people were gathered in a thick, noisy clump, loud enough to drown out the band. Beyond that group the throng thinned down rapidly—the land there was hilly and uncultivated, leading into a small wood.

The terrain and lack of chairs notwithstanding, most of the women were wearing nylons and heels. Two of them had come prepared, though—they were sitting on a blanket, stretching their long, tanned legs and taking innocent pleasure in their own beauty. As I passed they cried out to me in an enthusiastic chorus:

"Vic! Ernie told us you might be here. Come sit down. LeAnn's pregnant and we didn't want to spend the afternoon standing in the heat."

I obligingly stopped for a moment. If LeAnn was pregnant it could only be a matter of months before Clara started a new baby as well. The two had been inseparable since childhood and now, adult and married, they lived in adjoining Oak Brook mansions, were in and out of each other's houses all day long to borrow clothes, share a cup of coffee, or entertain their children together. And while Clara's light curls contrasted with LeAnn's straight dark hair, they looked almost indistinguishable in their Anne Klein shorts suits.

"You having a good time?" Clara asked.

"Great. When is the baby due?"

"Not until the end of March. We're only telling friends right now."

I smiled. That included about half the people at the picnic—anyone she knew by name.

I'd met them through Michael Furey. LeAnn was married to Ernie Wunsch and Clara to Ron Grasso. Michael's continued tightness with the pals of his youth never ceased to astound me. Since leaving South Chicago for college I've scarcely seen any of the people I grew up with. But in addition to Ernie and Ron, Michael had seven or eight boyhood friends who got together once a month for poker, went to Eagle River each October to shoot deer, and spent every New Year's Eve together with their wives. The pals were a major reason I'd never really clicked with Michael. Since I had gone out with him, though, LeAnn and Clara now treated me as if I were one of the girls.

I asked politely about the children, two each, and was gladdened to learn how much they loved school, how happy LeAnn was that they were in Oak Brook now and didn't have to worry about the public schools, an interjection from Clara on what a good time they'd had themselves as little girls in Norwood Park, but everything was so *different* now.

"Ron and Ernie here?" I said idly.

"Oh, yes. They went off *hours* ago to get us something to drink. But they know so many people here I'm sure they got waylaid or sidetracked or something."

I offered to bring them something, but they laughed and said they didn't mind waiting. LeAnn put a well-manicured hand on my knee.

"You have such a good heart, Vic. We don't want to interfere, but we know you'd be great for Michael. We were just talking about the two of you when you showed up."

I grinned. "Thanks. I appreciate the testimonial." I pushed myself to my feet, spilling my drink down my pants leg.

LeAnn looked at me anxiously. "I haven't offended you, have I? Ernie's always on my case for saying whatever comes into my head without thinking first." She reached into a large beach bag and pulled out a handful of Kleenex for me.

I dabbed at the khaki. "Nope. Trouble is, Michael's a Sox fan—I just don't think we could ever work things out."

They gave little shrieks of protesting laughter. I left to their chorus of "You *can't* be serious, Vic."

I turned back through the crowd to replace my drink. Near the entrance to the tent I caught sight of Ron and Ernie. They were deep in conversation with Michael and a couple of other men. Their heads were drawn together so that they could talk over the noise. They were so intent that they didn't notice my walking up. I tapped Michael on the arm.

He jumped and swore. When he saw it was me he put an arm around me, but he looked cautiously at the other men, as if to see how they took my entrance. "Hiya, Vic. Enjoying yourself?"

"I'm having a great time. You, too, by the looks of it."

He again looked doubtfully from his companions to me. "We're right in the middle of something now. Can I find you in about ten minutes?"

So much for gestures of reconciliation. I grinned savagely but tried to keep my tone light. "You can try."

I turned on my heel, but Ron Grasso put out an arm. "Vic, honey. Good to see you. Don't mind Furey here—he got out on the wrong side of bed today. . . . No business is more important than a beautiful lady, Mickey. And nothing's more dangerous than keeping one of them waiting."

The other men laughed politely, but Michael looked at me seriously. Maybe he was still pissed. On the other hand, he knows that kind of joke rubs me the wrong way, so maybe he was trying in turn for conciliation. I was barely willing to give him the benefit of the doubt.

Ron introduced me to the two strangers—Luis Schmidt and Carl Martinez, also in construction. And supporters of Rosalyn's campaign.

"Vic's an old friend of Rosalyn's, aren't you?" Ron supplied.

I nodded. "We used to work together in Logan Square."

"You were an organizer?" Schmidt asked.

"I was a lawyer. I used to help out on legal issues—immigration, housing, that kind of thing. I'm a detective now."

"Detective, huh? Like Sergeant Furey here?" That was Schmidt, a short, stocky man with arms the size of sewer pipes straining his jacket sleeves.

They were just interested enough to require an answer. "I work for myself. Kind of the Magnum, P.I. of Chicago."

"Vic looks into fraud cases," Ron put in. "She has quite a track record. Keeps Ernie and me on the straight and narrow, let me tell you."

Everyone laughed politely. His comment seemed so unanswerable that I didn't try. "I ran into LeAnn and Clara behind the tent," I said instead. "They thought you guys were bringing them something to drink."

Ernie hit his forehead. "Mind like cement after pouring it all these years. I'll take care of the girls, Ronnie—why don't you guys wait for me here."

He took my arm and hustled me away to the refreshment tent. "Buy you something, Vic?"

"No, thanks. I'm heading back to the city soon."

He looked at me seriously, eyes dark in a thin, weather-beaten face. "Don't take Mickey too seriously. He's got a lot on his mind."

I nodded solemnly. "I know that, Ernie. And I think this is a good time to leave him alone, let him get it sorted out."

"Could you at least wait until after dinner—go talk to the girls for a while?"

He was hoping I'd take their drinks to them. I smiled gently. "Sorry, Ernie. I know LeAnn would love to see you for a few minutes before you plunge back into it with the boys. She's sitting around back of here with Clara."

"Okay, Vic, okay." He shoved his way to the front of the line. Something in the set of his shoulders told me he was wondering what the hell Mickey saw in me.

7 SPEAKING IN TONGUES

On my way toward the parking pasture I saw Marissa standing near the back entrance to Boots's house. She was laughing heartily at some remark of the middle-aged man talking to her. He looked vaguely familiar, but I couldn't place him. Maybe it was just the avid look he was giving Marissa I recognized—with her head thrown back the décolletage of her peach dress sprang into dramatic relief.

Before returning to town I'd let her know I'd done my duty by showing up and that I hadn't laid tales of housing woes on any sensitive ears. I trotted up the path to the house.

Seen up close, her companion was older than I'd thought, perhaps over sixty, with a lot of distinguished gray in his dark hair. Tanned and still muscular, he bore his years gracefully. Probably was wealthy, too, if his camel-hair jacket and Texas boots were any sign. A good haul for Marissa.

"Great party, Marissa—thanks for inviting me."

She hadn't seen me come up. The smile on her dark face dimmed briefly, then glowed again. "Hi, Vic. Glad you could make it."

She didn't really look at me—I should have just let well enough alone. In fact, I should have followed my original impulse and stayed in Chicago. I didn't want to see any of these people and it was abundantly clear that none of them wanted to see me.

"Bye, Marissa. Thanks for letting me participate in this wonderful civic enterprise. Just wanted to let you know I didn't discuss housing with anyone."

At that she did look at me. "You leaving, Vic? Why not stay until after the speeches? I know Rosalyn would love to have a chance to see you again."

My party smile was wearing thin. "She's got a thousand palms to press this afternoon. I'll give her a call at campaign headquarters."

The man in camel hair looked at his watch. "They're talking right now— down around the other side where the pit is. Won't take more than fifteen minutes—Boots promised me he wouldn't go gassing on forever—come along—I should put in an appearance anyway." He held out a well-groomed hand and flashed a bright white smile. "Ralph MacDonald."

While I recited my name I shook his hand appreciatively—it's not often I touch flesh worth several billion dollars. As soon as he'd said his name I knew where I'd seen the face—in the paper a zillion times or so as ground was broken for this or that project he was financing or as he presented a gargantuan check to the symphony. My only question was what he was doing here —I'd kind of assumed he was a Republican.

When I said as much Marissa looked at me with cold disapproval but MacDonald laughed. "Boots and I go back—way back. The boy'd never forgive me if I voted Republican. And he won't forgive me now unless I listen to him blow smoke rings for a while. Marissa?" He held out his left arm. "And—Vic, is it?" He crooked the right.

Who knows, he might like to hear about some of my cases—maybe he needed a few million dollars' worth of investigations and didn't even realize it. Not only that, it would make Marissa steam—in itself a good reason to tag along. I took his arm and let him guide me toward the pit.

The barbecue had been installed on the far side of the house from the refreshment tent. A good-sized crowd was milling around the thick pungent smoke—I couldn't see the poor dead cow through the throng, but assumed she was roasting away.

People were standing in an informal horseshoe around a small platform— really a large tree stump with a few boards nailed to it—where Boots stood with his left arm around Roz's shoulders. A tall man, Boots has become majestic in late middle age—silver hair swept in leonine waves from his craggy face, broad shoulders usually encased in buckskin, and a deep hearty laugh. His head was tilted back now as he roared in amusement. It was his trademark look, the pose he affected for campaign posters, but even a nonbeliever like me found his laugh infectious, and I didn't know what the joke was.

The crowd near him included men and women of all ages and races. After Boots stopped laughing Rosalyn called out something in Spanish and got a good-natured hand. As I'd expected, she was in faded jeans, her concession to the party a crisp white shirt with a Mexican string tie. She looked just as she used to in Logan Square, her bronze skin clear, her eyes bright. Maybe I was too pessimistic—maybe she was smart enough to figure how to run with the regular Dems and keep her own agenda intact.

Rosalyn jumped down from a crate she'd been perched on and disappeared from view—she's not much over five feet tall. As she and Boots began pressing hands and exchanging quips, Marissa pulled MacDonald away from me. I smiled to myself. It had to be the first time I'd ever made Marissa downright jealous, and all for a billionaire I didn't have any interest in. At least, not much interest.

Farther back from them I caught sight of the two Hispanic contractors who'd been talking to Michael and the boys. They were watching me narrowly; when they saw me looking at them they smiled guardedly. I sketched a wave and thought maybe the moment had finally come when I could get back to Chicago. Before I could make an escape, though, Rosalyn and Boots materialized near me. Rosalyn caught sight of me and clapped her hands.

"Vic! How wonderful to see you. I was *ecstatic* when I heard you might be here." She hugged me enthusiastically, then turned to present me to Boots. "Vic Warshawski. She used to work for you, Boots, in the public defender's office. But you're working for yourself now, aren't you? They tell me as an investigator?"

I felt like a child prodigy being paraded around for the neighbors. I managed to mumble a species of response.

"What kind of investigator, Vic?" Boots poured his geniality over me.

"Private detective. Primarily financial investigations."

Boots gave his legendary laugh and shook my hand. "I'm sorry the county lost you, Vic—we don't do enough to keep our good people. But I hope your own work is successful."

"Thank you, sir," I said primly. "Good luck on the campaign trail, Roz."

Boots suddenly caught sight of Ralph MacDonald. Genuine pleasure warmed his smile.

"Mac, you old so-and-so. Knew your contribution would double if I didn't see your shining face, huh?" Boots stretched a hand over my head to smack MacDonald's shoulder. "And of course you found Marissa Duncan— you always could pick out the best in show, couldn't you?"

I ducked away from the arm and the hearty bonhomie. Marissa's face was frozen in the mannequin expression most women assume when they're getting the wrong kind of compliment. Reflexively she put a hand to pull the collar ends of her dress together. I even found it in me to feel a little sorry for her.

As I slid away from her I saw Rosalyn ahead of me talking to Schmidt and Martinez. To my surprise they were gesturing toward me. Rosalyn turned her head, saw me looking, and flashed a smile. The stainless-steel front tooth she'd acquired in her poverty-ridden childhood glinted briefly. She spoke earnestly to the contractors, then turned once more to me. She made extravagant signs for me to join her. Making a face to myself I shouldered my way through the eager hands stretched out to her.

"Warshawski! The boys and I were talking about you just now. You've met little Luis, huh? He's my cousin—my mother's sister married a German down in Mexico City and lived to be sorry ever after! You know those old love stories." She laughed gaily. "We could use your help, Warshawski."

"You've got my vote, Roz. You know that."

"More than that, though." Before she could continue, Boots came up with MacDonald in tow. He flashed a perfunctory smile at me and dragged Roz off to confer in the house.

"Wait for me, huh, *gringa*? I'll see you in the porch swing—oh, in an hour," she shouted hoarsely over her shoulder.

I was left glaring at her back. Because I'm a woman in a man's business people think I'm tough, but a truly tough and decisive person would have headed back to town at that point. Instead I felt the tired old tentacles of responsibility drape themselves around me. Lotty Herschel tells me it comes of being the only child of parents I had to look after during painful illnesses. She thinks a few years with a good analyst would enable me to just say no when someone shouts "I need you, Vic."

Perhaps she's right—the sour thought of my parents conjured by her remembered words mingled with the smell of roasting beef and nauseated me. For a moment I felt myself identifying with the dead animal—caught around by people who fed it only to smash its head in with a mallet. I didn't think I could eat any of it. When the head barbecuer suddenly sang out that they were ready to start carving, I hunched my shoulders and left.

I circled the house to find the porch swing Rosalyn had mentioned. What Boots treated as the back of the house had actually been designed as the main entrance when the place was built a hundred years ago or so. A set of shallow steps led to a colonnaded veranda and a pair of doors inlaid with opaque etched glass.

The porch faced a flower bed and a small ornamental pond. It was a peaceful spot; the band and the crowd sounds still reached me, but no one else had strayed this far from the action. I strolled over to the pond and peered into it. Clouds turned rosy by the setting sun made the surface of the water shimmer a silvery blue. A cluster of goldfish swam over to beg for bread.

I glared at them. "Everyone else in this country has a fin stuck out—why should you guys be any different? I just don't have any slush left today."

I felt someone come up behind me and turned as Michael put an arm around my shoulders. I removed it and backed away a few paces.

"Michael, what's going on with you today? Are you peeved because I wanted to drive myself? . . . Is that why you pulled that number on me at the gate and again with your pals back there? You can't muscle me aside and then come caress me back into good humor."

"I'm sorry," he said simply. "I didn't mean it like that. Ron and Ernie introduced me to those two guys—Schmidt and Martinez. They're breaking into construction, just getting a few good jobs, and their work sites are being vandalized. The boys thought they could use some free police advice. When you came up we were in the middle of it. I was afraid you were still mad at me and I didn't know how to handle it and not let them think I wasn't listening to them, either. So I blew it. Can you still talk to me?"

I hunched a shoulder impatiently. "The trouble is, Michael, you belong to a crowd where the girls sit on a blanket waiting for the boys to finish talking business and bring them drinks. I like LeAnn and Clara, but they'll never be good friends of mine—it's not the way I think or act or live or—or anything. I think that style—the segregated way you and Ernie and Ron work—it's too much part of you. I don't see how you and I ever can move along together."

He was quiet for a few minutes while he thought it over. "Maybe you're right," he said reluctantly. "I mean, my mother kept house and hung out with her friends and my dad had his bowling club. I never saw them do anything together—even church, it was always her taking the kids to Mass while he slept it off on Sunday mornings. I guess it was a mistake trying to see you at a function like this." The sun had set but I could see his smile flash briefly, worried, not cocky.

The surface of the pond turned black; behind us the house loomed as a ghostly galleon. It was Michael's ability to think about himself that set him apart from his pals. There was a time when it might have seemed worth the effort to work things out with someone who was willing to stop and think about it. But I'm thirty-seven now and no longer seem able to put the energy into dubious undertakings.

Before I could make up my mind what I wanted to say, Roz whirled up. I hadn't expected to see her—at a function like this she'd have so many demands on her time that a desire to meet with me could easily fade from her mind. Schmidt and Martinez were with her.

"Vic!" Her voice had faded to a hoarse whisper after a long day of talking, but it vibrated with her usual energy. "Thank goodness you waited for me. Can we grab a few minutes on the porch?"

I grunted unenthusiastically.

Schmidt and Martinez were greeting Michael in low-voiced seriousness. I introduced him to Rosalyn. She shook his hand perfunctorily and hustled me across the yard.

The lawn was smoothly trimmed; even at the pace she set we kept our footing in the dark. The porch was outlined by light coming from the other side of the opaque doors. I could see the swing, and Rosalyn's shape when she settled in it, but her face was in too much shadow for me to make out her expression.

I sat on the top of the shallow steps, my back against the pillar, and waited for her to speak. On the lawn behind us I could make out the shapes of Michael and the two contractors as dark splotches. From the other end of the house the band was revving up to a more feverish pitch; the increased volume and the noise of laughter drifted to us.

"If I win the election I'm finally going to be in a position to really help my people," Rosalyn said at last.

"You've already done a great deal."

"No soap tonight, Vic. I don't have time or energy for pats on the back. . . . I'm setting my sights high. Getting Boots to endorse me—it was difficult but necessary. You do understand that?"

I nodded, but she couldn't see that, so I gave an affirmative grunt. Anyway, I did understand it.

"This election is just the first step. I'm aiming for Congress and I want to be in a position for a cabinet post if the Democrats win in eight or twelve years."

I grunted again. The specific shape of her ambition was interesting, but I'd always known she had the ability and the drive to reach for the top. In eight or twelve years maybe the country would even be ready for a Hispanic woman vice president. She must have been born in Mexico, though—that was why she was thinking only of the cabinet.

"Your advice would always be valuable to me."

I had to strain to hear her, her voice had gotten so hoarse. "Thanks for the testimonial, Roz."

"Some people—my cousin—think you might do something to hurt me, but I told him you would never do such a thing."

I couldn't begin to fathom what she might be talking about and said as much. She didn't answer right away, and when she finally did I got the impression she'd chosen her words with great care.

"Because I'm working with Boots. Anyone who knows you knows you've always opposed everything he stands for."

"Not everything," I said. "Just the stuff I know about. Anyway, your cousin doesn't know me. We just met this afternoon."

"He knows about you," she persisted in her raw voice. "You've done a lot of significant work one way and another. People who are connected around town hear your name."

"I don't need soap any more than you do, Roz. I haven't said or done anything to make anyone think I'd stand in your way. Hell! I even paid two-fifty to support your campaign. What does your cousin imagine I'm doing? It may be chicken feed to a contractor, but that's a big outlay for me—I wouldn't do it frivolously."

She put her hand on mine. "I appreciate you coming out for me. I know it took a lot for you to do, both the money and the function." She gave a throaty chuckle. "I've had to swallow a few things, too, to be here—the sidelong looks from the party regulars. I know what they're thinking—Boots is getting a piece of Spanish ass and giving her a spot on the ticket as payment."

"So what is Schmidt worried about? That I'm from the Legion of Decency and I'm going to cook up a sex scandal? I'm *really* offended, Roz. Offended by the thought and by you thinking you had to sound me out over it."

Her callused fingers gripped mine. "No, no, Vic. Don't take it that way. Luis is my little cousin, my little brother, almost, the way he worries about me. Some men he was talking to told him how negative you are to Boots and he got worried on my behalf. I told him I'd talk to you, that's all, *gringa*. Boots has his flaws, after all, I'm not blind to them. But I can use him."

I didn't know if I was hearing the truth or not. Maybe she was sleeping with Boots for the good of the Hispanic community—there was very little Roz wouldn't do to help her people. It would turn my stomach, but I didn't really care. At any rate, prolonging the conversation wasn't going to buy me a copy of her thoughts.

"I don't like you tying your wagon to Boots's star, but I can't afford to be picky—I'm self-employed and it's a pretty small operation. And there's certainly something to be said for letting Boots do your dirty work. Pulling the plug on abortions at Cook County the way he did, he owes the women in this town something—why shouldn't it be you."

Roz gave a husky laugh. "I knew I could count on you, Vic." She summoned enough of her voice to call her cousin. "Hey, Luis, come on, we gotta go get a drink and shake a few more hands."

Luis ambled over to the porch with Michael; Carl Martinez apparently had taken off. "You get everything settled, Roz?" It didn't sound like a casual question.

"Coming up roses. You worry too much, you know—you're just like your mama that way."

We stood up. Roz hugged me. "I may call you yet, Warshawski. Get you to stuff envelopes or hold my hand if I freak."

"Sure, Roz. Whatever you want."

I followed her down the shallow steps. When Luis had hustled her around the side of the house, Furey took my arm.

"Let me meet you back at your place, Vic, get things talked out. I don't want to have matters go completely bust between us without at least saying good-bye in a friendly way."

I was staring at the corner of the house where Roz had disappeared, still trying to figure out what the hell that whole conversation had been about. I was so busy with my thoughts that I found I'd agreed with Furey without even realizing it.

8
A DEVOTED MOTHER

It was dark when I pulled up behind Michael's silver Corvette on Racine. I'd expected to be home long ahead of him—he'd run into Ron and Ernie after seeing me into my car. When I pulled out they were still talking. However, relying on superior police knowledge of city routes—and professional courtesy from the traffic cops—he managed to beat me. He climbed out of the Corvette when he saw me behind him and came over to me.

"Vic. This is not destined to be our best day. A call came in on the radio while I was driving over. I'm not supposed to be on duty until tomorrow morning, but Uncle Bobby doesn't care much about official rosters when there's been a triple homicide. Sorry. I'll give you a call tomorrow, okay?"

I tried to muster an appropriate expression of sorrow, but I was just as happy to be on my own tonight. The idea of a nice soak in the tub without having to be pleasant to an outsider had been tantalizing me during the long drive home. I barely waited to wave good-bye before heading up the walk to the front door. And the shattering of my dreams of solitude.

Elena was parked on the first-floor landing, her duffel bag at her feet. Next to her sat a young black woman. Even in the dim hall light I could see she was dressed with a stylishness that highlighted Elena's worn face and bedraggled clothes. When I saw them my guilty worries about my aunt vanished. My stomach knotted and I felt a cowardly impulse to shut the door and head back to Streamwood.

Elena sprang jerkily to her feet and opened her arms in a wide meaningless gesture. "Victoria, sweetie, your nice neighbor let us in so we wouldn't have to wait for you in the lobby. The old gentleman. He's a real gem, you don't find too many as chivalrous as him today. He told us you hadn't left town so I figured we'd just wait for you 'stead of coming back later."

"Hi, Elena," I said weakly. "I found a room for you. Over on Kenmore."

"Oh, Vicki, Victoria, I mean, family's family and I knew you wouldn't let me down. This here is Cerise. She's the daughter of a buddy of mine from the Indiana Arms. Cerise, meet my niece Victoria. Finest niece a woman could ever want. If anyone can help you, she will."

Cerise held out a slim, manicured hand. "Pleased to meet you." Her voice was almost inaudible.

"I can't put her up, Elena," I said grimly. "No amount of sweet-talking is going to make me turn my place into a way station for victims of Wednesday night's fire."

Elena pursed her lips in exaggerated hurt. "No way, sweetie. I wouldn't dream of it. Cerise here needs a detective. When I heard her story I knew you were just the gal for her."

I wanted to pull my hair out by the roots or scream or anything extreme that would keep me from pounding my aunt. Before I could formulate a nonviolent response, the door to one-north opened and the banker popped out again.

"Oh, it's you," he said disagreeably. "I might have known. Well, this time I am calling the cops. I saw your pimp pull off just now in that silver Corvette. What are these—your drug clients?"

"What do you do all day long at work?" I snapped. "Spy on the clerks to see who's taking five minutes too long at her coffee break? You must be one of the most popular guys around if all you do is peer over people's shoulders into their business."

"It's my business if you conduct your sleazy affairs at all hours—"

"No, no, honey," my aunt popped up. "She's a detective. A professional. We've come to consult her on business. You don't want to frown in that angry way—it's just as important for a man to keep his looks these days as it is for a girl, and you'll get terrible wrinkles around your eyes if you keep scowling like that. And you've got very nice eyes."

"Elena, just be quiet, will you? We can discuss Cerise's problem upstairs.

Take her on up, okay?" I wasn't going to resolve anything with the guy if Elena was mediating.

Elena protested, hurt, that she was just trying to help me get along better with my neighbors, but she finally agreed to start upstairs. I looked at the banker, debating whether I should say something conciliatory—it's not a great idea to have a vendetta with a neighbor in a six-unit building.

"Be sure to give the cops the Corvette's plates when you call, will you?" I told him. "The fellow who drives it is a detective with the Central District's Violent Crimes Unit. The beat guys'll enjoy razzing him about getting accused of being a pimp. If you didn't catch the plate, it's 'fureous'—that's F-U-R-E-O-U-S." Some days I'm just more conciliatory than others.

He scowled at me with dark angry eyes, trying to decide whether I was bluffing. Hearing the license plate spelled out apparently made him decide I wasn't. He stalked back into his apartment and slammed the door. From the south unit I could hear Peppy's insistent whimpering as she begged to join in the fray. I ran up the stairs two at a time to avoid Mr. Contreras's predictable harangue.

I ushered Elena and Cerise into my apartment. "Can I get you something to drink? Coffee? Soda?"

"I'll take a beer," Cerise said.

"Sorry. I don't have beer. Coffee, milk, or juice. Or I have seltzer and some Coke."

Cerise settled on a Coke while Elena asked for some of that wonderful coffee like my ma used to make. I served up the remains of the pasta salad I'd taken to yesterday's picnic and heated a couple of rolls. Neither woman seemed to have eaten much recently. Beyond Cerise's asking what the queer white things in the salad were, and accepting "calamari" with a wise nod, they both ate rapidly without speaking.

"So what's the problem that needs a detective?" I asked when they'd finished.

Cerise looked at Elena, asking her to speak for her.

"It's her baby," my aunt said.

In the bright light of my living room I could see Cerise wasn't as old as her sophisticated clothes had made her look downstairs. She might have been twenty, but any legitimate bar would card her.

"Yes," I said as encouragingly as possible.

"We think she died in the fire," Elena said.

"Died in the fire?" I repeated stupidly.

"At the Indiana Arms," my aunt said sharply. "Don't gape there like a carp, Vicki. You must remember it."

"Yes, but—you think? Don't you know?"

I'd spoken to Cerise. She shook her head and again turned to Elena. My aunt spoke briskly, using wild hand motions and pursing her lips periodically to underscore a dramatic point.

"The whole point of an SRO, Vicki, is that it's *single* resident occupancy.

Single means no one else in the room with you, not even a cockroach, if you get my drift. And certainly no babies. And here's Cerise, trying to get her life together, and she has the sweetest little baby you ever saw, fourteen months old and just starting to toddle, and what's she supposed to do with it while she's out hunting for work?"

Elena paused, as if waiting for an answer, but I didn't try to interrupt the flow.

"So she leaves it with her ma, same as you would if it was you. If Gabriella was still alive, I mean, being as how she always wanted the best for you. And Cerise's ma is just the same. Nothing too good for Cerise and she'll risk getting thrown right out on her rear end"—Elena smacked her own behind to emphasize the point—"if it'd help Cerise here make a decent life for the baby."

When I didn't say anything she repeated her last point sharply.

"Great," I managed.

Elena beamed. "So her ma is kind of a pal of mine. We've knocked back a few beers together, not that I drink, you understand, nor does she, just a few beers now and then in a sociable kind of way." She stared at me defiantly, but I didn't challenge the statement.

"So Zerlina—that's Cerise's ma—is watching the baby while Cerise is out of town Wednesday night when we have the fire. Now Zerlina's vanished— poof—and poor Cerise can't find out if her dear little baby made it out of the building alive."

She slapped her hands together for effect and watched me expectantly. All I could think was that it was Sunday night, almost four days since the fire— why was Cerise surfacing only now?

"So I told her you'd help," Elena prompted me impatiently.

"Help do what?"

"Well, Vicki—Victoria—she needs to find the poor little thing. She's afraid it'll get her ma in trouble if she goes to the police. You know, for keeping a baby in the room. Maybe she'd never be able to find another place. I said you were just the person for her."

"Why has it taken this long for Cerise to miss the baby?" I demanded.

"I been out of town." It was Cerise's first contribution to the conversation since she'd asked about the calamari. "Otis, he the baby's father, he took me up to the Dells. We trying to work things out, you know, I want him to marry me and make a home for me and Katterina and he don't want to do it. So he promised me a vacation."

I rubbed my forehead, trying to push the more harrowing images of her life out of my brain. "And you just got back today?"

"I went to the hotel," she burst out. "I went straight there. People say I don't love Katterina, leaving her with my mother and all, but I do. I just can't look after her and have my own life too, not twenty-four hours a day. I can't even get a job if I got to stay with her all the time. But I went there first thing, Otis dropped me there, you can ask him, that was yesterday. And I saw about the fire, and I hunted all over for my mama and finally I found Elena this afternoon. But she don't know where Mama is. Except maybe in the hospital where they took the people who was hurt in the fire."

"Maybe the fire fighters found Katterina," I offered. "Maybe she's with DCFS. Have you tried calling them?"

"I can't call them. They just want to take my baby from me, say I'm an unfit mother." She started to cry, her long red earrings bobbing into her shoulders.

"There, there." Elena put a soothing arm around her shoulders. "That's what we need you for, Vicki. We need someone who knows how to talk to all these people, who can handle it without getting Cerise or Zerlina in trouble."

It didn't sound to me as though there was much hope that Katterina had made it through the fire. If a baby had been found there, surely the newspapers would have trumpeted it.

"I'm sorry," I said helplessly to Cerise. "Sorry about Katterina. But you really are the best person to go to the police and to DCFS—you're her mother, you're the only one with a right to ask questions."

She kept crying without looking up at me. I tried explaining that the police were not going to care that Zerlina had had a baby in the room with her, that they couldn't keep her from renting a room ever again, but it washed over both Cerise and Elena like the tide.

I thought of the woman I'd talked to at the Emergency Housing Bureau, the despair she'd shared with the other people in the room, the few rooms and the many people to fill them. If you were that helpless, the police might become another bureaucratic menace, ready to use their power to keep you out of a place to live.

"Okay." I finally said. "I'll make some calls for you tomorrow."

Elena took her hand from Cerise's shoulder and came over to where I was sitting in the armchair. "That's my girl. I knew I could count on you. I knew you was too much your ma's daughter to say no to a fellow human being in trouble."

"Right," I agreed sourly. I looked at the clock on the bookshelves. It was ten. Even if I sent Elena over to the Windsor Arms this late she couldn't take Cerise with her. Gritting my teeth, I pulled out the sofa bed, dug around in my drawers for a long T-shirt for Cerise to sleep in, and locked myself in my bedroom.

9

THE LADY
IS INDISPOSED

I woke up early the next morning. My dreams had been of crying babies and fires; I'd jerked awake twice feeling suffocated by flames. When I got out of bed it was again with the feeling that someone had dumped a load of gravel in my head, this time without bothering to crush it too fine.

It was only six. Cerise and Elena were still asleep on the sofa bed, Cerise lying spread-eagled on her stomach, Elena on her back snoring. I felt like a captive in my own home, unable to get to my books or television, but if I woke them, it would be worse. I shut the door softly, put on my jeans, and went down the back stairs. It was too early to wake up Mr. Contreras to take the dog for a run. And even though exercise may be the best cure for a sandy head, running sounded like the last thing I was in the mood for.

I walked the half mile to the Belmont Diner, open twenty-four hours a day, and had the cholesterol special, pancakes with butter and a big order of bacon. I lingered as long as I could, following the saga of the search for the Bears new stadium through all three papers, even taking in every word on the latest zoning scandal to beset the mayor's chief supporters. It's boring to read about zoning scandals because their revelation never has any impact on election results, so I usually skip them.

Around eight I finally trudged back to my apartment. Life was stirring on Racine Avenue as people headed for work. When I got to my building the banker was leaving for the day, his thick brown hair lacquered to his head.

"Hi," I said brightly as we passed. "Just getting off the night shift. Have a good day."

He pretended not to hear me, crossing to the east side of the street as I spoke. Try to be neighborly and you only get stiffed for your pains.

Like LBJ or the Duke of Wellington, Elena could sleep anywhere, anytime. When I opened the kitchen door I could hear her snores oozing from the living room. I also caught my favorite smell, cigarette smoke. Cerise was at the dining-room table, staring moodily at nothing, chain-smoking.

"Good morning," I said as politely as I could. "I know you're really upset about your baby, but please don't smoke in here."

She shot me a hostile look but stubbed her cigarette out in the saucer she'd been using. I took it to the kitchen and tried to scrub the tobacco stains from it. After a few minutes she followed me in and slumped herself at the table. I offered her breakfast but she wanted only coffee. I put water on to boil and got the beans out of the freezer.

"What floor did your mother live on?"

She looked at me blankly and rubbed her bare arms.

"At the Indiana Arms. I'll probably need that information if someone is going to search for Katterina."

"Fifth floor," she answered after another long pause. "Five twenty-two. It was hard on her on account of the elevator didn't work, but she couldn't get nothing lower down."

"When did you leave the baby with your mother?"

Again she stared at me, but this time I thought there was an element of calculation in her gaze. "We did it Wednesday. Before we left town." She rubbed her arms some more. "It's too cold in here. I need to smoke."

It felt warm to me, but I was dressed; she was still in the outsized T-shirt I'd lent her. I went into my bedroom and got a jacket. She put it on but continued to rub her arms.

I ground the beans and poured boiling water through them. "What time Wednesday?"

"You trying to say I saw the fire and shouldn'ta left my baby?" Her tone was sullen but her eyes were still watchful.

I poured more water into the beans and tried to muster some empathy. Her baby was almost certainly dead. She was with a stranger and a white woman at that. She was terrified of the institutions of law and society and I was conversant with them, so to her I was part of them. She wanted to smoke and I wouldn't let her.

Thinking about all this didn't make me feel like running over to embrace her, but it did help me stifle the more extreme expressions of impatience. "Someone set that fire," I said carefully. "Someone hurt your mother and may have hurt your baby. If you were there Wednesday night, you might have seen the arsonist. Maybe he—or she—or they—were hanging around. If you saw someone, we could give the police a description, something to start an investigation with."

She shook her head violently. "I didn't see no one. We go there at three in the afternoon. We give Katterina to my mama. We leave for Wisconsin. Okay?"

"Okay." I poured out coffee for her. "Why are these questions upsetting you so much?"

She was trembling. She took the mug with both hands to steady it. "You acting like I did something bad, like it be my fault my baby's hurt."

"No, Cerise, not at all. I'm really sorry if that's how I sounded. I don't mean that at all." I tried to smile. "I'm a detective, you know. I ask questions for a living. It's a hard habit to break."

She buried her face in the mug and didn't answer me. I gave it up and went into my bedroom. The bed was still unmade. My running clothes had fallen on the floor at the end when I'd kicked the covers off in the night.

Untangling my sweats from the bedclothes, I stuffed them into the closet and pulled the covers back up onto the bed. The room wasn't exactly ready for *House Beautiful,* but it was all the housekeeping I was in the humor for.

I lay on the bed and tried to remember the name of the insurance man I'd met at the Indiana Arms on Thursday. It was a bird; that had struck me particularly at the time because his bright-eyed curiosity had made him seem birdlike. I shut my eyes and let my mind drift. Robin. That was it. I couldn't delve the last name from my memory hole, but Robin would get me to him.

I pulled the phone from the bedside table and put it on my stomach to dial. When the Ajax operator connected me with the arson and fraud division, I asked the cheery receptionist for Robin.

"He's right here—I'll put him on for you."

The phone banged in my ear—she must have dropped the receiver—then I got a tenor. "Robin Bessinger here."

Bessinger. Of course. "Robin, it's V. I. Warshawski. I met you at the Indiana Arms last week when you were digging through the rubble there."

"V.I. You the detective?"

"Uh-huh." I sat up and put the phone back on the bedside table. "You said if anybody's been killed, the police would have had a homicide investigation set up. So I assume everybody was rescued?"

"As far as I know." I'd forgotten how cautious he was. A bird making sure the worm wasn't really a rifle barrel. "You know anything to the contrary?"

"A baby was staying there Wednesday night. Staying with its grandmother on the fifth floor." He started to interrupt and I said hastily, "I know, I know. Against the rules. The grandmother has disappeared—maybe one of the smoke victims—so I don't know if they found the baby or not."

"A baby in there. Sweet Jesus, no. . . . I don't know anything about it, but I'll call someone at the police and get back to you. Was it your friend? The one you said had been burned out?"

I'd forgotten referring to Elena as my friend. "No, not her. The grandmother was sort of a friend of hers, though, and the mother just got back into town and found her little girl and her own mama both missing. She's pretty distraught." Or hostile. Or fried.

"Okay." He fumbled around for a moment. "I'm just real sorry. I'll call you back in a couple of minutes."

I gave him my phone number and hung up. I looked distastefully at my bedroom. Because I'm there only to sleep I don't usually pay much attention to it. The queen-size bed takes up a good deal of the available space. Since the closet is large I keep the dresser in there to have enough room to walk around, but it still makes me feel hemmed in to spend much time there during the day. More than ever I resented Elena's snoring presence down the hall, pinning me to one room in my own home.

I paced the short distance from the door to the head of the bed a few times but I kept banging my shin on the bedstead. I couldn't possibly practice my singing in these quarters, especially not with Cerise in the kitchen. Finally I lay on the floor between the window and the bed and did leg lifts. After forty or so with each leg Robin called back. He sounded subdued.

"V. I. Warshawski?" He stumbled a bit on my last name. "I—uh, I've been talking with the police. They say the fire department didn't bring out any children from that place last week. Are you sure the baby was in there?"

I hesitated. "Reasonably sure. I can't swear to it, though, because I don't know any of the people involved."

"They're going to send a team out to comb the rubble, to see if they can find any, well, any remains. They'd like you to be available to come downtown to meet with them, though."

I promised to check in with my answering service every hour if I left my apartment. Slowly hanging up the phone, I wondered what to say to Cerise. As I walked to the door Elena pounded on the other side.

"Yoo-hoo! Vicki! Victoria, I mean. Poor little Cerise isn't feeling too hot. Can you come out and help me settle her upset tummy?"

Poor little Cerise had vomited all over the kitchen table. Elena, at her brightest as she enjoyed the drama, wiped her face with a damp towel while I cleaned up the mess.

"It's the shock, you know," my aunt cooed. "She's worried sick about her baby."

I looked at the younger woman narrowly. She was sick, all right, but I was beginning to think a little more than shock underlay her behavior.

"I think we'll have a doctor take a look at her," I said. "Help me get her dressed and down to my car."

"No doctor," Cerise said thickly. "I'm not seeing no doctor."

"Yes, you are," I snapped. "This isn't a one-woman social agency. You just threw up all over my kitchen and I'm not spending the day nursing you."

"No doctor, no doctor!" Cerise screamed.

"She really doesn't want to go, Vicki," Elena stage-whispered at me.

"I can see she doesn't want to go," I said brittlely. "Just put her clothes on while I hold her arms still. And please don't call me Vicki. It's not a name I care for much."

"I know, I know, sweetie," Elena promised hastily. "It keeps slipping my mind."

Since Gabriella had driven home the point forcefully to Elena all through my childhood—"I didn't name her for Victor Emmanuel to have people talk to her as though she were a silly ingenue"—I didn't see how Elena could have forgotten, but this wasn't the time to argue the point.

Dressing Cerise made me glad I hadn't chosen nursing in a mental hospital as my career. She fought against my hold, screaming and thrashing around in the kitchen chair. I'm in good shape, but she strained my muscles to the utmost. At one point she raked open my left arm with a long fingernail. I somehow managed to hang on to her.

Elena worked with an ineffectuality that brought me close to the scream-ing point myself. She put Cerise's underpants on backwards and only man-aged to slide her skirt on after a good fifteen minutes of work.

"Just do her shoes," I panted. "She can wear the T-shirt on top. My keys are in the living room. I left them on the coffee table. Unlock the dead bolts."

I tried to explain which key worked which lock, but gave it up as Elena grew more confused. By some miracle she managed to undo them in less than an hour. Cerise had stopped fighting me by then. She hunched limply over the kitchen table sobbing to herself and offered no resistance as I es-corted her out the door. I took the keys from Elena.

"You'd best get your bag. I'm going to drop you off at your new place as soon as Cerise has seen the doctor."

Elena tried to put up a fight of her own, but I was past any feelings of guilt. I kept Cerise propped up against the wall and repeated my demand. My aunt finally shuffled back into my apartment. After an absence long enough that I wondered if she was back at the Black Label, she came out again. She'd taken a shower; her graying hair hung around her head in damp ringlets, but her makeup was complete and, for once, on target. The violet nightgown still hung out the side of the duffel bag. She let it trail along the floor as she followed me down the stairs.

10
A LITTLE HELP
FROM MY FRIENDS

Lotty Herschel's storefront clinic is about three miles from my apartment, near the corner of Damen and Irving Park. During the short drive Cerise threw up again in the backseat, then started shivering uncontrol-lably. I thought I might kill Elena, who knelt on the front seat watching Cerise and giving me minute-by-minute updates on what she was doing.

I jerked the car to a stop next to a fireplug in front of the clinic and jogged inside. The small waiting room, painted to look like the African veldt, was packed with the usual assortment of wailing infants and squabbling chil-dren. Mrs. Coltrain was keeping order, handling the phone and typing records with her usual calm. I sometimes suggest to Lotty that she found Mrs. Coltrain in a catalog offering to supply offices with old-fashioned grandmothers—not only does she have nine grandchildren, but she wears her silvery hair in a bun.

"Miss Warshawski." She beamed at me. "Good to see you. Do you need to talk to Dr. Herschel?"

"Rather urgently. I have a young woman in my car who's been throwing up and seems now to be going into shock. Can you ask Lotty if she'd see her now if I brought her in, or if I should take her to the hospital?"

Mrs. Coltrain refuses to call Lotty or me by our first names—we gave up urging them on her long ago. She relayed my message to Carol Alvarado, the clinic nurse, and after a couple of minutes Carol came out to help me bring Cerise in. Cerise's skin was cold. It felt thick, like wet plastic, not at all like living tissue. She was conscious enough to walk if we supported her, but her breathing was shallow and her eyes were rolling.

A murmur of resentment swelled around us as we brought Cerise past the waiting room into the examining area—people who've been waiting an hour or more for the doctor don't appreciate line jumpers. Carol got Cerise onto a table and wrapped her in a blanket. Lotty swept in a few minutes later.

"What are you bringing me now, Vic?" She didn't wait for an answer but went straight to Cerise.

I told her what little I knew about the young woman. "Suddenly this morning she started complaining about feeling cold, then she started throwing up. I don't know if it was pregnancy or drugs or some combination, but I didn't feel like dealing with her on my own."

Lotty grunted and pulled back Cerise's eyelids. "She's going to be here for a while. Why don't you come back in a few hours?" She turned to Carol with a request for a medication.

In other words, it was up to me to find out what to do with her when Lotty finished treating her. Not that I'd expected Lotty to do it, but somehow I'd managed to avoid thinking about Cerise's future.

My shoulders sagging, I walked on heavy feet back to the car. I'd forgotten Cerise's eruption, but the smell was a pungent reminder. I returned to the clinic and got some wet rags and a bottle of disinfectant from Mrs. Coltrain. All the time I was cleaning the backseat Elena kept chirping questions about Cerise.

"I don't know," I said wearily as I finally turned the engine on. "I don't know what's wrong with her or what the doctor will do or if she has to go to the hospital. I'll find all that out when I go back at noon and I'll let you know."

Elena put a tremulous hand on my arm. "It's only because her mother and me are pals, Vicki—Victoria. It'd be the same if it was you in trouble and I took you to Zerlina. She'd feel responsible for you because of me, don't you see."

I took my right hand off the wheel to pat her thin, veined fingers. "Sure, Elena. I understand. Your good heart does you credit."

We drove in silence for a while, then I thought of something. "What's Zerlina's last name?"

"Her last name, sweetie? Why do you care?"

"I want to find her. If she's in the hospital, I can't go to the reception desk at Michael Reese and ask for her by her first name. They don't keep track of patients that way."

"If she got hurt in the fire, sweetie, I don't know if she'd be up to seeing you."

"Not up to seeing me?" I tried to keep my tone conversational, but an overlay of a snarl came through anyway. "If you and Cerise want me to do anything more about the baby, she'd damned well better be up to seeing me. And you should do your best to help me find her."

"Language, Victoria," Elena said reprovingly. "Talking dirty isn't going to solve your problems."

"And dancing around the mulberry bush on this one isn't going to solve yours," I snapped. "Tell me her last name or kiss any help from me good-bye."

"When you scrunch up your face like that you look just like your grand-mother the last few months I was living with her."

I turned north onto Kenmore and pulled up in front of the Windsor Arms. My poor grandmother. If she'd had a stronger personality, she would have booted Elena out on her rump long before her thirtieth birthday. Instead, except for brief forays, my aunt lived with her until she died.

"Your own family is always the last to appreciate you," I said, turning off the engine. "Now why don't you quit screwing around and tell me Zerlina's last name?"

Elena looked at me craftily. "Is this the new hotel, sweetie? You're an angel to go to so much trouble for me. No, no, don't you go carrying that heavy bag, you're young, you need to save your back."

I took the duffel bag from her and escorted her into the lobby. She fluttered off to the lounge area to talk to some of the residents while I dug in my handbag for the room receipt. The concierge, coming from some base-ment recess when I tapped the desk bell, clearly remembered me but insisted on getting the receipt before she'd let Elena have the room. For a nerve-straining moment I was afraid I'd stuffed it in my skirt pocket on Friday, but finally found it stuck in the pages of my pocket diary.

I had intended to beard Elena in her room and force Zerlina's surname from her, but was thwarted by the concierge—this was a single-resident hotel and visitors were not permitted in the guest rooms. Elena blew me a kiss with a promise to get back in touch with me.

"And you will let me know what happens to poor Cerise, won't you, sweetheart?"

I forced a glittering smile to my face. "How am I to do that, Elena—by smoke signal?"

"You can leave a message for me at the desk, can't she do that, honey?" she added to the concierge.

"I suppose," the woman said grudgingly. "As long as you don't make a habit of it."

As they disappeared up the echoing stairwell I could hear Elena explaining that I was the smartest, sweetest niece a woman could ever hope to have. I ground my teeth and acknowledged defeat.

The pay phone for residents was in the lounge with the TV. I didn't want to compete with *The Price Is Right;* I walked up Kenmore looking for another phone. After a two-block circuit I decided I'd be better off going back to my apartment.

The super had finally gotten around to putting up the banker's nameplate. I stopped to look at it—Vincent Bottone. I felt vaguely affronted that an Italian could be treating me so rudely—didn't he know that we were compatriots? I glanced at my own nameplate—since my last name was Warshawski, maybe he hadn't been able to guess. I'd have to try speaking to him in Italian and see if that softened him. Or, I realized as I unlocked my apartment door, give me a chance to show him up.

Robin Bessinger was in a meeting, but he'd left word with the receptionist to get him if I called. I tucked the phone under my ear while I waited, and yanked the sheets from the sofa bed. I was just stuffing the mattress back into the sofa frame when Robin came on the line.

"Ms. Warshawski? Robin Bessinger."

"It's Vic," I interrupted him.

"Oh. Vic. I've been wondering what those initials stood for. Look—the lab says there isn't any trace of a baby's body in the debris. On the other hand, if it got caught in the fiercest part of the blaze, it might have been incinerated. So they've taken samples of the ashes and will get them analyzed, which'll take a few days. But Roland Montgomery—he's with the Bomb and Arson Squad—would like to talk to you, find out firsthand why you think the child was in there."

I wasn't sure I did think Katterina had been in the Indiana Arms. At this point I wasn't sure I believed Cerise had a baby, or even a mother. But I couldn't express any of this to Robin.

"The baby's mother told me," I said. "Where does Montgomery want me to meet him?"

"Can you make it at three in his office? Central District at Eleventh Street." He hesitated for a moment. "I'd like to sit in if you don't mind. A death would affect our insured. Dominic Assuevo will be there from the Office of Fire Investigation."

"Not at all," I said politely. I didn't know Montgomery, but I'd met Assuevo a couple of years ago when my old apartment had been torched. He was a pal of Bobby Mallory's and was inclined to look on me suspiciously by extension.

Before we hung up I asked Robin if he knew Zerlina's last name. He hadn't been given a list of the smoke inhalation victims but promised me he'd get it from Dominic at our meeting this afternoon.

I finished tidying up the sofa bed, then took the sheets down to the washing machine in the basement. I'm not normally so obsessive about cleanliness, but I wanted to get all traces of Cerise—and Elena—out of my apartment. If I washed the sheets, it was a clear commitment to myself that I didn't have to put the younger woman up here when I fetched her back from Lotty's. Although I didn't know what the hell I was going to do with her.

It was possible that Cerise had given Lotty her surname. If she hadn't, I thought Carol might call Michael Reese for me and get them to give her Zerlina's last name. I didn't want to meet with the police until I talked to Zerlina, assuming I could find her at Reese.

When I got to the clinic I learned that a chunk of my schedule had dropped out—Cerise had disappeared. Carol was worried, Lotty angry. Lotty had given her a mild tranquilizer and something to control her nausea. Cerise had slept for about an hour in the examining room. The third time Carol went in to check on her she was gone. Mrs. Coltrain had seen her walk out of the clinic but had no reason to stop her—she'd assumed since Cerise came with me that I had arranged to pay Lotty for her treatment separately.

Of course. I'd forgotten the money. A hundred dollars to pay Cerise's bill and help fund some of the clinic's indigent patients. Lotty, furious with me for interrupting her day with such a case, was in no humor to discount her services. I pulled my checkbook from my handbag and wrote out the check.

"I guess I should have taken her to the hospital," I said wearily, handing it to Mrs. Coltrain. "But she got sick so suddenly and so violently that I was afraid she might be dying on me. I didn't know if she had some neurological disease or was coming down from heroin or what. If something like this happens again, which I hope it doesn't, I won't bother you."

That pulled Lotty up short—she hates having her standard of care impugned. Her tone was a little less abrupt when she responded.

"It was a combination of heroin and pregnancy. If there's to be any hope for that fetus, Cerise needs to get into a drug program today."

"I wouldn't bet the farm on her doing it," I said. "I want to try to get in touch with Cerise's mother."

I explained that Zerlina might be in Michael Reese recovering from the fire but that I didn't have her last name. Carol went off to phone the hospital for me—she felt irrationally responsible for Cerise roaming the streets pregnant and addicted. Getting Zerlina's last name was something active she could do to help.

"Not your problem," I tried to tell her when she returned a few minutes later. "If Cerise is bent on destructing, you can't stop her. You should know that by now."

"Yes, Vic," Carol admitted. "I do know it. But I feel as though we let you down. That's partly why Lotty's so angry, you know. She tries to work at such a high level and then when she fails to save someone she takes it personally. And for it to be someone you brought in."

"Maybe," I said dubiously. The truth was, I was happy that Cerise had vanished. It was magic. I didn't have to look after her anymore.

"Anyway, the mother's last name is Ramsay." Carol spelled it for me.

"She's in room four-twenty-two in the main hospital building. I told the head nurse you were a social worker, so there won't be any problem you getting in to see her."

I made a face as I thanked her. Social worker! It was an apt description of how I'd spent my time since Elena showed up at my door last week. Maybe it was time for me to turn Republican and copy Nancy Reagan. From now on when alcoholic or addicted pregnant strays showed up at my door, I would just say no.

11

SMOKING GRANDMA

I climbed into the Chevy and slumped over the wheel. It was only noon, but I was as tired as though I'd been climbing Mount Everest for a week. A faint odor of vomit still hovered in the car, despite the twenty minutes I'd spent scrubbing the backseat. It slowly came to me that I was smelling my own clothes. My jeans were soiled where I'd been kneeling on the car seat—I'd just been too wound up with Elena to notice it earlier. Shuddering violently, I turned on the engine and drove south at a reckless pace, not even bothering to keep an eye out for the blue-and-whites. All I wanted to do was to get home, get my clothes off, get myself scrubbed as clean as I could manage.

I left the Chevy at a wild angle a yard or so from the curb and took the stairs up two at a time. Barely waiting to get inside to strip, I dumped jeans, T-shirt, and panties in a heap in the doorway and headed straight for the bathroom. I stood under the hot water for almost half an hour, washing my hair twice, scrubbing myself thoroughly. Finally I felt cleansed, that addicts and alcoholics were rinsed from my life.

I dressed slowly, taking time to put on makeup and to style my hair with a little gel. A gold cotton dress with big black buttons made me feel elegant and poised. I even burrowed through the hall closet for a black bag to go with my pumps.

On the way out I gathered my discarded clothes and took them to the basement. The sheets were ready for the dryer, but there are limits to my housekeeping fervor—I stuffed my jeans in with the sheets and started the cycle from the beginning.

It was a little after one by now. I wouldn't be able to eat lunch if I wanted to see Zerlina before my meeting with Dominic Assuevo. And I guess I wanted to see her, although my enthusiasm for the Ramsay family was at low tide. I headed over to Lake Shore Drive and joined the flow southward.

Michael Reese Hospital dominates the lakefront for a mile or two at Twenty-seventh Street. I circled the complex a few times until I found someone pulling away from a meter—I was damned if I was going to pay lot fees for this visit. A guard was stationed behind a glass cage in the entryway. She didn't care whether I was a social worker or an ax murderer, so I didn't have to use Carol's cover story to get a pass to the fourth floor.

The distinctive hospital smell—some combination of medication, antiseptic, and the sweat of people in pain—made me flinch involuntarily when I got off the elevator. I had spent too much time in hospitals with my parents when I was younger, and the smell always brings back the misery of those years. My mother died of cancer when I was fifteen, my father from emphysema some ten years later. He was a heavy smoker and there are days when I still get angry about it. Especially today, when I was feeling under siege.

Zerlina Ramsay was in a four-pack. Televisions perched high on facing walls were tuned to conflicting soap operas. Two women glanced indifferently at me when I came in but returned their attention immediately to the screen; the other two didn't even look up. I stood dubiously in the doorway for a moment trying to decide which of the three black women might be Zerlina. None of them bore any overwhelming resemblance to Cerise. Finally I saw a sign attached to one of the beds warning me not to smoke if oxygen was in use. The woman lying there had gauze covering her left arm. Short, her massive build amply displayed by the skimpy hospital robe, she would have been my last choice, but Zerlina had been brought in suffering from smoke inhalation so I supposed she'd needed oxygen. She was attached to what looked like a heart monitor.

I went over to the bed. She turned her gaze toward me reluctantly, her eyes narrowed suspiciously in her jowly face.

"Mrs. Ramsay?" She didn't respond, but she didn't deny it either. "My name is V. I. Warshawski. I think you know my aunt Elena."

Her dark eyes flickered in surprise; she cautiously inspected me. "You sure about that?" Her voice was husky from disuse and she cleared her throat discreetly.

"She told me you two hung out together at the Indiana Arms. Had a few beers together."

"So?"

I gritted my teeth and plowed ahead. "So she was waiting on my doorstep last night with Cerise."

"Cerise! What planet that girl come down from?"

I glanced around the room. As I'd expected, her companions were more interested in live theater than TV. They made no effort to mask their curiosity.

"Can you go out in the hall with that thing?" I gestured at the monitor. "This is kind of private."

"Those two took money from you, I don't want to hear about it. I can't even afford me a new place to sleep, let alone pay back all that girl's bills."

"It doesn't have anything to do with money."

She glowered at me belligerently, but heaved herself to a sitting position. Her substantial frame gave the impression not of fat but of a natural monument, maybe a redwood tree that had grown sideways but not too tall. She brushed away my hand when I tried to take her elbow. Grunting to herself, she slid out of bed, sticking her feet into paper hospital slippers lined up tidily under the edge. The heart monitor was on wheels. Rolling it in front of her, she made her way to the door and down the hall like a tidal wave—nurses and orderlies split to either side when they saw her coming.

She was panting a bit when we got to a small lounge stuck at one end of the hall. She took her time getting her breath before lowering herself onto one of the padded chairs. They were covered in cracked aqua oilcloth that had last been washed when Michael Reese himself was still alive. I perched gingerly on the edge of the chair at right angles to Zerlina.

"So Elena is your aunt, huh? Can't say you look too much like her."

"Glad to hear it. She's thirty years and three thousand bottles ahead of me." I ignored her crack of laughter to add, "I gotta say you don't look too much like Cerise, either."

"That's those thirty years you spoke of," Zerlina said. "I wasn't so bad-looking at her age. And I sure look better than she's going to when she gets to be as old as me, the rate she's going. What kind of story she tell you? She and that aunt of yours."

"Her baby," I said baldly. "Katterina."

Zerlina's face creased in astonishment. For a moment I thought she was going to tell me Cerise didn't have a baby.

"She's picking a funny time to care about that baby, being as how she hasn't paid much attention to it so far to date."

"Katterina wasn't with you Wednesday night when the Indiana Arms burned down?" I couldn't think of a gentle way to ask the question.

"Hm-unh." She shook her jowly head emphatically. "She left the baby with me on Wednesday, all right, but I couldn't keep her with me, not in an SRO, you know. They can be mighty strict about who you got with you, which Cerise knew. But that girl!"

She sat with her hands on her knees, looking broodingly at nothing for a moment. The heart monitor beeped insistently, as though in rhythm with her thoughts. She faced me squarely.

"I might as well tell you the whole story. I don't know why I should. Don't know I can especially trust you. But you don't look like Elena. You don't look like an alkie who'll do the best she can to make money out of your sad news to buy her another bottle."

I felt a little queasy at her words. It's one thing to think of your own aunt turning tricks with the old-age pensioners. It's quite another to imagine her blackmailing people for the price of a drink.

"Not that I haven't had a drink or two in my day, too, and I'll give Elena this, she makes you laugh. You can forget your troubles with her every now and then." She looked away again for a moment, as though her troubles had come too forcefully to mind.

"Well, Cerise had this baby. Last year it was. And this baby had all kinds of problems on account of Cerise is a junkie. She was using heroin all the time she was pregnant. I told her how it would be. She even pretended to be in a program that time they arrested her. She'd been out stealing, her and the boy she was with at the time, and they arrested her. And on account of it was the first time and she was pregnant, they let her go if she promised to go to the program."

She glared at me again, as if daring me to condemn her for having a daughter like that. I made what I hoped was a sympathetic sound and tried to look understanding.

"Then the baby was born—and my, what a time we had! Poor little thing was in the hospital, then Maisie—the other grandmother—took her home. I couldn't, you know. I just live on a little bit of savings I have. I don't have social security—you don't get it for cleaning houses, which is what I did all my life, at least until my heart started giving out on me. But I helped Maisie out as much as I could and by and by we got that baby to sleep at night and even laughing."

"So Cerise never took care of her?"

"Oh, no, she did. Finally she did when she got going with Otis. That was in June. Then suddenly on Wednesday, Cerise comes by saying she can't take it anymore, being home with the baby morning, noon, and night, and I tell her she should be thinking of that before she spreads her legs, you know, not two years later, but she leaves the baby and goes, saying her and Otis is off to the Dells. So I go to the pay phone but I can't find a number for his sister, so I call Maisie and she sends her boy over and gets Katterina. And if you think Cerise is worrying about her, think again, on account of she hasn't come near me here in the hospital."

Maybe it was my imagination, but it seemed to me the heart monitor was beeping faster by the end of her tale. I didn't want to ask her anything that might get her more upset. I also didn't think I had to be the one to let Zerlina know her daughter was pregnant again.

She demanded to know why Cerise had come to see me. When I explained that she was asking me to intervene with the fire department, Zerlina snorted.

"Maybe she does think the baby's dead. Maybe that's why she hasn't been to see me—she's too ashamed. But if her and Elena come to see you together, girl, I advise you to keep your wallet in the bottom of your purse and count all your money before you say good-bye."

I felt an uneasy twinge—I hadn't looked in my billfold before putting it into my black bag. Still, Cerise had been pretty sick, maybe too sick to go hunting for money or credit cards. Before I got up to go I asked Zerlina how long they were keeping her.

She gave a little smile that was half crafty, half embarrassed. "When they brought me in I was unconscious on account of the smoke. And they found my heart was kind of acting up. High blood pressure, high fat in my blood—you name it, I got too much of everything. Except money. So I'm kind of dragging it out, you know, until I can get me a place to stay."

"I see." I'd come across worse crimes in my time. I stood up. "Well, I'm glad the baby's okay, anyway. Cerise disappeared around noon today and I'm not going to put a lot of energy into hunting for her. But if I see her again, I'll let her know her kid is at Maisie's."

She grunted and got slowly to her feet. "Yeah, okay, but I got to call Maisie and tell her Katterina don't go off with Cerise again. You take it easy, girl. What did you say your name was? Vic. And you stay those three thousand bottles behind Elena, you hear me?"

"Got it." I walked slowly down the hall with her to her room door before I said good-bye. Back in the lobby I checked my wallet. The cash was gone and so was my American Express Card. The only thing left was my PI license and that was because it was stuck behind a flap. They'd even lifted my driver's license. I ground my teeth. Cerise might have cleaned me out while I was hiding out in my bedroom this morning. But for all I knew Elena had robbed me when I was struggling with Cerise in the kitchen. I felt my shoulders tighten from futile rage.

I found a pay phone in the lobby and called my credit-card companies to report the cards as stolen. At least I'd memorized my phone card number so I didn't have to stop all my phone calls. I usually keep an emergency twenty in the zip compartment of my purse; when I checked the black bag I found I'd left one in there. On my way out I used it to buy flowers for Zerlina. It wasn't enough, but it was all I could afford.

12

FIRING UP
THE ARSON SQUAD

Before leaving the hospital I tried to reach Robin Bessinger at Ajax. I was hoping to cancel our meeting with the Bomb and Arson Squad now that I knew the baby hadn't been in the Indiana Arms, but I was too late —the insurance receptionist told me he'd already left for the police department. I took a deep breath, squared my shoulders, and headed back to Ellis Avenue and my car.

It used to be you could go to Central Police Headquarters anytime day or night and park with ease. Now that development mania has hit the Near South Side, downtown congestion has clogged the area. It took me half an hour to find a place to park. That made me about ten minutes late for the meeting, which scarcely helped my frayed mood.

Roland Montgomery held court in an office the size of my bed. A regulation metal desk crammed with papers took most of the available space, but he squeezed in chairs for me, Bessinger, Assuevo, and a subordinate. Papers were stacked on the windowsill and on top of the metal filing cabinet. Someone should have told him the place was a fire trap.

Montgomery, a tall, thin man with hollow cheeks, gave me a sour look as I came in. He ignored my outstretched hand, pointed to the empty chair in the corner, and asked if I knew Dominic Assuevo.

Assuevo was bull-shaped—thick neck and wide shoulders tapering into narrow hips. His graying sandy hair was cropped close to his head the way the boys used to wear it when I was in third grade. He greeted me with a jovial courtesy not reflected in his eyes.

"Can't stay away from fire, huh, Ms. Warshawski?"

"Good to see you again, too, Commander. Hiya, Robin. I tried to get you a little bit ago but your office told me you were already here." I skirted my way past his long feet to the vacant chair.

Robin Bessinger was sitting in the opposite corner of the tiny room. He seemed a little older than he'd struck me when I first met him, but of course the hard hat had kept me from seeing that his hair had gone gray. He smiled and waved and said hello.

I squeezed in next to the uniformed man and held out a hand. "V. I. Warshawski. I don't think we've met."

He mumbled something that sounded like "firehorse whiskey." I never did learn what his name really was.

"So you think there was a baby in the Indiana Arms, Ms. Warshawski?" Montgomery pulled a folder from the stack in front of him. I had to believe he'd practiced it, that he couldn't know offhand what fire which folder referred to.

"I did when I spoke to Mr. Bessinger this morning. That was before I tracked down the baby's grandmother. I just finished interviewing her in the hospital and she says she had already sent the child to its other grandmother before the fire broke out."

"So we're wasting our time here, is that what you're telling me?" Montgomery's eyebrows rose to his sandy hairline. He made no effort to hide his contempt.

I gave a tight smile. "Guess so, Lieutenant."

"There were no babies in the Indiana Arms when it burned down?" He swung his neck cranelike across the desk at me.

"I can't say that categorically. I only know that the one I'd been told was there—Katterina Ramsay—had left the building earlier in the evening. For all I know there might have been others. You should check with Commander Assuevo here."

The young man next to me had started to write this in his open notebook but stopped at a sign from Montgomery.

"You have something of the reputation of a wit, Ms. Warshawski," the lieutenant said heavily. "Personally, I have never found your sense of humor entertaining. I hope this wasn't your idea of a joke, to turn police and fire department resources loose on a wild-goose chase."

"My comedic talents have always been greatly overrated by Bobby Mallory," I said coolly. I was feeling pretty angry, but it seemed to me Montgomery was provoking me deliberately. I wanted to be the last one to blink.

"Well, the next time you feel an urge to make a joke, call Mallory, not me. Because if you do abuse departmental resources again, Ms. Warshawski, believe me, I will be calling the lieutenant and asking him to give you a good lesson in legalities."

That seemed to be the end of the interview. Short of leaping over the desk and pummeling him with my bare hands, I couldn't think of anything to say or do to express my frustration effectively. I stood up slowly, aligned my belt buckle directly under the black buttons, pulled an imaginary hair from my dress, and shook out the skirt. I beamed happily at Firehorse Whiskey and sketched a wave at Robin Bessinger.

I kept the happy smile on my face all the way down the stairs. Once in the hall I let the waves of anger wash through me. What the hell was eating Montgomery? It could only be his relations with police lieutenant Bobby Mallory. Bobby talks about me one way and thinks about me quite another —he might easily have told the fire commander I was a pain in the butt and a wiseass—his publicly expressed opinion on many occasions. Missing would be Bobby's affection as an old friend of my parents'.

But that didn't excuse the squad commander's behavior. He could have asked me why I had called Robin to begin with. I certainly wasn't going to start piping out self-exculpation when treated to that kind of routine. And Bessinger—why didn't the guy speak up? I made a tight face and headed for the south exit.

"You look like a snake stood up and bit you. Can't you even say hi to your friends?" It was Michael Furey. I hadn't been scanning faces as I hunched my way down the hall.

"Oh, hiya, Michael. Must be sleep deprivation."

"What are you doing here? Helping us keep Chicago safe and legal?" His dark blue eyes teased me.

I forced myself to smile. "Something like that. I've just been meeting with Roland Montgomery about that fire in the Indiana Arms last week."

"The one where your aunt got caught? You oughta stay clear of arson—that's dirty, dirty stuff."

"Dirty work, but someone's got to do it. Since Montgomery doesn't want to, maybe I'll have a crack at it."

"Oh, Monty's not doing the investigation?" His eyebrows shot up and he looked thoughtful.

"Doesn't seem too interested." I kept my tone light.

"Well, in that case—" He broke off. "You don't want me telling you to mind your own business."

I bowed slightly. "Call the boy a mind reader."

He laughed a little, but there was a current of annoyance in it. "I won't, then. But keep it in mind that if Monty isn't touching it, there may be good reasons to stay away from it."

I looked at him steadily. "Like what? Well, it doesn't matter. Just to keep you happy, no one's asked me to look at the arson. But the more people tell me not to touch something, the more I feel like reaching out a hand just to see what's so special about it."

He hunched a shoulder impatiently. "Whatever you say, Vic. I gotta run."

He went on down the hall, greeting uniformed men with his usual good humor. I shook my head and went on outside.

Bessinger caught up with me as I was crossing State. "Slow down, Vic. I'd like to know what was going on between you and Monty in that meeting."

I stopped and faced him squarely. "You tell me. I wondered why you didn't say anything to explain why you thought it worthwhile bothering Montgomery based just on my phone call."

He held up his hands. "I've been around a lot of fires in my time. I don't step in between the accelerant and the kindling. Besides, I did try to talk to him. That's why I stayed after you. But I still can't figure out why he's so angry about this one. Other than manpower shortages, but he's taking it as a personal affront. Why?"

I shook my head. "I can see it would piss him and Assuevo to have the lab sifting through ashes for a nonexistent body. But I only called you in the first place to find out if you knew. When you didn't I took the long route, which meant getting the last name of the baby's mother and tracking down her mother. The grandmother, I mean."

"You didn't know that when you called?" His tone was puzzled, not accusatory.

"I never saw the young woman before—the mother of the baby—until she came to my place late last night. She'd left the kid with her own mother, Zerlina Ramsay, at the Indiana Arms, and she didn't want me talking to Mrs. Ramsay. She said if I knew their last name it would get her mother in trouble, that she'd never find another place to stay. She's a junkie, though—I don't know if that came from drug-related paranoia or real concern about her mother or what."

We were standing on the pavement near the curb. Patrolmen heading up State toward the entrance kept brushing against us. When I stepped aside to avoid a man being decanted from a stretch limo, I ran into a woman trotting down the street toward Dearborn.

"Can't you watch where you're going?" she snapped at me.

I opened my mouth to utter a guerrilla hostility back, then thought maybe I'd done enough fighting for one day and ignored her.

Robin looked at his watch. "I don't need to go back to the office. Want to get a drink someplace? I'm afraid if someone else bumps into us, Monty's going to have us arrested, the mood he's in."

I suddenly felt very tired. I'd been running since eight this morning cleaning up after Elena and Cerise. People as different as Lotty and Roland Montgomery had been chewing me out. A clean well-lighted place and a glass of whiskey sounded like doctor's orders to me.

Robin had taken a cab up from Ajax. He walked back to the Chevy with me and we headed through the early rush-hour traffic to the Golden Glow, a bar I know and love in the south Loop. We left the car at a meter down near Congress and walked the three blocks back to the bar. Sal Barthele, the owner, was alone with a couple of men nursing beers at the mahogany horse-shoe counter. She nodded majestically at me when I took Robin over to a small round table in the corner. She waited until we were settled and Robin had exclaimed over the genuine Tiffany lamps to take our orders.

"Your usual, Vic?" Sal asked when Robin had ordered a beer.

My usual is Black Label up. I pictured Elena's flushed, veined face and my missing credit cards. I remembered Zerlina's admonition to keep three thousand bottles behind Elena. Then I thought, hell, I'm thirty-seven years old. If I was going to get drunk every time life threatened me, I would have started in years ago. When I feel like having a whiskey, I'll have a whiskey.

"Yes," I said more vehemently than I'd meant.

"You sure about that, girl?" Sal mocked me gently, then went to the bar to fill our order. Sal's a shrewd businesswoman. The Glow is only one of her investments and she could easily afford to turn it over to a manager. But it also was her first venture and she likes to preside over it in person.

Robin took a swallow of his draft and opened his eyes in appreciation. "I've probably walked by here a hundred times going to the Insurance Exchange. How could I have missed this stuff?"

Sal's draft is made for her privately by a small brewer in Steven's Point. I'm not a beer lover, but my pals who are think it's pretty hot stuff.

I told Robin a little about Sal and her operations, then steered the talk back to the Indiana Arms. "You ever find any evidence that the owner was trying to sell the place?"

Robin shook his head. "Too early to tell. His limits aren't out of line, but that doesn't matter. It's really more a question of what's going on with the building and him and his finances. We haven't got that far yet."

"What does Montgomery say?"

Robin frowned and finished his beer before answering. "Nothing. He's not going to dedicate any more resources into investigating the arson."

"And you don't agree?" I drank a glass of water, then swallowed the rest of my scotch. The warmth spread slowly from my stomach to my arms and some of the tension the day had put into my shoulders disappeared.

"We never pay a claim when arson is involved. I mean, not unless we're a hundred percent sure the insured didn't engineer it."

He held up his glass to Sal and she brought over another draft. She had the Black Label bottle with her but I shook my head over the idea of seconds. Elena must have been affecting me after all.

"I just don't understand Montgomery, though. I've worked with him before. He's not an easy guy—not much looseness there—but I've never seen him as nasty as he was to you this afternoon."

"Must be my charm," I said lightly. "It hits some men that way." I didn't think it was worth explaining my theory about Montgomery and Bobby Mallory to a stranger.

Robin refused to laugh. "It's something about this fire. Why else would he tell me the file was closed? He said they'd only reopened it because you thought there might be a body in there. Now they want to put their manpower where it's more urgently needed."

"I've never worked with the Bomb and Arson unit, but I assume they're not too different from the rest of the police—too few people, too many crimes. It doesn't seem so unbelievable to me that Montgomery would abandon an investigation into an underinsured mausoleum in one of the city's tackier districts. The fire fighters and police may serve and protect everyone, but they're human—they'll respond to the neighborhoods with more political clout first."

Robin made an impatient gesture. "Maybe you're right. Insurance companies have to be more allergic to arson. Montgomery may want to concentrate on the Gold Coast, but we can't be so picky. Even if he's abandoning the Indiana Arms, we won't. At least not for the time being."

Or at least not until his boss also got his sense of priorities reorganized. But I kept that last unkind thought to myself and let the talk drift to the joys of home ownership. Robin had just bought a two-flat in Albany Park; he was renting out the ground floor while living on top and trying to rehab the whole place in his spare time on weekends. Stripping varnish and putting up drywall are not my idea of a good time, but I'm perfectly ready to applaud anyone else who wants to do it.

After his third beer it seemed natural to think about moving on to food. We agreed on I Popoli, a seafood restaurant near Clark and Howard. After that it seemed natural to drive up to Albany Park with him to inspect the rehab work. One thing kind of led to another, but I left before they drifted too far—I hadn't packed any equipment when I left my apartment for the day. Anyway, AIDS is making me more cautious. I like to see a guy more than once before doing anything irrevocable. Still, it's nice to get an outside opinion of one's attractions. I went home at midnight in a far better mood than I would have thought possible when I got up twenty hours ago.

13

WASHING UP

I slept late the next morning. Usually as soon as I wake up I get out of bed and get going—I'm not a napper or a snoozer. But today I felt a catlike languor envelop me, a sense of well-being that came from knowing I had my castle to myself. The street noises were subdued—the nine-to-fivers were long gone about their business—and I felt suspended in a little bubble of privacy.

By and by I padded into the kitchen to make some coffee. The remains of yesterday's shambles made a slight dent in my euphoria, enough to decide me not to skip my run two days in a row. I had cleaned up after Cerise, but the dirty rags were still in the sink, giving off a faint smell of Clorox mixed with old vomit. I needed to throw them in the wash and might as well do it at the start of my run.

Down in the basement after doing my stretches, my good mood deteriorated further on finding that someone had dumped my laundry on the floor —wet. A note scribbled in angry haste lay on top: "You don't own the basement too!" I knew Mr. Contreras would never have done such a thing.

The second-floor tenants were Korean; their English didn't seem up to the pointedness of the message. My third-floor neighbor was a quiet older Norwegian woman who almost never appeared. That left the banker, good old Vincent Bottone.

I put the clothes back in the washer, added the rags, poured in a double measure of soap and a good cup of Clorox, and left Westinghouse to do my dirty work. I stopped on the first floor for the dog, who was more than usually eager to see me—it had been several days since she'd had a good workout. Mr. Contreras was disposed to question me about my aunt and Cerise, but the dog was whimpering so loudly I was able to make my escape in fairly short order.

As I jogged up to Belmont and across to the harbor, my mind kept shifting to Vincent Bottone, trying to come up with some fitting response to his desecration of my laundry. Of course I shouldn't have gone off and left it all day, but did he really have to dump it on the floor and add a hostile note? My best idea was to break into his apartment some weekend when he was out and steal his briefcase for Peppy to chew to bits. But then he might poison the dog—he was just the type.

By the time Peppy and I got back home my early euphoria had evaporated completely. I turned the dog back to Mr. Contreras and pleaded a heavy work load to escape a second barrage of questions. Halfway up the stairs I remembered my laundry and stomped back to the basement to shift it to the dryer.

The washer was still in its final spin cycle. Propping my elbows on the vibrating machine, I tried to resolve on an action plan for the day. I had to get my driver's license replaced, which meant trekking up Elston by bus—I shouldn't even have been driving last night without it. After that—I wondered if it was worthwhile trying to confront Elena about my missing stuff. If she knew, she wouldn't admit it; anyway, the thought of dealing with her coy evasions nauseated me. If it was Cerise who had robbed me, I didn't have any desire to find her, even if I knew where to look.

Since I wasn't going to mess with those two anymore, there was nothing to stop my getting back to paying—and waiting—clients. I repeated some pretty stern orders to myself about going upstairs, getting dressed, and heading for the Loop, but something kept me planted in front of the washing machine.

The rhythm of the spin cycle was soothing. My mind relaxed while I stared at the dials. The niggling questions buried by Cerise and Elena's exigent needs came fluttering back to the surface of my brain.

Rosalyn. Why had she gratuitously sought me out at Boots's party? With a thousand people to meet—lots of them with lots of bucks—did she really want to assure herself that I was on her side?

I wished I could believe it. I just couldn't. She could see I'd shelled out for her; that should have been guarantee enough for someone who wasn't particularly close to her. Despite her and Marissa's soap, my public support wasn't particularly useful to her. I haven't been politically active for a long time. My name is getting better known in the financial world, but it doesn't count for anything in county politics. In fact, knowing I backed Roz—or any other candidate—could just as likely make people who know me from my PD days vote against her as for her.

I couldn't help believing she thought I knew something that might damage her. She had some secret and her cousin was worried I knew about it. It was after he'd pointed at me that she'd come back and asked me to meet her at the swing. She'd sought me out to scout the lay of the land.

"It doesn't matter, Vic," I said aloud. "So she's got a secret. So who doesn't? None of your business."

Grunting, I moved the heavy wet clothes from the machine to the dryer. I slammed the door shut and scowled at the knobs. The trouble was, she'd made it my business by seeking me out in that strange way. If she and Marissa were making a patsy out of me between them—I bit off the thought in mid-sentence and headed for the stairs. I was halfway up when I realized I hadn't turned on the dryer. I stomped back to the basement and set the wheel in motion.

I put on my newest jeans so I'd look tidy and respectable for the driver's license people. With it I wore a rose-colored blouse so I'd photograph decently.

All during the slow bus ride up Elston and the long wait while state employees processed applicants at a pace just short of total morbidity, I toyed with different ways of getting a fix on Roz's situation. My first thought had been to head to the Daley Center to see if she was being sued. But if someone were on her case, the papers would have the story—the first thing the eager reporters do when someone runs for office is check the public record on them.

With a start I realized my turn had come. I filled out the forms, handed over my three pieces of identification, waited some more, agreed to give away my kidneys and eyeballs if some cokehead totaled me, and finally got my picture taken. My care in dressing had been to no avail—I still looked like an escapee from the psycho ward at Cook County. Maybe I should lose this license, too, and try again.

I trudged back onto the Number 41 bus and endured the long trek south. The sight of my demented-looking photograph did make me think of someone who might know what Roz was up to. Velma Riter was a photographer whom I'd met when she was with the *Herald-Star*. She'd been assigned enough times to cover stories I'd been involved in that we got to know each other, at least by sight. Shortly before leaving the paper to go into business for herself, she'd done a big photo-essay for a special issue on "Fifty Women Who Move Chicago." I'd been included, as had Roz.

The artist was at home. She'd evidently been expecting some other call because she answered the phone eagerly on the first ring but seemed startled at hearing it was me.

"V. I. Warshawski," she repeated slowly, drawing out the syllables. "Well, well. To what do I owe the pleasure?"

"I just had my driver's license redone. I was wishing you could doctor the photo for me."

"Forged passports are my real specialty," she said dryly. "What are you up to these days?"

"Not much. I saw Roz Fuentes on Sunday, though, out at a big shindig Boots Meagher was throwing for her."

"I knew about it—she wanted me there, but I'm getting ready for a show. I wouldn't even have answered your call if I hadn't been expecting to hear from my agent."

I made appropriate noises of congratulation, wrote down the gallery name and opening date, and apologized for disturbing her work. "You keep up with Roz?"

"I'm doing some work for the campaign." A thread of impatience hit Velma's voice. "Vic, I really don't have time for a chat right now."

"I wouldn't be bothering you if I knew someone else to interrupt. Roz got me kind of worried, though. I wondered if she was digging herself into some kind of pit her pals ought to know about."

"Just what did she say to make you think that?"

"Not so much what she said but what she did." I told her about Roz breaking away from the crowd just to sound out how much I cared about her alliance with Boots.

"You worry too much about other people's business, Warshawski. Some people even think you're a pain in the butt. Go catch some real criminals and leave Roz's business alone. She's cool."

Her closing words made my cheeks flame. I hung up without even trying to reply. I had an ugly vision of myself as a crank and a busybody.

"She still shouldn't have come around asking if I was going to do anything to hurt her," I muttered aggrievedly to myself.

Hunching my shoulders, I went back outside. I was flat and I didn't have a cash card. The rest of the afternoon was taken up with errands to replace my missing credit—to the bank to cash a check and apply for a new card. To the grocery to get some food and a new check-writing card. At four I finally took some time to go to the Daley Center and dig around a little on a background check for an old client. Velma's words still stung so much I didn't even try looking Roz up.

The documents library closed at four-thirty. I walked across town to my office to see what new bills had come in since Friday, stopping at a deli to pick up a giant chocolate-chip cookie and a cup of bitter coffee.

While I finished the cookie I switched on the desk lamp and called my answering service. Both Michael Furey and Robin Bessinger had phoned. And one of the managers from Cartwright & Wheeler, the insurance brokers where I'd made my presentation last Friday.

I sat down heavily. A potential client. A paying client. And I had completely forgotten to make a follow-up phone call. After spending five hundred dollars and two days on a presentation to them.

Maybe this showed the beginning of senile dementia. They say the short-term memory is the first thing to go. Harassed though I'd been yesterday by dealing with Cerise and Roland Montgomery, I still should have remembered to make a phone call that important. I looked at my pocket diary— there it was. Call Cartwright & Wheeler. I'd even put in the number and the name of the contact person.

When I phoned it was to get bad news—they'd decided they didn't need my help at this time. Of course once they'd put off the decision the odds were against their choosing to hire me. But Velma was right—I spent so much time worrying about other people's business, I couldn't even keep track of my own. The vision of myself as a grotesque busybody returned. The outcome might not have been different if I'd remembered to call yesterday, but at least I'd feel like a professional instead of a fool.

14

CAUGHT
IN THE ACT

I returned Furey's and Robin Bessinger's phone calls, more for something to do to stop my self-flagellation than from any real enthusiasm to talk to either. Furey wanted to apologize for his comments to me at the department yesterday and arrange a final trip to the Sox, who like the Cubs had long since faded into the sunset.

"I didn't mean to criticize you," he added. "It's hard for us born-and-bred chauvinists to reform."

"That's okay," I assured him with what goodwill I could muster. "I wasn't at my best, anyway—Lieutenant Montgomery was jumping on my ass for the wrong reasons and it didn't leave me feeling very friendly."

After we'd talked a little about the meeting, and he'd given me some tips on the best way to handle Monty, he inquired about Elena.

I'd forgotten asking him to do a search for her. More dementia. More repellent busybodiedness. "Oh, nuts. I'm sorry—I should have told you— she showed up Sunday night safe and sound. With a truly hideous protégée."

"Sounds bad," he said with ready sympathy. "What was the protégée? Someone from the Indiana Arms?"

"Daughter." I gave him a thumbnail sketch of Cerise. "Now she's vanished into the woodwork, pregnant, addicted and all."

"Want to give me her name and description? I could ask the boys to keep an eye out for her."

"Ugh." The last thing I wanted was for someone to drop Cerise on my doorstep again. On the other hand, for the sake of the fetus she was working on, someone ought to try to get her into a drug program. Why not the cops? I gave Michael the details.

"I don't think this week is a good time for me to set a play date—I've been letting too many things slide and it's starting to get me down. I'll call next Monday or Tuesday, okay?"

"Yeah, Vic. Fine." He hung up.

Furey was fundamentally good-natured. Caring enough to look out for a pregnant junkie he'd never seen. Eileen Mallory was right—he was good father material. I just wasn't looking for a father. At least not for my unborn children.

I called Robin next. The lab they used had reported on the samples from the Indiana Arms. They'd confirmed his initial hunch on the accelerant—it had been paraffin.

I tried to force my mind to care about what he was saying. "Is it hard to buy?"

"It's common," he responded. "Easy to get hold of, even in large quantities, so I don't think we can trace the user by looking for a purchaser. What's interesting was the timing device they used to set the thing off. A hot plate had been plugged into it in the night man's quarters."

"So maybe the watchman had something to do with it." Hard to think he didn't if a timer was wired to his own appliance.

"The owner says he had only a night man at the desk, that he didn't think the building warranted a watchman. We haven't been able to locate the guy, though. . . . Vic, you've done a lot of work for Ajax in the past. Successful work. I wondered—I talked to my boss—could we hire you on this one?"

"To do what?" I asked cautiously. "I don't know a thing about arson—I couldn't tell an accelerant from a match."

He didn't respond directly. "Even though the building was underinsured, we're reserving over a million dollars. People were injured, and that means liability claims on top of the property loss. The police may not care, but it'd be worth it to us to invest several thousand in a professional investigation if we could save the big money. We'd like you to try to find the arsonist."

I watched the windowpanes vibrate at the continuous stream of rush-hour L's running just underneath. A little dirt shook loose, but not as much as whirled up to add to the glass's gray opacity. It wasn't a scene to bolster my low sense of competence.

"My fan club at Ajax doesn't exactly include a unanimous chorus of senior staff. Does your boss have the authority to hire me without a lot of other people getting involved in the approval process?"

"Oh, yeah. That's easy. We budget for outside investigators—they don't have to be approved on a case-by-case basis." He paused. "Could I interest you in dinner tonight? Try to help you make up your mind?"

I could picture his head tilted birdlike to one side as he watched to see if the worm would pop out of the ground. The image made me feel like smiling for the first time since finding my laundry on the floor this morning. "Dinner would be great."

He suggested Calliope, a lively place on north Lincoln that served Greek-style seafood. They didn't take reservations, but people could dance in the adjoining cabaret while waiting for their tables.

After hanging up I shut my office for the day. Another couple of inquiries had come in that I ought to deal with, but I didn't have the emotional energy for work this afternoon.

By the time I walked back to the north end of the Loop for my car and picked my way through the rush-hour traffic home, I just had time for a long bath before dressing for dinner. I lay in the tub a good forty-five minutes, letting my mind float to nowhere, letting the water wash away the sharpest edge of self-doubt.

When I finally got out and started dressing, the late-summer twilight was turning the evening air a grayish-purple. I watched Mr. Contreras working in the backyard. The tomato season was ending but he was cultivating a few pumpkins with tender care. He liked to do Halloween in style for the local kids. In the dim light I could just make out Peppy lying on the grass, her nose on her forepaws, gloomily waiting for activity that might include her.

I went down the back way to bid him and the dog good night. The old man was on his dignity, miffed at my shortness with him this morning, but the dog was ecstatic. I had to work hard to keep her from transferring leaf loam or manure or whatever Mr. Contreras was piling on the pumpkins to my black silk trousers.

He refused to be mollified by my light remarks. I felt myself on the verge of apologizing and bit back the words in annoyance—there was no reason for him to know every detail of my life. If I wanted to keep a few small segments private, I shouldn't have to say I was sorry. I gave him a cool farewell and slid through the back gate so that the dog couldn't follow. Her frustrated whimpering accompanied me down the alley.

I walked the short mile to the restaurant. Stepping around a wide hole in the concrete I slipped on a discarded hot dog. Just one more of the joys of city life. I dusted my trouser knees. The fabric was bruised slightly but not torn. Not enough damage to justify a move to Streamwood.

Robin was waiting for me outside the restaurant door, looking elegant in gray flannel slacks and a navy blazer. He had come early to sign up for a table and the manager was just calling his name when we walked in. Perfect. If you're born lucky, you don't have to be good. Robin ordered a beer while I had a rum and tonic and some of the cod roe mousse the Calliope was famous for.

"How did you become a detective?" he asked after we'd given our dinner orders.

"I used to be with the public defender." I spread some of the mousse on a piece of toast. "Trial division. It's hideous work—you often get briefed on your client only five minutes before the trial begins. You always have more cases than time to work them effectively. And sometimes you're pleading heart and soul for goons you hope will never see the light of day again."

"So why didn't you just go into private practice?" He scooped up some of the mousse. "This is good," he mumbled, his mouth full. "I never tried it before."

It was good—just salty enough to go down well with beer or rum. I ate some more and finished my drink before answering.

"I'd spent five years in the PD's office—I didn't want to have to start again at the beginning in a private practice. Anyway, I'd solved a case for a friend and realized it was work I could do well and get genuine satisfaction from. Plus, I can be my own boss." I should have given that as my first reason—it continues to be the most important with me. Maybe from being an only child, used to getting my own way? Or just my mother's fierce independence seeping into my DNA along with her olive skin.

After the waiter brought salads and a bottle of wine, I asked Robin how he ended up as an arson specialist. He grimaced.

"I don't know anyone whose first choice is insurance, except maybe the kids whose fathers own agencies. I majored in art history. There wasn't money to send me to graduate school. So I started work at Ajax. They had me designing policy forms—trying to make use of my artistic background"—he grinned briefly—"but I got out of that as fast as I could."

During dinner he asked me about some of the earlier work I'd done for Ajax. It was my turn to make a face—the company didn't know if it loved or hated me for fingering their claims vice president as the mastermind of a workers' comp fraud scam. Robin was fascinated—he said there'd always been a lot of gossip circulating, but that no one had ever told the lower-downs what their vice president had really been up to.

Over Greek-style bouillabaisse he spent a little time persuading me to go back into the Ajax trenches once again. I knew I needed a major job, not just the nickel-and-dime stuff that had come over the transom the last few days. I knew I didn't feel up to hustling for new clients right now. I knew I was going to say yes, but I asked him to call me at my office in the morning with some details.

"It's been a roughish day," I explained. "Tonight I just want to forget the detecting business and unwind."

He didn't seem to mind. The talk drifted to baseball and childhood while we finished eating. Dancing in the back room afterwards, we didn't talk much at all. Around midnight we decided the time had come to move the few blocks north to my place. Robin said he'd leave his car at the restaurant and pick it up in the morning—we'd both had too much to drink to drive, and anyway, it was a beautiful late-summer night.

We turned the six blocks into a half-hour trek, moving slowly with our arms locked, stopping every few houses for a long kiss. When we finally got to my place I whispered urgent warnings of silence on Robin—I didn't want Mr. Contreras or Vinnie the banker descending on us. While Robin stood behind me with his arms wrapped around my waist, I fumbled in my bag for my keys.

A car door slammed in front of the house. We moved to one side as footsteps came up the walk. A car searchlight pinned us against the apartment entrance.

"That you, Vicki? Sorry to interrupt, but we need to have a chat." The voice, laden with heavy irony, was almost as familiar to me as my own father's. It belonged to Lieutenant Robert Mallory, head of the Violent Crimes Unit at the Chicago Police's Central District. I could feel my cheeks flame in the dark—no matter how cool you are, it unsettles you when your father's oldest friend surprises you in a passionate embrace.

"I'm flattered, of course, Bobby. Two and a half million souls in the city, including your seven grandchildren, and when you have insomnia you come to me."

Bobby ignored me. "Say good night to your friend here—we're going for a ride."

Robin made a creditable effort to intervene. I grabbed his arm. "They'll put you in Cook County with the muggers and the buggers if you hit him— it's a police lieutenant. Bobby—Robin Bessinger, Ajax Insurance. Robin— Bobby Mallory, Chicago's finest."

In the searchlight Bobby's red face looked grayish-white; lines I didn't usually notice sprang into craggy relief. He was coming up on his sixtieth birthday, after all. I'd even been invited to the surprise party his wife was planning for him in early October, but I hadn't thought of the milestone as meaning he might be getting old. I pushed aside the stab of queasiness the idea of his aging gave me and said more loudly than I'd intended, "Where are we riding to and why, Bobby?"

I could see him wrestle with the desire to grab me and drag me forcibly to the waiting car. Most people don't know that if you're not under arrest you don't have to go off with a policeman just because he tells you to. And most people won't fight it even if they know it. Even a good cop like Bobby starts taking it for granted; a citizen like me helps him keep his powers in perspective.

"Tell your friend to take a hike." He jerked his head at Robin.

If I obeyed him on that one, he'd play by the rules. It wasn't a great compromise, but it was a compromise. I grudgingly asked Robin to leave. He agreed on condition that I call him as soon as the police were done with me, but when he got to the end of the walk, he stood to watch. I was touched.

"Okay, he's gone. What do you need to talk about?"

Bobby frowned and pressed his lips together. Just a reflex of annoyance. "Night watchman found a body near a construction site around nine-thirty. She had something on her linking her to you."

I had a sudden image of my aunt, dead drunk, getting hit by a car and left to die. I put a hand on the side of the building to steady myself. "Elena?" I asked foolishly.

"Elena?" Bobby was momentarily blank. "Oh, Tony's sister. Not unless she shed fifty years and had her skin dyed for the occasion."

It took me a minute to work out what he meant. A young black woman. Cerise. She wasn't the only young black woman I know, but I couldn't imagine any of the others dead near a construction site. "Who was it?"

"We want you to tell us."

"What did you find that made you connect her with me?"

Bobby pressed his lips together again. He just didn't want to tell me—old habits die hard. I thought he was about to speak when the door opened behind me and Vinnie the banker erupted into the night.

"This is it, Warshawski. This is the last time you get me up in the middle of the night. Just so you know it, the cops are on their way over. Don't your *friends* ever think—shining a light straight into a window where people are sleeping? And talking at the top of their lungs? Or are you trying to lure people inside?"

He had changed out of his pajamas into jeans and a white button shirt. His thick brown hair was combed carefully from his face. He might even have taken the extra time to shampoo and blow-dry it before dialing 911.

"I'm glad you phoned them, Vinnie—they'll be real happy when they get here. And so will the rest of the block when the squad cars cruise in with those new strobes of theirs painting the nighttime blue."

Bobby looked at Vinnie. "You call the cops, son?"

The banker stuck his chin out pugnaciously. "Yes, I did. They'll be here any minute. If you're her pimp, you've got about two minutes to disappear."

Bobby kept his tone avuncular. "Who you talk to, son—the precinct or the emergency number?"

Vinnie bristled. "I'm not your son. Don't think you can buy *me* off too."

Bobby looked at me, his lips twitching. "You been trying to sell him nickel bags, Vicki?"

He turned back to Vinnie, showing his badge. "I know Miss Warshawski isn't the easiest neighbor in the world—I'm about to take her off your hands. But I need to know if you called 911 or the precinct so I can cancel the squad cars—I don't want to waste any more city money tonight pulling patrol officers away from work they ought to be doing because you have a beef with your neighbors."

Vinnie bunched up his lips, not wanting to back down but knowing he had to. "911," he muttered, then said more defiantly, "And it's about time someone took her in."

Bobby looked toward the street and bellowed, "Furey!"

Michael climbed out of the car and trotted over. Just what I needed to complete the transformation of romance into farce—Michael must have seen me in a clinch with Robin at the door.

"This kid here called 911 when he heard me talking to Vicki—get on the radio and find out who's coming and cancel them, okay? And turn off the light. Guy needs his beauty sleep."

Michael, at his most wooden, ignored me completely and headed back to the car. Vinnie tried asking for Bobby's badge number so he could lodge a complaint with the watch commander—"your boss" as he put it—but Bobby put a heavy hand on his shoulder and assured him that everyone had better things to do with their time, and if Vinnie had to be at the office in the morning, maybe it was time he turned back in.

"Well, at least get this woman to stop conducting her business in the front hall in the middle of the night," Vinnie demanded petulantly as he opened the front door.

"Is that what you do, Vicki?" Bobby asked. "Lose your lease downtown?"

I gritted my teeth but didn't try to fight it as he took my arm and ushered me down the walk—Mr. Contreras would doubtless be out next with the dog if we stayed any longer.

"Elena," I said shortly. "She's come around a few times in the last week. Always after midnight, of course."

"I haven't seen her since Tony's funeral. Didn't even know whether she was still in town."

"I wish I hadn't seen her since then, either. She got burned out of her place last Wednesday—you know that SRO fire near McCormick Place?"

Bobby grunted. "So she came to you. Underneath it all you're not that different from your folks, I guess."

That left me speechless for the remainder of the short walk. Bobby opened the back door for me. I waved at Robin and climbed inside.

Michael was sitting in the front seat, John McGonnigal—the sergeant Bobby most preferred to work with—in the back. I said hello to both of them. They kept up an animated conversation about police business all the way to the morgue. Even if I'd wanted to, I couldn't have joined in.

15

AT THE RUE MORGUE

Some practical bureaucrat put the county morgue on the Near West Side, the area with Chicago's highest murder rate—it saves wear and tear on the meatwagons having to cart corpses only a few short blocks. Even during the day the concrete cube looks like a bunker in the middle of a war zone; at midnight it's the most depressing place in town.

As we walked up to the sliding metal doors marked "Deliveries," Furey began a series of morbid one-liners, a kind of defense against his own mortality I suppose, but still unpleasant. At least McGonnigal didn't join in. I moved out of earshot, into the entryway—a small box of reinforced glass whose inner door was locked. A knot of clerks at the reception counter inside looked me over and went back to an animated conversation. When Bobby materialized behind my left shoulder, the party broke up and someone unlocked the door.

I pushed it open when the buzzer sounded and held it for Bobby and the boys. Furey still wouldn't look at me, not even when I went out of my way to be superpolite. Last time I'd go to a political fund-raiser with him, that's for sure.

For the public brought in to identify their nearest and dearest, the county provides a small furnished waiting room—you can even look at a video screen instead of directly at the body. Bobby didn't think I needed such amenities. He pushed open the double doors to the autopsy room. I followed, trying to walk nonchalantly.

It was a utilitarian room, with sinks and equipment for four pathologists to work at once. In the middle of the night the only person present was an attendant, a middle-aged man in jeans with a green surgical gown thrown loosely around his shoulders. He was hunched over a car-and-track magazine. The Sox were on a seven-inch screen on the chair in front of him. He looked at us indifferently, taking his time to get up when Bobby identified himself and told him what we wanted. He sauntered to the thick double doors leading to the cooler.

Inside were hundreds of bodies arranged in rows. Their torsos were partially draped in black plastic, but the heads were exposed, arcing back, the mouths open in surprise at death. I could feel the blood drain from my brain. I hoped I wasn't turning green—it would put the cap to my night if I got sick in front of Furey and McGonnigal. At least Furey had shut up, that was one good thing.

The attendant consulted a list in his pocket and went over to one of the bodies. He checked a tag on the foot against his list and prepared to wheel the gurney into the autopsy room.

"That's okay," Bobby said easily. "We'll look at her in here."

Bobby took me to the gurney and pulled the plastic wrapping away so that the whole body was exposed. Cerise stared up at me. Stripped of clothes, she looked pathetically thin. Her ribs jutted ominously below her breasts; her pregnancy hadn't yet given any roundness to her sunken stomach. Her carefully beaded braids lay tousled on the table—I stuck a hand out involuntarily to smooth them for her.

Bobby was watching me closely. "You know who she is, don't you?"

I shook my head. "She looks like a couple of different women I've met briefly. What did she have that made you think I knew her?"

He compressed his lips again—he wanted to yell at me but he belongs to a generation that doesn't swear at women. "Don't play games with me, Vicki. If you know who it is, tell us so we can get moving on tracking down her associates."

"How did she die?" I asked.

"We don't know yet; they won't do a postmortem until Friday. Probably a heroin overdose. That help you distinguish her from the others?" Bobby's sarcasm is always heavy.

"What do you care, anyway? Dead junkies must be a dime a dozen around here. And here are three crack guys from the Violent Crimes Unit only three hours after she was found."

Bobby's eyes glittered. "You ain't running the department, Vicki. I don't account to you how I decide to spend my time."

The intensity of his anger surprised me; it also spelled in large block letters that he hadn't chosen to be here. I stared at Cerise thoughtfully. What about her life or death could bring heat from the top down to the Central Division in such a short stretch?

"Where was she found?" I asked abruptly.

"On the big construction project going up near Navy Pier." That was McGonnigal. "Watchman found her in the elevator shaft when he was making his rounds, called us. She hadn't been dead too long when the squad car got there."

"Rapelec Towers, right? What made him look down the shaft?"

McGonnigal shook his head. "One of those things. Why she was on the site we'll probably never know, either. Nice secluded place at night if you want to shoot up in peace, but awfully far from where you'd expect to find her."

"So what did she have that made you think of me?"

Bobby nodded at Furey, who produced a transparent evidence bag. Inside was a plastic square. My photograph was glued in the left corner, looking just as demented as the one I'd had taken this morning.

"Hmm," I said after I'd looked at it. "Looks like my driver's license."

Bobby smiled savagely. "This isn't Second City, Victoria, and nobody's rolling in the aisles. You know this girl or not?"

I nodded reluctantly. Like Bobby, I hate giving information across police barricades. "Cerise Ramsay."

"How'd she get that license?"

"She stole it from me yesterday morning." I crossed my arms in front of me.

"Did you report it? Report the theft?"

I shook my head without answering.

Bobby slammed his hand against the side of the cart hard enough that the metal rattled. "Why the *hell* not?"

He really was pissed. I looked at him squarely. "I thought Elena might have taken it."

"Oh." The fire went out of his face. He jerked his head at Furey and McGonnigal. "Why don't you boys wait for me in the car?"

When they'd left he said in quiet, fatherly tones, "Okay, Vicki, let's have the whole story. And not just the sections you think I'll find out anyway. You know Tony would say the same thing if he was here."

Indeed I did. It's just that I was too old to do things because my daddy told me to. I didn't have a client to protect, though. There wasn't any reason not to tell him the pathetic little I knew about Cerise, just as long as we didn't do it surrounded by cold bodies.

Bobby got the attendant to show us to a tiny cubicle where the ME's drink coffee or whiskey or something in between dissections. And I told him everything I knew about Cerise, including Katterina and Zerlina. "I can sign the papers if you want. Her mother's got a bad heart—I don't think it would do her any good to come down here."

Bobby nodded. "We'll see about that. What were you doing at Eleventh Street that rattled Roland Montgomery's cage so bad?"

The shift in topic was casual and expert, but it didn't make me jump. "Nothing," I said earnestly. "I don't understand it myself."

"He came to see me with a full head of steam and demanded I run you in if you showed up anywhere near the Indiana Arms."

Bobby's tone was neutral—he wasn't criticizing, just offering me information, telling me he couldn't protect me if I got powerful people mad at me. At the same time he'd make a stab at it if I gave him the inside track on why the Indiana Arms was a hot topic. Unfortunately I couldn't help, and in the end he got angry—he couldn't see that I wasn't being obstructive, that I was well and truly ignorant. He thinks I take on clients and cases just to thumb my nose at him, that I'm having a late-life adolescent fit. He's waiting for me to grow out of it the way his six children all did.

It was two when Furey, driving recklessly and wordlessly, dropped me at my apartment. I didn't make any attempt to be conciliating—I could understand why he was pissed, but at the same time it was just the luck of the draw that he'd seen me with Robin. It was farce, not tragedy—I wasn't about to pretend to be Desdemona.

I waited inside the front door until his car had screeched its way up Racine to Belmont. My Chevy was parked across the street. I climbed in, made a U, and headed south through the empty streets toward Navy Pier.

The Rapelec complex was a monster. It wasn't actually on Navy Pier of course—no development has been approved there because the aldermen can't figure out how to divide up the zoning payoff pie. The site was on the west side of Lake Shore Drive facing the pier, a strip of decaying warehouses and office buildings that has suddenly become development heaven.

The construction site took up the whole section between the river and Illinois Street. The foundations had been poured last May. They were up about twenty stories now in the towers, but the office/retail complex was going more slowly. The sketches in the papers had made it look like a giant high school auditorium. They were taking their time with the support structure.

Bare light bulbs slung around the top of the skeleton outlined its iron bones. I shuddered. I'm not exactly afraid of heights, but the thought of perching up there without walls around—not so much the height, but the nakedness of the building—frightened me. Even at ground level it seemed menacing, with black holes where windows should be and wooden ramps that led only to fathomless pits.

By now my skin was crawling. I had to fight an impulse to run back to the Chevy and head for home. Concentrate on putting one step in front of you, Vic, and curse yourself for a fool for leaving your party clothes on, instead of changing to sneaks and jeans.

I circled the site from the outside. The blue-and-whites had long gone, leaving behind a crime-scene barricade but no guard. There were at least a dozen ways into the grounds in the dark. Looking nervously above me, I selected an entrance lined with lights that didn't seem to have any steel beams poised to drop on it. My pumps made a soft *thwick* on the plank.

The boards ended at the third story. I stepped off onto a cement slab. Ahead of me and to the right shadows engulfed the floor and the beams, but the lights continued on the left where more wood had been dropped to make a crude floor cover. My palms were sweating and my toes felt ticklish when I forced myself down the corridor.

The lower floors were enclosed at this point, but no inner walls had been built. The only light came from the naked bulbs strung along the structural beams. I could see dimly into the recesses of the building. Steel beams stuck shadowy fingers upward to support the deck above. Inky splotches might be holes in the floor or maybe just some piece of machinery. I thought of Cerise coming here alone to die and the skin at the base of my neck prickled uncontrollably.

"Hello!" I cupped my hands and yelled.

My voice echoed faintly, bouncing from the steel beams. No one answered. Sweat now dropped from my neck inside my cotton sweater. A faint night breeze dried it, leaving me shivering.

The rough flooring suddenly ended in a nest of plywood cubicles. The door to the one on my right stood open. I went in. The room was dimly lit by the bulbs from the hall outside. I hunted around for a switch, finally finding a likely candidate in a thick cable. I touched it nervously, afraid I might be electrocuting myself, but the room lights came on.

Two large drafting tables were set up against one wall. Cradles holding books that looked like giant wallpaper samples covered the other three. I pulled one out. It was very heavy and didn't handle easily. Straining, I laid it across the cradle and flipped it open. It held blueprints. They were hard to follow, but it seemed to me I was looking at a corner of the twenty-third floor. In fact, this whole volume seemed to be devoted to the twenty-third floor. I shut it and slid it back into its nest.

A couple of hard hats stood on one of the drafting tables. Underneath them lay a stack of work logs. These documents were much easier to interpret—the leftmost column listed subcontractors. Next to them were slots to fill in billable hours for every day of the week. I studied the log idly, wondering if I'd see any familiar names.

Wunsch and Grasso figured prominently as the lead contractor in the joint venture that was building the complex. Hurlihey and Frain, architects, also had put in a bunch of hours. I didn't realize architects kept working on a project after construction started.

One name struck me as rather humorous—Farmworks, Inc. I wondered what agricultural needs a building like this had. Farmworks put in a lot of time too—they were submitting over five hundred hours for the week just ending.

A heavy step sounded on the wood flooring outside. I dropped the papers, my heart jumping wildly.

"Hello?" My voice came out in a quaver. Furious with myself for being so nervous, I took a deep breath and went out into the corridor.

A thickset black man in coveralls and a hard hat scowled at me. He held a flashlight. The other hand rested on the butt of a gun strapped to his waist.

"Who are you and what the hell are you doing up here?" His baritone was heavy and uncompromising.

"My name's Warshawski. I'm a detective and I'm here with some follow-up questions about the dead girl you found."

"Police left hours ago." He moved his hand away from the gun, but his hard eyes didn't relax.

"I just came from the morgue where I met with Sergeant McGonnigal and Lieutenant Mallory. They forgot to ask a couple of things I need to know. Also, since I'm here, I'd like to see where you found her."

For a tense moment I thought he was going to demand some police identification, but my fluency with the right names apparently satisfied him.

"I can't take you down to where I found her unless you have a hard hat."

I picked up one of the Hurlihey and Frain hats from the drafting table. "Why don't I just borrow this one?"

His cold eyes weighed me some more, not wanting to let me do it, but he seemed to be a man of logic and he couldn't argue himself into sending me back to Mallory empty. "If you people did your homework you wouldn't have to waste so much of my time. Come on. I'm not going to wait while you trip around in those ridiculous shoes of yours—our liability policy doesn't pay for police who don't dress right for the job."

I picked up the hard hat and followed him meekly back into the shadowy maze.

16

TENDER SITE

As I stumbled behind him in the dark I persuaded him to tell me his name—Leon Garrison. He was a night security man, head of a team working the Rapelec site. His firm, LockStep, specialized in guarding construction projects. It seemed to me part of his anger toward me was hurt pride that someone had climbed onto the premises to die without his knowing about it. He was further annoyed that I'd managed to come in undetected as well. When I explained I'd shouted a couple of times to try to rouse someone it didn't cheer him any.

He took me down to the bottom in a hoist that ran along the outside of the building, moving the levers with a morose efficiency. When we got off he shone the flashlight in swift arcs in front of him, uncovering coils of wire, boards, loose chunks of concrete. By staying half a step behind him I could see the obstacles in time to avoid them. I had a feeling that disappointed him.

He stopped abruptly in front of a deep square pit. "You know anything about construction?" he demanded.

"Nope."

That improved his mood, enough that he explained they put the elevators in last, after the shafts were built up to the height of the building and the machinery installed on top. The cradles they rest in go down a good way— they have to be able to cushion the elevators if the cables break or some other ghastly accident occurs.

This building had four banks of eight elevators each. Garrison moved along to the hole where he'd discovered Cerise's body, looking in each one to make sure no more unwelcome surprises awaited him. When we got to the right one he pointed the flashlight up so I could see the platform supporting the crane some twenty stories overhead. The crane took up the space that the elevators would fill once the place was finished.

Between the depth of the pit and the crane platform swaying gently overhead, I felt a rush of nausea. As I stepped back from the edge I thought I caught a little smirk on Garrison's face—he'd been trying to upset me.

"Why did you look in here, anyway?" I tried to sound forceful, not as though I was on the brink of throwing up.

"We had a fire in one of the cradles last week. Guys like to dump trash in here on account of it's an open hole. Someone flipped a butt in and things started burning. I just check to see what kind of rubbish we're piling up."

I asked him to shine the flash down into the pit again. A rough-hewn set of slats had been nailed down the side so that you could climb in and out if you wanted to, but it wasn't at all easy to get into. It was hard to believe Cerise, or any addict, would go to all that work just to find a private place to shoot up.

"How often do you check them?"

"Just once a night, usually. That was near the start of my shift. Since the fire I look in the pits first."

"And you saw her and called 911?"

He scratched the back of his head behind the hard hat. "Strictly speaking I called August Cray first. He's in charge of the site at night. He came down here, took a look, and told me to call the police. Then he called the contractor."

"Wunsch and Grasso?"

"You'd have to ask Cray—this project's got a bunch of contractors working on it. They need to know if anything special is happening on the site, and I guess you could call a dead body pretty special."

He seemed to be smirking again, although it was kind of hard to tell in the dark. I wondered where this Cray person had been when I was calling out on the third floor. Anyway, he phoned someone at Wunsch and Grasso, maybe Ernie himself. Then Ernie buzzed his boyhood pal Furey and told him to make sure the building site was clean, that they didn't get any adverse publicity or any liability suits. That was plausible, even likely, but it didn't explain why Bobby had been called in and why he was ticked about it.

Unless the boys had used their connection to Boots to get county heat on the investigation? But that didn't make any sense—they would want to keep the thing as quiet as possible, and getting Boots and the county involved would have the opposite effect. I prodded Garrison as best I could, but he didn't know whom Cray had called or why the city had sent the head of their Violent Crimes Unit in.

"You see everything you need?" Garrison asked roughly. "I don't want another relay coming from the cops tonight telling me they forgot one last diddle-shit question. There's plenty of work to do here."

"This should do it," I said. "I think you can feel safe from the police for at least twelve hours."

"I'd better be." He snapped off the flash and headed back toward the hoist. "I guess I'd better tell Cray you've been here—he likes to know who's on the site at night."

We rode back to the third floor. "You're dressed kind of funny for a cop, aren't you?" he said when we got off.

"I'm dressed funny for a construction site," I corrected. "Even detectives have private lives. Cerise Ramsay's death interrupted mine." The memory of Bobby shining his spotlight on Robin and me popped into my head. It seemed funnier now than it had at the time. I bit back a laugh as Garrison knocked on the door to one of the little cubicles.

Cray turned out to be a heavy white man in his late fifties. He eyed me suspiciously as Garrison outlined the reason for my visit.

"You didn't hear her when she came up here?" the security man asked.

"I was in the john," Cray answered briefly. "You get what you need here? Next time, call ahead."

I smiled brightly. "Next time I sure will. Who did you call—Ernie or Ron?—after Garrison told you about the body?"

Cray's frown deepened. "Does it matter?"

"It kind of does. A dead junkie shouldn't bring down a senior cop and I'm trying to figure out why."

"Why not ask your boss that?" He kept a heavy, unpleasant edge to his voice.

"Lieutenant Mallory? I did ask him—he wasn't saying. Just for the record, he's not my boss."

"Just a minute here." Cray got to his feet. "Let's see some ID from you."

I pulled out my wallet and took out the laminated miniature of my PI license to show him.

"You're not with the police? We went through all that for you and you're not a cop? Goddamn you, I ought to get your ass arrested."

I smiled at him again. "I can give you Lieutenant Mallory's home number if you want to ask him to do it. But I never said I was with the city. I told Mr. Garrison I was a detective. He could have asked for my ID up front. I know Ernie and Ron—I can phone up tomorrow and see who you called."

"Then do that. Get off my building. Fast. Before someone has an accident and drops a load of steel on your cute little head."

He was breathing hard. I didn't see any reason to be so excited, but it seemed to me that the prudent course was to vacate the premises. There are just so many dead bodies a construction site can absorb in one night.

Back in the Chevy I suddenly felt a wave of exhaustion wash over me. My feet were sore; they throbbed inside my pumps. It had really been stupid to subject the poor things to so much rough terrain. I slipped out of them and drove home in my nylons. The cold accelerator pedal felt good against my hot soles.

At the apartment I resisted the temptation to ring Vinnie's bell. Not out of any nobility of character—I wanted to sleep in and he'd be bound to retaliate in some awful way if I woke him now.

Peppy whimpered behind Mr. Contreras's door when she heard me go by but thankfully she didn't start barking. The old man was just deaf enough that he'd sleep through her crying, but not her barking. Upstairs I started shedding clothes as soon as I got inside. By the time I reached my bedroom I was naked. I climbed into bed and was asleep almost immediately.

I slept deeply, but my dreams were filled with Elena and Cerise chasing me through miles of steel beams. I'd think I was in the clear and then suddenly a giant elevator pit would open in front of me. Just as I was backing away Cerise would be there staring at me, naked as she'd been at the morgue, her braids tangled, stretching her arms out and begging me to save her. In the background Velma Riter's voice echoed against the steel, saying, Mind your own business, Vic, a lot of people think you're a pain in the butt.

When the ringing phone woke me at ten I came to heavily. I fumbled with the phone before getting the mouthpiece the right way up. " 'Lo," I mumbled heavily.

"May I speak to Victoria Warshawski, please."

It was the efficient voice of a professional secretary. I managed to get the idea across that it was me. When she put me on hold I sat up to grapple with a sweatshirt—in case it was a client I didn't want to be seen naked.

"Vic? Ernie Wunsch. Hope I'm not disturbing you—my girl said she thought she woke you up."

When he'd dated LeAnn she'd been his girl; now she was his wife and his secretary had become his girl. It was too confusing a concept to put across with my mind so heavy from sleep so I only grunted.

"I had a message a few minutes ago from the Rapelec site saying you'd stopped by there in the middle of the night."

I grunted again.

"Something wrong we can help you with, Vic? It gets me kind of pissed to think you were going on my site behind my back."

"Hang on a minute, Ernie, I'll be right with you." I put the phone down and went to the bathroom. I didn't hurry things and on my way back I stopped in the kitchen for a glass of water. By the time I picked the phone up again Ernie was well and truly pissed but my head felt a bit clearer.

"Sorry, Ernie—I was right in the middle of something when you called. You know a young woman was found dead at the site last night."

"Some black junkie. What business was it of yours?"

"She was a protégée of mine, Ernie. I promised her mother I would look after her and I failed pretty miserably." I could see Zerlina Ramsay's strong, anguished face in my mind's eye and it didn't cheer me any.

"So?"

"So when I heard she'd died at the Rapelec site I thought I'd better go check it out, see if I could learn any reason she might have gone there."

"You ever want to talk to my people again, Vic, you check it out with me first. Cray was damned angry that you came there impersonating a police officer. He was all for having you arrested. If I hadn't known it would embarrass the hell out of Mickey, I would have done it too. You want to play at detective you go do it someplace else." He sounded downright ugly.

"While I'm playing at detective, Ernie, there is one thing you can tell me —why was it so important to you that somebody really senior come and investigate? If you'd left it with the beat people, they'd have just reported a dead junkie and I probably never even would have heard about it."

Even as I asked the question, part of the answer came to me. Ernie called Furey because he was a pal and he was with the cops. Furey got Bobby involved. No, that didn't make sense—Furey would have wanted Mallory to stay far away, to minimize any fuss at the Rapelec site. Well, maybe he'd botched it and hadn't been able to keep it from Bobby. But that didn't make sense, because Bobby was pissed at being called in—someone had ordered him to go there when he hadn't wanted to.

While all this was spinning through my head Ernie said heavily, "Just learn to mind your own business, Vic. Everyone will like you better."

I was getting kind of peeved at this message. "Oh, go make ugly faces at someone who's scared of you, Ernie. You don't impress me any."

As he hung up I thought I heard him mutter, "I still don't see what Mickey sees in you."

And I couldn't see what a sweetie like LeAnn saw in him. What did she do when he started rattling his chains at her? Probably giggled and said, "Oh, Ernie, don't be such a crybaby."

I stumbled into the kitchen for some coffee, my feet tender and swollen from last night's escapade. Was Ernie angry because he felt I'd undermined his control of his project site? Or was there something specific about Cerise's death that was bugging him? I couldn't imagine what, but I couldn't come up with any reason why Bobby had been dragged unwillingly into the investigation. My brain was still woolly and remote, though, not churning ideas with any facility.

I resisted the temptation to take my coffee to the bathroom and while away the morning soaking my sore toes in the tub. I know that however unappetizing it seems, running is the best antidote to a thick head. Anyway, a big dog like Peppy depends on running for her mental health—it wasn't fair to leave her to the sedate walks Mr. Contreras could manage.

I grumbled my way to the living room to do my stretches. They took longer than usual. Even so I didn't feel fully fit when I pulled on my sweats and stomped down the back stairs.

Peppy heard me coming and raced up to greet me. She was always ready to move from deep sleep to intense action without taking time between to loosen up. Recognizing my sweats, she whipped herself into a frenzy, dancing around me several times, rushing to the bottom of the stairs, then darting back up to check my progress. Mr. Contreras came to his back door as we passed.

"Just taking Her Serene Doggedness out for a spin," I said.

He nodded without speaking and retreated into the kitchen. Still feeling wounded. I gritted my teeth, but didn't try calling to him. I wasn't ready to kiss and make up.

I moved up the alley to Belmont at a slow gait, calling Peppy back to me at the intersections, trying to avoid pulling a muscle. At the harbor I finally felt loose enough to actually run full out for the better part of a mile, but I kept it to a jog again as I started back.

I picked Peppy up at her usual spot by the lagoon. She'd found a family of ducks and was diving after them hopefully. Until they finally took off toward the lake she pretended not to hear me calling—a fit response for ignoring her the last couple of days. Then she came loping up to me, tongue out, grinning wickedly—I knew you were calling me all along, but you'll never be able to prove it.

My head felt a lot cleaner on the way home. Back at the apartment I even felt good enough to make up with Mr. Contreras. I knocked on his kitchen door, told him I'd been up till four on a case, and asked if he had any coffee ready. That made me feel totally virtuous—his coffee is foul, overcooked stuff, and it would be faster for me to brew a fresh pot than to chew the fat with him.

He allowed as how he had some left over from breakfast and opened the door, looking sternly from the dog to me. "Why'd you let the princess go in the water? Let alone it's only sixty degrees out, the water in that lagoon hasn't been clean since 1850."

Characteristic. In order to be forgiven I had to be scolded. I bared my teeth in the semblance of a smile. "I know, I know. I begged and pleaded with her, but you know how it is—lady wants to do something, she does it without taking advice from anyone."

He gave me a sharp look. "Seems to me I've known ladies like that, uh-huh. And then you got to just ride it out until they're ready to listen to you again."

I smiled significantly. "That's right. That's it exactly. Now, how about some coffee."

17

AN AUNT'S HOUSE
IS HER CASTLE

Mr. Contreras gets vicarious pleasure from my thrills. He'd heard the excitement last night when Bobby had accosted Robin and me, but he'd still been on his dignity—"I know you like to keep your own business to yourself, doll" was how he put it—and so he'd kept the slavering Peppy inside. And I hadn't thought I had blessings to count. By the time I'd stepped him through the morgue and the late-night tour of Rapelec Towers, he was palpably jealous.

"Should have taken me with you, doll. They threaten to dump a load of steel on you, I'd of known how to handle it."

"Indeed you would," I agreed, blenching slightly. The time or two he'd come to my defense with a pipe wrench still haunts my nightmares. "Thanks for the coffee. I've gotta go now—need to see a man about a dog and all that stuff."

Or a woman about the hair of the dog, I thought grimly as I ran up the stairs to my own place. Time to nail Elena down to some approximation of the truth. I took a perfunctory shower, patted myself dry while pulling on my jeans, tucked my rose silk shirt into the waistband, and headed for the door.

I was just starting to lock it when the phone rang. I sprinted back inside. It was Robin. Robin. I'd forgotten to call him, but he didn't seem to be bothered by it.

"Everything go okay last night?"

"Depends on what you mean. They wanted me to ID a kid whose body they'd found at a construction site."

He made sympathetic sounds. "Did you?"

"Yeah. She was black, poor, and an addict, so the odds were against a happy ending, but it was still a shocker."

"The cops could've acted a bit more human to you under the circumstances."

"I suppose under the circumstances they were trying to jolt me into telling the truth."

He hesitated a moment. "I don't want to be a pest, especially after you've had a bad night, but have you thought any more about taking on the Indiana Arms investigation? We need to get going."

I felt a warm little glow under my rib cage. Someone thought I was a competent human being, not a pain in the butt who should mind her own business. Even though I'd made up my mind last night to do the job, it just felt good to have someone—some man—call up and think first that I should be working, not that I should stay home and play with dolls.

"The only trouble is, I don't know anything about fires. And I don't think I can educate myself fast enough to do a technical investigation."

"We don't need you doing any of the engineering work—we hire a lab to handle that. What you can do is a financial check on the owner, see if he had any kind of motive to set the fire himself. What I hear, you're about the best for that kind of work."

The glow expanded from my ribs to my cheeks. "Fine." I took the owner's name and address: Saul Seligman on north Estes. He was in his seventies and semiretired, but he went into his office on Irving Park Road most afternoons. I conscientiously wrote down the phone number there as well.

"Could we try dinner again?" Robin asked. "Someplace near my house so the cops don't arrest you halfway through the evening?"

I laughed. "How about Friday? I'm pretty beat and I have a lot of work the next few days."

"Great. I'll call Friday morning to pick a place. Thanks a lot for taking on the case."

"Yeah, sure." I hung up.

It was past noon now. If my aunt was still the woman she used to be, she'd just be getting up. I drove with a reckless nervousness, covering the four miles in under ten minutes, and screeched to a halt across from the Windsor Arms. A couple was sitting on the sidewalk, their backs against the building, deep in an argument over whose fault it was that Biffy disappeared. I paused long enough to figure out that Biffy was a cat. The pair didn't spare me a glance.

I didn't get much more attention in the lobby. The chatelaine was watching TV in the lounge, her back to me. The five or six people with her were absorbed by the intensity of feeling pounding out of the high-perched screen. One of them looked up but went back to the show as I started up the stairs.

I took them two at a time and jogged down to Elena's room at a good trot. The door was shut. I tried the knob, then pounded loudly. No answer. I pounded again but didn't call out—if she recognized me, she'd play possum for the next twenty-four hours.

Finally she yelled in a sleep-thickened voice, "Go away. I've got a right to my beauty sleep same as you, you cloth-headed bitch."

I pounded some more, keeping it up steadily until she yanked the door open under my hand. She tried shutting it in my face as soon as she saw me but I followed her into the room.

"Sorry to break into your beauty rest, Auntie," I said, smiling gently. "Isn't it a little risky to call the manager a cloth-headed bitch?"

"Victoria, sweetie. What are you doing here?"

"I came to see you, Elena. I've got some bad news about Cerise."

The violet nightdress still hadn't been laundered. The mixture of stale beer and sweat it gave off was overpowering. I moved to the window and tried to open it, but it had been painted shut with a lavish hand. I sat on the bed. The mattress was about an inch thick; the springs underneath creaked and a little tendril of iron poked through into my buttock.

"Cerise, sweetie?" She blinked in the dim light. "What about her?"

I looked at her solemnly. "I'm afraid she's dead. The police came and got me at midnight last night to identify her body."

"Dead?" she repeated. Her face changed rapidly as she tried to decide how to react, moving from blankness to outrage. It seemed to me that one of the intermediate phases was cunning. Finally a few tears coursed down her veined cheeks.

"You shouldn't break news to people like this, it's really wrong of you. I hope you didn't go pounding your way into Zerlina's hospital room, waking her up and telling her terrible things about her daughter. Gabriella would be ashamed if she knew what you'd done. *Really* ashamed. Anyway, I thought you were keeping an eye on that poor little girl. Why did you let her run off and get herself killed?" She was clearly working hard to build up some anger.

"She kind of did it on her own. By the time I got back to Dr. Herschel's Monday afternoon she'd taken off. I called the cops and asked them to keep a lookout for her, but there's a lot of city and not enough boys in blue to patrol it. So she died of an overdose in the bottom of an elevator shaft at a construction site."

Elena shook her head, lips pursed together. "That's terrible, sweetie, terrible. I can't take news like that sprung on me so suddenly. Why don't you go away and let me digest it on my own? I'll have to see Zerlina, and what I'll ever say to her—you go on, now, Vicki. You were a good girl to come and tell me but I need to be alone."

I kept the gentle smile on my face and looked up at her earnestly. "I will, Elena. I'll go real soon. But first I need you to tell me what little scam you and Cerise had decided to run."

She pulled herself up and gave me a look of outraged dignity. "Scam, Victoria? That's a very ungenteel word."

"But it describes the process to a tee. What money-making scheme had the two of you fixed on?"

"The poor girl isn't even cold and you come here sullying her memory. I don't know what Gabriella would say." She plucked nervously at her gown.

The thought of my mother brought me a smile of pure amusement. "She'd say 'Tell the truth, Elena—it will hurt coming up but then you'll feel healthy again.' " Gabriella had held a firm belief in the value of purging.

"Well, irregardless, I don't know what you're talking about."

I shook my head. "Not good enough, Auntie. You and Cerise showed up on my doorstep full of fear over the fate of poor Katterina. Somehow overnight that evaporated—Cerise pulled a disappearing act and you were playing mighty coy yourself. If either of you had been that worried, you would have figured out some way to get back in touch with me."

"Cerise probably didn't have your phone number. She probably couldn't even remember your last name."

I nodded. "That wouldn't surprise me. But all she had to do was wait at Dr. Herschel's clinic and there I'd be ready—loyal, conscientious, and industrious, or whatever the Scout motto says. No. The two of you had something in mind. Or else you wouldn't have been so reluctant to tell me Zerlina's last name."

"I just didn't think you should go badgering her—"

"Un-unh. You told Zerlina last Wednesday she couldn't keep the baby at the Indiana Arms. What'd you do—blackmail her for the price of a bottle? Ugly stuff, Elena, but it saved the kid's life. You knew when you saw me on Sunday that Zerlina had sent the baby away. I want to know what the *hell* you were doing, and why you dragged me into it." The intensity of my feeling brought me to my feet; I glared down at my aunt.

The ready tears filled her eyes. "You get out of here, Victoria Iphigenia. You just leave. I'm sorry I ever even came to you after the fire. You're just a damned snot-nosed buttinski who can't show any respect to her elders. You may think you own Chicago but this is my room and I can call the police if you don't leave."

I looked around the room and my anger faded, replaced by shame and a wave of hopelessness. Elena couldn't back up her threat—she didn't even have a phone. All she had was her duffel bag and her sweaty filthy nightgown. I blinked back tears of my own and left. As I walked away under the empty light fixtures, I could hear her scrabble the key in the lock.

Out front the couple had stopped arguing and were making up over a bottle of Ripple. I walked slowly to my car and sat hunched over the steering wheel. Sometimes life seems so painful it hurts even to move my arms.

18

NOT DONALD TRUMP

What I wanted was to decamp for some remote corner of the globe where human misery didn't take such naked forms. Lacking funds for that, I could retire to my bed for a month. But then my mortgage bill would come and go without payment and eventually the bank would kick me out and then I'd have some naked misery of my own, sitting in front of my building with a bottle of Ripple to keep it all out of my head. I started the engine and drove north to Saul Seligman's office on Foster.

It was a shabby little storefront. The windows were boarded across the bottom; on the top right side "Seligman Property Management" was lettered on the pane in peeling gold scroll. Between the boarding and the grime on the glass, I couldn't see inside, but I thought a light was on.

The door moved heavily under my hand; it had caught on a piece of loose linoleum that worked as an effective wedge. When I got inside I tried to tamp it down but it curled up as soon as I took my foot away. I gave up and moved to the high, scarred barricade separating Saul from the world beyond. If he was rolling in loot, he wasn't putting any of it into the front office.

The back area held five desks, but only one was inhabited. A woman of about sixty was reading a library copy of Judith Krantz. Her faded blond hair was carefully sculpted in a series of waves. Her lips moved slightly as she slid one pudgy, ring-encrusted finger down the page. She didn't look up, though she must have heard me working on the linoleum. Maybe the book was due today—she still had about half to read.

"I can tell you how it comes out," I offered.

She put Judith down reluctantly. "Did you want something, honey?"

"Mr. Seligman," I said in my brightest, most professional tone.

"He's not in, dear." Her hand strayed for the book.

"When do you expect him?"

"He's not on a regular schedule now he's retired."

I found the latch on the inside of the gate in the barricade. "Maybe you can help me. Are you the office manager?"

She swelled a bit. "You can't come barging in here, honey. This is private. Public out front."

I shut the gate behind me. "I'm an investigator, ma'am. Ajax Insurance hired me to look into the fire that destroyed one of the Seligman properties last week. The Indiana Arms."

"Oh." She toyed with a wedding band that cut deep into her finger. "Is there some kind of problem?"

"Arson's always a problem." I perched on the corner of the desk adjacent to hers. "The company won't pay the claim until they're convinced Mr. Seligman didn't have anything to do with setting the fire."

She pulled herself up in her seat; her pale blue eyes darted fire at me behind her glasses. "That is an outrageous suggestion. The very idea! Mr. Seligman would no more . . . Do you have any proof to back this up?"

I shook my head. "I'm not accusing him of setting the fire. I just need to make sure that he didn't."

"He didn't. I can promise you that."

"Great. That means the inquiry will be short and sweet. How many properties does he own—besides the Indiana Arms, I mean."

"Mr. Seligman is the sweetest, most honest—look, he's a Jew, okay, and I'm a Catholic. Do you think that ever bothered him? When my husband left me and I had my two girls to look after, who paid their tuition bills so they could stay on at St. Inanna's? And the Christmas presents he gave them, not to mention me, if I said it once I said it a hundred times, he'd better not let Fanny see the kinds of presents he gave me, not if he wanted to stay happily married, which he was until she died three years ago. He hasn't been the same since, lost interest in the business, but if you think he would have burned down a building, you're the one who's crazy."

When she finished she was flushed and panting a little. Only a beast would have persisted.

"Do you collect the rents in here, Mrs. . . . ."

"Donnelly," she snapped. "The building managers do that. Look. You'd better show me some kind of authorization if you're going to come barging in asking questions."

I dug my license out of my billfold and handed it to her with one of my cards: V. I. Warshawski, Financial Investigations. She looked them over suspiciously, studying the photo, comparing it to me. For some reason my face had come out a kind of lobster hue in the picture. It always fools people.

"And how do I know you're with the insurance company?" It was a halfhearted snipe but a valid one.

"You can call the company and ask for Robin Bessinger in the arson division. He'll vouch for me." I'd have to get something in writing from them—I'd better walk a copy of my contract for services over tomorrow and pick up a letter of authorization.

Her eye strayed to the phone, but she seemed to decide it was too much trouble to fight me any further. "Okay. Ask what you want, but you'll never find any proof connecting Mr. Seligman to that fire."

"What's your position with the company, Mrs. Donnelly?"

"I'm the office manager." Her face was braced in fierce lines to deflect any attack on Mr. Seligman.

"And that means you . . . ?"

"People call in with complaints, I get the building super to check them out, or the property manager, whoever is in charge. I arrange for bids if any work has to get done, that kind of thing. Detectives come in asking questions, I talk to them."

It was an unexpected flash of humor; I grinned appreciatively. "How many properties are there?"

She ticked them off on her fingers—the one on Ashland, the one on Forty-seventh, and so on, seven altogether, ending with the Indiana Arms. I noted the addresses so I could drive by them, but judging by the locations, none of them was a big money-maker.

No, rents weren't down any. Yes, they used to have a lot more people in the office, that was when Mr. Seligman was younger—he used to buy and sell properties all the time and he needed more staff to do that. Now it was just her and him, a team like they'd always been, and you wouldn't find a warmer-hearted person, not if you looked through the suburbs as well as the city.

"Great." I got up from the edge of the desk and rubbed the sore spot where the metal had cut into my thigh. "By the way, where do you bank— not you personally, Seligman Properties?"

The wary look returned to her face but she answered readily enough—the Edgewater National.

As I was opening the gate something else occurred to me. "Who will take over the business for Mr. Seligman? Does he have any children involved in it?"

She glared at me again. "I wouldn't dream of prying into such a personal matter. And don't go bothering him—he's never really recovered from Fanny's death."

I let the gate click behind me. Wouldn't dream of it, indeed. She probably knew every thought Seligman had had for twenty years, even more so now his wife was dead. As I urged the door over the loose linoleum, I wondered idly about Mrs. Donnelly's own children, whom the old man had so generously educated.

Before getting into the car I found a phone on the corner to call Robin. He was in a meeting—the perennial location of insurance managers—but his secretary promised to have a letter of authorization waiting for me in the morning.

The afternoon was wearing on; I hadn't had a proper meal all day, just some toast with Mr. Contreras's foul coffee. It's hard to think when you're hungry—the demands of the stomach become paramount. I found a storefront Polish restaurant where they gave me a bowl of thick cabbage soup and a plate of homemade rye bread. That was so good that I had some raspberry cake and a cup of overbaked coffee before moving farther north to find Mr. Seligman.

Estes is a quiet residential street in Rogers Park. Seligman lived in an unprepossessing brick house east of Ridge. The small front yard hadn't been much tended during the long hot summer; large clumps of crabgrass and weeds had taken over the straggly grass. The walk was badly broken, not the ideal path for an elderly person, especially when the Chicago winter set in.

The stairs weren't in much better shape—I sidestepped a major hole on the third riser just in time to keep from twisting my ankle. A threadbare mat lay in front of the door. I skidded on its shiny surface when I rang the bell.

I could hear the bell echoing dully behind the heavy front door. Nothing happened. I waited a few minutes and rang again. After another wait I began to wonder if I'd passed Seligman somewhere on Ridge. Just as I was getting ready to leave, though, I heard the rasp of bolts sliding back. It was a clumsy, laborious process. When the final lock came apart the door opened slowly inward and an old man blinked at me across the threshold.

He must have been about Mr. Contreras's age, but where my neighbor had a vitality and curiosity that kept him fit, Mr. Seligman seemed to have retreated from life. His face had slipped into a series of soft, downward creases that slid into the high collar of his faded beige turtleneck. Over that he wore a torn cardigan, one side of which was partly tucked into his pajama pants. He did not look like the mastermind of an arson and fraud ring.

"Yes?" His voice was soft and husky.

I forced a smile to my lips and explained my errand.

"You're with the police, young lady?"

"I'm a private investigator. Your insurance company has hired me to investigate the fire."

"The insurance? My insurance is all paid, I'm sure of that, but you'd have to check with Rita." As he shook his head, bewildered, I caught a glimpse of a hearing aid in his left ear.

I raised my voice and tried to speak clearly. "I know your insurance is paid. The company hired me. Ajax wants me to find out who burned down your hotel."

"Oh. Who burned it down." He nodded five or six times. "I have no idea. It was a great shock, a very great shock. I've been expecting the police or the fire department to come talk to me, but we pay our taxes for nothing these days. Let it burn to the ground and don't do nothing to stop it, then don't do nothing to catch the people who did it."

"I agree," I put in. "That's why Ajax hired me to investigate it for them. I wonder if we could go inside and talk it over."

He studied me carefully, decided I didn't look like a major menace, and invited me in. As soon as he'd shut the door behind me and fastened one of the five locks, I began to wish I'd finished the conversation on the stoop. The smell, combined of must, unwashed dishes, and stale grease, seemed to seep from the walls and furniture. I didn't know life could exist in such air.

The living room where he took me was dark and chilly. I tried not to curse when I ran into a low table, but as I backed away from it I caught my left leg on some heavy metal object and couldn't help swearing.

"Careful, there, young lady, these were all Fanny's things and I don't want them damaged."

"No, sir," I said meekly, waiting for him to finish fumbling with a light before trying to move any farther. When the heavily fringed lamp sprang into life, I saw that I'd tripped on a set of fire irons mysteriously placed in the middle of the room. As there was no fireplace perhaps that was the ideal spot for them. I threaded my way past the rest of the obstacles and sat gingerly on the edge of an overstuffed armchair. My rear sank deep within its soft, dusty upholstery.

Mr. Seligman sat on a matching couch that was close by, if you discounted an empty brass birdcage hanging between us. "Now what is it you want, young lady?"

He was hard of hearing and depressed but clearly not mentally impaired. When he took in the gist of my remarks his sagging cheeks mottled with color.

"My insurance company thinks I burned down my own building? What do I pay rates for? I pay my taxes and the police don't help me, I pay my insurance and my company insults me—"

"Mr. Seligman," I cut in, "you've lived in Chicago a long time, right? Your whole life? Well, me too. You know as well as I do that people here torch their own property every day just to collect on the insurance. I'm happy to think you're not one of them, but you can't blame the company for wanting to make sure."

The angry flush died from his cheeks but he continued muttering under his breath about robbers who took your money without giving you anything in return. He calmed down enough to answer routine questions on where he'd been last Wednesday night—home in bed, what did I think he was, a Don Juan at his age to be gallivanting around town all night?

"Can you think of any reason anyone would want to burn down the Indiana Arms?"

He held up his hands in exasperation. "It was an old building, no good to anybody, even me. You pay the taxes, you pay the insurance, you pay the utilities, and when the rent comes in you don't have enough to pay for the paint. I know the wiring was old but I couldn't afford to put in new, you've got to believe me on that, young lady."

"Why didn't you just tear it down if it was costing you so much?"

"You're like everyone today, just considering a dollar and not people's hearts. People come to me, it seems like every day, thinking I'm a stupid old man who will just sell them my heart and let them tear it down. Now here you are, another one."

He shook his head slowly, depressed over the perfidy of the younger generation. "It was the first building I owned. I put together the money slowly, slowly in the Depression. You wouldn't understand. I worked on a delivery truck for years and saved every penny, every dime, and when Fanny and I got married everything went into the Indiana Arms."

He was talking more to himself now than to me, his husky voice so soft I had to lean forward to hear him. "You should have seen it in those days, it used to be a beautiful hotel. We made deliveries there in the morning and even the kitchens seemed wonderful to me—I grew up in two rooms, eight of us in two rooms, with no kitchen, all the water hauled in by hand. When the owners went bankrupt—everybody went under in those days—I scraped together the money and bought it."

His faded eyes clouded. "Then the war came and the colored came pouring in and Fanny and I, we moved up here, we had a family then anyway, you couldn't raise children in a residential hotel, even if the neighborhood was decent. But I never could bring myself to sell it. Now it's gone, maybe it's just as well."

Out of respect for his memories I waited before speaking again, looking around the room to give him a little privacy. On the low table nearest me was a studio portrait of a solemn young man and a shyly smiling young woman in bridal dress.

"That was Fanny and me," he said, catching my glance. "It's hard to believe, isn't it?"

I took him gently through the routine—who worked for him, what did he know about the night man at the Indiana Arms, who would inherit the business, who would profit by the fire. He answered readily enough, but he couldn't really think ill of someone who worked for him, nor of his children, who would get the business when he died.

"Not that it's much to leave them. You start out, you think you'll end up like Rubloff, but all I've got to show for all my years is seven worn-out buildings." He gave me his children's names and addresses and said he'd tell Rita to let me have a list of employees—the building managers and watchmen and maintenance crews.

"I suppose someone could burn down a building if you paid him enough. It's true I don't pay them much, but look at me, look how I live, I'm not Donald Trump after all—I pay what I can afford."

He saw me to the front door, going over it again and again, how he paid his taxes and got nothing and had nothing, but paid his employees, and would they turn on him anyway? As I walked down the front steps I could hear the locks slowly closing behind me.

19

GENTLEMAN CALLER

There was an errand I couldn't put off before going home. I squared my shoulders and drove south through the rush-hour traffic to Michael Reese. Zerlina was still in her four-pack, but one of the beds was empty and the other two held new inmates who looked at me with vacant faces before returning to *Wheel of Fortune*.

Zerlina turned her head away when she saw me. I hesitated at the foot of her bed—it would be easier to take her rejection at face value and go home than to talk to her about her daughter. "Quitters never win and winners never quit," I encouraged myself, and went to squat near her head.

"You've heard about Cerise, Mrs. Ramsay."

The black eyes stared at me unblinkingly, but at length she gave a grudging nod.

"I'm very sorry—I had to identify her early this morning. She looked terribly young."

She scowled horribly in an effort to hold back tears. "What did you do to her, you and that aunt of yours, to drive her to take her own life?"

"I'm sorry, Mrs. Ramsay," I repeated. "Maybe I should have tried to find her on Monday. But she left the clinic where I'd brought her and I didn't have any idea where she might go. I tried talking to Elena this morning; if she knew anything, she was keeping it to herself."

I stayed another five minutes or so, but she wouldn't say anything else, nor did her face relent. When I got back in the car I sat for a long time rubbing my tight shoulder muscles and trying to imagine a place I could go to find some peace. Not my apartment—I didn't want to confront either Mr. Contreras or Vinnie tonight. I was too tired, though, to drive out to the country, too tired to deal with the noise and distraction of a restaurant. What I needed was a club of the kind Peter Wimsey used to retire to—discreet, solicitous servants leaving me in total peace yet willing to spring into immediate action at my slightest whim.

I put the Chevy into gear and started north, going by side streets, dawdling at lights, finally hitting Racine from Belmont and coasting to a halt in front of my building. On my way in I stopped in the basement for my laundry. Some kind soul had taken it from the dryer and left it on the floor. My limbs heavy and slow, I picked it up one item at a time and put it back into the washer. I stayed in the dimly lit basement while the machine ran, sitting cross-legged on a newspaper on the floor, staring at nothing, thinking of nothing. When the washer clanked to a halt I stood up to dump my things once more into the dryer. Easily the equivalent of an evening at the Marlborough Club.

It was only when I got upstairs that I remembered giving the servants the day off, so there was no dinner ready. I sent out for a pizza and watched a *Magnum* rerun. Before going to bed I returned to the basement for my clothes. By a miracle I arrived before one of my neighbors had time to dirty them again.

Thursday morning I brought a contract down to Ajax, got a letter of authorization from them, and proceeded on my investigation. I spent Thursday and Friday tracking down Seligman's children—both in their forties— and talking to the different night watchmen, janitors, and building managers who made up the Seligman work team. Mrs. Donnelly—Rita to Seligman— even grudgingly let me look at the books. By the end of Friday I was reasonably certain that the old man had had no role in the fire.

His children didn't take any active part in the business. One daughter was married to an appliance dealer and didn't work herself. The other, a marketing manager with a Schaumburg wholesaler, had been in Brazil on business when the fire took place. That didn't mean she couldn't have masterminded it, but it was hard to see why. The two stood to inherit the business, and it was possible that they were going to torch the properties for their insurance money to increase the value of the estate, but it was a slow way to dubious wealth. I didn't write them off, but I wasn't enthusiastic about them as candidates, either.

My talks with Mrs. Donnelly left me scratching my head. She seemed loyal to the old man, but I couldn't help thinking she knew something she wasn't telling. It wasn't so much what she said as the sly look I got when the talk drifted to her children and what their expectations of Mr. Seligman might be. If it hadn't been for that occasional smirk, I would have given Seligman a complete pass to Ajax.

On Saturday I finally found the night man from the Indiana Arms. He was holed up with a brother on the South Side, trying to avoid any inquiry into his activities on the night of the fire. We had a long and difficult conversation. At first he assured me he hadn't left the premises for a minute. Then he came around to the idea that he'd heard a noise outside and gone to investigate.

Finally a combination of threats and bribes brought forth the information that he'd gotten a list of the races at Sportsman Park along with fifty dollars in betting money. They'd come in Wednesday's mail, he didn't know who from, he certainly hadn't kept the envelope. He didn't think it would matter if he left for an hour or two; when he got back late—after a snort with his buddies—the hotel was burning beautifully. He took one look at the fire trucks and headed for his brother's house on Sangamon.

It was clear that someone had cared enough about burning down the building to study the night man, find out he bet the races, and know he couldn't resist a free night at the track. But that someone wasn't Saul Seligman. I put it all together in a report for Ajax, wrote out a bill, and asked whether they wanted me to pursue the matter further.

If your primary goal is to find the arsonist, then I will try to discover who sent the money. Since no envelope exists and Mr. Tancredi claims never to have seen any strangers regularly lurking around the premises, finding who sent the money will be a long and expensive job. If all you want is a strong probability that your insured did not burn his own property, we can stop at this point: I believe Mr. Seligman and his subordinates are innocent of arson.

After putting it in the mail I walked the ten blocks to Wrigley Field and watched the Cubs die a painful death at the hands of the Expos. Although my hapless heroes were twenty games below five hundred the ballpark was packed; I was lucky to get a seat in the upper deck. Even if I could have gotten a bleacher ticket, I don't sit there anymore—NBC made such a cult of the Bleacher Bums when the Cubs were in the '84 playoffs that drunk yuppies who don't know the game now find it the trendy place to sit.

It was after five when I got home. A late-model black Chevrolet bristling with antennae was parked illegally next to the hydrant in front of my building. I looked at it with the usual curiosity you give an unmarked police car when it's next to your home. The windows were rolled up and I couldn't see through the smoky glass, but when the door opened I saw Bobby Mallory had been driving himself.

I was surprised to see him—it was the first time he'd ever come to my apartment without a formal escort. I hurried to the curb to greet him.

"Bobby! Good to see you. Nothing's wrong, is it?"

He ran a hand through my hair, a rare gesture of affection since I graduated from high school. "Just thought I'd come by and see you, Vicki, make sure you're not playing with some kind of fire that's likely to burn you."

"I see." I tried to keep my tone light while a wall of caution shut down part of my mind. "Is that something you can do in one sentence out here on the sidewalk or do you want to come up for some coffee?"

"Oh, let's go inside, be comfortable. If you've got decaf, that is—I can't take coffee late in the day anymore. I'm almost sixty, you know."

"Yeah, I know." I wondered if he was trying to pump me obliquely for word on what Eileen had planned for the big day, but I didn't think he'd treat me to such an elaborate routine for that. I politely held the door for him and let him precede me up the three flights.

Bobby, still on his good behavior, ignored the untidy heap of papers in the living room. I tried not to feel embarrassed at being caught in such chaos by an old friend of my parents and went to scrounge in my kitchen.

"I'm afraid I'm out of decaf," I apologized a few minutes later. "I can give you some juice or a Coke or wine. No beer, though."

He took a Coke. One of Bobby's fetishes, in addition to not swearing in front of me, is not to drink with me—he can't get over the idea that he'd be encouraging me in immorality. He drank a little, ate a handful of crackers, gestured at the piano, and asked if I was still working at my singing. My mother had been an accomplished musician, an aspiring operatic soprano whose career had been cut short when her family shipped her to America to escape fascism. One of Bobby's unexpected traits was to share her love of opera; she used to sing Puccini for him. He would be a happy cop if I'd fulfilled her dream and become a concert singer instead of aping my dad and turning into a detective.

I had to admit my voice was a little rusty. "Seen any rare birds lately?"

Another unexpected hobby of Bobby's was photographing birds. As he discoursed on taking his two oldest grandchildren to the forest preserve last weekend, I wondered how long we were going to pretend that this was just a social call.

"Mickey's coming out with us tomorrow," he said. "He's a good boy. Young man, I should say, but I've known him since he was born."

"Yes, he's told me you're his godfather." I sipped some Coke and watched him over the rim of the glass.

"Eileen and I were both hoping you two would hit it off, but she keeps telling me you can't force these things."

"He's a Sox fan. It would never work out."

"Even though you like sports and race around playing police, you want a guy who's more artistic."

I didn't know whether to jump down his throat for calling my work "playing police" or be amazed that he put so much thought into my character. "Maybe I just don't want to be married. Michael hangs out with a crowd where the wife is the little woman who stays home and has kiddies. That may be your dream for me but it's not my style, never has been and never will be."

" 'Never' is a long time, Vicki." He held up a hand as the blood rushed to my face. "Hold your fire. I'm not saying you're wrong. Just don't get yourself out on a limb where you'll saw yourself off rather than admit you changed your mind. But that's not what I came to say to you."

It made me downright mad to think of him and Eileen sitting at dinner, planning my marriage to his godson—"Maybe truelove will get her mind off wanting to be a boy and play boys' games with guns and baseballs"—as though my life and my choices were of no account. I bit back a diatribe. Yelling at Bobby could only put me at a severe disadvantage.

"I haven't asked Mickey anything about you," he went on. "I figure it's his business. But he's been like a cat on a hot stove since he saw you clinched with that kid the other night."

"I can't call up and apologize for being found necking at my own front door."

"Just go easy on him, will you, Vicki? I'm fond of the boy. I don't want an explosion on my staff because you're turning them on and off like faucets. I know there's been something between you and John, even though neither of you admits it; I don't want a blowup between him and Mickey. Or Mickey and you. You may not believe it, but I'm fond of you, too."

My cheeks flamed again, this time with embarrassment. "There's never been anything between McGonnigal and me. He gave me a lift home last winter in the middle of the night. I was beat, he thought I looked cute when vulnerable, we had one kiss and both knew we couldn't cross that line again. Since then it's been like I was Cleopatra's asp. And I'm damned if I'm going to apologize to him for that."

"Don't swear, Vicki, it's not nearly as attractive as you modern young women think." He put his glass down on the magazines covering the coffee table and got up. "I was talking to Monty yesterday afternoon—Roland Montgomery, Bomb and Arson Squad—he knows I know you. He says you're poking around in that Indiana Arms fire we asked you not to touch."

I gave a tight little smile. "Just playing police, Bobby—I wouldn't worry about it since it's only a game, not the real stuff."

He put a large hand on my shoulder. "I know you think you're a big girl —what are you now, thirty-five? Thirty-six? But your parents are both dead and they were my close friends. No one's so big they don't need someone else looking out for them. If Monty said to keep away from that fire, you keep away. Arson's about the nastiest thing on this planet. I don't want to see you messed up in it."

I closed my lips in a tight ball to keep my ugly words in. He'd touched about ten raw nerves in five minutes and I was too angry to give any kind of coherent response. I saw him to the door without telling him good-bye.

When I heard his car start I sat at the piano and vented my feelings in a series of crashing, dissonant chords. Yeah, I ought to practice, ought to keep my voice limber before I got too old and my vocal cords lost their flexibility. I ought to be everyone's good little girl. But for my own self-respect I needed to solve the arson.

I got up from the piano and jotted a second note to Robin:

I sent you a report this morning, but as I've thought over the case during the day I believe it is critical to locate the person who sent Jim Tancredi the money for the track.

It was only when I'd mailed it that I calmed down enough to wonder why Bobby had come to see me—to talk to me about Michael Furey? Or to warn me off the Indiana Arms investigation?

20
HEAVY WARNING

Bobby's visit left such a bad taste in my mouth that I wanted to tell Eileen I couldn't make it to her party. But Bobby was right about one thing—you shouldn't saw off the limb you're sitting on just to salve your pride.

I called a couple of friends to see if anyone wanted to take in a movie but everyone was out. I left messages on various machines and stomped off to the kitchen to scramble some eggs. Normally sitting home alone on Saturday doesn't trouble me, but Bobby's visit made me wonder if I was doomed for an old age of crabby isolation.

I turned on the TV and moodily changed channels. You'd think Saturday night they could offer something enticing for the stay-at-homes, but the networks thought all America was out dancing. When the phone rang I turned off the set eagerly, thinking maybe someone was returning one of my messages. I was startled to hear Roz Fuentes's husky voice.

She didn't even say hello before she started lambasting me for butting my nose into her business. "What are you trying to do to me, Warshawski?" Her voice had recovered its usual rich, throaty timbre; the vibration through the phone made my ear tingle.

"I'm not doing anything to you, Roz. Don't you have a campaign to run? Why are you picking on me?"

Her rich chuckle came, but it lacked mirth. "Velma called me. She said you were trying to get her to spill some dirt on me, that she put you in your place but she thought I ought to know. What kind of dirt are you looking for, anyway?"

I bared my teeth at the phone. "Hey, Roz—Velma put me in my place. Relax."

"Vic, I gotta know." She spoke softly, urgently—it was like listening to the Chicago Symphony string section. "This campaign means *everything* to me and my people. I told you that last weekend. I can't afford to have someone lying in the bushes waiting for me with a shotgun."

It had been too long a day for me to make any great display of subtlety. "Roz, I don't care if you've been sleeping with Boots and the whole county board to get yourself on the ticket. What bugs me is you going out of your way to ask me if I was sandbagging you. What would even make you *think* such a thing unless you're getting me to sign on to something I'm going to be very sorry about later? I'm thin-skinned, Roz; it gets me itzy if someone is trying to make a monkey out of me."

"I came to you as a show of respect for our old relationship," she said indignantly. "Now you are twisting my friendship into something evil. Velma was right. I should know better than to turn to a white girl with my concerns."

"A white boy is okay, though?" I was thoroughly riled. "Boots can be your ally but I can't? Go save the Chicago Hispanics, Roz, but leave me out of it."

We hung up on that fractured note. I was mad enough to call Velma to demand chapter and verse on not trusting me just because I was white, but a conversation like that can go nowhere constructive.

Sunday morning I got a further indication that the Fuentes-Meagher pot had something cooking in it when Marissa invited me to stop by for drinks that evening. Something spontaneous and casual, was how she put it, for people she hadn't spent enough time with at Roz's campaign. I told her I was truly overwhelmed to be remembered by her and that the thought of such an evening was irresistible. Marissa had herself well in hand, though, and refused to be ruffled.

At five I set out for her Lincoln Park town house, one of those three-story jobs on Cleveland where every brick has been sandblasted and the woodwork refinished so it glows warmly. Marissa rented out the ground floor and lived in the upper two.

When I got to the top of the first flight she met me in the landing to escort me into what she called her drawing room. As usual Marissa looked great, her idea of casual being bulky red silk trousers, a matching pajama-style top, and lots of silver jewelry. I hadn't worn jeans, but I couldn't help feeling she'd dressed with the intention of making me look dowdy.

The drawing room, which had once been the two front bedrooms, ran the width of the building, its row of mullioned windows looking out on Cleveland. Whatever negative thoughts I had about Marissa didn't include her taste—the room was simply but beautifully furnished, a high-Victorian look predominating, complete with red Turkish rugs scattered at strategic places. An exotic array of plants gave the whole scene warmth.

When I complimented her she laughed and said it was all due to her sister, who owned a plant rental business and rotated fresh shrubbery for her every few weeks. "Let me introduce you to some of the folks, Vic."

Some fifteen or twenty people were chattering with the ease of familiarity. As she led me toward the nearest group the doorbell rang again. She excused herself, telling me to help myself to a drink and see if I knew anyone.

I'd half expected to see Roz, or even the Wunsch and Grasso contingent, but the only person I recognized was Ralph MacDonald. I tipped my hat to Marissa—she must be even better connected than I'd realized for the great man to spend a Sunday evening at such a low-profile function as this.

He was talking to a couple of banker-looking types who'd dressed down for the weekend in open-necked shirts and sport jackets. Two women in their little group were talking sotto voce to each other so as not to disturb the boys. This sample of good wifely conduct made me gladder than ever I hadn't stood by my own man, a lawyer who now lived in palatial splendor in Oak Brook.

The bar, set in the far corner behind one of the trees, had just about anything one's heart could desire, including a bottle of indifferent champagne. The whiskey was J&B, a brand I can take or leave, so I poured myself a glass of the chardonnay. It made me feel too much like a Lincoln Park native for comfort, but it wasn't a bad wine.

I took it over to an armchair and watched Marissa return with the newcomers, a thirty-something couple I also didn't recognize. She brought them to a clump not too far from me where they were greeted enthusiastically as Todd and Meryl. Marissa, the perfect hostess, stayed to chat, then moved to the MacDonald group before responding again to the buzzer.

By and by two women in black slacks and white blouses came in with trays of hot hors d'oeuvres. Ralph MacDonald moved over with the two women from his huddle just as I was helping myself to a couple of spinach triangles.

"Vic? I'm Ralph MacDonald—we met at Boots's shindig last weekend."

"I remember you, of course—but I'm surprised you know me." I tried to sound suave while hastily swallowing the last of my pastry.

"Don't be modest, Vic—you're a pretty memorable gal."

The comment was innocuous but the tone seemed charged. Before I could question him he introduced me to the two women, who obviously were as enthusiastic at meeting me as I them. They filled small plates with a sample of treats and retired to the bankers as Marissa brought another unaccompanied man over to us. She introduced him as Clarence Hinton; he and MacDonald clearly knew each other reasonably well.

"You remember Vic from last Sunday, Ralph," Marissa stated.

"I was just telling her not to undersell herself." He turned to me. "Actually I probably wouldn't have remembered you if I hadn't run into Clarence here after you left."

I shook my head.

"Clarence and I were both friends of Edward Purcell."

I flushed against my will. Purcell had been chairman of Transicon and the mastermind of a major fraud I'd uncovered in my first big investigation. It wasn't my fault he'd committed suicide the day before the federal marshals were coming to pick him up, but I had to fight back a defensive retort.

I forced myself to ask Clarence in a neutral voice if he was a developer too.

"Oh, I play around with putting projects together. I don't have MacDonald's energy for that kind of thing. Ralph, I want a drink and the lady here needs a refill. I'll be back in a minute."

"Mine's bourbon on the rocks," MacDonald said as Hinton turned to the bar. To me he added, "I'm glad you came, Vic—I've been hoping to have a chance to talk to you."

I raised my eyebrows. "About Edward Purcell? It's been almost ten years."

"Oh, I've always felt sort of disappointed with Teddy for that. There's no lick so hard you can't fight it in court."

"Especially in this town," I said dryly.

He flashed a smile to let me know he got the joke without finding it particularly funny. "I don't hold Teddy against you. No, I wanted to talk to you about something more contemporary."

Maybe this was going to be my big break—detective to the stars. My chance to fund an international enterprise that would make my uncle Peter swoon with envy. Before I could ask, Clarence returned with the drinks and Ralph shepherded us down the hall to a small back room. It had probably been a maid's room in the old days of the house, but Marissa had decorated it in white on white and used it for watching TV.

I sat in one of the hard-upholstered chairs and smoothed my challis skirt over my knees. MacDonald stood across from me, his foot on the rung of the couch, while Hinton leaned against the door. There was no special menace in their faces but the poses were meant to intimidate. I sipped a little wine and waited.

When it was clear I wasn't going to say anything, MacDonald began. "Donnel Meagher has been chairman of the Cook County Board for a lot of years."

"And you think the time has come for him to pack it in?" I asked.

MacDonald shook his head. "Far from it. He's developed a political savvy in that time that no one else in this area can match. I expect you don't agree with all his positions, but I'm sure you respect his judgment."

"If I respected his judgment I'd agree with his positions," I objected.

"His political judgments." MacDonald smiled thinly. "After Clarence pointed out who you were I asked around about you. The consensus is, you consider yourself a wit."

"But with good judgment," I couldn't help saying.

He declined the gambit. "Boots picked Rosalyn Fuentes for the county slate based strictly on her political merits. That's the kind of decision I understand you may have a hard time with."

In my secret heart I hadn't really expected he wanted to hire me, but it was still a letdown to think he only wished to warn me off Roz. "I don't have any trouble with that kind of decision. Boots is clearly a political mastermind, and if Roz can get his backing, her future looks golden."

"So you're not trying to sandbag her campaign?" That was Hinton's first contribution to the discussion.

"You guys are making me awful, awful curious," I said. "Marissa put the arm on me to go to Roz's fund-raiser in the name of a decade-old solidarity. I shelled out more money than I've ever given a candidate, was bored out of my head, and was getting ready to leave when Roz talked to me just to make sure I wasn't going to do anything to hurt her. Now you two lock me in a little room to pick my brain. I don't know anything about Roz's secrets and I wouldn't care what they were if people weren't going out of their way to make me wonder."

"It really would be better if you minded your own business this time around," Hinton said in a toneless voice more ominous than a shout.

MacDonald shook his head. "She's not going to listen to threats, Clarence—her whole history makes that clear. . . . Look, Vic—Roz needs Boots's support if she's going to win her first county-wide contest. But Boots needs her too—the Hispanic wards pretty much vote the way she tells them to."

That wasn't news to me so I didn't say anything.

"Roz committed a major indiscretion in her youth. She confessed it all to Boots when they were talking over the slate and his opinion was that it wouldn't hurt her if it came out in five years, when she had a big base, but that it could be pretty damaging to her home support if they learned about it now. So someone said something to her at the barbecue that made her think you were probing and she was trying to assure herself that you weren't."

"And what was that youthful indiscretion?"

MacDonald shook his head. "Even if I knew, I couldn't tell you—Boots is an old political hand and he doesn't share secrets with people who don't need to know them."

"Well, you know my reputation—I don't care if she was screwing the village goat, but I don't sign on for fraud."

MacDonald laughed. "You see, Vic, everyone has a different notion of morality. There are plenty more people in Humboldt Park who would care about the goat than any money she'd siphoned off a public works project. So don't set up your own standards to run the county by, okay?"

I smiled sweetly. "Just as long as no one is making *me* the goat. That's probably what I most care about."

He came over and helped me to my feet. "It would take a smarter crew than us to do that. Let's go back to the party—I want some of those little salmon things before the ignorant mob gets them all."

When we returned to the drawing room Marissa caught Ralph's eye anxiously. He nodded fractionally to telegraph all's well, that I'd been convinced. But of what?

21
AUNTIE'S TURNING TRICKS AGAIN

When I got home the sun had just set and the air was still softly lit. I went slowly upstairs to my living room and stood at the window looking out. Vinnie the banker emerged from our building and climbed into his car, a late-model Mazda. A gaggle of teenage boys headed south, yelling raucous slogans and dumping their potato-chip bags onto the sidewalk.

I let the curtain fall and went to sit in my armchair. I didn't want to learn something awful about Roz. I really didn't. I wanted strong women in public office and she was better than most. So why did she keep rubbing my face in it?

I hadn't turned on any lamps. In the twilight the room seemed ghostly, a place where no living creatures moved. The image of Cerise's dead face came into my mind and I felt an unbearable sadness for the waste that had been her life. And again, unwanted, came the nagging question about what Bobby was doing at the site within hours of her body being discovered. And what was he doing coming to see me yesterday? Off and on all day I'd worried over it like a sore tooth, but couldn't put it to rest.

I had one client, Ajax, to look into one issue—had Saul Seligman burned down his own building. As a host of people from Bobby Mallory to Velma Riter and Ralph MacDonald kept reminding me, neither Cerise nor Roz was any of my business. Of course the cops thought the Indiana Arms wasn't any of my business, either.

By and by I got stiffly to my feet and went down to Mr. Contreras's apartment to borrow the dog. Sometimes he has enough sensitivity to spare me an intrusive barrage. Tonight, mercifully, was such a time. He handed Peppy over to me with a stern adjuration not to feed her cheese or anything else dangerous to her delicate GI tract and returned to the tube.

I walked Peppy around the block before returning to my own apartment. She thought that was a pretty miserable excuse for a workout, but when I fixed her a plate of spaghettini with dried tomatoes and mushrooms to go with my own, she cheered up. She wolfed it down and came to lie on my feet while I turned to the phone.

Murray Ryerson was Chicago's leading crime reporter. He'd been with the *Herald-Star* for almost eleven years, moving from covering the city wire stories to nickel-and-dime stabbings to now where he was a leading authority on the frequent intersection of crime and politics in town.

He didn't show any particular enthusiasm at hearing from me. At times we've been friendly enough to be lovers, but both of us covering the same scene and having strong personalities make it hard to avoid conflict. After the latest clash between our jobs Murray had been furious. He still hadn't warmed up. He believed I'd held back significant chunks of a story until it was too late to use them. Actually I'd held back significant chunks that he never even knew about, so he probably had a right to a grievance.

Tonight he told me astringently that he was very busy and if it was business it could wait until he was in the office tomorrow.

"Does she have a name?" I asked hopefully.

"Make it snappy, Warshawski. I'm not in the mood."

It was easy to be brief since I didn't have much to say. "Roz Fuentes. She's on the county ticket and she thinks I think she's hiding something. Is she?"

"God, Vic, I don't know. If you had to bother me at home to ask me that—"

"I wouldn't have," I interrupted him. "Do you know who Ralph Mac-Donald is?"

"You're wasting my time, Warshawski. Everyone knows MacDonald. He's the leading contender to put together the package for the new stadium-retail-housing complex."

I hadn't heard that. Murray told me loftily I didn't know everything, that it was just county scuttlebutt because of Boots being tight with MacDonald.

"And I don't need you calling me at home catechizing me to remember what an inside track Ralph MacDonald has in county building projects. He and Boots grew up together. They got big together. Everyone knows that. So come to the point or hang up."

I scowled at the phone but plowed ahead in my best Girl Scout style. "Ralph is hanging out with a lady I sort of know—Marissa Duncan. She's kind of a political PR woman, fund-raiser, that type of thing. She trotted him out for me tonight at her Lincoln Park town house to tell me to lay off Roz."

"Yeah, I know Marissa. She's at all the right events. If she and Ralph want you to leave them alone, it's not news—they must know what a pain in the ass you are. It still could have waited until morning."

When I didn't say anything he grudgingly allowed that he didn't know of anything about Roz that the paper was holding back. They do that more often than the trusting public likes to think—they don't run a juicy story because it will stub an important advertiser or religious figure's toe. Or even worse, they want to wait and drop it like a stink bomb when it will hurt the most people.

"But you'll check tomorrow for me?" I persisted.

"Only if I get an exclusive on your obituary, Warshawski."

I made a face at the phone. "The number of french fries you eat I'm bound to outlive you, Murray. . . . Did you see anything about a dead junkie picked up at the Rapelec construction site?"

I could feel him trying to figure it out on the phone—which was the real reason I'd called, Roz or the junkie. "I missed that one," he said cautiously. "Friend of yours?"

"In a way." Peppy got up and started sniffing around the corners. "I ID'd her. It just seemed strange to me that some of the city's top cops were there—thought you might know about it. Well, sorry to have bothered you at home—I'll talk to you at the paper tomorrow."

"Warshawski—oh, the hell with you. Go find someone else to run your errands." He hung up with a bang.

Peppy had found some dust balls behind the piano that she was bent on eating. I retrieved them from her mouth and hunted around for a tennis ball to play a little indoor fetch with her. She likes to sit on her haunches and catch the ball without letting it bounce. The hitch is, I have to go scampering after it if she doesn't make it. I was lying on my back pulling it from under the piano when the phone rang. I clambered upright to answer the phone and bounced the ball to Peppy. She watched it go by her with a look of pure disgust and slumped dejectedly onto her forepaws.

It was Michael Furey. I stiffened at once, thinking Bobby must have given him a little godfatherly advice on the best way to handle stubborn women.

Furey was ill at ease. I didn't do anything to make him relax. "Sorry to bother you so late in the day. Do you have a minute? I need to talk to you about something. Can I come over?"

"Is this Bobby's idea?" I demanded.

"Well, yes, I mean not that I come over, but—"

"You can tell him from me to butt out of my business. Or I'll tell him myself."

"Don't make this harder for me than it already is, Vic. She's not just your private business, even if you wish she was."

I held the receiver away from my face and looked at it for a minute. "You're not calling about—about Tuesday night?" I asked stupidly.

"No. No, nothing like that. Though I admit I owe you an apology. This —it's about your aunt and it's not real easy talking about it on the phone."

My heart squeezed shut. "Is she dead?"

"No, oh no, it's just—look, I hate being the one to do this to you, but Uncle Bobby—the lieutenant—he thought you and I were, well, since we'd been friends it would come better from me than anyone else."

Wild thoughts of Elena's somehow being responsible for the fire at the Indiana Arms clashed with the fear of a drunken stupor turned to disaster. I sat on the piano bench and demanded to know what Michael was talking about.

"There's no easy way to say this. But she's been spotted a couple of times soliciting in Uptown, mostly old guys, but a couple of times young ones who were pretty affronted."

Relief that it was so trivial made me laugh—that and the image of Elena taking on someone like Vinnie the banker or Furey himself. I hooted so loudly that Peppy came over to see what the trouble was.

"It's not as funny as all that, Vic—the only reason she hasn't been arrested is because of the connection between your family and the police. I was hoping you could go talk to her, ask her to stop."

"I'll do my best," I promised, gasping for breath, "but she's never paid much attention to anything anybody said to her." I couldn't help it, but started laughing again.

"If I came along?" he suggested tentatively. "Uncle Bobby thought it might make more of an impact if someone from the force was there to back you up."

"Tell me the truth—he was too chicken to confront her, wasn't he?"

Michael hedged on that one—he wasn't about to slander his commander, even if Bobby was his godfather. Instead he asked, even more hesitantly, if I might be free to do it tonight. I looked at my watch. It was only eight-thirty; might as well get it over with.

"If she's in, she's probably drunk," I warned him.

"She won't be the first one I've seen. I'll pick you up in twenty minutes."

I still had on the red rayon challis skirt I'd worn to Marissa's party. I changed it for jeans—I didn't want Furey to think I was dressing up for him. When he rang the buzzer, right on time, I took Peppy back down to Mr. Contreras. She was totally miffed—no run, no games, and now she had to stay inside when I was setting out on an adventure that would doubtless include chasing a lot of squirrels and ducks.

Michael had recovered a certain amount of his breeziness. He greeted me jauntily, asked if I'd gotten over the shock of identifying Cerise, and solicitously held the door of the Corvette open for me. I gathered my legs together and swung them over the side, the only possible way to get into that kind of car—I've always wondered how Magnum leapt in and out of that Ferrari.

"Where does she live?" he asked, starting the car with a great roar.

I told him the address of the Windsor Arms but left him to find his own way. You never have to give a Chicago policeman street directions. Maybe we should require a year of patrol duty for all would-be cabdrivers.

Michael used police privilege to block the hydrant in front of the hotel. A couple of drunks came over to inspect the Corvette but slid into the night when Furey casually let them see his gun. When he got inside no one was at the desk. I had headed toward the stairs, Michael behind me, when a voice shouted from the lounge, "Hey! No one up those stairs but residents."

We turned to see a man in green work clothes push himself out of a chair and head toward us. Behind him some mindless sitcom was blaring from the high-perched TV. In his youth the man had been muscular, maybe played high school football, but now he was just big and sloppy, his belly straining the buttons on his green work shirt.

Michael flashed his white teeth. "Police, buddy. We need to talk to one of the inmates."

"You got some ID? Anyone can come in here saying they're police."

He might be three-quarters drunk and run to seed, but he had some spunk. Michael seemed to debate playing a police heavy, but when he caught me watching him he pulled his badge from his pants pocket and showed it briefly.

"Who you after?" the night man demanded.

"Elena Warshawski," I said, before Michael could put out the police none-of-your-business line. "Do you know if she's in?"

"She ain't here."

"How about if we go upstairs and see for ourselves," Michael said.

The man shook his head. "Wouldn't do you any good. She took off three days ago. Packed up all her stuff and took off into the night."

"Thursday?" I asked.

He thought for a minute, counting backward. "Yeah, that'd be right. She in some kind of trouble?"

"She's my aunt," I said. "She gets lonesome and tries to find people to keep her company. I want to make sure she's okay. You know where she went?"

He shook his head. "I was setting in there, watching the two A.M. movie, and seen her sneaking down the stairs. 'Hey, sis, ain't no law against you coming downstairs in the middle of the night. You can walk upright,' I calls to her. She gives a gasp and asks me to go outside to see if the coast is clear. None of my business what business people get up to, so I goes out and watches her head over to Broadway. No one was bothering her so I come back inside. And that's the last I seen her."

That was an unsettling scenario. Something had rattled her badly enough to make her scoot from a secure bed, badly enough to keep her from landing at my door.

"Can I go up and look at her room?" I asked abruptly. "Maybe she left something behind, some sign of why she bolted."

The night man scrutinized me through drink-softened eyes. After asking for a look at my driver's license, he decided I passed whatever internal test he was running. We went back to the stairs and followed him as he trudged heavily to the third floor. Michael asked me in an urgent whisper if I had any idea where she might have gone.

"Hm-umh." I shook my head impatiently. "Probably the only friend she had from the Indiana Arms is in the hospital still and doesn't have a place to stay anyway."

The night man laboriously fiddled with the keys at his belt until he found one to unlock Elena's room. He flipped a switch that turned on the naked bulb overhead. The room was bare. Elena had left the nylon bedding jumbled. It hung over the end, trailing on the floor, exposing the thin pad of a mattress as a tawdry indictment of the whole room.

I shook out the bedding. The only thing concealed in it was a bra turned gray and shapeless with age. Elena had emptied the plastic chest. Nothing remained in the box under the bed. Since the night man had a master key it was always possible he'd been there already to clean it out, but as far as I knew Elena didn't have any valuables to leave. The bra seemed like such a forlorn relic that I folded it and stuffed it in my shoulder bag.

I shook my head uselessly. "Maybe I could talk to some of the other residents. See if any of them know why she might have left."

The night man rubbed his big hands along the sides of his pants. "You can, of course, but when they see your boyfriend here is a cop, they probably won't want to talk to you. Besides, I don't think your aunt knew anyone here that good."

When she was drunk she might have said anything to anyone, even people she'd never seen before in her life. Someone she'd shared a bottle with would seem like a lifelong friend. I asked the night man when he came on—he would be easier to work with than the daytime chatelaine.

"Six. I'm off tomorrow and Tuesday."

So if I wanted to question the residents, I should do it tonight. My shoulders slumped dejectedly.

Michael was watching me sympathetically. "Look, Vic. Why don't you put together a good description. I'll get it out to the uniforms. If we're looking for her hard, we have a good chance of turning her up and it'll save some wear and tear on you."

"Thanks." I smiled gratefully. It was that kind of concerned gesture that had always been his most attractive trait.

We followed the night man back downstairs. Before we left I decided to secure Elena's room for her through October. The night man—I finally got his name—Fred Cameron—took my money and wrote out a receipt in a large clumsy hand.

Back in Michael's Corvette, I gave a careful description of Elena, including what I could recall of her wardrobe. He relayed it through the radio, underscoring the urgency of finding her, and asking that any sighting be reported directly to him.

As we turned south I asked when Elena had been seen soliciting. "If she's been seen since Thursday, the places she's been spotted are probably close to where she's hanging out."

"Good point. I'll check the reports when I get back to the station." He swooped around a car in an intersection and speeded into the southbound Broadway traffic. It's that kind of maneuver I've always liked least in him.

"You don't have any idea why she would have taken off like that, do you?" he asked.

"No. Something must have scared her, but I don't know what. She was kind of friendly with the young woman who died at the Rapelec site. I know she was shaken when I told her about it, but she didn't take off until late the night after I told her. I don't have a clue. I suppose I will have to talk to some of the residents."

He pulled up in front of my building and gunned the engine a bit. "Despite what that guy Cameron said, Vic, I think people will talk to me. Why don't you let me handle it—you're too close to the situation and that always makes for a bad interrogation."

I agreed readily, even willingly. After a pause I asked if they'd turned up anything on Cerise to explain why she'd chosen the Rapelec site to shoot up.

"Nope. We only came out because Boots has some money in the project and he wanted to make sure there wasn't anything funny about a dead body there. He's sensitive to scandals around election time. Uncle Bobby was plenty mad about being dragged into it, I can tell you. And Ernie was pissed that you came around afterwards."

"I know—he called and told me."

Michael fiddled with the ignition key. "Look, Vic—I'm sorry I acted so dumb that night. It was just jealousy seeing you with another guy when you told me you were too busy to go out last week."

"He was a potential client. One thing kind of led to another."

Vinnie's Mazda pulled up in front of us. He got out with another man, a tall, loosely knit fellow who seemed to be on pretty friendly terms with him. Well, well. Who would have thought it.

"I was wondering if I could come in with you, sort of patch things up."

"No," I said as gently as possible. "We've been spinning around too much this last week, Michael. I can't put it all back together right now."

"So you'll be off screwing this other guy, this client," he said bitterly.

"None of your business, Michael—you know that."

He slapped the steering wheel but didn't say anything. "Ah, hell, Vic. If I make another scene now, you'll never give me the time of day again. I'll let you know when we run your aunt to earth."

I got out of the car. I'd barely shut the door when he was off down Racine with a great roar from the engine.

22

TEARING UP
THE RYAN

I slept badly, my dreams again haunted by Elena. I was searching for her through the barren corridors of midnight Chicago. I could hear her whining "Vicki, sweetie, where are you when I need you?" but I never actually saw her. Michael Furey stood nearby shaking his head: "I can't help you, Vic, because you wouldn't let me inside."

I got up around seven, my neck stiff from my restless sleep. I moved sluggishly through my morning routine, wondering if I should have invited Michael up last night. Would he still question Elena's hotel mates as thoroughly since I'd sent him packing? Should I try to do it myself? Did I even care where my aunt had gone, let alone why? Even as the last bitter thought went through my head I felt ashamed. Who else did she have to care about her, if not me?

Maybe Zerlina Ramsay. I considered her. Of course relations between the two were a bit peculiar, but she might be someone Elena would consider a friend. I drank a second cup of coffee, then took Peppy on a hurried mini-run to the lake. By the time I showered and changed into a respectable pair of trousers, a cotton-ramie beige sweater and a good jacket, it was still just shy of nine.

The penalty for rising and shining early is lolling in traffic. If I'd had a proper breakfast instead of toast while I dressed, I'd have gotten to the hospital just as fast. As it was I only met with disappointment—Zerlina had checked out on Friday. No, the hospital didn't know where she'd gone, and even if they did, they really couldn't tell me.

I stomped back to the Chevy in annoyance. How the hell would I ever find her? All I knew about her was that her granddaughter's other grandmother was called Maisie. Cerise's boyfriend's first name was Otis. That gave me a great starting point—comb every apartment in Chicago asking for Otis or Maisie and when people answered to those names find out if they knew someone named Zerlina.

Zerlina's knowing anything was a long shot, anyway. I'd only gone zooming down to the hospital because it was something to do. Otherwise I was better off leaving the search for Elena to the police. They had the resources; Michael had broadcast her description. Someone would find her.

I drove back north to the Loop, parking my car in the underground garage. Until Ajax asked me to proceed I couldn't justify any further work on the Indiana Arms. It was time to do some of my bread-and-butter financial work and to send out query letters to small or midsize firms who could use my expert advice. After going to my office to pick up the client letters with the names of their would-be executives, I headed to the Daley Center.

Somehow, though, instead of looking up John Doe and Jane Roe, I found myself checking on Rosalyn Fuentes and her cousin Luis Schmidt. No one was after Roz, but Luis had started several actions a couple of years back. He'd sued the city for turning down his bid to repave the parking lot at the Humboldt Park Community Service Center. He claimed that they had discriminated against him as a Hispanic in favor of a black contractor who was a crony of the mayor's. That action went back to 1985. More recently, in 1987, he had sued the county on similar charges, this time for not getting the job to build a new court building in Deerfield. His partner, Carl Martinez, had been a party to both suits. He'd withdrawn the complaints about six months ago without a settlement. That sounded as though someone had slipped him a few bucks to soothe his hurt feelings.

I shrugged. If it had happened that way it wasn't savory, but it was just too common to be the kind of dynamite that would cost Roz an election. If Chicago has one law that everyone obeys, it's "Look out for your own." Still, thinking back over Boots's party, it seemed to me it was Luis who had warned Roz about me—it was only after he'd been talking to her, pointing at me, that she'd come back and sought me out.

I went upstairs to look at partnership and corporation filings. Roz owned a minority interest in Alma Mejicana, her cousin's contracting business, but no one could conceivably imagine that as even a venial sin. If Ralph MacDonald had been telling the truth and Roz was hiding a youthful indiscretion, then maybe something had happened in her Mexican childhood. If so, I didn't give a damn and I didn't see why she would expect me to.

"None of your business, Vic," I said aloud. "Remember—some people think you're a pain in the butt."

A man using the microfiche reader next to me looked up, affronted. I stared intently at the screen in front of me, pursed my lips, scribbled a note, and pretended I hadn't heard—or said—anything.

It really was time to get to my clients. Still, I made a genuine note, writing down Schmidt's name, Alma Mejicana, and the address on south Ashland. Maybe there was a way to get a look at his sales figures. Or I could go over to the county side and see if any contracts had been going to Schmidt recently.

That turned out to be a fruitless idea. They did keep a list of contracts, of course, but I had to know the project name to find out who'd gotten the bid. They were not going to let me go through the myriad files looking for one contractor. I sucked on my teeth. Now it was *really* time to get to work.

As I turned to leave, the door at the end of the corridor opened and Boots came in, a handful of men listening as he made a forceful point. He caught sight of me and gave the legendary smile and a wave on his way into his office. He hadn't remembered me personally, but knew he knew me. It was a strange sensation—against my volition I felt myself warmed by his recognition and smiling eagerly in return.

Perhaps to dispel the hold his magic had on me I butted one step further into Roz's business. I called Alma Mejicana, said I was with OSHA, and wanted to know where they were pouring today. The man who answered the phone, speaking minimal English in a heavy accent, couldn't understand my question. After a few fruitless exchanges he put the phone down and went to fetch someone else.

I'd met Luis Schmidt only once, but it seemed to me that the suspicion-laden voice belonged to him. Just in case he had an acute aural memory, I sharpened my tone to the nasality of the South Side and repeated my pitch.

He cut me off before I could get my whole spiel out. "We have no problems; we don't need anybody coming to watch us, especially not OSHA spies."

"I'm not suggesting you do have problems." It was hard to be glib and nasal at the same time. "We've been told that minority contractors in Chicago are allowed sloppier safety practices than white-owned enterprises. We're doing a random spot check to make sure that isn't the case."

"That is racism," he said hotly. "I do not allow racists to look at my work. Period. Now disappear before I sue you for slander."

"I'm trying to help you out—" I started with nasal righteousness, but he hung up before I could finish the sentence.

Okay. Alma Mejicana didn't want OSHA hanging around their construction sites. Nothing bizarre about that. A lot of businesses don't want OSHA crews. So leave it alone, Vic. Get back to projects for people who are paying you.

It was that sage advice that took me over to the University of Illinois library to look up Alma Mejicana in the computer index to the *Herald-Star*. And to my joy they had gotten part of the Dan Ryan reconstruction. In a February story the paper listed all the minority- and women-owned businesses participating in the project. The suits Luis had filed must have made an impression on the feds when they handed out the Ryan contracts. I remembered the protest from black groups over the small number of minority contractors involved; given Chicago's racio-ethnic isolationism, I didn't suppose they were appeased to see Alma Mejicana eating part of the pie.

With a certain amount of self-deception I could make myself believe that I would pass the Ryan construction anyway on my way back to the Loop. It wouldn't really count as an additional detour from my legitimate business to check out Luis.

I went on down Halsted to Cermak, then snaked around underneath the expressway's legs looking for a way to get at the construction zone. Cars and trucks were parked near the Lake Shore Drive access ramp. I pulled the Chevy off the road into the rutted ground below the main lanes of traffic and left it next to a late-model Buick.

Once again I was badly dressed for a construction site, although my linen-weave slacks weren't quite as inappropriate as my dress silk pants had been. I picked my way through the deep holes, around pieces of convulsed rebars that had fallen down, past the debris of ten thousand sack lunches, and hiked up the closed southbound ramp.

As I got close to the top the noise of machinery became appalling. Monsters with huge spiked arms were assaulting concrete, driving cracks ten feet long in their wake. Behind them came an array of automated air hammers, smashing the roadway to bits. And in their wake rumbled trucks to haul off the remains. Hundreds of men and even a few women were doing other things by hand.

I surveyed the carnage doubtfully from the edge of the ramp, wondering how I could ever get anyone's attention, let alone find one small contractor in the melee. Now that I was here I hated to just give up without trying, but I should have worn work boots and earmuffs in addition to a hard hat. Dressed as I was, I couldn't possibly climb around the machinery and the gaping holes in the expressway floor.

When I moved tentatively toward the lip of the ramp, a small man made rotund by a layer of work clothes detached himself from the nearest crew and came over to me.

"Hard-hat area, miss." His tone was abrupt and dismissive.

"Are you the foreman?" I asked.

He shook his head. "Dozens of foremen around here. Who you looking for?"

"Someone who can point out the Alma Mejicana crew to me." I was having to cup my mouth with my hands and yell directly into his ear. As it was he needed me to repeat the request twice.

He gave the look of pained resignation common to men when ignorant women interrupt their specialized work. "There're hundreds of contractors here. I don't know them all."

"That's why I want the foreman," I screeched at him.

"Talk to the project manager." He pointed to a semi trailer rigged with electric lines parked beyond the edge of the road. "And next time don't come around here without a hard hat."

Turning on his heel, he marched back to his crew before I could thank him. I staggered across the exposed rebars to the verge. Like the area underneath the expressway, this had become a quag of mud, broken concrete, and trash. My progress to the trailer was necessarily slow and accompanied by a number of catcalls. I grimaced to myself and ignored them.

Inside the trailer I found chaos on a smaller scale. Phone and power lines were coiled over every inch of exposed floor. The rest held tables covered with blueprints, phones, computer screens—all the paraphernalia of a big engineering firm consolidated into a small space.

At least a dozen people were crammed in with the equipment, talking to each other or—based on shouted snatches I caught—to the crews in the field. No one paid any attention to me. I waited until the man nearest me put down his phone and went up to him before he could dial again.

"I need to find the Alma Mejicana crew. Who can tell me where they're working?"

He was a burly white man close to sixty with a ruddy face and small gray eyes. "You shouldn't be on the site without a hard hat."

"I realize that," I said. "If you can just tell me where they're working, I'll get a hard hat before I go out to talk to them."

"You got any special reason for wanting them?" His small eyes gave away nothing.

"Are you the project manager?"

He hesitated, as if debating whether to claim the title, then said he was an assistant manager. "Who are you?"

It was my turn to hesitate. If I came up with my OSHA story or a similar one I'd have to produce credentials. I didn't want Luis to know I'd been poking around his business, but it couldn't be helped.

"V. I. Warshawski," I said. "I'm a detective. Some questions have come up about Alma Mejicana's work practices."

He wasn't going to field that one on his own. He got up from his table and threaded his way to the back of the trailer where a tiny cubicle had been partitioned off. His bulky body filled the entrance. I could see his shoulders move as he waved his arms beyond my field of sight.

Eventually he returned with a slender black man. "I'm Jeff Collins, one of the project managers. What is it you want?"

"V. I. Warshawski." I shook his proffered hand and repeated my request.

"Work practices are my responsibility. I haven't heard anything to make me question what they're doing. You have a specific allegation I could respond to?" He wasn't hostile, just asserting his authority.

Since I didn't know anything about construction practices I could scarcely talk about their equipment. My brain raced in search of an idea. "I do financial investigations," I said, putting it together as I spoke. "My client thinks Alma's way overleveraged, that they've taken on projects they can't handle just so they can claim they're eating at the same table with the big boys. He's worried about his investment. I wanted to look at their equipment to see if they own it or lease it."

It sounded woefully thin to me, but at least Collins didn't seem to find it bizarre. "You can't go on the site looking for that kind of thing. I've got several thousand men out there. Everything they're doing is carefully coordinated. I just can't allow unauthorized civilians out there."

I was going to argue my case, but he frowned in thought. "Chuck," he said abruptly to the ruddy white man, "call down there and ask about their trucks. Give the lady the report." To me he added, "That's the best I can do for you and it's more than I should."

"I appreciate it," I said with what sincerity I could muster. It actually didn't satisfy me at all—I wanted to *see* Alma at work, see if anything strange jumped out at me just by looking at them. But I had no choice. The Dan Ryan construction zone was not a location I could infiltrate.

Collins returned to his office and Chuck got on the phone again. After ten or fifteen minutes of shouted conversation with a variety of people, he beckoned me to his table.

"I thought they were in sector fifty-nine but they'd been moved to a hunnert and twenty-one. I don't think you have to worry about them paying for their trucks—all the stuff they have on site belongs to Wunsch and Grasso."

When I looked at him blankly he repeated the information in a louder voice. I pulled myself together, gave him my sweetest smile, and thanked him as best I could.

23

STONEWALLED

By the time I got back to the Loop it was too late to use any of the Daley Center reference rooms. I parked illegally in front of the Pulteney so I could check my messages. When I got into the elevator it took a few minutes for me to realize it wasn't moving, so lost in thought was I. As I climbed the four flights I kept turning it over in my mind.

How strange was it really for Luis to be using Wunsch and Grasso machinery? It had hit me like a bolt at the trailer, but it might not mean that much. Luis and his partner knew Ernie and Ron, that was clear from their close confab at Boots's party. If Alma Mejicana was struggling to find a toehold in the Chicago construction business, they might well lease equipment from a bigger firm.

"Mind your own business, Vic," I chanted out loud as I unlocked my office. "If Roz is hiding dirt from her girlhood, it's not your affair."

I turned on the lights and checked in with my answering service. Robin had called, as had Darrough Graham, wanting to know where in hell his report was. I called Graham first, since he was a promptly paying customer, told him I'd been away for a few days and that I'd get the job done tomorrow. He wasn't happy but we've been working together a long time—he wasn't going to break up over this. Still, I could not continue ignoring my good clients.

While I waited for the receptionist to hunt down Robin—he'd asked to be interrupted for my call—I pulled a pad of newsprint out from behind my filing cabinet. Using a thick Magic Marker, I drew up a list, with time lines, of all my current assignments. Still propping the receiver under my ear, I took the sheet and taped it to the wall facing my desk.

"That's your work," I lectured myself sternly. "Do not do anything else until all those tasks are accomplished."

"Vic?" Robin's voice cut into my lecture. "Are you there?"

"Oh, hi, Robin. Just thinking aloud. When you work by yourself you can't tell the difference between speech and thought."

"Oh. I wonder if isolation is too big a price for working alone." We chatted for a few minutes, about that, and about whether I'd like some company for dinner. When I agreed he switched to business.

"Your report came in today—your two reports. I went over them with my boss—we decided we want you to do some more checking. I'm not questioning your assessment of the old man's character, but somebody got that night watchman out of the way. It was clearly someone who knew his habits, so it had to be either a resident or a person in the Seligman operation."

"Or an outside party who was watching him," I put in.

"Yeah, I suppose. The trouble is, the only person who really benefits from the fire is the old man—or his children if he dies. Before we pay the claim I want to make sure Seligman didn't send the guy money for the track. Can you give us another week?"

I looked at my time lines. If I did Graham's project tomorrow morning, I could stretch the rest of my work around the Ajax job and still get it all done by the end of Friday—as long as I didn't take any more time to worry about Roz, about why my call to Velma had prompted her to sic Ralph MacDonald on me, and all the rest of it.

"You still there, Vic?"

"Yup. Yeah, I guess I can give you guys another week. Are you going to pay my current bill or do you want me to give you a new one with all my hours after I finish this next stint?"

"We've already sent that one through for payment—you'll get a check in ten days or so. . . . You say Seligman's not losing money but he's not making much, either."

I drew a circle on the newsprint with my Magic Marker. "I don't think he cares that much. I can try to find his old books, see how profits compare with fifteen or twenty years ago, but he just doesn't strike me as a guy pining over his lost billions."

"Well, do some more hunting, see what you can find. I know you won't let your bias for the guy cloud the way you look at the evidence. . . . See you at seven-thirty, right?"

"Right." It was couched as a compliment, but it was really a warning. Impetuosity is the detective's worst enemy.

I added eyes and a nose to the circle and gave it some whiskers. Despite Robin's warning, I couldn't believe in the old man's guilt, not unless he had some personality aberration that hadn't come through the two times I'd spoken with him. Robin was right, though, Seligman had the glaring financial motive. Of course his children would inherit the estate and maybe they were savvy enough to torch the building now so that they wouldn't come under suspicion when he died.

I gave the face a floppy suit and a hand held out asking for money. Someone at the Indiana Arms might have seen something she was too circumspect to come forward with—when you live in the margins you learn not to make yourself conspicuous. If I could locate any of these former residents, maybe I could persuade them to talk to me. Maybe I should get photos of the younger Seligmans from the old man and show those—although of course they could easily have hired someone to do the legwork. It didn't matter that the daughter had been in Brazil—she still could have engineered the fire.

The problem with this plan was that even if Rita Donnelly would give names of any of the old inhabitants, it would take an army to find out where they'd moved after the fire. Of course I had two residents—Zerlina Ramsay and my aunt. I didn't know where either of them was, but that was a trifling problem for an intelligent investigator.

It dawned on me that I might find Zerlina through the morgue. If she had collected Cerise's body, they would have a record of her address. What I needed was someone who could get that for me. A police officer could do it, but I could hardly call Furey for help and then deny him the chance to spend personal time with me. Bobby would rather see me dead than help me with an investigation. At least he'd rather see me in jail. John McGonnigal was acting kind of aloof to me these days.

There was someone on Bobby's staff who didn't feel particularly hostile toward me. Terry Finchley. I wouldn't say we were friends, but all our interactions in the past had been pleasant. And once a few years ago he'd told me he liked the way I stood up for my friends. It was worth a try.

By a miracle Finchley was at the station. He expressed cautious pleasure at hearing from me.

"I need a favor," I said abruptly.

"I know that, Miss Warshawski. You wouldn't have called otherwise. It's not about Furey, is it?" He had a light pleasant tenor with a hint of humor in it.

"No, no," I assured him. Of course everyone in Bobby's unit would be aware of the ups and downs of Michael's and my relationship. I told him about Cerise and my wanting to find Zerlina.

When he answered again his voice was cold as he said he didn't think that was an appropriate use of his time.

"It probably isn't. But I think they'd respond to a query from you where they wouldn't from me."

"Ask Furey. Or McGonnigal." He spoke with finality.

"Detective," I said quickly, before he could hang up, "I called you because I didn't feel able to call them. I know I know them better than you, that we don't know each other that well, but I thought you wouldn't mind. It's not a—a menial task, it's one the police can do and I can't. I need to find Mrs. Ramsay to see if she saw anything . . ." When he didn't respond my voice trailed away in a tangle of hopeless syntax. "I'm sorry. I won't bother you another time."

"You say you didn't feel able to call Furey or McGonnigal. Why?"

I was starting to get annoyed myself. "It's not really your business, Detective. It's totally personal and I know personal business is a happy topic for public discussion in the squad room."

"I see." He was silent for a minute, thinking, then he said abruptly, "It's not because I'm black?"

"Oh." I felt my cheeks flame. "Because Mrs. Ramsay is? No. I wasn't thinking about that. I'm sorry. It didn't occur to me it would look that way."

"I forgive you," he said with a return to his easier tone. "This time, anyway. Next time look before you leap. And go easy on Furey—he's not a bad guy, just rough around the edges. What's your number?"

I gave it to him and he hung up. I went to the window and watched the L cart commuters past. I couldn't make up my mind whether I'd been out of line or whether Finchley overreacted. The problem was, he probably got so many slights so many hours of the week that it didn't matter what my intentions were—they came out sounding like the crap he was used to hearing.

I looked at the pigeons checking each other for lice regardless of the color of their plumage. On the surface the animal kingdom looked healthier than us humanoids. But one day last summer when a gull had joined them on the ledge the pigeons had pecked and squawked at it until it left, its neck bloody.

I went back to my desk and read the junk mail that had come in the last few days. Seminars on how to manage my office better, seminars on improving surveillance techniques, special offers on weapons and bullets. I swept it all into the garbage impatiently. Finally, irritated with myself for neglecting my business too much the last few weeks, I went through my file of potential customers and started typing query letters.

I'd done three when the phone rang. It wasn't Finchley but someone from the morgue—he'd asked her to call me directly. Cerise's body had been released to Otis Armbruster at an address on Christiana.

I thanked the woman and pulled out my city map. Sixteen hundred south Christiana is not in the happiest part of town. It's not a great place for any woman to be alone at night, especially a white one. I considered putting it off until the morning, then my discomfort over my talk with Finchley returned. If Cerise or Zerlina navigated those streets, I could too.

Just as I was turning out the lights Furey called. I tensed at first, thinking Finchley might have been discussing our conversation with him, but he was calling about Elena.

"You haven't heard from her, have you?" he asked. "Because we got another soliciting complaint last night—from a bar in Uptown that's trying to cater to yuppies—and it sounded like it might have been her."

I rubbed the back of my neck, trying to ease out some of the stiffness. "I haven't heard from her, but I'm leaving now to see a woman she knew pretty well at the Indiana Arms. I'll see if Elena's checked in with her."

"You want me to come along?" He tried unsuccessfully to cloak his eagerness.

"No, thanks. She's not going to be real eager to talk to me to begin with. The sight of a police officer will cause a total shutdown."

"Give me a call later, okay? Let me know if you learn anything?"

"Sure." I stood up again. "I've got to go. Bye."

I hung up before he could ask anything more, like Zerlina's name and address, and left quickly to avoid any more calls. I took the stairs down two at a time—when going on an unpleasant errand do it as fast as possible.

The Chevy had a parking ticket stuck under the wipers. Crime does not pay in Chicago, especially for Loop parking offenders.

I went down Van Buren, took a look at the slow line of cars on the Congress, and elected to go by side streets. Wabash to Twenty-second Street was a good run. Once I was clear of the expressway interchanges the westbound traffic also moved well. It was only a few minutes after six when I turned north onto Christiana.

At this point I was about seven miles southwest of the Rapelec complex on Navy Pier. If Cerise had been living here, why had she gone all that way to find a quiet place to shoot up? I couldn't make sense of it.

Vacant lots interspersed with gray stone three-flats made up the street. Their broken or boarded windows showed the buildings tottering on the edge of collapse. During the day it looked like Beirut. Now the purple twilight softened the worst outcroppings of rubble in the lots, muting the abandoned cars into soft dark shapes.

The only businesses seemed to be the taverns sprinkled liberally on every corner. There were few cars out. Someone rode on my tail from Cermak to Seventeenth, making me rather nervous, but when I finally slowed and moved to the right, he darted around me with a great blaring of horn. It was a ghost town, seemingly uninhabited except for the occasional knot of young men arguing or joking in front of the bars.

I pulled up across from the Armbruster apartment. It was another stone three-flat. Lights shone yellow through the sheets covering the first- and second-story windows. The third floor was boarded up. As I walked up the crumbled sidewalk I could hear a radio blaring loudly.

Inside the entryway a strong scent of Pine-Sol showed someone making an effort to overcome the urine. It was almost successful, but the stench still lingered underneath, turning my stomach. Presumably the same hand had screwed a grate over the sprung mailboxes. The postman could get letters through, but you had to unlock the grate to get them out.

The Armbrusters were on the second floor. No stairwell lights existed. I picked my way slowly in the dark, testing each stair before putting weight on it. Twice a major portion of the tread was missing and my heart lurched as nothing but air met my foot.

At the second-floor door an infant's howling mixed in with the radio. I pounded on the door with the side of my closed fist. On the second try a deep-voiced woman demanded to know who was there.

"It's V. I. Warshawski," I yelled. "I've come to see Mrs. Ramsay."

The door held a peephole; I positioned myself so that my clean honest face would be visible from the other side. For a while nothing happened. Then the radio and the baby stopped almost simultaneously; I could hear someone undoing a series of locks.

When the door opened a thin middle-aged woman faced me holding a baby. The child's soft cheeks were still wet with tears. She turned her head away when she saw me watching her and buried her chubby hands in the thin woman's tight bun. Something about the immovable tidiness of the woman's hair and the severe ironing of her dress made me think she was responsible for the Pine-Sol in the lobby.

Zerlina stood behind her, overshadowing her both in girth and in the rich blackness of her skin. I presumed the other woman was Maisie and that she held Katterina.

"How did you find me?" Zerlina demanded.

"The morgue gave me the address of the person who took Cerise's body. It was just a guess that you'd be here, but you'd talked about Otis and about Katterina's other grandmother, so I thought you might all be together."

All the light was behind them. I had to squint to see their faces, but I thought it would be better if I waited to be invited in. No one seemed in a hurry to do so.

"You can't come around hounding people in the privacy of their homes," Maisie growled, jiggling the baby to let her know the anger wasn't for her.

I rubbed my face tiredly. "Someone burned down a big hotel two weeks ago. No one died but a lot of people were hurt, including Mrs. Ramsay. She's the only person I know who might be able to give me some help in finding out who did it."

"I'm not the only person you know, little white girl, as you're well aware," Zerlina said. "Ask that precious aunt of yours."

"The last time I talked to Elena I told her about Cerise. That scared her so much she ran away from home. She's been hiding on the streets ever since. I figure you're made of sterner stuff."

Her strong face set into stubborn lines. "You figure what you want to. Between the two of you, that aunt of yours and you got my daughter dead. I don't have *nothing* more to say to you."

Before Maisie could slam the door in my face I pulled out a card and gave it to Zerlina. "If you change your mind, you can call me at that number. Someone takes messages twenty-four hours a day."

Before she'd bolted the first lock the radio started again. The insistent beat of the rap music followed me down the stairs and into the night.

24

ASLEEP IN A BASEMENT ROOM

I spent the night at Robin's. He was a sweet and thoughtful lover, but he couldn't wipe the decay of north Lawndale from my mind. Falling into a fitful sleep around one, I was jerked awake by a dream in which I was walking up Christiana while a car trailed me. I woke up just before it ran over me.

I fumbled around on the night table for my watch. Squinting in the dark, I could just make out the hands: four-ten. I lay down again and tried to go back to sleep. In a strange bed, though, with the memory of a bad dream lingering, I couldn't relax. Finally, a little after five, I gave it up and tiptoed into the bathroom with my clothes.

In the kitchen I found a spiral notebook next to the phone. I tore out a page and scribbled a note to Robin, explaining why I was taking off, and slipped out quietly.

At five-thirty the city was barely coming to life. Lights burned in a number of apartment windows—this was a neighborhood of hard workers who started the day early—but I was alone on the road until I hit a main artery.

When I got to my own place I felt tired enough to go back to bed. This time I managed to sleep until eight. When I got up again I felt groggy and disoriented. I pulled on a sweatshirt and a pair of underpants and sat in the kitchen reading the paper and drinking coffee until past nine when Furey called.

"I thought you were going to phone me last night, Vic."

I didn't like the angry impatience in his tone. "I thought so, too, Michael, but it slipped my mind. If I'd had anything to report, I might have remembered, but the woman wouldn't even let me in the front door."

"Why don't you give me her name and I'll give it a try?" He dropped the anger for indulgent coaxing.

"Why don't you give it a rest, Furey? Elena isn't doing anyone any harm out there. You must have a godzillian murders and rapes and stuff to keep you happy. She'll turn up in due course, drunk and repentant, and in the meantime I don't think she needs all this city money lavished on her."

"The only reason we're doing it is because Uncle Bobby wanted to save you the embarrassment of bailing her out of women's court," he said stiffly. "If I had any say in the matter, I wouldn't be wasting time looking for her."

"Then I'll call Bobby and tell him I don't care." I caught sight of the clock and suddenly remembered my time lines. *Damn* it all. I should have been at Daley Center twenty minutes ago to get a jump on Darrough Graham's project.

"Sorry, Michael—I've got to run."

"Wait, Vic," he said urgently. "Don't tell the lieutenant. He'd take a stripe off my butt if he knew I'd been complaining to you."

"Okay," I agreed, irritated, "but in that case, stop riding me. The second I see her or hear from her I'll let you know. Good-bye."

I slammed down the receiver and ran into my bedroom. As I was zipping my jeans the phone rang again. I let it go at first, thinking it was probably Furey, then gave in to the pressure of the bell.

"I want Victoria Warshawski." The accented voice belonged to the man I'd spoken to yesterday at Alma Mejicana.

He pronounced it "Warchassy." After saying it correctly I asked who wanted her.

"This is Luis Schmidt, Warchassy. A little bird told me you been prying into my work crew down at the Ryan. I'm calling to tell you to mind your own business."

"I think you have the wrong number." I took the phone from my ear while I pulled a yellow cotton sweater over my head. "There's no one here named Warchassy."

"This ain't Victoria Warchassy? The private dick?" he demanded angrily.

"I'm a private investigator, but my last name is 'Warshawski.' " I kept my tone affable.

"That's what I been saying, bitch. I'm talking to you. If you know what's good for you, keep your damned nose out of other people's business."

"Oh, Looey, Looey, you just said the magic word. I surely hate it when strange men call me a bitch. You just bought yourself a whole lot of interest in what Alma Mejicana is doing down at the Ryan."

"I'm warning you, Warchassy, to butt out of what don't concern you. Or you could be very, very sorry." The phone slammed in my ear.

I tied my running shoes and took the stairs two at a time. Behind Mr. Contreras's door I could hear Peppy whining. She recognized my step and wanted to come with me. It wasn't fair to make her hang out with Mr. Contreras all day—he couldn't run her properly. But I just couldn't stop for her.

I felt close to screaming at the pressure of all the demands on me. The dog. Furey. Elena herself. Graham. My other clients. And now my bravado to Luis Schmidt. Well, damn him anyway for calling up with stupid threats.

If only I could get a few bucks ahead of the game, I'd take some time off, just get clean out of this town for six months. I ground my teeth at the futility of the idea and savagely jerked the Chevy into gear.

By three o'clock I had finished an exhaustive search into the life and loves of Graham's prospective marketing vice president. In the report I included the fact that the guy had a steady girlfriend along with his wife and infant son —not that Graham would care. It would make me run ten miles in the opposite direction, but Graham didn't think what happened below the belt had any bearing on job performance.

Not until I had typed up the report and sent it across the Loop by messenger did I break for lunch. By then hunger had given me a nagging headache, although I felt better mentally for being able to cross a major task off my time chart.

I went to a vegetarian café around the corner for soup and a bowl of yogurt. That took care of the hunger, but my headache grew more intense. I tried ignoring it, tried to make myself think about Luis Schmidt and his anger at my visit to the Ryan construction site. My head hurt too much for logic. When I retrieved the Chevy from the underground garage, I wanted just to drive home and go back to bed, but all the time I'd wasted lately was still haunting me. I slogged north to Saul Seligman's house.

He wasn't happy to see me. Nor did he want to let me have pictures of his children. It took every ounce of energy I had to keep being gentle and persuasive through the blinding pain thudding in front of my eyes.

"In your place I'd be angry too. You have a right to expect service for the premiums you pay. Unfortunately, there are just too many dishonest people out there and the good guys get stuck as a result."

We went on like that for forty-five minutes. Finally Seligman made an angry gesture. He moved to a massive secretary in one corner and opened its rollaway top. A pile of papers cascaded to the floor. He ignored those and pawed through a drawer behind the remaining papers until he found a couple of photos.

"I suppose you'd stay here until dawn if I didn't give you these. I want a receipt. Then go, leave me alone. Don't come back unless you're telling me you've cleared my name."

The pictures were both group shots, taken at some kind of family party. His daughters stood in the middle, on either side of his wife, while Rita Donnelly and two other young women flanked them. Those two were presumably her daughters, but I didn't much care at this point—I was having too much trouble seeing.

I pulled a small memo pad from my bag to write out the date and a description of the pictures for Seligman. The letters danced around the page as I wrote; I wasn't sure my note made sense. Seligman stuck it in the secretary, rolled the top back down, and hustled me out the door.

I drove home more by luck than skill. By the time I got there I was shivering and sweating. I managed somehow to make it upstairs to my bathroom before being sick. I felt a little better after that, but crept off to bed, putting on a heavy sweatshirt and socks before crawling under the blankets. As I got warm my tense neck and arm muscles relaxed and I drifted into a deep, drugged sleep.

The ringing phone brought me slowly back to life. I was buried so far down in sleep that it took some time to connect the noise with something outside me. After a long spell of weaving the ringing in with my dreams, my mind finally swam lazily back to consciousness. I felt newly born, the way you do when an intense pain has been washed out of your system, but the insistent bell wouldn't let me enjoy it. Finally I stuck out an arm and picked up the receiver.

"H'lo?" My voice was thick and slurred.

"Vicki? Vicki, is that you?"

It was Elena, crying extravagantly. I looked at the clock readout in resignation: one-ten. Only Elena would rouse me at this godawful time.

"Yes, Auntie, it's me. Calm down, stop crying, and tell me what the trouble is."

"I—oh, Vicki, I need you, you've got to come and help me."

She was well and truly panicked. I sat up and started pulling on the jeans I'd left on the foot of the bed. "Tell me where you are and what kind of trouble you've got."

"I—oh . . ." She started sobbing heavily, then her voice disappeared.

For a moment I thought I'd lost the connection, but then I realized she was covering up the mouthpiece. Or someone else had covered it. She'd been running away and her pursuers had caught up with her? I waited in an agony of indecision, thinking I should hang up and summon Furey, not wanting to hang up until I was sure I'd lost her. Since I had no idea where to send police resources I waited, and after a couple of heart-wrenching minutes she came back.

"I ran away," she sniffed dolefully. "Poor little Elena got scared and ran."

So she hadn't been in mortal terror, just rehearsing her act. I kept my voice light with an effort. "I know you ran away, Auntie. But where did you run to?"

"I've been living in one of the old buildings near the Indiana Arms, it's been abandoned for months but some of the rooms are still in real good shape, you can sleep here and no one will see you. But now they've found me. Vicki, they'll kill me, you've got to come help me."

"Are you in the building now?"

"There's a phone at the corner," she hiccoughed. "They'll kill me if they see me. I couldn't go outside in the daylight. You've got to *come*, Vicki— they *can't* find me here."

"Who will kill you, Elena?" I wished I could see her face instead of just hearing her—it was impossible to sort out how much truth she was spouting along with the rest of it.

"The people who've been after me," she screamed. "Just *come*, Vicki, stop asking so many goddamn questions, you're like a goddamn tax collector."

"Okay, okay," I said in the soothing voice one uses with infants. "Tell me where the building is and I'll be there in thirty minutes."

"Just kitty-corner to the Indiana Arms." She calmed down to a quavering sob.

"On Indiana or Cermak?" I tied my running shoes.

"In-Indiana. Are you coming?"

"I'm on my way. Just stay where you are by the phone. Call 911 if you think someone really is coming."

I turned on the bedside lamp. Dialing Furey's home number, I carried the phone over to my closet. It rang fifteen times before I gave up and tried the station. The night man said Michael wasn't in. Neither were Bobby, Finchley, or McGonnigal.

I hesitated, undoing the safe in the back of my closet where I keep my Smith & Wesson. Finally I explained that Bobby wanted Elena found and that Michael had been assigned to look for her.

"She just called me from an abandoned building on Indiana. She says she's in trouble—I don't know if she is or not, but I'm on my way down there to get her. I'd like Furey and the lieutenant to know."

He promised to put out a call on the radio to Michael for me with the address. I set the phone on the closet floor while I checked the clip. It was full and the ninth bullet was chambered. I carefully made sure the safety was on, put a shoulder holster over my sweatshirt, and left.

When I got to the bottom Peppy started barking anxiously behind Mr. Contreras's door. She hadn't seen me all day, she'd missed her run, and she was determined I wasn't going to leave without her. Her barking followed me down the walk to the street.

As I was getting into the Chevy, Vinnie stuck his head out his front window. He yelled something, but I was already rolling and didn't hear him.

I headed for Lake Shore Drive. The Dan Ryan would decant me closer to the site, but I wasn't up to dealing with the construction and detours in the dark. For the same reason I left the Drive at Congress and went down Michigan Avenue instead of negotiating the spaghetti behind McCormick Place.

The moon was nearly full. Once I'd slid past the streetlamps onto south Michigan its cold light created black-and-white stills: objects highlighted with unnatural clarity, their shadows pitch black. I was feeling a little weak still, from being sick and from having eaten only once in the last twenty-four hours, but my mind was wonderfully clear. I could make out every drunk on the benches in Grant Park, and when I turned onto Cermak and up onto Prairie, I could even see the rats slithering through the vacant lots.

In the moonlight the Near South Side looked like postwar Berlin. The lifeless shells of warehouses and factories were surrounded by mountains of brick-filled rubble. When I got out at Twenty-first and Prairie, I was shivering from the desolation of the scene. I took a flashlight from the trunk and stuck it in my jacket pocket.

I took the Smith & Wesson from my shoulder holster and crept along the shadows on Twenty-first, holding it in my right hand. The cold metal brought me little comfort. I was wound up enough to take aim at a passing alley cat. It snarled at me, its eyes glinting in the moonlight as it passed.

Even as my heart pounded I wondered how much of Elena's panic to believe in. I remembered all the times she'd gotten Tony out of bed with urgent alarms, only to have them dissolve—revealed as the phantasms of her drinking. This might easily turn into another such evening—maybe I shouldn't even have roused Furey.

My lingering doubts didn't make me careless. When I got to Indiana I stayed awhile in the shadow of an abandoned auto parts dealer, straining my eyes and ears for any kind of movement. I'd worried about finding Elena's hideout from her vague directions, but there was only one hotel on the street besides the Indiana Arms. The moonlight picked out the dead neon lights of the Prairie Shores Hotel, halfway down the block on my side of the road.

I heard a rustling across the street and knelt, the gun cocked again, but it was a large plastic bag dragged loose from the rest of the garbage by the ubiquitous rats. Against my will I saw their yellow teeth tearing my exposed hands; they felt tingly and uncontrolled and I hugged them under my armpits, the gun digging into my left breast. I gritted my teeth and headed down Indiana.

Across from me loomed the burned-out hull of the Indiana Arms. The sharp night air carried the acrid scent of its charred beams to me and I fought back a sneeze. When I got to the corner I could see the pay phone but not my aunt. I prowled around the street for a few minutes, tempted to return to my bed. Finally I squared my shoulders and went over to the Prairie Shores Hotel.

Its front was boarded shut; I cautiously circled around to the back. The door there was heavily chained, but on the north side a broken window provided an easy entrance.

I shone my flashlight through the missing panes. I was looking at part of the pantry for the old kitchen. I trained the light around as much as I could see of the interior. No one was there, but a rustling and the sudden darkening of shadows along the top of the broken cabinets told me my yellow-toothed pals were.

I wished I'd worn a cap. I tried not to think of the red eyes watching me as I climbed carefully over the bent metal frame. A glass shard caught in the crotch of my jeans. I stopped to loosen the fabric and listened some more before moving again. Still no human sounds.

Once inside I picked my way carefully from the pantry to the kitchen. The old smells of grease still hung heavily there; no wonder the rats were so interested. I got lost in a maze of service rooms but came at length to a door that opened on a flight of steep stairs.

Before starting down I stopped to listen again. I shone the light on each step, not wanting to tumble through the rotten boards. Every few treads I called out softly to my aunt. I couldn't hear her.

A hall led from the bottom of the stairs to another rabbit warren. I checked each of the rooms whose door opened but saw nothing except decayed furnishings. At the end of the hall another corridor led to the right. When I stuck my hand out to steady myself as I peered around the corner, I clawed at open air. I gulped and jumped back, but the light showed me nothing more menacing than a dumb waiter.

I called to Elena again but still got no reply. I turned out the light to make my ears work harder. I could hear nothing except the scrabbling and squealing of the rodents.

Tiptoeing, straining my ears, I moved down this side corridor. A series of rooms lined it. I tried each in turn, shining the light around, calling softly to my aunt. Some were empty, but most were stacked with rotting refuse from the old hotel—abandoned sofas with stuffing sticking out at all angles, mattresses, old iron springs. Every now and then I'd catch a movement, but when I stopped to look all I saw was red eyes glaring back.

Finally I reached the far end of the corridor, where a lifeless phone hung. It was an old black model with a dial face lined with letters, not numbers. When I replaced the receiver and lifted it again, no dial tone came. It was as dead as the building.

Anger gripped me. How *dare* she do this to me, call me out on a bootless errand to a rat-infested shell? I turned and began marching at a good clip back up the corridor. Suddenly I thought I heard my name. I stopped in my tracks and strained to listen.

"Vic!"

It was a hoarse whisper, coming from a room on my left. I thought I'd looked in there but I couldn't be sure. Flinging the door open, I shone the flash around the heap of old furniture. A large mass lay on a sofa wedged in the corner. I'd missed it on my first cursory scan of the room.

"Elena!" I called sharply. "Are you there?"

I knelt next to the couch. My aunt was lying on her side, wrapped in a filthy blanket. Her duffel bag leaned against the wall, the violet nightdress still poking from one side. Relief and anger swept through me in equal measures. How *could* she pass out after calling for me in such a way?

I shook her roughly. "Elena! Wake up. We've got to go."

She didn't respond. Her head lolled lifelessly as I shook her. My stomach churning, I laid her gently down. She was still breathing in short shallow snorts. I felt her head. Along the back was a tender swollen mass. A blow—from a fall or from a person?

I heard someone move behind me. Panicking, I pulled the gun from my holster again. Before I could get to my feet the night around me broke into a thousand points of light and I fell into blackness.

25

THE LADY'S NOT FOR BURNING

My headache had returned full force. I tried desperately to be sick. My empty stomach could produce only a little bile, which left me more nauseated than ever. I was so sick I didn't want to move, but I knew I would feel better if I went to the kitchen and put some compresses on my aching head and drank some Coke. My mother had always spoon-fed me Coke for a stomachache. It was a miracle cure.

I sat up and got so fierce a stab of pain that I cried out. And realized beneath the pain that I wasn't home in bed—I had been lying on a couch, one that smelled so bad I couldn't lie back down even with my aching head.

I sat with my head on my knees. I was on a couch with no cushions. When I stuck out a gingerly hand I could feel the tufts of padding spring out. My groping hand came on a leg. I recoiled so fast that the lights danced in front of my eyes again and I retched. When the spasm subsided I reached out tentatively and felt it again. A thin bony knob of a kneecap, the hem of a thin cotton housedress.

Elena. She'd called me, gotten me to the burned-out shell of the Indiana Arms. And then? How had I come to be unconscious? It hurt my head to think. I stuck up a hand and touched the locus of the pain. A nice lump, the consistency of raw liver and about as appealing. I'd been hit? Or had I fallen? I couldn't remember and it was too much work trying.

But Elena was hurt too. Or maybe passed out. I fumbled in the dark to find her chest. I could feel her heart beneath the thin fabric. It kept up a shallow, irregular beat. And she had a head injury. She'd been hit, someone had called my name so I'd think it was she calling, and all the while she was lying in here unconscious. And then he (she? that hoarse whisper had sounded like Elena) had knocked me out.

I was so pleased with remembering the evening's events that I sat for a bit without moving. My memory wasn't quite right, though. I hadn't come to the Indiana Arms but an abandoned hotel across the street from it. It was only the acrid smell of smoke that made me think I was in Elena's old building.

I leaned against the foul remains of upholstery to rest my eyes. The acrid smell didn't diminish. I hadn't thought the wind was so strong tonight as to blow ash across the street, and anyway, how intense would the fire smell be a week later? Something else was burning, some other part of the Near South Side going up in smoke. Not my problem. My problem was to feel well enough to get out of here.

I'd brought a flashlight with me. Pushing back my nausea, I got down on my hands and knees to hunt for it. Crawling on the malodorous floor, I stumbled against a piece of hard metal. My gun, I realized after a moment or two of blind groping. I picked up the Smith & Wesson. In the dark my fingers automatically checked the safety before fumbling it into my shoulder holster.

I couldn't find the flashlight, only pieces of chewed-up cushion. When I touched a warm little body I couldn't keep back a scream. I stumbled upright, my head spinning. I couldn't force myself to get back down on the floor to hunt further. We'd have to make our way out in the dark.

I blundered around the room, tripping on nameless forms, running into some bedsprings with enough force to jolt my ribs and make tears stream down my face. Good. That's good, V.I. The pain in your side will keep you from harping on your stupid head. It's doing you no good so just disregard it. Better still, unscrew it and leave it on the couch.

When I finally found the door I couldn't open it. I pulled with all my might but couldn't get it to budge. Maybe I had it wrong, maybe it opened outwards. But all my shoving didn't move it. I was locked inside.

I wanted to sit on the floor and cry in frustration, but the thought of the warm little fur balls kept me on my feet. It's okay, Vic, it's a fixable problem. You're just feeling sorry for yourself because your head hurts.

I pulled the Smith & Wesson from my holster, turned off the safety, held it against the keyhole, and fired. The recoil went up my arm, jarring my shoulder. The sound in the small room echoed frenziedly in my sore head, making spirals cartwheel in front of my closed eyes.

When I tried the door again it shook but didn't open. "Come on, dodo brain, think," I urged aloud. If blowing the keyhole didn't open the door, it was because it was nailed shut, not locked. I was too tired to figure out how to find where the nails were and shoot around them. I plowed four shots into the hinges where they attached to the wall, bracing myself each time for the recoil, for the sound. By the last shot the air was so smoky and my head ringing so badly that I had to go down on my knees. I vomited more bile and rested, gasping for air, trying to force my vibrating head to stillness.

When I finally got back to my feet I pushed against the door. I was so feeble at this point that I couldn't put much into my thrust, but I felt the paneling give a little. I tucked the gun back into my holster, sucked in a deep breath, and flung my right shoulder against the edge of the door. Something splintered on the other side. I pushed again and felt the whole thing give. I put out an arm to explore and found that the rotted wood had fractured, leaving a large jagged opening.

Leaning against the jamb to catch my breath and steady my head, I thought the smoke seemed more intense in the hall than in the room. It wasn't gun smoke, but fire.

The reason I'd been smelling smoke since I came to was because the damned building was on fire. Not left over from the Indiana Arms. Fresh, new fire created just for me. The building I was in was on fire. Someone had knocked me out, locked me in a room, and set fire to the place. The Prairie Shores Hotel, that was its name. In my mind's eye I saw the dead neon sign swaying a little in the night air.

That's so helpful, your last thought can be congratulations on dragging the name from your slug brain. Instead of that, maybe try to do a little work. Otherwise, Robin Bessinger is going to be picking through debris for your charred bones in the morning.

I went back to my aunt, trying to figure out a way to move her. My whole head hurt from the effort of thinking. I had to fight an overpowering impulse to lie back down and rest, to take my chances on waking up again in time.

Elena didn't weigh much, but even if I'd been totally myself, I couldn't have carried her far. I was afraid dragging her might jar her too much in her injured state and finish her off, but what other choice did I have? If I left her on the mattress, though . . . It might be more awkward, but the mattress would make a good barrier if we had to go through fire.

It had handles on the sides but not along the narrow end. I took my keys from my pants pocket and made some gashes in the cover. If they didn't rip off completely, they'd be good enough. I stumbled over to Elena's duffel bag and ripped the strap free. Even that much effort made me pant and brought another wave of pain crashing across my brain to the front of my head. I had to lean against the wall until it receded enough that I could walk.

I ran the strap through the gashes I'd made in the mattress cover. Before starting to haul it, I knelt again to feel Elena's heart. It maintained its erratic beat.

I slipped the duffel strap over my head and shoulders and pulled the ends around my waist. Stooping slightly against the weight behind me, I began dragging it toward the door. When I got that far I put the strap down and gently maneuvered the mattress by hand out to the hall—I didn't want to bang Elena's head into the splintered door.

Once in the corridor I began a nightmare journey. Around us in the dark the rats were twittering, unnerved by the fire and trying to delve deep into the bowels of the building. They kept running over my feet. I knew they had to be crawling around the mattress, crawling on my aunt's body. That thought made me shudder and start to black out.

I leaned a hand against the wall and forced my mind to clear, forced the thought of what was happening behind me out of my head, forced the swells of pain to the back of my brain. Smoke was starting to drift toward me down the hall, further fogging me. I wanted to sit but was too scared of the rodents clamoring for air on the floor to be able to.

I was almost at the basement stairs. If the smoke was getting thicker, it meant the fire was at the top of the stairs and I wouldn't be able to make it through the maze to an exit.

My eyes were streaming. My throat was raw and I could feel a searing tightness in my chest when I tried to inhale. I might have been able to run up on my own with my sweatshirt around my head, but if I tried it with Elena, we'd both die.

So move, Vic. Don't stand there, go back, put your harness back on, that's a good cow, turn around and pull. A door stood open at the bottom of the stairs. I had just enough sense to heave it shut before taking up my burden again and heading back down the hall.

My arms were beginning to tremble from overexertion. I couldn't remember any real poems so I started chanting jumping-rope rhymes to give some rhythm to my movements and take my mind from my fatigued body.

"Dance, girl, dance, girl, hop on one foot." But hop to where? I didn't remember any other doors in the section of basement we were trapped in. Then, at the intersection of the two corridors, I thought of the dumbwaiter I'd inadvertently found.

I stuck a hand in and explored it. It was a large space, originally used for hauling furnishings from the basement. When the hotel had been built it stood in Chicago's most exclusive neighborhood. They'd needed lots of linens and things, and before a widespread use of electricity this made an ideal passageway.

If the fire was inside the building, the shaft would also be an ideal conduit for flames. But if it had been started on the outside and was working inward, we might have a grace period. It was possible, of course, that rats had long since chewed through the cables. Anything is possible, Warshawski, my old Latin teacher used to say. I want to know what *is*.

I slipped Elena from the mat and hoisted her, straining, over one aching shoulder. "Up we go, Auntie. Just relax and breathe normally."

I slid her into the box. It was high enough that she could have sat up, but I laid her on her side. I looked at where the mattress lay. Travel light or keep my only tool? I hoisted it up and folded it into an awkward bundle next to my aunt, checking to make sure she had breathing room. Finally I stuck a foot into the box and hiked up to the top.

It was covered with greasy dust and little things that were probably rat droppings. "But there are no rats here, Auntie, because they've all been clever enough to burrow underneath the building. We will rise above it all."

I fumbled in the dark for the cables, found one and tugged. It creaked ominously but the box didn't move. There was tension on the line, though— it was still connected somewhere. I pulled again and felt the box sway a little. Maybe I had the wrong cord. I held on to it with my left hand and waved my right around in the dark air. Finally I found another rope on the other side of the shaft.

I shifted my weight across the box and tugged with both hands. The dumbwaiter jerked underneath me and started to move. It was slow, tedious work. The rope burned my bare palms. My biceps had pretty much turned to water by now and strongly resisted the idea of more exercise. "You're at the wall now, Vic—go for the burn," I mocked myself, then returned to rope chants.

I'd been through my repertoire twice when we finally came to the opening onto the ground floor. The door was shut. When I put a hand on it, it was scalding to the touch. A poor exit choice. I tried looking up but it was a futile exercise. Even adjusted to the dark, my eyes could make out nothing.

I started hauling again, sticking a hand up every few pulls to see if I was going to run into ceiling. The pain in my head had passed beyond agony to some light, remote feeling, as though the top of my head were floating some miles from my body. Every time I stopped working to feel about, though, it came crashing down with a pounding thud. Was this what it was like to use heroin? Was this what Cerise had crawled off to the Rapelec site to feel—her head buoyant above her body?

"Last night and the night before, twenty-four robbers came knocking at my door. Asked them what they wanted, this is what they said"—the words kept spilling out, against my volition, long after I couldn't stand the sound of them. In the dark I was seeing pinwheels spinning through the elevator shaft, flashing strobes of light from my burned-out retinas. Future and past disappeared into an endless present, presence of rope, of muscles beyond fatigue, of hand over raw hand, and the unbearable sound of my own voice spewing out childhood chants.

The rope abruptly stopped moving. For a few seconds I kept tugging at it, frustrated at breaking my liquid crystal movements. Then I realized we were at the end of the line. If we couldn't get out here, we were—well, at the end of our rope.

I sat down on the box. My knees were stiff from the long haul upward and gave me little protesting stabs at my abrupt bending. I leaned down and felt for the dumbwaiter door. It was cool to the touch. I turned around, climbed down the front of the box, and twisted around to sit against the bulk of the mattress.

The door was stiff but not locked, as I'd first feared. I leaned against the mattress and pushed as hard as I could with my wobbly legs. The door creaked. I drew my knees to my chest, ignoring their throbbing, and kicked hard. The door popped out of its frame.

I slid out and turned around for my aunt. Years of abusing her body had given it great resilience—she remained unconscious, but her shallow uncertain breaths still came snorting out.

I propped her against the wall and forced my tired legs down the hall. Now that we were above ground, faint light from the full moon and streetlamps gave a pale glow to the walls, enough that I could walk without feeling my way. In the distance I could hear the deep excited honking of fire engines. All I had to do was find a window where they could see me.

"Love will find a way," I sang softly to myself. "Night or day, love will find a way." I was skating, moving so smoothly I was almost floating. My cousin Boom-Boom and I were on the forbidden frozen lagoon, circling round and round until we slid dizzily onto the ice. We weren't supposed to be there, no one knew how thick the ice was, if it gave way, we'd drown for sure because no one would rescue us. The first one to give up was a chicken and I wasn't going to be a chicken to my cousin. He was a better skater than me but he wasn't tougher.

He was near me someplace, I knew that, but I couldn't quite find him. On and on I skated, calling his name, opening every door but not seeing him. I got to a window and stared through it at a metal platform. I thought Boom-Boom was behind me, but when I turned he was gone. When I looked back at the window all I found was my own reflection. Beyond the glass lay a fire escape.

I struggled with the window but it was painted shut. I looked around the room for a tool, but it was completely bare. I lifted my trembling right leg and kicked as hard as I could. The ancient glass shivered and cracked. I kicked again and the whole bottom pane gave way.

I looked down. Below me the building was burning steadily and fire was licking upward. We'd come up three stories and we'd better get back down them fast. The fire escape was at the back. Whatever firepower belonged to the distant engines was around the other side of the building.

I lurched back down the miles of corridors I'd traveled until I came to Elena, still snorting away under the dumbwaiter. I pulled her pallet from the box and got her settled on it again. At some point my body must surely give out, no longer respond to the senseless commands of an imperial brain. I flogged myself onward, a good warhorse, old and near collapse but responding to one last call to arms.

Back at the fire escape I wrapped my sweatshirt around my right arm and knocked out the remaining shards. Then I slid Elena to the floor, moved her pallet to the fire escape, and lifted her again, my hamstrings and back shrieking in dismay, and laid her out on the mattress.

"You'll have to wait here for me, Auntie. I'll be back, just breathe deeply and don't be afraid. I've got to get help, I can't carry you on my own."

Slowly, each leg weighing a thousand pounds, I dragged myself down the stairs, down through the cloud of smoke, past the point of feeling, to the place where breath and sight were collapsed into one solid pinpoint of agony, finding the end of the escape, swinging down, feeling the bottom flight fall loose and my feet dragging on the ground.

I rolled through the smoke and staggered around the side of the building. A multitude was there. Firemen, onlookers, cops, and a man in uniform who came to me and told me sternly the building was dangerous, no one was allowed beyond the police barricades.

"My aunt," I gasped. "She's up on the fire escape around the side. We were in the basement when the fire started. You've got to get her."

He didn't understand me and I turned to a fireman helping guide a heavy hose. I tugged on his sleeve until he turned in annoyance. I pointed and gasped until someone understood and a little troop jogged off into the smoke.

26

DOCTOR'S ORDERS

"What are you doing with your clothes on?" Lotty Herschel was sharp to the point of unfriendliness.

"I'm going home." Getting dressed with both hands taped in gauze had been a chore. "You know I hate hospitals—it's where they send people to die."

"Someone should have burned those," Lotty said coldly. "They smell so bad, I can hardly stand to be in the same room with you."

"It's the blood and the smoke," I explained. "And I guess stale sweat—I worked up a pretty good meltdown hoisting myself up those ropes."

Lotty's nostrils curled in distaste. "All the more reason to remove them. Dr. Homerin cannot possibly examine you with that stench coming from you."

I'd noticed a slender middle-aged man standing patiently behind Lotty and assumed he was another resident seeking education at my feet. At my head, actually.

"I don't need another goddamn examination. Twenty-four hours here and I feel like a pot roast every housewife in Chicago has taken a poke at."

"Mez Homerin is a neurologist. You got a nasty blow to the head. I want to make sure that that thick Polish skull of yours hasn't taken any irremediable harm."

"I'm fine," I said fiercely. "I don't have double vision, I can tie my shoes with my eyes closed, even with these baseball mitts covering my fingers, and if he sticks pins in my feet, I'll know about it."

Lotty came over to stand next to me, her black eyes blazing. "Victoria, I don't even know why I bother. This is the third time you've been hit hard enough to knock you out. I don't wish to spend my old age treating you for Parkinson's or Alzheimer's—which is exactly where you're heading with your know-it-all reckless attitude. If you don't get your clothes back off this minute—this instant—you may be sure of one thing—I will *never* treat you again. Do you understand?"

Her anger was so intense it made my knees wobble. I sat back on the bed.

I was pretty angry myself, enough that my head started pounding savagely as I spoke.

"Did I send for you? This is Michael Reese, not Beth Israel—you came barging in without so much as a by-your-leave, at least not a by-my-leave. Someone tried to murder both my aunt and me. Getting out of that building was one of the most harrowing experiences of my life and you scream at me about my clothes and Alzheimer's disease. If that's your attitude, leave with my blessing—I don't need your kind of medical care."

Dr. Homerin coughed. "Miss Warshawski. I can understand your being upset—it's a natural side effect of concussion and the other experiences you went through last night. But as long as I'm here, I think I might as well examine you. And it would be easier to do if you could take your clothes off and put on your hospital gown."

I glowered at him. He turned to Lotty and said apologetically, "Dr. Herschel?"

"Oh, very well," she snapped. She whirled on her heel with the precision of a figure skater and swept out of the room.

Dr. Homerin pulled the curtain around my bed. "I'll wait out here—give me a call when you're ready."

I could go ahead and leave, but it would make me feel incredibly stupid. Angrily I kicked my running shoes off. With thick clumsy fingers I unfastened the buttons of my shirt and unzipped my jeans. I took as much time as I possibly could before sullenly calling out that I was ready.

Dr. Homerin sat on the chair next to the bed. "Tell me a little about your injury—what happened?"

"I was hit on the head," I muttered churlishly.

He refused to acknowledge my ill humor. "Do you know who hit you or what was used?"

I shook my head and saw black circles swirl around. "No. He was hiding in the room. I was looking at my aunt, who was drunk." I frowned. "No. I thought she was drunk, but it turned out she had been coshed. That's right, I realized someone had hit her and that he might still be there and as I was jumping up to protect myself I got hit from behind."

He nodded, like a professor at a promising pupil. "It's very good that you have so much recall—very often the memory immediately before such an incident is blocked out by what we call protective amnesia."

I rubbed the tender spot on the back of my head. "What I don't remember is what happened afterwards. I know I was climbing a rope in an elevator shaft but I can't remember how I got Elena up with me. And then we came out. The fire fighters had to bring my aunt, but I think I got out on my own. . . ."

My voice trailed off as I tried to focus the blur of memory. Mallory had shown up along with Furey when I was in the emergency room, but someone had been in the crowd around the fire who didn't belong there. I remembered a faint inflection of surprise mixed in with a sense of my imminent death as the paramedics carried me through the barricades. The face swam on the edge of my consciousness. Tears of frustration pricked my eyelids when my aching head refused to concentrate.

"I can't remember," I said helplessly.

"Do you have any idea of why this happened?"

His gray eyes looked harmlessly genial behind their thick lenses but I stiffened at once. "Did Bobby—Lieutenant Mallory—tell you to ask that?"

There'd been quite a scene in the emergency room, with Bobby roaring at me like a bull elephant on a rampage. Dominic Assuevo and Roland Montgomery from the Bomb and Arson Squad had joined him, but it was only because I kept passing out that the resident on call finally threw them out of the examining area.

Homerin shook his head. "The police haven't spoken to me at all. I'm just checking your ability to answer logical questions."

In the intervals between sleeping and tossing in pain I'd been testing that skill myself, without any happy answer. Maybe someone arriving to torch the building had seen Elena come out. He followed her, heard her phone me, then when she went back inside he knocked her out and waited to get me, too, before setting the place on fire. It could have happened that way, but it seemed awfully elaborate: Why not just torch the place while she was out of the way? Maybe she'd seen him clearly enough to recognize him again, so he felt she had to die. But then why go for me too? My head was starting to disintegrate. I couldn't figure it all out. I wanted to go home and I was starting to feel too helpless even to get out of bed again.

Seeing my fatigue and frustration, Homerin switched to a general interrogation—did I know who the President was, the mayor, people like that? I wished I didn't but rattled off the names. After that we went through the pins-in-the-feet routine and he banged on my knees and elbows and felt my head—all the usual medical stuff that lets the doctor know all your pieces are still attached to your aching body.

When he finished looking at my eyes and rotating my head around a few times, he sat back in the visitor's chair. "I know you want to leave, Miss Warshawski, but it would be better if you stayed another day."

"I don't want to." I was close to breaking down and sobbing.

"You live alone, don't you? I just don't think you're up to looking after yourself right now. There's nothing wrong with you that I can see, barring the side effects of concussion. They did a CAT scan of your head in the emergency room Wednesday morning and nothing alarming showed up. But you'll manage better if you let us look after you another day."

"I hate being looked after, I can't stand it." I didn't want to be like Tony, reduced to such helplessness he couldn't even breathe on his own at the end. The sound of his harsh wheezing breathing cut through my brain and against my will I found myself crying.

Homerin waited patiently for me to dry my eyes and blow my nose. He asked if there was something specific I wanted to talk about, but the memories of my dying parents were too painful to mention to a stranger.

Instead I blurted out, "Is Lotty right? Am I going to get Alzheimer's disease?"

A smile twitched at the corner of his mouth. "She's worried about you—that's why she dragged me down here and got the house staff to agree to let me see you. I'm not a prophet, but three blows in seven years—it's more than you need, but you're not taking the regular pounding that a boxer does. I'd worry more about feeling better now. And give me a call if you have any unusual symptoms."

He fished a card from his wallet and handed it to me: Mez Homerin, boy neurologist, with an address on north Michigan and another in Edgewater. "What kind of symptoms?" I asked suspiciously.

"Oh, blurred vision, trouble with your memory, any tingling in your fingers or toes. Don't lie around worrying about them—I'll be startled if you have any. Concentrate on getting your strength back. But please call me if you want to talk about any concerns."

He put a gentle stress on "any" and I stupidly felt like crying again. "There is my aunt," I said as assertively as I could. "Do you know how she's doing?"

"Your aunt? Oh, the woman you rescued. . . . She'd been hit on the head, right? Do you know if she's here?"

I didn't, but he said he'd find out and get a progress report for me. I'd been planning on getting up and dressing as soon as he left, but my crying bout had put the finishing touches to my fatigue. I was asleep almost before his hospital coat disappeared behind the curtain.

27

WE SERVE AND PROTECT

It was Saturday before the pounding in my head receded completely. I'd gone home on Friday, admitting—only to myself—that Mez Homerin had been right: I was better off for the extra day of people waiting on me. As it was, Friday involved so many difficult encounters that by the time I went to bed I was wishing I'd stayed in the hospital. The worst was with the police—Homerin had shielded me from Roland Montgomery of the Bomb and Arson Squad.

Of course the cops were most anxious to speak with me. Montgomery had been in the emergency room with Mallory and Furey early Wednesday morning and he'd sent a subordinate to Reese both Wednesday and Thursday. Since I'd slept through most of Wednesday I only learned about the subordinate's visit on Thursday. When Mez left me he encountered the detective in the hall. Their altercation led to a big red notice on my chart proclaiming "No visitors" and a lot of excitement among the orderlies and nurses who reported the episode to me in dramatic detail later.

I took a cab from the hospital to my car, which started with a reproachful groan that it kept up all the way to my apartment. Mr. Contreras saw me pull up a bit after noon. While I was sponging myself off as best I could without soaking my gauze mitts, he came to the door laden down with food.

"You shoulda let me know when you was coming home, doll. I could've come and got you—you shouldn't be driving with your hands all wrapped up like that."

"I just wanted to be by myself for a while. In the hospital you're a twenty-four-hour-a-day freak show for every medical student in the city."

"You shouldn't try to do so much on your own, cookie. No shame in asking for help every now and then. And I know darn well you wouldn't eat *nothing* this afternoon if I didn't bring it to you, so you want to be alone, you say the word and the princess here and I'll go, but not till we see you eat something."

I gave up trying to hint him away, but made him wait in the living room while I finished washing and changing. Peppy, feeling no inhibitions, stayed next to me until I was done.

Lotty'd been right about one thing—my clothes stank so badly I could scarcely stand being in the same room with them, let alone the same body. I didn't even want to wash them. Although it was my newest pair of jeans I stuffed them into a bag and put it outside my back door to cart down to the garbage.

Finally clean from my bra to my socks, I joined the old man. He'd prepared a special feast, much more food than I could deal with in my sickly state, but he was miffed that he'd had to hear all my news secondhand.

"If you was going off into danger like that, you might of notified me," he grumbled. " 'Stead the first thing *I* know about it is the morning paper. That oversize teenager Ryerson putting in a story about 'Chicago's most troublesome private eye' and I start reading and of course there you are, rescuing bodies from burning buildings, hit on the head, and not even a phone call to me from the hospital. I says to the princess here, I says, 'You could be an orphan and you'd be the last to know.' "

Peppy thumped her tail to corroborate his story. Her liquid amber eyes gazed at me with unwavering intensity as I slowly chewed a piece of steak.

"Ever since my aunt came prancing into my life two weeks ago you've been riding me for getting you up in the middle of the night. I figured if I woke you up to tell you where I was going, I'd just get another lecture."

"That's not fair." He was hurt and astonished that I could think such a thing. On top of that he was pretty darned tired of me leaving him standing on the sidelines while I went out and had all kinds of fabulous life-threatening adventures.

"It's not the first time, doll. You forget how I helped you and Dr. Lotty out that time her clinic was attacked. You don't remember how I took on them guys trying to break into your place. I may be seventy-seven but I'm in good shape, I'm still a good man in a fight."

It was precisely because I *had* remembered his assistance that I tried never to involve him in the livelier aspects of my work. If I told him that, though, it would be just too painful for him. I skated around it, saying Elena was so prone to drunken fables, I hadn't taken her claims of endangerment seriously. By the time I finished he was nodding portentously.

"I know just what you mean, doll. I used to work with a guy like that. Of course he was a danger to the whole shop, showing up drunk most days, and the ones he arrived sober he didn't stay like that past lunchtime. There was the day he didn't turn off the surface grinder, and Jake—you remember Jake —lost most of the little finger on his left hand, but Crenshaw—Crenshaw was the drunk—he claimed it was me using the machine when I wasn't supposed to . . ."

His good humor restored, Mr. Contreras went on in this vein at some length. The happy drone of his voice, the weight of the meat in my stomach, the warm pleasure I felt at being back in my own home, sent me drowsing in my armchair. I held my hand down and let the dog lick my fingers while I nodded sleepily in tune to the old man's speech.

The shrill burr of the phone startled me awake. I stretched an arm out to the piano and picked up the receiver.

"Tried to write your obit for you, Warshawski, but you made it through one more time. How many lives you got left, anyway? Three?"

It was Murray, with more vibrant energy than my head could handle. "I hear you called me the most troublesome detective in Chicago."

"Private eye," he corrected. "Nothing libelous in that—I checked with the legal department. You can sue me only if it's not true. What I want to know is, who did it? Did it come out of Roz Fuentes's camp or your dead junkie, Cerise?"

"Ask the cops—the city pays them to investigate arson and attempted murder."

"And you're just going to stay home and watch TV while they sort it out?" He guffawed. "Between us ace investigators, what were you doing down there?"

Black spots were starting to dance in front of me from the resonance of his voice. I moved the earpiece away from my head. "Performing feats of derring-do. I understand it was in all the papers."

"C'mon, Warshawski," he said, trying to wheedle. "I do lots of stuff for you. Just a few little words."

He was right—if I wanted help from him, I had to throw him the occasional quote. I told him everything from the moment Elena called me to my drop from the fire escape.

"Now it's your turn—what was the fire department doing there so pat?"

Mr. Contreras looked at me as intently as the dog, miffed I was telling my tale to Murray but wanting all the juice. I took the phone over to the couch where I'd dumped my bag and pulled out my memo pad. "Anonymous phone call," I scribbled on it for Mr. Contreras as Murray boomed the news at me. Someone had called 911 from a pay phone at the corner of Cermak and Michigan. The police didn't have a clue as to who phoned, except for its having been a man.

"So you think it was someone after your aunt?" Murray asked. "How is she, by the way?"

"I don't think anything right now. My head hurts like all the cement trucks on the Ryan just ran over it. And my aunt, who has the system of a goat, sat up and took nourishment yesterday. She refused to talk to me, though, when I started asking her pointed questions, and is acting sick enough that the docs are stonewalling the cops for her. You can call Reese and see if the medicine men will let her talk to you, but don't set your hopes too high. Now you know everything I do. I'm going to bed. Good-bye."

I hung up before he could say anything else and ignored the phone when it started ringing again. Mr. Contreras solicitously offered to fix me up with pillows and a blanket on the couch, to leave me the dog, to make me tea, to do a thousand things that made the black spots grow into giant spirals.

"I need to be alone in my own bed. I can't take any more people now. I know you mean well, I know you're helping like mad, but I'm going to faint or scream or both if you don't take the dog and leave."

He was a little hurt but he'd seen concussion cases before, he knew it took time before you really felt yourself, and in the meantime the smallest things got you down—sure, doll, sure, he'd leave me alone, sleep was the best thing for me right now. He gathered up the dishes, clicking over the small amount of steak I'd eaten—gotta get your strength back up, doll, you look like you lost ten pounds the last few days—finally collecting the dog and heading down the stairs. I locked the triple dead bolts and stumbled to my bedroom.

The spirals receded back to spots as I thrashed around in an uneasy doze. The image of Elena, her face sunk into deep canyons, drips in her malnourished arms, kept swarming into my half sleep. She was a pain in the ass but someone had tried to kill her; I couldn't just abandon her at this point.

I'd tried talking to her before I left this morning but she'd pretended to sleep. "It's no good playing possum, Auntie—you're going to have to talk to me sometime," I'd warned her.

Mez Homerin interrupted my lecture to her, taking me by the arm and hustling me from the room.

"She's had a severe shock to a system that wasn't in the best shape to begin with. She needs to be completely free from any kind of stress or harassment if she's to recover. I've forbidden the police to question her. Do you want me to bar you from the room too? She needs your support, not your abuse."

"Bar me from her life," I'd snapped at him. "Keep her from calling to demand that I help her one last time—write it on her hospital forms. Make sure she doesn't put my address in as her own or list me as the guarantor of her bill. Do all those things and you can keep me out of her room with all the righteousness you want."

Homerin looked at me steadily during my outburst and then said in a gentle voice that he thought I ought to consider bringing her home to convalesce when she was a little stronger. That was when I'd left the hospital —before I gave in to my urge to take his stethoscope and strangle him with it.

Now, though, tossing restlessly, I was tormented wondering how much I owed my aunt. Would my uncle Peter thrash in guilt for saying no? Of course not. I hadn't even called to ask him—my tired brain wasn't up to rebutting his smugness. Did I have a duty to Elena that overrode all considerations of myself, my work, my own longing for wholeness?

I'd held glasses of water for Gabriella when her arms were too weak to lift them herself, emptied wheelchair pots for Tony when he could no longer move from chair to toilet. I've done enough, I kept repeating, I've done enough. But I couldn't quite convince myself.

Such unquiet sleep as I achieved was broken up for good at four when the police came, represented by Roland Montgomery and Terry Finchley. Montgomery kept a finger on the bell until I couldn't ignore it, and then said through the intercom that if I didn't let them up to talk, they'd get a warrant and take me downtown. It was Montgomery who did all the bullying. Terry Finchley, sent by Bobby to represent Violent Crimes, was clearly unhappy with Montgomery's approach but was too junior to protest very forcefully.

I shuffled into the living room with a blanket wrapped around me. I'd been sweating heavily in my uneasy dozing and felt a chill run through me when I got out of bed. The black spots had gone away but my head was thick, as though someone had stuffed it with wool. I sat on the couch with my legs curled up underneath me.

"Let's have the whole story, Warshawski. What were you doing in that building? How did it come to catch fire while you were there?"

"The force of my fiery personality," I mumbled, my tongue thick.

"What was that?" Montgomery demanded angrily. Finchley shook his head slightly, trying to warn me without the arson expert seeing.

"I called Furey," I said, suddenly remembering. "He wanted to know where my aunt was and I left a message with the night man saying where I was going. Did he get it? Is that why he and Bobby were at the fire?"

"I'm asking the questions," Montgomery snapped. "Why did you call the station?"

"Get the chip off your shoulder, Lieutenant, and listen to me. I just explained why I called the station. Did Detective Furey get my message?"

Finchley spoke swiftly, before Montgomery could bellow at me. "Furey was at a poker game; he left his beeper in his coat pocket and didn't get the message until he went over to get a cigar and found the thing vibrating away. Then he called the station, got your message, and went roaring down to the Near South Side. By that time, though, someone had already reported the fire. Lieutenant Mallory gave the night operator a pretty good going-over for not notifying someone else in the unit, but you hadn't said anything about an emergency."

"So Furey and Bobby stormed the hospital. How come you're here now?"

"*Miss* Warshawski," Montgomery interrupted frostily, "Detective Finchley is here to help with an investigation. Why the department sent him is none of your business."

I wanted to make a grandiose statement about how the police worked for the citizens and how I was one, and therefore one of Montgomery's bosses, but I felt too sick to fight. I just wrapped the blanket closer about me and continued to shiver. And when Montgomery asked me I went back through all the tired old details. About Elena disappearing, about Furey coming around hunting for her, her early morning phone call, and on and on.

"So why did someone want to leave the two of you there to die?" Montgomery asked.

"You're the bomb-and-arson whiz, Lieutenant. You tell me. All I know is, she called up scared, I found her on a pallet in the basement barely breathing, got knocked out myself, and am lucky to be here enjoying this scintillating conversation with some shred of my wits intact."

Finchley started a sentence, then changed his mind and made an industrious note in his pocket diary. In the dim lamplight his closely cut hair merged with the black smoothness of his face.

Montgomery scowled at me but only said, "The Prairie Shores Hotel is across the street from that fire you were so excited about last week."

I gave the thread of a smile. "Amazing."

"I'm wondering if you set the fire yourself, to try to get the department to respond to your demands for an investigation into the Indiana Arms."

I felt a jolt, the way you do when the earth goes on hurtling through space and you haven't quite moved with it. Finchley's jaw dropped. He clearly hadn't been privy to Montgomery's theories. "I didn't know we were considering that possibility, Monty," he said softly.

"And I would never have suspected you of so extravagant an imagination," I put in. "Sounds like you read too much Tom Clancy on your days off."

Finchley hid a smile so fast I wasn't sure I'd seen it. "Monty, what evidence do we have that points to Miss Warshawski?"

Montgomery ignored him. "You tried to waste police resources last week, claiming there had been a baby in the Indiana Arms that was never there. It's one of the hallmarks of arsonists that they can't stand to have their handiwork ignored."

"Hunh-unh." I shook my head. "You go away and do some real work on this problem before you bother me again. You find out about the accelerant and who had access to it, and you come up with a reason for me knocking myself out and then setting the fire and then scrambling to get away. Then we'll talk some more."

"Accomplice," Montgomery said smugly. "You must have run afoul of your partner in this."

I leaned back in the corner of my couch and shut my eyes. "Good-bye, Lieutenant. The door will lock automatically behind you."

He started shouting at me. When I didn't respond he got up and shook my shoulder until my head throbbed in earnest.

"You're one step away from a complaint of police brutality," I said coldly. "Unless you have a warrant with my name on it, you get the hell out of my place now."

If Finchley hadn't been there, I think Montgomery would have slugged me, but he could see whose side the detective was on—he wasn't nearly as dumb as he looked.

"Just watch your ass, Warshawski. I'm going to be sticking to you like your underpants. If you're up to something, next time we'll catch you red-handed."

"Thanks for the warning, Lieutenant. It's a help to know who your enemies are before you hit the streets."

When the door shut behind them I did up all the bolts again and checked the back door for good measure. I was too tired to think about what it all meant, too tired even to call Bobby and chew his ear off about it. I staggered back to my bedroom and fell back into a deep, unrestful sleep.

28
A FEW KIND WORDS
FROM A FRIEND

Robin phoned later that evening, concerned that he hadn't been allowed to see me in the hospital and glad I was still in one piece. He was eager to drive down for a convalescent visit. I was too worn out for more company but said he could stop by on Saturday if I felt better.

Before he hung up I remembered a question. "By the way, did Ajax insure the Prairie Shores Hotel—the place I was in?"

"No. It was the first thing I looked at, but of course we don't cover abandoned buildings. And if it's any comfort to you, it wasn't owned by your pal Saul Seligman. So it's either a vendetta against that block of Indiana or someone with a grudge against the Warshawski family."

The last comment was meant as a joke, but it reminded me again of Elena, her red-veined face slack and empty. I muttered something to Robin about feeling too feeble for jokes and hung up. I did not have to be a Victorian angel and go sit with her. I didn't, didn't, didn't.

I stumbled into the dining room and dug around in the cupboards hunting for stationery. It had been so long since I'd written any personal letters that the box had landed behind the fondue set and silver salad servers left over from my brief marriage. I stared at the pieces in bewilderment: Why had I carted those particular items all over Chicago with me for the eleven years since my divorce?

I wasn't up to making a decision about them today; I thrust them back into the cupboard and sat down with the yellowed stationery to write my uncle Peter. It was a difficult letter—I had to overcome my dislike of him enough to plead Elena's case with conviction. I described the accident, made much of my own decrepitude and the fact that I'd saved her life, and concluded with a plea that he either take her in himself or put her up in a convalescent facility. In the morning I'd express it to Mission Hills. It was the best I could do for Elena.

In the bathroom mirror my face looked sunken, nothing left but cheekbones and eyes, their gray looking almost black against the pallor of my skin. No wonder Mr. Contreras had been eager to fill me with steak. I stepped on the scale. My weight had fallen below a hundred and thirty pounds. I couldn't afford to be that light if I wanted to have the energy to do my job. I wasn't hungry but I'd better eat something.

I wandered moodily to the kitchen. After all this time any resemblance between the stuff in my refrigerator and human food was purely coincidental. I smelled the yogurt. It was still okay, but the vegetables and fruit had passed the point of no return while the orange juice smelled both rotten and fermented.

I took a bag of fettucini from the freezer and sawed off a hunk with my big butcher knife. While it boiled I ate the yogurt directly from the carton, trying to put some order into the chaos that enveloped me.

Several people had been annoyed with me the last week or two. Ralph MacDonald had descended from his throne to hint me away from Roz Fuentes's affairs. Saul Seligman was upset that Ajax wouldn't honor his claim. Zerlina Ramsay blamed me and Elena for her daughter's death. It was quite a list, but I didn't know that any of them would express their annoyance by leaving both Elena and me to die by fire. Of course Lotty was angry with me, too, but she preferred to do her scorching directly.

Then there was Luis Schmidt. He'd called me a bitch on Tuesday and told me not to ask any more questions about Alma Mejicana or he'd make me sorry. I'd flipped back some good macha retort and he'd hung up on me. So if I was going to go pawing around any of these people, Luis was the place to start.

The hissing of water on gas startled me back to the present—the fettucini had boiled over, extinguishing the pilot. Of course I couldn't find a box of matches among the jumble on the stove. I started slamming doors open and shut. I just couldn't take this life anymore, living alone, no one to pet me when I came home from the wars, nothing to eat, no matches, no money in the bank. I grabbed a handful of spoons and spatulas and flung them as hard as I could at the kitchen door.

When the clatter died down the grate over the door vibrated in a mournful bass for a few seconds. My shoulders sagged in defeat. I shuffled over to the door to collect my utensils. A wooden spoon had landed on the refrigerator. When I reached up for it I knocked a box of matches down. Okay, good. Have fits. They get results. I stuffed the implements back into a drawer and relit the stove.

Besides Luis and the possible problems of Alma Mejicana, I had to consider my aunt's affairs. I didn't want to think about her anymore—and not just because I didn't want Victoria the Victorian Angel nudging me to look after her. Her tales of woe had sucked me into a series of hideous events lately, starting with my hunt for her new home and culminating in my near death. I couldn't take much more probing into her life.

I still wasn't hungry, but I was starting to feel light-headed from lack of food. I drained the pasta and grated some rock-hard cheddar onto it. It was slow work with my padded hands. My arm muscles were still sore enough that I gave it up, panting, with only a few teaspoons of cheese for my effort. My right palm stung so violently I was afraid I might have rubbed the scab off through my mitt.

I carried the plate in my left hand into the living room. After forcing several mouthfuls down I leaned back in my armchair and made myself think about my aunt. Elena ran away when she learned about Cerise's death. It's possible something else had frightened her—I didn't know much about her day-to-day life. With her character she could easily have stubbed more than one toe.

But I had to start somewhere. Linking her flight to Cerise's death made sense. It would take a strong compulsion to force her from a secure berth. Since losing the Norwood Park bungalow she'd lived precariously on the small annuity scraped out of the remains of the sale. Even though the Windsor Arms was a desolate place, she'd had too much experience of hand-to-mouth living to turn her back on it lightly.

She and Cerise had been working some scam together. When I told Elena that Cerise was dead she'd been both crafty and uneasy. So she'd gone to their mark. That made sense too—twenty-four hours had lapsed between my telling her about Cerise and Elena's disappearance. She'd had time to talk to their target and find out . . .

My thought trailed away. She'd found out that Cerise had been murdered? Was that possible? What else could frighten her into running away, though? Someone saying, Look what we did to your friend. The same thing could happen to you. A quart of whiskey inside you and death by exposure on Navy Pier and who'd be the wiser.

I rubbed my aching head. Romance, Victoria. You need facts. Just say for starters that Cerise and Elena had a tiger by the tail. To find out what it was I needed Elena to start talking. Or Zerlina Ramsay—it was remotely possible that Cerise had confided in her mother.

My phone books were buried under a stack of music on the piano; I'd been singing more recently than I'd been looking up numbers. No Armbrusters were listed on south Christiana. I called directory assistance to make sure. So I'd have to make another trip to north Lawndale. I gritted my teeth in anticipation of this treat. And after that I should find out where everyone on my list of annoyed patrons had been early Wednesday morning. Although if Ralph MacDonald or Roz's cousins had tried torching me, they'd probably hired someone else to do it. Still, it would be worth finding out where they'd been. It wasn't exactly a job for a convalescent. Maybe I could wait until Sunday to start working on it.

My eyes were too sore for television or reading. My body ached too much for anything else. After I force-fed myself the plateful of fettucini I went back to bed. Lotty capped my wonderful day by phoning at eight-thirty to see if I was still alive.

"I'm doing okay," I said cautiously. If I told her I hurt like hell, I'd only get a lecture on my just deserts.

"Mez told me he'd released you today. He didn't think you were ready to go home, but I assured him you had an iron constitution and would be ready to do something else life-threatening next week."

"Thank you, Lotty." I lay down in the dark with the phone propped on a pillow next to my mouth. "If I turned my back on people who came to me in need, I can imagine how loudly you'd cheer. And if I avoided all risks—stayed home watching the soaps or something—you'd really be leading the applause meter."

"You don't think you could find some point of balance between doing nothing and putting your head in the noose?" she burst out. "Do you know how I feel every time I see your body come in on a stretcher not knowing if you're alive or dead, not knowing if this time your brain is ruined, your limbs paralyzed? Do you think you could manage your affairs so that you stopped a few feet short of the point of death, maybe even ask the police to take those risks?"

"So someone else's friend or lover can do the worrying, you mean?" I wasn't angry, only very lonely. "It will happen inevitably, Lotty. I won't be able to jump through hoops or climb up ropes forever. Someone else will have to take over. But it won't be the police. Not when I have to fight them every inch of the way to look into arson and they still won't do it. Or when their only answer to my near death is to accuse me—"

I broke off. Maybe Cerise and Elena had seen who set fire to the Indiana Arms and were going after him. Or her. Or them. Still, if that was so, it could be the arsonist was disposing of her by his favorite means. And maybe assumed she'd confided in me so I had to go too? And—but had they murdered Cerise? The police said it was an overdose, pure and simple.

"I know I shouldn't be losing my temper with you. It's only my fear of losing you, that's all." Lotty said.

"I know," I said wearily. "But it just puts that much more pressure on me, Lotty. Some days I have to fight a hundred people just to be able to do my job. When you're the hundred and first I feel like all I want to do is lie down and die."

She didn't say anything for a long moment. "So to help you I have to support you doing things that are a torment to me? I'll have to think about that one, Victoria. . . . One thing I don't support, though. That you dedicate your life to your aunt. Mez mentioned that part of your conversation to me. I suggested that if you were a man, he would never even have raised the topic with you except to ask if you had a wife to do the job."

"What did he say?"

"What could he say? He hemmed and said he still thought it was a good idea. But there's a limit to how much of yourself you have to immolate for people, Victoria. You almost killed yourself for Elena. You don't have to sacrifice your mind as well."

"Okay, Doctor," I muttered. I blinked back tears—I was so weak that one little sentence of support made me feel like crying.

"You're exhausted," she said curtly. "You're in bed? Good. Get some sleep. Good night."

When she hung up I switched my phone over to the answering service. I fumbled around with the switch in the dark to turn off the bell. When my thick ungainly hands had managed that I finally fell into a deep clear sleep.

29

HEAVY FLOWERS

When I woke up on Saturday it was past nine-thirty. I'd slept more than thirteen hours and for the first time in a week I felt rested for my time in bed. I let myself come to slowly, not wanting to bring on black spots by jerking my head.

In the bathroom I unwrapped my hands. The palms had turned an orangey-yellow. I flinched in nausea—their swollen discoloration made a sickening wake-up call. When I gently pushed the blood blisters lining my hands like railroad tracks, they seemed to be healing. I tried to remember that injuries always look their worst when they're on the mend, but the squishy mass still made my stomach turn. I also wasn't sure I could wrap them back up again myself. The hospital had given me a salve and some dressing but hadn't included a manual on how to apply them with my teeth.

Still, if I kept my hands on the edge of the tub, I could take a proper bath. I turned on the water, threw in some milk bath, and toddled off to the kitchen to make coffee. Since I could use only my fingertips to handle the kettle, it was a slow and tiresome experience. By the time I had a cup poured the bath was close to overflowing. I climbed in carefully, holding the coffee in my fingers. When I sank down cross-legged a great wave swept over the side of the tub but my hands stayed dry.

I lay soaking until the water became tepid, thinking of nothing at first, then going back to my painful headwork of the previous night. I still couldn't understand why Cerise's death had terrified Elena into flight, unless someone had pumped Cerise full of heroin and left her to die. I couldn't move on that idea, though. I didn't have any evidence—it was just the only explanation that I could come up with. And how had Elena known? She'd found it out in the twenty-four hours between my visit to her and her panicky exit in the middle of the night. While she was lying mute behind a protective barricade of doctors and nurses I didn't have any way of finding out. I'd have to drop it for now.

What I could do was take a look at Alma Mejicana. I put the coffee cup up on the windowsill and looked at my palms again, grimacing. Tomorrow would be the ideal time to slide into their offices, but I didn't think I'd be much more healed by then than I was this morning.

I soaped down and pulled myself cautiously from the tub. Drying off presented more difficulties. It's only when you can't use them that you realize how much you need your hands. The third time I dropped the towel I left it on the floor and climbed back into bed to finish drying.

The front doorbell rang just as I was trying to hoist jeans over my still-damp rump. I'd forgotten Robin was coming. I slid my arms through a zip-up jacket and managed to have it closed by the time he got to the third-floor landing.

"Vic! Good to see you in one piece." He looked me over critically. "You don't seem nearly as battered as I figured from the news reports. How you feeling?"

"Better than I did a few days ago. My head's clear, that's the main thing."

He held out a bunch of late-summer flowers picked from his own tiny, carefully tended plot. I got him to carry them into the kitchen and fill a pitcher for me. Something about the bright gold daisies on the table suddenly gave me an enormous appetite. I wanted pancakes, eggs, bacon, a whole farmer's breakfast.

Even though he'd eaten several hours ago, Robin obligingly agreed to go to the corner diner with me. He even overcame his own nausea to dress my hands for me. I thought with my palms padded I could manage a bra, but the hooks still were too much for me. It was one thing to get my hands dressed, another to need help with a bra. I put on an outsize sweatshirt and headed downstairs without one.

Mr. Contreras and the dog were coming in the front door as we left. He looked Robin over with critical jealousy. Peppy jumped up on me and started licking my face. I played with her ears and introduced the two of them to Robin.

"Where you off to, doll?"

"Breakfast. I haven't had a proper meal since Monday night."

"I told you yesterday you was looking peaked. The princess and me would have brought you breakfast if you'd asked, saved you a trip out. I only didn't come up because I figured you was still asleep."

"I need the exercise," I said. "Robin here will make sure I don't overdo it."

"Well, you call me if you need help. You be sure and give him my number, doll. You pass out or something in the restaurant, I don't want to see it in the papers first."

I gave him my solemn word that he would have the honor of providing me smelling salts if needed. He scowled at us but went on inside with Peppy.

"Who is he?" Robin demanded when we were out of earshot. "Your grandfather?"

"He's just my downstairs neighbor. He's retired and I'm his hobby."

"Why's he so rattled about you going out to eat?"

"It's not breakfast—it's breakfast with you. If he was twenty years younger, he'd be beating up any guy who came visiting me. It's tiresome, but he's essentially so good-hearted I can't bring myself to punch him down."

The four blocks to the Belmont Diner wore me out. I've been through convalescence before. I know the early part is slow and then your strength comes back pretty fast, but it still was frustrating. I had to work to get the tension in my stomach to subside.

Most of the waitresses at the diner know me—I probably catch at least one meal a week there and sometimes more. They'd all read about my misadventures and crowded around the table to find out how I was doing and who the talent I'd come in with was. Barbara, whose section I was in, shooed the others away when they started offering juice and rolls. When I ordered a cheese omelet, potatoes, bacon, toast, and a side of fruit with yogurt, she shook her head.

"You're not going to eat all that, Vic—it's twice what you get when you've just run five miles."

I insisted, but she was right. I got through half the omelet and the potatoes but couldn't even make a pro forma effort with the fruit. My stomach strained uncomfortably; all I felt up to was napping, but I forced myself to talk a little shop with Robin.

"You know anything about the fire at the Prairie Shores? What kind of accelerant they used, whether things looked the same as at the Indiana Arms?"

He shook his head. "The Indiana Arms job was more sophisticated because there were people on the premises. It looks as though they put a fuse in the wires in the night man's quarters when they'd gotten him off to the track. They had a trailer going down to a stock of paraffin in the basement and a timer so they didn't have to be anywhere near the place. The fire you were in they didn't have to be that careful—they just dumped gasoline in the kitchen and at the doors to the basement, set the thing off, and took off." He looked at me soberly. "You were lucky, V.I. *Damned* lucky."

"That's what gets the job done. Napoleon wanted lucky generals, not theoretical whizzes." It gets me edgy when people lecture me on a narrow escape. I *had* been lucky, but all the luck in the world wouldn't have helped if I didn't also keep myself in top physical and mental shape. Why didn't my skill count for anything?

"Yeah, but he was beaten in a big way in the end. . . . Do you have any idea who did this to you? My management is concerned that it came out of your investigation into the Indiana Arms—that you're sitting on information you haven't shared with us."

I tried to keep my temper even. "I don't know who did it. It's possible it's connected to your claim, but the only person who can tell me is lying doggo. If I had that kind of information, I wouldn't be so unprofessional as to keep it to myself."

He hesitated, toying with the salt shaker. "I'm just wondering—my boss and I were talking yesterday—we work with a lot of investigators. Maybe we should bring someone else in on the Seligman case."

I sat stiffly in my booth. "I realize I don't have the results you want, but I've done the financial checks and a pretty good rundown on the organization. If you want someone else to talk to the night watchman or explore what Seligman's children may have been doing, that's your call, of course."

"It's not your competence, Vic, but—well, this assault on you just has people questioning your judgment."

I tried to relax. "I went down there because I got an SOS from my aunt. Since she has a strong proclivity for alcoholic histrionics I wanted to see her myself first rather than share that part of my family life with outsiders. If I'd had any serious inkling of danger, I would have handled things differently. But I am really, really fed up with being chewed out by everyone from doctors to the police to you for saving her and escaping from danger with my own life intact."

By the time I finished I was panting. I leaned back in my chair with my eyes shut, trying to head off the incipient pain in my head.

"Vic, I'm sorry. I'm glad you're alive. You've been doing a marvelous job. But we wonder whether someone else could bring a different perspective. Just the fact that your aunt *is* involved may be affecting your detachment."

"That's your right," I repeated stiffly. "But if you bring someone else in, I will not work in a subordinate capacity to him. Or her. I'll be glad to share my notes and my ideas, but I won't continue working for Ajax."

"Well, maybe we don't have to hire someone else at this point. There is a city Bomb and Arson Squad . . ." Robin offered tentatively.

"Who wouldn't even look at the Indiana Arms for you. Don't put your faith in them just because I've gotten some licks—it'd take more than that to get Roland Montgomery to look at the case seriously. He's even spinning a little story about me setting the fires myself."

Robin looked startled. "You're joking!"

When I told him about my meeting yesterday with Montgomery, he made a sour face. "What the hell is with that guy? He hates outsiders horning in on arson inquiries—I know—we've clashed before—but this is outrageous even for him."

His mention of outsiders brought the elusive memory of a face at the fire swimming back to my mind, but I couldn't place it. "You don't know who called in the alarm, do you? If the fire trucks hadn't been there, I don't think my aunt would have made it out."

Robin shook his head again. "I have pals in the fire department who let me see everything they have on both fires, but the call to 911 was anonymous."

I ran my fork around in the congealed grease on my plate, trying to come up with questions I should ask about the fire. Did the police have a list of the onlookers, for example, or had anything been left behind at the site that might point to the arsonist?

My heart wasn't in it, though. The questioning of my professional judgment wounded me as few other criticisms could. At the same time I saw myself in a shameful light, clattering off to the Prairie Shores Hotel like a giant elephant thundering through the veldt. If I'd called the cops—of course, I had called Furey. Still, a full police battalion might have saved both Elena and me a knock on the head. But the truth was, if it happened again tonight, I would do it the same way all over again. I couldn't expose Elena to the ribald indifference of the police. I have to solve my private problems privately. I don't even know if it's a strength or weakness. It just is.

I paid my bill and we set off silently for my apartment, neither of us pretending the conversation hadn't occurred. Outside my building Robin played with the bandages on my right hand, choosing his words.

"Vic, I think we'll let the Seligman investigation go on the back burner for a few days. We'll get someone to talk to the night watchman in more depth, but we won't ask him to take over the case. Next week, when you're feeling better, we'll see what he's turned up and you can decide how you feel about going ahead with the rest of it."

That seemed fair to me. It didn't stop me feeling depressed as I slowly hiked upstairs, but it did ease the tight knot between my shoulder blades.

As I was unlocking my door Mr. Contreras and the dog came bounding upstairs. When they reached the second landing I could hear him scolding her gently—he couldn't see where he was going; did she have to keep racing back and forth under his feet? Trip him up and then where would she be with me gone all the time. I felt the knot come back to my neck and faced them without a welcoming smile.

Mr. Contreras was hidden behind a giant parcel wrapped in the striped paper florists use. "This came while you was out, doll," he panted. "I thought I might as well accept it for you so they didn't bring it by when you was asleep or something."

"Thanks," I said with what politeness I could muster—I just wanted to go into my own cave and hibernate. Alone.

"It's okay, doll, I'm happy to help. What happened to your friend? He leave you high and dry?" He set the parcel down gently and wiped his forehead.

"He knew I wanted to rest," I said pointedly.

"Sure, cookie, sure. I understand. You want some time by yourself. You need me to do anything for you?"

I was about to utter a firm denial when I thought of the letter I wanted to express to my uncle Peter. I needed to sleep so badly I couldn't get to the post office before their early Saturday closing.

Mr. Contreras was more than pleased to mail it for me. He was ecstatic that I'd chosen him for the errand. He was so thrilled I wished I'd fought back my fatigue and taken the damned thing myself.

When he bustled off with the letter—"Don't give me no money now, doll, I'll settle with you later"—I dragged the flowers inside. It was a magnificent bouquet, reds and golds and purples so exotic I hadn't seen them before. They were arranged in a handsome wooden bowl lined with plastic. I fished around among the foliage for a card.

"Glad you're out of the hospital," ran the round unformed writing of the florist. "Next time try to pick quieter work."

It was signed "R.M." I was so tired I didn't even want to try to decide if it was a good-natured gibe or a warning. I locked all the bolts, turned off both phones, and stumbled into bed.

30
PREPARING FOR
THE HIGH JUMP

When I got up on Sunday I knew I'd turned the critical corner toward recovery. I wasn't back to my full strength, but I felt clear-headed and energetic. The lingering depression from my breakfast with Robin resolved itself to a manageable problem—my ability to handle the Seligman investigation was in doubt, not my entire career and personality. Even my hands were better. I didn't take off the gauze, but I could do simple household chores without feeling that the skin was splitting open to the bone.

The early detective gets the worm. Although it was unlikely that anyone would come into the Alma Mejicana offices at all on Sunday, they were less likely to do so first thing in the morning.

Before taking off I went into the living room to do a modified version of my exercises—I wasn't ready to start running yet, but I needed to keep limber. Ralph MacDonald's flowers dominated the room. I'd forgotten them. As I stretched my quads and tightened my glutes, I eyed the tropical rain forest balefully. Whether meant as a threat or a humorous compliment, they were overwhelming, too big a gesture from a man who scarcely knew me.

When I finished my leg lifts—twenty-five with each leg instead of my usual hundred left me breathless—I scrambled into my jeans and a sweatshirt. Straining, I carried the flowers down to my car. I drove over to Broadway and picked up a bagel, an apple, and some milk at one of the delis.

My attempts to eat and drive at the same time showed the state of my healing—two-handed, the steering wheel was manageable. With one hand my palms started smarting and my wrist ached. I pulled over at the corner of

Diversey and Pine Grove to eat. The tropical flowers stained the car with their heavy scent, making it hard to eat without queasiness. I rolled the window all the way down, but the smell was still heady. Finally I gulped down the milk and started south without finishing the bagel.

Sunday morning is the best time to drive in Chicago, because there isn't any traffic out. I made the nine miles to Michael Reese in fifteen minutes without pushing the speed limit.

Getting the massive bouquet up to the fourth floor taxed my healing palms and shoulders almost beyond endurance. When I got off the elevator a sympathetic orderly offered to take it from me.

"These are gorgeous. What room you want them in?"

I gave him Elena's room number. He carried the pot as easily as if it were a football—as easily as I could have done a week ago. I followed him down the hall and into Elena's room. A woman about my own age in a yellow nylon gown was sitting in Elena's bed reading the *Tribune*.

My jaw dropped slightly, the way it does when you're taken unawares. "My aunt," I said foolishly. "She was here on Friday."

"Maybe she checked out," the orderly suggested.

"She wasn't in very good shape. Maybe they moved her." I scurried back to the nursing station.

A middle-aged woman was making elaborate notes in a chart. I tried interrupting but she held up a warning hand and continued writing.

Finally she looked at me. "Yes?"

"I'm V. I. Warshawski," I said. "My aunt, Elena Warshawski, was here—she'd been hit on the head and was unconscious for a day or so. Did they move her or what?"

The nurse shook her head majestically. "She left yesterday."

"Left?" I echoed, staggered. "But—they told me she was in bad shape, that she ought to have a month or so of convalescent care. How could they just let her go?"

"They didn't. She took off on her own. Stole the clothes belonging to the lady she shared a room with and disappeared."

My head started spinning again. I gripped the countertop to steady myself. "When did this happen? Why didn't someone call me?"

The nurse disclaimed all knowledge of the particulars. "The hospital called whoever was listed on her forms as next of kin. They may not have felt you needed to know."

"I am her next of kin." Maybe she'd given Peter's name, though—I shouldn't push my rights as her nearest and dearest too hard. "Can you tell me when she took off?"

She snapped her pencil down in exasperation. "Ask the police. They sent an officer over yesterday afternoon. He was pretty annoyed and got all the details."

I was close to screaming from frustration and confusion. "Give me the guy's name and I'll talk to him with pleasure."

She sighed audibly and went into the records room behind the counter. The orderly had been standing behind me all this time holding the flowers.

"You want to take these, miss?" he asked while I waited.

"Oh, give them to the person who's been here longest without any visitors," I said shortly.

The nurse came back out with a file. "Michael Furey, detective," she read without looking up. She went back to the chart she'd been working on when I interrupted. The interview was clearly over.

Back in my car my arms trembled—carrying Ralph MacDonald's flowers in had overstrained them. So Elena'd done another bunk. Should I care? The police knew about it. Presumably they'd keep an eye out for her. I had better things to do.

Instead of driving over to the Alma Mejicana offices on south Ashland, I took the Chevy back to the Prairie Shores Hotel. It started groaning again as I turned onto Indiana.

"You think *you* feel bad," I grumbled. "I don't want to be here, either. And my hands hurt."

The palms were sore under my mitts. They throbbed against the hard steering wheel. Next car I got would have power steering.

The Prairie Shores made a fitting neighbor now for the Indiana Arms. The two blackened shells leered at each other across the street. Not even Elena could be hiding out in one of them. But there were other abandoned buildings on the block—an old warehouse, a boarded-up school, the remains of a nursing home. She could be in any of them. I didn't have the energy to hunt through them all. Let the police do it.

I headed down Cermak at fifty, weaving in and out of traffic, sliding through red lights. I was just plain pissed. What kind of cute little game was she playing, anyway? And how much time did I have to spend playing it with her? She'd gotten someone rattled enough to try to kill her. And instead of talking to me about it she was skulking around town thinking she was a smart enough drunk to keep out of his way. Or her way, I amended conscientiously.

I turned left on Halsted in front of a madly honking, braking semi. That cooled me down pretty fast. The worst thing in the world to do with a car is use it when you're angry. Tony had told me that, as close to angry himself as he ever got, when he took my keys away from me for a month. I'd been seventeen and it was the worst punishment I'd ever endured. It should have cured me of this kind of outburst.

I kept up a sober, alert pace the three miles to the Amphitheater. Alma Mejicana's offices were behind it on Ashland. Tony used to take me to horse and dog shows there, but it had been a good twenty-five years since I'd been in that part of town. I'd forgotten the maze of dead-end streets between Ashland and Halsted. Even having to double back to Thirty-ninth and make my way on the main streets brought me to the contracting company in twenty minutes.

I drove slowly past their drab brick building. The door was padlocked shut. The high-set dirty windows reflected the gray morning air—no lights were on behind them. I made a careful circuit down the alley behind the building. The rear metal doors had a heavy chain slung through their handles clamped together with a businesslike American Master padlock.

I drove on through the alley and went up Ashland again to Forty-fourth. I left the Chevy at the corner, across from a handkerchief park where an old man was walking a lethargic terrier. Neither of them paid any attention to me. I walked down the alley with my head up, purposeful, I belonged there. When a Dumpster lid clattered shut behind a nearby gate, I didn't jump, at least not very high.

With an American Master you need either an acetylene torch, a high-quality saw, or the key. I didn't have any of those. I studied the chain regretfully. It was bigger than me too. After a complete circuit of the building I didn't think I could get to the windows without a ladder. That left the roof, which also meant coming back and doing it at night.

Down the alley a telephone pole stood close enough to a building that I could shinny up and make my way across to Alma Mejicana. I stretched my arms up against it. The first spikes were about four feet out of reach. Still, some kind of footstool should make the climb possible.

Three flat-topped cubes of varying height lay between the pole and my target. I paced the distance. I'd only have to manage five feet at the widest jump. Even in my feeble state I ought to be able to do that in the dark.

I looked for a landmark that would let me know I'd reached Alma. The buildings facing the alley were lined with undifferentiated high wood fencing, but a garage had been built into the wall catty-corner to the contractor. I should be able to spot that with my flashlight.

The old man and the terrier were sitting on a bench reading the morning paper when I got back to the Chevy. Neither of them looked up even when I slammed the car door shut. I headed over to the Ryan at a brisk clip. The Chevy started its hideous grinding when I pushed it to sixty on the expressway but quieted down at forty. I made it home in time to catch the Bears' opening kickoff against the unbeaten Bills. Like all good Chicagoans, I turned the TV sound off and caught the radio commentary—we like Dick Butkus's knowledge and his partisanship.

With the Bears cruising at halftime, I looked at the Sunday papers. I was flipping idly through the *Star*'s "Chicago Beat" section when the Seligman name jumped up at me. The company offices on Montrose had been burgled. Mrs. Rita Donnelly, fifty-seven, a thirty-year employee, had been killed.

Behind me Jim Hart and Butkus were carrying on about the fine points of Dan Hampton's first-half play. I switched the radio off and read the story slowly.

The *Star* had only given it five inches. I went through the *Tribune* and the *Sun-Times* and finally found enough detail to let me know the time the police thought it had happened—late Friday afternoon—the mailman's discovery of her body on Saturday when he went in through the unlocked front door with a registered letter, and Mr. Seligman's shock. Mrs. Donnelly had left two daughters, Shannon Casey (thirty-two) and Star Wentzel (twenty-nine), both married, and three grandchildren. Mass would be at St. Inanna's parish Tuesday afternoon; visitation at the Callahan Funeral Home Monday evening. In lieu of flowers money should be sent to the St. Inanna scholarship fund.

The Bears and Bills were stacked in a violent heap on the silent TV screen —the second half had started without me. I switched off the set and went to the window to look out. It could have been random violence—money came into the office. Someone knew that, staked it out, killed her before she could get to the bank.

"Just don't forget that's possible," I lectured myself out loud. "Don't get so wound up in your favorite theories that you ignore the amount of random ugly violence in this town." How could it have been random, though, with Cerise dead, the attack on Elena and me, the two fires. It all connected someplace. The murderer had ransacked the files, but no money had been taken, either from the office or from Mrs. Donnelly's own bag.

Mrs. Donnelly's death made me do something I had felt too churlish to do earlier—call Furey to see what he knew about Elena.

He sounded pleased enough to hear from me, although I could tell by the background noise I'd interrupted a party. "You got us all kind of worried, Vic. You doing okay?"

"I was feeling better until I went to the hospital this morning to visit my aunt. They told me you'd come around to talk to her and that they gave you all the details."

"Yeah. I tried calling you a few times but just got your answering service. I was hoping you might have some idea where she went. She's our only real lead on Wednesday's fire."

"Besides me." I told him about Montgomery's theory.

"Oh, Monty—he gets a little off balance sometimes. Don't pay any attention to him. What about your aunt? I checked that hotel on Kenmore, but she hasn't been back there since she skipped ten days ago."

I suggested the abandoned buildings on the Near South Side and he promised to get a patrol unit to check them out. The pals had all come over to watch the game—he kind of wanted to get back to it, but he'd talk to me later in the week.

The phone rang as soon as I'd hung up. It was my uncle Peter, frothing because of my letter: What did I think he was, some cretin that he'd expose his children to someone like Elena?

"It's okay, Peter—she's vanished. No one's going to ask anything of you." Actually I was planning on calling Reese tomorrow to make sure they had his name and address as Elena's financial guarantor, but I didn't see it would help him any to learn that this afternoon.

The news didn't mollify him. "Just get this through your head, Vic—if I'd wanted to stay tied to a bunch of losers, I wouldn't have moved away from Chicago. If that offends you, I'm sorry, but I want more for my children than Tony wanted for you."

I was about to launch a full-scale counterattack on how Tony wouldn't have wanted sleaze for me, but even as I started it I realized the futility of saying anything. Peter and I had been around this track together a good many times. Neither of us was going to change. I hung up without saying good-bye.

I went back to the window and looked down at the drab bungalows facing my building. Maybe Tony would have wanted a mansion in Winnetka for me, but he'd only known bungalows and walk-ups—he wouldn't think they were any disgrace for me.

My fight with Peter had exhausted me more than carrying around that tropical rain forest had this morning. If I wanted to prance around the rooftops tonight, I needed some rest. I switched off the phones and fell into my bed.

31

HOUSE CALLS

It was six when I woke up again. My shoulder muscles had stiffened from the aftermath of carrying Ralph MacDonald's flowers up to Elena. I wanted to soak them under a hot shower. That was impossible with my gauze mitts. Anyway, I needed to keep my hands protected for my upcoming labors.

Although I'd had a little peanut butter while watching the Bears, I hadn't eaten a proper meal yet today. I still didn't have any real food in the house. I'd planned to ask Robin to drive me to the store yesterday, but after his squib about taking me off the case it had gone out of my mind. I didn't think I could do my Santa Claus imitation without dinner.

I pulled on the top to my long underwear and put a black cotton sweater on over that. It might be cool on the rooftops and I didn't want anything as bulky—or as visible—as a jacket. Jeans and my black basketball high-tops completed the ensemble that the well-dressed burglar was wearing this year. I also needed some kind of dark cap or scarf to keep light from reflecting from my face or hair. I rummaged through my drawers and came up with a soft black linen square Eileen Mallory had given me last Christmas. I didn't think the green and blue design woven into it would show up at night.

If I'm carrying my gun I usually wear a shoulder holster. Since I wanted to bring a few tools with me tonight, I dug out an old police-style belt with a holster and holes for slinging handcuffs or a truncheon.

My best flashlight was buried in the Prairie Shores rubble, but I had another one someplace. After rooting through the dining-room cupboard and the hall closet, I found it at the back of the refrigerator top. Although a little greasy to the touch, its battery still worked. I strung some twine through the hook on its end and tied it to my belt. A small hammer, a screwdriver, and a dark hand towel completed my supplies. I used to have a set of picklocks given to me by a grateful client in my PD days, but the police had confiscated those several years ago. I picked up my rolling footstool from behind the refrigerator and headed out.

I managed to slink out of the apartment without rousing Mr. Contreras, Peppy, or even Vinnie the banker. The fall twilight had set in, purply-gray and changing quickly to black. No passerby could make out my equipment belt. I stuck it in the Chevy's trunk with the footstool and drove the four blocks to the Belmont Diner for dinner. After a bowl of hearty cabbage soup and a plate of roast chicken with mashed potatoes, I felt too stuffed to move.

Gluttony is a terrible enemy of the private detective. I'd have to wait a good hour before starting my trek, maybe even longer. You're disgusting, I admonished myself privately as I paid the bill. Peter Wimsey and Philip Marlowe never had this kind of problem.

Back in the Chevy I drummed my fingers on the steering wheel. If I returned to my apartment, the chances were good I'd run into the old man. If his jealous sixth sense warned him I was setting out on an adventure, I might not be able to get away without him. I didn't want to go to a movie. I didn't want to sit in my office with a novel.

I put the car into gear and went north, up to Estes. The Chevy seemed to be behaving itself again—maybe I'd been imagining the groan in its engine.

It was only eight when I got to Saul Seligman's house, not too late for visiting even an old man. I could see a dim glow of light behind the heavily draped windows. A late-model Chrysler stood immediately in front of the house. I parked just behind it and went up the walk to ring the bell.

After a long wait the locks turned back. Seligman's elder daughter, Barbara Feldman, answered the door. She was close to fifty, well groomed without being fashionable, her reddish hair dyed and carefully set, her sweater and slacks tailored but comfortable.

She looked at me vaguely, not remembering me from the visit I'd paid to her Northbrook home.

"I'm V. I. Warshawski," I said loudly enough to penetrate the glass. "The private investigator who came to see you last week about the fire at the Indiana Arms."

Mrs. Feldman cracked the door so she could speak without shouting back at me. "My father isn't well this evening. He's not up to seeing anyone."

I nodded sympathetically. "Mrs. Donnelly's death must have upset him terribly. That's why I've come. If he's really ill I won't stay long, but it's possible he knows something that would help me get a line on her killer."

She frowned. "The police have already been here. He doesn't know anything."

"They may not have known the right questions to ask. I think I do."

She thought it over, sucking on her upper lip, then shut the door. At least she didn't rebolt the myriad locks. While I waited for her to come back I did some gentle quad stretches. I didn't want to face a five-foot jump and miss because I hadn't loosened up. A couple passing by with a small dog on a leash eyed me curiously but didn't say anything.

Mrs. Feldman came back after about five minutes. "My father says you can't help, that all you do is bring trouble. He thinks you caused Auntie Rita's death."

There's always something unsettling about a grown person using childhood names to discuss friends and relations—as if the world around her is so kaleidoscoped that Auntie Rita or Mummy or Daddy means the same thing to everyone listening to her.

"No," I said patiently, "I didn't do that. It's possible, though, that Mrs. Donnelly knew something the person who torched your father's hotel didn't want disclosed. She may not even have known it was a terrible secret. If I talk to Mr. Seligman, maybe we can find out what they'd discussed the last time they were together. That might give me a lead on why she was killed. And that can help us figure out who killed her."

Mrs. Donnelly had known something. I was sure of that. I hadn't thought it had anything to do with the arson—more about her children, it had seemed, in some way that had made me wonder vaguely if Mr. Seligman might have been their father. I hadn't thought it concerned either me or Ajax, but now it seemed I'd been mistaken.

Mrs. Feldman trundled back into the recesses of the house with my message. I felt a little absurd communicating this way, as though she were the wall and I was Thisbe. After a shorter wait she returned to tell me her father would see me.

"He says you're like one of the plagues and if he doesn't talk to you now, you'll just hound him until he does. I don't think he should, but he never listens to me anyway."

I followed her into the stale hallway. We went down to the end of the passage into the kitchen, a room even more cramped and dingy than the musty living room where I had seen the old man before. He was huddled at the Formica table in a shabby plaid dressing gown, a mug of tea in front of him. Under the dim ceiling bulb his skin looked like a moldy orange. He kept his eyes on the tea when we came in, stirring it relentlessly.

"I'm sorry to bother you, Mr. Seligman," I began, but he interrupted me with a snarl.

"The hell with that. If you were sorry to bother me, intrude on me, make my life miserable, why do you keep coming around?" He didn't lift his eyes from the mug.

I sat down across from him, banging my shin against the refrigerator as I pulled one of the grimy chairs away from the table. "I suppose it does look as though I'm the one assaulting your life, since I'm the only stranger you see. But someone out there doesn't like Seligman Property Management. They torched the Indiana Arms and they killed Mrs. Donnelly. I'd kind of like to see they get stopped before they do anything else, such as come after you."

"I just want to stop you coming after me," he muttered sullenly.

I held up my gauze mitts and spoke harshly. "Someone tried to do that last Tuesday, tried to burn me to death so I'd never go after anyone again. Was that your idea?"

He finally looked up at me. "Anyone can wrap bandages around their hands." The words were truculent but he couldn't hide the little hiss of breath when he saw the gauze.

I unwrapped the left hand without speaking. Now that the palm was healing it looked worse than before, yellow pustules surrounding the angry red line down the middle. He glanced at it, then looked away, scowling. He couldn't keep his eyes from sliding back to it. Mrs. Feldman made an uneasy noise in the background but didn't speak. Finally I put the palm down on my lap.

"After I came by here on Tuesday did you *see* Mrs. Donnelly or just talk to her on the phone?"

When Mr. Seligman hesitated his daughter answered. "She came by most evenings, didn't she, Pop? Now that you've stopped going into the office every day."

"So she came by after I was here? And what did you talk about?"

"My business. Which is none of your business, young lady."

"When you told her I'd asked for a photograph, why did it upset her?" I kept my body completely still, my voice monotonous.

"If you know so much about it why are you asking me?" He muttered the snipe to his tea mug.

"Was it your children or her children she was worried about? Or is that the same thing?"

Behind me Mrs. Feldman gasped. "What are you trying to say? What's wrong with you, anyway, to come around badgering him when he's had such a shock."

I ignored her. "How many daughters do you have, Mr. Seligman?"

I was way off target. I could tell by his look of outraged disgust. "I'm just glad Fanny didn't have to live to hear this kind of garbage in her own kitchen."

"So why did it bother her that you gave me the picture?"

"I don't know." It was a sudden, frustrated explosion. "She came by, we talked, I told her you'd been around, hounding me, still not letting me have my money, but you wanted a picture of Barbara and Connie. Then, when I told her I let you have the one taken at our fortieth anniversary, Fanny's and mine, she got all excited. She wanted to know which picture it was. Of course I only gave you one I had a copy of, I don't expect someone like you to return something sentimental, that's why I picked that one. I told her all that and she started carrying on about how I was desecrating Fanny's memory letting you have something from such a personal time."

By the time he finished his orangey cheeks were spotted with red and he was panting. "Now are you happy? Can you leave me in peace?"

"I think so. Probably. When is the service for Mrs. Donnelly? Tuesday afternoon?"

"Don't you go barging in destroying her funeral. I still think it's all because of those questions of yours she's dead."

I met his angry glare sadly. I had an uneasy feeling he was right. I got to my feet, wadding the discarded gauze from my left hand into a tight ball.

"I'll give you back your picture, Mr. Seligman, but it won't be for a few more days. I won't come back here again, but I would like to get into your office. Can you arrange that for me?"

"You want the keys? Or you want to just break in like those hoodlums that killed Rita?"

I raised my eyebrows. "I didn't read about a break-in. I thought the door was open for normal business and they walked in."

"Well, it's locked now and you can't have the keys. You'll just have to do your grave robbing someplace else."

Fatigue was starting to hit me. I didn't have any more energy to give to arguing with him. I stuffed the wadded gauze into my jeans pocket and turned without speaking.

Mrs. Feldman bustled me down the hall. "I hope you can leave him alone now. I shouldn't have let you in in the first place, but he's never listened to me. If my sister'd been here—she looks just like Mother. Don't come back again. Not unless you have his check for the Indiana Arms. It's just a fire to you, but it meant something special to him."

I started to say something about my own warm and wonderful character but broke it off—she wouldn't care. I'd barely stepped across the threshold when she began snapping the locks shut.

32

A LEAP
IN THE DARK

I didn't feel like an overstuffed goose anymore, that was one good thing. At the same time, my bravado had cost me the dressing to my left hand. I tested it gingerly against the steering wheel. The blisters rolled and squished a bit.

I got out and opened the trunk and pulled out the towel I'd stuck in my equipment belt. I wrapped it around my left hand, using my teeth to hold it in place while I tucked the ends inside. It made a slippery glove, but I could manage driving now.

As I drove across Touhy to the Edens, I was so tired and depressed that I wondered if I should abandon my project at Alma Mejicana. Often when I feel like quitting I hear my mother's voice in my head, exhorting me. Her fierce energy was tireless—the worst thing I could ever do in her eyes was to give up. Tonight, though, I heard no echoes in my head. I was alone in the dark city with my sore palms and bruised shoulders.

If you're going to sink into self-pity, go home to bed, I scolded myself. Otherwise, your mission is bound to fail. For acrobatic derring-do you need to be at the peak of self-confidence, not down in a well.

I didn't want to dwell on the scene in Seligman's musty kitchen, but I forced myself at least to think about what he'd told me. Rita Donnelly had been sitting on something. I should have probed her harder about her daughters at the time, but it had seemed so purely personal. If it wasn't their paternity she'd been hiding, what was it about them she didn't want people to know?

The light at McCormick stayed red so long I was only roused from my musings by the violent honking behind me. Startled, I leapt forward through the intersection, barely clearing it on the yellow and getting a finger from an irate driver accelerating past me.

Going sixty on the Edens, I found managing the steering so difficult with my towel-wrapped hand that I couldn't think about anything except the car and the traffic. I moved into the right-hand lane and slowed to fifty. As I maneuvered past the construction zone at Roosevelt, the damned engine started grinding again. I had to slow to forty before the noise subsided.

I drove straight to Ashland without mishap and once more circled the Alma Mejicana building through the alley. No lights showed. This time I parked on Forty-fifth near the mouth of the alley in case I needed to get to my car quickly.

I tied Eileen's scarf around my head and pulled the equipment belt from the trunk to strap around my waist. With the weight I'd lost recently it hung a little low; the flashlight and hammer banged unpleasantly into my thighs when I walked. I hugged the footstool close to my chest. It was an unpleasant sign of my weakened state that a weight I would normally find negligible slowed me down tonight.

Even though the night air was pleasantly cool the streets were empty. Most of the buildings on the east side of the alley were commercial; the residents behind the fence on the west side probably hung out on the street behind.

It was just after nine-thirty when I reached the telephone pole down the alley from Alma Mejicana. I looked up at it dubiously in the starlight. Behind their wrappings my palms tingled. I undid the towel on my left hand and stuck it in my waistband at the small of my back. On the footstool my outstretched fingertips were just shy of the first set of spikes. I planted my feet firmly on the stool, bent my knees, and jumped.

The first time I was too scared about slicing open my left palm and didn't hang on. The clatter I made knocking the footstool across the alley woke the neighborhood dogs. I lay in the shadow of the fence, rubbing my thigh where the hammer had dug in when I crashed, waiting for angry householders to appear.

When no one came I picked up the rolling stair and carried it back to the pole. The dogs were thoroughly roused now; I could hear various shouts at them to shut up. Their unified chorus apparently made the owners think they were barking at each other.

Back on top of my stool I took some diaphragm breaths, leaning my head against the pole. The pole is an extension of my arms. It welcomes me as a sister. It will not fight me as an intruder.

I repeated this litany a few times, bent my knees, and jumped without waiting to think it out. This time I grabbed hold of the spikes and wrapped my thighs around the pole, ignoring the sharp bite of the hammer and the twinge in my shoulder blades. I moved fast, still not thinking about my hands, shinnying up the rough wood until I could reach the second row of spikes and hoist myself up standing.

Once I'd done that it was easy to climb the remaining ten feet so I was level with the building top. When I stepped onto the roof I felt exhilarated with my achievement, so much so that pain and fatigue lay shielded behind a wall in my head. I ran lightly across the rooftop, judged the three-foot gap, and jumped it easily. The next break was wider, and upward, but confidence was now carrying me in an easy tide. I turned off my mind and made the jump, my left foot scraping the side of the wall but the right landing clear on the asphalt.

I went to the edge facing the alley and cautiously shone my flash. My garage marker lay in front of the next building; Alma Mejicana was the one beyond that. The jump this time was the five-footer, but downward. The building where I landed was close enough to my target that they almost shared a common wall.

I stepped across and explored the surface. Sure enough, a trapdoor lay behind the vent pipes. I pried at it gently with the claw end of the hammer. As I'd hoped, they didn't bother locking it; it came up heavily. I laid my towel on the asphalt behind it and hoisted it slowly open, my shoulders sending out little white-hot sparks of pain that I tried to ignore. I had to strain to get the door to a balance point and then drop it softly on the towel beneath.

I lay down next to it, catching my breath and making sure no alarms sounded. The moon was in its dark phase. The stars were chips of cold glass in the black sky. Despite my exertions and my long underwear, I shivered.

Before the night demons could approach me I sat up and shone my flashlight into the building. Opening the trap had released a set of hanging stairs. I climbed softly down in my black high-tops. I was in a small attic where the heating and cooling apparatus was set up. Some rough stairs, wide enough to handle equipment, led to the main part of the building.

Even though the streets were empty I didn't want to risk rousing someone by turning on the building lights. Stuffing the scarf in my back pocket I started exploring the interior. A frugal use of my flashlight showed that the two floors of the building had been divided into a series of offices. For the most part they were bare of furniture. One was set up with a metal desk and an Apollo computer.

On the ground floor Schmidt and Martinez had separate offices equipped with a certain degree of luxury. Schmidt liked the sleek Milan style while Martinez favored a heavier baroque Spanish look. Because the ground-floor rooms were windowless, I could turn on their office lights and explore to my heart's content.

I whistled a little under my breath as I opened and shut desk drawers and filing cabinets. I didn't have time to go through all their papers. I just wanted some obvious clue left out on a desktop, something like "Kill V. I. Warshawski and her aunt Elena tonight by torching the Prairie Shores Hotel."

Someplace they should have a big chart showing all of Alma Mejicana's projects. Even after going through the premises twice I didn't find any obvious sign of work in progress. It could be that it was all stored on the Apollo, but that meant any time someone wanted to check their commitments to see if they could bid on a new job, they'd have to crank up the machine and get a printout.

Maybe they were such a small operation they could work on only one project at a time. If that was so, how had they been able to get part of the Ryan contract? Even if they were leasing equipment from Wunsch and Grasso, they couldn't get involved in projects that size without substantial resources.

I made a face and started hunting for ledgers. Maybe all the bookkeeping was done on the computer upstairs, but they still had to have some kind of hard copy of their transactions. Anyway, I didn't believe they used that machine: the room it was in was completely empty except for the metal desk it sat on—it held none of the papers and manuals you expect to find around a machine in active use.

It was midnight when I finally located the books in the bottom drawer of a filing cabinet. By then my eyelids had started to swell with fatigue. One thing I hadn't thought to bring was a flask of coffee, but I found an electric machine and a can of Mexican coffee in the storeroom and recklessly helped myself to a pot. I carried the ledgers into Luis's office and sat at his glossy black desk with my coffee. It was the heat more than the caffeine that kept me going.

The books were perfectly straightforward. Payments were received from various project owners, such as the U.S. government in the case of the Dan Ryan, and payments were made for heat, cement, and other necessities of contracting life. But the biggest consistent payees were not suppliers. They were Wunsch and Grasso and Farmworks, Inc.

I shut my swollen eyes, trying to remember why I knew that name. When I woke up it was three o'clock. My neck was stiff from where I'd slumped over in Luis's chair and my heart raced uncomfortably—I could have slept until morning and been surprised in here by the Alma Mejicana employees.

When I glanced back down at the ledgers, though, I remembered Farmworks, Inc. perfectly—that was the bizarre name I'd seen on the time sheets at the Rapelec site the night Cerise was found dead there. I rifled through Luis's desk drawers for a pad of paper. Not finding any, I ripped a blank sheet from the back of the ledger and jotted some of the numbers down. I had an inkling of what they meant, but with morning near I didn't have time to think, just to copy and get going.

I put the ledgers back in the drawer where I'd found them, cleaned the coffeepot, and tiptoed back upstairs to shut the trapdoor to the roof, pulling my towel in first. The front door could be unlocked from the inside. I wouldn't be able to lock it again, but they would just think they'd forgotten to shut it properly on Friday night. Even if they suspected a break-in, I hadn't left any personal signs behind. Anyway, I was far too beat to go back the way I'd come.

I undid the bolts and stepped out onto Ashland. I was about ten feet from the door when the alarms went. I'd been going to circle through the alley for my footstool, but this seemed like a good time to buy a new one. I moved up the street at a brisk walk—never let anyone see you running when an alarm sounds.

A car heading up Ashland to Forty-fifth slowed. I fished in my back pocket for the scarf—I should have put it on before I left the building. It wasn't there. I dug in my jacket pockets, my waistband, my belt, but somewhere in the recesses of Alma Mejicana I'd lost it.

My hands trembled and my legs turned rubbery. I made myself walk naturally. If the police or Luis Schmidt found it, who was going to know it was mine? Bobby Mallory probably didn't keep track of the presents his wife handed out and it was most unlikely he'd ever be shown this evidence.

Reciting this high-level logic didn't calm me, but it occupied enough of the front of my mind to keep me from total panic. It helped that the passing driver, while still going slowly, didn't stop. For all I knew he wasn't concerned about the alarm but was debating whether to try to assault a woman carrying as much weaponry as I had strapped to me. I kept facing straight ahead, trying to make him invisible. When I turned left at the corner he continued north.

My control broke; I jogged the remaining half block to my car and headed for the Ryan without waiting to see if anyone responded to the alarm.

33

DRESSING FOR WORK

"For she's a jolly good sister, Though her hands are a giant blister," I sang in the bath. It was eleven Monday morning; I had risen from a sleep as sound as if I were one of the just, instead of a moderately successful burglar.

The morning papers contained no news of my break-in. Of course they'd probably been at the printer as I was driving home, but I didn't think an alarm at a small business on the South Side would get a mention when they couldn't find any signs of damage. My late-night panic had vanished. I'd left a piece of evidence behind, it was true, but that scarf was sold by the dozen at various Irish import shops around the city each week. It was only my own guilty fears that had made me think it could be traced to me. The one thing I should *not* do was call Furey or Finchley or any of my other police pals to inquire about Alma Mejicana.

I'd unwrapped my right hand before climbing into the tub. The blisters on the left had broken and reshut with a lot of oozing. They stung sharply when I cautiously put my hand in the water. The right, protected behind its gauze shielding, was starting to look like real skin. Nothing makes you heal faster than good genes. Good work, V.I., good choice of parental chromosomes.

Even though my shoulders were stiff and my neck sore, I felt pretty happy. "Music is the voice of love," I crooned, soaping my armpits.

I didn't know what Farmworks, Inc. was. I hadn't found proof that Luis Schmidt had tried to murder me. I wasn't any closer to knowing whether Cerise had been killed, or why Elena had run scared, but my successful burglary proved better than a tonic.

I bounded out of the bath, did a more vigorous exercise routine than I'd managed yesterday, and put on my jeans and a shirt to borrow the dog from the old man. Peppy had set up a barking when I came in last night, but neither Mr. Contreras nor Vinnie the banker had popped out to see me so I'd hoped I'd gotten home free.

Mr. Contreras's suspicious scrutiny when he answered my knock made me wonder, but I didn't volunteer anything—when I was a public defender I was always having to caution my clients against boasting out of euphoria. The easiest way to get caught is to pull off a slick job, then feel so full of yourself that you have to brag about it. Then one of your pals gets pissed at you and squeals, and there you are at Twenty-sixth and California talking to the PD.

"You musta been tired, cookie, to sleep this late," Mr. Contreras said severely.

"Yeah, but I'm much better this morning. I'm going to take her royal heinie out for a walk." I showed him my healing palms and got grudging consent to take the dog. It would have been cruel to turn me down, considering that she was practically wriggling out of her skin in her eagerness.

I wasn't up to running her, but I drove her over to the lake and threw sticks into the water for her. A pair of winter gloves seemed to provide enough protection for my hands. Since golden retrievers are born knowing the backstroke, my only difficulty came in persuading Peppy to get back into the car when my shoulders grew too sore to throw anymore.

I parked the car illegally by the hydrant in front of our apartment and ran in to drop her off with Mr. Contreras. He refuses to believe that lake water won't ruin her delicate constitution, but before he could get well into the body of his complaints I smiled and said good-bye.

"You'll be able to remember it all to tell me later," I assured him as he glared at me in the doorway.

I ran upstairs to my own place and dug my hiking boots out of the hall closet. I pulled my gun from the belt where I'd draped it on a chair early this morning and stuck it in my waistband. The phone began ringing as I was shutting the front door but I let it go. Despite my sense of urgency, I took the time to lock all three dead bolts—someone had wanted to kill me, after all, and there was no reason to invite an ambush.

I pulled my gloves back on and headed for Lake Shore Drive. Although the grass in the lakefront parks was brown and sere, the soft air and sparkling water eased the memory of the harsh summer. As I drove south I sang "We're on the way to Grandma's farm" and other selections from childhood.

The underground garages were full, but even having to park in one of the pricey Wabash Avenue lots didn't seriously dampen my spirits. I whistled under my breath as I took the feeble Pulteney elevator to the fourth floor.

Our building management doesn't believe in such unnecessary expenses as hallway lights. Only the emergency bulbs at either end of the corridors provide a faint illumination, enough to fumble your keys into your lock. As I got off the elevator I could see a dim shape outlined against the wall across from my office. I don't get much walk-in business—most of my corporate clients prefer that I come to them. It's one of the reasons I can run my business from such dismal surroundings.

If someone wanted to shoot me, this was the perfect opportunity. I thought about racing for the stairwell and fetching help, but Tom Czarnik, the building super, was waiting for a chance to prove me an unfit tenant. And getting the cops would take so much time that my visitor would probably be long gone before they got there.

And the real truth, V.I., is that you can't stand asking people for help. This cold thought came to me even as I was trotting down the hall, moving from side to side and hunching my shoulders to minimize my size. When I came up to the shadowy figure I gave a little gasp of laughter, release from my fears—Zerlina Ramsay was waiting for me.

"I didn't know if you was ever coming in here, girl. I've been here since eight this morning." It was a comment more than a complaint.

"I've been under the weather," I said, wrestling clumsily with the keys in my gloved hands. When I finally turned the right one in the lock the door opened slowly—a week's accumulation of mail was blocking it. I scooped it up and held the door open for Mrs. Ramsay.

"You could have called me at home if you needed me—I'd have been happy to go see you."

Under my office lights her skin color looked healthier than when she'd been in the hospital. Her dour hostess apparently was looking after her well.

"Didn't want to do that. I didn't know who you lived with, whether they'd let you talk to me." She lowered herself carefully into my utilitarian guest chair. "Anyway, I didn't want Maisie to hear me on the phone to you."

I dumped the mail on my desk and swiveled in the desk chair to face her. My desk faces the window with the guest chairs behind it so that a steel barrier won't intimidate visitors.

"I heard on the news you'd been hurt in that fire last week. Across from the Indiana Arms, wasn't it?" She nodded to herself and I waited patiently for her to continue. "Maisie says leave you to yourself—you got Cerise in trouble, leastways your aunt did, let you get yourself out by yourself."

I didn't feel responsible for Cerise's death, but I also didn't see what purpose arguing about it with her would serve. Anyway, she could well be right about Elena, at least partially right.

"It seemed to me the two of them had some scheme going," I ventured.

"I thought maybe they wanted to pretend Katterina had died so they could collect a big award from the insurance company."

"You could be right." She sighed unhappily. "You could be right. Blaming you doesn't take away the pain of having a child like that, one that uses heroin and crack and God knows what-all else, and steals and lies. It's just easier to blame you than lie in bed asking myself what I should of done different."

"Elena's no prize, either," I offered. "But my dad was her brother and they didn't make 'em any better than him."

"Yeah, but you didn't bring her up. If I hadn't a had to work so hard, be gone all the time—" She broke herself off. "No use talking about it now. It's not why I came up here. Took me three buses too."

After a brooding silence in which her full lips disappeared into a narrow slit in her face, she said, "It's no news to you that that aunt of yours, that Elena, likes to tell a story or two."

She waited for my agreement before continuing. "So she claims she saw someone talking to Jim Tancredi a few weeks before the fire, and then she came over to my room the night the place burned down telling me he'd been there again."

She smiled in embarrassment. "You gotta understand, the kind of life we lead, any new face is excitement. Maybe you wouldn't of been interested, but I was. And that was when she saw I had my little granddaughter with me, Cerise and Otis dropped her off, you know, and she gets real righteous about how no children can be in the building and she'll talk to Tancredi about it, so I give her the price of a bottle and she goes off, but I figure I'd better get our little princess over to Maisie. With an alkie like Elena you can't trust her to keep her mouth shut just because she *says* she will."

When she looked at me defensively I grunted agreement—I knew that chapter and verse on Elena too well to argue the point. "What did she say about the man she'd seen? Black, white, young, old?"

She shook her head regretfully. "He was white, I'm pretty sure of that, even though she didn't say it in so many words. But she said he had the most gorgeous eyes, that was her expression, and I can't see her using it about a black man."

That was really helpful—Elena thought every man under eighty-five had the most gorgeous eyes. Still, she'd used it in my hearing. The night of the fire. Vinnie the banker, he came to chew me out and she told me not to upset a boy with such gorgeous eyes.

That memory brought the elusive face in the crowd at the Prairie Shores to the forefront of my mind. Vinnie. Vinnie, who shouldn't have been within fifteen miles of the Near South Side. I'd opened my eyes as the paramedics were carrying me through the crowd and seen him looking down at me. It was a slide shown so briefly on my retina that I only now remembered opening my eyes for that brief flash.

I came slowly back to the room. At first I thought I'd have to revise my agenda for the day and go racing off to see him. But as the rushing in my head subsided and reason returned, I remembered I didn't know which bank he worked for.

"You okay?" Zerlina asked anxiously.

"I'm fine. I think it's just possible I may know who she was talking about." Although would Elena have hidden the fact that she'd seen Vinnie before? Wouldn't it be more in keeping with her to issue sly hints? There hadn't been time, though—we'd been fighting about whether she could stay. That could have driven Vinnie from her mind. And then that night she and Cerise showed up together, they started with a story about Katterina, but after they were in bed together Elena suggested blackmailing Vinnie as a better idea. At that point of course she wouldn't say anything about him to me.

"Elena's disappeared again," I said abruptly. "Took off from her hospital bed Saturday morning. She'd taken a pretty good blow to the head and shouldn't have been walking, let alone running."

"They didn't say nothing about her on TV, just you on account of you being a detective. And that you'd rescued your aunt, which I was pretty sure had to be Elena. I didn't come here today because of her, but I'm sorry for her. She's not an evil person, you know, nor Cerise wasn't, either. Just weak, both of them."

She brooded over it in silence for a bit. When it was clear there wasn't anything else she wanted to say, I asked if I could give her a lift.

"Um-unh. I show up in some white girl's car everyone on the street's going to be up telling Maisie about it. No, I'll just go back the way I came. It doesn't matter, taking three buses, you know—I don't have anything else to do with my time these days."

The rush of excitement I'd felt over remembering seeing Vinnie at the fire died away after Zerlina left, and with it much of my earlier euphoria. It was hard to think about her life and that of Elena and maintain a great flow of good cheer. Then, too, the more I considered Vinnie as an arsonist the less sense it made. Maybe he was a pyromaniac sociopath, but it seemed too incredible a coincidence that he would move in below me and then turn out to be torching my aunt's building. Of course even sociopaths have to live someplace, and he couldn't have known that my aunt lived in one of his target buildings. And that might explain his being awake and irritable so soon after the fire.

My mind kept churning futilely. Finally I willed myself to turn it off. I flipped quickly through the mail. Two checks, goodie, and a handful of get-well cards from corporate clients. The obvious junk mail I pitched. The bills could certainly wait, but the incoming money would defray my expenses this afternoon.

I stopped at a cash machine to deposit the money and withdraw a couple of hundred. Armed with that I walked west on Van Buren, hunting for a place that carried work clothes. The systematic mowing down of the Loop to make room for glitzy high rises has driven most of the low-rent business away. Van Buren used to be jammed with army surplus outlets, hardware shops, and the like, but only the peep shows and liquor stores have kept a tenacious hold on the area. They would probably go last.

I had to walk the better part of a mile before I found what I was looking for. I bought a hard hat and a heavy set of coveralls and work gloves. At five-eight I'm tall for a woman, but I still fit easily into a man's small.

Everything looked too new to convince anyone I was a seasoned construction worker. Back in my office I laid the coveralls on the floor and scooted across them in my desk chair several times. Now they looked new but covered with grease.

I keep a set of tools in my filing cabinet to work on the women's toilet, which goes out an average of twice a month. Since Tom Czarnik would like to get rid of all women tenants, not just me, I've learned to do plumbing basics over the years. I took out the wrench and pounded my hard hat a few times. It still looked too new, but I was able to add a few artistic dents and scratches to it. It would have to do.

I pulled the coveralls on over my jeans, moving the gun to one of the deep side pockets, and added my small supply of office tools to the others. Useless on the Ryan, but I thought they gave me a touch of authenticity. I emptied the contents of my handbag into various other pockets and shut off the office lights. I'd left my hiking boots in the car. I wouldn't put them on until I got to the Ryan—they were too hard to drive in. Tucking the hard hat under my arm, I took off again. This time it was my office phone that I ignored as I locked the dead bolt.

The elevator, which had been running with great difficulty when I got back with my work clothes, had given out completely. I squared my shoulders and headed for the stairs.

34

HEAT FROM
THE TOP

I laced up my boots and hiked up the broken on ramp I'd slid across in my street shoes last week. A good set of boots with treads made a big difference; I moved at a good clip to the top. In my hard hat and coveralls I fit in well enough that no one spared me a glance.

As I tramped along the shoulder I realized I shouldn't have worried about how new my clothes looked—concrete dust soon enveloped them. I pulled my sunglasses out of one of the front pockets to protect my eyes but I didn't have any way to keep the dust out of my lungs. Still, my hacking cough gave me an added touch of authenticity. The only thing I lacked was a bandanna at the throat—in red or yellow it could be pulled up over the mouth when one was actually bent over an air hammer.

Actually I was missing something else—a union card. Even if I'd wanted to risk recognition by the men in the trailer, I couldn't go asking for the Alma Mejicana site without showing I belonged to the fraternity. I kept trudging along, looking for the bright red and green Wunsch and Grasso logo.

I was stronger than I'd been two days ago, but the longer the hike became, the less enthusiasm I felt for my project. I realized, too, that the compleat construction worker ought to have strapped a water jar to her belt loops. It was cooler today than it had been for a while, but walking along in heavy overalls, lugging my wrenches, breathing the dust, turned my face hot and my throat scratchy. My shoulders sent up sympathetic warning shouts.

Earplugs would have been a help too—the noise was staggering. Air hammers, giant earth movers, cement trucks, bulldozer-like things with evil-looking spikes attached to a front claw, combined with the shouting of several thousand men to raise a discordant chorus. Few of the genuine workers wore earplugs—it's better to go deaf than display an unmanly weakness.

I was walking south along the west side of the road. To my untutored eye this was the most complex part of the project, since they were adding a whole new lane for traffic merging south from the Eisenhower. I scanned that part of the construction, then strained to see around the traffic using the middle four lanes to make sure I didn't miss the Wunsch and Grasso logo on the northbound side.

I was almost at the I-55 turnoff before I found their equipment, mercifully on my side of the expressway. I hoisted myself up onto the guard-rail to wait for my second wind while I surveyed the territory. The Alma Mejicana part of the operation involved about a half-dozen machines and perhaps twenty or thirty men.

Their contingent wasn't pouring concrete. Instead, as nearly as I could figure out, they were readying the roadbed, using giant rollers to mash rock into tiny pieces, then coming along after with another machine to smooth it down. The men not operating the machines were walking alongside them with picks and shovels, correcting flaws at the edges. Several stood by surveying the work.

It was a busy, industrious scene, and despite the modern machinery, one that harked to an earlier era. None of the crew was black, and as far as I could tell none of them was Hispanic, either. Most of their hard hats were decorated with the Wunsch and Grasso logo. It's one thing to borrow someone's equipment, but even a small firm ought to be able to spring for their own hard hats.

I hopped down from the fence and went up to one of the men surveying the work. Close to the rock crushers the noise was so intense that it took some effort to get the surveyor's attention.

When he finally looked up at me I bawled in his ear, "Luis Schmidt here today?"

"Who?" he bellowed back.

"Luis Schmidt!"

"Don't know him."

He turned back to the road, signaling to one of the men. I thought he was going to pass my inquiry on, but instead he wanted to point out something that had to be done to the roadbed. I tapped his arm.

He jerked around impatiently. "You still here?"

"Is this the Alma Mejicana site?"

He rolled his eyes—dumb broad. He pointed at the machine nearest him. "What do *you* think?"

"I think you're with Alma Mejicana and leasing equipment from Wunsch and Grasso."

He was beginning a scathing put-down when another one of the surveyors came over. "What's going on here?" he demanded, silencing the first man with a commanding arm wave.

"I'm looking for the Alma Mejicana crew," I bawled. "I was told they were using Wunsch and Grasso equipment."

The second man dragged the first off to the side. They had an animated conversation that I couldn't hear, but it involved a lot of gesturing—at the roadbed and at me. Finally the first man went on down the road another ten yards while the second came back to me.

"Rudy's new on the site. The crew are A-M men, but the foremen and the equipment are all from Grasso. He didn't know that. What do you need here?"

He thrust his weather-beaten face close to mine so I could hear him. Maybe I was being fanciful, but behind the film of white dust his expression seemed cold, almost menacing.

"I'm looking for Luis Schmidt." It was the only line I had so I stuck to it.

"He's not on the site. I'll take a message for him."

I shook my head. "I don't mind waiting."

"He won't be here today, lady. Or tomorrow. So if you have a message, let me have it. If you don't, get off the site."

He looked at a couple of men with picks and jerked his head. When they ambled over he said, "Lady got on the site by mistake. You want to see she gets off and stays off."

I held up my hands placatingly. "It's okay, big guy—I can find my own way out. Anyway, I got what I came for."

I trotted northward at a good clip. The pick bearers trotted along next to me, keeping up a line of small talk that I fortunately couldn't make out. No one could possibly attack me right here on the Dan Ryan with two thousand men to witness it. Assuming my screams penetrated the sound of the machinery, or they didn't think I was a scab and join in mauling what was left of my body.

About a half mile up the road, when I thought I might throw up from exertion, they decided they'd fulfilled their mission. One of them poked me playfully in the side with his pick. The other told me he guessed I'd learned my lesson but they could really make it *stick*—ha, ha—if I came back.

I nodded without speaking and staggered clear of the roadbed to collapse on the slope rising up on its west side. I lay there for half an hour, sucking in great mouthfuls of chalky air. They couldn't have known who I was. If there was some red alert out on me, they could easily have knocked me accidentally under one of the rock crushers. But they must have some general cautionary warning against anyone prying around about Alma Mejicana.

What if I'd been with the feds? Would the second foreman still have behaved so precipitously? Massive bribe-taking doesn't seem to have penetrated federal bureaucrats yet, but maybe Roz—through Boots—had some other source of protection for her cousin's firm.

From where I was lying the Sears Tower dominated the near horizon. The sun was low enough in the sky to turn its windows a fiery copper. It was too late for me to go to the Daley Center to look for any background on Farmworks, Inc. I lay there watching the fire on the tower mute into soft oranges, then darken.

Finally I got to my feet and began the long trek back to my car. My legs were a bit wobbly—too much exertion too soon, I told myself sternly. Nothing to do with the surge of fear over the guys with the pickaxes.

Day crews were starting to pack it in. Night shifts hadn't started yet. There was a lull in the noise and a general relaxation in the work frenzy. The machines were still moving doggedly, but the ground crews were standing around laughing, drinking longnecks that they somehow spirited onto the site.

It took over half an hour to move the mile to my car. By then most of the other vehicles parked around it had left. Alone among the detritus under the giant stilts of the expressway, I shivered. When I got in the car I carefully locked the doors before starting.

It was after five-thirty. I turned up Halsted instead of joining the packed throngs on the expressway or the drive. No one on the site knew who I was, but I didn't take the hard hat off until I was north of Congress.

When I got home I dumped the overalls and the hard hat in the hall closet and headed straight for the tub. I longed for sleep but I still had several errands to run. I tried to convince my wobbly legs and sore shoulders that a long bath would do them as much good as twelve hours of sleep. More good. It might have worked when I was twenty, but when you're closer to forty than thirty there are some myths the body won't believe.

Carbohydrate packing was my next great idea. Although there was no fruit or meat in the house I still had onions, garlic, and frozen pasta. Just the kind of dish my mother thought adequate for a Saturday dinner, while my father, who could never bring himself to criticize her, longed privately for chicken and dumplings.

I found a can of tomatoes in the back of my cupboard. I couldn't remember buying this brand and studied the label dubiously, trying to figure out if they were still any good. I opened the can and sniffed. How do you tell if something is full of botulism? I shrugged and dumped them in with the onions. It would be fairly entertaining if I escaped the ravages of mad killers only to die of food poisoning in my own kitchen.

If the tomatoes were poisoned they didn't affect me immediately. In fact, the bath and the dinner did make me feel better—not as good as if I'd had my sleep, but good enough to go on for a bit. I was even whistling a little under my breath when I went into the bedroom to change.

My only lightweight black dress has big silver buttons down the front. With black stockings and pumps I looked more as though I were on my way to the theater than a funeral, but I thought white stockings wouldn't be much of an improvement. It would have to do.

While I was looking up the Callahan Funeral Home, the phone rang. It was Terry Finchley from the Violent Crimes Unit.

"Miss Warshawski! I've been trying to reach you the last few days. Did you get my message?"

I thought of all the ringing phones I'd let go lately and realized I hadn't checked in with my answering service for some time. "Sorry, Detective. What's up? Any new evidence linking me to the Prairie Shores or Indiana Arms fires?"

I thought I heard him sigh. "Don't make my life harder than it is, Vic, okay?"

"Okay, Terry," I agreed meekly. "To what do I owe the pleasure of hearing from you?"

"I—uh—discussed our interview with the lieutenant. You know, the talk Lieutenant Montgomery and I—"

"Yes, I remember that particular conversation." I had sat on the piano bench with the phone book in my lap, but I stopped searching the Callahans.

"He, the lieutenant, Lieutenant Mallory, I mean, was—uh—quite astonished that Montgomery would suggest such a thing—linking you with the arson, you know—and he went and had a talk with him. I just thought you'd like to know that you probably won't be hearing from him again."

"Thank you." I was pleased and surprised, both at Bobby's going to bat for me and at Finchley's taking the time to phone me about it. That took a little extra courage.

"Well, check in with your service in the future—don't leave me sweating it out for three days. See you Saturday."

Saturday. Oh, right. Bobby's sixtieth birthday. Yet another item on my burgeoning to-do list—a present for him. I rubbed my tired eyes and forced myself back to the phone book. The Callahan Funeral Home was on north Harlem. I dug around in the accumulated papers on the coffee table for my city map. The address put it just north of the expressway there; it should be a pretty easy run across town.

I was packing up my good handbag when the phone rang again. I was going to let it go, but it might be someone else who'd been leaving messages for three days.

"Miss Warshawski. Glad I caught you in."

"Mr. MacDonald." I sat back down on the piano bench in astonishment. "What a surprise. I'm sorry I haven't sent you a note yet for the flowers—I'm moving a little slowly with my convalescence."

"That's not what I hear, young lady—I hear you barely rose from your sickbed before you started prancing around town prying into business that's no concern of yours."

"And what business is that, old man?" I just cannot stand being called "young lady."

"I thought we had an agreement that you'd leave Roz Fuentes alone."

I put the receiver in my lap and stared at it hard. It could only be my invasion of Alma Mejicana that he was referring to. But he couldn't know about that—my only link to them was a scarf that could scarcely be traced to me—no one had ever seen me wear it because I never did. So it was my trip to the construction site. But what was his connection with Alma Mejicana that he'd know about that so fast?

"Are you there?" His voice came scratchily from my lap.

I put the receiver back to my face. "Yeah, I'm here but I'm not with you. I don't know what I've done that you think is harassing Roz. And I don't know why you're so protective of her, anyway."

He laughed a little. "Come, come, young la—Miss Warshawski. You can't go blundering all over the Ryan without people hearing about it. Construction's a small community—word gets around fast. Roz is hurt that you're looking at her cousin's business behind her back. She mentioned it to Boots —he asked me to take the time to give you a call."

"So all this stuff is going on at Boots's command? You work for him or something, Ralph? Somehow I thought he and the whole county were in *your* back pocket."

"All what stuff, young lady?" he demanded sharply.

I waved a vague hand. "Oh, arson, murder, attempted murder, that kind of thing. Boots says—go git me a dead alkie and you say, yessir, Chairman Meagher. And you find you someone to do it? Is that what's been going on around town lately?"

"That would be offensive if it weren't so ludicrous. Boots and I go way back. We're involved in a lot of projects together. Over the years the press has decided on a prolonged smear campaign about our relationship and business methods that *you* apparently have bought into. I'm disappointed in you, Vic—you seemed like a sharp young lady to me."

"Gosh, thanks, Ralph. And did you mastermind the fire that almost killed me last week? Was that how you and Boots decided to respond to Roz's hurt feelings?"

His breath came in a little hiss in my ear. "For your information, not that I owe you a *damned* thing, the report in the *Star* was the first I knew about that fire. And I'd go on oath with that. But if you've been treating other people around town the way you've been behaving toward Roz, it wouldn't surprise me that one of them tried to put you out."

"That sounds strangely like a threat to me, Ralph. You're sure, you're absolutely positive, that you didn't order that arson last week?"

"I said 'on oath,'" he snapped. "But if I were you, I'd watch my step, young lady—you were lucky to get out of that alive, weren't you?"

"No, I wasn't, old goat," I yelled, fear disguising itself as anger. "I was skilled. So go tell Roz or Boots or whoever is yanking your chain that I rely on my wits, not my luck, and that I'm still trucking."

" 'Bulldozing' would be a better word, young—Miss Warshawski. You don't know what you're doing, and you're liable to cause a major mess if you don't stop blundering around in the middle of things that don't concern you." He spoke in a crisp, no-nonsense tone that no doubt ended debate with subordinates.

"Is that supposed to make me snap a salute and shriek 'Yessir, Mr. M.'? I'm going to the papers with what I've learned so far. If I don't know what I'm doing, they've got the resources to look into it in a lot more detail." I wasn't going to tell him I'd noticed a striking absence of any minority workers at the Alma site—they could ship in a few dozen before Murray showed up with a photographer.

MacDonald thought this one over for a few minutes—it obviously hadn't been in the script when he called. "Maybe we can change your mind on that one. What would it take?"

"Not money, I can assure you." Or a new car, despite the ominous noises the Chevy was making. "But a complete story on Alma and Roz and what you all are so jumpy about could persuade me that you're right—that I don't know what I'm doing there."

There was another long pause. Then MacDonald said slowly, "We might be able to arrange that. Just don't go to the papers until we've talked again."

I ground my teeth. "I'll give you a day, Ralph. After that all bets are off."

"I don't like threats any better than you do." He gave a humorless chuckle. "And I'm not scampering around to meet your timetable. You'll wait until I have something to say and like it. And if you think you can go off to your friends at the *Star* or the *Tribune* in righteous indignation, just remember that both publishers are personal friends. It's time someone in this town had the guts to stand up to you."

"And you're just the man to tame the wild mare, Ralph? Maybe it's time someone taught you that playing Monopoly on Michigan Avenue doesn't mean you own the world." I slammed the receiver down hard enough to make my palm tingle.

35
DAUGHTERS IN MOURNING

One good thing about MacDonald's call—getting angry had given me an adrenaline rush. I felt charged with energy as I drove up the street to Belmont.

It was past eight now. The September sky was completely dark, and in the dark, chilly. I should have picked up a jacket on my way out, but I'd been too annoyed to think properly. Should have brought my gun, too, although I didn't think Vinnie would follow me around hoping to ambush me.

I made it to the funeral home by a quarter to the hour. It was a small stone building, with a discreet sign identifying it as a chapel. A few cars still dotted the parking lot when I pulled in. I jogged to the front entrance in my pumps in case they were going to shut down the viewing at nine sharp.

The door shut with a faint whoosh. Beyond a small vestibule with a place for coats and umbrellas lay a larger reception area paved in thick lilac pile. Dark paneled walls hung with a few pious prints created an atmosphere of heavy Victorian mourning. I found myself walking on tiptoe even though my shoes made no sound on the dense lilac. No one came out to greet me, but they couldn't have heard me come in.

A small square card behind a glass at the end of the reception room told me that the Donnelly visitation was in Chapel C. A hall to the right led to a series of rooms. I didn't check their labels, but went to the one door where light was showing.

A handful of women were sitting on folding chairs near the door talking, but softly, out of deference to the open coffin along the far wall. They looked at me, decided they didn't know me, and went back to their conversation. I recognized Mrs. Donnelly's daughters from the picture Mr. Seligman had given me, although I didn't know which was Shannon and which Star.

A man materialized from one of the corners. "Are you here for the Donnelly viewing, miss?"

He was short, and his plump bald head made him look about fifty. Close up, though, I saw he must be younger than I. I nodded, and he took me over to look at Rita Donnelly. They had put her in a two-piece dress, white with a tasteful pattern of blues and greens on it, and her face was as carefully made up as she'd done it herself the times I'd spoken with her. Dressing the dead for burial, from brassiere to panty hose, robs them of dignity. The makeup, including shadow and eyeliner on her closed lids, made it impossible for me to think of her as anything but a china doll on display.

I shook my head, which the young man took as a sign of respect. He led me back to the front of the room and asked me to sign the guest register. At this point one of Mrs. Donnelly's daughters detached herself from the chatting group and came over to shake my hand.

"Did you know my mother?" She spoke softly, but her voice had the unmistakable nasality of Chicago's neighborhoods.

"We were business acquaintances. She talked a great deal about you and your sister—she was very proud of you. Of course I know Barbara Feldman."

"Oh. Uncle Saul's daughter." Her blue eyes, slightly protuberant like her mother's, looked at me with greater interest. "She was too much older than us to play with when we were little. We knew Connie better."

Her sister, seeing us talking at some length, got up to join us. Even with them standing side by side I couldn't tell which was the elder—at thirty a year or two either way doesn't show the way it does when you're three.

I held out my hand. "I'm V. I. Warshawski, a business friend of your mother's."

She shook my hand without volunteering her name. The boorish manners of the younger generation.

"She knows Uncle Saul, too, Star."

That solved the name problem—I'd been talking to the elder, Shannon. "I know your mother hoped to get you involved in Mr. Seligman's business. Do you think you might want to now that she's—gone?"

I'd started to say dead, the real word, but remembered in time that most people don't like to use it. The two sisters exchanged glances that were part amused, part conspiratorial.

"Uncle Saul's been very good to us," Shannon said, "but his business is really too small these days. Mother only stayed on there out of affection for him. There really wasn't even enough for her to do."

I wasn't sure what I was after, but something had made Mrs. Donnelly not want me to show pictures of her daughters to anyone connected with the Indiana Arms arson. I couldn't ask them outright if they knew Vinnie Bottone, or if they were involved in arson for hire.

I tried a delicate probe. "But she got you interested in real estate, I understand."

"Are you a buyer?" Shannon asked. "Is that how you knew Mother?"

"Really more of a seller," I said. "Do you work for a firm that might be interested in buying?"

"I don't, but Star might."

Star blinked her blue eyes rapidly. "I don't really work for a real estate firm, Shannon, you know that. It's just a holding company."

"Farmworks, Inc?" I asked casually.

Star stared open-mouthed at me. "Mother must have really liked you if she told you that, but I don't remember ever hearing her mention your name."

"Word gets around," I said vaguely. "Was it through you that Farmworks hooked up with Seligman?"

"I don't think it's respectful to discuss business here at Mother's viewing." Star looked pointedly at Mrs. Donnelly's open casket. "You can come by the office if you want, but I don't think we do anything that you'd be interested in."

"Thanks very much." I shook hands with both sisters. "I'm sorry about your mother's death. Call me if I can do something to help."

I turned around as I left the chapel, hoping for signs of consternation, but the two had rejoined their small circle of friends. As I was wading through the lilac pile the bald young man caught up with me.

"You didn't sign the register, Miss—the family would appreciate knowing who was here."

I took the proffered pen. In a spirit of malice I signed "V. Bottone" in a large dark hand. The young man thanked me in a soft sober voice. I left him standing under a print of a Pietà.

It was ten by the time I got back to my own building. The Chevy behaved itself as long as I kept below fifty. Maybe nothing major was wrong.

It was kind of late for neighborly visits, but the lights were still on in Vinnie's living room. I ran up the stairs two at a time, changing quickly into jeans before racing back down again. On my way out I thought of my gun. If Vinnie really was a pyromaniac, it might be a good idea not to talk to him unarmed. I dashed back in, stuck it in my waistband, and took off again.

I was panting by the time I got to the bottom, but fortunately it took

Vinnie several minutes to answer my knocking. I was on my way to the lobby to ring his bell when I finally heard the lock turning back. He was in sandals and jeans with a Grateful Dead T-shirt—I hadn't known he could dress for comfort.

When he saw me his round smooth face puckered up in a frown. "I might have known it could only be you disturbing me this late in the evening. If you're trying to sell some coke or crack, or whatever you deal in, I'm not interested."

"I'm buying, not selling." I stuck my right leg between the jamb and the door in time to keep him from slamming it shut. "And you'd better have something very good to give me or the next people here will be police detectives."

"I don't know what you're talking about," he said angrily.

From the living room behind him a man called out, asking who was at the door.

"If you don't want your friend to listen to our conversation, you can come up to my place," I offered. "But we're going to keep talking until you explain why you were at the Prairie Shores Hotel last Wednesday."

He tried shoving the door against my leg. I pushed back and slid into the vestibule. He glared at me, his brown eyes tiny specks of fury.

"Get out of my apartment before I call the cops!" he hissed at me.

A tall young man came out of the living room to stand behind Vinnie, topping him by a good four or five inches. It was the same guy I'd seen getting out of the RX7 with Vinnie a week or so ago.

"I'm V. I. Warshawski," I said, holding out my hand. "I live upstairs, but I haven't had a chance to get to know Mr. Bottone very well—we keep pretty different hours."

"Don't talk to her, Rick," Vinnie said. "She pushed her way in and I want her to leave. She's the one we—the one who conducts her *business* in the stairwells at three in the morning."

Rick looked at me interestedly. "Oh! *She's* the one we—"

Vinnie cut him off. "I don't know what she's doing butting in here, but if she doesn't leave in ten seconds, I want you to call the cops."

"Do that," I urged with savage cordiality. "Only make it the Central District, not the local station. I want some of the guys who were at the Prairie Shores fire last week to come by and make an ID. Your friend Vinnie was there and I bet someone will recognize him."

"You're making this up," Vinnie snapped.

I knew I was right, though—the anger had gone out of his face and he was looking worried.

I pushed my advantage. "In fact, I bet they could match his voice with the one on the tape calling the fire into 911."

"You're lying," he blurted. "They don't make tapes of those calls."

"Sure they do, Vinnie. You gotta learn a few police procedures if you want a life of crime. What did you do—force Elena to phone me, then knock her out and wait for me in the dark? You call my name when I didn't see her right off?''

"No!"

"Don't lie to me, Vinnie—I can put you at that fire. The police have got you on tape. And Elena recognized you. She's run away again, but she described you to a friend when she saw you hanging out at the Indiana Arms.''

"I don't know who this Elena is!" he bellowed.

"You know, Vinnie, I think you ought to tell her what happened." Rick looked at me. "Vinnie thinks you've been harassing him. If you two are going to be neighbors the best thing you can do is clear the air between you.''

"Whose side are you on, anyway?" Vinnie muttered, but he didn't offer any resistance when his friend took his arm and gently propelled him back to the living room.

I followed. His apartment was pretty much a copy of mine in terms of layout, but his style—and budget—were way out of my league. The living room was done in textured contrasting whites. The long wall backing onto the stairwell was covered by an abstract oil in different blues and greens. That was the only color in the room—the bookshelves and coffee table were a clear glass or acrylic or something.

I lowered myself carefully into one of the low-slung nubby armchairs, hoping that my jeans wouldn't leave any telltale dirt streaks behind. Vinnie sat as far from me as he could get, in a matching chair near the front window, while Rick leaned against the wall near him.

"So tell me what happened," I invited.

When Vinnie didn't show any inclination to answer, Rick spoke for him. "This was a week ago tomorrow night, right? We were asleep—" He broke off to look at me guardedly, to see if I was going to scream and yell at this revelation. When he saw I wasn't reacting he went on.

"The dog was barking her head off—that woke us up. The bedroom is next to the hall, you know."

In my place it was on the outside and the kitchen was next to the hall, but they were reversed on the first floor because of the way the back stairs came down—I knew from all the times I'd been in Mr. Contreras's kitchen picking up the dog.

"We got up and saw you leaving. And Vinnie said it was the last time you'd wake him up in the middle of the night. He said you did something illegal and had the cops paid off but he was going to track you down, catch you in the act, and go to the police with hard evidence that would make them arrest you." He cocked his head on one side. "Just out of curiosity, what is it you do? You don't look like a dealer or a hooker.''

I couldn't help smiling. "I'm a private investigator, but that doesn't have anything to do with why I've been waking him up. Actually it's an aunt of mine—she got burned out of her home and came to me for late-night assistance a few times. But Vinnie reacted so violently I couldn't bring myself to confide in him. So what did you do when you saw me leave?"

"We got in the Mazda and followed you."

Rick had a cool poise that made me wonder what he saw in Vinnie. Still, it wasn't the first ill-matched couple I'd ever met. I thought back to my cautious approach down Indiana to the Prairie Shores. I didn't think I'd been followed.

"We waited on Cermak," Rick explained. Neither of us was paying any attention to Vinnie, who sat hunched inside his Dead T-shirt. "If you were really meeting a drug dealer, I didn't want to be caught in the middle. And that was the eeriest street I've ever seen. We drove up and down Cermak a few times; we saw you come down Indiana and disappear behind that building, the one that burned. So we turned up the street and watched and after about twenty minutes we saw the place start up in flames and some guy running off. That really freaked us, but we thought we'd better call 911. Is it true that they tape the calls?"

I nodded abstractedly. Of course this could be a romance cooked up to appease me, but it had the ring of truth to it. Vinnie looked too sulky, for one thing, and the bit about not wanting to leave Cermak Road sounded authentic.

"Could you describe the man you saw running away from the building?"

Rick shook his head. "It was dark and he was dressed in dark clothes. I think he had a leather jacket on, but I was too nervous to pay much attention. I'm pretty sure he was white; I think I saw the lamplight reflect off his cheekbones, but I'm not sure if I really remember that."

"Then you stayed around to see if someone came to put out the fire?"

He looked a little ashamed. "I know we should have rushed into the burning building to save you, but we didn't know what you'd been up to— whether you'd set the fire yourself, maybe you'd gotten out however you came in. And the fire got going fast."

"Because of the accelerant," I said absently. "But Elena told Mrs.—told someone that she'd seen the man who torched the Indiana Arms and that he had the most gorgeous eyes. And that's what she said when she saw Vinnie the first night she woke him up. So I thought maybe she'd recognized him and had been blackmailing him."

My voice trailed off as Rick began to laugh. "This is pure Restoration, Vinnie. Come on, lighten up! You think she's running a crack house upstairs all the time she's tracking you down as a pyromaniac. I want you two to shake hands and have a drink together."

Vinnie didn't want to and I wasn't much in the humor for it, either, but Rick went off to the kitchen and came back with a bottle of Georges Goulet. It seemed churlish not to have at least one glass. In the end Rick and I drank that bottle and part of another one while Vinnie stomped angrily off to bed.

36

TREASURE HUNT

I didn't have a clear memory of getting back to my own apartment. Ten hours later I wished I didn't have a clear sense of waking up, either. Someone was running an artificial surf machine inside my head. It swooshed and swirled when I tried standing. Even if I hadn't drunk the champagne, I would have felt awful—my hike around the Ryan had stiffened up my legs. My shoulders felt as though I'd spent the night on a circular saw. With the better part of a bottle swelling my cytoplasm, I wished I could spend the next twelve hours unconscious.

Instead I staggered into the kitchen looking for orange juice. The maid or wife or whoever looked after these things hadn't been to the store yet. I thought about going out myself, but the idea of being in direct sunlight made me feel so ill that I had to sit down. When the spasm passed I went into the bathroom, located the Tylenol, and took four, extra-strength, with a couple of glasses of cold water. After a long soak in the tub with the water as hot as I could tolerate, I shuffled back to bed.

When I woke up again it was past noon. I didn't feel like running a mile but I thought I could manage getting dressed and going to the grocery. When you feel really lousy, puppy therapy is indicated. I stopped at Mr. Contreras's to pick up Peppy.

"You look terrible, doll. You doing okay?" He was wearing a red shirt so brilliant it hurt my eyes.

"I feel like death. But I'm going to get better. I just want to borrow the dog for a while."

His faded brown eyes were bright with worry. "You sure you even oughta be dressed? Why don't you go back to bed and I'll fix you something to eat. You shouldn't of got out of the hospital so soon. I don't know what Dr. Lotty would say if she could see you."

I swayed slightly and caught hold of the doorjamb. Peppy came over to lick my hands. "She'd say I got what was coming to me. This is just cork flu —it doesn't have anything to do with my injuries, or at least not much."

"Cork flu?" He cocked his head to one side. "Oh. You been drinking too much. Don't do that, doll. It's no way to solve your problems."

"No, of course it isn't. Who should know that better than you? I'll bring Peppy back later."

I wobbled off with the dog while he was squawking righteously about how knocking back a few with the boys was not the same as me drowning my sorrows in whiskey, I should know by now it was bad for my system. Peppy was totally uninterested in these fine points of ethics, or the different morality prevailing for men who drink than for women. She was staggered that we weren't going running. She kept looking up at me to see if I was watching her, then looking very pointedly to the east to say we should be going that way.

When she saw it wasn't going to happen she took it like a lady, waiting sedately outside the grocery on Diversey and staying fairly close going home. She'd run half a block ahead of me, come back to see if I was still there, tree a squirrel a few yards back, then move ahead again. Back at my apartment she placed herself on the kitchen floor between the stove and the table. In my stupefied condition I kept stepping on her tail but she didn't move—what if some food fell?—she wanted to be able to get to it before I tripped on it. That's what a guard dog is for.

I squeezed some orange juice and fried hamburgers for the two of us, hers without rye or lettuce. The hamburger raised my blood sugar to the point that I thought I might even manage to live another few days.

I'd intended to go back to the Recorder of Deeds office to look up Farmworks; if it wasn't a partnership, I'd have to drive to Springfield to see whether they'd been incorporated. Halfway through the second bottle last night, though, as Rick described in hilarious detail the collapse of a set he'd designed for the *La Brea Tarpit Wars,* I'd remembered the Lexis system. If you had a pal who subscribed to it, you could find out who the officers of a closely held company were as long as it had filed to do business in Illinois.

I wasn't up to taking the first step, visiting the Recorder's office in the old county building, but I went to the living room to call Freeman Carter. He's my attorney, not exactly a pal, and he wouldn't get me the information for nothing, but it still beat driving to Springfield.

Freeman expressed himself pleased at hearing from me—his secretary had brought in the news clips about my near death. He'd been waiting for me to feel better before seeing if I wanted to start a civil action against anyone.

"You mean the way you have to do if the Klan murders your kid?" I asked. "What is it you do—sue for being deprived of your civil right to life?"

"Something like that." He laughed. "How are you feeling?"

"I'm coming along, but I was too ambitious yesterday—I'm not going out today. I was wondering if you'd do something for me."

"Maybe, if it relates to my proper professional role in your life and if it is very clearly marked 'legal.' "

"When have I ever asked you to do something illegal?" I demanded, stung.

He responded more promptly than I really enjoyed. "There was the time you asked me to give you financial details on one of Crawford, Meade's other clients. That's not only illegal but highly unethical. Then when you wanted me to get a restraining order against Dick you could hardly stand it when I turned you down. Then ten or twelve months ago—"

"Okay, okay," I interrupted hastily. "But those were all things I would have done myself if I'd been able to. Name something illegal I *wouldn't* do myself."

"I don't have that much imagination. And anyway, you wouldn't give away confidential client records to anyone. Probably not even to me. Still want to ask me something?"

"Just for some information out of Lexis." Peppy, giving up on the idea of more hamburger, started exploring the room to see who had been there since her last visit.

"You still don't have a computer? Christ, Vic, when are you going to join the eighties?"

"Soon," I promised. "Very soon. As soon as I get four thousand dollars that isn't marked rent or mortgage or insurance or something. Also I need a new car. The Chevy has ninety-five thousand miles on it and is starting to make horrible grinding noises at high speeds."

"Don't drive it so fast," he advised unkindly. "What do you need off Lexis? Just the officers of a corporation? Spell it for me, okay—one word, right, 'works' not capitalized. One of the paralegals will call you back this afternoon or tomorrow morning. Drink some chicken soup and get a good sleep."

The sleep idea sounded inviting, but first I checked in with my answering service to see how many people I'd kept hanging since Saturday. Lotty had phoned once, as had Furey. Robin Bessinger had called a couple of times.

Maybe Michael had some word on my aunt. I tried both the station and his house and left a message on his machine.

After hanging up I went to the window to stare down at the Chevy. The real reason I'd been skipping my calls was my aunt. Her condition had been pretty marginal when she left the hospital; every time the phone rang I was afraid it was someone with bad news about her.

If she did turn up alive, she'd probably need some nursing care. Maybe I could get Peter to shell out for it, but history didn't make me want to bet on it. Where would I put that kind of money together, though? You'd better not be blowing your transmission or anything really irreplaceable like that, I warned the car. 'Cause it's you and me, babe, for the foreseeable future.

At least I could call Robin. It might be that we'd killed the personal side of our life together, but I ought to be friendly—if I could only play the corporate politics right, I could turn Ajax into a major account.

Robin was in a meeting. With her usual bouncy good cheer the reception-ist promised to give him my message. I fiddled with the cord to the blinds. What I really ought to do was call Murray and talk to him about the lack of any Hispanic or black workers at the Alma work site, even though they'd won part of the Ryan contract because they were a minority contractor. But MacDonald had promised me more details about Alma and Roz and I thought I should give him another day before going public. Waiting wasn't my style, though. Why was I being so patient now?

"You're getting old, Vic," I told my wavery reflection in the window. "People didn't used to scare you so easily." Was it his phone call last night or my being trapped in the Prairie Shores last week? It had to be the phone call —I didn't have any reason to connect him with my near death. Except, of course, for the note he'd sent with his greenhouse.

Behind me Peppy was whimpering in frustration. I pulled on the cord to the blinds impatiently, then flicked them shut and looked to see whether she needed to go out. She came over to me, pawed my leg, then went back to the sofa, got down on her forepaws, and whimpered again, her tail waving gently.

"Whatcha got there, girl?" I asked. "Tennis ball?"

I lay down on my stomach and peered underneath but couldn't see anything. She refused to give up. Despite all my assurances that nothing was there, she continued her impatient mewing. Once she got going on something like that she could easily keep it up for an hour. I bowed to her superior concentration and hunted for my flashlight.

When I finally remembered dropping it with my other tools on the floor of the hall closet Sunday night, Peppy was still trying to burrow her way under the couch. I hoped she hadn't found a dead rat, or worse yet a live one. With some foreboding I got back down on my belly to peer underneath. Peppy was crowding me so closely I couldn't see anything at first, but at least no red eyes stared back at me. Finally I saw light glinting off metal. Whatever it was lay out of the reach of my arm.

"Naturally you've seen something that involves moving the couch," I grumbled to the dog.

When I pulled it away from the wall she danced hurriedly around to the back, tail wagging vigorously. She raced in front of me when the object came into view, sniffed at it, picked it up, and laid it at my feet.

"Thank you," I praised her, rubbing her head. "I hope you think it was worth all that effort."

It was a gold link bracelet, a heavy piece, big enough to be a man's. I pushed the couch back against the wall and sat down to examine the trophy. Two amethysts were set among the links. I turned them over but the backs of the stones hadn't been inscribed.

I tossed it from one hand to the other. It looked vaguely familiar, but I couldn't think of any recent male guests who might have lost it. What men had visited me lately? Robin had come over on Saturday but he hadn't gone near the couch. Terry Finchley and Roland Montgomery had sat there when they came to accuse me of torching the Prairie Shores Hotel on Saturday, but it was hard to imagine how they could have dropped it so it fell underneath. It would be so much more likely for something someone dropped to land in the cushions if one of them had lost it. Still, it wouldn't hurt to ask Finchley.

The only way I could really see it getting down underneath like that was if someone had been sleeping on the sofa bed—when it was pulled out there was a gap between the end of the springs and the floor. Guests of mine had occasionally forgotten a watch or a ring that they'd absently laid on the floor after going to sleep.

Cerise and Elena had been my only recent overnight guests. I thought I'd know if Elena had been carting around such a valuable knickknack, but maybe not. She could have stolen it, after all, hoping to trade it for liquor. Maybe it had belonged to Cerise's boyfriend and she wore it the way girls did when they went steady in my high school. Maybe I should drive down to Lawndale and show it to Zerlina since it was much likelier that Cerise had owned it than Terry Finchley. But would Zerlina know? And if Maisie was standing militantly in front of her, would she even say?

I was feeling better but not nearly well enough to deal with Maisie. Anyway, the bracelet was scarcely the most urgent item on the agenda. I stuffed it in my jeans pocket and looked down at Peppy's expectant face.

"You've been treated badly the last few days by the people who ought to be worshiping you. You'd like to go to the lake, wouldn't you?"

She thumped her tail happily.

37

HUNTING FOR RABBITS

I walked along the beach, Peppy dancing around me, dropping sticks for me to throw. It was almost October. The water had grown too cool for me, but she could swim happily for another month if we didn't get any heavy storms.

I ambled along to the rocky promontory jutting east into the water. When I sat to stare at the water Peppy jumped down the rocks to explore for rabbits. It was a pretty steep drop, but she occasionally found them burrowing in the boulders along the shore.

The water had a flat silvery sheen, a flinty shade that you don't see in summer. You can tell the seasons by the color of the lake, even if nothing else in the landscape changes. When it's calm the water seems infinitely enticing, offering to hold you, to caress you until you sleep, as though there were no cold depths, no sudden furies that could dash you helpless against the rocks.

It was helplessness I feared. A life like Elena's, bobbing along without any channel markers to guide it. Or my own the last few days, nibbling circumspectly at the edge of the dam but not daring to dive clean in. Letting myself wait on Ralph MacDonald, for instance. I didn't even know if it was out of fear of him, fear of his veiled threats I'd been doing so. Maybe I was just too worn by my aunt's recent escapades to have energy left for taking charge of my own affairs. It was an ego-salvaging theory, at any rate.

I should overcome my repugnance and pay some attention to Elena's problems, though. It wasn't fair to her or to Furey to just hand her affairs over to him. At least I could hunt out Zerlina to ask again if she knew anyone who would shelter Elena. My shoulders drooped at the prospect.

I could stop by the Central District to see if Finchley recognized the bracelet—and to check on whether Furey had turned up anything on Elena. If he hadn't, I'd organize my own search in the morning, maybe call in the Streeter Brothers to help out. And I could go see Roz—it was time I went on the offensive with Ralph MacDonald. Whether he was connected personally with the fire or not, he had something on his mind; I'd stood passively by far too long.

I stood up abruptly and called to the dog. Peppy gained the top in three easy jumps and danced around eagerly. When she saw we were getting in the car instead of returning to the beach, her tail sagged between her legs and she slowed to a painful crawl.

The Chevy was crawling pretty painfully too. I'd put in more transmission fluid, checked the oil, looked with a semblance of intelligence at the plugs and the alternator. Tomorrow I'd have to make the time to bring it to a garage. And make the money for paying a mechanic and hiring a rental car in the interim.

"Keep moving," I ordered the engine.

The top speed it allowed me this afternoon was thirty-five. I had to stick to side streets, irritating the traffic behind me by keeping below twenty. It took over half an hour to get to the Central District.

"I'm stopping here first because Finchley will be gone later," I explained to Peppy, in case she was accusing me of cowardice. "I'm still planning on finding Roz."

I went in through the entrance to police headquarters on State Street. If I used the station door around the corner, I'd have to explain my business to the watch commander. Of course there's a guard at State Street, but he didn't take as much persuading as a desk sergeant would—especially since he recognized my last name. He'd known my dad years ago and chatted with me about him for a bit.

"I was just a rookie then, but Tony took an interest in the young men on the force. I've always remembered that and try to do the same for the new guys coming up. And gals, of course. Oh, well. You want to go up to the lieutenant, not stand around reminiscing. You know where his office is, don't you?"

"Yes, I've been there hundreds of times. You don't need to call up."

Bobby's unit shared quarters on the third floor at the south end of the building. The detectives had desks jammed behind waist-high room dividers lining the fringe of the room while the uniformed officers shared desks in an open space up front. Bobby held the reins of command in a minuscule office in the southeast corner.

Terry Finchley was finishing a report, banging on a typewriter almost as ancient as my own. Mary Louise Neely, a uniformed officer who worked with the unit, was sitting on the edge of his desk talking while he typed. The typewriter was so noisy, they didn't hear me come in.

Most of the desks were empty. The shift changes at four, so roll call and assignments had long been disposed of. Five is a slow time in the crime world. The cops take it easy then, too, getting dinner or waiting for witnesses to come home from work or whatever else you do when you have a little breather on the job.

The door to Bobby's office was shut. I hoped that meant he'd gone home. I went over to Finchley's cubicle, interrupting Officer Neely as she was describing the interior of an XJS she'd chased down last night. I didn't know if it was the black leather seats or the three kilos of coke she'd found underneath them that impressed her more. Usually ramrod stiff, she was gesturing and laughing, a tinge of color in her pale face.

"Hi, guys," I said. "Sorry to butt in."

Finchley stopped his one-handed banging on the machine. "Hi, Vic. You looking for Mickey? He's not in right now."

Officer Neely retreated behind her colorless facade. Murmuring something about "putting it in writing," she marched stiffly off to the desks in front.

"Only partly—to see if he'd turned up anything on my aunt. She's been missing four days now, you know. I found something at my place this afternoon and stopped by to see if you might have dropped it."

"I didn't know your aunt was missing. The lieutenant must have given Mickey the assignment on the side." Finchley gestured hospitably to the metal chair by his desk. "Take a pew. Want some coffee?"

I shuddered. "My stomach isn't strong enough for the stuff you guys drink." I sat down. "I never saw Officer Neely look so human. I kind of wish I hadn't interrupted."

The policewoman was sitting at a typewriter clattering away with flawless precision, her back straight enough to satisfy a West Point inspection.

"She's the first female in the unit," Finchley explained. "You know how that goes, Ms. W. Maybe she's afraid you see her acting natural, you'll squeal to the lieutenant."

"Me?" I was outraged.

Finchley grinned. "Okay, maybe she's afraid if she acts friendly around you, the lieutenant will think you've corrupted her. You like that better?"

"Much," I said emphatically. I pulled the bracelet from my pocket and showed it to Finchley.

"I found it under my couch," I explained. "You and Montgomery are the only men who've been sitting there lately. I wondered if you'd dropped it."

Finchley looked at it briefly. "Ain't mine. That's pimp jewelry—I hate that kind of stuff. And give Monty his due, it's not exactly his style, either." He scanned my face. "I'll ask him for you if you like."

I hesitated. I hated to admit I couldn't stomach facing the arson lieutenant. On the other hand, how many difficult confrontations did I need to prove I wasn't a chicken? I accepted ruefully.

Finchley was sliding the chain through his fingers. "You know, this really looks more like—" He bit himself off. "I'll ask around."

"Can you just do it with a description? The other person it might have belonged to is the dead girl—the young woman whose family you helped me locate last week. I want to take it down to show her mother in the morning."

"Conscientious little thing, aren't you? You ever think of hiring someone to do some of your legwork for you?"

"Every day." I gestured toward Officer Neely's stiff back. "Maybe I should talk to her. The pay isn't great but it'd make a change from typing reports on cokeheads."

"Hey, if you don't have to type reports, start with me," Finchley protested. He made a careful note of the number of amethysts in the chain and handed it back to me. "I'll ask Monty and—and give you a call tomorrow if I can."

His phone started ringing. "Take it easy, Vic."

"Thanks, Terry. Can I use a phone before I leave?"

He picked up his own receiver and gestured to the desk behind him. I went around the divider and called my answering service.

Lucy Mott had phoned from my lawyer's office with information on Farmworks, Inc.; she hadn't left details with the answering service. Lotty had called. So had Robin.

I tried my lawyer first. Lucy Mott was gone for the day but Freeman Carter was still there, in conference with a client. The man answering the phone offered to take a message, but when I explained I was at police headquarters and couldn't ask for a callback, he went to get Carter.

Freeman thought I'd been arrested, of course, and wasn't too thrilled to learn I was just borrowing a phone. "It's that kind of tactic that burns your name around town, V.I.," he grumbled. "But since you've taken me out of my meeting I'll show you how much better my manners are than yours and dig the stuff out now instead of making you wait."

"I know you've got better manners than me, Freeman—that's why I always stand quiet and serious at your side when I have to go before the judge."

He left me dangling for five minutes or so. A few more detectives wandered in, people I didn't know who stopped to talk to Finchley and eye me curiously. Just as Freeman got back on the line Sergeant McGonnigal walked in. When he saw me his eyebrows shot up in surprise. He didn't wave or detour to see me but kept on his way to Mallory's door, where he knocked and stuck his head inside. I turned my attention to Freeman.

Farmworks, Inc. was an amazing company—it existed without officers. The only name associated with it on the Lexis system was the registered agent, August Cray, at a Loop address. Freeman hung up on my thanks. I sat with the receiver in my hand until the police operator came on asking if I needed assistance. I hung up abstractedly.

I knew that name. I'd heard it fairly recently. I just couldn't place it. It was too late to go traipsing over to the LaSalle Street address Freeman had given me. Anyway, I was too tired tonight to undertake many more errands and I kind of wanted to go see Roz. I'd get over to the north Loop in the morning. When I saw Cray I'd probably remember why I knew his name.

"Can I help you find something, Vic? That's my desk you're burrowing in."

McGonnigal's voice at my elbow made me jump. He was trying for a light note but his voice held a brittle undercurrent.

I held up a hand. "Pax, Sergeant. I wasn't delving into your deepest secrets. I came by on an errand and Detective Finchley told me I could use this phone. . . . Can't we go back to being friends, or at least nonenemies, whatever it was we used to be?"

He ignored the bulk of my comment and asked what kind of errand I had. I rolled my eyes in disgust but pulled the bracelet out of my pocket and went through my saga.

McGonnigal picked it up, then flung it to the desk. "We can go back to being friends or at least nonenemies when you stop playing little games, Warshawski. Now get lost. I've got work to do."

I stood up slowly and looked at him stonily. "I'm not playing games, McGonnigal, but you sure are. You little boys give me a call if you ever decide to let me in on the rules."

Officer Neely had stopped typing to watch us. "You get tired of the Boy Scouts, come see me," I said as I passed her. "Maybe we can work something out."

She flushed to the roots of her fine sandy hair and resumed typing at a furious rate.

38
RUNNING INTO
A CAMPAIGN

When I got into the Chevy, Peppy looked at me expectantly. I'd forgotten I had her. It wasn't fair to make her sit while I tried to track down Roz, but I was afraid if I took her home I wouldn't be able to goad myself back into action.

"Sorry, girl," I said, turning on the ignition. "Terry and John both know who owns that bracelet, wouldn't you say? So why won't they tell me?"

Peppy looked at me anxiously—she didn't know, either. A small procession of cars was moving north up State Street. I waited for them to pass so I could make a U. The tail of the procession was Michael's silver Corvette. I tried honking and waving, but he either didn't see me in the fading light or chose to act as though he hadn't. I could try to catch up with him to ask him about Elena but I didn't feel like running into McGonnigal again tonight.

I drove north to Congress. The potholes and derelict buildings gradually melted into the convention hotels fringing the south rim of the Loop. After I turned west on the Congress and speeded up, the Chevy gave an ominous whine. My stomach jolted again.

"Not at thirty," I lectured the car. "You gotta get me around town a few more years. A few more days, anyway."

The car paid no heed to me but increased its nerve-wrenching noise as I took it up to forty. When I brought it back down to twenty-five, the engine quieted some, but I really couldn't drive it on the Ryan. I left the Congress at Halsted and plodded my way north and west to Logan Square.

Roz Fuentes's campaign headquarters were in her old community organization offices on California Avenue. The front window held flags of Mexico, the U.S., and Puerto Rico, with the Mexicans on the left and the U.S. in the middle. Underneath the Mexican flag hung a huge portrait of Roz, beaming her two-hundred-watt smile, with the slogan in Spanish and English: "Roz Fuentes, for Chicago." Not original, but serviceable.

The office was still brightly lighted. We were five weeks from election and people would be working into the dawn at different headquarters all over the county. On top of that Roz was still functioning as a conduit for community problems with the city on housing and crime. According to the papers, that was a thorn for the alderman—a gent of the old macho school—but Roz was too popular in the neighborhood for him to try going head-to-head with her.

Beyond the plate-glass window people were working with the noisy camaraderie a successful campaign brings in its wake. A dozen or so men and women sat at desks in the big front room talking, answering the wildly ringing phones, shouting questions at each other in Spanish or English. No one paid any attention to me, so I wandered past the campaign workers to the back, where Roz used to have a small private office.

Another small knot of people was sitting in there now, a nice landscape of Roz's multiracial appeal: a white man of about thirty and two Hispanic women—one plump and fiftyish, the other not long out of high school—were deep in conversation with a wiry black woman in horn-rims. I didn't recognize the white man but I knew the woman in horn-rims—it was Velma Riter.

The four of them fell silent when I came in. Velma, who was seated behind the beaten-up desk in Roz's swivel chair, looked up at me fiercely. To call her expression hostile was about as descriptive as calling Niagara Falls wet —it didn't begin to convey the intensity she was putting out.

After a puzzled glance from Velma to me, the fiftyish woman asked, "Can we help you, miss?" She wasn't unfriendly, just brisk—they were conducting business and needed to get back to it.

"I'm V. I. Warshawski," I said. "I was hoping to find Roz."

The plump woman held out a palm toward the high school grad without speaking; the young woman handed her a typed sheet of paper. She scanned it and said, "Right now she's finishing a community meeting on gangs in Pilsen. After that she's going to Schaumburg for a fund-raising dinner. If you tell me what you need I can help you—I'm her chief assistant."

"You're not content with trying to stab Roz in the back—you're coming in here to put poison in her coffee, is that it, Vic?" Velma spoke up venomously.

The young woman looked flustered at Velma's open anger. She stood up hurriedly and picked up a stack of papers. Murmuring something about getting them typed before she went home, she excused herself.

"Are these people so close to you that you want me to talk in front of them?" I asked Velma.

"They know you've been trying to smear Roz."

I leaned against the door, my shoulders too tired to keep me upright without a prop. "Have you seen some kind of smear story in the papers or on TV that you can trace to me?"

"People are talking." Velma held herself rigidly. "Everyone on the street knows you want to stab her in the back."

"That wouldn't be because *you* told them that, would it, Velma?" I couldn't bear to look at her angry face; I turned my gaze to a peeling poster on the wall showcasing a quote from Simón Bolívar that proclaimed liberty for all peoples.

"Why don't you tell us why you've come, Ms. Warshawski? We're all close to Roz, we don't have any secrets from each other," Roz's chief assistant said.

I moved uninvited onto the metal folding chair the young woman had vacated. "Maybe first you can tell me your names."

"I'm Camellia Maldonado and this is Loren Richter. He's managing the finances for Roz's campaign."

Richter flashed a perfect Ipana smile. "And I can assure you there's nothing amiss with them."

"Splendid." I put my arms on the desk and propped my chin on my hands. "I'm really exhausted. If Velma's told you all about me, you know I almost died in a fire in an abandoned hotel last week. I'm still not quite over it, so I'm not going to make any effort to be subtle.

"Two weeks ago at a fund-raiser out at Boots's place Roz made a special point of taking me to one side and asking me not to sandbag her campaign. Since that was the farthest thing from my mind, I was irked to say the least. And it made me think she must be hiding some secret."

"If it was secret, then it was none of your business, Warshawski," Velma interjected.

I sat up at that. "She made it my business. She—or anyway, Marissa Duncan—got me to put my name to a public roster announcing my support. And I backed it up with more money than I gave to all other political candidates this year. If Roz was pulling off something illegal or unethical behind my name, I damned well did have a right to know about it."

I was panting by the time I finished. I took a minute to calm myself and focus my thoughts. Camellia and Loren were sitting stiffly, willing to hear me out but ready to slam the door on me as soon as I'd finished.

"When I started asking questions a long list of people began telling me I was a pain in the ass and to mind my own business. The first, of course, was Velma here, followed by Roz. And then, interestingly enough, Ralph Mac-Donald, the big guy himself—Boots's pal, you know—warned me off. A little more subtly than Velma and Roz, but a warning nonetheless. And after the fire he warned me again, this time not nearly as subtly."

Ralph's name took them all by surprise. If Boots had told Roz he was siccing MacDonald on me, she'd kept it to herself.

"Well, when I was at Roz's fund-raiser she had her cousin with her—Luis Schmidt—and Carl Martinez, his partner in Alma Mejicana. And it seemed to me that it was they who pointed me out to her, suggesting I was up to no good."

I stopped. Something in that picture, the scene of Wunsch and Grasso huddled with Furey and the two men from Alma Mejicana, was tugging at my brain. If I wasn't so tired, if Velma wasn't so hostile, I'd get it. It was because he'd been talking to Wunsch and Grasso that Schmidt warned Roz. They were all connected, Wunsch and Grasso, Alma, Farmworks. And Farmworks was connected to Seligman, through Rita Donnelly's daughter

Star. Did that mean that Wunsch and Grasso were connected to the arson? My brain spun around.

"We're waiting, Vic." Velma's cold voice interrupted my flurried thoughts. "Or are you trying to embellish your story to make it more credible?"

I gave a bitter smile. "I'll wrap it up fast. And believe it or not as you please, but worse is going to follow soon. Alma Mejicana was on the fringes of the construction business up until two years ago. They had a couple of suits against the county, claiming discrimination in the matter of bids, but they were strictly small potatoes—parking lots, a few sidewalks, that kind of thing. They really weren't big enough for the projects they were bidding on.

"Run the cameras forward. Suddenly they've dropped their suits and by a remarkable coincidence they pick up a piece of the Dan Ryan action. You've got to be a heavy roller to play at that table. Where did they come up with the equipment and the expertise?

"Now Roz is a partner in Alma Mejicana. I'm just guessing this part—" I ignored an explosive interruption from Velma. "I don't know whether she went to Boots or he came to her. But his support has eroded badly in the Hispanic wards. They've been backing Solomon Hayes to oust Meagher as board chairman. As long as they're going with Hayes and the blacks have a different candidate, Meagher can scrape by. But lately it's been sounding like the old Washington coalition is perking up again. And if the Hispanics got together with the black coalitions and united on a black candidate, Boots could kiss his forty years of power and patronage good-bye."

Velma was muttering to my right, but Camellia Maldonado sat with a look of glassy composure, much as an Edwardian lady might have watched a drunk in her living room.

Loren Richter was tapping his pencil rapidly against the chair leg. "That's not news. It's not even a crime."

"Of course not," I agreed. "Coalitions, changing loyalties, that's the name of the game. But Boots isn't ready to turn in his chips yet. So say he went to Roz. If he put her on the ticket, she'd bring in Humboldt Park and Pilsen for him—she's gold here. In return he'd see that Alma got a big piece of county action. They drop their discrimination suits, tie in with a dummy corporation, the work will really go to Wunsch and Grasso, who will share out the profits and everybody's happy. Alma doesn't do a lick of work on the Ryan—I've been there and seen it. They got the bid, they pay everything out to a dummy corporation, and let Wunsch and Grasso supply the equipment and the personnel."

"You don't have any proof of this, none at all. It's a total fabrication," Camellia Maldonado said hotly. "Whatever Velma said of you you're ten times worse."

I got up. "I'm not going to stay to fight it. I'm beat. I just wanted to give Roz a chance to answer before I go to the papers. There's one thing I don't understand, though."

"One?" Velma spat out. "Just one? I thought you understood the whole universe, Warshawski."

I ignored her. "I don't know why Roz thought a story like this would hurt her chances on the ticket. It's just business as usual in this old town. When the story finally breaks the good old boys will breathe a collective sigh that she's not a flaming radical, that she's one of them after all."

I turned on my heel, not listening to the three of them shouting at me. Camellia ran to the door on pencil-heels and grabbed my arm.

"You must tell us what proof you have of this terrible allegation. You can't come in here and drop such a bomb and then just walk off."

I rubbed my eyes tiredly. "It's all there. You just have to go to the Ryan and look at their part of the zone. Although maybe now they know I've been there they'll bring in a few minority or women workers for the photographers. But the real kicker is to visit their offices. They're a sham. There're only three desks occupied in the whole place. You don't run a big business out of a cubbyhole, at least not a contracting business."

Camellia looked at me with such anger that it made my knees feel wobbly. "I've worked for Roz's success for a long time," she hissed. "You're not going to be able to ruin her with your lies."

"Great," I said. "Then you don't have anything to worry about."

I glanced back at Velma, sitting in the swivel chair. She didn't say anything, but dropped her gaze to the desktop. Camellia followed me to the big front room. She was too savvy a campaigner to let the hired hands see a crisis was in the works. She shook hands formally with me at the door, gave me a big smile, and said she'd be sure to let Roz know we'd spoken.

39
DEATH RATTLE

When I got back to the Chevy I was exhausted past the point of feeling or thinking. In some recess of my mind I knew I needed to see August Cray, to try to understand the connection that apparently lay between Farmworks and Seligman. Even if it hadn't been too late to visit his Loop address I couldn't have gone—I just didn't have the stamina left to talk to anyone else today. All I wanted was to get home to a bath and my bed.

Peppy, curled in the front seat, gave me a look of disgust when I got in. She didn't deign to lift her head—after three hours in the car she didn't think I was good for much.

"Sorry, girl," I apologized. "We'll go home now, General Motors willing."

The Chevy was grinding horribly even at twenty-five. I forced it forward like a knight with a battle-shy horse. It went about as happily. With the car whining and screaming I couldn't follow the frantic line of thought I'd started at Roz's any further. Aside from the noise, I was too nervous that the car might stop altogether to be able to think about anything else.

When I turned onto Racine it went on me, going from a brain-shattering whine to a lurching rattle to a final dead silence. I turned the ignition key. The engine ground horribly but wouldn't catch. Behind me cars were honking furiously—it's well known that the best cure for a stalled engine is for a hundred thousand drivers to blow their horns in unison.

I was less than three blocks from home. If I could push the Chevy to the curb, I could leave it there for a tow truck and walk home with Peppy. Peppy had other ideas. When I opened the door she bounded across the seat divider and outside so fast I was just able to grab a hind leg before she hurled herself in front of a delivery van. I wrestled her to the ground and dragged her back into the front seat.

"You gotta wait five more minutes," I told her. She wasn't buying it. Usually the most docile of dogs, she snarled at me now and I had to wrap her leash around the seat divider to keep her in the car. She stood on the passenger seat barking at me furiously.

My legs had cramped up from tensing them so hard while I drove. When I stood up I almost fell over. I steadied myself against the car door.

"Neither of us is in very good shape, are we?" I murmured to the Chevy. "I promise I won't sell you for scrap if you'll do the same for me."

Cars were moving around me now that they saw I was stalled, but the ones farther back kept up their honking. I was too tired to react to the insistent blare. With one hand on the steering wheel and the other on the doorframe, I tried pushing the car to the curb. Too much strain in the last few days had left my shoulders so weak that I couldn't urge the extra force into them to muscle the car forward.

I leaned my forehead against the roof. Someone across the street was adding to the cacophony on Racine. I ignored him along with the rest until finally over the din of the traffic I heard my name.

"Vic! Vic! You need some help?"

It was Rick York, Vinnie's friend, at the wheel of a VW. I darted across the traffic to explain my plight to him. Vinnie was sitting in the passenger seat with his head pointedly turned away—he clearly didn't think Rick should have tried so hard to get my attention.

"Do you think you could push me up the street? If I can get it back to our place, I can leave it for a tow in the morning."

"Sure, just let me turn around," Rick said, in the same breath that Vinnie announced they were going to be late if they waited around any longer.

"Aw, don't be a turdhead, Vinnie. This'll take us five minutes."

I sprinted back to the Chevy, feeling refreshed just by an offer of help, and waited for Rick to come up behind me. Peppy didn't like this new development at all. She left off barking to leap into the backseat and whimper, then plunged back into the front seat. I undid her collar to keep her from choking, but she jumped around so much that I had a hard time keeping an eye on traffic at the intersections.

I coasted into an empty patch across from my building. Rick honked twice and took off without waiting for my thanks. In the morning I'd find out where he lived and order a bottle of champagne for him. His kindness took the edge off my fatigue, enough so that I was able to give Peppy her due and walk her over to the inner harbor and back.

When I finally returned her to Mr. Contreras it was past eight. He was beside himself: "Let alone I don't know if you're alive or dead, I don't even know where you've gone to come bail you out. And don't tell me you don't need my help. Where would you of been last year if I hadn't a known where to come hunting for you? Even if you don't want me, you might spare a little thought for the princess here. And when people come calling on you what am I supposed to tell them?"

I ignored the bulk of his diatribe. "Just say I'm a secretive bitch who doesn't give you a printout of my agenda every day. Who came calling?"

"Couple of guys. They didn't leave their names—just said they'd be back later."

His disclaimers to the contrary, my neighbor could identify any man who'd come to visit me in the past three years. If he didn't know these guys, they were strangers.

"Probably Jehovah's Witnesses. How'd you come to let them in? They ring your bell?"

"Yeah, they said they got the floor wrong."

"And the side of the building?" I asked affably. "Did they leave or are they still upstairs?"

His tirade changed rapidly to remorse. "My God, doll, no wonder you don't want to trust me with any of your secrets. Here I am falling for the oldest game in the world. They left, but what if someone else let them back in, that Vinnie guy across the hall or Miss Gabrielsen upstairs?"

Berit Gabrielsen, who lived across the hall from me, was still at the cottage in northern Michigan where she spent her summers. Mr. Contreras refused to listen to this idea but insisted on bustling me into his living room while he went up with the dog to check out my apartment. He wanted my keys but I resisted.

"You'll be able to tell if the locks have been tampered with. They're more likely waiting outside the door if they're there at all. And if they are, I don't want you waltzing into their arms—I don't have the energy to carry you to the hospital. Besides, my car is broken."

He was too agitated to pay any attention to me. If I'd thought there was really any danger I would have gone with him, but if my visitors had been sent by Ralph MacDonald they wouldn't come back when they knew they'd been ID'd. I let Mr. Contreras usher me into his badly sprung mustard armchair.

I leaned back in the soft musty cushions, my mind drifting on the verge of sleep. My neighbor's living room wasn't that different from Saul Seligman's —the same soft, overstuffed furniture, the same relics of their dead wives filling every available inch. And except for Seligman's fire irons, the relics were also remarkably similar, down to the studio photos of their weddings.

I felt a tender kind of pity for the two of them, each struggling in his own way to maintain the intimacy their wives' deaths had stripped them of. Seligman had accused me of being like everyone else, wanting him to sell his heart for a dollar, but I—

I sat up in the mustard chair. But I hadn't been paying proper attention to him. That was my problem. Someone had been trying to get him to sell the building. I hadn't heard that; I'd just been letting his plaints flow over me. Mrs. Donnelly knew, though, because it was Farmworks that wanted to buy it.

Her daughter worked there. To help boost her career she'd let them know the building might be for sale? Or she'd given them access to Mr. Seligman? At any rate, something about the sale, or at least about the fire, had brought that little smirk to her face because it reminded her of some special benefit to her daughter Star. But when she went to the man (woman?) she knew at Farmworks, worried because I had a picture of Star, he (she?) had killed Mrs. Donnelly and torn up the place to find any documents relating to their sale offer.

I got up and started pacing around the room, knocking my shins into a shrouded birdcage. Swearing briefly, I ran into the curio case Mr. Contreras kept in the middle of the room under an old bedspread.

Saul Seligman didn't have anything to do with the property management company anymore. He told people he went in most afternoons, but he didn't really leave his home to do much of anything. I'd never seen him with shoes on, only his worn bedroom slippers. Still, he hadn't given Mrs. Donnelly a power of attorney or anything. She would have needed his agreement to sell.

Whoever killed her had left him alone because everyone knew he wouldn't be able to make the necessary connections. He didn't have any documents—those had all gone to Rita Donnelly. She might even have portrayed him as mentally incompetent to her principals.

But why had they wanted the Indiana Arms? What was it about that building that someone cared so much about? It was just a derelict property in the decayed triangle between McCormick Place and the Ryan. Of course that was where MacDonald and Meagher wanted to put their stadium; if they got the bid, the value of any property there would skyrocket.

I came to a stop in front of the birdcage before I could bang into it again. I couldn't believe it. I couldn't believe I could have been so dense for so long.

Old MacDonald had a farm. Of course. He had damned near every other piece of land in Chicago, why not a farm too? He'd have a little holding company that could do deals on the side without drawing the public scrutiny that MacDonald Development inevitably attracted. And why not call it Farmworks? Just the name for someone with a macabre sense of humor. And if the Indiana Arms was the last, or one of the last, bits of property standing in the way of his development, then just burn that sucker down.

Wunsch and Grasso, they did a lot of business for the county. Ernie's daddy had grown up in Norwood Park alongside Boots and the two of them had just naturally kept in touch. Ernie and Ron had started out doing favors for the Dems—in Chicago that could mean anything from hustling votes to breaking the legs of tavern owners who didn't pay off the right people. So when they took over Ernie's daddy's business it expanded along with Boots's career. So if Boots and his pal Ralph wanted them to supply Alma Mejicana with trucks and compressors and manpower for the Ryan project, they'd be happy to help out.

"What's wrong with you, doll?" Mr. Contreras's severe voice behind me made me jump. "You know I ain't had a bird in there in ten years. I only keep it because Clara loved canaries. You thinking of getting a bird, don't. You may not think they need a lot of looking after, like the princess here, but you can't be gone all the time and have any kind of animal."

"I wasn't planning on a canary," I said meekly. "Anybody upstairs?"

"We went up outside your kitchen besides going up inside here, in case you wondered what kept us. Nobody there. Seemed to me someone might have been trying to get past those locks of yours, but they held okay. Maybe you should spend the night down here, though. I'm not going to be real happy wondering what's happening to you."

"I'll be fine upstairs," I assured him. "They know you saw them. They won't come back. Even if they could field a different crew, they'd be too worried that the cops would trace them through you. I'll lock all the bolts and tie a rope across the upstairs landing, okay?"

He didn't like it and went on at some length to explain why. I couldn't tell if he was genuinely worried or if he just wanted a bigger role in my affairs. Whichever it was, I preferred the possibility of a break-in to spending a night on his sagging couch under the empty birdcage.

"I'm sleeping in here, then, cookie. The princess'll bark if anyone comes in and we'll be upstairs in a wink."

I wondered briefly if they'd have a jolly confrontation with Rick and Vinnie in the middle of the night. It might be worth getting out of bed for. I thanked him gravely for his concern and made good my escape.

40

SCARED OUT OF HOUSE AND HOME

I turned on the bath when I got into my own place but my mind was racing too hard for me to relax. I got out of the tub and tried Murray. He wasn't in, either at the news office or his home. I thought about calling Bobby but I could just imagine his reaction. Accusations against the chairman of the county board and his wealthy sidekick? Much worse than stirring up the officers of his regiment. Just not done, Vic old thing—if you had a touch of class you'd understand.

I went to look out the window. Despite my brave words to Mr. Contreras, I felt lonely and vulnerable by myself. I wondered if the two men who'd come calling had indeed meant to waylay me or if they were, in fact, a harmless duo of salesmen. Were they the answer Ralph MacDonald had promised to give me within twenty-four hours? Was that man idling across the street really waiting on his dog or waiting for me to come out?

I dropped the blind and went back to the phone to call Lotty.

"Vic! I've started to become quite worried, not hearing from you for so many days. How are you?"

"I'm not sure. I've got a tiger by the tail and I don't think I'm quite strong enough to wrassle with it."

"What kind of tiger?" Lotty asked.

I told her where my thinking had been leading me. "I'm just a little scared, Lotty. And I keep worrying about my aunt. I think she must have seen whoever they hired to set the fire. She probably tried a little genteel blackmail, she and Cerise between them, and now she's hiding out someplace not very safe. I don't know how to find her. The cops are helping. At least a cop is helping," I amended, remembering that Finchley hadn't even known Elena'd skipped again. "And now my car is dead so I can't . . ."

My thought died and my voice with it. A cop knew Elena had done a bunk because he'd gone to Michael Reese specifically to see her. Just as he'd gotten me to reveal her address two weeks ago so he could go see her then.

The police didn't give two hoots if an aging drunk on her uppers tried to pick up young men in Uptown. Michael did.

McGonnigal's reaction to that gold bracelet came tumbling through my head and I saw it laid out for me in such complete detail that I thought my whole insides would come up through my mouth. I remembered now where

I'd seen it before, the time he'd worn it last February when I'd gone to a birthday party the pals had put on for him. McGonnigal thought I'd brought the bracelet around to flaunt my long-cooled affair with Michael. That's why he hadn't told me it was Furey's.

Only Furey hadn't left it at my apartment. Elena and Cerise had. The night they slept there they'd laid it on the floor under the mattress, the way people do. And in the morning, when Cerise was so sick, they'd forgotten it.

"Vic—what's gone wrong? You haven't fainted, have you?" Lotty spoke sharply; I realized I was standing like an idiot with the mouthpiece in my hand.

"No. No. I just suddenly am seeing something that ought to have hit me long ago."

"What you need most right now is a hot meal and a night's sleep. Why don't I come for you—you can have some soup and sleep in my guest room. Then tomorrow you'll have the strength to think of an advanced design in tiger traps."

It was so enticing an offer I couldn't turn it down, even as my mind was churning over Michael. I pulled my jeans on again and flung a few things into my backpack—including an extra clip for the Smith & Wesson.

The night Elena brought Cerise to my apartment was the night of Boots's barbecue. Michael had driven back to my place and was waiting for me there when I pulled up. He'd had a police emergency and couldn't stay, that was what he'd said. A triple homicide. I could check that sometime, if I lived past tonight, but I doubted it had ever occurred.

No—he'd gone into the lobby and found Elena and Cerise sitting there on Elena's duffel bag. They'd come with their tale of Cerise's baby, hoping they could use me to screw a little money from the insurance company. Then they'd seen Michael, put some heat on him. They'd seen him hanging around the Indiana Arms before the fire, had to be. He had the connection to Roland Montgomery. He'd be the one the pals would turn to when they wanted a building torched. Why the pals were involved I couldn't say, except that they did favors for Boots in exchange for contracts. And Michael did favors for the pals because they were all good old boys from the neighborhood.

So Elena recognized him when he came into the lobby after Boots's party. She told him she loved boys with gorgeous eyes and she wouldn't tell anyone she'd recognized him if he'd just help her out, give her a little something so she could buy a drink.

He gave them the bracelet, that was the payoff, but the next day he hunted out Cerise and took her to the Rapelec site, got her shot full of heroin, left her to die. No, that wasn't quite it. He'd gotten the heroin to someone—maybe to the pals or to their night manager. August Cray! The registered agent for Farmworks was also the night manager at the Rapelec site.

Anyway, Michael thought he could get the bracelet back but Cerise didn't have it. That was why Bobby's unit was there so fast once the night watch-man had spotted her—he had to be the first person to see her. Another police officer might be able to identify the bracelet if she had it on her.

But then? It didn't explain everything, but it made a certain amount of horrible sense. He needed to find Elena to get her quiet, too, but she'd skipped. When I told her about Cerise she'd hunted him out someplace and he'd said enough to make her know he'd killed Cerise. She'd run for cover. So his whole story about her trying to turn tricks in Uptown, that was made up. Bobby never asked him to find her. That was why Furey had made such a big deal out of my not calling to ask him.

My legs were cotton. They kept bending when I tried walking on them. I had to get to the Streeter Brothers fast—I couldn't leave Elena out on the loose for Furey to find and pick off at will.

I forced myself to wobble over to the phone. When I dialed their number I reached their answering machine. I left a message, trying to sound urgent without being hysterical, and gave them Lotty's number to use in the morn-ing.

When I'd hung up I tried Murray again; he was still out prowling some-place. I checked the street from my window. The man with the dog had disappeared. A few other people were strolling along the block, coming back from their workouts or heading for dinner. I didn't believe any of them were emissaries of Ralph MacDonald with orders to garrote me on sight, but I still waited behind the blinds until I saw Lotty's new Camry screech to a halt in front of my building.

Before going downstairs I called Mr. Contreras to let him know his vigi-lance wouldn't be required.

He was a tad miffed that I would sleep at Lotty's but not with him. "Anyway, just because you're not home don't mean someone won't try to sneak in to hit you on the head when you get back. I think me and the princess'll keep up our patrol anyway."

Calling to tell him my plans was the farthest I could stretch my humani-tarian impulses—I couldn't summon the courtesy to thank him for immolat-ing himself so unnecessarily. It's true he'd saved my life last winter, but it didn't make me any more eager to include him in my work. I trotted down-stairs, waved cursorily at the dog and Mr. Contreras when they popped their heads into the hall, and got quickly into the car. I hate feeling scared—it makes me run when I'd much rather be walking.

"So you've ruined that Chevy of yours with your reckless driving?" was Lotty's greeting.

I opened my mouth to retort, then shut it as Lotty made a rakish U in front of a *Sun-Times* delivery van. The driver braked so hard that a bundle of papers flew onto the sidewalk. Lotty ignored his mad honking and cursing with an imperiousness worthy of her ancestors—she once told me they'd been advisers to the Hapsburgs.

Lotty drives as if she were responsible for an ambulance during the Blitz

—she sees the roads filled with enemy aircraft that she's either dodging or beating to a likely target. She insists on buying standard transmissions because that's what she grew up with, but she strips the gears so mercilessly that this was her third new car in eight years. Like all rotten drivers, she thinks she's the only person who has a legitimate right to the road. By the time we'd gone the two miles to her apartment, I was thinking I should have stayed at home and taken my chances with Ralph MacDonald.

When we stopped the Camry hiccoughed softly—it knew better than to complain too loudly to her. I followed her meekly into her building, up to the second floor, where a brilliant display of color always knocks me back on my heels when I haven't been there for a time. Lotty dresses in severely tailored clothes—dark skirts, crisp white shirts or sober black knits. It's in her home that her intense personality emerges in rich reds and oranges.

Even though I've stayed there a number of times, Lotty always treats me as a real guest, taking my bag, offering me a drink from her limited repertoire. She almost never uses alcohol herself and keeps brandy on hand only for medical emergencies. I turned it down tonight—my stomach still had a strong memory of the bottle of Georges Goulet I'd put away last evening.

Lotty had a stew simmering on the back of the stove, some kind of Viennese dish reconstructed from her childhood memories. Hearty and simple, it brought back the comforts of my own childhood.

"You must have known I'd be coming when you made this," I said gratefully, cleaning the last carrot from my plate. "Just what the doctor ordered."

"Thank you, my dear." Lotty leaned over to kiss me. "Now a bath for you, and bed. You have black circles the size of craters around your eyes."

Before I went to bed she checked my hands. The blisters were a bit tender from my gripping the Chevy's steering wheel too hard, but they continued to heal. She put more salve on them and tucked me into her cool scented sheets. My last thought was that the smell of lavender was the smell of home.

When I woke up again it was past ten. The sun stuck little fingers of light around the edges of the heavy crimson curtains, striating the walls and floor. In the empty apartment all I could hear was the hum of the bedside clock, an oddly comforting noise.

I pulled on my sweatshirt and padded into the kitchen. Lotty had left a glass of orange juice for me and a note to help myself to food. My long sleep had left me with an enormous appetite. I boiled a couple of eggs and ate them with a great stack of toast.

While I was eating I tried to come up with a design for a perfect tiger trap, but as soon as I started thinking about Ralph MacDonald and Furey and the rest of the gang, I got too nervous for logic or design.

I wished I had the beginning of an idea of where to look for Elena. Maybe she did have some cronies who she could turn to when she hit the bottom of her considerable depths. If she had been in any of the other abandoned buildings on the Near South Side, Furey would have found her by now.

I got up abruptly. Maybe he had. He could have put a bullet through her or strangled her—her body wouldn't be found until the wrecking crews came through a year or more from now.

I went into the living room to use the phone and tried the Streeter Brothers again. The Streeter Brothers—Tim and Jim—operate a security firm called All Night—All Right. I've used them in the past when I had surveillance work too big for me to handle alone. Tim and Jim operate the firm as a collective with a handful of other guys, all big, all with beards. They move furniture as a sideline and most if not all of them spend their spare time reading Kierkegaard and Heidegger. They do a respectable job, but they also make me nostalgic for the dear dead days of yesteryear.

I got Bob Kovacki, whom I knew pretty well, and explained my situation to him. "I need to find her before this mad police sergeant does, but right now I've got a sickening idea he may have flushed her in one of the old buildings on the Near South Side and left her body there. I'd like you guys to look down there first, then we can go over some of her old hangouts."

"God, Vic, we're pretty booked now." I could hear him drumming his fingers on the desktop. "I'll talk to Jim, see if we can shift the schedule any. You going to be around this afternoon?"

"I may be doing errands, but I'll call my answering service every hour. Look—I—well, I don't have to spell it out for you. This is urgent. I know you'll do the best you can, though."

Once I'd arranged a tow for the Chevy I'd rent a car and go to the Near South Side myself. I called my garage and described what had happened. Luke Edwards, my mechanic, tisked lugubriously.

"Doesn't sound good, Vic. You shoulda called me when it first started making that grinding noise. You probably drove the transmission dry. I'll send Jerry over with the truck in an hour or so, but don't hope for too much."

I made a face at the phone. "Don't be so cheerful, Luke—you'll build up your endorphins too high and your brain'll blow."

"You saw what I see every day and you'd be sober too."

Luke always makes his garage sound like the county morgue. I gave it up and told him I'd be waiting for Jerry with the car keys. I quickly washed the dishes and made up the bed. Leaving an effusive note for Lotty, I hiked to my own home.

41
UNLIT FIREWORKS

I felt honor-bound to stop at Mr. Contreras's and inquire into any dark doings in the night. He was intensely disappointed—nothing had happened. Peppy had wakened him around three barking her head off, but it turned out to be just a couple of guys climbing into a car across the street.

I finished the conversation as quickly as I tactfully could and went up to the third floor. No one was lurking there. I called a small local rental company to arrange for a car. They had an '84 Tempo, no power steering, fifty thousand miles. It sounded like a clunker but it was only twenty dollars a day, including taxes, usage fees, franchise charges, and all the other items the big chains stiff you for. I told them I'd be by around one.

My long deep sleep had worked wonders on my sore shoulders. They were stiff but the needles of pain had gone. While waiting for Jerry I got out my small hand weights and did a light set of exercises to loosen them further.

The bright yellow tow truck finally honked in front of my building a little before one—I should have remembered the laws of relativity that apply to garage time and multiplied Luke's estimate of an hour by three.

I couldn't find my car keys. Finally I remembered stuffing them into the backpack, where they'd clattered against the Smith & Wesson. I picked up the whole pack and fished the keys out on my way down the stairs. Mr. Contreras stuck his head out the door.

"Just turning my car over to the tow service," I said brightly, waving good-bye. Sometimes it was easier to tell him everything than to fight him.

Jerry was a small, wiry guy in his late twenties. He owned a towing service but had a contract with Luke and did most of the garage's work. In his spare time he raced slot cars. We chatted a few minutes about an amazing race he'd won in Milwaukee the previous weekend.

"Let me see if she'll turn over this morning, Vic. Save you the price of a tow."

"The car's dead, Jerry. I had to push it the final three blocks home last night." Why can't a car jock admit that a woman might at least know whether her own automobile starts or not.

"Well, maybe we can jump it then. Just open the hood a minute, okay, Vic?"

"Oh, all right." I stomped ungraciously across the street and undid the hood release. It was already loose, which seemed odd. I wondered if I might have pulled it by mistake while I was fumbling around trying to push the car last night.

Jerry turned his truck around and backed up parallel with the Chevy. Whistling between his teeth, he pulled a set of cables from the back of the truck and came over to join me.

It was the looseness of the catch that made me look inside the engine before he hooked up the cables. Still whistling, Jerry was moving to attach one of them to the battery when I yanked his arm down.

"Get that thing away from the engine."

"Vic—what—" He broke off when he saw the twin explosive sticks laid near the coil.

"Vic, let's get the fuck out of here." He spoke with a casualness belied by his white face. He grabbed my arm and shoved me into the truck. Before I'd shut the door he was at the corner of Belmont.

I was trembling so violently, I'm not sure I could have moved without his pulling me. I tried to stop my teeth chattering long enough to tell him to get the police on his truck radio.

"We can't leave that bomb there for any passerby to touch," I said through clenched jaws. "We've got to get the cops."

His face was still so white that his brown eyes looked black, but he coasted to a stop in an empty loading zone near a hardware store. "I don't want to go near that thing again. Dynamite scares the shit out of me. Who you get so pissed off at you, Warshawski?"

While he dialed 911 I opened the truck door and threw up my eggs and toast in a neat little heap on the curb.

It was three-thirty by the time I finished with the cops. After a squad car duo had taken a quick, fearful look at the bomb, Roland Montgomery showed up with young Firehorse Whiskey, whom I'd seen briefly in his office two weeks ago. As the day wore on I never did get the young man's real name.

Montgomery sent for a bomb-removal team. They arrived after half an hour or so in something that looked like a moon mobile. In the meantime a half dozen more squad cars roared in to seal off the area. For a few hours the street had more excitement than it usually gets in a year, what with police cordons and lots of guys in space suits moving in on my car. The networks all sent their vans, and children who should have been in school appeared miraculously to wave at their playmates on the four o'clock news.

When he saw the TV crews pull up, Montgomery got out of the car where he'd been questioning Jerry and me and went over to talk to them. I ambled over to join in. He liked that so little that he tried grabbing the mike away from me when I started to explain how Jerry and I found the bomb.

"We don't have anything to report to the media yet on this device," the lieutenant said roughly.

"You may not"—I smiled limpidly for the camera crews—"but I'm the owner of the car and I have a lot to say about it. I think my downstairs neighbor heard them putting the bomb in around three this morning."

Of course they lapped that up and wanted more. There wasn't anything Montgomery could do about it. "It was the dog who really heard them," I said. "She probably saw them at my car—that's why she started barking. You can ask him all about it."

I gestured broadly at Mr. Contreras, who was standing on the periphery of the crowd with Peppy. Peppy bounded over to me while Mr. Contreras made his way to the eager reporters. Montgomery backed away from the dog and demanded I get rid of her.

"Don't shoot her, Lieutenant," I said. "It'll be on three networks all over the country."

Dogs make a welcome addition to any picture, especially a golden retriever as beautiful and heroic as Peppy. While Montgomery frowned horribly I told the reporters her name and got her to shake paws with a couple of them. They were naturally enchanted.

I fondled the dog's ears and listened to Mr. Contreras explain at excruciating length exactly what it was he'd heard and seen. He also told them how the dog had saved my life last winter when she found me bound and gagged in the middle of a swamp. I was glad I wasn't the one who'd have to listen to it all in order to find one usable comment.

Once the experts had removed the dynamite from the car and whisked it away in a special sealed container, the TV crews departed too. Montgomery's demeanor changed immediately. He sent Jerry off and informed me we were going downtown for a real talk. A trace of sadism in his expression as he took my arm roughly made my stomach churn. Mr. Contreras pawed anxiously at him, demanding to know what they were doing with me. Montgomery brushed the old man back so roughly, I was afraid he might knock him over.

"Take it easy, Lieutenant, he's seventy-eight. You don't need to prove you're bigger and more powerful."

"Bobby Mallory puts up with a lot of shit from you I don't have to take, Warshawski. You button up now and speak when you're spoken to or I'll have you in on an assault charge fast enough to make your smug little head spin."

"Whew, Lieutenant, you been watching too many Dirty Harry movies."

He yanked my arm hard enough to jar the shoulder socket and hustled me to the car. As he was pushing me inside I turned to scream at Mr. Contreras to call Lotty and get my lawyer's name from her.

Down at Eleventh Street, Montgomery took me to a small interrogation room and began demanding to know how I'd gotten hold of a supply of dynamite. When it dawned on me that he was trying to accuse me of rigging my own car, I was so furious that the room swam in front of my eyes.

"Get a witness in here, Lieutenant," I managed to get out in a voice below a scream. "Get a witness in here to what you're saying."

He swallowed a triumphant smile so fast I almost missed it. "We've got a pretty good case, Warshawski. You've been involved in two suspicious fires in the last month. We figure you for a sensationalist. When you couldn't get the kind of attention you wanted out of those fires, you rigged a bomb up in your car. All I want to know is where you got the dynamite."

I wanted to jump up from behind the table and seize his long stork neck and pound his head against the wall, but I had just enough reason left to know he was hoping to goad me over the brink. I shut my eyes, panting, trying to force my temper down—the first time I let it go he'd have me in the lockup for assaulting an officer.

"You've been hiding behind Bobby Mallory for years, Warshawski. It's time you learned to fight on your own."

I felt him moving toward me just in time to back my chair away. The blow he'd aimed for my head got me on the diaphragm.

"I presume this room is wired. Please let the record show that Lieutenant Montgomery just hit a witness in a bombing case," I shouted.

He aimed another fist at me. I slid from my chair under the legs of the table. Montgomery got down on his hands and knees to pull me out, shouting abuse at me, calling me names out of porn flicks. I scooted away from him. He went flat on his abdomen and grabbed my left ankle. I twisted away and got to my feet on the other side of the table.

Just as I staggered upright Officer Neely walked in. Her professional mask cracked at the sight of a lieutenant on his belly scrabbling around under an interrogation table.

"He lost a contact," I said helpfully. "We've both been down there looking, but he started confusing my ankle with his eyeballs so I thought I'd get out of the way."

Neely didn't say anything. By the time Montgomery had climbed awkwardly back to his feet, she had her face composed in its usual rigid lines. She spoke in a monotone. "Lieutenant Mallory heard you were questioning this witness and wanted to talk to her for a few minutes."

Montgomery glared at her, furious at being caught looking like a fool. I felt sorry for her, her career buffeted by being the wrong person to show up at a bad moment.

"I don't think the lieutenant here has anything else useful to say to me. He's got his facts without asking a single question. Let's go, Officer." Unfortunately I didn't feel sorry enough to keep my mouth shut.

I opened the door to the interrogation room and headed down the hall, not waiting to see what Officer Neely would do. She caught up with me on the stairs. I wanted to say something helpful and sisterly to her in support of her law-enforcement career, but I was too badly rattled to think of anything very chipper. She was looking rigidly ahead, making it impossible to know if she was embarrassed, disgusted, or just not very responsive. On the third floor we silently crossed the Violent Crimes area to Bobby's tiny office along the far wall. Officer Neely knocked and opened the door.

"Miss Warshawski, sir. Did you want me to take notes?"

Bobby was on the phone. He shook his head and motioned me to a chair. Officer Neely shut the door behind her with a sharp snap.

Bobby's desk and walls were crammed with photographs—pictures of yellow birds in flight, gap-toothed children grinning as they sported his dress uniform cap, Eileen hand in hand with her eldest daughter as a bride. He liked to shift them around every so often so he could see them with a fresh eye. Ordinarily I hunt for the shots of Tony or Gabriella—or even the one of me at five sitting on Tony's lap. Today I didn't really care. I sat gripping my hands on the side of the metal chair, waiting for him to finish his conversation. Next to Montgomery, Bobby was the last person I wanted to see today.

"Okay, Vicki, tell me what's going on and make it fast. I had a call from your lawyer, which is how I knew you were down here, but it doesn't make me happy to run interference for you with another man on the force."

I took a deep breath and came out with a tolerably coherent version of the day's events. Bobby grunted and asked a few questions, like how come I knew it was a bomb and how long it had taken Monty to get there after Jerry called in the report on his car radio.

When I got to the end Bobby made a face. "You're in an awkward spot, Vicki. I keep telling you not to play around in police business and this just proves my point. You came to me to get you out of hot water you boiled up yourself—"

"What do you mean?" I was so furious, my head seemed to rise a foot from my body. "I did *not*, repeat *not*, put that bomb in my car engine. Someone did, but instead of trying to get a description of the men who did it —who may have done it—from a pretty good witness, the police are trying to charge me with attempted suicide."

"I'm not saying you planted that device, Vicki. I know you well enough to realize you're not that unbalanced. But if you hadn't been playing around with arson and a whole lot of things I told you to stay out of, you wouldn't be in this mess at all."

He looked at me sternly, daddy to naughty child. "Now I'm going to use a few chips on your behalf, Vicki, with a guy who's not too easy to work with. In return I want you to promise me that you are not going to touch this business any further. Let alone the trouble you've got yourself into, since you started in on that fire three weeks ago you've got my whole unit stirred up. You were in last night with some damned piece of jewelry that has the boys in an uproar now. I just can't have it. Do you understand?"

I pressed my lips together. "I brought in a man's bracelet I found under my couch because I though Finchley might have dropped it when he and Montgomery were in last week. McGonnigal flipped out when he saw it because he knew it was Furey's and thought I was flaunting it at him. It was only late last night that I realized it belonged to Furey and came to see what it was doing in my apartment.

"He'd given it to Elena, Bobby, to Elena and the dead junkie you went to see at the Rapelec site two weeks ago. It was just a little extortion, something to keep them from reporting that they'd seen him—"

Bobby slammed his palm hard on the desk. One of the pictures teetered and fell over the side. "I've had enough out of you!" he roared. "That's a loathsome suggestion. You've been treated too easy for too long, that's your problem, so when things don't go your way you manufacture conspiracy theories. You ought to know better than that, than to come in here and try to lay that kind of sh—something like that on me. Now get out and go home. I told you two weeks ago to stop stirring up my department and I meant it. This had better be the last time I see you around here."

I got up and looked steadily at him. "You don't want to know what I've learned? If I'm right, Montgomery and Furey could be involved in one of the ugliest little scandals to hit this department in a long time."

Bobby scowled ferociously. "Spare me. I hear enough trash in here every day without listening to you fling garbage around about one of my own men. I've told you dozens of times that you're in a line of work that's bad for you, and this is perfect proof of it. You don't know how to reason, how to follow a chain of evidence to a conclusion, so you start making up paranoid fantasies. If I tell you I think you need a good man and a family, you get on your high horse, but women your age who don't marry start getting strange ideas. I don't want to see you ending up like that crazy aunt of yours, propositioning young men for the price of a bottle."

I stared down at him not knowing whether to scream or laugh. "Bobby, that psychology was old before you were born, the old repressed-spinster routine, and even if it were true, it sure wouldn't apply to me. I just hope you aren't laying that line on Officer Neely, or about the time I hit West Madison you're going to be facing a harassment suit so big it'll make your head spin. Anyway, if you have to think of me as a crackpot virgin to keep your faith in the department intact, remember when the pieces come breaking around you that I tried to warn you."

Bobby was on his feet now, too, panting, his face red. "Get out of my office and don't come back here. Your parents were two of my best friends, but I'd have broken every bone in your body if you talked to me the way you spoke to them, and look where it's led—how dare you talk to me like this. Get out!"

The last few words were on a crescendo so loud that they must have heard them on the street, let alone in the adjacent room. I managed to keep my head up and my steps steady and even to shut the door gently behind me. Everyone in the room turned to stare as I made the long walk from his office to the unit-room exit.

"It's okay, boys and girls. The lieutenant got a little excited, but I don't think there'll be any more fireworks this afternoon."

42

MOURNING BECOMES ELECTRA

I walked slowly up State Street. Anger dragged at my steps, anger and depression both. Someone laid a bomb in my engine and no one in the police department had tried to get a word from Mr. Contreras about the men he'd seen. Instead, Roland Montgomery assaulted me physically while Bobby did it mentally. Break every bone in my body. Oh, yeah. That's how you get people to stop asking questions and do as you say, you break every bone in their bodies.

I was angry with myself too—I hadn't meant to talk to Bobby about Furey until I had some proof. Of course Bobby wouldn't listen to me spreading stories about his fair-haired boy. It would be hard enough to get him to listen when I could really back them up. And even though I was furious right now with Bobby, I didn't look forward to bringing him that much pain.

Maybe I'd feel better for food. It had been six hours since I'd eaten and I'd thrown that up. I wandered into the first coffee shop I came to. They had a variety of salads on the menu but I ordered a b.l.t. with fries. Grease is so much more comforting than greens. Anyway, my weight was still down—I needed to pack a few carbs to build myself back up.

Because I'd come during off-hours they made up the fries fresh just for me. I ate them first, while they were still hot and crisp. Halfway through the fries I remembered I was supposed to check in with my answering service every hour to see if the Streeter Brothers could fit me into their schedule soon. I carried the last handful of potatoes to the pay phone at the front of the coffee shop.

I got Tim Streeter this time. "We can start for you first thing in the morning, Vic, but we'll need you to brief the boys, give them a description, and maybe show them the kind of place your aunt would likely pick."

My stomach fell. Morning seemed an awfully long time away just now. I couldn't protest, though—they were doing me a mighty big favor. I told Tim I'd meet him at the corner of Indiana and Cermak at eight and hung up.

Maybe it would still be light enough for me to do some hunting on my own tonight. I could stop at August Cray's office and then head home to pick up the Tempo. I called my neighborhood car rental. They closed at six but said they'd leave the Tempo out front for me with the keys taped underneath the front bumper. If someone stole it before I got there they weren't going to be out much.

I paid my bill—under ten dollars, even though I was perilously close to the upscale part of the South Loop—and took the sandwich to eat on my way to Cray's office.

The address Freeman Carter had given me for Farmworks was on north LaSalle. I took a bus up to Van Buren and then got on the Dan Ryan L—it would take me around the Loop faster than any taxi this time of day. It was just on four-thirty when I got off at Clark and walked the three blocks to Cray's building. I hoped someone was still in the office, even if Cray himself wasn't.

I was going against the tide of homebound workers. Inside the lobby I had to move to the wall and scoot crablike around the outgoing throng to the elevators. I rode in splendid isolation to the twenty-eighth floor and made my way on soft gray carpeting to Suite 2839. Its solid wood door was labeled simply "Property Management." They probably ran so many different little firms out of there that they couldn't list all their names on the door.

The knob didn't turn under my hand so I tried a buzzer discreetly imbedded to the right of the panel. After a long pause a tinny voice asked who was there.

"I'm interested in investing in Farmworks," I said. "I'd like to talk to August Cray."

The door clicked. I walked into a narrow reception area, a holding pen really, with a couple of stiff chairs but no table or magazines—or even a window for waiting customers to gaze through.

A sliding glass window in the left wall allowed the inmates to look at visitors without exposing their whole bodies. This was shut when I came in. I looked around and saw a little television camera in a corner of the ceiling. I smiled at it and waved and a few seconds later Star Wentzel opened a door next to the glass panel. Her blond hair was combed back and gathered into a jeweled white clip. She wore a long narrow skirt that highlighted her gaunt pelvic bones. She looked like a high school student from the fifties, not a participant in a development scam.

"What are you doing here?" she demanded.

I smiled. "I might ask you the same question. I came here to find August Cray—Farmworks's agent of record. And here you are, mourning your mother, but putting a brave front on it by coming into the office."

"I can't bring Mother back to life by staying home," she said pettishly. "I don't need you to tell me how to behave."

"Of course you don't, Star. Can we go inside? I'd still like to talk to August Cray."

"He's not here. Why don't you tell me what you want?"

This was clearly a rote line—she rattled it off without the hostility of her earlier remarks. I smiled.

"I came to invest in Farmworks. It's such an up-and-coming company. I hear they're going to get a huge piece of the new stadium project—I want to be a millionaire just like Boots and Ralph.''

She smoothed a hand over a jutting hipbone. ''I don't know what you're talking about.''

''Then I'll explain it to you. Let's go sit down—this will take awhile—your feet are going to start hurting in those spiky heels if we talk out here.''

I opened the door and shepherded Star into the inner office. It was a small room with a blond wood desk about the color of her hair. A couple of portables covered the top—one seemed identical to the Apollo I'd noticed in the Alma Mejicana offices on Sunday. Wood filing cabinets filled the windowless walls and spilled over into the narrow hallway. It was a working person's office all right.

I dumped a stack of prospectuses from a chair in the hall and moved it into the office while Star sat in her padded swivel chair behind the desk. Her mouth was set in a mulish line. I expect I looked about the same.

She lifted a thin wrist to examine a weighty gold timepiece. ''I don't have much time, so make your spiel and let me get home. My sister and I have to entertain some of Mother's church friends tonight.''

''It's partly about your mother that I came to see you,'' I said.

''You claimed to be a friend of hers but no one at the church had ever heard of you,'' she said sharply.

''That's because I only knew her in the narrow context of her work at Seligman. Since the fire at the Indiana Arms—I'm sure you know about that, don't you?—I'd been talking to her, hoping to get some idea about who might have set it. She obviously was sitting on some kind of secret. And that secret had to do with you or your sister. After I talked to you at the funeral home on Monday, I was pretty sure that you working here was what she was so pleased about—and so eager to withhold. And that's what I want you to tell me—why she couldn't tell people where you worked.''

A ghost of her mother's smug look flitted across her face. ''That's none of your business, is it?''

She said it in a saucy little singsong, the way young children do. It got under my skin, goading me to act like a child myself. I put both hands on the desk and leaned forward between the two computers. ''Star, sugar, I want you to be real brave about this, but you should know your boss killed your mother.''

Little red spots burned in her cheeks. ''That's a lie! Mother was killed by some awful mugger who thought the office was empty and—''

''And broke in and stole only the documents relating to Farmworks's offer to buy the Indiana Arms,'' I cut in. ''Come off it, Star. Ralph and Boots are spinning you a line. Your mother learned I'd gotten hold of a picture of you and she was afraid you'd get linked to the fire when I started showing it around. She went to Ralph and told him she was going to have to tell me all about his offer to purchase—she didn't want you taking the fall in case someone *could* connect you with that arson. And he killed her. Or he got someone to kill her. How bad do you want to protect those cretins? Bad enough to let them get away with your mama's death?"

"You're making this up! Ralph and Gus told me you might be around to harass me. He told me what you might insinuate. You think you're so smart, but he's smarter than you."

"Gus?" I started to ask, then realized she must mean August. "One thing's for damn sure—he's smarter than you! Don't you realize that I didn't *know* MacDonald was involved in Farmworks until you told me just now? It was a guess, but it sure was right on target. Shall I guess everything else that happened and you let me know if I'm right or wrong? Or do you want to tell me yourself?"

She pulled herself up in her swivel chair. "You'd better get out of here before I call the police. You're harassing me in a private office and that's against the law."

"Let me make another guess." I pulled her Rolodex toward me and started flipping through it. "You'll call Roland Montgomery's private number and he'll send some uniforms hopping to drag me away. And Star! What a coincidence! Here it is."

"I . . . uh . . ." She started a sentence several times but didn't finish it. "You don't have any proof."

"No," I had to admit. "It's just another guess. But he—or at least Farmworks—is at the center of a whole lot of different action that he'd just as soon the FBI didn't see. They're going to, though, Star, because the *Herald*'s going to print the whole story. And then the feds will come subpoena your files and they'll charge you with conspiring to commit fraud and arson and murder. And then you won't just be a poor little orphan, you'll be a poor little orphan in jail. Only if a jury hears how you let your own mother take the fall for you, they're not going to treat you like a helpless waif."

"Just because my employer tried to buy a building belonging to Mother's employer does not mean he killed her." Her voice was scornful.

"Ralph and Boots really wanted the Indiana Arms, didn't they? Really badly. I know about their stadium bid—that's not a secret. And it won't take too much work to do a proper title search for the stuff back there, so you might as well tell me."

She thought it over carefully, then finally conceded that Farmworks had been buying up property in the triangle behind McCormick Place and the Dan Ryan for several years now, positioning themselves for a bid on the stadium. The Indiana Arms was one of the few occupied buildings they hadn't been able to acquire. Star had been keeping Seligman's books for him at the time—she was a CPA. She thought he was foolish not to sell and tried to pressure him.

"He acted like that place meant more to him than his own children," Star said resentfully. "You'd think he'd of been glad to get what they were offering—it would have been so much better for Barbara and Connie than inheriting that run-down junk heap. Even after—after things started going really wrong, like when the elevators broke down and no one would come fix them, he couldn't see it was a losing proposition."

"It had some sentimental meaning for him. So what happened next? You went to August Cray and Ralph and said if they'd hire you, you'd keep up the pressure on Seligman through your mom?"

She tossed her golden hair scornfully. "They made me an offer. They could see I was good, that I was wasted in that nickel-and-dime place."

"What were you supposed to do? Forge a title transfer? Were you good enough to do that? Or just get your mother to keep the heat on the old man to sell?"

She smiled at me coldly. "You'll never know, will you?"

"But then Rita learned that Mr. Seligman had given me a photo that had you and Shannon in it along with his own daughters. And she came to you, panicked. She was afraid if I started showing it to someone who had lived or worked at the Indiana Arms that they would recognize you. What had you been doing down there? Sabotaging the elevators yourself? Or just guaranteeing that no repair company would come fix them? So you told Ralph your mom was getting cold feet and he did the only decent thing—he got someone to kill her."

She sucked on her lower lip, but she didn't shake that easily. "You're in here with guesses and stories. If that's your idea of fun, I'm not going to stop you."

"Yeah, they're guesses and stories, but they're pretty volatile. A more innocent woman might be hollering for cops or lawyers or witnesses or something. But you're taking it all in to see how much I know, aren't you? Well, Boots may have the local cops in his hip pocket, but I don't think he owns the FBI yet."

I got up to go. Star had a strange little smile on her face. "Of course you have to talk to them first, don't you? And even if Boots doesn't have much influence with the FBI, he can make sure they don't listen to you."

My stomach jolted a bit but I said calmly, "Oh, did Ralph and Boots tell you about their joke on my ignition? I found it and I'll be extra careful looking for others. I remember LeAnn Wunsch telling me what a kidder Boots was. I'm only just beginning to really appreciate it."

She barely waited for me to leave before she picked up her phone. I didn't shut the door all the way and stood with my ear against it. She asked for Ralph and said it was urgent and that she'd wait at her desk until he called back. I guess her mother's church friends weren't that important.

43
THE EYE OF
THE HURRICANE

I stood in the middle of LaSalle Street trying to quell a rising tide of panic. I needed some allies and I needed them fast. It was luck, pure and simple, that had kept me from disintegrating into my component parts today. If I had, Roland Montgomery would have closed the investigation for lack of leads—or painted me as a bizarre suicidal maniac. I'd miraculously sidestepped my fate, but it wouldn't be Ralph MacDonald's last effort to present me with his side of the story, as he'd put it on Monday.

Maybe I was jumping to conclusions in putting Ralph behind the dynamite in my car. Perhaps it was Roland Montgomery—he had ready access to all kinds of incendiary stuff. Or Michael, getting it from Wunsch or Grasso. Michael. My stomach twisted some more. He couldn't have tried to blow me up. We'd never been in love, but we'd been lovers for a brief sweet time. Can you want to think of a body you've caressed torn into jagged chunks of bleeding bones? Or did my rebuff make him want to see me so?

I shook my head, impatient with myself. This was hardly the time or place to sink into a melancholy reverie. I needed to get myself organized. The Smith & Wesson was in my backpack, that was one good thing. Of course I couldn't very well pull it out in the middle of LaSalle Street, but I didn't think anyone was likely to try to shoot me during the evening rush hour. I was just lucky that Montgomery had been so hot to get me in the interrogation room and break my jaw that he hadn't bothered with the usual formalities at the police station. No one had searched me; I hadn't had to surrender the gun and go through the tedious process of producing my permit and getting permission to pick it up again.

I needed to get to a phone but I was too scared of what direction MacDonald—or Montgomery—or Michael—might next attack from to go to my office. That was an easy place to lay a trap. For the same reason I didn't want to go home—or to Lotty's. If MacDonald's mind was running to dynamite, I didn't want him to kill Peppy or Lotty in the effort to destroy me.

I finally flagged a cab to ride the nine blocks to the Golden Glow. Sal would let me use her phone and I wouldn't mind a little Black Label to settle down some of the more extreme lurches my stomach was giving.

As the taxi wove recklessly through the end of the rush-hour congestion, it occurred to me that Ralph probably hadn't ordered the dynamite in my car. Most likely it had happened just like Becket—him running his fingers through his well-cut silver hair and asking tragically if no one would rid him of this meddlesome priestess. It's always that way, I thought bitterly, from Henry II to Reagan—your barons or Oliver North or whoever does the dirty work and you wrap yourself in a mantle of bewilderment and lawyers. I never knew about it, they misinterpreted my instructions.

"You say something, miss?" the cabbie asked.

I hadn't realized I'd been angry enough to mutter aloud. "No. Keep the change."

Murray Ryerson was sitting at the mahogany horseshoe bar drinking Holstein and talking to Sal about the upcoming college basketball season. Neither of them broke off a spirited debate about the NCAA sanctions on the KU Jayhawks when I climbed onto a stool next to Murray, but Sal reached behind her for the Black Label and poured me a glass.

Sal's cousin was taking care of customers at the tables. I sipped my whiskey without offering any opinion on Larry Brown's perfidies or Milt Newman's abilities now that Danny Manning wasn't leading the squad anymore. When Sal and Murray had run out of ideas on the subject, Murray casually asked me what was new.

I swallowed the rest of my drink and accepted another from Sal. "You almost got your wish to write my obituary today, big guy—someone laid a bomb across my ignition coil."

At first Murray thought I was joking. "That so? How come you're here to tell about it?"

"Really happened." When I got to the part where the head of the Bomb and Arson Squad refused to conduct a proper investigation, he shut me up and went to his car for a tape recorder. He was somewhat aggrieved at missing the story. He'd been at a conference out at the airport all day so he hadn't seen any of the wires or the sensational reports the networks were trumpeting.

I told him everything I knew, from Saul Seligman and the Indiana Arms to the little scam among Farmworks, Alma Mejicana, and Wunsch and Grasso, to Roland Montgomery's strange theory of me setting fire to the Indiana Arms and then blowing myself up in remorse.

When I finished Murray put an arm around me and gave me a sloppy kiss. "You're wonderful, Vic. I forgive you for holding out on me last winter. This is a great story. All it needs is a little proof."

"You don't call a hunk of dynamite proof?" Sal snapped a bottle of Holstein's down in front of Murray. "Her dead body would impress you more?"

"It shows someone wanted to kill her, but not who." Murray drank directly from the bottle. "You didn't copy any of the stuff you found at Alma's offices or at Farmworks did you?"

"I took notes at Alma's offices, but I didn't see any of the books at Farmworks. But can't you track some of this stuff down through Lexis and the Office of Contracts and so on? And get someone in the county to tell you what Roland Montgomery owes Boots? That scares me more than almost anything—you get a big cop dogging you and he can kill you or frame you or any damned thing he wants. I'm shaving my head and growing a beard until this sucker blows up big enough that I'm not the only figure tap-dancing in the spotlight."

Sal offered me the bottle again but I turned it down. I couldn't spend the night at the Golden Glow and I wouldn't survive if I left here too drunk to notice who was walking up behind me.

Murray went into Sal's private office to make some phone calls. It was too late in the day to look up any records in the county building, but he was going to initiate a more thorough search through the Lexis network than Freeman Carter had done for me—now that we were looking for a tie-in between MacDonald or Meagher and Alma Mejicana, Murray could ask the system to pull together combinations of names that hadn't occurred to me earlier.

"So what do you do now?" Sal asked. "Lay low until the storm passes?"

"I think I go home." I interrupted her voluble protest. "I know, I came in scared, crying for help. I'm still scared but—" I broke off, trying to think my inchoate feelings into a semblance of logic.

"It's like this. Now Murray has the story—he can get enough going by tomorrow even maybe to print something Friday or Saturday—if the *Star* isn't too scared of Boots and Ralph. So as soon as Boots and MacDonald see things are coming into the open, they'll be shredding documents like mad, be covering their tracks on the Ryan. They're probably rounding up a truck-load of Hispanic and black workers right now with documents proving they've been working there since the first of March.

"If they think it's still just me on my own, maybe they'll try to come get me. And then at least we can nail a few of them in the act."

"You and Murray?" Sal pursed up her face in high disdain.

"I'll do the story—Murray'll make the pictures," I said with a lightness I was far from feeling. "No. I think I'll be okay at home. I was panicking earlier, wondering if Ralph might dynamite the whole building just to get me. But really, he's much more likely to wait until I'm on my own and try something different. My old guy downstairs has been on all the stations talking about the men he saw yesterday—the pair who came calling on me in person and the pair who probably put the bomb in the car. So I can't believe they'll risk anything there again, at least not so soon." I hoped.

A couple of guys in business suits came in and sat up at the mahogany bar on the opposite side from me. Sal went over to fill their orders.

I played moodily with my whiskey tumbler. The one name I hadn't given Murray was Michael Furey's. It wasn't that I wanted to protect Furey, but I didn't have proof—just a string of guesses supported only by logic. His name hadn't even been in *Star*'s Rolodex.

Before I started my own offensive I wanted to know how deep Furey's involvement went with his neighborhood pals—whether he'd just put some of his daddy's life insurance money into Farmworks when they gave him the opportunity—or done more. Like maybe borrowed heroin from police evidence stores so Cerise could kill herself.

If he'd done something like that—I couldn't imagine trying to break the news to Bobby. I'd tried today without evidence. If proof came in—I shuddered. It just better not be me that lets Bobby know about it, that was all.

When Murray came out of Sal's office I went in to call Lotty to let her know what I was doing. She'd heard the story of my bomb from her clinic nurse, who'd called after watching the six o'clock news and was well and truly alarmed. She wanted me to come stay with her, wait in seclusion until the police caught my assailant, but when she heard what response they were giving me she reluctantly agreed I was making the right decision.

"Only, Vic—be careful, all right? I couldn't bear it if you got killed. Will you think of me before you stick your head in front of a gun?"

"Christ, Lotty, I'll think of me before I do that. Don't. Don't think I'm that careless of my life. I'm more frightened now than I can remember being in a good long while. If Bobby Mallory were paying the least attention to me, I wouldn't touch this business with a barge pole."

We talked a little longer. By the time we hung up I was close to crying. I got up slowly from Sal's desk and went back through the mahogany door to the bar. My palms were tingling with nervousness, but a warm afterglow from the whiskey kept my stomach in place.

The bar had cleared out. Sal was washing the empties as her cousin brought them in from the tables. She finished sticking a row of glasses in their slots above the bar and came over to me.

"You sure you want to take off now, girl?"

"Yup." I stuck my hands deep in my pockets. My right fingers ran into metal. I pulled out the Cavalier keys—I'd forgotten putting them there. The sight of the Chevy logo stamped into their heads increased my nervousness.

Sal isn't given to demonstrativeness but she came around to the front of the bar to hug me tightly. "You be careful, Vic. I don't like this at all."

"It's a far better thing that I do now than I have ever done," I recited in attempted bravado.

"If you die you're not going to land in a better place than you've ever been, so just watch yourself, you hear?"

"Do my best, Sal."

Murray offered me a lift north. "Then maybe I'll just cruise around the block every now and then to see whether you're still alive."

"Shut up, Ryerson," Sal said roughly. "Gallows humor isn't going down well tonight."

We stood awkwardly silent for a few minutes. A late customer came in, breaking the spell. Murray and I left while Sal stirred a martini for him.

Murray and I have a style of banter together that somehow precludes true intimacy. Tonight I was too nervous to respond in kind to his jokes. Too nervous to respond at all. I kept rubbing my palms dry against my jean legs and trying not to imagine what MacDonald might do next.

44

AN OLD FRIEND CATCHES UP

Murray dropped me at the neighborhood car rental. He waited while I checked the engine—whether out of courtesy or because he was hoping for another dynamite story, since he'd missed the first, I didn't ask. No one could have known I'd called Bad Wheels for a car; it was just my jangling nerves that made me look.

The Tempo's engine ignited with a lurching rumble, but no flames shot out from under the hood. When Murray saw I wasn't going up in smoke, he tore off in his battered Fiero, leaving me drumming my fingers on the wheel in indecision.

The sun had set. It would be light for another half hour or so, not really long enough for me to go hunting Elena with any confidence. If Michael had found and killed her, would it matter that her body lay waiting for me until morning? Of course she wouldn't be alone, exactly—there were all those rats I'd seen last week.

It made my palms and feet tremble when I remembered the little ball of fur I'd encountered groping for my flashlight in the dark. I drove home, parking on Nelson west of Racine and going down the alley to the back of my building.

Peppy set up a terrific barking when I came in the back gate. Mr. Contreras appeared at the kitchen door, holding her on a short leash with his left hand and carrying a pipe wrench in his right.

"Oh, it's you, doll. Gave me a start. I thought maybe someone was sneaking up on you."

"Thank you," I said meekly. "I was just creeping up on myself. I didn't want to be ambushed in the stairwell."

"No need to worry about that. Her highness and I are keeping a sharp eye out."

He let go of the leash—the dog was whimpering in her eagerness to greet me. Her tail was whipping up a great circle—not the portrait of a fierce guard dog. I kissed her and fondled her ears. She danced with me back to the stairs and clattered up with me, convinced this was the prelude to a major run. Mr. Contreras trudged up behind us as fast as his stiff knees would allow.

"What are you doing now, doll?" he asked sharply when he'd invited himself into my apartment.

"I'm trying to remember where I left my flashlight," I called from the bedroom. It had rolled under the bed, I finally saw. Peppy helped me lie flat to pull it out. She ate a Kleenex she found underneath and started to work on an old running sock half buried under the bedclothes.

"Yummy, is it?" I pulled it away from her and went back to the kitchen.

"I mean, where are you going?" the old man demanded severely when he saw me checking the clip to my gun.

"Just to see if I can locate my aunt. I'm worried that she might be dead and lying in one of those vacant buildings behind McCormick Place." Come to that, she'd left the hospital in bad shape—she could be dead without anyone lifting a finger to make it happen. Or lying there unconscious.

"I'm coming with you—me and the princess here." His jaw set in a stubborn line.

I opened my mouth to argue with him, then shut it again. Here was a perfect errand to restore his good humor with me—he could see the action without causing any major havoc. Not only that, Peppy could kill the rats. I accepted his escort graciously and was rewarded with a big smile and a resounding slap on my still-weak shoulders.

"Just don't swing that pipe wrench around," I warned him, locking the grate across the kitchen door. "You're under a peace bond because of that thing, remember?"

He slung it decorously through one of his trouser loops and headed happily up the alley to the car with me. All the way to Lake Shore Drive and the McCormick Place exit he kept up a happy flow of talk.

"You know, your Chevy's still out front with the hood up. Didn't no one want to touch it. I tried getting that young fellow, the one with the tow truck, to take it off, but he was too chicken. I said, 'Let me do it. I'll hook it up and drive it to the garage for you, you're too yellow to do it,' but he just took off like a bat outta hell, if you know what I mean."

"I know just what you mean." Besides having steering as stiff as an old-fashioned shirt collar, the Tempo roared rather loudly. Bad Wheels didn't pay much attention to exhaust systems—"Drive 'em Till They Drop" was their motto. The noise spared me most of Mr. Contreras's conversation until I parked on Prairie.

Peppy was thrilled to be part of the expedition. She strained at her leash, sniffing every pile of rubble, investigating trash heaps with the solemnity of Heinrich Schliemann. Mr. Contreras was only a hair less enthusiastic in commenting on the general decay around us.

"Been a lot of fires down here."

"Yep," I said shortly. Elena being a creature of rather tiresome habit, she would most likely select a place close to the Indiana Arms, as she had when she'd chosen the Prairie Shores. I was going to look at only one or two of these in the fast-fading light. The rest could wait until morning.

We went first into the warehouse two doors down from the shell of the old hotel. Mr. Contreras's pipe wrench came in handy in knocking out the boarding around the entrance—annoying, since it would make it impossible to get him to leave it at home in the future.

Once inside we let Peppy take the lead. She had a field day chasing rats. I kept my gun out in case one of them turned on her, but there were enough escape routes to keep them from becoming bellicose. After five or ten minutes of sport I called her off and kept her close to me while I explored what was left of the premises.

The interior walls had crumbled, making it easy to go from room to room without hunting for doors. Chunks of plaster lay everywhere. Wires dangled from the exposed ceiling studs. When I ran into one I let out a muffled shriek, it felt so much like a hand trailing through my hair. Mr. Contreras came stumbling through the rotted flooring to see what was wrong.

A giant tractor tire propped against one wall was the only sign that humans had ever been around. I guess it didn't even prove that—only that tractors had been around.

When we got outside it was dark, too dark to make hunting in rotting buildings very smart. And it was too evocative of my near baking at the Prairie Shores for my taste—my clothes were wet with sweat, my hands grimy from touching the decayed walls. I was glad I'd had the dog's support in the warehouse.

Even Mr. Contreras had been subdued by the expedition. He put up a token protest that we shouldn't leave now, just when we were getting our bearings. When I said it was too dark to look farther, he agreed readily, volunteering to return in the morning with the Streeter Brothers.

"Sure," I said heartily. "They'll love the help."

I returned the gun to the back waistband of my jeans and bundled him into the car with Peppy. On the way home he kept shaking his head and muttering comments that drifted to me only sporadically over the roar of the engine—he hoped Elena—roar, roar—not a place for a—roar—you really should do something, doll. I gave the car more gas to drown out what it was I should do.

I found a parking place on Wellington and left the Tempo there. I didn't want to make it too easy for anyone watching me to connect me with the car. I turned down the old man's invitation to dinner and headed up the stairs, shining my flashlight on the treads above me.

Furey was waiting at the top of the third flight. I dropped the flashlight and fumbled for my gun. When he launched himself down the stairs at me, I turned to race back down. Fatigue and injuries slowed me. He got my feet and grabbed my head in a brutal armlock.

"You're coming with me, Vic. You're going to kiss your aunt good-bye and then have a farewell party yourself."

He was sitting on my back. I tried twisting underneath him, biting into his leg. He yelped in pain, but grabbed my hands and cuffed them together. Seizing the handcuffs, he started pulling me down the stairs. I let out a great cry that brought Mr. Contreras and the dog to the door of their apartment.

"I'm going to shoot both of them, Vic," Furey hissed at me. "Interfering with the police in the performance of their duties. You want to watch? Or stop fighting and come along with me."

I gulped in air, trying to quiet my heart enough to talk. "Go in," I quavered at Mr. Contreras. "He'll shoot Peppy."

When the old man came into the hall anyway, brandishing his pipe wrench, Furey fired at him. The wrench flew to the floor as the old man crumpled. As we left I saw Peppy race over to lick Mr. Contreras's face. I was choking on my tears, but I thought I saw him put up an arm to pet her.

45

A WALK ON
THE WILD SIDE

Furey's car was parked halfway up the block. He jerked the driver's door open and shoved me across the gear box into the passenger seat. I flung up my cuffed hands to protect my face as I fell against the door. My left leg was tangled in the gear stick. I was twisted at an awkward angle, unable to kick at Michael when he thrust my leg onto the passenger side.

At least he hadn't bothered to pat me down. Maybe he didn't know I sometimes carry a gun. If I kept my wits, I might still be able to use it.

A handful of people were out on the street, but they turned studiously the other way when they saw me struggling against him—no one wants to be involved in domestic quarrels. I kept biting off the cry to call the cops. After all, Michael was the cops. What would the patrol units do when they showed up and Michael told them I was a violent prisoner?

"I'm not taking any chances with you, Vic—Ernie and Ron were right about you all along. You're not interested in the things a normal girl is—you just play the odds and wait your chance to jump on a guy's balls."

I leaned back in the leather seat. "You're so brave, Furey, shooting a man old enough to be your grandfather. They have special sessions on that at the Police Academy?"

"Shut up, Vic." He took a hand from the wheel and slapped my face.

"Gosh, Michael, now I *am* scared. You and your friends really know how to keep your women in shape. How about fastening my seat belt so I don't go headfirst through the windshield—you'd have a hard time explaining it to Bobby."

He ignored my request and took off with such a burst that I was flung against the leather. I squirmed awkwardly to fish the seat belt from where it was wedged against the door.

"They kept laughing at me, all the kowtowing I did to you—Ernie said LeAnn talked back to him that way just once and he taught her who was boss. That's what I should have done with you from the start. Out at Boots's barbecue they warned me you were acting sweet just so you could nose your way into our business. Carl and Luis took them seriously—but me! I just couldn't listen!" He pounded the steering wheel, his voice rising and cracking.

I finally managed to snap the metal tongue into its holder. "Three weeks ago, when you told me Elena had been seen soliciting in Uptown, that was a lie, wasn't it? That's why you were so insistent I not call Bobby to talk to him about it."

He turned onto Diversey and moved into the oncoming traffic lane to swoop around the traffic backed up from the light at Southport. "You're so sharp, Vic. That's what always attracted me to you. Why couldn't you be smart and sweet at the same time?"

"Just luck of the draw, I guess." I tried to brace myself against his sudden braking as he cut back into the right lane. "You said you had my aunt. Where did you find her? Down in one of those abandoned buildings on Cermak?"

He laughed. "She was right under my nose. Can you beat that? Right around the corner in my own neighborhood. Eileen had seen her and told my mother and Mother mentioned it to me at supper last night. She'd gone to hide out with one of her old cronies, but her thirst got to her—she just had to go get herself a bottle. I knew sooner or later, if she wasn't dead, she wouldn't be able to put up with that thirst anymore. I just didn't expect it to be around the corner from me. So I hung out all afternoon and sure enough, round about eight o'clock, there she came. I just helped her into the car. She tried sweet-talking me. It was loathsome."

He did sixty through the park to Lake Shore Drive. I suppose the beat cops knew his license plate, or at least called it in and saw it belonged to a detective. The local traffic didn't have that inside track and honked ferociously as they had to swerve out of his way.

"Was she loathsome because of her age or her drinking or both?" I asked.

"Women who think they've got sexual powers that they don't are disgusting."

"She appeals to some guys. Just because she's not your type doesn't mean everyone finds her repulsive."

He turned onto Lake Shore Drive so fast I was flung against him. When I was upright again I said conversationally, "Touching you seems loathsome to me, but I'm sure some women would disagree."

He didn't say anything, just took the Corvette up to ninety, diving in and out of lanes around the other cars, making them seem to stand still in a blur of light. I was afraid I was going to throw up when he braked into the curve at the Michigan Avenue exit. He slowed down then—the traffic was too thick for him to keep up so mad a pace.

"You're cracking, Michael. You're leaving a trail a mile wide. Even if Roland Montgomery's your clout in the department, he can't protect you from the mayhem you're manufacturing tonight."

In the streetlamps along the Drive I could see sweat beaded on his forehead. He made a violent gesture with his right hand but the car swerved; he fishtailed and got us back in our lane by a miracle.

"What is it that Roland owes Boots?" I kept my tone level. "And why did he get you to set the fire—why couldn't he do it himself?"

Furey bared his teeth at me. "You're not that fucking smart, Vic. *I* went to Montgomery. I found him for Boots. All he had to do was get me the accelerant and make sure no one investigated too closely."

"What a good boy," I said, marveling. "Is that when they gave you the Corvette?"

"You don't understand anything, do you? I was prepared—I was willing —you could have lived like LeAnn and Clara—had whatever you wanted— but you—"

"I have what I want, Michael. My independence and my privacy. You've just never understood it, have you, that all those things, those diamonds and stuff, just don't turn me on."

He got off at the Grand Avenue exit and whipped around the curves to the Rapelec complex. He parked the Corvette well away from the street, behind one of the wooden walls blocking the site.

He jumped out and came around to the passenger door. I had thought I might be able to kick him as I got out of the car but he'd handled a lot of rough arrests in his time—he stood well away from the frame and waited for me to wrestle with the seat belt and get my legs out myself. He put an arm around me in a savage mockery of chivalry and hustled me into the building.

I shivered involuntarily when we moved into the inky corridors. We were on the plank-covered ramp I'd walked three weeks earlier up to the management offices. Beyond the naked bulbs lay the gaping hole of the complex. I wondered where my aunt was, if she was still alive, what tragic end was destined for us.

Furey hadn't said a word since we'd gotten to the site. I began to feel boxed in by the silence as much as by my cuffs.

To regain my composure I said conversationally, "Was it because McGonnigal told you I had the bracelet? Is that why you came to get me tonight?"

He bared his teeth again in a violent parody of a smile. "You left your scarf at the Alma offices, Vic. I saw you unwrap it when Eileen gave it to you the day we met. You don't remember it but I do because I thought you were the hottest little number I'd ever laid eyes on. I do want my bracelet back, but I'm not in any hurry."

"That's good," I said calmly, even though my cheeks burned at the idea of being a hot number. "I left it in my apartment. You're going to need a wrecking crew to get in there. You don't get it, do you? Not even being a cop can cover your tracks for you when you've created this much carnage. Not even Bobby will do it. It'll break his heart, but he'll let you go."

Michael hit me across my mouth with the back of his hand. "You need to learn a few lessons, Vic, and one of them is to shut up when I tell you to."

It stung a little but didn't hurt. "I don't have a long enough lifeline right now to learn new tricks, Mickey, and even if I did, yours just purely make me throw up."

Michael stopped in the middle of the gangway and shoved me against the wall. "I told you to shut up, Vic. Do you want me to break your jaw to make you do it?"

I looked at him steadily, marveling that I'd ever found those dark angry eyes engaging. "Of course I don't, Michael. But I have to wonder if beating me while I'm defenseless would make you feel powerful or ashamed?"

He held my shoulder with his left hand and tried to slam his right into my face. As he came forward I kicked him as hard as I could in the kneecap, hard enough to break it. He gave a sharp cry and dropped my shoulder.

I ran down the ramp, terribly hampered by my bound hands. Above me I heard Furey crying out, and then Ernie Wunsch calling down asking what the fuck was going on. I darted into the shadowy interior, stumbling over boards in the dark. I was making too big a racket—no one would have any trouble finding me.

I stopped running and moved cautiously forward until I came to a big pillar, steel with concrete poured around it. I sidled around behind it and stood there trying not to breathe out loud, scrabbling behind me trying to reach my gun. My arms were crossed in their cuffs, though, and I couldn't reach far enough around.

A powerful flashlight stuck fingers out on the floor around me. I didn't move.

"Let's not play hide-and-seek here all night," Ernie said. "Go get the aunt. She'll flush her out."

I still didn't move. A couple of minutes later I could hear Elena's breathless voice, squeaky with fear.

"What are you doing? You're hurting me. There's no need to hold me so hard. I don't know how you were brought up, but in my day a true gentleman did not squeeze a lady's arm hard enough to bruise it."

Good old Elena. Maybe I'd find a happy death, laughing at her incongruous scolding.

"We have your aunt here, Warshawski." It was Ron Grasso speaking now. "Call out to your niece, Auntie."

He did something to make her scream. I flinched at the noise.

"Louder, Auntie."

She screamed again, a cry of genuine pain. "Vicki! They're hurting me!"

"We just broke a finger, Warshawski. We'll break her bones one by one until you decide you've had enough."

I swallowed bile and stepped out from behind my pillar. "Okay, he-men. I've had enough."

"That's a good girl, Vic," Ernie said, moving toward me. "I always told Mickey there was a way to manage you if he just looked for it. . . . Keep the light on her, Ronnie. Little bitch maybe broke Mickey's knee. I don't want her clawing at me."

He came up to me and took my arm. "Now don't you try anything, Vic, because Ron there will just start breaking your auntie's fingers again if you do."

"Vicki?" Elena quavered. "You're not mad at poor old Elena, are you?"

I held out my cuffed hands to her. "Of course I'm not mad at you, sweetie. You did the best you could. You were very smart and brave to hide so long."

What good would it have done to chew her out for not sharing the whole story with me from the beginning—or at least from her bed at Michael Reese.

"They hurt me, Vicki, they broke my little finger. I didn't mean to scream and make them find you, but I couldn't help it." Her face was in shadow but I sensed the tears beginning to fall.

"No, no, sweetie, I know you couldn't." I patted the thin bones in her hands. They were fragile, exposed, as easy to break as sticks of china.

Behind Ron and Elena stood August Cray, the night project manager. "What happened to your security guard? He not in on the kill?" I asked. "And I don't see dear little Star, either. She and I had such a nice chat this afternoon."

Nobody answered me. "We're just going to go for a ride, Vic," Ron said. "You take it easy. There are three of us here and we can make it mighty unpleasant for both of you if you try any of your cute tricks on us."

"Just three of you? What happened to Furey? Did I really get his kneecap? A shot like that takes a lot of practice." I was amazed to hear myself sounding as chipper as a cheerleader. "You know, if he's gone to the hospital, you've got a little problem—if my body's discovered with his handcuffs on, I mean—it's going to be awkward for the poor boy to explain that one away."

"You're not the only one around here with a brain, Warshawski, so don't get your underwear in a bundle over that one." Ernie's sharper voice came from behind me. "Mickey won't leave us holding the bag."

"That's right," I said approvingly. "You're all pals and pals gotta stick together, even unto death, at least the death of a whole lot of innocent bystanders."

"You're no little innocent, Vic, so don't get me shedding tears for you."

We got to the hoist and they bundled us in. Cray operated the controls while Ron and Ernie hovered close to Elena and me. I wished futilely that I'd learned enough Polish to do more than greet my grandmother Warshawski at

Christmas. I could have told Elena about the gun and gotten her to slip it out of my back before Ron or Ernie found it, but if I muttered the news to her, they'd hear me and disarm me.

As we rode slowly up my terror and helplessness increased. I could imagine our end, tipped over the side of the building, the accidental death of an unstable wino and her eager but unhelpful niece. I stopped trying to goad the boys with my bright chatter and slumped down on my heels against the elevator wall, my head in my hands.

"What's she up to?" Ron demanded.

"I'm sick," I groaned. "I'm going to throw up."

"Be my guest," Ernie said sardonically.

I made retching noises and collapsed on the floor of the hoist, clutching my stomach with my cuffed hands. Elena fluttered down next to me. "Oh, my poor baby, what would Gabriella say if she could see you? She'd never forgive me. I hope I don't go to heaven when I die, I couldn't bear to see the look on her face for knowing I got you into trouble like this. Come to Elena, baby, come here, Vicki, just lean your head against old drunk Elena and maybe you'll feel a little better."

I sat up and leaned my head against her shoulder. With my voice muffled against her scrawny neck, I told her about the gun. "Wait until we're out of here and in the dark, then pull it out and hand it to me."

Fear had sharpened her wits. She didn't give a sign of having understood me. "Oh, Vicki, yes, whatever you say, baby, just don't cry. That's a good girl."

Maybe she hadn't understood me. I wondered if I should try to repeat the message, but the hoist had slid to a stop and Ernie was urging me to my feet. Still clutching my stomach and moaning, I lurched on the way out and stumbled against the concrete.

We were on the open deck at the top of the building. Around us steel beams sent blacker fingers against the dark sky. We were up twenty-five or thirty stories. A stiff wind made the girders sway and froze my marrow. The sight of open air in all directions brought on a genuine attack of nausea. I fell down, almost swooning.

Elena was on me like a shot, weeping over her poor little Vicki. While Ron tried to wrestle her away her bony hands felt behind me for my gun. He pulled her up, but she had the Smith & Wesson loose and dropped it in front of me. The sharp sound of metal on concrete echoed a thousandfold in my ears.

Ernie and Ron didn't immediately realize what had happened. The only light came from the hoist. I could just make out the glint of the metal and scrabbled madly for the gun. I reached it just as Ernie yanked me to my feet. Fumbling it into my right hand, I slid the safety off with my thumb. I wrenched myself from Ernie and turned and shot him.

Cray was still standing in the hoist. When he heard the shot and saw Ernie fall, he closed the doors and started back down. Ron started dragging Elena toward the edge of the platform. I couldn't make him out except as a bundle of darkness moving along the paler sheen of the concrete. I forced myself to follow him, to fight down the spinning in my head, to place the muzzle in his back and pull the trigger.

A yard from the edge Ron collapsed, falling on top of Elena. I had never killed a man before, but I knew from the way his body lay, crumpled as a dark blob on the concrete deck, that he was dead. I couldn't bring myself to walk close enough to check—but what would I have done even if he had been alive? My hands were still cuffed and the hoist was somewhere below us.

My aunt began thrashing about, trying to move away from him. That finally brought me over to the body. Even a yard from the edge of the deck my head swam. I shut my eyes and managed to roll Ron from my aunt's torso. I brought her with me to the center of the platform.

Behind us the crane loomed up. The pale light of the midnight sky glinted from its long swaying arm. I thought of the hole underneath, going down thirty stories to the bottom of the elevator shaft, and shuddered.

Ernie was still alive. I'd shattered his shoulder. He was losing enough blood to want to get help, but he told me there wasn't any way to bring the hoist up myself. Ernie wasn't inclined to talk much. I tried asking him about his relations with Boots and MacDonald and why he and Ron did so much for them, but he told me I was a nosy interfering bitch and to mind my own business before it was too late. At the same time he was peeved with me for not climbing down to the ground—he told me they nailed ladders into the openings where fire stairs would eventually be poured.

"You could at least try to get some help," he complained. "You shot me —you owe me something."

"Ernie, sweetie, I shot you because you were going to throw me over the side of the building. I'm not climbing down thirty stories of ladders in the dark, especially not with my hands not working."

At that Wunsch cursed some more, this time at his partners. It seems Furey had given Cray the key to my handcuffs—he'd been supposed to undo me right before I went over—they didn't want to run the risk of not getting to me before some passerby did. "Now look at that jerk. Takes off and leaves us alone up here to die."

"I thought you were a real macho kind of guy," I said disapprovingly. "John Wayne would never have lain around pissing at how rotten his pals were just because he'd taken a bullet."

Ernie swore at me, then asked me to take off my sweatshirt to wrap him up, he was getting so cold with blood loss.

"Ernie, I can't get it over my hands. Remember? They're locked together. Anyway, I don't want to hang around up here all night with nothing but a bra between me and the cold cruel wind."

Ernie flung a few more unimaginative epithets at me, then lapsed into silence. I wished Elena would too. Playing a heroine's role for once in her life, my aunt grew loquacious. She went on as though shot full of pentobarbital, talking about her childhood, her quarrels with her mother, what Tony —my father—said when he cut all the hair off her dolls when she was eight.

After a while I thought I might scream at the emotional, inconsequential torrent. Ernie found it so intolerable, he demanded I shut her up.

"She's driving me round the bend with that drivel," he announced. In his own living room this probably got instant results. I could picture LeAnn giggling and saying, "You're so cute, Ernie," but taking her offending friends or children or mother off to the kitchen. I wondered what LeAnn and Clara would do now.

"She's not doing anything to you, Ernie. Listen to her—it'll take your mind off your troubles." I asked Elena to repeat a particularly tangled narrative involving my uncle Peter, a dog, and the neighbor's flower garden.

I don't know how much time passed that way when I heard the hoist returning. It can't have been long, but in the dark, surrounded by the wounded and the babbling, it felt like hours.

I persuaded Elena to stop talking and move with me behind one of the girders. "Just be quiet, Auntie. They may have come back to shoot us and we don't want to give them any help finding us."

"Sure, Vicki. You know what you're doing. Whatever you say. I was never so scared in my life as I was when that boy with the gorgeous eyes picked me up at the liquor store—"

I put a hand over her mouth. "Shut up, darling, for now. You can tell me about it later."

The hoist groaned to a stop. My hands were thick with cold. I was having trouble remembering which was the right and which the left. I counted painfully in my head, trying to figure out how many shots were in the clip. I tried to subdue the tremor in my right hand so I could make all of them count.

I waited for the noise of doors opening or feet on concrete. When a minute had gone by with no sound, I peered around the edge of the pillar. I couldn't see the box-like car inside the frame. Over the wind in the girders and Elena's nervous whispers, I strained to hear. Finally I moved away from her in the dark, ignoring her piteous cry.

To my left I suddenly saw a bobbing point of light. I moved toward it cautiously, keeping my weight on my back foot with each step until I was certain I hadn't come to some unexpected hole.

The light flickered again and went out. Ernie had mentioned a ladder in the stairwell opening. This must be Cray or some other confederate hoping to climb up and surprise us from behind.

My eyes were so accustomed to the dark that I saw the stairwell opening loom in front of me as a darker patch in the black night. I lay on my stomach and watched until the black changed again, a blob crawling up the side to the top. When a hand emerged on the deck I smashed the butt of the Smith & Wesson into it with all my strength.

Cray cried out but leaned against the ladder and brought his other hand up and fired. The bullet went wide in the night but I slid back, away from the opening, as he hoisted himself one-handed to the deck.

I aimed at the dark shape in front of me and fired. Lying awkwardly as I was, the recoil wrenched my right shoulder. I fell over but managed to hang on to the gun. Light shone on me, blinding me, and I rolled instinctively as he shot.

Somehow I managed to get to my feet and around behind one of the girders. Cray kept the light on for a moment but realized when I fired again that it made him as much a target as it did me. When the light went out I dropped to my knees and elbows and scooted to the next girder. I stopped there and listened. Elena had started talking again, in an undertone, the sound just audible above the wind.

"You can get the old woman, Cray," Ernie called in the thread of a voice. "She's jabbering away over here. You can find her by the babble."

Elena whimpered but couldn't make herself shut up.

"You still there, Wunsch?" Cray shouted back. "Keep the faith—I'll have you down in no time."

Cray started circling around behind me in the dark. I couldn't keep track of where he was. I was tired and disoriented and I clung to my girder without trying to figure out his next move. Suddenly he gave a cry, a scream of such panic that my heart thudded violently.

"What happened? Where are you?" Ernie called out.

From the middle of the deck I could hear Cray screaming, his voice muffled, coming from a distance. He had fallen down the opening for the crane, but the safety nets around it had saved him.

46

ON THE SCALES OF JUSTICE

I have a hard time remembering what remained of the night. I managed somehow to climb down the slats connecting the deck to the floor below. My arms trembled so violently that I don't know how I made it— more by will than by muscle. And I got the hoist up, after a painful round of trial and error. It wasn't easy to run at the best of times; with one hand it was pure bloody hell. And I got Elena and Ernie into the cage and lowered us down to the ground.

Furey was waiting there but he'd been joined by some uniformed cops. A passing blue-and-white had heard the gunshots and swung over to the site. They were keeping Furey company until the hoist came down. I spent a good chunk of what was left of the night in a lockup at Eleventh Street—I was in cuffs and Furey persuaded the uniformed boys that I'd resisted arrest.

Furey went off to the hospital to get his knee attended to. He had bravely stayed at the construction site in excruciating pain waiting for his pals to come down—it was just his bad luck that the patrol car had shown up first.

I couldn't get the cops who were holding me to understand that another man was on top of the building, in the nets around the crane, and that he had the key to my handcuffs. After a while I gave up trying. I didn't say anything at all except to tell them my name. When they shut the lockup on me I lay on the floor and went to sleep, oblivious to the clamor of the drunks around me.

They got me up about a couple of hours later. I was so sleepy and disoriented, I didn't even try to ask where we were going—I assumed it was for early morning court calls. Instead they hustled me to the third floor, to the Violent Crimes area, to the corner office where Bobby Mallory was sitting behind his desk. His eyes were red from lack of sleep, but he'd shaved and his tie was neatly knotted.

"Is there some reason she's still in cuffs?" Bobby asked.

The men who'd escorted me didn't know anything about it. They said they'd been told I was dangerous and to leave me locked up.

"Well, get them off before I make a report to your commander."

He didn't speak again until they'd found a key that would work on those cuffs. When I was free, rubbing my sore arms, he laced into me with scorching bitterness. He went on and on about me playing at police, ruining his best men, screwing up his department until nobody knew what he was supposed to be doing. I let it wash over me, too tired, in too much pain, too overwhelmed by his fury, to try to form a response. When he'd finally exhausted himself he sat still, tears coursing down his ruddy face.

"May I go now?" I asked in a thread of a voice. "Or am I still facing charges?"

"Go. Go." The word was a hoarse squawk. He covered his face with his right hand and shoved the left in the air as if to drive me from the room.

"The boys here wouldn't listen to me, but there's a man named Cray trapped at the top of the Rapelec building. He fell into the nets around the crane." I stood up. "Can you tell me where my aunt is?"

"Leave, Vicki. I can't stand the sound of your voice tonight."

When I left his office and got to the Eleventh Street entrance, Lotty was waiting for me. I fell into her arms, beyond surprise or question.

47 IN LOTTY'S NEST

Lotty took the day off on Thursday to look after me. She wouldn't let anyone near me, not Murray nor the networks, not even the federal district attorney. Good Republican appointee that he was, he was slobbering at the possibility of bringing down the Democratic county chairman. With her characteristic flair for detail, Lotty called my answering service and told them to switch calls for me through to her—but she wouldn't let me take any.

When I woke up finally around five I remembered Mr. Contreras. Lotty bundled me into some blankets on the daybed in her living room and insisted I eat some soup before she told me her end of the adventure.

The shot and our scuffle had brought Vinnie and Rick York to the hall. They'd been busy in the back bedroom or they might have arrived soon enough to help out—or maybe to get shot themselves. Anyway, Mr. Contreras had taken the bullet in his shoulder and was able to give Rick Lotty's number.

"He's all right," Lotty assured me. "It would take more than a broken shoulder to stop him—as soon as we got someone to patch him together he had to be sedated to keep from racing off to hunt for you."

"How did you find me?" I asked from my nest on the daybed.

"I called Lieutenant Mallory. Your tiresome neighbor knew who had shot him—I gather he monitors all your male visitors?" She flashed a wicked grin. "A full-time job for him, my dear. Anyway, the lieutenant was not at all disposed to intervene, but he could scarcely ignore the evidence of a man who'd been shot. He finally agreed to call me when they'd located you. I was afraid he wasn't going to push hard enough—you had me very frightened, my dear."

She compressed her lips and turned her head away to regain her composure.

"I was damned scared myself," I said frankly. "I just didn't understand how desperate those boys were getting."

"At any rate, I had done a difficult delivery for the chief assistant federal prosecutor, or whatever her title was, so I rang her up and told her what I knew. I think she organized some resources to look for you, but by then you'd surfaced at police headquarters. What a loathsome place. I tried hard to get in to fetch you, my dear, but they were quite—quite physical in keeping me out."

I got out of my nest to hug her. Lotty has an antigen against police stations—they played too terrifying a role in her early childhood—so it made her effort doubly precious to me.

I asked her about Elena. My aunt had been treated for exhaustion and had her broken finger set, but the hospital released her around noon. After telling me about Elena, Lotty tried to get me to think of other things, like the possibility of a vacation. She pulled out a giant folder of travel brochures —trips to Caribbean islands, to the Costa Brava—various warm and friendly climates that would make me forget the Chicago winter closing in on us.

On Friday, Lotty finally let the rest of the world loose on me. She laid down the law with all her imperial force: Anyone who wanted to see me had to do so on Sheffield Avenue. Unfortunately there were any number of people eager enough to talk to me to meet that condition.

First in line was Alison Winstein, the deputy prosecutor whose life Lotty had saved last year. She took me through what I knew and what I surmised. Like all prosecutors, she didn't feel like giving much back but she did let me know that they had obtained warrants for Alma and Farmworks. They had wanted to subpoena the county contract files but Boots was a pretty wily fighter—neither he nor Ralph would turn over records without a pretty good battle.

After Ms. Winstein left I went through the account of my escapade in the papers. Murray had put together a pretty strong story without talking to me —he'd gotten an exclusive with Mr. Contreras and managed to track Elena down before the hospital released her. I grinned to myself over the interview with my neighbor. Of all the men I know, Murray is the one Mr. Contreras likes least—thinks of him as a snothead and a hot dog. Murray earned his byline on that one.

When I'd finished with the papers I called Robin Bessinger at Ajax. He'd seen the stories and was in a chastened frame of mind. "I'm sorry we questioned your judgment, Vic. You were the pro on this one. I—could we have dinner again?"

"I don't know," I said slowly. "I'll take to think about that. But you could do one thing for me—cut a check for Saul Seligman. I'll take it over to him in the morning."

"We'd kind of like to subrogate against MacDonald and Meagher," Robin said.

"Be my guest. But don't keep the old guy hanging. He's had a rough three weeks, with his favorite old building going and his chief lieutenant getting murdered. I know you can grease those bureaucratic wheels. Drop it off for me on your way home and I'll take it to him tomorrow."

Robin agreed, somewhat unwillingly. It was perhaps the hope of dinner— et cetera—with me that made him agree at all. I was going to have to build up my strength and get over a lot of wounds before I was in the humor for much et cetera.

Lotty had gone to Beth Israel to see her more pressing patients, but she came back at lunch to heat some homemade chicken soup for me. "You're too thin, *Liebchen*. I want to see those purple circles disappear from your eyes."

I obediently ate two large helpings and a few slices of toast. While I was finishing the toast Murray showed up. I didn't much feel like talking to him, but the sooner I did it the faster it would be behind me. And when I'd done I was glad because he knew what had happened to Furey—suspended without pay, out on $100,000 bond for felonious assault on me, Elena, and Mr. Contreras.

"They're never going to prove a case against him with that young girl— what was her name? Cerise? Sergeant McGonnigal did tell me off the record that they're missing some heroin they'd copped in a drug raid a month or so ago. He also figures the department's going to sit on that one."

"What about Boots?" I asked. "How do things look for the election next month?"

Murray made a face. "This is Chicago, sweetheart, not Minneapolis—he got a standing ovation at last night's meeting of the County Board. And the campaign funds are still coming in—too many of those contractors owe the old guy too much. They're not going to jump ship unless he falls below the waterline."

"Has he backed away from Roz?"

"Same story—she's just too popular in the Hispanic wards. Boots lets her go he can kiss the Humboldt Park–Logan Square vote good-bye. And don't forget there's a sizable Mexican population out in the Mount Prospect area —her support isn't all in the city."

"So why did she bother?" I burst out. "Why did she care what I did or who I talked to? That's what burns me. The way people were carrying on I thought she was sitting on bigamy or illegitimate children tucked in an orphanage. Turns out it was just business as usual in this town. I'm sick to death of it, but it's so goddamn usual, why did she think it would matter?"

Murray shrugged his massive shoulders. "Maybe she felt vulnerable. First woman Boots has backed in a big way. First Hispanic. Maybe she was afraid the rules would be different for her. You of all people ought to be able to figure that one out."

"Yeah, maybe." Suddenly I was very tired, so tired that I started drifting off to sleep while Murray asked me something about Elena. I tried to answer coherently but he saw I was struggling.

"You go back to bed, kid. Once more Wonder Woman saves the city. Go to sleep." He patted me on the shoulder and took off, magnanimous because I'd let him garner so much glory.

It was late in the afternoon, after I'd slept a while, that Velma Riter dropped in. When Lotty told me who had come I wanted to dive back under the covers. Instead I staggered to the living room on woolly legs and braced myself for her onslaught.

She stood in the middle of the room twisting a copy of the *Star* around and around in her hands.

"Quite a story you were digging up," she finally said in a voice like dry soil.

I looked at her warily. "It doesn't seem to be hurting Roz much. Of course there's still a month till the election."

"I don't know who I'm madder with—Roz for doing all this or you for turning on a sister and making it all public."

I rubbed my face with the heels of my hands. "I don't have a pat answer for that, Velma. Does being a feminist mean you have to support *everything* your sisters do? Even if you think they're abusing you?"

"But talk to her in private, couldn't you do that?"

"She wouldn't let me. I tried. She just wants those golden apples too bad, Velma. I'm sure she'll do a good job. She'll be better than most, I expect. But she isn't enough of a risk-taker to try for the apples without getting some worms to help her."

Velma flung up her arms. "It's too much. Too much for me, anyway. I should have stayed with photography—it's safer."

I looked at her directly. "Velma—your pictures are honest—and they involve a lot of risk—emotional risk. I'd think you'd want that in any woman you came out in public for. Well, I do. And I won't take it, to be spun around—by *anyone*. And especially not by someone like Roz, trading on old loyalties and asking us to countenance—well, worms."

"She didn't do it for the money, you know," Velma said.

I made an impatient gesture. "I know—she did it for her cousin, family loyalty, wanting Hispanics to have a bigger piece of county action. Just because her motives were so damned wonderful doesn't make me like it any better."

Velma stared at me unblinkingly for a minute. "Well, anyone looking at your body knows you take risks, Warshawski. I'll give you that. I did resign from her staff today. She—she—" The wide, generous mouth crumpled. "She talked to me so sweet, you'd think that voice was every mother in the world singing a lullaby. That hurt. I had to quit."

I looked at her and nodded without speaking. She winked back her tears and left abruptly.

48

THE BIRTHDAY PARTY

On Saturday, before I took old Mr. Seligman his check, I stopped at a Pontiac dealership on Western and bought myself a bright red Trans Am. I've never owned a new car before, especially not one with twin exhausts and horsepower. I didn't know what I was going to do for money to pay for it, but when it moved up to fifty with just a whisper of gas it seemed like the car I'd been waiting for all my life.

After that I took my time going north and west to Norwood Park. Eileen had decided to go ahead with the party for Bobby. So much planning had gone into it, involving so much of the neighborhood, that she didn't feel she could turn it off now. The people on either side were lending their yards so there'd be a place for a refreshment tent and for some pipers.

I'd called Eileen to tell her I wasn't up to seeing Bobby, but she'd begged me to come.

"Vicki, try to understand. Michael is his godson. He was like a seventh child to Bobby and his great hope in the department. He was only yelling at you out of his hurt for Michael."

"It doesn't work for me, Eileen. Michael wanted to kill me and he damned near did it. By the time Bobby finished with me I felt he wished it had happened."

"No, no, don't ever think such a thing." Her warm rich voice cracked in distress. "Tony's child? Gabriella's? It was himself he wanted to attack, for letting himself be so betrayed. He—Bobby's a good man, Vicki. A good cop too. You know that. Tony would never have taken him up if he wasn't. But—he's not good at thinking through these things, figuring out why he lashed out at you the way he did. He has other strengths, but not that one. I'm asking you—begging you—to understand and be better than him. It would mean so much. Not just to him, but to me. So if you can't do it for him, will you do it for me?"

And so I found myself ducking under the billboard of Boots Meagher at the corner of Nagle—a smiling year-round fixture proclaiming that "Boots Is Chicago"—and crossing into Bobby's neighborhood. Bobby's neighborhood. Michael's neighborhood. Where my father and uncles and Aunt Elena grew up. Where Boots and Ernie and Ron came from. Where they all grew up together and helped each other out because the one thing you must never forget in Chicago is to look out for your own.

Usually when I cross the invisible line into Norwood Park I feel as though I've gone into Munchkin land, a place of tidy tiny bungalows on minuscule well-tended lots. It's a mirage of a neighborhood—it seems to have nothing to do with the sprawling, graffiti-laden, garbage-ridden city to the south-east.

Today, though, it seemed dead. The October air was gray and the houses looked drab and colorless. Even the bursts of fall flowers in the tidy yards seemed drained of vividness, the bronze mums looking brown, the gold ones merely sickly. I wished I was anywhere in the world but here.

I pulled my new toy into a line with other cars blocking the street. No one would be out ticketing today. I dragged myself slowly up the short drive. Laughter and the sound of bagpipes were coming from the back. A few knots of people had spilled over into the front yard. They smiled and waved at me in the happy camaraderie of a big party and I dutifully waved back.

When I got to the back the crowd was packed into every inch of turf, not just in Eileen's yard but in the two adjacent. A canopy with Bobby's name done up in lights stood in the middle. I couldn't see the pipes or anyone I knew. I stood awkwardly on the fringe until Eileen suddenly came from nowhere and pulled me to her large soft breasts.

"Oh, Vicki, oh, it's so good to see you. Thank you so much for coming. I was afraid . . . Anyway, Bobby's over here. He'll be so pleased—he hasn't said—but you know . . ." Tears sparkled on her long black lashes. She took my hand and made her way through the throng to the densest part, where Bobby stood. Beyond him a piper was playing and the crowd was urging Bobby to dance.

Eileen waited until the howl of the reel had ended before thrusting me forward. "Bobby. Look who's come."

When Bobby saw me the smile died from his face. He looked at me with some combination of embarrassment and rigidness.

"You guys gotta excuse me," he said abruptly to the group around him. "I need to see this young lady for a few minutes."

He took me into the house, a slow procession through the jam of happy neighbors, fellow cops—I even saw Officer Neely looking flushed and re-laxed in a bright fuchsia dress—and screaming grandchildren.

Inside the house two of Bobby's daughters were constructing a giant cake. They squealed when they saw him. "Daddy! You know you're not supposed to come in here."

"It's okay, girls—I ain't seen nothin'. I'm just going down to the family room with Vicki for a few minutes. You keep everyone out, okay?"

"Sure, Daddy, but go on before you see something!" They shooed us down the steps.

Bobby had finished the basement himself, installing a bathroom, real floors and walls, building in bunk beds for his two sons when there'd been six children in seven rooms upstairs. Only two of their daughters were still at home, but he'd left the beds for his grandchildren to sleep in—he loved having them stay over.

He turned on a lamp and sat on the red plaid couch next to the bunk beds. I sat in the shabby armchair facing him, next to the fake fireplace. He moved his big hands uncomfortably, trying to think of something to say. I didn't help him.

"I didn't expect to see you here," he said at last.

"I didn't want to come. Eileen talked me into it."

He looked at the floor and muttered, "I said a lot of things I shouldn't have last week. I'm sorry."

"You hurt my feelings, Bobby." I couldn't keep my voice from cracking. "Your golden boy damned near killed me and you talked to me like I was some kind of street scum."

He rubbed his face. "I—Vicki, I talked to Eileen about it, she tried to make sense out of it for me. I don't know why I did it, that's God's truth. Dr. Herschel called me. That's how I knew you were in trouble. You know about that part, don't you?"

I nodded without speaking.

"I knew by then it was Mickey. Well, you'd tried to tell me, but it wasn't until she told me he'd shot the old man that I—don't look at me like that, Vicki, you're making it hard to say this and it's hard enough to start with."

I turned my head toward the cowboy coverlets on the bunk beds.

"I called John and the Finch. They weren't as upset as I was—they knew Mickey'd been acting queer since the day before when you brought that damned bracelet of his in. And they'd wondered about some other things. Of course they'd never told me—I was the lieutenant and he was my fair-haired boy." He gave a harsh laugh. "What was the story on that bracelet? Why did it send him into orbit?"

I explained. "I tried to tell you Wednesday. I didn't know what it was—I don't think he'd worn it around me more than once or twice. He thought— you know, as long as Elena was alive she could link it to him. Well, not just that. She could tie him to the fire at the Indiana Arms. He was the person, too, who knocked us both out and tried to burn us at the other place." I started shivering as the memories hit me. I tried to push them aside but I couldn't.

Bobby grunted and stood up to reach for one of the cowboy coverlets. He tossed it to me and I wrapped myself in it. After a bit my shivering stopped, but both of us sat lost in our own reveries.

At least my last visitor yesterday was benign—Zerlina, again taking three buses, wanted to know how her daughter came to die. She shared a Coke and more of Lotty's chicken soup and wept with me. She shook her head in amazement when she learned Elena had saved my life: "Thought she'd pickled her brain too good years ago to come up with something like that, but the Lord provides when you least expect it."

As if following my thoughts, Bobby asked abruptly about my aunt.

"It's like it all never happened. I stopped by the Windsor Arms—the hotel where she's living now—last night. She was out front with a bottle and a crowd of greasy old men, showing her little finger in a splint and bragging over her heroics. Some people even a whirlwind won't change, I guess." I laughed mirthlessly.

Bobby nodded a couple of times to himself. "I want you to understand something, Vicki. Try to, anyway. Tony, your daddy, took me under his wing when I joined the force. He must have been a good thirteen, fourteen years older than me. A lot of guys were coming back from the war then, they didn't make it easy on us rookies. Tony looked out for me from day one.

"I thought I could do the same for Mickey and it hurts me, hurts my pride Eileen tells me it is, that I could be so wrong. I keep thinking to myself, what would Tony think, he saw me making such a colossal mistake?"

He didn't seem to want an answer but I gave him one anyway. "You know what he'd say, Bobby, that anyone can make a mess but only a fool wallows in it."

Bobby smiled painfully. "Yeah, well, maybe. Yeah, probably. But here's what you gotta understand, Vicki. I thought the best thing I could do to pay Tony back for all he did for me was look out for you. I never could understand the way Tony and Gabriella brought you up, not making you mind the way my own girls did. And you just didn't seem like a real girl to me, the things you wanted and wanted to do. I'm not even sure I liked you all that well. I just thought I owed it to Tony to look after you."

I thought he'd finished, but he only stopped to crack his knuckles, get himself over the hump. "So you're not like other girls. Eileen—Eileen never minded a minute, she always loved you like you were her own daughter. But I just couldn't deal with it. And then when you exposed Mickey—he was like my son and you were like an alien monster. But if he'd had your guts and your honesty, he'd never of gone along with those buddies of his to begin with. Never dug himself that kind of hole.

"So I've had to think about it. Think about you, I mean. Start from the beginning. I love my girls. I don't want them any different from how they are. But you're the daughter of the two people I loved best, next to Eileen, and you can't do things different than you do, shouldn't do them different, not with Gabriella and Tony bringing you up. Do you understand?"

The door at the top of the stairs opened and Bobby's daughter Marianna called down. "Daddy! People are waiting for you!"

"Be up in a jiffy, sugar!" he yelled back. "Don't let them start without me."

He got up. "Okay? Is that enough?"

I stood up too. "Yeah, I think that's enough." I fished in my pocket and handed him a small parcel. "I brought that along for you. Just in case, you know—just in case I felt like giving you a present."

He undid the paper and opened the little box. When he looked inside and saw Tony's shield lying in the cotton, he didn't say anything, but for the second time that week I saw him cry.

ABOUT THE AUTHOR

SARA PARETSKY is *The New York Times* bestselling author of eight books about private detective V.I. Warshawski, including *Guardian Angel, Bitter Medicine, Killing Orders, Deadlock,* and the stories in this omnibus, *Indemnity Only, Blood Shot,* and *Burn Marks.* She lives in Chicago with her husband and their golden retriever.